I0721654

STORM

A DARK & DIRTY SINNERS' MC: EIGHT

SERENA AKEROYD

Copyright © 2021 by Serena Akeroyd

All rights reserved.

No part of this book may be reproduced in any form or by any electronic or mechanical means, including information storage and retrieval systems, without written permission from the author, except for the use of brief quotations in a book review.

❀ Created with Vellum

DEDICATION

TO YOU, intrepid reader.

For your faith in me.

For your trust in Storm.

For your belief in a happily-ever-after.

As well, of course, to the people who had my back while making this happen—the real life Posse and my very own Snopes, you all know who you are. Hope you enjoyed seeing your road names in the flesh.

And finally, to Stacy. For having the balls to be herself, for having the courage to strike it out on her own, and for giving me Coshocton and allowing Storm to have his own stomping grounds—even if they're in between a bunch of cornfields. ;)

TRIGGERS

IMPORTANT INFORMATION
PLEASE DO NOT IGNORE

Hey you,

Have you:

A) Grabbed your favorite blanket,

B) Got a box of chocolates to hand,

C) Have some tissues,

D) Removed your eye make-up (this is at an ARC reader's suggestion,)

E) {And if booze is your jam} Have a glass of wine close by—or three?

If you're prepared… here are the trigger warnings:

- Suicide,
- Drug abuse,
- Addiction,
- Self-harming,
- Violence,

- References to child neglect,
- References to child abuse,
- References to euthanasia.

I almost didn't write this book. Now, as I sit here, I can't tell you how tragic that is to me.

The notion that with every mistake we make, there's a karmic chopping board that means we don't deserve happiness, *ever*, is pretty damn depressing but the hate Storm was shown by a lot of readers made me want to back away from his story.

I was scared.

I admit it.

Scared about the hate, scared about the one stars.

But Anne, my EA, has pretty much fought for Storm since I started having doubts about whether I could write his story. She shored me up when my confidence was low, when readers attacked Storm in FB groups, tearing both him and Keira down. The reaction to him has been intense to say the least.

But here, now, I can tell you this.

This is the book I'm the proudest of.

This book is everything.

This book—*this* is why I became a writer. To make you feel, to make you hope, to make you love, and to make you need.

If you loathe Storm, but are reading to make sure you don't miss the Sparrows' continuity storyline, then you don't need to worry. Please, back away from the book if cheating is a trigger and the NWS is why you're reading it. I wrote it specifically without the Sparrows' series arc so it could be skipped.

If you loathe Storm but are reading so you can tell me in a one-star review that I'm a terrible human being, please, just put the book down. *I get it.* Cheating is a trigger. But forty percent of marriages are impacted by infidelity. This is as real as it gets.

I hope, if you're still reading, and if you're going to dive in, you'll know one thing—I know Storm did wrong. Hell, *Storm* knows he did wrong. I never excuse what he did. Just provide explanation.

Storm is one of the most broken men I've ever written. Maybe even more so than Nyx.

I hope you love him as much as I do.

Hopefully happy reading,

Serena

xoxo

UNIVERSE READING ORDER

FILTHY
FILTHY SINNER
NYX
LINK
FILTHY RICH
SIN
STEEL
FILTHY DARK
CRUZ
MAVERICK
FILTHY SEX
HAWK
FILTHY HOT
STORM
THE DON
THE LADY
FILTHY SECRET
REX
RACHEL
FILTHY KING

<u>FILTHY DISCIPLE</u>
<u>THE CONSIGLIERE</u>
<u>THE ORACLE</u>
<u>LODESTAR</u>
<u>SILENCED</u>
<u>END GAME</u>
<u>FILTHY RICHER</u>

PLAYLIST

If you'd like to hear a curated soundtrack, with songs that are featured in the book, as well as songs that inspired it, then here's the link:

https://open.spotify.com/playlist/1GLvN8qS0uY2v6BmlhwkXK?si=1c09fd91c14246eb

DEAR DIARY

SENIOR YEAR

I saw this guy today.

It was weird. Weird in a good way though.

I don't think he noticed me, but I couldn't help but notice him.

He has really long hair, and I mean, I hate long hair on guys, but his was unusual. He has this long streak at the front, and it's silver. A whole streak of silver. I've never seen anything like it.

He's not ashamed about it or anything, not that he needs to be, but it just made him stand out even more. I googled it. It's a condition called poliosis. It sounds kinda ugly, but trust me, it's not.

That wasn't the only thing unusual about him.

He wore a cut.

He's a Sinner.

How crazy is that?

I'm not sure why he was at Jackson High, but it looked as if he were waiting on someone.

Mostly, he stuck out like a sore thumb, and I knew I wasn't the only one watching him.

People say that Jimmy Dane is a Prospect at the Sinners, but I don't know how true that is.

There's a lot of nonsense floating around about the local MC. I don't believe half of it to be honest. They can't be that bad, can they?

Dad wouldn't agree with me.

He keeps pushing members of the country club to do something. I'm not sure who he thinks he is. He's a church minister, not a gazillionaire who can put pressure on the mayor and get them to toss out the local motorcycle club…

When he goes on one of his diatribes, I want the ground to open and swallow me up. His hypocrisy is disturbing in someone who is preaching to people about 'loving thy neighbor.'

Sometimes, I look at Mom and Dad and just pray that when I'm their age, I'm not so bitter.

Is that sad?

To have 'don't be bitter' as a life goal?

He looked sad. The guy, I mean. He looked real sad. Bone deep. Tired too. Of all the things I noticed about him, that resonated the most.

I'm not sure how he looks like he could go to sleep for a decade and still wake up looking exhausted when he's as gorgeous as he is, but it's a miracle he achieves.

He's way too old for me to even be thinking about, but, I don't know, that sorrow. I feel it for him. His eyes are so… Man, it sounds dumb, but they really are like the windows to his soul.

I think that's why I saw him.

His face, his beauty, it's irrelevant.

His soul called to me.

I wonder what his name is.

Maybe it's best if I don't find out. I know he's trouble, and trouble isn't something Keira Miller's allowed.

Even so, I'd like to make him smile. I really would.

DEAR KEIRA

Jimmy told me that's your name. It suits you.

I saw you the other day after class broke out and the light hit your hair, just so. I wish I had my camera with me. The crappy one on my phone won't do you justice, won't capture your smile forever like I need to.

You're way too young for me.

Way too innocent for a man like me.

I should leave you alone.

I'm just not sure that I can.

That smile, damn, I can't stop thinking about it. No malice, no manipulation—just pure joy. I'm not sure I've ever seen a woman smile like that before. With an innocence that makes every filthy part of me stand up and take note.

The shit I've done... The things I've seen... The people I've hurt... My hands are dirty. My soul is black. My heart is a shriveled mass in my chest.

You're so clean, Keira.

So fucking clean, and I'm so dirty. So unworthy.

You're the kind of woman a man should worship. That he should get on his hands and fucking knees to serve. In my world, men don't do that. But you deserve it.

You deserve everything, and everything isn't something I'm able to offer.

For you, I'd try, but I don't think you'll ever notice me. Maybe that's for the best.

Storm

ONE

KEIRA

PAST

West End Girls - Pet Shop Boys

"TAKE ME SOMEWHERE."

Asher tilted his head to the side in surprise. He'd watched me walk over to him from the entrance to the school, but clearly, he hadn't anticipated my request. After my birthday party last night, however, I could think of nothing else but him.

He'd been on my mind all night and all day, and it had nothing to do with seeing him here this morning and now. It hadn't helped my stupid crush on him that was for sure.

"Where do you want to go?"

I shrugged. "Anywhere but here?"

"Are you okay?" he asked carefully. "Did that Leinster prick hurt you? Or say shit about you today?" His nostrils flared as if just the prospect agitated him.

"No, he wasn't in school today." I bit my lip. "What did you do to him?"

He arched a brow. "You don't want to know."

"Take me somewhere," I repeated softly because he was right—*I didn't want to know.*

By his own admission, he hadn't killed Ray. Not if he thought the school's QB would be able to spread rumors about me. There was some solace to be found in there.

"Anywhere?"

I nodded.

"I don't have a helmet for you."

"You won't crash, will you?"

"Not with you riding bitch." When I flinched, he soothed, "That's what it's called when a woman rides behind you. Only a man's Old Lady or his wife is supposed to ride behind him."

I frowned at that. "Seriously?"

"Yes. Seriously." He smiled, and it lit up his eyes. They were still sad, just… *less*. "I'll get you a helmet so if you want to ride with me again, I'll be prepared."

That had me blinking at him. "You'd do that?"

"Of course."

He said it so easily, so simply. A helmet had to cost a hundred bucks. That was insane to me that he'd just drop a hundred dollars on me like that.

A thought occurred to me. "Is that why Kendra always rides behind Jimmy? Because she's his Old Lady?"

His brow puckered so fast that I almost missed it when he relaxed it the next second. "No. She's not his Old Lady."

She was eighteen, so that didn't come as a surprise. *Sons Of Anarchy* had taught me Old Ladies weren't old in years, but Jimmy never so much as looked at Kendra. If anything, he studied her ass.

"Is she a sweetbutt?"

"Lemme guess. *Sons of Anarchy*?"

I shot him a sheepish smile. "Yes."

He rolled his eyes. "She's on the way to becoming one."

A part of me wanted to grimace, but another part didn't want to be disrespectful. Whores existed everywhere, after all. Even in my father's church.

I wasn't sure why anyone would want to have sex with a lot of bikers, but if they looked like Asher, and if they weren't raised like I was, maybe that would be an interesting career trajectory. Who was I to judge?

"Do you still want to get on the back of my bike, baby girl?"

Scowling at that, I retorted, "I'm not a baby."

He smiled. "You are to me. It's okay to be afraid. You should be, even though I'll never hurt you. I'd hurt myself first."

Why did I believe that?

Swallowing, I whispered, "Ray was going to hurt me last night."

"Yes. He was. That's why I stopped him."

I gnawed on my bottom lip. "I feel like…"

"You feel like?" he prompted when I fell silent.

"Like you had no right to protect me, but I'm glad that you did," I blurted out.

He didn't tell me that he'd protect any woman from a predator like Ray. He didn't tell me that he was relieved he'd saved me.

He just looked at me.

Our eyes tangling.

And a strange feeling burst inside me.

Warmth and… *want*.

I licked my lips.

"Is your mom waiting on you?"

"How do you know she's waiting on me?"

"I know most things about you, Keira." He tapped his nose. "Made it my business to know."

"Why?"

"Because you're fascinatin'."

"Me?" I whispered, pointing at myself.

"No one else around here, is there?" He smiled a little, then he reached out, and his finger tangled in a lock of hair that I let dangle by my cheek. "You sure you want to play with monsters, baby girl?"

"I'm not a baby," I repeated. "I'm nineteen."

He grunted at that. "That reminds me. I got you a present."

Shocked, my mouth gaped. "You got me a gift? But you don't even know me!"

He ignored that and leaned over, unfastening a latch on a satchel on the side of the bike. "Saw it in a store and thought of you."

He handed me a box, tied with a simple ribbon, that I immediately unfastened to reveal a pendant on a necklace.

It was a thin, silver obelisk, engraved with words that made a liar out of him.

Love looks not with the eyes.

This wasn't something you 'found.'

This was something you had engraved.

"Just to clarify, I think you'd have made a better Hermia in the school play, but the quote..." He shrugged. "Well, let's say it resonated."

"You really were there at the play that night. I thought I saw you but—" I smiled sheepishly. "I couldn't imagine you wanting to see that."

"Always did like Shakespeare."

"You?" I sputtered. "You liked Shakespeare?"

"Are you stereotypin' me, Miz Keira?" he teased, making me laugh.

"No. But... you have to admit, you don't look like the kind of guy who'd love Shakespeare."

"That's the joy of the Bard. Fans where you least suspect them." He dropped his chin, motioning to the gift. "It's okay if you don't like it—"

"No!" I declared. "I love it!! Would you put it on for me?"

"Of course." His smile was soft. *Pleased.*

I passed him the box, then gathered my hair in my fist and raised it so that he could loop the chain around my throat and fasten it. I swore I felt his breath against my nape, but the cold chill of the metal against my skin made me think I was mistaken.

Peering down at it, I whispered, "I can't thank you enough."

It was the most thoughtful of all my gifts. Even from Laurie and Josse who'd grabbed me a couple CDs. Not that I was being ungrateful, just... this held a message. I hadn't received a gift like this before.

"You really like it, huh?" he questioned sheepishly, a warm grin making his lips twitch up at the corners in a way that made his beautiful face softer, more boyish. More approachable.

"I love it." I leaned into him because the desire to kiss his cheek in thanks was strong, but I held back, muttering instead, "I was dumb to approach you here. Would you meet me around the corner at JayJay's?"

He blinked. "Why?"

"Because my dad…" My mouth worked. "He's not a nice man."

Temper flared in his eyes. "Does he hurt you?"

"No." But he might if he thought I was interested in a biker.

"Why don't I believe you?"

"He doesn't," I promised. *He just hurt my mom.* "JayJay's? I'll walk there now. I have a couple hours until curfew."

"You have a curfew at your age?"

"Thought you said you knew everything about me," I mocked, but before he could say another word, I just explained, "They're strict."

"Apparently." His brows surged. "I'll meet you at the coffee shop."

"Thank you." I smiled at him, and somehow, that made the frown that had formed on his brow disappear. "I'll see you in ten?"

He nodded as I backed off, and twisting away, a blush surging on my cheeks, I heard him start his engine, then ride off.

Excitement flushed through me, but that was nothing to what I experienced over the following week.

That first day, he didn't ride us far. We stopped off at a park and ate the sandwiches he bought from the coffee shop where we met up.

The second day, he appeared with a helmet, and rode us all the way to New York and back. I swore, nothing beat the energy that came from clinging to him with all my being yet made me feel as if I were flying at the same time.

The third day, we went to East Orange and ate in a coffee shop there. We talked about life. Nuts, right? But it felt so good.

I got the impression that he whitewashed his version plenty, but it was nice to talk about my concerns regarding my lack of a scholarship and the pressure it put me under to do as my father wanted.

Then, we talked about politics, of all things. Religion—both of us were atheists—Pascal's wager, anyone? And there was even a dose of ethics.

It was, in a word, dreamy.

Absolute heaven.

Each day, he took me somewhere different, all without breaking my curfew. And I learned so much. He was kind and gentle, and when I was with him, I felt safe.

From the outside, he might look big and burly, but my father was small and rather petite but he whupped my mom where I knew, point blank, Asher would never do that.

Ever.

Life changed people, that I'd come to see over the years, but there was an intrinsic part of someone's character that defined us, and a kind of wholesomeness registered in my being whenever I was with Asher that put me at ease.

We carried on like that for a few weeks.

Stolen moments in an afternoon that couldn't be classed as dates, not after Josse and Laurie had described their idea of a date to me, but that I cherished nonetheless.

One evening, he rode us along a tract of land that took us out past West Orange, while somehow staying near it. I figured he was taking us to his clubhouse, and though I started to get nervous, I knew he'd never put me in danger.

My mom would shriek at me, anyone else would too—the red alert would be flashing as he took me higher up a hill that I'd never even seen before, never mind walked up—but the part of me that had lost faith in people the day I'd caught Dad cheating on Mom for the second time, rang true with Asher.

And he didn't disappoint.

"Peace and quiet," he murmured softly, once his bike stopped rumbling and we were left with exactly what he said.

I smiled as I unbuckled my helmet and hopped off the bike with his help. He grabbed food out of the saddlebags, even unraveled a blanket, then laid it flat out on the ground about twenty feet away.

Watching him make a picnic for us, I laughed a little, then whirled around, my skirt catching in the wind as I twirled.

I'd never have done that with anyone else, but the sun was shining on our heads, it was warm and pretty, and I was with one of my favorite people in a secret place where no one was watching.

When I stopped twirling, I found Asher watching me. His lips were curved with amusement, but in his eyes there was something new.

Something… hot.

It surprised me, but it didn't scare me.

It didn't have me backing away to the bike and demanding he take me home.

If anything, it had me stepping closer to the blanket he was kneeling on.

I slipped off my UGGs, letting my toes curl into the grass before I sat down on the blanket at his side.

Unsure of what to expect, I waited, only realizing when my lungs started burning that I'd held my breath.

He had a way of looking at me that transcended anything I'd even read about in books, and it made no sense. I wasn't anything special, but *he* was. He was beautiful. Absolutely stunning. And that hair… I just wanted to stroke him all over.

I bit my lip as he murmured, "Come on, Keira, let's just relax, huh?"

Nodding, I carefully unfolded my limbs so that I was lying down on my side, pleased when he did the same. It was… strange.

Good, but strange.

I'd never wanted to do this before.

Never wanted to just be with someone, to have their eyes on mine, to feel the brush of their breath, for their scent to be filling my senses.

Moreover, I'd never felt the power of silence before. It was like it made the space between us vibrate, energy ping-ponging back and forth between us, ratcheting up the tension more and more.

When he reached out, he broke the tension, but his thumb came to rest on my chin.

"You know you're always safe with me, don't you, Keira?"

My eyes widened at the question, but the truth spilled from my lips. "Yes. I know I shouldn't, but I do know that."

"No, you shouldn't feel that way, but I'm glad you do. If you didn't, we wouldn't be here, would we?"

I shook my head. "How did you find this place?"

"You don't want to know," he said dryly. "But I come here when the noise in my head keeps me awake at night."

"You come out here in the dark?" I whispered, surprised.

A soft laugh escaped him. "I do."

"What if there are bobcats or possums?"

That had him snickering. "They're more than welcome to come snack on me."

I scowled at him. "Don't say that."

"I sit on my bike," he appeased. "I thought you'd like it here, that's why I brought you."

"I'm glad you did."

After that, he brought me there every evening without fail, only not on the weekends when I had things to do for my parents.

Obligations—they sucked.

I wanted to spend every moment with him, every minute of every day as ridiculous as it sounded.

I felt like I couldn't get close enough, because something about him remained distant.

He looked at me in a way that made me feel as if I were the only thing he saw, but there was that sorrow in him I'd recognized that first day.

I wanted to raze that sorrow into dust.

I wanted to burn it to the ground and replace it with joy and happiness.

Bikers could be happy, too, couldn't they?

A couple of weeks after Spring Break, which had been torture as I couldn't see him, I laid in his arms in our spot on the hill. It was getting warmer, but he was like a furnace anyway, and he told me about how his family worked.

The club lifestyle sounded intriguing, a little scary, especially after *Sons of Anarchy*, but I listened because there wasn't a single damn thing I didn't want to know about him.

He explained about how his foster father was a guy called Bear, whose Old Lady was called Rene, and how he had several men in his life who weren't blood brothers but were regardless. Kinda complicated, but I got it.

Mostly, I was just happy he was sharing this with me. It had taken him a long time to open up about what really mattered to him, and I was content to soak it in like a sponge.

Pressing my face into his throat, I let out a soft sigh as I placed a kiss there.

It was instinctive.

Natural.

As easy as breathing.

But it made him tense up like I'd punched him in the throat.

I stiffened, for the first time realizing how invasive that had been, and I pulled back, cheeks flushing, until he grabbed my hand to stop me from moving away and rumbled, "Keira?"

Mortified, my shoulders hunched in on themselves as I replied, "I'm so sorry, Storm. I shouldn't have—"

"You should have," he corrected, reaching over to grab my chin and to urge me to look at him. "You have every right to do that, but I wanted to check in with you first."

Surprised, I peeked up at him, and when I saw the banked fire in his eyes, I knew I'd done it.

The sorrow was gone.

At that moment, I was all he thought about, not whatever put that unhappiness in those beautiful green eyes of his.

A shaky breath escaped me as I clambered onto my knees. He tugged on my hand, clearly thinking I was about to leave, but then he stopped when I moved over to him.

Cupping his cheeks, I whispered, "I want you to look at me like that all the time."

His nostrils flared. "I do, I just temper it because I don't want to scare you."

"You could never scare me, Asher. Haven't we had this conversation already?"

"I don't think you're ready for what I feel for you."

That had a shallow breath escaping my lungs. "Maybe I'm not, but that doesn't mean I can't learn to be ready."

His lips quirked up at the edges. "You want me to teach you, huh?"

"I wouldn't be averse to that particular lesson," I told him primly, but I knew my flushed cheeks gave the game away. And if it didn't, then I pressed a hand to his shoulder and pushed him back onto the blanket.

He eyed me warily, but I ignored his wariness and instead, straddled him the second he was lying flat.

As my ass settled on his thighs, a feeling of empowerment whirred through me.

This strong, powerful, badass biker was letting me sit on him like he was a chair.

I knew I should be nervous. I knew I should be scared. I knew, point blank, I shouldn't be excited.

With anyone else, I probably would have been a bag of nerves.

But this was Asher and I wanted to unwrap him like a candy bar.

I was more curious about what went on underneath the Henley he wore constantly than I was afraid of what was about to happen.

Because something was definitely about to go down.

Something that I really, truly wanted to be with him.

I rolled up his Henley, revealing abs that I'd only ever seen on posters and in movies, and he let me undress him. Let me unwrap him.

Lifting up so that I could tug his cut off, then his top, I left him bare from the waist up on the blanket. His hair was loose, splayed over the plaid cover, and I trailed my fingers through the silver streak that so fascinated me.

All the while, he watched me with hot eyes when I leaned over him and finally joined our mouths together.

He wasn't aggressive, didn't push things, in fact, he surprised me with how placid he was. He let me kiss him and caress him and touch him, then I reached between us when I was feeling brave, and I palmed his dick.

The second I did, his body locked up with tension, his nostrils flaring, and his voice was an octave deeper as he rasped, "Are you sure you want to do that, Keira?"

Butterflies invaded my stomach. "I'm sure."

"We can go. I can take you home—"

The butterflies disappeared. "Why would I want that?"

"Because you're testing the waters. Seeing if I'll bite."

"You're mixing metaphors."

His lips curved. "I'll mix them some more. You're not ready—"

"Are you really going to tell me that I'm not ready? Are you in my body? My head?"

"I know you're innocent and that you're not used to—"

"Used to what?" I snapped, pissed that he was putting words in my mouth. "I've been going to bed thinking of this for months. Touching myself, thinking it was you, wishing it were you, knowing that soon, it would be you—"

Before I could say another word, he surged upward and bound our mouths together.

There was no more docile Asher, this was the man I knew was waiting behind the strict control he'd erected as he lay there, suffering, I realized, through my ministrations.

His hands held my cheeks, holding me close as his tongue thrust between my lips, dragging against mine and jolting me with a sensation that powered through me. I groaned with the joy of it, of feeling his need for me, need that wasn't tempered, but that was full throttle.

Now I knew what he held back from me.

With this one kiss, I saw what that distance was.

Him being a gentleman.

And they said chivalry was dead.

I fought back, playing with him, taunting him as much as he did me, all while my hands went to the buttons on my shirt, and I dragged it then my bra off. He didn't so much as break my kiss but he must have felt my struggles because his hands went to my breasts and he palmed them once they were bare.

A shocked, stunned gasp escaped me at his first touch, and as his fingers plucked at my nipples, my knees clenched down around his thighs, hugging him close as I sought something I didn't really understand.

One hand stayed on my breast, the other slid down over my waist and to my jeans. He gently stroked along my waistband as his tongue plunged into my mouth, then his fingers slipped along the seam on the denim and I shuddered against him, that one touch already enough to make me feel empty.

When I reached between us and opened my fly, dragging the zipper down, he moved into the space I made and cupped me through my panties. One finger moved between the folds and I squirmed against him even as I groaned against his mouth.

His reverent touches made me realize how this felt a thousand times better than when I did it on my own.

I groaned again when he found my clit, and as he concentrated on it, bringing me quickly to a release, the shockwaves had my back arching in delight.

I had no idea why, but though I gasped against his lips as pleasure wormed its way through me, it wasn't enough. It would never be enough.

I needed him.

More of him.

All of him.

On a shaky breath, I pulled back, letting my teeth bite down on his lip, rasping, "More, Asher, please, more."

A grunt escaped him as he pressed his face to my throat, nipping and sucking there as that devilish finger slipped under my panties. When he circled my slit, I tensed as he gently thrust it into me.

God, he was…

That was big.

And I'd felt his dick.

Nerves hit me, but it was replaced with hunger. It'd hurt at first, sure, but then the good stuff would happen. I couldn't even imagine how wonderful that would feel.

Excited, I clung to him as he twisted us around so that he was on top of me. The heavy weight of him settled on me, feeling so beautifully right that I sighed with delight.

Overhead, the dying sun gleamed purples, pinks, and golds, making the shadows of twilight dance over us like a patchwork quilt while the birds serenaded us with their final song for the night.

It was perfect.

He was perfect as he loomed above me, so dangerous, so beautiful.

So mine.

I groaned when he moved away, but I didn't complain for long. He dragged my jeans off me, then jerked to his feet, pulled something out of his pocket, then dragged his off too.

Maybe I should have felt self-conscious, but I was more focused on the beast between his thighs, as well as the fact that I was seeing him naked.

Dear Lord, he was perfect.

Absolutely perfect.

He made me wish I were good at art because he needed to be painted, or drawn, or both. I wished I could do that, just so I could savor him forever, but instead I'd need to remember him like this. Imprint him on my memory banks.

It wouldn't be a hardship.

The hair on his legs was both soft and prickly against my legs as he dropped to his knees between them.

When I watched him open the condom wrapper, then cover himself, I determined that next time, I'd do that. It looked hot. Although, maybe that was just watching him touch himself?

I guessed I was a little shy about all this, but mostly, I was intrigued. I wanted to know everything, and I wanted to know it now.

How to please him and be pleased, how to touch him and be touched… there was so much to learn and I was an eager student.

He pressed a kiss to my lips, but didn't let me play, instead he worked his way down my body, kissing my breasts, tonguing the nipples, biting one and tweaking the other with his fingers.

All the while, one hand was between my legs, touching me and caressing me, until I could hear how wet I was as he thrust it into me. A second finger made itself known, followed by a third.

That pinched.

I squirmed, gasping as he sucked on my nipple, his other hand drawn to my clit now as he rubbed there while he stretched me.

"Oh, God," I ground out, my head flinging from side to side as he hit me with pleasure and discomfort simultaneously.

Ass rocking, hips shaking, I tried to stay still but it was impossible not to squirm beneath him.

That fourth finger had me tensing up, shoulders bucking as my back arched. A hiss escaped me, but I sighed once the pinch of pain died down. He stretched me again, his fingers scissoring, until I ground out, "Asher, please, please."

I didn't realize that I said that word over and over, my hunger for him there, a solid entity between us.

Then he growled under his breath which set off a welter of sensation along my nerve endings, pulled his fingers out of my pussy, sucked them clean with a fervor that had my cheeks heating up—especially when he groaned like he was slurping down a really great, cold beer—and then he moved over me. His forearms settling on either side of my head, his dick landing against my sex.

His mouth above mine, he whispered, "You sure you want this, baby girl?"

I groaned. "Yes!"

"You can say no."

"Dammit, no!" I grumbled, lifting my legs so I could dig my heels into his ass. "Stop with the chivalry, Asher. I need you!"

He nipped my chin, then pressed several kisses down my jawline. When he reached my ear, he whispered, "Then you can have me. All of me, baby girl."

Ugh, his words made me melt into a puddle, which probably helped when he pressed the tip of his dick to my entrance because it stopped me from pulling back in shock at how much bigger he was than his fingers.

I gulped, a little nervous, then he bridged both of our hands together and raised them over my head, pinning them to the blanket.

When he settled on top of me, his eyes on mine, slowly, he pushed into me.

Nostrils flaring as his thickness invaded me, I breathed through it, relaxing when he whispered, "Do you know how fucking beautiful you are, Keira? Everything about you. From the inside out."

I nuzzled my cheek against his, not unaware that he thrust another inch into me.

"I've been dreaming about touching you and tasting you from the minute I saw you."

I moaned, but not because another inch filled me.

"I've been dreaming about what your pussy tastes like."

A mewl whispered from me.

"God, it's better than fucking coke. Your pussy's like crack, baby girl. All of you is."

My heels dug into his ass.

"You gonna take all of me? I bet you can. You're so fucking beautiful. I know you can do it—"

I whimpered.

"So proud of you, sweetness. So fucking proud of you."

A high-pitched wail escaped me as his pelvis finally met mine. It wasn't founded in pain, just need.

My fingers tightened on his and I rasped, "Oh God, Asher. Oh God. Oh God."

"It's okay, baby, it's okay. Let me take you there."

And he did.

As the sky turned to night and the stars began to twinkle, he made love to me. He cherished me. He made my first time unforgettable.

But that was Asher.

He was unforgettable.

Intoxicating.

Beautiful. Inside and out.

As I clung to him and he clung to me, he showed me what it meant to be with someone you loved. He made me realize, without us having to say a word, that he loved me and that I loved him and that was what made this perfect.

I screamed with the wonder of it as he made me come, as the pleasure burst through my being when I couldn't contain it anymore, but what really added to the perfection of the moment was when his cries entangled with mine.

When his release and mine joined together in a wonderful harmony that, I recognized, I was only supposed to feel with him.

TWO

STORM

PRESENT - DAY AFTER CHRISTMAS

Savin' Me - Nickelback

YOU EVER STARED at nothing for so long that it made your eyes burn?

That was me today.

With my feet propped up on the desk, my ass settled in a chair that only recently had been the throne for another Prez, and my hands resting on my abs, I stared out of the window as I watched snowflakes drift to the ground.

I wasn't where I wanted to be.

I was neither in my family home, sitting with my woman and my kid as they watched cartoons and Christmas movies while I handled some work on my phone with a piece of pie in front of me, nor was I in West Orange. I was stuck in Coshocton, Ohio. The one advantage was this office—I was Prez here.

Rex, the Prez of the New Jersey Chapter of the Satan's Sinners, lived up to both his birth and road names.

He was the fucking *King* of that place, and when I'd ruled at his side as VP, I'd admit that shit was too easy. Things flew by me because

Rex was the kind of fucker who had everything under control, and because I could slack under his watch, I had.

I'd grown lazy.

Weak.

Here?

Nothing was under control.

Everything was chaos.

I hated it because addicts like me functioned best with monotonous, controlled schedules, but it was a challenge that I guessed I needed too. I couldn't rest on my laurels here. There was no Rex to save my ass.

I had to man up. In more ways than one.

I'd kill to be playing games with my kid right about now. To be eating leftover pie with Keira on my lap as we watched some dumb movie.

A knock sounded at my door, rupturing my contemplative state of mind, and I called out, "Come in."

I didn't bother twisting around to see who it was, just stayed staring out at fucking nothing because until tomorrow evening, that was the sum total of my life.

Nothing.

I was allowed in through the gates to my personal paradise once a day. I broke bread with the two girls who were my world. We sat and talked about our day as we ate, and then I was tossed out once again.

My whole day revolved around dinner. Twenty-four hours boiling down to a two-hour meal that I always dragged out because leaving added to the cracks in my soul, creating more and more pressure on the other splinters in my spirit.

Which rammed home the one truth I was learning to live by—there was no Storm without his girls.

"Prez?"

I recognized the voice as Little. Quite naturally, he was the size of a fucking mammoth. I pitied his hog, that was how goddamn big he was.

"What's up?" I asked tiredly, swiping a hand over my face.

God, I wanted nothing more than to climb into Keira's bed and just go to fucking sleep. I was so tired of being tired. So tired of missing what kept me awake.

"Bitch outside the gates, asking to come in."

"Bitch?" I frowned as he ambled into my line of sight, then my temper stirred and I growled, "That'd better not be my wife you're fucking talking about, Little."

His eyes flared wide, a smart prey reacting to the sudden awakening of a predator in its midst, as he quickly shook his head. "Naw, Prez, it ain't Keira. I'd never talk smack about your woman."

As his eyes widened further, *mine* narrowed more. "Good. You'd better fucking not."

Though Keira and Cyan had been living down here for a good six weeks, they'd only come to the clubhouse three times. That was enough for the guys and the clubwhores to recognize them, and for Keira to have left a great impression.

Not.

I didn't blame her, not with our history, but I wished she'd made an effort—even if it was only for her sake.

Before she'd thrown me out, she'd said she wanted to be a part of the Sinners. Here was her chance to merge into club life and she was snubbing it and the people under the clubhouse's roof.

Heaving a sigh, I asked, "What bitch, then?"

"She says she knows you. MaryCat's her name."

I straightened up and jerked to my feet. "MaryCat?"

My phone buzzed as I strode toward the door.

A quick glance at the Caller ID revealed that Lodestar, the latest addition to the Sinners' cyber armory, as well as a massive pain in the ass, was on the line.

As I connected the call, I barked, "I ain't got time for your games, Lodestar—"

"Fucking nerve," she ground out. "I know MaryCat arrived. Let her in, dumbfuck. She's got her kid with her."

Surprise filtered through me as I strode down the hall toward the front door, passing the bar which housed a lot of brothers smoking joints and cigarettes, drowning themselves in alcohol and pussy. All of those things were my goddamn vices and dragging my ass away from them was hard.

My addictions had me spending most of my time in my office. At least there, I got into less shit, but it meant I wasn't getting to know my brothers too.

Worse still, it meant they weren't adapting to me and the way that I worked. Which, pain in the ass that it was, would be something I'd have to fix soon.

Technically, they weren't supposed to smoke weed, but I allowed it. Anything harder I'd have to nip in the bud.

Butch, the Prez before me, had been hooked on coke, but so far no one else had revealed themselves to be addicts. Until they did, I'd let them get away with smoking pot, just because I liked secondhand sniffing it.

"You listening, asshole?" Star grumbled in my ear.

"No," I retorted even as I shoved open the door and found myself staring at a cab behind the gates. A quick glance at the back of the cab revealed a face peeking out of a hooded sweater, a swaddled baby in her arms that she had propped up against her shoulder. "What the fuck is she doing here? Has she left Digger?"

Christ.

If she had, I'd have to send her back to West Orange...

Unless he was beating on her.

But I couldn't see it. Digger'd never do that.

No.

He wouldn't.

I knew all my West Orange brothers. It was these fuckers here I didn't know.

"No, she's left her mother."

"Who the hell leaves their mother? Ain't she already left her considering she's branded up to her eyeballs?"

Considering the piece of work that MaryCat and my brother, Sin's, bitch egg donor was, I couldn't fucking blame them for pulling a disappearing act either.

Reaching up to rub the back of my neck, I stepped out into the snow, uncaring that I wasn't wearing a jacket and that heavy snowflakes were starting to fall.

Behind me, Little stomped while my booted feet merely crunched through the white covering the stone flags on the driveway. I swore the dude'd cause an earthquake if he were ever knocked out. Most of his mass was muscle and just sheer height. I'd never seen a fucker this tall be anything other than lanky, but not Little. Nope, he was like a human grizzly bear, especially with that massive beard of his.

"MaryCat can explain, but she called to tell me your fuckwits weren't letting her onto the compound. She doesn't have your phone number."

"Shame you do," I grumbled, even though I was relieved for Mary-Cat's sake. "What the hell's going on, Lodestar?"

"Her mom was trying to take the kid away from her. Digger's on a run for the club. I decided to help stage a breakout."

"A breakout?"

"You're dumber than usual, Storm. What's the problem? What aren't you understanding? I'm sure I'm speaking English."

I growled under my breath. "I swear to fuck I don't know how Maverick puts up with you."

"No one puts up with me," she growled back. "I don't need to be put up with, so fuck you."

Rolling my eyes, I motioned at Little. "Open the gates."

He ambled off, his Hulk ass moving far faster than it usually did, and I turned, watching as the gates opened. The taxi's engine stopped idling, and the driver carefully pulled into the driveway, braking to a halt at my side.

"Grab whatever's in the trunk," I called out to Little as I opened the door to the backseat and bent down to peer at MaryCat. "Honey, what the hell are you doing here?"

"Didn't you hear? Her mom tried to steal her kid? You've been in Coshocton too fucking long. You must have goddamn corn in your ears—"

Before Lodestar could keep on bitching at me, I cut the call, shoved my cell back into my jeans' pocket, ignored it when it immediately started ringing again, and prodded, "MaryCat?"

She swallowed, all big eyes and trembling mouth as the kid in her arms began to wail. "I had nowhere else to go."

Her evident fear had me pausing. "You leaving Digger? Is that what this is?" Had she lied to Lodestar to get her help?

"Oh, my God, no! I love Digger! I don't want to leave him!"

Her fervor surprised me, but I fell quiet as I studied her. "Lodestar wasn't bullshitting me then? Your mom really is trying to take the kid away from you?"

She nodded, but tears pricked her eyes. "I-I've not been doing too well." Her mouth trembled some more, and I cringed because I'd never been good with tears. Cyan's tears were one thing, Keira's another, but anyone else's? Nope.

My mom had been harder than fucking nails, and my baby sister, Scarlet, was much the same. I wasn't used to women who cried, so that had been another clusterfuck with Keira. I'd adapted over the years, probably badly, but MaryCat just made me want to dart back into my office.

Of course, the old Storm would have done that.

He'd have fucked off and left MaryCat to the clubwhores, getting one of them to settle her in, but this was Storm 2.0.

I was a different man.

A drug-free, sex-free, alcohol-free Storm.

The only contaminant that went into my body now was second-hand smoke from pot and tobacco, oh, and meat. I couldn't give that up, even though Cyan had turned vegetarian since she'd moved down here and bitched at her mom and me if we ate it.

I had no idea what that was about, but I wasn't going to question it, not when the alternatives were worse.

Sucking it up, I muttered, "Come on, let's get you inside." As she started to turn on the seat, I pulled back and saw Little was empty-handed. I frowned. "Where's your shit?"

"I don't have anything with me," she whispered rawly. "I had to get out of there. Fast. The taxi came with the car seat."

My brow puckered some more, but inwardly, I was cursing.

Fucking Lodestar.

Uncertain of what to do next, I did the sensible thing and moved over to the driver door.

The guy lowered his window and asked, "You gonna give me trouble over the bill?"

"Surprised you took the fare," I murmured as I cast a glance at the screen.

Jesus, a first-class flight would have cost less.

"I got kids to feed," was all the cabbie said.

I grunted. "Give me five minutes. We're good for it."

"I-I'm so sorry about the fare, Storm. I'll pay you back—"

Raising a hand to silence her, I muttered, "MaryCat, you need to chill out."

She bit her lip, then her eyes watered some more as she awkwardly grabbed a hold of her diaper bag and stacked it on her shoulder. That was when the kid started crying—he had some lungs on him, that was for sure.

"Come on, he must be cold."

Bobbing him up and down, she did her best, only the more the kid cried, the more she did too.

I kept an eye on her as we walked back up the path to the door, my hand on her elbow. It wasn't ideal moving her past the bar where there were all kinds of shit in the air, and I didn't want to raise attention to her or the kid just yet, so I murmured, "Want me to try? I used to get Cyan to sleep in a flash."

She blinked up at me, her eyelashes spiked up with tears. "Y-You wouldn't mind…?"

"Like I said, I used to be good with Cyan." Awkwardly, I shrugged. "It's okay, you don't have to—"

Her eyes were pretty much wild with desperation, which spoke of how damn long that car journey had been. So when MaryCat shoved the kid at me, I wasn't surprised. Just grabbed a tight hold of the swaddled bundle.

God, it had been a long time since I held a baby.

Long time since I'd had to deal with the weird scent of powder and lotion and soap and the soft remnants of piss and shit from a soggy ass.

My lips curved, though, as I tucked him against me, and immediately the little dude calmed down.

I shot MaryCat a look, saw her shoulders were slumped as she took us both in, and I asked, "What's his name?"

"Maddox."

I nodded. "Strong name."

"Digger picked it." Her tone was wooden as she stared at us both. "I-I think he misses his dad."

"Probably," I told her softly, aware of the cocktail of emotions in her voice. Jealousy and relief, misery and fatigue.

Keira hadn't had to deal with postpartum depression or anything that awful, but I remembered how quick to cry she'd been back then. How tired.

Jesus, I'd been just as bad.

Cyan had barely slept for the first three months. At least, it felt that way at the time. After twelve weeks of sleep deprivation, my ass had barely been able to function, never mind do math.

With the warm bundle now napping in my arms, I muttered, "Right, let's get to my office."

She gulped, nodded, and followed me to the back of the building. Once in there, I headed to the safe, and though with another brother, I'd have told them to fuck off while I opened it up, she wasn't another brother.

She belonged to the West Orange chapter.

That made her family—in a way the Coshocton guys might never be.

The office was larger than Rex's, consisted of a battered desk that barely survived the weight of my laptop or my legs when I propped them on there, a solid desk chair that was actually comfortable, a sofa on the back wall, a beaten-up coffee table, and some highly questionable artwork on the walls where a bunch of dogs played poker—real classy shit.

In the back corner, there was a free-standing safe for cash and another cabinet that housed the few weapons on the compound that were 'legal.' As for the rest, the corner opposite that one, in the window nook, was home to a bunch of houseplants.

I hadn't changed the room that much since moving in. Nothing except a quick paint because the walls were spattered with what looked like dried blood and cum, and even I couldn't live with that.

Either way, new paint job or not, that wasn't enough to combat over a decade of substance abuse. It stank of smoke, with a little hint of weed that made me crave a joint in a wicked way, one which the houseplants did nothing to combat.

All in all, it wasn't ideal bringing a newborn in here, and I really didn't want MaryCat to sit on the sofa, but she did, holding the diaper bag on her lap, clinging to it like it was a life raft.

Sin's half-sister was sitting on my fucking sofa.

The realization hit home just as I squatted down with Maddox still in my arms, opened up the safe, and grabbed the couple of Gs the taxi driver needed.

Activating the lock, I stood up, then asked, "You okay with me taking him outside?"

Her eyes were on her knees, and she nodded but stayed quiet.

"Hey," I chided softly, "it's okay to be tired."

Her mouth wobbled as she caught my gaze with hers. "He just... he was crying all the way down here."

"Could you feed him?"

She shook her head. "I breastfeed. I didn't want to—" She cleared her throat, then whispered, "Not with the driver able to see. We stopped once, but Maddox wouldn't take..."

"He's probably just hungry then, huh?" I shot her a calm smile. "I bet he starts crying for missing you the second I step out of the room."

"Maybe," she muttered, her misery clear to a blind man.

"I'll be two minutes," I told her quietly, aware that she was staring at her knees again.

When she didn't answer, I headed out of the office and started down the hallway again.

A clubwhore tripped out of the bar, her pupils dilated, her tits out.

"Back in there, Lolly," I ordered.

Last thing I wanted was for MaryCat to see that.

Of course, Lolly had other ideas.

She blinked, once, twice, before she puked in the hall.

Growling under my breath, I ducked my head into the bar, and hollered, "Get someone to clean this mess up."

And I wasn't just talking about Lolly.

Surprised the kid didn't utter a squawk at my roar, I peered down at him and saw his eyes were closed.

Babies were a conundrum sometimes.

Sitting in a moving car for eight hours, tucked up safe and sound in a car seat, his ma at his side, the kid didn't sleep. Take him to a clubhouse, past a bar full of bikers and bunnies fucking and partying, the little man rested.

Go figure, I thought with a laugh.

It took the kid of a biker to be so fucking difficult.

Grim staggered upright and hauled one of the clubwhores off her knees. As he zipped up his dick, he caught my eye and nodded, telling me he'd deal with it.

Grim wanted to be my VP, but I wasn't so sure. He hadn't been on the old council, but that didn't mean I trusted him.

Long story short, the last Prez's Old Lady had run the show more than he had, and because of her ties to the Italian mafia in New York, had compromised the Sinners by getting us involved with them. Which, as we were at war with the fucking *Famiglia*, was a goddamn problem.

Earlier in the year, when Sin had been exiled to Coshocton for failing to protect Giulia from the fucker with a death wish who'd attacked her, he'd found a way to get back home—he'd uncovered a pedophile's whereabouts.

Pedophiles were Giulia's Old Man's version of candy. So, with news of fresh meat, to Ohio Nyx had come, Old Lady at his side, along with Rex and, if memory served, Link and Steel.

It had been a real fucking road trip, one that ended with Nyx quieting his demons, Rex uncovering the truth behind the Ohio Chapter's pussy-whipped Prez, and Sin being able to return home despite his sins.

Of course, with a Prez-shaped hole in Coshocton, someone needed to fill the fucker, and that schmuck was me. Surrounded by men I didn't trust, trying to cobble together some form of leadership when I couldn't even cobble together my goddamn marriage. Talk about a match made in hell.

Blowing out a breath, I headed past the bar and back out into the cold. The kid shivered in my arms so I tucked my cut around him, which immediately made him coo—little dude really did miss his dad —and I shoved the money at the taxi driver who was starting to look nervous.

At least the bastard was smart.

He snatched the cash, then with a heavy roar of his engine, reversed out of the driveway with a squeal of his tires.

Behind me, on my way back to the clubhouse, Little closed the gates. Upon my return, I found Cinnamon cleaning up the puke, making gagging noises as she did so. Lolly was dead to the world, snoring at her side while Cinnamon glared at her.

Ever since I'd made it down here, the clubwhores had been giving me shit about fucking them, so I wasn't surprised when the gagging stopped as soon as Cinnamon caught a glimpse of me, and was doubly unsurprised when she started jiggling her tits some more.

Rolling my eyes at the sight, I strolled down to the back office, then heaved a sigh when I found MaryCat fast asleep on the sofa.

Peering down at the kid in my arms who was also fast asleep, I grunted under my breath.

"Today just keeps getting better and better."

THREE

KEIRA

THE FOLLOWING AFTERNOON

This Love - Camila Cabello

"CYAN? YOU WANT SOME LUNCH?"

When I received no answer for my pains, I felt the nerve in my left eye start to twitch.

I loved my baby girl.

I did.

I really did.

I just wished she weren't intent on driving me crazy.

When Storm was around, she was an angel.

When he left, she was a nightmare.

In fact, no, screw that.

Nightmare, capitalized.

Nudging through the freezer's contents, I took out my rage on a bag of carrots that were squished between a pack of chicken and the wall.

When a bunch of ice came flying out, followed by the pack of chicken which, of course, landed right on my toe, I growled under my breath as I did the 'of all the toes, in all the world, it had to drop onto mine' dance.

Hissing under my breath, I snatched up the chicken, grumbled at it, then called out, "Cyan?"

No answer.

Six weeks after she'd gotten into that pervert's car and somehow, things weren't much better between her and me. Now that Storm was eating here every night, I'd finally figured shit out—Cyan blamed me for us splitting up.

She blamed me when he was the two-timing, cheating—

I ground my teeth together as I shoved up the sleeves on my over-sized hoodie. I'd been living in the damn thing since we moved down here, *for her*, and I just couldn't seem to get my groove back.

In Jersey, I'd finally felt like I was starting to find my place. My position back in the real world—even if it was on the sidelines of the Satan's Sinners' MC.

Now, though, I felt the exact same way I did the day after I'd tossed him out.

I wanted to cry in bed, wanted to wallow and stare at the ceiling and have the TV on and just… God, just do nothing.

I wanted to just do nothing again.

But I'd already let her down once before by turning into a robot after I dumped him.

I couldn't do it again.

If she hated me for leaving, then I had actual concrete evidence that life really wasn't fair.

I'd only triggered our separation because I wanted to break the old ways, wanted her to know that a woman didn't have to take that kind of shit.

That she could and should leave when a man wasn't good enough for her.

And Storm wasn't.

He really wasn't.

Even if he was my darn soul mate, that didn't mean we were meant to be together.

Soul mates didn't get a free pass. They had to earn it. Personally, I needed self-respect more than I needed him to lie beside me in bed.

But God, *how* I missed him in my bed. His heat, his warmth, the way he didn't take up too much space—just enough. How he'd lie behind me, barely moving all night, curved into me, big spoon to my little.

How was I supposed to sleep for the rest of my life without that?

My throat choked up, and I closed my eyes.

Self-respect.

That was my new mantra.

How can you expect her *to respect* you *if you let a guy treat you this way? And what's to stop her from letting a man do the exact same thing to her as Storm did to you if you don't show her another way?*

Which led me to a simple conclusion—I was doing the right thing.

My mom had taught me the opposite. She'd taught me that it was okay for men to cheat so long as they kept it quiet, she'd taught me that men had urges a wife didn't want to withstand. Maybe if Kendra hadn't… My mouth tightened. I could have forgiven the cheating. It was the betrayal I couldn't forgive.

Whatever my reasons, I didn't want her to be like me. Didn't want her to grow up believing that cheating wasn't wrong.

If that meant suffering right now, well, I'd suffer.

But I'd probably get an ulcer in the process.

It'd be a righteous ulcer though, right?

Turning away from the fridge where I was trying to figure out what we were eating for the day, I hollered again, "Cyan! What do you want to eat?"

My refrigerator had morphed into a Whole Foods' store. Everything was vegetarian this and vegan-friendly that.

For someone who loved a good, old-fashioned beef burger, my kid was definitely trying to kill me with all this meat-substitute stuff, but I'd do anything to buy peace.

"Nothing!" she hollered over *High School Musical*, reminding me that she was still a preteen for all that she had the sass of a sixteen-year-old.

"God help me when she really *is* sixteen," I mumbled under my breath.

Grabbing some hummus—frickin' hummus when my ass was alllll about nacho cheese dip, none of this garbanzo bean crap—that was on the brink of going bad, I also hauled some sweet potato chips out of the cupboard and shoved them on the counter.

I couldn't make her eat.

Only Storm could do that.

Only Storm made her act like the little girl she used to be.

It was annoying and worrying and tiring, all at the same time.

We'd gone from being close to, in the span of a couple months, being enemies.

I knew I was her safe space. I guessed it was a compliment that she could offload onto me, because she knew I'd do my best not to let her down, but the truth was, she was only 'in the building' when her dad was.

I was starting to resent the hell out of Storm for that.

He was the reason for our break-up, not me, but I was the one dealing with the fallout. Something that meant that he had to be around if I wanted Cyan to do anything other than be a pain in the butt. That was beyond bittersweet. Being around him when he was like this *hurt*.

Take Christmas, for example. He'd been fun, Cyan had cheered the heck up, and it had been nice.

Really nice.

It had been like any other holiday before we'd split up.

Except, actually, it had been better.

I knew the truth now.

I knew why his eyes sometimes looked glassy. Why, sometimes, he looked like he felt as if his skin were crawling.

He was hyperactive at those times, moving fast and twitching—God, I should have seen the signs. I should have noticed that wasn't normal. I'd just thought that was his way.

We all possessed quirks, didn't we?

I got snappish when I had my period, but when he'd hugged me and held onto me like he'd never let me go, that always burned off my hormonal moods.

Food was a comfort, so I always sank into that when I was grumpy, too, and God forbid the laundry room was messy when I was feeling nervous because I'd organize the heck out of it to clear my mind.

Quirks.

Not addictions…

A whole world apart as I was coming to learn.

But he'd shown none of those signs two days ago. He'd been the Storm I'd fallen for.

The Storm that made me pine for him in the worst way.

He'd been *Asher*.

I closed my eyes, trying not to get upset, trying not to get angry. I bottled my emotions up and snuggled into my hoodie, the Sinners' one Storm had given me years ago, one that had a salsa stain on the front from last night's late-night binge session.

My cell buzzed, rupturing my pity party, and Storm's ringtone echoed through the kitchen.

Praying Cyan didn't hear it over the TV she was blasting in the family room—the only place she was allowed access to screen time now—I quickly silenced my phone and stared at the image that flashed on my phone.

It was of him and Cyan together, a picture I hadn't changed even when we'd split up. They were both grinning at each other, and I'd caught them just as Storm was kissing her on the nose.

Happier times.

Better times.

Or was that just a part of the larger charade?

Another lie that kept me quiet, another falsehood that made me think we were a happy family when we weren't.

I bit my lip, tempted not to answer. If he was calling now, that could mean he was going to cancel.

God, Cyan was going to be a nightmare if he didn't come over for dinner.

He hadn't done it before, but maybe six weeks was the period of grace? Maybe now, this was when the real Storm would show his true colors?

Tears pricked my eyes, based on fatigue, loaded with misery. I swiped my hand over them, tempted to toss the hummus and shitty sweet-potato tortilla chips all over the goddamn place just to mimic the chaos raging inside me.

A storm that was shaped like one man.

My ex-husband.

The man I craved. The man I missed. The man who'd ruined me and who'd broken me…

The man who, despite it all, I still loved.

What a moron I was.

My jaw clenched as I stared at the cell, at that picture, that goddamn smile. His devotion to Cyan was clear. It always had been.

Toward the end, before we'd broken up, that was when I'd known something was going on—he'd been distant.

He'd been skipping time at home, disappearing for weeks on end when the man, before, had only not slept in our bed when he was on a run.

That was why I'd gone hunting for answers, and Kendra, that bitch, had given them to me.

I reached for my cellphone, my hand aching as I clenched down on it. The desire to slam that into the kitchen counter was even stronger than the one that made me want to toss hummus everywhere. But the memories, the rage, the *hurt*, shored up my attitude like nothing else could.

So what, I didn't know anyone here in Coshocton. So what, I was floundering, wondering what to do here. That didn't take away from who and what I was.

A woman who deserved respect.

A woman who deserved to be loved.

A woman who deserved a faithful man.

Nostrils flaring after reading myself the riot act, I hit the connect button, and before I could say a word, before I could snap at him in self-righteous anger, he rumbled, "Keira, I need your help."

If I hadn't just been working myself up like a pro athlete before the big game, I'd have sighed at his voice.

That rumble.

That fucking rasp.

Everything about him was designed to make me weak at the knees.

That streak of silver in his hair, the soft strands on his chest that my fingers tangled with as I traced the 'Cyan' tattoo on his pec, that voice that could convince a saint to sin.

"Keira? You there, baby girl?"

My brows lifted even as I squirmed at the endearment. He hadn't called me that in ages, and I missed it.

Jerk.

Bastard.

Lying, cheating, disease-ridden, padlocked-dick prick!

Don't you dare forget, Keira. I won't let you!! He was getting blowjobs when you were bedridden. Yeah. BED. RIDDEN. Don't you dare forget. Don't you dare—

"What kind of help?" I preempted his reply with a growled, "I'm not telling Cyan you're not making it for dinner. If that's why you're calling—"

"Keira!"

"—you can do your own dirty work," I finished, ignoring his bark of my name.

"I wasn't asking for that. Of course, I'll be there for dinner."

Even as relief sank into my bones, a relief that wasn't just for my kid, I snarked, "I'll make sure it's veggie burgers then."

'Of course, I'll be there for dinner.'

Like we were his priority.

If only we'd been that before.

He groaned. "You're a cruel woman. When's she going to get out of this phase? I miss beef."

God, so did I. I couldn't even bitch at him about that. I was so sick of meat substitutes.

"I think it started with Katina and Lodestar, you know they're both vegan, but Dr. Janowicz does say it's a way for Cyan to control her environment. Better this than bulimia," I reminded him softly of what our therapist had said, even as panic whirred in my brain.

How was it Cyan was at a risk for this stuff? How had my life derailed so much? She was eleven, not seventeen!

He heaved a sigh. "Of course, it is. It's just those burgers are fucking gross."

My lips formed a half-grimace, and a half-smile—I understood his pain entirely.

Rather than commiserate with the adulterous bastard, I demanded instead, "Okay, what is it? What do you need help with?"

"You know MaryCat?"

Surprised, I tilted my head to the side. "Yeah?"

MaryCat, or her nickname MC, was one of the West Orange Old Ladies. I'd never really gotten to know her.

From the start, I'd fitted in badly with them, the differences between my upbringing and most of the Old Ladies had been too stark, and when I'd made no attempt to get to know them, Storm hadn't forced the issue. Especially when I'd allowed Rene into our lives. She and Bear had been the only ones I'd really opened up to.

"She's here."

"She's here? In Coshocton?" I frowned. "Thought she was in Manhattan. Didn't she give birth there?" I lifted my hood up, covering my hair with it, trying to hide from the fact that I wished to hell I was in Manhattan and not Ohio.

You knew your homesickness was bad when you actually frickin' missed Manhattan.

I'd begun to fit in with the new wave of Old Ladies, and despite the move, I was still included in their group chat. There, Tiffany, Mary-Cat's sister-in-law, had sent us a photo of mother and baby in a fancy clinic in the city.

"She did, but she's here now. She ran away."

"Ran away? She's a little old for that, isn't she?" I teased, thinking he was joking.

"Something to do with her mom trying to steal the kid or something," he muttered, then he made this hushing sound, a sound that made my ovaries twinge because I remembered it.

"You're holding the baby, aren't you?" I whispered, reaching up and rubbing at my forehead.

He fell silent. "How the hell did you know that?"

Because that sound was reminiscent of the times he'd put Cyan to bed. When she'd been a baby, he'd been all in. Every night, apart from when he was on a run, he'd danced her to sleep.

I'd watched him.

Even when I was exhausted, I'd watched him.

Usually it was Motown—Storm liked Marvin Gaye—sometimes it was something more modern.

Every frickin' night, he'd danced with her, and every frickin' night, I'd fallen harder for him.

Our marriage had a rough start, but how he'd been with Cyan had calmed me down, had helped me see that he was in this for the long haul.

Of course, I'd only *thought* he was all in.

He'd been banging clubwhores while I'd fallen hook, line, and sinker deeper into love with him.

The bastard.

The shithead—

Before I could condemn him some more, the baby fussed and he started humming.

Seriously, my heart broke open.

'Blurry' by Puddle of Mudd.

I knew that song. It was one of his favorites and one of mine as a result.

Excuse me while I bawled my eyes out.

Feeling choked up and resentful for it, I rasped, "What do you want me to do?"

"MaryCat's been asleep ever since she arrived last night, and she's still stone cold on my sofa in the office and we both know how funky that is. Plus, the kid's being a kid." He heaved a sigh. "Babe, I'm sorry to ask, but I got church in an hour. I can't go in there with a baby."

"You want me to come sit there?"

"Yeah. If you don't mind. I'll drive you back if we finish late. Lots of Old Ladies are here with their kids as well, and I'd ask them but she doesn't know them—"

"Why are they there?" I questioned, my brow furrowed.

"It's a tradition here." I heard the shrug in his voice. "Apparently, when the men have church, the women and kids get together too."

"What about emergency church? Do you call them in for a quick potluck dinner?"

"Mockery, Keira? *Et tu, Brute?*"

Smirking, I commented, "You're okay with all that? The family vibe?"

"Already changed a lot about the place. Ain't interested in changing that shit up, not when I'm as much of a family man as they are.

"If I were Rex, then maybe it'd piss me off, but I ain't him. Plus, it comes as no surprise. I told you what happened to the other Prez, didn't I?"

I hummed, well aware that the last guy to hold Storm's position had let his woman worm her way into power over the MC.

So accustomed to the Sinners in West Orange, the very notion was alien to me, but I almost applauded her for her balls.

It was so easy to get pushed aside, to have to stick to the perimeter when these men of ours were one foot in jail and one foot out.

Even as I thought she was smart, I knew she was also dumb.

Getting the Sinners to fraternize with the enemy against the Mother Chapter's orders? That was more than just asking to get your ass killed, it was begging for it.

Of course, that was something I'd come to learn recently. During our marriage, I'd barely known what he did for a living, aside from the fact riding with the MC took him away from the house for days on end.

He'd kept Cyan and me and his life at the club completely separate, but I couldn't blame him for that—I'd started that, and over the years it had snowballed out of control.

I blamed my naïveté and youth for failing to settle in.

Maybe things would have been different if I'd been a more integral part of club life?

"Cyan's being difficult so I don't know if she'll want to come," I said with a sigh, dragging a lock of hair behind my ear. "Anyway, I'm not—"

"Did Daddy call? Is that him?"

Sitting bolt upright, I twisted around and saw my daughter, all five feet of her, skidding toward me, her glee quite clear.

She made grabby hands for the phone, and I winced as she

snatched it from me, almost dropping it in her haste to get the damn thing before squealing, "Daddy!"

When she started to turn away, I reached for her shoulder and held her in place. She scowled at me, but then her bottom lip popped out. "Are you calling to cancel dinner?"

I didn't hear his reply, but I felt it. That low rumble called to me even over the sound waves.

A part of me wanted to cry at somehow being the enemy in this situation, but her joy at speaking with her father had happiness welling up inside me.

Before I'd had her, I'd believed my mom was inherently weak. There'd always been a distance between us, and I'd watched her take Dad's criticisms, had frowned over the way he treated her and controlled her.

The older I got, the more he'd done the same with me, until I'd begun testing the bonds of his control.

It had made my rebellion with Storm seem even sweeter… which, of course, was how I found myself in this position all these years later. It was only now, however, that I recognized the truth.

Mom had done her best.

Just as I had.

Was doing.

It wasn't enough.

Some days, I was pretty sure it'd never be enough.

Christ, being a mom was hard. Harder than I could have imagined. Harder than they talked about in home ec.

"Daddy wants to talk to you," she said, her tone less surly than before but the resentment was still there.

"We need to work on her attitude," Storm rumbled, and my ear drums melted, as did the ice around my heart. "She's turning into a real little bitch with you."

I winced. "She's not a bitch."

"A little one—I modified it because I love her."

Snorting, I muttered, "You're all heart!"

"Don't I know it." He huffed out a breath. "Goddammit, this kid has just shit again. I swear, there's some kind of evolutionary tactic that makes you forget how much babies crap."

Despite myself, I chuckled. "You remember Cyan? How she was in one cloth diaper for about ten minutes then we had to change it?"

"Always had a goddamn bottle in her mouth," he agreed. "I remember. Attitude or not, I prefer it now that she can deal with the bathroom herself."

Amusement growing, I asked, "Why don't you just wake MaryCat up? I don't know if she'd want me looking after her baby.

"I was really possessive after I gave birth to Cyan. If anyone other than you or I went near her, I was pretty feral. I didn't even like Rene holding her."

"I remember those days," he murmured softly, something catching in his words that ensnared me, just for a moment, before he reasoned, "She was okay with me taking care of him, and anyway, I want her to sleep. She looks exhausted.

"Plus, I called Digger. He says he's on his way here ASAP, but he's on a run so I don't know when that'll be, and he told me she has post-partum depression."

Wincing on MaryCat's behalf, I shoved away my selfish desire to never go anywhere near the clubhouse as that made up my mind for me.

Still...

"You sure you want me there?"

He hesitated. "What do you mean?"

I worked my bottom lip between my teeth. "You sure you want me there?" I repeated, not willing to change the question, not willing to elaborate.

A hiss escaped him, and I heard jangling, like his keys were dancing as his agitation grew. "Keira, that had better not be an ass backward way of asking if I don't want you here because there are clubwhores I've fucked."

It was stupid of me, so stupid, but I reached down and grabbed the key I'd hung on a leather strip that I wore around my neck.

The act of wearing it like a necklace was ridiculous enough, but the need to touch what he claimed belonged to me was impossible to avoid.

Not when I was so insecure where he was concerned.

So pathetically insecure.

The thought had me closing my eyes even as I fingered the key he claimed was the singular way to open up the goddamn padlock on his dick.

Yes, the man had put a padlock on his dick.

I still couldn't get over it.

Still couldn't deal with it.

My ex-husband, the cheating rat bastard, had gotten a piercing, then instead of threading a ring through it like any other normal person, he'd slipped a padlock through the tip.

A heavy one.

An uncomfortable one.

One so large that it made me wince when I glanced at his crotch which, of course, I did every time he visited.

Now that I knew it was there, I couldn't stop playing peekaboo with it.

God help me.

He claimed the only key to that padlock was the one I wore around my neck.

He'd lied to me a lot over the years, so I had to question whether I could believe that now or not, but for whatever reason, I was wearing the damn thing. So that meant I *did* believe him, didn't it?

"Keira? I know you're there."

Licking the lips I'd just been worrying with my teeth, I rasped, "I don't know what to believe anymore, Storm."

He grunted. "Trust is earned, Keira, I know that."

He sounded disappointed, not angry, which had my shoulders straightening, a weird relief filling me. I'd half-expected him to be resentful, but he was surprisingly patient with me too. It wasn't something he bestowed solely on Cyan.

I didn't apologize, even though the words were on the tip of my tongue, instead, I mumbled, "They're going to treat me like the Prez's wife."

A soft laugh escaped him. "That's because you are, Keira. Whether you decide to go through with the divorce or not, you know Sinners don't work that way.

"The wedding was for your parents—not that it ever got them to approve of me—but you're my wife—"

"Until you pick someone to fill my shoes," I sniped.

"Ain't gonna happen," was his calm, resolute response to that.

"If you say so."

"I do."

His resolve didn't fill me with peace, just confusion. "Why couldn't you have made this decision all those years ago?"

He made a soft noise that told me the baby was fussing again. "Because I was young, foolish, and to be frank, an asswipe.

"If Cyan comes home with a dipshit like me when she's eighteen, don't worry, I'll handle him."

A shocked laugh escaped me. "Going to feed him to the pigs?"

"Yeah," he said gruffly. "I deserve worse, but I—" He hesitated. "I'm not sure how to make this right, Keira. You know that. We've talked about it. Maybe there's no way I can, and that's on me. I just... Never mind, you don't need to hear that.

"Can you come, honey? I need your help. MaryCat *really* needs your help. If she don't want you looking after him, can't think she'd want a fucking sweetbutt holding her kid."

I hadn't needed that particular trigger to be pulled, but the mention of sweetbutts holding an Old Lady's child was like a cattle prod to my spine. I stiffened and informed him, "I'll be there in less than an hour."

"Thanks, babe."

Babe.

He cut the call.

Babe.

Even though I needed to rush, I opened the messaging app that had my group chat with the West Orange Old Ladies and typed out:

Me: *Storm asked me to look after MaryCat's baby.*

Lily: *Huh?*

Tiffany: *MaryCat? As in OUR MaryCat? My sister-in-law MaryCat?*

Me: *Apparently, yeah. She's here.*

Tiffany: *Sin didn't tell me she was coming to visit with you.*

Me: *Sounds like it was a surprise all round. She's passed out cold in Storm's office.*

Tiffany: *What the hell happened?*

Giulia: *I hear gossip.*

Me: *More than just gossip. I'll report back when I know more.*

Lily: *You doing okay down there, honey? You've been quiet.*

Me: *It's crazy to me that I miss West Orange when I hate the place… I guess I miss you guys and everything.*

Giulia: *Is Cyan still acting up?*

Me: *In front of everyone but her dad. Lol.*

Giulia: *Is Storm dealing with it?*

Me: *He mentioned just now that her attitude is getting out of hand.*

Giulia: *Good, he needs to get that under control. She okay with everything else?*

By everything else, she was talking about the fact that my baby girl had been goddamn groomed by a fifty-year-old pervert.

That she'd willingly gotten into a car with him.

That she'd done so because the bastard had promised to take her to her daddy after they visited Disney World together.

The thought was more than just a knife to the gut. It was like someone stabbed me, twisting the knife over and over and over and over again, forcing that goddamn blade deeper, making the hole ten times bigger until the gut rot overtook me, killing me from the inside out.

I'd done that.

Somehow, I'd made her this way.

It had to be my fault, right? They always blamed the parents…

Rather than write it all out, I sent them an audio note.

"Ladies, I'll let you know what's going on with MaryCat. As for You Know Who, she's doing okay, as much as she can be, I think. Therapy's hard, mostly for me, but, yeah, it's all good." It was. Technically. I just felt like shit. "I gotta go help MaryCat. Speak later."

Before I could be convinced to speak with them further, before I could really open up about how tense things were at home, how Storm was fucking with my head by being so understanding and pleasant and not blaming me for anything all while being, well, *him*, alongside how much I hated Coshocton, I slipped my cell into my pocket.

"Cyan, get your things together. We're going to spend some time at the clubhouse," I hollered as I left the kitchen.

Of course, like the little biker princess she was, the news had her hooting with glee.

Of course, the last thing *I* was was a biker princess.

As I climbed into the shower to wash up and to change out of my dirty clothes, I wished I felt half as happy about a trip to the clubhouse.

DEAR KEIRA

You smiled back at me today. Not like before. Where it was accidental. We shared the smile. We shared a look.

It was... weird.

I loved it.

You saw me.

You really saw me.

I know you did.

You were smiling at that fucker in front of you, one of those teen pricks who probably can't keep his dick in his pants, and when he does, makes a two-pump chump look good in the sack, but then you saw me.

Your smile faltered, turning hesitant, before it widened some.

You don't know how that smile kept me going.

You don't know what it stopped me from doing.

Today was not a good day.

Mom OD'd.

I know what you're thinking.

Why would I want to score the same fucking thing that could have killed her?

But Christ, I wanted... I don't know what I wanted. I really don't.

I'm not just saying that. You're never going to see this fucking letter. I can be honest with you. I just... I guess I wanted some peace.

I find some of my own when I look at you.

I felt it today when you looked at me.

And your smile? That made me feel like I was fucking flying.

Maybe together, we will.

Who am I kidding?

As if you'd ever look at a loser like me.

Did you know that five grams of crack could get me a five-year federal prison sentence? But five-hundred grams of powdered cocaine would have me serving the same time? It's the same shit, but rich city boys sniff cocaine and poor bitches like my ma use crack.

She was hooked on crack both times she gave birth to both my sister and me. Lucky ol' me, she was in jail at the time of my birth.

Rene—she's the Prez's Old Lady—helped look after us whenever Mom got shoved behind bars. That's probably why she's more like my mother than my own. If anything happened to Rene, I'm not sure what I'd do.

I guess it's sad that I hate my own flesh and blood so much that I'm kinda annoyed she didn't die. I wouldn't miss her or grieve for her if the doctors hadn't managed to resuscitate her.

She's a reminder. One I don't want or need of who I am. What I am.

You're so pure, Keira. Do you know that? Do you see that in yourself?

I'm so fucking dirty in comparison.

You deserve more than a guy who was hooked on crack before he even took his first breath.

So I'll watch you.

I'll crave your smiles.

I'll dream of something that'll never be.

And maybe, just maybe, it'll stop me from heading to my dealer.

Storm

FOUR

STORM

PRESENT

Welcome To The Jungle - Guns & Roses

KEIRA SHOWED up with ten minutes to spare, early like usual. That was Keira.

Solid.

Punctual.

Earnest.

A good girl.

One I corrupted by breathing the same air as her.

One I loathed corrupting, and one I was compelled to corrupt even more.

Just the memories of us together had my dick twitching. The discomfort that triggered filled me with a blessed relief.

I kept upping the gauge on my padlock piercing, needing the pain to combat the sweetness of the lust I felt.

It made even the beginnings of a semi excruciating.

That bite of agony was my atonement.

She'd never know, of course, but she didn't have to.

I did.

The pain stopped the pleasure, but it kept me on the straight and narrow. A path that would never guide me back to Keira, but that didn't mean I had to stop trying to be worthy of her.

My kid, ever exuberant, barreled her way out of the car like she was being chased by rabid dogs. I watched as her feet got tangled up in her backpack, but she didn't go flying—nope, she was way too flexible for that.

Instead, she hit the ground running as she rushed toward me, squealing, "Daddy!"

Cy's voice was so high pitched that Maddox squirmed in my arms. I'd have dealt with him bawling his eyes out though because I loved how excited she was to see me.

Some days, I felt like she was the only person who was happy to be a part of my life.

Some days, she was the only reason I got out of bed.

Years of self-destructive thoughts plagued me, but a smile from my baby girl, a soft huff of laughter from her mother as Cyan collided into me, enough force behind the move that I staggered back a half-step, kept those thoughts at bay.

She squealed some more as I swept down, tucked my arm under her butt and hauled her up.

Cy was a tiny thing still, fragile, all long limbs and skinny bones that she somehow managed to contort for gymnastics.

She giggled as she clung to me much as she had when she was a toddler, and when her arms went around my neck and she nuzzled into me, I swore I wanted to cry.

Christ, what a pussy.

But if I was gonna melt, then I figured it was fitting that the baby girl I could have lost was what triggered those goddamn tears.

Put me in the middle of a fucking showdown between two bikers who had guns cocked at each other's heads and I'd be fine.

Absolutely fine-and-fucking-dandy.

Throw my kid at me, remind me what had almost happened to her, have that memory plague me while fear swirled around my being as I thought about how easy it would have been for her to have been killed…

Yeah, you had a broken man on your hands.

No shame in that when the stakes were so high.

"What are you going to do when you're too old for me to pick up?" I teased, squeezing her tighter because I didn't want her to let go while I clung onto a squirming Maddox just to make sure he wouldn't fall from my arms.

Not that I had to worry for long. Keira was there, hers outstretched, and as the kid settled against her tits, I found myself envious.

Envious.

What I'd give to rest my head against those tits.

Keira had the best tits. She was all self-conscious about them, usually wore those push-up bras that made my dick weep precum, but when she was at the house, when I caught her alone and she thought I wasn't around, I saw her go braless.

I'd sacrifice my left hand for a titty fuck. Those ripe curves of hers jiggling all around my flesh—

I grunted as the pain slammed into me.

Rightful pain.

Cleansing pain.

It took a second for me to focus on what Cy was saying as she chided me with another giggle, one I felt in my soul.

"I'll never be too old for you to pick me up, silly."

My mouth twisted into a rueful grin as her belief in me settled in my gut. "How about when I get too weak to lift you?"

She pshawed. "You're the strongest man in the world!"

My gaze clashed with her mother's.

How I wished that were true, I told her silently, just as she told me that right back. *How I wished you'd been strong enough to be the man I deserved…*

God, she was beautiful.

Just as beautiful as when she was eighteen and I'd first seen her at West Orange's high school. I'd been there to pick up a Prospect whose ride had died on him, and I swore to fuck, I still felt the power of that first look between us.

Sometimes, whenever we stared at one another, it still felt like it did back then.

Her hair had been a lot lighter at eighteen, now it was a hundred shades of gold, some dark, some light. It framed her face, the shape that of my heart goddamn breaking whenever I looked at her.

Hazel eyes that erred more toward brown than green and were like living quartz gemstones gleamed back at me. She had the smallest button nose that Cyan had inherited, a delicately pointed chin, and high cheekbones that gave her the air of a fairy.

I was pretty certain that was why Cyan looked the way she did—as if she could fly away at any given moment with those bird-like arms and legs of hers.

Keira, on the other hand, was all curves. Always had been, and I prayed, always fucking would be.

Back when I was a teenager, I'd fallen hard for Shannon Doherty in *Beverly Hills 90210,* and Keira had that same kind of look without the resting bitch face and was somehow a thousand times hotter as a result.

She was born to make my dick detonate—if my head wasn't so far shoved up my ass that I managed to fuck everything up, of course.

I squeezed Cyan while I could, while she wasn't too cool to do this, while she was insecure and vulnerable about what had happened and was in need of this kind of reassurance, as I murmured, "I really appreciate this, Keira."

She didn't answer that, just peered down at Maddox. "Goodness, he's young."

Goodness.

That was Keira, a minister's daughter.

It was only recently that she'd started dropping F-bombs, and they came few and far between.

When we were first married, every time I swore, she flinched like I'd hit her. It'd made me curb my language around her, made me curb a lot of stuff.

That was when things had started to go wrong, when it had begun to resonate that angels didn't mate with demons for a reason…

"Well, he just popped out," I answered her with a soft smile.

Her nose crinkled. "If only it were that easy."

"Yeah, unlike you, ladybug," I teased Cyan, hugging her harder again. "Forty-two hours of torture."

Cyan grinned. "All good things are worth waiting for."

Laughter barked out of me at that comment, surprisingly adult in contrast to the way she was clinging onto me like she'd done when she was tiny. Well, tinier than she was now.

Shaking my head, I told her, "You know you owe your mom, right?" I squinted at her, an intentness to my gaze that I knew she registered because she tried to look away. "All that pushing and heaving just for you to be mean to her now." I clucked my tongue. "We're all trying here, ladybug. Everyone apart from you."

Her brow puckered. "I *am* trying."

"You need to be kinder to your mom."

Though Cyan had found out that I'd cheated on Keira while she was pregnant, for some reason, she still blamed her mom.

I was at a loss at how I could make this better.

I was totally at fault, but not in Cyan's eyes. This wasn't something I could have foreseen, and it concerned me.

As grateful as I was that she didn't hate me, her irrational need to be close to me at all times freaked me out. I deserved her hatred. Yet she focused her displeasure on her mom.

The unfairness of it made me want to fix things, but I didn't know how.

A squawk escaped Maddox who shoved his face harder against Keira's tits, who said around a laugh, "There's no milk there, baby."

Though I laughed when he carried on nosing her chest, on the hunt for milk, I felt Cyan stiffen up at my side. "That's so gross."

"Why is it?" I queried, cocking a brow at her. "That's what you did."

"It's still gross."

"Hey. It isn't. It's completely natural. He wants his mom."

"Yeah, well, she isn't *his* mom, is she? She's mine."

I frowned when she untangled herself from my hold and went rushing into the clubhouse, veering toward the bar.

That was when I called out, "Cyan! Do *not* go in there! Family room only!" Turning back to Keira once I saw she'd obeyed, I arched a brow. "You know what that was about?"

"She doesn't want me to be her mom but doesn't want me to be anyone else's mom either?"

My frown only deepened. "She doesn't feel that way."

"Doesn't she?" Her mouth tightened even as she bounced Maddox. "Okay, I'm here, you can go do Prezidential stuff."

I snorted at her emphasis on the 'Z' sound, but rather than take off like she said, I stepped closer to her and cupped the back of Maddox's head. "He's fussy."

"Probably misses his momma."

"Maybe."

"Is she still sleeping?"

"Yeah. Going on thirteen or so hours now."

Her eyes widened. "Holy shit, she must be in agony!"

"Agony? Why?"

"Don't you remember? She needs to express her milk."

"Babe, the last mom I was around was you and that was eleven years ago," I said dryly.

"Take me to your office," she stated, with enough command to her tone that my dick twitched again.

Ouch.

I swept a hand out, much like Prince Charming might have done, then murmured, "This way, Madam First Lady."

Her brow puckered with annoyance, but I saw the sliver of amusement in her eyes before she turned her head away and stepped ahead of me.

Keira knew exactly where my office was, had been inside the first time I'd brought her here. She didn't need to wait on me, and she didn't. Simply stormed down the hallway like the queen she was.

When she shut the office door in my face, I barely refrained from laughing, but relieved that she was okay with handling MaryCat, I backtracked to the family room, wanting to check in on Cyan.

Along the way, I saw the bar was quieter than usual.

The clubwhores were under orders not to suck dicks or fuck in public with the kids and Old Ladies around, and that had nothing to do with me.

The last Prez's Old Lady might have been scum, but she knew how to keep the bunnies in line so that was something I didn't have to waste time on.

The family room was the largest communal area in the whole building, which told me that at some point, a Prez had a large family, one that mattered to him.

There were several seating areas, blocked off with how the sofas and armchairs were clustered together in squares, circles, or rectangles. Hell, there was even a fucking triangle.

One corner was dedicated to younger kids, with all kinds of toys and shit for toddlers and upward—at least, I thought I remembered Cyan playing with something similar to that plastic crap when she was tiny.

Another corner had more grown-up games and a long bench table where older kids were currently playing what looked like Monopoly and Clue together. When it wasn't school break, I'd seen them doing their homework there as well.

The vibe was decidedly different than in West Orange where, after the death of Rex's mom, everything had changed.

Maybe that was why I couldn't seem to settle here.

What I knew was at odds with what I was experiencing.

Corruption had run rife in this chapter, to the point where Rex had had the last Prez killed, while a good chunk of the council, and the rest of the fuckers involved with the *Famiglia,* had either run off or gotten their asses handed to them.

For all that, family still mattered here.

The concept smacked of a dissonance that didn't gel with me, even as I was relieved for that family vibe because I saw Cyan over by the table, already playing Monopoly with Slayer's kid.

At least, I thought it was Slayer's.

Could have been Jump's.

These fuckers bred like rabbits down here.

There were barely any kids in WO, but the Coshocton chapter was rammed full with them.

Guessed that was what happened when you were in a state that taught abstinence in health class...

Snorting at the thought, I determined that Cyan would know what a fucking condom was before she hit fifteen, and that she was on the pill even if it meant having to ride up to goddamn New Jersey to get the prescription from Stone.

I retreated from the family room, content that she was busy, and headed toward the other end of the hall for the room where church was held.

That was another difference.

Church went down in Rex's office.

Not here.

A massive table ran down the center of a room that was named after the meetings held there, 'church,' and the space around it was large enough that I could call all the brothers into it if required.

I wasn't sure if it had been like this when Rex had come down, and to be frank, I wasn't bothered enough to question it. I had a feeling that changes had been made without a Prez's presence, and I wasn't about to argue the difference either.

I didn't mind more communal meetings, especially when I didn't know the brothers, didn't know what made them tick, and sure as fuck didn't know whether to trust them.

As far as I'd gathered, the ones on the up and up were the guys with kids. They couldn't afford to pick their families up and run from the Sinners' Mother Chapter.

That didn't mean I trusted them blindly though.

I might have been an idiot for most of my life, but where business was concerned, I was as sharp as a tack, and for the first time, I was being allowed to shine so I wasn't about to let Rex down.

Church today was different, that was why I had thirty men in here rather than the whole chapter.

I had some decisions to make, and I couldn't put it off any longer, which was why I'd brought Keira in.

God, I wished she were here just so I could bend her over my desk.

Fuck.

Her hair was getting longer, tangling around her face in messy waves. I'd loop that around my wrist, arching her back while I shoved my dick into her…

A hiss escaped me as my padlocked prick responded to the stimuli, and I forced myself to stop thinking about her crying out my fucking name, begging for my cock, begging for *me.*

Thoughts like those would get me nowhere other than the ER with a mangled cock for my pains.

Taking the safer option, I dipped my chin in response to the few brothers who greeted me while I moved over to the head of the table, taking a seat and settling in for a meeting that was going to be tedious as hell.

Most of the guys plunked their asses down after I did, sitting on one of the hodgepodges of chairs that filled the space.

This chapter was run down, the furniture old, and it spoke of how the last Prez had shortchanged his men. Refurbishing this place was on my to-do list, but I was putting it off, hoping Keira would take over and do it for me.

Maybe, just maybe, I could start getting her to do shit like that.

She'd stormed over to MaryCat like that was her problem. Like any good Prez's wife would have…

She was born for this job, much as I was. I'd just never thought we'd be doing this in Coshocton, much as I'd never really been able to imagine myself leading West Orange when that was Rex's territory.

Weird, huh?

Casting a glance over the men, I rumbled, "You guys know why you're here. You've been patient with me, and I appreciate it, but learning the lay of the land, getting to know you all, it took some time—"

"Didn't help you spent a good couple of weeks over in West Orange," someone grumbled.

The interruption had me scowling. "Who the fuck do you think you are interrupting me like I'm some bitch?" I snarled, shoulders bunching with outrage, slamming to my feet. "Show your fucking face."

Belligerent to the last, Grim straightened into a standing position, living up to his name by flashing his miserable mug to the rest of the room. "You should have stayed here. You're our fucking Prez now, man. Not their VP."

Well aware that he wanted to be *my* VP, I squinted at him. "The Mother Chapter needed our help. *My* help."

"They got other brothers to do that."

"Only thing *you're* doing right now is proving that you shouldn't sit at this goddamn table."

"I ain't afraid to speak up when you're wrong," he countered, his jaw firming. "You were wrong to leave."

Some mutterings snapped up, and because there were so many men watching, I knew I couldn't let it slide. I shoved my fists to the table and loomed over it. "You forget, fuckers, because your last Prez was a piece of shit, that the Sinners are family.

"Whether they're in West Orange, Butte, or here, we're all on the same goddamn side. We all help each other out, and if you've got a problem with that, then you're in the wrong place and need to fuck off.

"The Mother Chapter's clubhouse was bombed. There wasn't a fire in the kitchen, a raid didn't go down. There was a fucking blast. It was destroyed. Completely obliterated.

"We had a moral obligation to help out, just as they'd do the same if we needed them. The construction guys who came with me got that, but if you don't, Grim, then again, I repeat, you're proving yourself unworthy of the position of VP."

His eyes narrowed upon me. "That so-called Mother Chapter came in here and slaughtered our brothers—"

"Who were helping scum out," I retorted, not appreciating the way he was hurling shit at me. "Again, I repeat, if you've got a fucking problem, you know where the door is."

Grim hitched a shoulder. "I ain't going nowhere, but a man's got a right to say his piece, and that's my piece."

Surprised, I glowered at him as I moved around the table, well aware that he tensed up as I leaned my ass back against it. "So you wait until the day I announce my councilors?" I asked him softly.

"Why not? Best to get grievances out, no? Better to air them than let them fester."

"You for real? Sit your ass down, man. No one asked for you to stand up like you're Nancy fuckin' Pelosi."

His chin butted out. "Never been realer. I ain't gonna lick your ass, Storm. Sure, you're from the almighty West Orange chapter, and sure, you're the Prez, but it ain't in my nature. I told you my issues—"

I was in his face before he could take his next breath. Not about to take any shit, from him or any of these fuckers, my hands snapped to the edges of his cut and I hauled him against me, shoved my face into his space and snarled, "Sometimes, it's wiser to keep your mouth fucking shut."

Tension soared through the air like a bad smell, but I didn't fail to notice that not a single brother stood up for Grim or tried to get me to back off.

He shoved me away, or tried to, but the pussy couldn't get me to let go. I tightened my hold on his cut until the chokehold began to take effect on his neck.

His face turned bright red fast, and as he tried to scramble away and started spluttering, I rasped, "You come to me with this kind of shit in private. You do *not* disrespect me in public."

"If I were your VP, I wouldn't hold back if I didn't agree with you," he gasped, fingers prying at mine, trying to get me to let go of him. His eyes began to bulge as my hold tightened, not lessened, and he choked, "Seems to me that everyone in this room sides with me but ain't said shit."

"Ain't no one stood up for you, period," I scoffed, throwing him down against his chair. The legs buckled under his weight, but mostly, he just skidded backward, his arms flying as he tried to stabilize himself. "Stay the fuck in your seat and make sure that goddamn mouth of yours keeps shut.

"You're right—I don't need someone who'll kiss my ass. What I do need is men on my council who've got fucking sense. Unlike you, dipshit."

Turning my back on him, well aware that he could attack but not believing he had the balls to do so, I returned to the table then scanned the men.

Most of 'em looked uncomfortable. On edge. Not angry. Not even as if they were in agreement, but maybe they were too pussy to say anything like Grim made out.

Either way, now he'd raised this subject, I wasn't about to let it drop.

The guys in here were the ones I was interested in ruling at my side. We were still missing some brothers who were working on rebuilding the clubhouse back home, but from Grim's bitterness, I knew I could have a problem on my hands.

This was the first time I'd noticed something amiss, but it was also the first time I hadn't just been going through the motions of ruling the place, trying to get it back on track. After everything with Cyan, I just hadn't had the energy to make waves.

Having pissed six weeks away, though, and just before the new year, I knew that I had to get my ass in gear.

I narrowed my eyes at the men as I folded my arms across my chest. "Anyone else got a problem with helping the Mother Chapter? Anyone else got a problem with them weeding out rats from the sinking ship?"

When no one said dick, I didn't smirk at Grim, because maybe they *were* too chicken shit to speak and he was the only one stupid enough to say a fucking word.

Letting my gaze dance along the brothers, I zoomed in on GIF. The SOB never sent me a message without at least eight GIFs. Lucky for him, they were usually funny. I swore the guy could write a conversation with GIFs alone.

"What about you, GIF? You got something to say?"

His eyes widened as he shook his head. "No."

"You sure about that? Because seems like Grim's speaking for all of you and he ain't got a right to."

GIF licked his lips as he cast a glance at his still-gasping brother who was rubbing his throat like I'd garrotted him. "We've been without a decent Prez for a while. It was hard at first, then it got easier, but you left again." He shrugged. "It was weird, but okay. Better now you're back."

Was the fucker saying they'd missed me?

Heaving a sigh because I guessed they deserved an explanation, I rasped, "What do you know of the *Famiglia* in New York?"

The guys frowned at me.

"Not a lot. It ain't our business to know, is it?" Mash rumbled, getting to his feet. He had a beard as well, one that was more like pussy hair than anything else, but even I knew why he kept the thing grown out—he had a pretty face. Way too pretty for a biker.

"Ain't your business? Your fucking Prez and his bitch Old Lady made it your business when he got the MC involved in it.

"They run pussy, brothers. Sell bitches as if they're fucking meat on a slab. Having a stable of whores is one thing, but they treated them like dogs. Hell, I wouldn't want an animal to be treated the way those women were. And a lot of us here have daughters. I know I sure as fuck don't want my kid ever being sold like she's a leg of fucking lamb from the store.

"We helped liberate some in West Orange, and I got to know a few of those women. A couple are even Old Ladies now.

"You heard about those cunts, the New World Sparrows?" I got some nods, a couple of shakes of the head which immediately ruled those dimwitted fuckers out of the running of serving on the council. There was nothing but shit about the NWS in the news, and these asswipes hadn't heard about them? "The *Famiglia* were their front."

Quickly, I scanned the crowd, eyeing the faces, studying their responses. Not only did I want to check for surprise or shock, but also, a glimmer of goddamn intelligence.

Pursing my lips afterward, not exactly happy with what I learned from that experiment, I barked, "Those fuckers were what your old Prez got into bed with. That's on him *and* on you. You got involved whether you voted on it or not.

"Now, me? I won't lead you into a war with the Mother Chapter's enemies, not because they're my family, but because I'm not a bitch like that. I don't want to see any of you on the wrong side of things when shit hits the fan." I smirked. "Ain't I kind?"

When they all squirmed in their seats, I watched them some more, taking in their reactions.

"Selling pussy ain't never been the Sinners' way. Neither is being a goddamn traitor to the people who put a roof over your fucking head.

"Peggy was an O'Byrne." On the receiving end of a ton of blank looks, I ground out, "She was the sister of Johnny O'Byrne. He was a Five Pointer. You know them, right? The most powerful Irish mob in the goddamn country?" At last, I got a response. "Johnny was a junkie, and he turned on the Five Points when the *Famiglia* sold him Colombian marching powder at a cut rate. Peggy was who he used to get shit done for those Italian fuckers, manipulating Sinners in jail to get them to protect their guys on the inside.

"The second Butch got involved with that, the second he let Peggy pussywhip him into shape, was the day he signed his death warrant.

"You bet your ass the Mother Chapter dealt with him *and* her. He was a rabid goddamn dog. But I ain't rabid. I'm a smart fucker and I can guarantee that after a year in this place, you'll no longer be in the red."

"We're in the red?" Grim sputtered. Whether that was out of shock or from the choking I'd just served him, I didn't know.

I frowned back at him. "Is that a joke or a serious question?"

He blinked at me. "A serious question."

Because I was nonplussed, I reached up and rubbed the back of my neck. "Look around you. The place is falling to pieces. Didn't you realize business wasn't going well? Everyone had fucking jobs outside of the MC. You dipshits know that's not normal, right? Brothers work for MC businesses, not outsiders."

For my pains, I got some shrugs, that was when I saw Slayer heave a sigh.

"You got something to say, Slayer?"

The brother grimaced. "I was telling Butch that he wasn't running shit right. Bitched at the council about it too when I saw the books and realized there was money going missing—"

"You were on the council? Thought they'd all gone on their merry ways." That was, of course, code for 'were dead or wished they were dead right now.'

"They did, and I wasn't on the council. Just did the bookkeeping because none of them could deal with figures like me." He shrugged. "I didn't mind. Always been good with numbers."

"What did you learn from the books?"

It was a rhetorical question. I already knew from what I'd seen. Half the council had been on the take.

How sister chapters worked was they paid a tithe every month to the original chapter. That meant, so long as Rex received his payment from the branch, he'd never question the running of the place. Well, unless they went against the club's bylaws.

Yeah, even a one-percenter club had rules we had to abide by or there'd be goddamn chaos. Each chapter did its own thing, paid its dues, but answered to West Orange. Their enemies were a sister chapter's enemies. Same went with their allies.

"The Prez—" He cleared his throat. "*Ex*-Prez, the VP, the Secretary, and the Road Captain were on the take."

"You didn't think to contact West Orange?"

"And do what? Snitch?" He scoffed. "Yeah, right."

"You know why?"

"They had bad coke habits," he admitted gruffly.

"Why didn't you say anything?"

Slayer gritted his teeth. "Which part ain't you understanding, Storm? I'm not a goddamn snitch."

I respected that, more than he'd probably comprehend, especially as he looked like he was bracing himself for a reprimand. "How'd you feel about becoming my Secretary?"

He reared back, his surprise clear. "Huh? Me?"

"Yeah, you." *Fuck, don't be a dumbass and make me take back the offer,* I thought to myself, suddenly weary with how slow this process was going.

He swallowed. "You sure? I ain't got no schooling or nothing. Just learned what I know on the job."

"Even better. I'd prefer goddamn experience over letters after your name."

Well, that wasn't exactly true.

Look at Cruz—more degrees than a doctor and a wicked chemist as a result.

Sometimes, ya needed the letters when it came down to destroying dead bodies and turning them into goop so the authorities couldn't find dick.

Slayer blinked. "Well, sure, then. I mean, I'd love to be Secretary."

I waved my hand at the table. "Come and take your place."

Glancing back at the group of men, I decided to get on with this before they ended up pissing me off even more.

Plus, I had Keira and Cyan here, I'd prefer to spend my time with them than these assholes.

Okay, brothers.

Not assholes.

Brothers.

Maybe if I said it enough, then I'd fucking feel that way.

Barely refraining from grinding my teeth, I disregarded the idiots who hadn't recognized the Sparrows when I'd mentioned them. Then, I discounted the ones who were morons and hadn't come to the realization that this place was falling down around them.

That left twelve.

Pursing my lips, I asked, "Slayer, did any of the guys in here question what Butch was doing? Make noises about Peggy's authority over the MC?"

He wiggled uneasily in his new seat. "It ain't my place to say, Storm."

"You're on the council now, fucker. If you want to be Secretary, start acting like you're a councilor. Your loyalty is to the brotherhood first, then the individual. If you can't deal with that, then that's your fucking problem and, I repeat, you know where the goddamn door is."

Slayer gritted his teeth, but murmured, "Mash, GIF, Techie, Sweet Lips, Picasso, DD, and Shadow. They questioned shit."

I dipped my chin, relieved that those names aligned with my earlier assessment. "Okay, all of you, come and take your place at the council table."

As their eyes widened with shock, that was nothing to Grim's reaction. "The fuck? You know I should be VP!" Once again, he was on his goddamn feet.

"I don't know dick about you being VP. Thinking you deserve it and deserving it are two separate things entirely," I snarled back, before I lifted my hand and ticked off, "You didn't know about the *Famiglia*, or the Sparrows, didn't even question shit about Peggy, for fuck's sake.

"VPs need a functioning brain," I mocked. "They need to have critical thinking skills and shouldn't be afraid to speak out for the good of the club—none of which you just did. In fact, you spoke up about the only fucking thing that this chapter has done right for years by the sound of it.

"Now, get your ass back in that chair and stop bitching like a pussy before I make sure you take your last breath." He plunked his ass down like I'd smacked him in the face. "If you got shit to say, then there'll be a time and a place that ain't here or now. This is church. This is for councilors."

I scanned a look over the rest of the room, taking in all the brothers, and found mostly relieved looks, some confused ones, but only Grim was mega pissed.

The problem with his anger, when tangled with a bruised ego and his dumbfuck brain, I knew he'd be trouble along the way.

Scrubbing a hand over my chin as I tucked keeping an eye on him onto my mental to-do list, I muttered, "If any of you don't like that you ain't been chosen today, it's tough shit.

"If you decide that the way to get back at me is to hurt the MC, or to act against the chapter, then just know, I'll make the Spanish goddamn Inquisition look friendly when I respond to whatever infractions are taken against the Sinners." I made sure to slam that threat home by staring at Grim, long enough for him to reach up and rub his throat. When he bowed his head, finally breaking eye contact with me, to everyone else, I stated, "Right, as for the rest of you, thank you for coming here but you can go and hang out with your families now."

As they scampered off, leaving me with my new council, I rubbed my hands together, turned to face them, and declared, "Let the Hunger Games begin."

FIVE

STORM

PAST - TWENTY-TWO YEARS AGO

"YOU'RE gonna break your fucking hand you keep on doing it that way, boy."

I twisted around to smirk at Bear. "I ain't gonna break shit."

"How many times I gotta tell you? Thumb out, not tucked in."

"That's how Coot lost his fucking thumb," I argued.

"He lost it because he's a dipshit, Asher. Not because he had his thumb tucked in or out. Boy couldn't keep his bones together if his skeleton was taped up."

King laughed. "Dad has a point."

I glowered at him, then shoved him in the side. "Fuck off."

He smirked. "That sounds like you think I'm right."

"Storm's always gotta be right, so it's a shame he's always fuckin' wrong," Nyx retorted.

King snickered, but Bear huffed out a sigh as he trudged over to me, grabbed a hold of my hand and properly fixed up my form. "Remember, hand out, fingers straight, thumb cocked. Curl your fingers in, curve your thumb and press against your index and middle finger. Keep your hand and forearm straight, and make sure you punch with your knuckles.

"Got high hopes for you, son. They don't include the insurance nightmare with the surgery you'd need to get your hand working again when you break it."

"It feels better with my thumb inside my fist," I complained, even though I appreciated his advice.

I had… *issues*. That was the kindest way to phrase it, and beating the shit out of stuff put me on a more even keel.

That was why my brothers and me were always down here.

If I didn't work out, I lost my shit.

A broken hand wasn't something we could afford, and it had nothing to do with health insurance.

"Won't when you snap your goddamn thumb," he retorted. "But hey, you carry on doing you and I'll make sure I don't cover your surgery when you get a compound fracture."

I grunted as I made to jab at him, but he was quick enough to back off before he grabbed my arm, jerked me around, then twisted it up along my back.

He tutted. "Don't pick fights with bears that are bigger than you."

Eyeing us both in the mirror in the gym in the clubhouse's basement, I grumbled, "One day, old man, I'm gonna put you on the floor."

He grinned at me. "I can't wait for that fuckin' day, kid."

Of course, that was when Nyx let loose a holler and hurled himself at Bear. King went low, tackling his dad's legs out from under him, and cackling, while I twisted around, eager to get in on the action.

With Bear hooting away like a fucking lunatic, somehow, he managed to get out of the tangle of arms and legs we'd pinned him in.

As all three of us were left panting on the ground, he loomed over us and retorted, "How many times?"

As one, we all sang, "Don't pick fights with bears that are bigger than you."

His smirk wasn't that of a power-hungry prick, not like his brother. Grizzly was a jackass. Meaner than his namesake, a real jerk when he was drunk. Bear was always fair, though.

I sometimes wondered at that.

Sometimes wondered how it was two kids could be raised the exact same way, and yet, could be so different.

Me, I wanted to fit in. I wanted to belong. My anger issues, my aggression, didn't help matters, but they were out of my control.

Whereas Scarlet just wanted to cause trouble. She lived for it. I was pretty fucking sure it was the reason she got up in the morning.

As he leaned down and held out a hand for me, the way he hauled me into him had me tensing up. "Rene wants to talk to you 'bout something, boy. She's in my office," Bear rumbled in my ear so Nyx and King who were wrestling on the floor like wild animals couldn't hear.

I blinked up at him, trying to read his expression.

Bear didn't do pity. It wasn't in his nature.

He was old school—strong, hard, determined. He was also fucking smart. He didn't rule with an iron fist, but everyone respected him. Well, apart from Scarlet.

But what I saw in his eyes had me tensing, because, no, Bear didn't do pity, unless it came time to dealing with my mom, sister, and me.

He nodded slightly, like he knew what I was thinking, and I was grateful that he told me without Nyx and King being able to hear.

I stepped away, already dreading the upcoming conversation, but though my ears weren't working too well, I heard him holler something that had the guys grunting.

Knowing they'd be fighting, that they were occupied, I found myself doubly grateful because maybe I wouldn't have to talk about my fuck up of a mom with them after.

Nyx, King, Matt, Jameson, Rob, and I didn't keep much from one another. We shared how Matt had a massive crush on Cherry, and how he was hoping to lose his V-card to her, we knew Jameson liked dicks as well as pussy, and then we also knew about Nyx—about what was going on with his fam.

Nyx was actually why we were in the gym today. Helping him burn off his aggression was imperative because Caleb, his baby bro, wasn't doing too good in the hospital.

As for the others, Matt was with his grandma, Jameson was studying for a test tomorrow, and Rob was fixing his bike while Stone 'supervised,' otherwise we'd have been a full group and I'd have had to hide this convo from them all.

Thankful for small mercies, I headed up the stairs toward Bear's office, snagging a towel on the way out and trying to dry myself off.

Scrubbing it over my hair, I passed Hot Lips fucking Grizzly in the hall, and because it wasn't that unusual a sight, I didn't really even bother to look.

What I did notice? The sweet scent of weed in the air.

Anything related to my mom always made me want to smoke pot, but Rene didn't like it, and Bear always shook his head at me when I came home stinking of it.

They were the only real family I had so I didn't like it when they were disappointed, but sometimes, I didn't know how else I'd cope.

Knocking on the office door, I headed inside when Rene's soft voice called out, "Come in."

I frowned at the sight of Scarlet who was popping gum while swinging on the edge of Bear's desk, muttering, "You shouldn't sit on there like that."

"Don't worry about it," Rene replied from her place on the sofa.

Though I cast her a quick glance, I ignored her and moved over to Scarlet, then dragged her off the desk.

She pulled her arm out of my hold, snapped a bubble in my face, and retorted, "Just because you're so far up Bear's ass that you can't tell his shit stinks don't mean I am."

"Take that back," I growled, stepping into her.

Scarlet and I weren't good for each other. With a year between us, we should have been joined at the hip, but it felt like I'd been at odds with her since she'd been born.

Maybe that was because we'd both been born addicted to crack?

Even when we were inside our mom's belly, we'd been fucking fighting for a high, which gave us no room for anything else in our lives… not even a sibling.

Although, that was bullshit, wasn't it? I had a family made up of brothers and Rene and Bear. They weren't bound to me by blood, but I'd kill for them. Scarlet alienated every fucker in sight. Me included.

"I ain't taking shit back," she sneered at me, shoving me aside.

Barely managing to remember that she was a girl, I struggled to hold off from smacking the fuck out of her. "I don't give a shit what you do, but you don't disrespect Bear and Rene."

"What you gonna do to stop me?" she snarled, smirking when I just glared at her, no answer tripping from my tongue because, in all honesty, I didn't have one. I never did where she was concerned, and she knew it.

"Kids, come on, I have something to tell you both."

Scarlet rolled her eyes. "So, Mom's back in jail. So fucking what?"

I tensed. "She is?" I turned back to Rene. "Is she right?"

The woman who was more of a mom to me than my own sighed. "Yes, Asher, she is."

"For how long this time?" I grumbled, bored more than anything else.

Mom was in and out of jail like she had a bungee cord tied around her waist.

I knew Bear had told her that he wouldn't bail her ass out anymore, and I didn't fucking blame him.

"It's a little more complicated this time, Ash," Rene told me calmly, but the sympathy in her eyes told a different tale.

"Why?"

"It's looking likely she'll serve a lot more than a couple of weeks. With the way it's shaping up, our lawyer's saying her sentence could be eight years, maybe more."

My eyes flared wide, but the sweetest sensation filled me.

Relief.

I almost sagged back against the desk, my shoulders slumping as it overtook me.

Eight years of peace.

Eight years of fucking freedom.

Maybe more.

Maybe longer.

"Oh, my God, you're happy about it," Scarlet shrieked, then she hit out at me.

Slapping me across the face, I hissed when her nails caught my cheek, drawing blood like the fucking animal she was.

"Scarlet!" Rene barked, jumping to her feet to wade in. "You stop that now!"

Because I didn't want Rene to get hurt, I quickly drew away from the little bitch before I hit back, but I didn't answer her accusation, didn't even bother catching the drips of blood. Instead, I turned to Rene, asking, "What did she do?"

"She got charged with intent to distribute." She winced. "Crack."

"Of course." My jaw worked as I looked at Scarlet, saw she was still glowering at me, her hands balled into fists like she was waiting for me to do something that would let her off the leash again.

She hated Mom as much as me, so why she was defending her, I didn't have a clue.

"Thank you for telling me, Rene. Is that everything? Can I go back to the gym?"

Rene hesitated, but then, she queried, "Scarlet?"

My sister's mouth pursed up like a fucking prune, but when she didn't answer, I snapped, "What have you done now?"

Like mother, like fucking daughter.

"I'm pregnant," she muttered. "I don't know why it's such a big deal. I'll just get an abortion—"

Rene shook her head. "Honey, I don't want you making any rash decisions—"

"Who's the father?" I rumbled, temper whipping at me at just how fucking blasé she was about this.

That was Scarlet's problem. Life was one big game. I almost wished *she* were the one heading off in a sheriff's car. Maybe she wouldn't get into so much trouble in juvie.

"Like you care," she sneered.

"I do, actually. You're fucking fourteen, Scarlet. You're a kid. Who the hell screwed you?"

She smirked. "Wouldn't you like to know?"

Rene sighed. "She won't tell us, Ash. Maybe you can talk to her? See if we can... I don't know, get something arranged with the father?"

"I just want an abortion. Mom said she'd sign the form. I don't see what the problem is."

No, because just like her, our whore of a mother was more than willing to use abortion as family planning. Condoms existed for a fucking reason.

I never wanted kids. Ever. If there was a pill for a guy to take, I'd swallow that shit down if it meant I didn't get any bitch pregnant. The cunts in my family didn't share the same philosophy.

I worked my jaw a second, trying to contain my annoyance, before I snapped, "Didn't you use a condom, Scarlet? What the fuck is the matter with you? Why can't you do anything right?"

"Fuck you," she hissed.

"Yeah, bite back because you're in the wrong and you know it."

"Asher, honey, this isn't..." Rene heaved a sigh. "You can't blame your sister for this. She's only a child."

"Old enough to be screwing someone. Was it that douche in your class? That prick Alex?" When she popped her gum, I grumbled, "You're just like Mom, and if you ever do have a kid, I'd bet that that poor bastard would be just as happy as I am at the thought of you rotting in jail." I shook my head. "Rene, there's no point. If she ain't gonna tell us who raped her—"

"It wasn't rape," Scarlet retorted. "I wanted it."

"I'll just bet you did," I sneered. "But you're fourteen. It's statutory rape, dumbass. Probably a good thing you're not talking about who the father is because he'd be sitting in jail right this second too."

With that, I turned away, and for the first time in my life, I ignored Rene when she called me back. Instead, I headed past Grizzly who was still getting it on with Hot Lips and moved toward the front door.

I needed to run.

Fucking Scarlet.

Why did she always have to give Rene and Bear shit?

I needed to clear my head.

Why did she always have to make Rene worry?

Why couldn't she just be grateful that they looked after us like we were their kids?

God.

I needed pot.

I needed to get away from her.

Mom was inside. She'd forget about us for eight years. But Scarlet was trouble. Always trouble.

I ran.

But instead of running around the compound like my friends and I usually did to build our endurance, I found the break in the chain link fence that King had made last year, and I slipped through it. It cut my shoulder, but I didn't care. I'd wash it later.

For now, I had to find Johnny Regis—the only fucker dumb enough to sell marijuana in Sinners' territory. The only jackass with fewer brain cells than Scarlet who'd sell pot to a Sinners' kid—because I needed to escape.

The day, my life, the world.

I needed all of it to be one big blur.

SIX

KEIRA

PRESENT

THE SECOND I stepped into Storm's office, my nose crinkled with distaste.

It stank in here.

Not only of old soft furnishings that had way too much stuff spilled on them, stuff I didn't want to even question, but there was the faint scent of faded tobacco and weed.

Of course, until Storm, I'd never known what weed smelled like, but he'd come home drenched in the sickly/sweet notes far too often for me not to recognize it now.

Dumb me, I'd thought his brothers smoked it. Never thinking he'd be getting high as well.

I really had been too stupid to live.

In the weeks since I'd first visited this place, I'd expected him to make changes here, but he hadn't. Maybe a splash of paint on the walls, but if anything, it was as shitty now as it was then.

Seventies' era in style, the place wasn't exactly prezidential. The only thing in any way luxurious about it was a bunch of houseplants squatting over in one corner.

The sight had something inside me churning. Storm had never been green-fingered, and I couldn't imagine a brother tending to them. That meant a clubwhore probably did it.

A clubwhore came in here, shook her ass in his face, waggled her tits at him, and he...

He, what?

I didn't know what. I'd never know, either.

I'd heard a bunch of stuff, tales of Storm's apparent prowess in the sack, and yet, the guy who'd apparently fucked around with half of West Orange had padlocked his penis up like it was the door to a garage that contained an expensive frickin' ride.

I guessed the intention with the whole padlock thing was to stop him from being able to get his cock *in* anyone.

Did it work?

Was the key around my neck really the only way to release him?

To believe that, I'd have to trust him.

Wasn't it ironic that the one thing I trusted him with was the only thing of value to me? My kid.

Well aware that I shouldn't be jealous about the clubwhores because he wasn't mine anymore, well aware that the imagery of that long, fat shaft with the obscene padlock wasn't something that should have me drooling, I forced myself to shift focus.

Those damn houseplants kept catching my eye…

What was he doing with so many? They were probably another sign that I'd never understand him.

Glancing at MaryCat, I winced at the sight of her on the wrecked sofa. Partly because it was gross, mostly because it was a sign of how fatigued she was if she could sleep on that shitty, old thing.

I was, however, relieved to see that Storm had misunderstood the situation.

Didn't come as much of a surprise. And I meant that with zero shade.

For all that he'd been hands on as a dad, that didn't take away from the fact that some of the minutiae of day-to-day care for a small infant had escaped him and fallen on my shoulders.

Beside the sofa, he'd evidently gotten one of the Old Ladies to bring in a bassinet, and on the rickety coffee table in front of her, her diaper bag was open and there were full bottles in there which told me she'd been expressing milk.

Not enough to take her through the night, mind, and as Maddox wasn't fussing too bad, I figured she'd been feeding him every couple of hours.

Was she asleep now? Or just pretending?

Cuddling Maddox closely to my chest, smiling when he nuzzled my boobs again, I headed over to the sofa and though it icked me out to sit on it, I rested against her and peered over to see her face which she had turned away, her back to the room.

"You must want to shower," I told her softly, aware from her tension that she was awake.

She didn't answer.

Maddox fussed harder.

She heaved a sigh then, despondently, whispered, "I wish he liked me."

The words weren't what I expected, but I hummed under my breath as I bobbed Maddox in my arms. "Of course he likes you."

"He likes my boobs."

I snorted. "I think you'll find he likes a lot more than that. Did you know babies still think they're in the womb at his age?"

She tilted her head back so she could look at me. "Really?"

I nodded. "You want to hold him?"

"I always want to hold him," she whispered miserably. "He's the one who doesn't want me to hold him."

I clucked my tongue, then carefully handed the baby over to her. When Maddox settled against her, he immediately started bawling, which had MaryCat sobbing too.

Goodness.

"He can feel your tension," I tried to soothe her. "You need to relax, honey. You're his mommy. Of course he loves you."

"Why does he always cry? I'm so tired of him crying." She released a soft, grief-stricken sob. "He won't stop. Not unless someone else holds him."

"That's because you're tense around him," I told her calmly, even though I felt her pain like it was my own. "You're stressing him out with your stress."

Well, I really hoped that was the reason why.

It was a long darn time since I'd had home ec and had learned about babies, and about as much time since Cyan had been this age.

Apparently, my softly-spoken, non-judgmental words worked. "You really think so?" she asked, the plea in her voice so strong that it hurt me to hear it. "Mom says it's because he hates me. She says it's because I'm a shitty mother."

My eyes bugged. "She said what?" MaryCat's mouth wobbled a bit as she awkwardly edged her way into a sitting position. I held out my arms to help her upright, and murmured, "They're super sensitive to how you're feeling, MaryCat. Storm said something about your mom trying to take him away?"

A sardonic laugh hiccuped from her. "Yeah, Moms are supposed to help, aren't they? Not try to steal your baby away from you." Maddox fussed but then stopped squirming when she adjusted her shirt and started feeding him.

When a relieved sigh escaped her as she tipped her head back against the sofa, a soft laugh escaped me. "I swear, there's no pain like it, is there?

She pulled a face. "No."

"No better feeling either."

"Agreed. Oxytocin FTW."

I smiled, but then a thought occurred to me that had it dying. "Why did your mom do that? Try to take him away from you?"

"I'm not being paranoid!" MaryCat barked at me.

"I never thought you were," I replied quietly, well aware that the other woman desperately needed more sleep and to chill out a little.

Of course, that wasn't so easy with a newborn, when you were on the lam, hundreds of miles from home, and the man you loved was only God knew where in the country.

Frickin' bikers. I remembered those days so well.

As VP, Storm hadn't gone on as many runs, but back in the early days of our relationship, I'd hated it when he went off for days at a time.

My friends had left for college but they'd stopped talking to me months before that; my family had cut me from their lives; I didn't fit in with the Sinners, and my status as a biker's wife had made people who'd known me almost all of my life suddenly turn their backs on me in town… I was alone.

So isolated and lonely that it made me shiver just to remember those times.

No wonder I'd grown to depend on Storm for everything.

No wonder our relationship hadn't been healthy.

MaryCat broke into my troubled thoughts with: "I was diagnosed with postpartum depression."

"Lots of women are," was my calm response.

"Not according to my mom. The way she was talking to me, it was like I was going to hurt him or something." Her voice broke. "As if I'd ever do that."

Mind whirring, I questioned, "Digger's on a run?"

"Yes."

"Do you know when he's coming back?"

"He said four days, but you know what they're like."

My nose crinkled. "Time flies."

"Exactly," she said with a sigh, before she tipped her chin down against the crown of Maddox's head and gently hugged him. "I wish he were here."

"He can be. I'll bet he'll ride here and not back to the other chapter."

"Do you think?" she warbled hopefully.

"Why would he go to West Orange *or* Manhattan," I amended, "when you're here?"

"Maybe Rex wants him there?"

"I'm sure Rex will get it." I reached over and with a finger, softly traced the fuzzy hairline at the back of Maddox's head. "If he doesn't, I'll make him get it."

MaryCat shot me a watery smile. "You will?"

"Men aren't the only ones with balls. I had to grow a pair of my own."

"When you left Storm?"

"It took a lot of courage." God, understatement.

"But you did it."

"I did." I smiled back at her. "Best thing I ever did. Shocked the hell out of him, though."

"I heard about Cyan," she whispered. "I'm so sorry, Keira, but I'm relieved she's safe."

"She's definitely that, but… things are hard right now." My smile was rueful. "Not unlike Maddox, she's acting out. That doesn't get easier. Being a mom doesn't either.

"At first, *after*, I thought everything was going to go back to normal, but then I realized there is no normal. Not without Storm, and I don't know what to do about that. I don't know how to fix things for her when the solution isn't feasible for me."

MaryCat blinked. "She wants you back together again?"

"And she makes that abundantly clear every time he comes home for dinner."

"You have to do what's right for you."

"For her too." I smiled down at Maddox. "I didn't mean to change the subject, just… I guess I wanted you to know that having kids and being a mom, well, it's okay to feel like it's impossible some days. Because it really can feel that way. I didn't have PPD and some days, I bawled my eyes out.

"Either way, you're one of us. You're a mom, and you know that they become a part of you. You're not just on your own. You'll always be split in half."

"Or thirds. Or fourths," she agreed, "depending on how many you have."

"Cyan's more than enough of a handful. I don't know if I could deal with more than one of her right now," I told her, knowing I was lying. Storm had been the one who didn't want more kids. Not me. "She's Storm's kid through and through. I was a good girl."

MaryCat pulled a face. "I wasn't. Digger didn't sound like he was a good kid either."

I snickered. "Something to look forward to."

Our eyes clashed, held, before we both started giggling.

Her grin, when it made an appearance, was genuine, and I was glad to have broken some inner tension inside her.

As our laughter died, I told her, "You're safe here, MaryCat."

"Do you know who my dad is?"

"Irish Mob, isn't he?"

That had her mouth gaping. "How do you know that?"

"I hear things. Storm talked business when he was at home." I corrected, "Not with me. Just on the phone. I used to listen in."

"Do you know how powerful the Irish mob is?"

"I can imagine," I said softly. "But you're in Ohio—"

"It's not exactly the other side of the world, Keira," she rasped, hefting Maddox higher against her chest to burp him after he'd finished feeding and I'd handed her a soft cloth from the diaper bag. "They could come for me at any time."

"And if you think the Sinners will allow that, you're nuts." I grinned at her. "Honey, you might as well be in Timbuktu."

She didn't look convinced, but before I could try to comfort her more, I heard a phone ringing.

"Is that yours?" I asked, twisting around, but when she shook her head, I got to my feet, and realized it was the landline on the desk.

I knew I shouldn't pick it up, but I didn't want it to disturb Maddox further, so I held on tight to my big balls, feeling ridiculously brave as I lifted the receiver.

"Hello? Storm isn't here right now, but I can take a message."

"Keira?"

I stiffened. "Rachel?"

Rachel Laker was the club's lawyer. We'd always had a prickly relationship, mostly because Rachel had that kind of effect on most people.

Some might call her an ice-cold bitch but, when my daughter had been abducted, Rachel had been the one to hold my hand while I waited for some news about Cyan. In all honesty, she'd kept me from losing my mind.

She'd also been the only person who'd ever told me the whole truth about Storm. Not just as my husband, but as a man. That meant that anyone who called her an ice-cold bitch in my presence would have to deal with me afterward.

"Yes. I—" She heaved a sigh. "Storm isn't there?"

"No. He's in church."

A soft sound escaped her, one that had my brows lifting.

Was Rachel crying?

What the hell was going on?

Tension flittered through me as I thought about all the shit that had happened in the club's recent past. God, I—

Then it hit me.

Tears welled in my eyes. "Bear?" I choked out.

She let out a sob. "Yes."

Pressing my fist to my mouth, I tried to hold back the tears but it was impossible.

While I didn't know West Orange's last Prez as well as I had his wife, especially since her death when he'd been AWOL for so long, I knew what he meant to Storm. Knew he'd been like a father to him.

Oh, God, this was going to destroy Storm.

First Rene, now Bear…

"Rachel, I hoped—" My words waned with grief, and when I shot a look at MaryCat, noticing she was cuddling Maddox a little more than before and that her eyes were wet too as she read between the lines, I covered my face with a hand.

"We all did," she whispered, her voice raw and gritty, like she'd been crying for hours. "I-It happened on Christmas Day. Rex is..." She gulped. "He's gone missing. We don't know where he is, so everything kind of got—" A choked cry escaped her. "Tell Storm I'm sorry."

"Is Rex back?"

"No," she whispered. "Not yet."

"Do you think he's coming down here?"

"I don't know. He could be anywhere." She swallowed. "Would you mind telling Storm? He'll probably take it better coming from you."

Even through my tears, I grimaced, but nodding, said, "I will. I'll tell him."

Her voice was husky as she whispered, "Thanks."

"Not a problem." I pressed my knuckles along the curve of my cheekbone to gather the tears that were falling. "When's the funeral?"

"I'll let you know. There's going to be an autopsy—"

"There is? Why? Isn't it obvious what killed him?" God, the blast at the clubhouse had torn him limb from limb.

"They're… they think there might have been foul play."

For a second, I couldn't process what she was saying, but when it resonated, I couldn't hold back the words as I blurted out, "You're saying the cops think Bear was murdered?"

DEAR DIARY

SENIOR YEAR

This sounds so dumb, but we looked at each other today.

I've been waiting to see him again, hoping he'd show up at school, and he did.

He looked so tired again, so sad.

Does nobody else see that?

I felt like I was the only one who noticed.

Most of the guys were just drooling over his ride, and the girls were drooling over him. Don't get me wrong, there's plenty to drool over, but how can't they see his sorrow?

I wish I could unsee it.

It makes me think about him all the time.

I downloaded 'Love Story' the second I realized he makes me think of that song. Which, actually, is pretty hilarious. No way should a biker make me think about Taylor Swift songs, ha.

I think I might make a mixed CD. I watched this really old movie the other night, Say Anything, and it seemed like such a cool idea to give to someone. I'd never give him the mixed CD, but instead of thinking about how sad he looks, maybe I could think of songs for him?

Gah, that sounds dumb. So dumb.

His smile… I wish I could forget it. Forget him.
Some people, though, are just unforgettable.

DEAR KEIRA

Your name is as beautiful as you. I looked it up. It means 'little dark one.'

Why can't I stop thinking of you?

You saw me watching you tonight. You probably think I'm a creep, a fucking lech, but I'm not. I don't mean you any harm. You're just so pure that it hurts to look at you and because I'm a masochist, I can't stop.

I'm going to see you every morning and every afternoon, and it's going to be bittersweet.

It's going to hurt.

Maybe that's the kind of hurt I need though.

This kind of wanting isn't something I'm used to.

I take.

That's what I do.

I take and I take.

You're a giver. I can see that. If I needed proof I'll be toxic to you, I have it already, but I'm addicted now.

Yeah, I am.

I'm addicted to you.

Watching you laugh... do you know how carefree you look? How you make the air around you dance when you're happy?

When I saw you that first time, I looked at you and wondered if it was possible to be that perfect. I'm not sure if it is. I'm not sure if it's a lie. I hope it isn't. Even as I know you're not an angel, I want to believe you are.

Tonight, afterward, I fucked a clubwhore because I couldn't have you. It's a bitter pill to swallow, this need. I want you, but I can't have you because I'm dirty. But I'm dirty because of these clubwhores I fuck to get over wanting you.

I need to leave you alone because I stain everything that comes near me.

I'm poison, Keira.

I'm living death.

I don't want that for you.

But I'll still be there in the morning, watching you walk into school, making sure you're safe.

Yours,

Storm

SEVEN

STORM

PRESENT

BY THE TIME church was over an hour later, I had my new councilors, except for one.

Mash had refused to be my Enforcer, but had agreed that, when I picked my guy, he'd work under him and make shit copacetic.

Not all of them were happy about it, but I actually was.

Having eliminated the others the way I had, I figured that I had men on my side with at least some awareness of current events.

With President Davidson squawking all over the news about how he was going to eradicate the New World Sparrows, I had no idea how those brothers had never heard of them. I mean, there was living in a clubhouse, then there was living under a fucking rock.

That goddamn Davidson was never off the TV, and the bitch of it was his approval ratings had never been higher. That meant another four fucking years of the jackass.

Pulling a face as I stretched my arms in front of me, I watched as the others trudged out. I'd known one or two of them would lag behind, so I arched a brow at Sweet Lips in question when he stuck around.

"Everything okay, SL?"

I wasn't sure I wanted to know how my goddamn VP was called

Sweet Lips, but fuck, we all earned our road names in many varied and disturbing ways... Who was I to judge? But I sure as fuck wouldn't be calling him that.

For a second, he scratched his chin where his stubble was growing out, then he muttered, "You sure you want me as VP?"

I shrugged. "Gonna give you a shot. No harm, no foul."

"You say that now. What if I fuck up?"

"We all fuck up," I countered, because truer words had never been spoken, especially coming from me. "I told you your duties."

He pulled a face. "Yeah."

"Yeah?" I laughed. "What's that supposed to mean?"

"It means I understood what you were saying, but not necessarily what you were saying. I'm not sure how to do what you want me to."

"We need to start investing in businesses that brothers can work in."

"Yeah, but it's not like I can make them appear out of thin air."

"Not asking you to."

"No? Well, where am I supposed to find them?"

"Locally?" I sank my ass against the side of the table. "Where else?"

"You want me to takeover businesses that are already open?"

"Not necessarily."

"See, this is why I'm confused. You're saying shit I understand, but you're saying shit I don't know how to resolve."

"We need jobs. Find us jobs. You know, the usual places. A garage? A bar? A strip joint? In West Orange, there's a fucking diner. Replicate them all, find something new, I don't give a fuck.

"I spoke with Rex before Christmas, he's willing to float a loan to the Coshocton chapter to get us underway. I just need you to bring me proposals."

"I ain't into real estate, man," SL muttered, rubbing the back of his neck.

"Naw? Well, you're about to be. Find businesses that are for sale, check into how much it'll cost to start from scratch. Work with Slayer to cost shit up. See if it'll be profitable."

"What if I don't?"

I narrowed my eyes at him. "What if you directly disobey a goddamn order?"

He shook his head, quick enough to tell me that, somehow, my reputation had traveled all the way over to Ohio.

There was a reason I was called Storm.

Figured that 'show and tell' with Grim had helped some too.

"What if we pick shitty businesses?"

"Try not to," I retorted. "The last decision will rest with me. So you're off the hook."

His grin, when it came, was lightning quick. Was that why he was called Sweet Lips? "Gotcha. I can deal with the fault lying with you if it's a disaster. I'll try not to let you down."

I grunted. "Good. Now fuck off."

Straightening up, I followed him once I'd shut off the lights and headed into the hall.

Though I wanted to see Keira, I knew she'd be talking to MaryCat, and, to be honest, I had no idea in hell what to do with her so I was glad to leave it to my wife.

Preferring to go and visit with Cyan, maybe hang out with her until her mom came looking for her, I returned to the family room. Only, when I got down to the end of the hall, I heard hoots and hollers coming from inside.

With a frown, I peered around the corner, then barked, "Cyan O'Shea! What the hell are you doing?"

Because she was too busy in a cat fight, hands burrowed away into the hair of a girl I recognized as GIF's kid, she didn't hear me.

Elbowing through the small crowd that had gathered, I growled at the Old Ladies, "Why the fuck aren't you stopping this?"

Christ, they looked as if they were going to start taking bets!

All of 'em bitching and talking behind their hands as small sheets of Monopoly money fluttered in the air like confetti, while chairs groaned and squeaked as they were shoved aside from the brawl.

With a snarl, I dipped down, snagged each kid by the hoodies they were both wearing and tugged them apart.

The little shits didn't even fucking realize I was separating them.

Their arms and legs kicked in extra wide circles and they growled at each other like wild beasts.

"The hell's going on?" I snapped, enough temper in my voice to trigger Cyan's awareness of who was doing the separating.

She peered up at me, slowly drooping in my hold as she winced when she saw the annoyance on my face. I always kept my temper in check around her, but apparently my facial expression revealed exactly how pissed I was with her.

"She started it."

The soft, frightened whisper had me narrowing my eyes at GIF's kid, before I turned back to mine. "Did you?"

Her mouth tightened and she wriggled in my hold. I let go of GIF's daughter but kept a firm hand on Cyan's hoodie even as I let her stand on her own two feet again.

"I didn't do nothing," Cyan sniped. "She was the one who—" She broke off, and her nose tipped up, straight into the air. "I ain't no snitch, Daddy."

Was it weird to be proud of her?

GIF's brat had caved in the second she'd recognized who I was. My kid? Nah.

Should have fucking known I'd breed a rebel.

I tugged her into my side, clamping my arm around her shoulder as I frog-marched her out of the room, barking, "Clear up the mess they made."

Not letting go of her, I moved over to the front door and marched us outside.

"It's cold, Daddy!" Cyan complained as she wrapped her arms around her middle.

Though her glower was all me, I wasn't her mom, and it didn't do shit to make me back off.

"I can't take you to the office. Your mom's there with MaryCat."

Her eyes lit up. "MaryCat's here?"

I arched a brow. "You know her?"

She shrugged. "'Course. I know all the brothers and the Old Ladies." She straightened up, chest puffing out as she declared, "They know me too. All of 'em. They know my name and my birthday."

"Went out of your way to introduce yourself, huh?" The thought had me smiling a little.

"Well, I didn't want to be like Mom." She huffed out a breath, unaware I winced at her words, before she whined, "It's cold!"

"Then answer fast, because you apparently need to cool down." I zoomed in on her statement from before. "What do you mean? Be like Mom? She's a good woman. Why wouldn't you want to be like her?"

Cyan's small mouth tightened. "She isn't a part of the MC. I don't wanna be like that. I want to be a biker princess. I decided."

"You did, huh?" Surprised, I rubbed my chin. "Your mom wasn't raised like you."

"No. I know."

"You do?"

She gritted her teeth. "I do."

Still confused, I asked, "What was that fight about?"

"I ain't a snitch."

Though I used 'ain't' too much, I corrected, "'I'm not a snitch.' Don't be dropping your grammar, baby girl."

"You say it all the time," she contested with a glare.

"Yeah, but I'm not gonna be the MC's next... whatever. Lawyer?" I smirked at her as I carefully tipped her chin with my knuckles. "Doctor? Bookkeeper?"

"You think I could work for the MC?" She beamed up at me like I'd just told her we were going to frickin' Six Flags.

"Don't see why not." I folded my arms across my chest. "Now, a good brother—"

"I'd be a sister," she corrected with a scowl.

"Well, we don't have sisters here, do we? So I can only tell you from experience.

"Now, a good brother doesn't back talk to his Prez. He sure as hell doesn't hold back an answer when his Prez wants info." Though obstinacy had her tensing up, she was too sly not to figure out where I was going with this. "Because if you wanna be a part of the MC, you gotta remember I'm more than just your daddy, I'm your Prez. So, tell me why you were fighting in there."

Her jaw worked a second, her gaze darting from me to the snow beneath her boots to the car.

I knew she had anger issues. Had known for a while. Long before that fucker had kidnapped her, I'd known she had shit going on in her head. Shit that was likely my fault.

I was scum, wasn't I?

The purity of Keira's soul, of her DNA, wasn't strong enough to counteract the crap I brought to the table.

Was I surprised when she dropped down and scooped up some snow then started battering the SUV with snowballs?

Nope.

I just watched her.

I let her work out her anger, unsurprised when she released a frustrated yell that encompassed all the exasperation and outrage her eleven-year-old self could contain.

When she turned to me, her face was bright pink, her eyes wet, like liquid emeralds, and her mouth was quivering as she finally admitted, "S-She said that you and Mommy would never get back together again."

I wasn't sure why she was so mad at Keira, but that she called her Mommy right then gave me a clue. Even if her attitude stank sometimes, and even if I forgot she was still a preteen and not a goddamn teenager, she was a baby.

In this life, she would always be mine to protect, and I'd already let her down so fucking badly. When she'd been taken, I was in goddamn Manhattan, visiting an NA meeting because I was a weak ass pussy who had put his addiction before his kid.

Was it any wonder she was raging at the world after what she'd been through?

How I'd failed her?

I just didn't understand why she was directing her shit at Keira and not me. So it was on me to fix this. To fix my girl.

Squatting down in front of her, I leaned one hand on the cold ground, the snow smushing between my fingers as I murmured, "If we don't, it's because your mom's a wise woman. I hope that, if one day, a guy treats you like I treated her, that you leave his sorry ass."

Cyan's eyes rounded, much as her mouth did. "Don't you say that, Daddy! Why would you say that?" she snapped. "You're the best!"

"I'm really not, honey. And I say it because it's true." I shot her a sad smile. "I've been a bad husband. A decent-ish father, because I know you love me, so I can't have let you down too much. But as for your mommy? No. She should have tossed me out a long while ago."

Her small hand slapped across my mouth, not to hurt, just to shut me up. Her fingers were wet and cold from the snow and smelled faintly of Kool-Aid. Strawberry Kiwi—her favorite. "Don't say that, Daddy," she repeated, this time her voice was harder though, as if she were trying to make me believe it.

But walking away from addiction wasn't as easy as turning your back on it. It was a constant shadow, plaguing everything and anything.

Wherever I looked, I had regrets.

Wherever I looked, there were apologies to make.

Wherever I looked, there were things that I needed to make amends for.

Here was one of them.

I reached up, cupped her delicate wrist, then squeezed it gently. "I know who I am, ladybug, and that's why I can say it, because I'm going to change that. I'm going to be the man your mom and you deserve."

"You already are—"

Shaking my head at her indignant interruption, I murmured, "No. No, honey. You don't have to say that. How many nights wasn't I at dinner? Huh? How many nights wasn't I there to tuck you in bed, to read you those stories you liked when you were younger?" I let my thumb swipe over the back of her hand. "I let you both down. Admitting that is the hardest part. Did you know that?"

She bit her bottom lip, those liquid emerald eyes of hers making me feel like my soul was being shredded from the faith she had in me.

But I hadn't earned such blind faith.

If anyone had, it was Keira.

She wasn't the bad guy here. She was just being smart. No right-minded woman would want me as is. I was a fucking mess. But time healed all wounds, didn't it? At least, that was what they said. That was what I had to pray for.

"Admitting to anything you do wrong is hard," she whispered sullenly.

"Especially when you like to be right all the time."

"Who doesn't like to be right all the time? That's normal."

I snorted. "You won't make friends with a sucky-ass attitude, baby. You want to roll with the Sinners, you gotta befriend their spawn."

A glimmer of something whispered behind her eyes. "I don't care if they don't like me."

"But do you want their respect?" I questioned. "There's a fine line between both, after all. You know who I aspire to be?"

She blinked. "Who?"

"Rex."

Her grin turned dopey. "Uncle Rex is awesome."

"He is."

"I miss him. I miss everyone in West Orange." She sighed. "This is home now, though. This is where you are. Why did you have to leave? I wanna be back there."

"Because aspiring to be like Uncle Rex ain't enough for me anymore, honey. I had to go out and act as if I were him, not just talk about it. I had to stop running my mouth and start doing.

"You know we call each other brothers?" At her nod, I told her, "To me, Rex, Nyx, Link, Steel, and Maverick are like we all popped out of the same mom. We grew up together, we were like this." I crossed my middle and pointer finger. "I miss 'em every day I wake up here.

"I don't know these guys. I don't know 'em, but I'm supposed to trust 'em. I have to have faith in the fact that they're Sinners, and that they're looking up to me, wanting me to be their leader.

"They don't have to like me, but they gotta respect me. You have to be that way too. You earn the kids' respect because you're the Prez's daughter."

"I'm a biker princess," she told me proudly.

My lips twitched. "You are now, that's for sure."

She peered at me, those green eyes of hers making and breaking my heart as she pondered my words. Then, she blurted out, "Is Mom a whore?"

My eyes widened. "What? Why would you ask that? Of course she isn't."

Cyan didn't cower from my harsh tone, just firmed her chin. "I knew she wasn't."

Confused, I frowned at her. "What's going on, Cyan? Did someone call your mom names?" Had that little bitch in there dared to call my woman a whore?

Her top lip curled up. "I dealt with it."

For a second, I was too taken aback at her very adult response to figure out what she was talking about, then I shook my head. "What did you deal with? Who the hell called your mom that?"

Who did I need to go beat the crap out of?

"It was some guy at the community center back home, where I took gymnastics class." She shrugged, but I saw the turmoil she couldn't hide in her eyes when she ducked her head.

Considering she'd met that bastard London there, as well as this jackass who'd apparently called her mom a whore, was it wrong of me to never want her to do goddamn gymnastics ever again?

Jesus Christ.

When she shivered, I knew the adrenaline had died down, and though I was too livid to feel the cold, I wrapped this up fast.

"What did you do to him?" When she bit her lip and her sneaker started to toe into the snow, I smiled. "It's okay, honey. Whatever you did, I won't punish you for it."

She sniffled. "Martin saw me do it—"

My heart sank.

"—he told me I was naughty and that I was a bad girl—"

My temper surged.

"—that was when he started talking to me more."

Nostrils flaring as I inadvertently uncovered the reason that pedophile bastard had targeted my kid, I rasped, "Baby, what did you do?"

"I got one of your screwdrivers, started carrying it around until I saw his car in the center's parking lot. I sneaked out and poked it in the man's tires." Her expression turned earnest. "He deserved it, Daddy. No one should be allowed to call an O'Shea that."

I reached over and grabbed her shoulder, then squeezing it softly, murmured, "You did the right thing." Well, for our world, she had.

A small welter of pride filled me. Sure, it wasn't the legal way to go about this, but retaliation was rarely on the books.

I just didn't have the heart to tell her that the guy who'd called her mom a whore was, in all likelihood, Derek Miller.

Only the promise I'd made to Keira to never harm her family, no matter how they blocked her out, how they dissed her, stopped me from pulling out my phone and calling Nyx and getting him to send a bunch of Sinners around to the Millers' house to make that bastard pay for his words.

Because Cyan, without knowing it, had met her grandfather for the first time in her life, and the way he'd chosen to use that introduction was to call his daughter a whore... how wasn't that deserving of a beatdown?

EIGHT

KEIRA

PRESENT

WHEN I FOUND them outside in the cold, I frowned past my tears, rubbed at my eyes as I stepped outside, huddling into my coat as I trudged over to them.

"What's going on? Why are you guys out here? It's freezing!"

I had no idea why, but Cyan burst into tears. She started to move, and I was pretty sure she was going to head back into the clubhouse, leaving me alone with Storm, but she didn't. She barreled into me, her skinny arms going around my hips as she pushed her face into my throat, hiding away from the world like I was her calm in the eye of a storm.

Of course, that phrase held more meaning than it usually did.

Only difference was, this Storm was over six feet of gorgeousness who just happened to be my estranged husband.

As I held her tighter, I stared at him in confusion, wondering what had triggered this.

He surged to his feet with a grace that always surprised me for a man this tall and muscled, and I tipped my head back to look at him.

One thing they never told you when you got married young? Watching that person grow old was never tiring.

Sometimes, when we were in bed together, even if things were bad and we'd argued, and he'd come back home after a run where Cyan and I hadn't seen him for days, I would look at him while he slept, tracing every single one of the differences between then and now.

That streak of gray was as full length as the rest of his hair, and it offset the pure black of the rest of his mane, making it seem even more luxurious. I loved feeling that silk against me, loved when he was on top of me and it spread around my face in a curtain.

His golden skin was pale from the cold, his strong jaw clenching like he was angry, something that was visible through the short beard he had. A strong nose led to a tightly pursed mouth that, after the few dates I'd had this year, I knew were perfect kissing lips. Soft, yet giving, I'd even come to miss the tickle of his beard when I kissed another guy.

His wide eyes, dark green, rumbled with a fire that was born of outrage as he looked at our kid. I saw the little nerve flickering at his temple and took in the rest of his expression as I watched him deal with an anger that apparently affected Cyan.

I knew my kid, knew my ex-husband. Well… recent revelations made a liar out of me, but I knew him as a father. Her tears weren't related to his temper as in, I knew he hadn't made her cry, but that didn't enlighten me much further.

Having come out here to share the news about Bear, Cyan's state didn't exactly make me want to reveal the truth to either of them. I didn't think she knew Bear all that well anymore. Before Rene's death, they'd been like two peas in a pod, but after Rene passed away, he'd distanced himself from everyone. Not just close family, but the entire MC.

Regardless, now clearly wasn't the right time to share Bear's passing so, instead, I asked, "Baby, what is it? What's wrong?"

Storm straightened up. "She's upset because we had words."

"Why? What did she do?" Storm wasn't exactly a disciplinarian. That shit fell to me. Which was, I assumed, why I'd turned into the Hans Gruber of our household.

Even though he was stricter now after that bastard, you couldn't change eleven years of parenting overnight.

"She got into a fight with one of the kids in there."

My eyes flared wide as shock slammed into me and almost knocked me on my ass. "Cyan? Our daughter, Cyan, got in a fight?"

Said daughter sobbed a little harder, and Storm's already tight mouth pursed some more. "We should get inside. It's cold."

"It is," I agreed, but before he could make a move, I tacked on softly, "Storm, I think it'd be best if you came and stayed at the house tonight."

Brow puckering, he mouthed, "Why?"

I grimaced, but Cyan stopped sniffling as she turned her face away from where she was hiding it against my neck, and whispered, "Daddy can stay the night?"

Humming, I said, "He sure can."

It was the first time I'd let him, and I did so for one reason—learning about Bear's passing would destroy him.

Storm didn't question crap, not like I'd thought he would. But his concerned frown didn't die as he said, "I'll grab my stuff."

I cleared my throat. "MaryCat's coming home with me, too, Storm. Are you okay with sleeping on the couch?"

He shrugged like it made no difference to him. "Of course."

When he walked past me, the aftershave he'd worn as long as I'd known him wafted along too.

God, he smelled good.

How was it that hadn't changed, the basic layout of his face hadn't either, even if he was a lot older now, and yet, the man was so different.

I half expected to receive a cocky smirk, one that told me he'd charm me out of my pants the second he could. I thought there'd be heat or expectation in his gaze—there wasn't. There was just the acceptance that I needed him at home tonight.

The thought had me biting my lip as I squeezed Cyan. "You okay, baby? What made you get into a fight?"

She sniffled some more as she peered up at me. "Why can't you and Daddy get back together, Mommy? Daddy says it's because you're smart, but I miss him. I-I don't want him to be at the clubhouse. Why can't he stay with us all the time?"

'Mommy' was still my kryptonite word. The one she'd stopped using, so whenever it came out, it felt like both a hug and a bullet.

And yet, for all that it had the power to stop me, what resonated the most was her words.

Daddy says it's because you're smart.

What was that supposed to mean?

She'd talked about our separation, and Storm had told her I'd done the right thing?

As much as when a cold front bashed into a warm one, I felt the stirrings of a hurricane brewing, but I wasn't sure why.

The key lay heavily around my neck, suspended there as if it were a trophy, much like it were a precious gem in a pendant I could show off when it was the opposite. In reality, it was bulky and heavy and industrial, but oddly comforting for all that.

If he accepted that I was right to have dumped his ass, why had he gone to all this effort?

Property of Keira.

I thought about the tattoo he'd shown me back at Rachel's house in West Orange. I'd seen his junk a thousand times before, but it was different now. So different. Enough that, despite the frigid temperature, the grief, and the situation, I squirmed a little inside.

He'd branded his dick with my name, for God's sake. Had padlocked it and handed me the key.

That sure as hell beat the gesture of him giving me damn flowers and a limp apology for 'accidentally' falling into some slut's pussy, didn't it?

"Mom?"

Cyan tugged at my focus, and I blinked down at her. "Do you want to know a secret?"

Confusion flittered into her eyes. "Okay."

"I fell in love with your dad the second I laid eyes on him." My lips curved as memories bombarded me. "I was walking out of the auditorium at school. I was in the theater group and we'd been rehearsing for a play. *A Midsummer Night's Dream*." I tugged on a piece of hair that had fallen into her tear-slick face and slipped it around to tuck it behind her ear. "I walked through the entrance, and he was there. Perched on a bike, looking bored as heck.

"He didn't know that I saw him, not at first, but I did. I watched him watch me." My lips quirked up. "I started school older than everyone else until I skipped two grades. So, for a while, the boys around me weren't just young in maturity but in age too. Your daddy was so different by comparison. He stuck out like a sore thumb to me.

"In all these years, he hasn't changed that much. Still wears Henleys and jeans and that cut, but he was younger and dangerous and when I saw him, seated on his hog, he was the most terrifyingly beautiful man I'd ever seen."

She peered up at me, all bewildered curiosity even as she was hungry for more. "What happened?"

"Nothing." I shrugged but I softened it by squeezing her into a hug. "I smiled at him. He watched me go."

"That's it?" she complained, which made me grin.

"That's it." I didn't tell her that he'd been there every day for the remainder of the school year.

I didn't tell her that he'd been sitting outside, whenever I left weather be damned, and that, each and every time, we'd smiled at each other.

Instead of telling her any of that, I just whispered, "I loved him then, I love him now, but baby, life isn't simple. I wish it were, I wish I could give you what you need, but I can't." I sucked in a breath as I gave myself a moment. Nothing about today had gone how I expected, and yet, for all that my head was here, there, and everywhere, I had no desire to malign her father. Not when it seemed as if he were the one source of joy she had amid this welter of changes in her life. "Your dad and I, we can love each other without being together."

"But I want you to be together," she whispered, her voice soggy with emotion. "I-I want to go to sleep at night knowing Daddy's down the hall. I want him to be there all the time. I want—"

When she broke off, even though her words killed me, I whispered, "What do you want, baby?"

"I-I want to be safe. Daddy keeps us safe. If he's there, no one can get into the house."

Tension whipped up inside me, but as calmly as I could, I asked, "Did—" I almost choked on the bastard's name. "—Martin get into our place?"

"Just once." Her eyes were wet. "I-I didn't like it, but he was..." She swallowed. "I-I don't want to feel unsafe anymore, Mommy. Can't Daddy come and live with us again?"

A million thoughts whirred to life inside my head.

Some mean, some bad, some evil.

I wanted to know exactly how long that evil fucker had been grooming her. I wanted to know what had gone on under my roof without me knowing it. And, more than that, I wanted to know, word for word, what had happened to him. I needed to know the details.

I needed to know he'd been made to pay.

I needed to know that he'd suffered.

I said none of that, however. I just hugged her close and rasped, "We'll work out a way to make you feel safe, baby girl."

And if that meant moving Storm into the spare room permanently, then that's what I'd do.

Even if that would kill me, slowly, I'd bear the burden, because making Cyan feel safe again was my top priority.

My *only* priority.

Right now, she mattered more than Storm or me or anything else, and getting her back on track, correcting the wrongs that had seen her take solace in a man nearly double her father's age...

Perhaps I'd never understand how the bastard had wormed his way into her defenses, but truthfully, for all the therapy in the world, I didn't have to understand.

I just had to make sure it never happened again.

Ever.

NINE

KEIRA

PAST

I HATED it when Storm slept at the clubhouse.

Four years together, and I'd grown so used to it that I never slept right without him.

I knew why, as well.

Rene.

I blew out a breath as I rolled onto my side.

We'd gotten the call at five PM that she'd been found on the roadside like she was trash, the victim of a hit-and-run accident.

I'd always kept myself apart from the Sinners, had never really known how to fit in with them or the women, had never known how to act around them and Storm had never made me get involved. Rene, though, I'd come to know better than most. Bear, not so much as his woman, but enough for it to count. I knew them both not as Prez and his Old Lady, but as the people Storm considered family.

Sure, Nyx, Rex, Link, Steel, and Maverick were his brothers, but Rene and Bear were different. He thought of them as his parents and, to be honest, I was raising Cyan that way. They were her only grandparents and, last night, someone had stolen Rene from us all.

I should have been with Storm. I should have been there for him, but getting into my car, driving over to the clubhouse… it was like a weird form of social anxiety.

Everything about that place sent shudders rolling up and down my nerve endings.

It had always been that way, *always*.

I wished it weren't, wished I could relax there, but I'd just never been accepted by them. The few times I'd visited, they always looked at me funny, like I was a cop or something rolling through their gates, sitting on their turf…

If I felt weird there, it was something they'd helped perpetuate.

Still, today was different.

Today was…

Rene was dead.

I released a shaky breath as I sat up, staring at the empty side of the bed, wishing he were there, wishing yesterday hadn't happened, but I knew I was going to have to grow a pair. Knew that, today, I was going to have to go to the clubhouse to help out.

Showering and getting dressed took a half-hour longer than it should because I dawdled so much.

I knew Cyan wanted to see her dad, and I knew he'd missed her as well, but I dropped her off with a neighbor, deciding that would be easier all round seeing as we hadn't shared the truth about Rene's passing with her yet.

So, when I rolled up the road to the compound, I was on my own, and it made me even more nervous.

The gates opened up and I crept through them, edging along as I smiled at a Prospect I didn't recognize but who apparently knew me, and when I parked, there was a lull to the clubhouse.

An odd atmosphere that spoke of the hazy shadow that grief cast over a building.

Bear might be the head of the Sinners, but Rene was his heart, which meant she was the soul of the place.

Everyone loved her.

Everyone.

She was sweet, so kind. Loving and giving and…

She was none of those things anymore. Someone had taken her from us.

Gnawing on my lip, I grabbed my purse and jumped out of my car. The creaking of the gates, the slamming of my door, it seemed to echo around the yard, and it was weird. So weird. The clubhouse was always the opposite of silent, but right now, it was eerily so.

Though I'd been here relatively few times, I knew where Storm's room used to be and figured he still had a bedroom that he slept in when we argued or when he had to work late.

A part of me had always wondered if he'd used it for other things —I was naive but those clubwhores were around for a purpose—yet he'd never given me a reason to worry. His clothes were never peppered with the scent of another woman's perfume, and he didn't come back with hickeys or anything like that.

Mom had once told me that men had urges a wife couldn't always satisfy, and that she should be grateful when they went 'elsewhere' to appease them.

If that were true, then I was just curious what kind of urges those would be. Storm never did anything weird, and we'd watched porn together, so I didn't think he was going to pull out a fetish from his bag of magic tricks.

Funny how the state of my marriage was the only thing I was confident about when I entered the clubhouse, and not even that was enough to make me feel at home here. To feel accepted.

I heard a game of pool being played in the bar, heard low mutterings, even heard the soft sounds of tears as someone cried, and they all made me anxious. But when I headed up the stairs, I zeroed in on Storm's room, entering it and finding him in bed. He was fully dressed, his eyes were open, and he was…

My brow puckered.

Was he drunk?

That was when my anxiety soared.

Storm rarely got drunk.

"Keira?" he rumbled, but his head didn't tilt toward me. "Keira?" he repeated.

I licked my lips. "I'm here, Storm," I said softly, slipping out of my shoes and heading toward the bed.

Whatever I'd anticipated from this morning, be it making a lot of food for the brothers, or just holding Storm's hand, or even helping to organize the funeral, it wasn't that I'd be climbing into bed with him.

The place stank of something weird, I wasn't sure what. It was kind of fruity. A little like tobacco but funky.

Pot?

No. Storm didn't smoke pot.

Still, had he last night because of his grief? He'd certainly been drinking, but I couldn't get angry when he was trying to cope with the loss of a woman who he loved like a mother.

Clambering onto the mattress, I slipped my arms around him. He was a very tactile man for a big, burly biker, always hugging me and curling around me like he couldn't stand for there to be an inch of space between us. I'd grown to crave it, much as I craved him. We were like oil and water, but I liked to think we worked.

Then he stunned me. His mouth collided with mine, but there was none of the patience I was used to.

No delicate kisses, no soft pecks that made me hunger for him.

This was raw.

Brutal.

Edgy.

He thrust his tongue against me so fast and so hard that it stole my breath, leaving me winded and reliant on him for air as he—there was no other word to describe it—fucked my mouth.

"Need you, baby girl, need you, always fucking need you," he chanted, his desperation penetrating the air much as that weird smell did, making me high on it, high on him.

His hands shaped me, but with none of the cherishing that I was used to. There was no tenderness here, only raw need. It branded me in a way his usual touches didn't, and that was how I knew something really was going on with him. Even drunk, he'd never touched me like this.

When his fingers went between my legs, I let out a sharp cry because he didn't caress me and tease me, he plundered. He stole. But it felt good. So good. The tips moved over my clit with all the finesse I was used to, but it was different. So different and so wonderful.

In no time at all, he had me gasping into his mouth as I came, orgasming from the hard touches and his possessive hold on me. Exploding faster than I ever had before, and Storm wasn't exactly a slouch in the bedroom.

I clutched at nothing, at everything, stirred and ravished as well as ravaged. Stunned by his manner, yet not overwhelmed. Just hurled into the eye of the storm and enjoying the adrenaline high.

He grabbed my pants, tearing and tugging at the waistband, not stopping until I was bare from the waist down, then, he climbed off the bed.

At first, I thought he was leaving me, about to abandon me because he thought he was being too rough only, he didn't drift away.

No, he grabbed a condom from the nightstand, handling his dick more aggressively than anything he'd done to me. He held his cock as if it were a snake and he was terrified of them, but as he covered himself up, he clambered back onto the bed and fell between my thighs.

As his dick found its way home, I let out a soft scream as he moved into me, fast and hard.

And though he was blowing my mind, I recognized the difference —Storm didn't make love to me. He was screwing me.

I should have felt dirty, used, but it was too good for that. Too good to feel ashamed when he worshipped me like I was a pagan goddess instead of an angel.

I cried out again, but his mouth stopped me, his tongue plunging into me, grinding against mine, making my heart race even harder as my body burned when he set me alight.

"Need you, baby girl, need you," he chanted. "My home, my every-thing." The words were feverish, filled with a rapture that had my heart soaring. "Always. Always, baby girl."

His fingers found my clit again and he tweaked me there before he did the damnedest thing—he pulled back, grabbed my hips and hauled me higher into him, allowing a globule of saliva to drop down so it splashed against my clit, and he used that to get me off faster.

Not just that, but harder too.

I screamed again, loud and high, as he took me somewhere he never had.

He worked me like he was an animal in full rut, and I'd never even known that I needed that before. That I needed him to break, for his control to be lost, thrown to the wind.

When I came the second time, it shuddered through me with the power of the elemental force he was named after.

My climax tore me apart and built me back together again, but that was nothing to when he tipped back his head, all the veins and cartilage visible as he roared out his release.

"Keira!"

My name seemed to reverberate in my head, echoing and echoing like we were in the middle of a mountainous valley, before he slumped on top of me.

His dick ground deeper inside my pussy, and he arranged me so that I was half covering him, but there was enough force to keep me clasped around him. Then, he hugged me so tightly that my eyes bulged a little, and his mouth burrowed against my throat as he broke down.

As if, after the pleasure, he could allow his tempestuous emotions to rumble free.

He cried.

After that insane display, he cried, and like that, even though it was racing a mile a minute because of what we'd just done, my heart broke for him.

He never cried, but it fit that Rene's death would trigger this.

I swallowed back my own feelings and held him through the emotional deluge that battered him.

"Asher, baby, it's okay. It's okay," I soothed, holding him tight, loving him for letting down his guard with me, rocking him as he dealt with his grief.

He didn't say anything, just let me care for him, and eventually when he fell asleep, I almost did too, but unlike him, my brain was wired, my body still humming in the aftermath.

I asked myself why this was the first time I'd seen him act like this.

Then, when that thought occurred to me, I pondered if I satisfied him. If the way we made love pleased him. He never complained, but, would he? He loved me. I knew that. But this was…

Night and day.

Did he seek this out with other women? Did he…

I swallowed as I thrust the thought away.

I didn't want to know.

Mom had said that men had dirty, depraved urges but I'd never imagined that I'd like those urges.

That I'd want them.

Maybe, if he'd asked me, I wouldn't have, but having seen it, experienced it? I knew I needed more. I just wasn't sure if I could handle it.

Did I want to be fucked? Or did I want him to make love to me?

What would I be inviting into our lives if I unlocked that door? Would it break me, and ultimately, tear us apart if I realized I couldn't give that to him?

Then, of course, a noise from downstairs had me feeling selfish. When someone slammed a door and I heard the sounds of sobbing, my brain shifted gear once more.

I could only imagine what Rex and Bear were going through, and that they needed me too resonated strongly. I was different than the other Old Ladies. I was Storm's wife. My kid was their grandkid. We all acted like it was biological, not just by choice.

After a good hour of letting my mind race, I tugged at Storm's grip on me, and he was so deeply asleep that he actually let go, curving onto his other side and relaxing as I gently clambered off the bed.

Flushing when I saw my pants strewn on the floor like they were trash, I grabbed them and reached for a tissue from the box on his nightstand.

I could have showered but he needed the sleep, and I… well, I needed to get out of here. I didn't want him to wake up while I was still around, while my mind was whirling like a hurricane.

I felt like a coward, but there was a reason the old adage existed— *best to let sleeping dogs lie.*

So, shoving the tissue between my thighs, I dragged on my panties then my pants, and fussed with my hair in the vanity in the bathroom.

When it no longer resembled tumbleweed, I stepped out into the hall, which was where I found Link sitting on the top step of the staircase.

When he saw me, he shot me a sad smile. "Hey."

Link was the nicest of Storm's brothers. Whenever they came to the house, he was the one who always played with Cyan, never left crap on the coffee table, cleared up after himself, and somehow managed to remember I wasn't a servant.

I slipped onto the step at his side, and turning to him, asked, "Is everything handled?"

"Bear's drunk. Rex destroyed the office and went for a ride yesterday—" He sucked in a breath. "Not sure what we're gonna do without Rene, Keira. She kept Bear together."

Had she?

Bear always seemed so strong. Just like Storm, I guessed. Although... he'd just cried for her.

Was that how powerful a woman Rene was?

That all these men, these mean bikers who'd make the Reaper Crew look real friendly, would sob and breakdown and mourn the Prez's woman, messed with my head.

I'd loved Rene like she was family, but this went deeper.

The sorrow in Link's eyes, my husband's sobbing, the muted atmosphere here, that Bear was drunk when he never got drunk... all for Rene.

She deserved nothing less, don't get me wrong, but it still surprised me.

She'd been integral to them, a cog in a wheel that wouldn't spin without her. I was just a moving part.

It was my fault, of course. I'd stayed on the outside looking in...

Was it too late to make a change?

Did I want that?

"They just left her there to die, Keira. I saw her. It was..." Link shook his head.

"I wish you hadn't been there to see that, Link," I told him softly.

"I want to kill the fucker who did that to her."

"Does the sheriff have any clue who was driving?"

"'Course not. Dumbfucks couldn't organize a party in a nightclub."

He scrubbed a hand over his face. "Look, I wanted to catch you before you left."

"Okay, why?"

"Storm might..."

"He'll be grieving," I finished for him. "I know."

Link's mouth twisted. "Not sure you do, but yeah. Just... I dunno, Keira. Maybe remember that Rene was like a mom to him?"

"Can I ask you a question?"

He sighed. "Don't see why not."

"Is his birth mom dead?"

His stillness had me frowning before he turned to me, muttering, "You mean he didn't tell you?"

"No. We don't really talk about our parents."

"She's as good as dead to him," he confirmed.

"That bad, huh?" I asked sadly.

"Worse. Storm lived half the time with Rene and Bear, then Ellen would get released and she'd draw them back into her web. I never used to get why she did that. Rene would have looked after them all the time." He cleared his throat. "Storm's mom and Rene are, *were*, cousins."

"Really? I didn't know that."

"They didn't like each other, but Ellen knew Rene would have killed her if she'd dumped the kids in foster care." He picked up the end of the rosary he always wore and started twisting it through his fingers as he muttered, "Never been gladder than when he cut her out of his life."

"What did she do?"

"What didn't she do? You think Scarlet was a cunt by nature?" He scoffed. "More like nurture. Ellen was Scarlet's model. She just made everything worse by 2.0."

My nose crinkled at the bridge. "I hate Scarlet."

"Everyone fucking hates that skank. Even Storm." He shot me a look. "She ain't been around for a long time. Did Storm say what happened that last time he went to bail her out?"

I knew when he meant. "No." I grimaced. "I-I..."

Link patted my hand. "I remember. You ran away again."

I winced. "God, you make me sound like a puppy in a movie."

"You did take off a lot that first year, Keira," he chided.

"Because I was scared! Because I was going to be a mom, because Storm was going to be a dad and he kept taking off for days on end and wouldn't tell me where he was going or—" I blew out a breath. "I still hate it when he goes on runs, but at least I understand it now. He's not that great at explaining himself, Link," I grumbled.

"You left, then Scarlet got arrested, and the day after, you got rushed into the hospital, right?" he asked. "I think that was the order of shit. Maybe there was some time in between."

"Does it matter?"

He hummed. "What did she say to you? It was Scarlet, right? That made you leave that time? You'd started to settle in—"

"How do you know that?"

"I remember him being happy," Link said wryly. "Ain't you noticed? When you're down, he's down."

"It's not that simple."

"Isn't it? My boy's whipped for you, honey," Link teased softly. "Rene said she ain't never seen a boy so in love as he is with you."

My cheeks turned pink. "Well, I love him too," was my prim response.

"You love what you know. You should remember, Keira, still waters run deep." Before I could ask him what the hell that meant—although, I guessed I'd just dealt with some of that back in my husband's bedroom —he queried, "Why did you leave him so much that first year?"

"I didn't just leave because I'm flighty. Something happened or went wrong and I just, well, I got scared. That time, Scarlet told me I should get an abortion."

"So? You didn't have to leave Storm. Wasn't like he was asking you to get one."

"Do we have to talk about this?"

"I'm curious."

"Why are you?"

"Because Bear was asking where Scarlet was. He wants her here for the funeral. I just wondered why Storm ran her off."

"Scarlet… she's…"

"A bitch?"

"Yes, but she's cruel. She scared me. She looked at me like she could push me down the stairs and make me lose the baby." I shuddered. "It felt so real—"

"Christ," Link muttered. "I wonder if it's because she couldn't have kids?"

This was the first I'd heard of that. "Why couldn't she?"

"She was pregnant and when she lost it, she had a really bad—" His words waned. "Well, I don't know what happened, but I know they took all those parts out."

"Good God, that's terrible!"

He grunted. "Maybe. If any woman wasn't made to be a mother, it's her and that skank Ellen. You really thought she was going to hurt you?"

I nodded. "It's dumb now."

"But you were nineteen then. Newly pregnant. Newly graduated. Newly married. Newly adult."

"Yeah."

"I'm glad he cut her out of his life."

"Me too." I pulled a face. "Will Bear really want her around for the funeral?"

"Yeah. Rene spent years raising her. Wasn't her fault she was like the kid from a horror movie, was it?"

Despite myself, my lips curved. "That pretty much sums her up."

"The antichrist." He mock-shuddered, then slung his arm around my shoulders. "Just remember, Keira, even if Storm pulls away because of his grief, he loves you."

My brow puckered. "You're scaring me, Link. Why should he pull away?"

He squeezed me. "Just in case he does."

Concerned and confused, I stared up at him. He meant it. No 'just in case' about it.

And though he warned me, when Storm spent most of the next three weeks at the clubhouse, I was still underprepared for it.

I barely saw him, barely heard from him, then, one day, he just came back.

Looking like hell, his face white, his skin sallow. He'd dropped at least twenty pounds and was walking around as if he'd had the crap beaten out of him even though he had no bruises.

But things reverted to normal, and because I was a chicken shit, I didn't press.

Maybe Link was right about still waters running deep and, maybe, I didn't want to look beneath the surface. Maybe I liked things just as they were...

TEN

STORM

PRESENT

I FOLLOWED Keira's SUV at a leisurely pace, watching her, watching the road ahead, making sure all was well.

From the corner of my eye, I saw one of the brothers I paid to guard her permanently tailing us both, and even though I was here, I didn't bother to call him off. He lived opposite Keira and Cyan now, neither of them the wiser that he only lived there because of them.

Almost all of our married life, I'd had someone tailing her, and she'd never noticed. This wasn't her world, though. Even after eleven years of marriage, it still wasn't.

Looking back, I knew I should have pushed things, shouldn't have let her settle into her bubble, should have drawn her into the Sinners' world but... Christ. It had been in my best interests that she stayed away from the MC, and I hadn't done dick to discourage her dislike of the clubhouse or my family.

One mistake... one mistake was all it took to worm away at the foundations of our marriage.

My hands tightened around the handlebars of my ride as we trudged along the snow-dusted road toward her house in a nice subdivision on the other side of Coshocton.

It was the kind of place where her SUV was the common ride, not a hog, but though I got some side eye, and Jump did as well, nobody had said anything yet.

'Yet' being the operative word.

As we rolled through the gates of the community, I tipped my head at the security guard who didn't bat an eye at me or Jump even though, ordinarily, security would be all over us like flies around shit in a subdivision like this one. The fact that I slipped him and the other guard a thousand a month to keep him happy, to make sure he kept me in the loop about her comings and goings, lubed things up, of course.

Bribing was the way to go when you had a wife you wanted eyes on twenty-four-seven.

Heading into the subdivision, I rolled past houses that, as a kid, I'd craved as a permanent address.

Money wasn't a problem for me anymore, hadn't been when I was VP, and though shit was tighter here because the club wasn't making as much money, I wasn't a complete asshole. I had a fuck ton of savings which I'd spent a small chunk on getting this address, the SUV —one of the safest on the market—and sending Cyan to a local private school.

I'd stayed low key in West Orange because of Keira's father. Not sent her private, kept our addresses nice and middle class.

Here, I could do whatever the fuck I wanted.

I was fresh.

I was new.

I was a clean page that was ready to be written on, and I intended to start the first chapter of my redemption story right.

That meant giving Cyan what she needed, and it meant ensuring her mom was happy too.

Keira and I still hadn't had a conversation about her own schooling, but I knew that was on the cards. I'd encourage it too.

I'd been such a dumbass before.

So many fucking mistakes. I felt as if I were buried in them. Like they were shit that I needed to dig my way out of.

Would I ever be free?

No.

But that didn't mean I didn't have to keep on trying, did it?

When her BMW rolled up the driveway, I pulled onto the side of the road. I could feel the neighbors' curtains twitch at the sound of my half-pipes, but I didn't give a damn. I'd selected this house because it was a corner lot with a massive yard all around the property.

The location meant riding past a good chunk of houses, but when I parked, we were away from nosy fucking Karens who'd call 911 just for me showing up, with the nearest houses being a vacant one and where Jump was living with his woman and kid.

I stretched as I climbed off my bike, ignoring the sound of Jump's half-pipes, too, then grabbed the small bag I'd packed and had stored in my saddlebags.

Heading up the path toward the SUV, I helped gather Maddox's baby gear, not that there was much, and most of it borrowed, but I grabbed it all without a word, popping the trunk without asking, before trudging over to the front door to wait on the women.

Cyan had been quiet ever since I'd gone into the clubhouse to gather my shit together, but whatever had been said, it seemed to have been more cathartic than angry because the second she was out of the car, she was her mom's shadow.

Only after Keira had let us in did she trail into the family room, which kind of surprised me because I thought she'd be all over Maddox, but she wasn't.

Following the women, I left the gear in the spare room, then retreated to the kitchen to grab two sodas before I went to find Cy who'd switched on the TV.

Slumping into the sofa beside her, she giggled when I nosed into her space, shoving her up against the side, giving her no room at all.

"You're squishing me!" she complained with another giggle that melted my heart.

Truth be told, I'd never imagined the love I felt for Keira could be overtaken by another, but Cy had done that. She'd wrecked me too. It was why I didn't want another kid. I couldn't afford to feel this way for another child. I just... it was too much.

Much too much.

"I'm totally not squishing you," I countered as I popped the tab on the soda can and shoved her even more into the side.

She huffed, but grabbed my arm, dragged it high, then shoved herself under it so she was cuddled into my side. Neither of us said anything after that though, just tuned into Disney+.

It took me a second to figure it out, but then I muttered, "Why do they have to redo everything?"

She peered up at me. "Huh?"

"When I was a kid, *The Mighty Ducks* was a movie. That was fine. Why do they have to change it?"

Cy sniffed. "Because it's old."

"Yeah, well, so am I."

"You're not old."

I grinned. "You know that logic don't work, right?"

"My logic is perfect."

"Well, I wouldn't go that far." My eyes twinkled as I glanced down at her. "You're pretty high up there, but no one's perfect, honey."

"I am." She grinned back. "Did I show you what I learned last week?"

She'd been going to a ton of classes while waiting to start school in January, most of which another brother, Peanut, shadowed her on. It was to my detriment that I'd only stalked my wife all our married life. I fucked up with Cy, but never again.

Never.

Fucking.

Again.

I didn't give a shit if she bitched about it when she was thirty-fucking-three.

She was going to have an MC shadow for the rest of her goddamn life.

"Which class?" I questioned after I sipped my drink.

"Gymnastics." She squirreled out of the seat, then cried out, "Watch!"

I was surprised that she was still so eager where gymnastics was concerned, seeing as that was where she'd met that fucker—make that two fuckers when you counted her grandfather—but I wasn't about to discourage her, so I watched as she did some kind of weird handstand thing which morphed into a backward flip, before she mirrored that and tumbled forward.

Clapping, I asked, "You dizzy now?"

Her smile was, in a word, luminescent. "Nope." Then she did it four more times until I was the one who was dizzy.

"Storm?"

I twisted around at Keira's call. "Yeah?"

"Want to come help me make dinner?" she asked from the doorway.

"Can't we order takeout, Mom?" Cy wheedled, but Keira just smiled.

"Nope."

I got to my feet, then winked at her. "Let me work some magic, kiddo."

Cy bounced on her feet then proceeded to do more cartwheels and all kinds of funky shit across the family room floor.

Shaking my head at her, I left her to it before I traipsed after Keira and followed her into the kitchen.

This was one room I loved about this house. It was closed off with a barn door. Kept all the funky smells inside and usually, whenever Keira and I needed to talk, it meant we could shut things off without Cyan overhearing.

The second I slid the door closed, I saw her leaning over the kitchen counter, her hands braced against it, head bowed.

Trepidation filled me. "Baby girl? What is it?"

Her shoulders tensed a second, before she looked up and I saw the tears on her face, tears that were new but somehow had made her pink and red and all kinds of in between. I knew why—she'd been holding this back. But what the fuck had happened?

Her eyes were bloodshot, her cheeks slick as she whispered, "Storm, I'm so sorry."

Fear hit me, but the truth was, my whole fucking world was inside this house...

Had something happened at the clubhouse? Had some bitch said something? Did she want to go back to West Orange?

Prepared to fight for my life, I rasped, "Who is it? What's happened?" I knew it'd be a who. It always was.

"B-Bear didn't make it, honey. H-He's gone."

She might as well have dropped a bomb in here for all my brain imploded with the news.

Like I'd been hit with ten bullets, my back thudded against the door. "No. You can't know that!" It was a sweetbutt who'd upset her.

It had to be.

"I answered your phone in the office. It was Rachel." Mouth quivering, she whispered, "Rachel told me h-he's gone."

Eyes unseeing now as, slowly, I slid down against the door, my knees unable to hold my weight as I sank into a puddle of bones.

Rationally, I'd known this day was coming.

Rationally, I'd known a man like Bear would never have the will to live when he was so torn to shreds in the blast that had destroyed the Sinners' clubhouse.

As far as I knew, he'd never woken up, but if he had, he'd have been unable to ride, would be unable to do what he loved the most— be on the back of a bike. That wasn't the kind of life he was born to have, but that didn't mean I wanted to lose him. He was my father in everything but biology.

Fuck.

He couldn't be dead.

Only, Keira's soft sobs told me otherwise.

Regret hit me.

Remorse next.

Guilt followed.

Then shame.

Shame. Always fucking shame.

I bowed my head, hiding my face in my hands as I propped my elbows on my knees.

"I-I didn't see him that day we left," I whispered rawly. "I never got to say goodbye."

Footsteps sounded, tapping against the tiles, and when she slipped down to the floor beside me, her arms awkwardly twisting around me, I sank into her hold.

I sank into my home.

My haven.

I'd admit, I took advantage. Her embrace was awkward, so I slipped down further onto the ground, then dragged her onto my lap and tucked my arms around her. She tensed for a second, then immediately relaxed when I pushed my face into her throat.

I was a grown man.

A biker.

Grown-assed bikers didn't fucking cry.

But when the man who was like a dad to them passed away, that was a time when the rule book was thrown out, tossed aside like the toxic masculinity bullshit it was…

ELEVEN

KEIRA

PRESENT

WHEN STORM STARTED CRYING, I'd admit, I lost it.

I'd seen his eyes wet with tears twice in our marriage, and each time, it had killed something inside me. Something that made me want to make things better, made me want to fix the problem, but some problems couldn't be fixed.

When I'd given birth to Cyan, he'd held her, and tears had made his eyes glassy. He hadn't sobbed or anything, but he'd pressed his lips to my sweaty forehead, and he'd rasped, "Thank you, baby girl. Thank you for her."

Back then, I'd been so scared, I'd clung to him like a life raft. At first, I was terrified that he'd run off, leave me with the baby like my parents threatened he would. Instead, he'd married me. He'd set me up in a house the second my dad threw me out. But I'd been so scared that giving birth would be too much of a reality check.

Ironically enough, he'd never really let me down as the father of my kid.

It was just as a husband, he'd sucked.

But I still remembered that day. The scent of blood, salty perspiration from how hard labor had been, his fading deodorant, the tang of ozone in the maternity ward, the bittersweet stench of cleaning fluids...

all of it was as strong as the memory of him kissing my temple in thanks.

Then, there was the day Rene had died. When her broken body had been found on the road like she was trash...

The memory had me clinging to him, not arguing about the way he was holding me, how I was sitting on his lap like this was 'before,' when it most definitely wasn't.

Three times in our marriage now.

Three.

Three sets of tears.

Was it wrong that I wished he'd cried when I told him we were through?

Was it wrong that I wanted him to mourn the death of our marriage as much as he did Bear and Rene's passings?

I shoved that thought aside, mostly because it wasn't helpful. If anything, it was the opposite. It was also irrelevant.

Instead, I held onto him, clinging to him tightly as he clung to me.

God, he felt good in my arms. He felt right. Why did he have to feel so right? Why did he *always* have to feel so right?

My eyes prickled with tears as his shoulders shook, his body trembling, and I just held him. That was the only thing I could do.

For all the shit he'd done, he was still my baby daddy, and he'd lost the equivalent of his father. I wasn't that much of a bitch that I could reject him, that I could turn away from him as he dealt with his grief.

When, minutes, maybe hours later, a knock sounded at the door and it slid open a little, I answered for us both when Cyan asked, "Mom? Dad? What's going on?"

"Daddy's had some bad news, baby. We'll be out in a minute." If I sounded choked, so be it. I could no more stop that than I could fix things for Storm.

"Oh." Her voice turned small. "Is there anything I can do?"

He croaked, "No, Cy. I promise, we'll be out soon."

Christ, Storm sounded like living death.

My visceral reaction to that was as if he'd punched me in the gut.

Hurting for him, I squeezed him tighter, thankful he'd answered her because I didn't think she'd have stopped asking questions until she had something to work with.

She hovered outside the door, before slowly, I heard her walk away, her feet padding against the tiles as she retreated. Walking when, I knew, she'd have cartwheeled down it if her dad hadn't sounded so wrecked.

After a few minutes, Storm pulled back, and I let him. His head tipped against the door and for a second, those gemstone-like eyes of his were hidden from me until, slowly, he opened them. They were drenched, shot with redness, the pupils stark against the crystalline nature of his irises.

"I didn't say goodbye," he repeated.

I reached up and cupped his cheek. "I don't think he even woke up, Ash."

A heavy sigh escaped him. "It don't matter. If I'd said the words, at least he'd know—" His jaw clenched as his words waned. "Rex... I need to call him." He dipped his chin, inadvertently dislodging my hand. He snagged it in his with a move that was as natural as breathing, bridging our fingers together before, with his free one, he scrubbed it over his face. "Jesus, this'll break him."

"Rex is—" I winced, unsure of what to say, but after he rubbed at his eyes then looked at me, I couldn't lie to him. Not wholly, anyway. "He's taken some time out."

"Time out?" Storm repeated, blankly staring at me as if I'd started talking in Mandarin.

Nodding, I didn't say anything to incriminate myself further. 'Time out' and 'taking off' had a similar definition.

He stared at me, his eyes narrowed like he'd scented something funky about what I'd said, but then he heaved a sigh. "We need to make arrangements to ride over for the funeral."

God. More complications. More explanations.

I cleared my throat. "They're doing an autopsy."

"An autopsy? Ain't it obvious why the poor bastard died? A fucking bomb ripped him to shreds!"

I felt his agitation stirring to life beneath me, much as if he were an earthquake that was beginning to take hold.

"It's standard procedure."

I didn't want to lie to him, but I figured this was the kindest thing to say. No way in hell would anyone have murdered Bear. Jesus, not unless they wanted to be killed, brutally, by the Sinners.

It'd be some kind of political maneuvering with the Sheriff's office or something.

At least, I hoped it was or I'd just lied to him for real about a man he considered his dad.

Praying my desire to break it gently to him wouldn't bite me in the ass, I accepted that I wasn't just being selfless here as anxiety started choking me.

He sounded so broken.

So destroyed.

Grief was one thing, but he wasn't just a regular guy, was he?

He had… *problems.*

Which was why I whispered, "Y-You're not going t-to start on the drugs again, Storm? Are you?

His eyes tangled with mine, and his shock was clear as he shook his head. "No, Keira. No."

He sounded so sure, but I wasn't.

For so long, he'd done stuff I'd never been able to understand, reckless things, crazy things, and I'd just thought that was his nature. He was Storm, and I was living in the eye of the tempestuous soul of the man I loved. I thought it was because he was a biker, because that was a part of the lifestyle, but maybe it wasn't.

Maybe it was because he'd been hooked on drugs.

All our married life, I'd been naive. Then Kendra had given me some home truths. Then our daughter had been kidnapped. Then I'd learned about his addictions.

There was no diminishing the harsh reality of the world I lived in now. No putting those blinders back on.

He reached out, hesitating when I flinched as he cupped my chin. "How do you know about the drugs?"

I hadn't told him that I knew. In the aftermath of Cyan's return home, I'd had no need to, especially when, after closely monitoring him, I'd seen that he was clear-eyed, focused, and intent on righting the wrongs he'd done to his family.

Sorrowful, penitent—the expression in his eyes was enough to break me, but he was too different to the Storm of before so I'd known he was clean.

"Rachel told me before we came here."

His mouth tightened with displeasure. "She had no right to do that."

"She wanted to explain something to me."

"What?"

"It doesn't matter. She was trying to make me see you in a different light—"

"The worst kind?" was his bitter retort.

"The opposite if anything. She was trying to open my eyes to the real you."

He gritted his teeth. "Do you know Rach and me *used* to be friends? Emphasis on *used to be*." His nostrils flared. "Goddammit. I didn't want you to know—"

Reaching over, I squeezed his shoulder. "She was being a friend, Storm. You've always done some crazy things, pulled some weird stunts, and I was too goddamn blind to realize what was going on. At least now I know."

Our gazes clashed, held, and for a small segment of time, we were bound to one another. Bound in a way I knew I'd only ever feel with him.

On my dark days, I railed at that. Railed at a world, a fate, that tied me to a man who could treat me how he did.

Sitting here, now, I didn't hate on kismet. I just felt sad, a little defeated. As if, all this time, I'd been blaming him, but maybe I shouldn't have. Maybe I should have been blaming us instead.

Now wasn't the time for this conversation, but I couldn't stop myself from asking, "What else don't I know, Storm? What else have you kept from me?"

My teeth burrowed into my bottom lip as I looked at him, seeing the raw pain in his eyes, accepting that there was a lot of hidden truths he'd buried. I didn't get angry, even though it was my right to be angry. I just decided, then and there, that if I was ever going to have a decent relationship with him, one that wasn't toxic, one that didn't stain my daughter's childhood, I needed to learn the real man.

Flaws, weaknesses, addictions and all.

He bowed his head, hiding his glance from mine, before he whispered, "You can't—" I tensed up, expecting him to tell me that I couldn't possibly handle whatever it was he was keeping a secret, but he didn't. Instead, he continued, "—expect me to remember all the shit that's gone on throughout our marriage, Keira. Not when I was high at the times you're talking about."

Though my heart sank, I refused to let that sway me. "Can't I?" I reached over, grabbed his chin. His beard tickled the pad of my thumb as I forced him to look up at me. "Can't I?" I repeated, my voice harder. "Don't I deserve to understand, Storm? Don't I?

"We need to make this work for Cyan's sake. I can't keep on hating you for what you did when I didn't understand it, and you can't keep shit from me when all it's doing is making me think the worst of you."

I stared him down, absorbing his surprise and disregarding it. I'd been a pushover for such a long goddamn time that it was no wonder he looked astonished. I'd been so eager to bury my head under the covers to keep everything peaceful at home.

Just like my mom.

A goddamn Stepford Wife.

It was time, however, that I took a firm hold of my backbone and made it mine again. The process had begun when I'd thrown him out, but that didn't mean it wasn't a work-in-progress.

Only, he didn't say a word, so I informed him, "Now isn't the moment to start confessing your sins, Storm. I'm not asking you to. But I want you to bear it in mind over the upcoming days.

"If you want us to have a decent relationship, one with mutual trust and respect, then you can't hold back, because all I'll think is that you haven't changed one bit."

"Even if you never take me back, Keira, I'm not going to stop working on trying to convince you we're meant to be," he rumbled eventually.

"Then you know what you have to do." I softened the harshness of my words by reaching forward and pressing a kiss to his temple. "You can stay here for the next few days. I don't want you on your own while you're dealing with this—"

"I won't fall off the wagon, Keira. I won't."

My smile was sad, but my pain went too deep to believe him. I was learning about all this in the aftermath, but that didn't make the secrets he'd kept hurt any less.

As I looked at him, I wondered if I'd ever really known him.

Somehow, that made the hurt even more brutal.

I'd have gasped if I'd been alone, as I accepted the repeated knife to the gut that was each secret he'd kept from me.

Voice husky, croaky with his betrayal, I told him, "I don't believe you, and for Cyan's sake, I need to make sure you stay strong." Maybe I should have wanted to hurt him, to wound him with my words like he'd staggered me with his actions, but at that moment, he was my kid's daddy. A son mourning. So, I squeezed his shoulder as I carefully climbed off his lap. "That doesn't mean I don't have faith in you. It just means I know what Bear was to you, and that this would be a blow to anyone, never mind a surrogate son."

He peered up at me, all big eyes and vulnerability, pain and distress and need.

Need for me.

Why couldn't he have looked at me like that before?

Why had I never been enough for him?

Why, when he could look at me like that, why, when he put me on some kind of pedestal, could he look as if he were dying when I stopped touching him, but could easily fuck some random ho as if I weren't waiting back at home for him in our bed?

Mouth tight, I asked, "What is it?"

"No one's ever called me that before," he admitted softly.

I frowned. "Never called you what?"

"A surrogate son." Storm swallowed. "But I was. He wasn't my dad, but he was like my dad." He swiped a hand over his face, then carefully clambered to his feet. "So many nights, I used to go to bed wishing I'd wake up the next day and he would be."

"I know," I told him, which was why I was going to let him stay here. Not just to keep an eye on him, but because I knew what Storm felt for anyone he considered family.

When I held out my hand, he eyed it with confusion. "Why—" He motioned at me.

"Because we need to tell Cyan this. Together."

As our fingers tangled, I prayed I wasn't making a mistake here. But even as I lowered the barriers around my heart a little, I remained cautious.

Maybe, I thought sadly, I always would be that way around him.

TWELVE

STORM

PAST

"HE DID IT AGAIN LAST NIGHT."

I heard Nyx's mutter and shot him the bird. "Fuck off."

"I won't," he retorted, folding his arms across his chest. "Where the fuck do you think I can fuck off to? I live here."

"What did he do?" Link asked, ever late to the party.

"Did that hyper thing." Nyx wriggled his shoulders uneasily. "We were dealing with that fucker, Jonny Laramie, trying to beat him down for the money he owes the club, when out of nowhere, his fucking fists are flying. I swear they moved so fast it was like a goddamn blur."

"Shut up. It wasn't that fast."

Nyx's eyes bugged out. "Wasn't that fucking fast? Steel, since when have you known me to exaggerate?"

"Never?" He scratched his balls. "But then, I'm not used to you talking this much so I'm not sure."

"The fact he has words to spill is indicative of the peculiarity of the situation."

I sniffed. "Indicative, is it, Rex?"

He grinned at me. "Sorry. Was cramming law textbooks last night with Rachel."

"When you gonna bang her?" Link grumbled. "She's the only thing that puts a smile on that ugly fucking face of yours."

Ignoring him, Rex turned to me, "Lightning, what's with you?"

I grunted. "Nothing."

"You taking that shit again?"

"No."

"Fuckin' liar," Nyx muttered. "You're taking something, prick. Like something from a sci-fi movie."

"So I got him squealing faster than you did, so fucking what, Nyx? Instead of bitching at me, you should be grateful. You got to go home earlier. Got to fuck Lipstick, didn't you? Why you giving me all this crap?"

He huffed. "Because, fucker, it ain't right. Can't walk into a shake-down with you high as a kite."

His words had the jitters rolling through my system taking another toll for the worst.

"He's right," Link said softly. "He's gotta be able to trust you."

"If I was unreliable," I argued, "then I'd fucking—"

"Unreliable? You're as fickle as the fucking weather. Worse than lightning. You're more like a goddamn storm rolling in out of fucking nowhere.

"This shit has to stop. Dunno what got you high yesterday, but you need to stop taking it before it messes with your system too much."

Rex eyed Nyx with no small amount of surprise, and it wasn't like I could blame him. Nyx was the kind of guy who said a lot in ten words. He never rambled into mini speeches. Never made declarations about shit.

That he was spooked said a lot for how wired I'd been yesterday, but Prince had gotten me some meth from this new kid who was cooking it over in East Orange.

It slipped through my veins like a knife through butter on a hot day. Went straight into the system as clean as neat whisky, and I'd felt the hype all goddamn night.

It was eleven AM, and I hadn't come down yet. It was starting though. I could feel the withdrawals. Could feel the hunger crawling around my system.

Not yet.

Not yet.

This was our ritual.

Most of us dragged our asses out of bed to eat breakfast together at eleven AM every day.

Cherry made us our breakfasts, we ate it together, before we fucked off and did our own thing.

It was a weird tradition we'd taken to doing since Maverick's last leave.

Eleven AM was six-thirty PM in Kabul, which was when he ate dinner. For whatever reason, he made sure to eat then, and for some other dumbfuck reason, we ate then as well.

We all missed the fucker. It was crazy to follow this tradition, but hell, we'd done crazier shit in our time.

"I swear to fuck, he's been making Sin look chilled when we do our rounds," Nyx groused.

Rex's brows soared again, because we all knew Sin had anger management issues. I'd never have said that I did...

"You're still high, aren't you?" Rex murmured softly, leaning closer to me, peering at my eyes.

I shoved him back, not even that hard, but Rex went flying off the breakfast stool.

Christ.

My mouth worked as I tried to figure out how I'd done that. Rex wasn't exactly fucking small.

I stared down at my hands like they'd transformed into the Hulk's fists as silence fell in the kitchen which, thankfully, housed only my brothers. Either way, I was screwed.

Nyx rumbled, "See what I fucking mean? Don't know what the hell he's taken but Marvel must have been doctoring it. Fucker's turning into Peter Parker."

Pretty goddamn poetic that I'd just likened myself to the Hulk.

"Parker's DC Comics—"

"Shut the fuck up, Link. Spider-Man's goddamn Marvel," Steel spat.

"Whichever the hell it is," Nyx argued. "We gotta do something about him."

Rex ambled to his feet, brushing down his cut, studying me like I hadn't just shoved him off his chair. That was when my heart started pounding, sending adrenaline chugging through my system.

I didn't know what Rex was thinking, but I didn't like that look in his eyes.

I jumped to my feet, just as Rex ground out, "Get him."

Like they were all on a goddamn leash, and even though Link and Steel were still bickering about comic books, they surged on me.

Fuck, it was like being taken down by a goddamn bomb as four guys, each over two hundred pounds, barreled into me.

After a childhood of my mother's boyfriends trying to use me as a punching bag, I was used to scrapping dirty. Though they tried to take me down, I fought hard and fast, even as the sluggish crawl of need slinked through my veins, sped up, I thought, by the unexpected surge of adrenaline.

As I kicked them aside, using tricks that Bear had taught me, blood spurted and bones crunched—some of my own included—I almost made it out of there, which was when Rex called out, "Stand down."

"Fuck," Link panted, rubbing his side where I'd punched him.

Steel shoved a hand to his nose that was bleeding freely. "Motherfucker's fast."

"See?" Nyx ground out, breathing hard from his bent over position as he caught some air.

"I see it," Rex muttered.

I backed away from them all, muttering, "Just leave me the hell alone—"

A gasp escaped me as the sudden gnawing hunger overwhelmed everything else, buckling my bones, making me topple over so I had to prop myself up on my knees.

The pain of their hits, the concern about their conversation—nothing mattered.

I didn't give a shit about anything other than the call in my body.

I needed more meth.

Fuck, I'd die without it.

"That's the beauty of withdrawals," Rex murmured grimly. "They'll do the work for you."

"Guess I got confirmation he *is* on something, huh?" Nyx grumbled as he finally straightened up, his breath in order.

I ran out of the room, surprised when they didn't stop me. I heard Link reply, "See why you said he was like a fucking storm, Nyx. Jesus Christ. Feel like I just got swept up by a goddamn tornado."

Steel grated out, his voice nasal as he stemmed the blood flow, "The fuck is he on?"

"Meth, probably."

I tuned out after Rex spoke, hurrying down the hall. As expected, Prince was in his bedroom, banging Popsicle, and I demanded, "You got some more of that meth from last night?"

He grinned at me. "Good shit, right? Never tasted Hot Ice like it."

The best.

But I wasn't about to tell him that.

He'd charge me double.

"I got work in a couple hours. I need something to take the edge off."

His eyes narrowed at me as he stopped thrusting. "Tell you what, Lightning. I'll hit you up if you give me fifteen percent of your cut."

I blinked at him, nostrils flaring as the need for the sweet relief hit me.

At that moment, I realized I'd have offered him my fucking kidney if he'd asked for it.

"Yeah. Deal."

He pointed at the chair where his cut lay. "Got a baggy in my jeans. Grab it then get the fuck outta here."

I got the shit, hurrying out without a backward's glance. I heard Prince's chuckle as I scurried out like a fucking rat with cheese in its paws, but I didn't think anything of it. Wasn't thinking of anything but getting this nectar into my veins.

I never imagined that my fighting under the influence would gain me a rep that would tear away my short-lived road name and would replace it with one that Nyx had come up with.

Storm.

My temper. My fists. My rage.

THIRTEEN

STORM

PRESENT

WHEN I WOKE up on the couch, it was because a bony elbow somehow dug its way into my stomach and a knee nearly castrated me.

Surprise and pain had me yelping, then when Cyan squeaked and almost tumbled off the cushions, I reached out and grabbed her and stopped her from falling.

"Cy?" I rasped dopily. "What are you doing here?"

"I couldn't sleep, Daddy."

How could I chastise her when it had taken me six hours to finally drift off? *This* was why I needed pot. And the kid in my arms, the woman sleeping down the hall, were the reasons that was no longer an option open to me.

Pot to mellow down, meth to wake up.

Rather than say another word, I got to my feet and held out my hand. Mutely, she took it, her shoulders slumped as I walked us down to her bedroom.

Hers was the only room that was truly decorated. The same color as her eyes, the walls were a rich jewel-like green, and she had bookcases loaded down with stuff she'd been collecting since she was a kid. Her bed had a canopy and, thank God, was a double.

When I let go of her hand and rounded the other side, I told her, "Climb in."

"But I don't want to," she said, tone teary.

"Cyan," I rumbled, "get in."

She huffed a little but did as asked, then I hauled the bright blue comforter over her, grabbed the furry blanket that sat at the foot of her bed, and plunked my ass down on top of the covers.

Quiet a second, I laid back, then she heaved a sigh. "That's better."

A smile curved my lips at the innocent reply, and I closed my eyes, letting her lift my arm so she could burrow into my side. She curled up into such a small ball that her toes dug into my thigh.

Why did kids have such bony toes?

As her tension ebbed, I thought she was close to sleeping, and I allowed the chase and hunt of my thoughts to start up again as I tried to process the many things that had happened today.

Just as I thought she was falling asleep, she whispered, "Daddy?"

I hummed.

"I love you."

It wasn't like she never told me that, but after the evening I'd had, fuck, those words hit me hard.

If my voice was a little choked when I replied, "I love you too, lady-bug," then so be it.

With us huddled together, we fell asleep, but as usual, even without my kid somehow managing to kick me in all the soft places on my body, I woke up when it was still dark.

Disentangling myself from the chokehold of the blankets that she'd tossed over me as she wriggled around, I somehow got to my feet without disturbing her and padded out and over to the kitchen.

This place was the nicest room in the house so far and without need of renovating. With creamy white cabinets, marble countertops, a station island in the middle that was a breakfast bar, I loved being here because it was so different than the kitchens I'd had as a kid.

It belonged in a magazine, and Keira and Cy deserved that.

I headed over to the double-wide fridge, grabbed the bottle of milk, retrieved a glass from a cupboard, then plunked my ass on the stool after I dragged out my cell from my pocket.

I had some messages from a couple of guys back at the clubhouse, then there were some from my brothers, my real family, in a group chat that had been surprisingly silent for the last couple of days.

Figuring that was because it was Christmas, I'd not suspected anything, but now I opened it and saw the hundreds of messages that were unread.

Quickly perceiving that Bear had died on the night of Christmas Day, that the guys were all mourning him as much as I was, I just read through Nyx, Link, Steel, and Maverick's comments. Rex hadn't said a damn thing.

Me: *You could have told me sooner.*

It was an accusation. I knew that. But I didn't care.

Nyx: *We didn't fucking know until yesterday.*

Me: *What? Why not?*

Nyx: *Rachel didn't tell us. When we started asking about Rex, then she keyed us in.*

What about Rex?

Me: *What the fuck? Why didn't she?*

Nyx: *Dunno. I'm looking into it.*

Me: *She had no right to keep that from us.*

Link: *Agreed.*

Me: *What are you doing awake, anyway?*

Nyx: *Same thing as you, dipshit.*

Me: *Fuck you.*

Nyx: *You wish you could.*

Me: *Don't joke, Nyx. This is serious. Fuck, Bear's dead.*

Nyx: *I know, Storm. I know. It's like a fucking bad dream.*

Link: *When's this year gonna end, huh?*

Me: *You couldn't sleep either?*

Link: *No.*

Link: *Where do you think Rex is?*

Nyx: *I'm hoping he's riding to Ohio.*

Me: *To see me? Why would he do that?*

Me: *He's been gone since Christmas Day?*

Nyx: *Yeah. That's why we started asking questions.*

Nyx: *You were close to Bear, I figure you could talk about old times.*

Me: *So? We were all close to Bear.*

Nyx: *You know you're different. Why wouldn't he want to be with you?*

Me: *Well, it only takes eight hours to get here. If he's coming, then he's gone via fucking Alaska. Why the hell did he take off?*

Nyx: *He did the same when Rene died, remember? Anyway, not saying you're the only place he's heading, just that I bet you're his end destination.*

Uncertain of his logic, I didn't reply, just asked:

Me: *When's the funeral?*

Link: *You coming back for it?*

Me: *What the fuck do you think? Of course I am. Even if it's just for the day, I have to be there.*

Link: *I wasn't sure. Rex said you were having issues with the club.*

Me: *I picked a council yesterday. Things should even out soon enough.*

Nyx: *They're saying there was some kind of foul play with the body.*

Me: *What?! Is that why're they're going ahead with an autopsy?*

Nyx: *It's a load of asshole, bullshitting, fucking insanity. I don't know what that asswipe sheriff is doing, but if he doesn't fix this fast, I'll work on getting another one in our pocket.*

Me: *That'd be a stupid move to make. Just let the investigation run unheeded. Nothing happened.*

Me: *He was involved in a fucking blast and died as a result of his injuries.*

Me: *They'll figure that out as soon as they… Jesus.*

Link: *Yeah. As soon as they, you know what.*

Bear was gonna be cut up soon. Christ.

Nyx: *He's dead, guys. I can't believe it.*

Me: *I can't either.*

I reached up and grabbed my glass of milk. Taking a deep sip from it, I sighed.

Me: *You know where Digger is? I've been trying to get in touch with him.*

Link: *Heard about MaryCat.*

Me: *How?*

Link: *Keira.*

Christ, I'd forgotten they were close friends.

How that had happened, I still wasn't sure, but Link used to have all the bitches swarming around him like fucking flies. Why wouldn't my wife be the same?

Me: *Of course.*

Link: *Storm. Shut up.*

Me: *Never said anything.*

Link: *You didn't have to.*

Nyx: *Are we gonna start talking about our feelings or something?*

Me: *Fuck off.*

Link: *Keira told the Posse, and Lily told me over dinner.*

I wished that didn't make me feel better.

Nyx: *Think Digger's in Canada.*

Me: *Why?*

Nyx: *Rex knows...*

Me: *Not you?*

Nyx: *I know why, not where. Plausible deniability or some such shit. I'm not happy about being out of the loop. Trust me.*

Me: *Why?*

Link: *Yeah, you never said.*

Nyx: *Rex thinks the Rabid Wolves are on the take.*

My brows soared upward in surprise.

MaryCat and Digger had created a little union of sorts between the Irish Mob and the Satan's Sinners. One that had been cemented in place by the fact that Sin, the Sinners' Enforcer, was also her half-brother. Sin and Rex were cousins, because his dad was Grizzly, Bear's brother, and Sin shared an egg donor with MC.

Complicated, sure.

Ever since Digger had branded MaryCat, the Five Points had been using the Sinners to traffic goods up to the Canadian border. There, the Rabid Wolves took over the transporting.

They were ruthless fuckers, because they were dumbasses.

Arming stupid with a gun was never a wise equation.

Me: *Who's with Digger?*

Nyx: *Couple of brothers. It was just a scouting mission.*

Me: *He gonna get his ass killed? Not like Rex to send the dad of a newborn into a fucking bloodbath.*

Nyx: *Like I said, I don't have details. I just know why. But you're right. I don't think Rex expected trouble.*

Link: *Is that what he got?*

Me: *Fuck, I hope not. MaryCat's already wrecked over here. Don't think she'd be able to deal with her Old Man getting shot.*

Nyx: *Look, when Rex took off, he didn't exactly leave his cell behind for me to monitor everything. I'm as blind as you fuckers.*

Me: *Get Maverick onto it. Have him crack Rex's phone.*

Link: *Maverick's all over the place right now.*

Me: *Still in and out of the hospital?*

Link: *Yeah. It's looking better though. They've got him on some kind of alternative therapy course. Alessa was telling Lily about it. Costs a fortune. They're gonna run through their money trying to fix him.*

Me: *No, they won't. Rex'll open up the Sinners' coffers before he lets that happen.*

Nyx: *You know that's right.*

Link: *I hope so. Either way, Lily won't let them bankrupt themselves.*

Nyx: *Can't believe that fucker took off like this.*

Link: *We're all worried about him.*

Me: *You'll tell me when you know about the funeral?*

Nyx: *'Course.*

Me: *Thanks. I'm gonna get some sleep.*

Nyx: *Me too. Giulia's all over the place right now. Pregnancy hormones on top of this, it's the opposite of what she needed. Night.*

Me: *I'll bet. Night, guys.*

Link: *Night.*

As we all signed off, melancholy swirled inside me.

My family was under this roof.

My family was also in West Orange.

Torn in two directions, I knew there was only one place to go—the refrigerator.

I pulled out the pie Keira had bought with takeout, and I cut myself a huge slice. As I sank back onto the stool again, I heard footsteps padding down the hall, and braced myself for whomever was incoming as I took a massive bite of strawberry lattice pie—Keira's favorite.

When the under-cupboard lighting flared into being, I squinted a little.

"Couldn't sleep?" Keira questioned.

"Cyan woke me up a few times."

Her brow furrowed. "Is she sick?"

I shook my head. "Just..." I blew out a breath when I really thought about what had woken my kid up. "She's hurting." A sorrowful cast overtook her features. Instead of letting it fester, I murmured, "Want some dessert?"

"Yeah. I really do." She stepped over to me, sat on the stool at my side. I handed her my fork, she didn't even question it—just took it, cut off some pie, raised it to her mouth then ate it. Before she passed it back to me.

When she took a sip of my milk as well, a warm feeling overwhelmed me. A sense of rightness.

We belonged together.

"Can I tell you something?" I asked after a couple minutes of silence.

"Sure," she said with a shrug.

"It's about what we were discussing earlier."

"Figured it wasn't about the weather."

I snorted. "Sassy."

"It's five AM, Storm. What else can I be?"

"It's not... *nice.* To hear, I mean."

"If it's honest, then I'm good with it."

"You say that now..."

As my words waned, she turned to me as she snatched my fork and dug into the pie. "Storm, right now, I think you're a cheating piece of shit. I also think you're insane.

"You've got a biker following me, and according to you, you've had a biker following me since I was eighteen years old." Her jaw clenched. "I'm still not over that by the way.

"You tattooed your dick then had it pierced and both your cock and the padlock say, 'Property of Keira.' I know you're a drug addict, I know you were born addicted to crack. Have I said anything there that sounds in anyway good?"

"No," I choked out, pissed that Rach had even shared that sordid truth with her—that I was a crack baby.

Goddammit to hell.

"No," she confirmed gruffly. "And yet, here you sit. In my kitchen. You put my kid to bed. You're staying here for the next however long. When MaryCat sorts herself out and Digger gets his ass down here and they figure things out, into my spare bedroom you'll go... I know a lot of stuff about you, most of it bad, but I haven't tossed you out on your ass."

"Because of Cyan."

"Because of Cyan," she confirmed. "But she's my daughter, Storm. I'd kill for her. I'd fucking die for her. Do you think I'd place her with someone I don't trust to love her back? To keep her safe? Especially after what she's been through?"

"No." My throat grew thick with emotions again. "I do love her, Keira."

"I know you do." She snatched the fork back when I didn't make a move to take another bite. "You got a biker watching her as well?"

"Yes."

She sighed. "I wish I weren't relieved about that."

"When she went into school, I was going to do something then. Bribe a janitor or something, but I didn't go through with it. I regret that now. I regret not having someone tail her."

"Must cost you a fortune in bribes."

"It does."

"You don't care?"

"I don't give a fuck if it bankrupts me."

"From the size of this house, I'd say you're far away from bankruptcy."

"I am." I cleared my throat. "You are as well."

"Good to know."

"Told you, when you're ready for school, I'll cover it. No matter the cost."

She disregarded my words with a hum. "You going to tell me, or what?"

All night long, her words had been churning in my head. As had reprimands Bear had given me along the way. They'd tangled together, forming knots that made it hard to close my eyes because I was pretty sure those knots were in my optic nerves.

The question really was... how deep down the rabbit hole did I go?

"I didn't cheat on you intentionally."

Though she tensed up at first, her tone wasn't bitter, just cold as she stated, "Just fell in her pussy, did you?"

It was weird hearing Keira swear. Until we'd split up, I'd never heard her say anything worse than 'gosh darn' when she cut herself while chopping fucking tomatoes.

"You want to hear this or not? I'm not asking for forgiveness, just telling you facts."

"Nothing is fact. It's all about perspective."

"Yeah, and in your mind, I got off on cheating on you. I didn't."

"Sure as hell did it enough."

My mouth tightened. "Do you want me to tell you this or not? I won't ask again, and if you say no, then I won't share shit with you."

She glowered at me, but though the nod she gave me was tight, she dipped her chin in assent.

"You know I struggle to get to sleep most nights. I'm wired and I can't calm down. When I was younger, like twelve? I realized pot helped." I reached for the milk, took a deep sip. "I started using it when shit was bad, when I really couldn't switch off.

"I don't know if it's to do with what I went through as a baby, but they say if you're born addicted to drugs, it fucks with you long term.

"It makes sense, I guess. All those chemicals in your system when you're in the womb... why wouldn't it mess with your development? Scarlet was just as bad, but she used alcohol to numb it.

"I started using more and more pot to the point where, eventually, I couldn't fucking function without it. There was this brother, he was VP for a while." I rubbed my thumb along my bottom lip. "Prince was hooked on meth. He used to get me the shit I needed to sleep. One day, he slipped me some of his stuff, and for the first time in years, I felt awake. It was surreal." I closed my eyes. "I know that sounds crazy, but I felt alive."

"And that's how you got addicted?" she asked, her tone wooden.

"Yeah."

"I think I knew about the pot, to be fair, but I just didn't realize how habitually you were using it. What made you take meth the first time?"

"Scarlet."

A growl escaped her. "Should have known."

I licked my lips. "She's dead, Keira. Been dead for years."

"Rachel told me that too." Her tone wasn't exactly warm, but she reached over and covered my hand with hers. "She was a bitch."

I nodded. "She was."

"You never did think the sun rose and set on her, did you?"

"No. Though she had most people fooled for a while. Apart from Bear and Rene, of course."

"Why?"

"Because they saw her at her worst. She even wrapped Rex around her pinkie finger until her true colors shone through." The notion still boggled my fucking mind. I guessed it was because we'd all grown up together. He'd seen her before she turned into the bitch tyrant.

"I'm sorry she's dead, but not sorry she can't ruin things for us anymore."

I twisted my hand over in hers. "She didn't deserve what she got."

"She's the reason you got hooked on drugs, Storm. That's what you just said. You also agreed that she's a bitch."

"Her death wasn't necessary," was pretty much all I could say.

Somehow, Scarlet had gotten tangled up with the *Famiglia*. It was the ex-Don, Benito Fieri, who'd had her killed. She hadn't been back in West Orange for years, but for whatever reason, had been there long enough to get her ass brutally murdered.

"You know she told me to abort Cyan?"

My hand tightened around hers as my teeth clenched with my anger, but I didn't say anything. Scarlet's bitch mouth was one of the reasons why I'd cut her out of our lives.

"That was just the first of many suggestions from her. So forgive me if I don't start wearing black and saying the world is a worse place without her because you won't get that from me."

"I didn't expect to," I countered, and I meant it.

Family was family.

You tolerated them.

Put up with their shit.

I'd done that for so long with Scarlet that I hadn't even smelled the stench when she came around. Until I'd realized blood *wasn't* thicker than water and that my life *was* better without her in it.

"Good thing, because I'd hate to disappoint." She snatched her hand away, which made me mourn its loss, before she reached for the fork again and dug out some more pie for herself.

"What did she do that made you try meth that first time?"

"She got pregnant at fourteen. She never said who the father was—" I grimaced at the memory. "—but I know he had to be an older guy just because of what he did to her. She never did tell us, not even after he nearly beat her to death."

"She made a habit of nearly getting beaten to death, huh?"

"Keira," I reprimanded gruffly, aware that she didn't even know how my sister had died but was right anyway.

It *had* been a habit of Scarlet's. She'd ruffled feathers and her nose had met many another woman's fist as a result.

She shrugged. "What? It's true."

It sadly was.

"Scarlet admitted she tried to blackmail him."

"And there you have it. Knew there'd be something like that going on," she muttered unsympathetically.

"Wherever there was a buck to be made, she was sniffing around it… that's for sure," I agreed.

"She lost the baby?"

"Yeah."

She blew out a breath. "Poor thing."

I knew she meant the baby, not Scarlet.

I'd always been aware that there was no love lost between my sister and her, but still, her venom came as a surprise because Keira was a sweetheart, in possession of a *sweet heart.*

I knew Scarlet too well to be offended on her behalf though. Some people came into this world kicking and screaming, and they left that way too. That was my sister—a pain in the ass from the beginning until the end.

If she'd been a regular sister, I'd have wanted to avenge her death. As it stood, mostly I was left wondering what she'd done to deserve it and, all told, I just hoped she finally found some fucking peace.

"Link told me once that she had to have a hysterectomy... was this the same pregnancy? Or did she get pregnant again?" Keira asked, breaking into my thoughts.

"This was the only kid she had."

She grimaced, but questioned, "You seriously never found out who the guy was?"

"She never said," I hedged.

"You didn't have any suspicions?"

I heaved a sigh, because I didn't want to think about this, never mind talk about it. She was right, though, earlier. She did deserve for me to be less reticent. "I thought it might have been Kevin. Nyx's uncle."

"The one who..." She gulped, freezing in place. "You know?"

"Yeah." *I knew.*

The one who'd abused Nyx's sister until she'd killed herself to escape his claws.

The one whose head Nyx had blown off by messing with his uncle's shotgun, and whose murder Bear had helped cover up.

"Did you never ask her?"

"She never told me."

"Did she love him? Or just want to hold it against him?"

"Who the hell knows with Scarlet?" I grumbled, reaching up and rubbing at my tired eyes. "I just know that only that creep would fuck around with a fourteen-year-old girl and get her pregnant then beat her ass."

"God, that's terrible," she rasped, the story finally penetrating her hatred of my sister. "Fourteen... Cyan..."

Yeah. The ramifications were worse when you had a daughter approaching that age.

The little girl who watched Disney like it was her crack, who needed a nightlight still... how could she be a few years away from having sex and getting pregnant?

"When she was in the hospital, that first night, it was so bad, K. Seriously. I thought she was going to die. She bled out because of the baby, had to have an emergency hysterectomy..." I scraped a hand through my hair. "It was crazy. I didn't sleep for days, and I was just so fucking tired. Prince, he was the VP by that time, hooked me up."

"You took drugs to stay alert?"

I nodded. "Dumb, huh? Not for fun, not to escape, not to party all night, just to stay awake."

"I wouldn't say that was dumb. Sad, but not dumb. Why didn't you just get some sleep? You didn't have to be awake all the time, surely?"

"Scarlet and I, well, you know we didn't get along great. I have no idea why, but she'd start sobbing whenever I tried to leave. So I didn't. I stayed with her. But the beeps, the noises, I couldn't ever rest.

"Plus she'd wake up at all hours and was manic as hell. Sometimes, she'd start screaming at me, other times she'd break down in tears. That went on for seven days. I took the meth, it made shit a lot easier until she was discharged four days after that."

"And by then, it was too late?"

"I had the taste." I nodded again, and even after all these years, I still savored those first highs.

Nothing beat that initial hit.

Every other time, you just chased a fucking rainbow for the pot of gold at the end of it.

"You're lucky you still have your teeth."

My lips curved. "I didn't stick with meth."

"No?"

"Prince died. It got harder to source it."

"You went clean?"

"For a time."

"Meaning?"

"After Prince died, Bear might as well have turned into the DEA. We could push 'em, but we couldn't take 'em. He had a few brothers tossed out for breaking that law."

"MC and drugs, don't they go together like a horse and carriage?"

Though I smirked at her play on words, I merely said, "Prince's death was nasty."

"What happened?"

"It might not have been meth-related, but Bear blamed it all the same. This, man, I don't even know what it was, but it burst in his brain."

"An aneurysm?"

"No. I don't think. Blood came pouring outta his nose like it was a fucking fountain." I grumbled. "It was pretty sick. Unfortunately, it happened at one of the family BBQs, in front of all the kids."

"Jesus."

"Yeah. It left an impression watching him keel over into the grill like he was a sack of potatoes."

"He fell onto the hot grill?"

"Uh-huh. Smelled like bacon." I made an oinking sound which had her gagging.

"Ewww."

Despite myself, despite the situation, I had to grin. Even if it died shortly after, I'd smiled. That was Keira for you. She always did make me feel lighter.

Talking about the grimy shit that fell in our laps on the regular wasn't something I ever did with her, either. Maybe she could ease the burden if I trusted her with it.

"He didn't really," I corrected apologetically. "But the blood stuff, the nose stuff, that was true."

"Still sounds gross."

"It was. Left enough of an impression for Bear to turn into the MC's personal alphabet agency." I shrugged. "Maybe I was the reason for that too. He made me go cold turkey."

"How?"

"Tough love."

"Not sure that works."

"He had the sheriff arrest me."

"On what grounds?"

I wafted a hand. "Something dumb. Parking tickets or some shit. Two weeks in county jail before I got bailed out. It was obviously a setup. The sheriff's always been in our pocket. By the time I got out, the withdrawals were over."

"That's a hard way to get clean," she choked out.

"The hardest. Taught me a lesson, though."

"Until the next time you scored."

I winced but found myself surprised by the lack of accusation in her voice. "Mom got out of jail. That was the next time. She scored some for me. I think she liked that we were both weak."

She gulped. "God, I'm so glad that I never met her."

"Me, too, honey. Me fucking too."

"How did you get clean?"

"Rex."

"What did he do?"

"He wasn't as kind as his dad. Locked me in the Fridge when shit got really bad."

"The Fridge?"

"It's where…" I winced. "…things disappear."

"Oh." She blinked. "Ohhh."

I hummed. "Been in there more fucking times than I can count over the years."

"They just left you there?"

Smiling a little at her indignation, pleased because those occasions had been hell on earth, I told her, "Nah. Someone always stayed with me. They just camped outside."

"How many times have you gotten clean?"

"Four. But the last time, I didn't get clean. I transferred addictions."

"What does that mean?"

"When you go clean, and you do the twelve steps, you're not supposed to have sex or drink or anything like that in case you switch addictions."

"I guess that makes sense."

"It does."

"You didn't listen, did you?" Her voice was sorrowful.

"No. I didn't."

"You're addicted to sex, aren't you? Because I've seen you with booze. You don't drink that much."

"I drank more at the bar at the clubhouse than I did at home, but never to excess. It's not my vice."

"Fucking whores is, though, huh?"

Her bitterness raked at me worse than Bear's passing did. I closed my eyes, and admitted, "I didn't want them, Keira."

"You still fucked them."

"I didn't want them. I always wanted you."

"Is that supposed to make me feel better?" she snarled. "Is that supposed to make everything okay? I was goddamn there, Storm. I was there." Her anger faded. "Why didn't you— I was there." She gulped, and I knew she was holding back her tears. "I was there," she repeated. "You put me on some kind of pedestal. I see that now. I just don't get it." She shook her head. "That night, after we got Cyan back, and I saw the tattoo, you said that you think I'm an angel. I'm not, Storm.

"I'm just a woman. I'm not perfect, I make mistakes. I don't have wings. I don't pretend to be holier than thou. That's not who I am. You put that label on me. You did. Nobody else. I'm flesh and blood."

I wasn't surprised when she got to her feet, the stool scraping against the floor as she shoved it back.

Her words resonated with me in a way that didn't make me feel bad, just angry. It wasn't her fault. None of this was, but that didn't lessen my anger.

As she started to walk away, I snatched her hand and hauled her against me. She yelped in surprise because I never touched her in anger, *ever*, and when she slalomed into my side, her other hand came up against my chest. As she pushed, I didn't let go. I held on tighter. Not letting her budge.

"You are perfection," I rasped. "You are everything that is beautiful in this world. You are a goddess," I snarled. "Don't you dare ever say anything less in my presence."

In the lowlights from beneath the kitchen cabinets, I saw her wide eyes, saw her mouth tremble, and it would have been so easy to press my lips to hers.

I didn't.

But I didn't let go either.

"I'm not a goddess. I'm not perfect. I'm not everything that's beautiful in this world," she replied miserably. "I was a stupid girl who gave everything up for a man who fucked his way through a soccer team of clubwhores rather than be with his wife, a stay-at-home mom who somehow messed everything up so bad that her daughter willingly got into a pedophile's car—"

My brain whirred as I thought about how she looked upon what I'd done. She was taking it as if it were her failing, but it wasn't.

It was mine.

All of this was my fault.

What had I done that made both my woman and kid blame *her* rather than me?

"Keira, you need to listen to me," I growled, unable to bear hearing her talk shit about herself. "Cyan was groomed. That's what pedophiles do. She didn't get into that car because she hated you or hated me. She got into that car because those bastards are clever. They're fucking smart.

"For years, Kevin lived under the MC's radar. He was so goddamn arrogant, so fucking sure of himself that he raped Sinners' kids. If anyone is gonna be more street smart than the regular kid, it's ours. But they didn't say shit. They never said anything until it was too late. Because they get groomed.

"These fuckers are good at what they do because they have to be. Cyan didn't want to run away—"

"She wanted to be with you. She thought he was going to take her to be with you. I could have stopped all this if I'd just come here when you asked," she whispered, but I heard the tears that were coming. "Why did I have to choose that moment to be independent?"

"Because you were standing up for both of you. The day you tossed me out on my ass was a day you made me proud of you, baby girl. I was so, so proud. I was hurting and grieving and terrified but I was glad that you did that because you deserve so much better than me."

"I only ever wanted you," she cried out, and this time, she started sobbing. "Why didn't you want me enough? Why?" When her fist pounded on my chest, I let her. "Why did you have to break us apart? Why couldn't you have just come to me? I would always have been there. Always."

My teeth clenched at her words, words that were like magic to my dick, but the pain it triggered had me tensing up, freezing in place.

"I can't make things right, Keira. I can't change the things I've done," I rumbled, "but I can work to be a better man—"

Her hand dropped to my dick and she shaped my shaft through my jeans. "Why did you do this to yourself? Why, Storm? Why did you brand yourself when the only woman you didn't want to fuck was me?" Her mouth quivered. "At the end, there were months where you never touched me. Christ, I was so sure that—"

"It wasn't you," I muttered rawly. "It was me. It was always me. I couldn't touch you, Keira. I couldn't. I was so dirty, and you were so clean.

"I'd look at you and Christ, I just wanted to take one big bite out of you, but—" I needed her not to touch my dick, but I could no more stop myself from pressing my forehead into hers than I could stop her from doing that. "Some days, I was jacking off twenty to twenty-five times, Keira." I'd never admitted that outside of a meeting before. "I was getting fucking calluses on my goddamn dick. But I still did it. It was a compulsion. How was I supposed to—" My mouth worked. "What was I supposed to do?"

"You could have come to me," she mumbled miserably. "I could have helped."

"How?" I countered. "It was ridiculous. Crazy." I pulled back. "I got weak. I got stupid. I got reckless. When shit got hard, and I wanted to get high, I'd jack off instead. The sex…" I ground my teeth. "It didn't happen as often as you think. When it did, it was after a meltdown, after I got high.

"I'll never be able to earn your forgiveness, Keira. Never. And that's okay." I released a shaky breath. "I realized that tonight. You don't have to forgive me, but that doesn't mean I'll stop trying. I won't. I'll never stop. If I have to spend the rest of my life— It doesn't matter. Nothing does apart from you and Cyan."

"Does it hurt?"

I frowned. "Jacking off twenty times a day?"

"No." Her voice was small. "I asked you before and you said no, but I don't believe you. The padlock… does it hurt?"

It hadn't back then. But I'd upped the gauge with another custom-built device.

"Yes." It fucking ached like a son of a bitch.

"So, instead of drugs, and rather than jack off or fuck to escape the drugs, you're self-harming?"

"It's working."

"You're self-harming," she repeated grittily.

"I haven't had sex in months. I haven't jacked off in months either. It's working, Keira."

"It's not a sustainable solution."

"It's breaking the habit. I won't cheat on you again. I won't. I can't."

"Even if I never take you back? Even when I get a boyfriend?"

My jaw ached with how hard I clenched down. "Even then."

A shocked breath escaped her. "Why are you doing this? Why now?"

"Because you leaving me… I hit rock bottom. I've been there so many fucking times, K. So many times. I'm so sick of being on the ground, looking up. Trying to fix my fuck ups, to make shit right. I can't do it again. I can't. I can't want to end it all again—"

"Suicide?" she interrupted, a horrified gasp to her words.

"You've no idea how many times I almost tried. I don't want you to know. I just… I did the best I could, and that was nothing in comparison to what you brought to our family. I let you down. I let Cy down. But I won't do it again."

The sound of an engine rumbled to life, half pipes with it, and when a solitary light pierced the kitchen window, I wasn't altogether surprised that the biker was coming to our house. I'd given the security guard a heads up to let a brother through the gates, just in case Rex or Digger arrived, but now wasn't the best timing.

Not when, finally, I felt like Keira saw me for what I truly was.

A nothing.

A nobody.

An addict.

Worthless.

Trash.

And yet she still held me.

She didn't push away from me.

She didn't act as if my touch were poison to her.

I swallowed, affected more than she could know by her generosity, her selflessness.

How didn't she realize how perfect she was?

How beautiful a person she was?

It hurt me. It physically hurt me. Which was why, there and then, I vowed that would be part of my recovery too.

I'd fix me, I'd try to fix us, but I'd fix her as well.

She was the priority.

She was always the priority.

When the knock sounded at the door, she murmured, "I'll go get that."

"No. It's okay. Go and get MaryCat. Digger's here."

She blinked. "How do you know?"

I shrugged. "I know Rex's knock."

A soft, shocked laugh escaped her, breaking the tension between us. "No way."

My lips curved a little. "Yes way."

I leaned away from her, removing my forehead from hers, and she finally let go of my dick.

As she backed off, I watched her until she made it to the door. That was when she looked at me over her shoulder, a strange gleam in her eyes, an odd expression on her face, before she disappeared.

I deserved for her to disappear for good.

But I knew my angel. She'd never do that to me, even if I deserved it.

FOURTEEN

KEIRA

PRESENT

Nothing Compares 2 U - Sinead O'Connor

MIND WHIRRING, brain buzzing, heart racing, and body shaking, I felt like I'd been put through the emotional and physical wringer by the time I made it to the door of the spare bedroom.

I heard Storm move along the hall, open the door, and greet someone. Heard them slap their hands on each other's backs because that's what 'bros' did.

Even though I rolled my eyes, I smiled a little too because the house had been so quiet without him. Without his brothers stopping by, without him and Cy messing around after dinner.

I'd missed him.

And it wasn't only to do with breaking up with him, either.

I'd been missing him for years.

And now that I was coming to learn about other facets of his nature, I was also realizing that I didn't know him well. He'd held so much back from me, so much that a sane woman would back the hell away but if I was Storm's angel, then he was my devil.

My temptation.

A blessing and a curse.

Who dared me to be bad.

Who allowed me to be free.

Clearly, he didn't realize that.

I knew why too... My bad, my free, by comparison to his, were pathetic. But when you were raised in a household with a minister as a father, one who'd gone on missions, taking it doggy style was unorthodox.

Pathetic, I was so pathetic.

As I tapped my hand on MaryCat's door, I had to admit that his admission he jacked off twenty-plus times a day came as a shock.

Twenty times?

How the hell did he get hard so often?

And how often did he need sex to feel sated?

Or, by that point, was it not about the fulfillment but something else?

Confused and, weirdly enough, turned on, I decided I needed to research sex addiction more. Nothing about that sounded sexy, but Storm... he always made me burn. I'd never seen him jack off either. He'd never done that in front of me.

Truth was, I'd spent the last weeks trying to acclimate to Ohio, getting Cyan registered at school, making sure she had everything she needed because Storm insisted she go private.

In the meantime, I'd signed her up for some after-school activities, well aware that she had a lot of energy to burn, was used to being active, so being stuck at home would do her no good at all.

Since moving, it had all been about Cyan. Rightfully so. But now, with the winter break eking out, the new year beckoning, I recognized that I needed to understand the man I'd called husband if we were ever to take some steps forward instead of backward.

Storm was right—he might never earn my forgiveness, but I deserved for him to work hard in redeeming himself. I was owed that. It didn't take away from the fact that I wanted to understand, however. That I needed to.

Fucking for the sake of fucking was one thing. Having a girlfriend behind my back for years was another. Because he needed to get off twenty times a day? That was more of a sickness than lust.

His admission changed everything, and he didn't even know it.

When MaryCat didn't answer, I opened the door and stepped inside. The bassinet we'd borrowed was on the floor, but in the meager dawn light, I could see she was asleep, sitting up, Maddox nuzzled between her breasts, both of them resting after an early morning feed.

I wasn't sure why he fussed so much, unless it was just because he sensed all wasn't well with his mom, but right then, they both looked so sweet. If it hadn't been creepy, I'd have taken a picture for her to see how he was cuddling into her.

For some reason, I'd come to learn that MaryCat truly believed Maddox didn't like her. This was proof of the opposite.

Carefully, I stepped over to them both and murmured, "MaryCat? Digger's downstairs."

She sighed, her nose wrinkling a little as she muttered, "Huh?"

"Digger's here."

It was only a single bed, so I wasn't sure if they'd be staying or if they'd be heading off as soon as MaryCat and Maddox were ready to be on the road.

Although… Digger had arrived on the back of a bike. You couldn't exactly fit a car seat on one of those.

"Digger's here?" MaryCat whispered, her voice morphing between sleep-laden, rawly relieved, and joyous.

Maddox squawked when she sat upright, but she bounced him a bit as she straightened up, then clambered to her feet.

"Want to button up your shirt, honey?"

She blinked tiredly. "Oops."

I snorted. "It's easier when you just sleep naked."

"God, it is," she said on a sigh. "But I didn't like to… thought it might be weird."

"Well, there's no need to worry about that. If you stay a little while, be sure to make yourself comfortable." I pointed to the floor. "Your shoes are there if your feet are cold."

She obeyed, which made me smile as I could tell she only did it because she was half-asleep. When a yawn cracked her jaw, I grabbed her arm and steadied her before she fell back asleep or something.

I knew how it felt when your man came back from a run the first time after you had a kid. The relief was unreal. The excitement was strong. But then you were just so damn tired because you knew he was safe, and by extension, so were you and your kid, that you really wanted to take a long nap.

Apparently, however, Digger wasn't willing to wait on her making it downstairs. I heard footsteps and then MaryCat cast her eyes upon him and immediately started sobbing. Which, of course, triggered Maddox.

Digger laughed though, not meanly, just in a way that said he was happy. Happy to be back with his family. Happy that they were together again.

As he stormed forward, he hauled Maddox into his arms which shut the little guy up, and after juggling him to the side, dragged his woman against his chest.

"Don't you dare scare the hell out of me like that again, MC," he chided gruffly as he squeezed her tight. Her arms funneled around his waist as she burrowed into him.

"She was gonna take him away, Dig. I had to do something. She was—"

"She couldn't have done shit. You had no need to fear. I'd never have let that happen."

"You weren't there," I said softly, not wanting to intrude upon this tender moment, but needing him to hear the truth too.

He'd had to go on a run. I got it. Business was business and bills had to be paid, but I didn't want him to discount what she'd gone through.

He caught my eye and nodded. "You're right. I wasn't there." His lips brushed over MaryCat's temple as she snuggled into him, still weeping but clearly happy to be back with him. "Is it okay if we stay for the rest of the night... well, day, Keira?"

"Stay all week if you want." I shrugged. "No skin off my nose."

His brow puckered. "Really?"

"Really."

When he blinked, and combined with his surprise, I knew the exact reason why. So I grumbled, "I never hated the club, Digger. By the end,

I was just never invited to half of the events that went down and didn't feel welcome there."

His brow furrowed with surprise, but I didn't let him reply.

"Okay, I'll leave you to it. I'll make sure Cyan's quiet in the morning so she doesn't disturb either of you. Her room is at the other end of the house so it should be okay. The bathroom's through there, Digger," I told him, pointing to a door. "Hope you get some rest."

I slipped out, then, and found myself hovering in the hall. Not because I wanted to know what they were talking about, but because I wanted to keep on talking with Storm. I wanted more answers.

But as I thought about what I'd learned, I recognized that maybe the answers he'd given me were enough for tonight.

I already had a lot to process. Too much, truth be told. And really, I knew there was nothing good that would come from me extending the conversation, not until I understood more of what he was going through and dealt with how I was going to handle him in the upcoming weeks.

So, I went back to bed after I opened Cyan's door and peeped inside. She was fast asleep, the covers all over the place, and though I'd have liked to sort them out, I knew from experience that would wake her up.

As quietly as I'd peeked in, I slipped back out and headed to my room.

When I got into bed, I reached for my phone, and I did the smart thing that any woman in my position would do.

I googled, 'Sex addiction. The facts.'

DEAR DIARY

SENIOR YEAR

It felt soooo good to sneak out last night, but I have to be careful. I think Dad's suspicious, and I really don't want him to catch me. He's so mean lately. I don't know what's up with him, with Mom too. She's drinking again, so I know something's going on.

Of course, they won't tell me.

I don't count.

At least, that's how it's starting to feel.

I wish I were one of those girls who disobeyed to get their parents' attention, but I'd prefer to just stay under the radar. Thank God I'll be out of here soon.

I'm still not sure what I want to study. Dad says that I shouldn't be stupid —why become a nurse when I have the grades to be a doctor? But I don't want to be a doctor. I don't want to have to make life and death decisions for someone. I just want to help people. That's all I've ever wanted to do. But Dad says that I'd be wasting myself.

Would I?

Really?

Helping people get better? To overcome illnesses? Is that a waste? When we were in Haiti, nurses helped me more than the doctors did.

I don't think he's being fair, but he's the one who'll be paying for it seeing as I never got a scholarship. That's what happens when you don't play sports anymore.

Anyway, enough about him and college, that's too depressing and last night was great. We went to that dive bar on the edge of town. The Pig & Whistle. I have no idea why it's called that but it was grungy and dark and really kinda skanky, but they played the best music.

Laurie, Josse, and I hung out and danced for hours. Laurie's ID card is a work of frickin' art, so we managed to get our hands on some tequila as well.

It was nerve-wracking being there, a little like an adrenaline rush. I guess it's weird to admit that it made me feel really young and really adult all at the same time. Young because I was surrounded by older men and women who were drinking hardcore, kissing and, well, touching each other up as if they were in their bedrooms. But adult too because, next year, I'll be able to do this as often as I want. Maybe not the drinking, but the clubs. The dancing. I can't wait!

It really shouldn't have been the highlight of my night, but that guy with the streak of silver in his hair showed up. I'm not sure why. He was alone, not with his brothers—I watched Sons of Anarchy *so I could learn some of the words—and I felt certain he was watching me. But why would he be?*

As long as I watched him, he never once glanced my way, but I saw how many women were all over him. They touched him like they had a right to as well.

It made me jealous.

Crazy, I know.

I have nothing to be jealous about.

Why would I want to be with a biker anyway? They're dangerous and they do bad stuff... So why does that just make him more interesting? Haaaaalp!

STORM

PRESENT - JANUARY

"PRETTY DRASTIC MOVE, DIG," I pointed out as I watched him pacing from one side of the office to the next.

"What other choice do I have, man? Every time I fucking mention going back to West Orange, MaryCat loses her shit." Air gusted from between his lips as he rumbled, "I'm not even sure how they were gonna do what they said they were, but she's got it in her head that they're going to take Maddox away from us."

"You know Rex'd never let that happen."

"I do, but where the fuck is he? How the hell can he keep my Old Lady and my kid safe when he's in the fucking wind?"

I winced because, unfortunately, he had a point.

Seven days, and we still hadn't heard a peep from him, which was not only unlike him, it was worrying too.

I scraped a hand over my beard, smoothing it down before I scratched it. "You sure you want to transfer here permanently?"

He grimaced. "Buttfuck, Ohio ain't exactly our style."

"Not mine either," I said wryly. "But it's good for hiding out. Laying low."

"I need to assess the threat but, either way, threat or not, I know she wants to be as far from her mom as physically possible, and I don't fucking blame her. So, if Buttfuck, Ohio keeps my woman happy, then I've no problem with staying.

"She's been better since she got here. I really need to thank Keira, Storm. She's been a champ." He scrubbed his jaw. "Helping her buy all the shit she and Maddox needed, keeping her calm, I'm pretty sure she's cried less this week too."

That was my Keira. A fucking angel.

Eyeing him, I commented, "Got a space on the council, Dig. Enforcer. Nobody I'd prefer taking that spot, having my back, than a West Orange brother."

Digger gaped at me. "You shitting me?"

"Nope. That's the only spot I ain't filled yet."

"How come?"

"The guy I offered it to didn't want it, and he was the only one I didn't think his parents were siblings too."

Digger snorted. "They ain't that bad here."

"No?" I rolled my eyes. "If you say so."

"GIF and Techie are okay. That Grim's a bit of a prick. He's got a real attitude problem, and he treats the whores like shit." He grunted. "Now you come to mention it, I wondered why I hadn't seen an Enforcer. Just thought there was a run going on that no one was talking about."

"Well, now you know. No one would take the job."

He snorted. "This is getting to be a habit. You hauling my ass in on jobs that no one else will do."

I grinned a little. "At the time, you were the only Sinner Keira liked."

"Don't think she liked me that much that she wanted me to officiate her wedding," he retorted with a soft shake of his head.

Jimmy had only been a Prospect at the time. I'd have preferred Rex to officiate, but Keira would have shit a brick if he'd been the one marrying us.

"Is it dangerous?" Digger asked, changing the subject.

"Ain't being a Sinner dangerous?"

"I got a kid now, Storm. I wanna make sure I'm around for graduation."

Nodding, I replied, "I know, man, I know. What can I say? Nyx did the job in West Orange for a long enough time without croaking it, and it's not as chaotic here. Mostly I'm trying to get the legit side of shit set up.

"You and I both know that Rex uses this place more as a halfway home on runs."

Digger hummed his agreement. "True. You want to change that?"

I shrugged. "Probably. Why not, huh? Makes it more challenging, and God knows, it's boring by comparison." Stretching my arms out, I cracked my knuckles. "I know there's a house down the road from mine available to rent. It's cheaper than West Orange. You'll get more bang for your buck."

"Not sure that hoity-toity subdivision will cope with three brothers living in it."

"Infestation alert," I said with a smirk. "Not like they can do anything. You want to live there, you can. Might be a good idea. MaryCat and Keira seem to get along okay, and I know my wife—" I faltered there, because it was still way too easy to call her that when she wasn't. Our conversation in the kitchen made me see that.

Dig winced. "I know what you mean, man. And I swear, Keira's been the real MVP with MC. I'm grateful as fuck."

"Keira'll carry on watching out for MaryCat and Maddox if you're happy with that."

"MaryCat can be trusted with Maddox," he argued, folding his arms across his chest. "I don't understand why her mom would think otherwise, so don't believe MC's bad press, okay?"

"I don't, not particularly." My lips twisted. "I wasn't even talking about the PPD. I just remember how isolated Keira was back when she first gave birth." Hell, until Cy had gone to preschool. Only Rene had consistently checked in on her. "Encourage the friendship or don't, I don't give a fuck. It'd be good for them though. At least they both know each other."

"Sorry, Storm," Digger muttered with a sigh. "Didn't mean to get all defensive."

"If my mother-in-law had tried to take Cyan away from us, I'd have been more than fucking defensive, bro. I get it.

"You do you though. You wanna stay, you stay. The Enforcer's position was only a suggestion. You and I both know there's no movement on the council in West Orange unless, God forbid, something happens to one of my brothers."

Dig flinched. "Hell, nah. I don't want that. I like the chapter as is."

"So this is your one shot at a promotion." I studied him. "Do you want more? More money in your pocket? More authority? More of a fixed position?"

"I don't know the lay of the land. Is it wise to have a rookie to the area as your main security?"

"Mash, he's the guy I asked to take the job, said he'd help out whoever I decided on."

"Why didn't he want to take it?"

"His Old Lady's sick. Needs the dough, but ain't got time for the responsibility. Got a couple kids, you know?"

"It'd be good if you could get Keira onto that."

"Helping out? Remember Rene? She was always there, her nose in everyone's business." I smiled at the memory. "Bear was fucking lucky that she put up with his ass."

"Keira will stand by you, too, Storm. It'll just take time. You've both been nuts for each other since day one," was Digger's gruff retort.

If anyone would know, it'd be him, seeing as he'd inadvertently started all this.

Well, his shitty bike breaking down had.

"Might take more time than any of us have," I said softly. "It's all good. Anyway, I know she's going up to North Canton today. Cyan's enrolled in a private school there, and today's the first day of class. But it works out well because there's a state college in town too.

"She wants to be a nurse, and I want her to have whatever she needs to be happy. She won't have time to do all the shit Rene did, and I wouldn't blame her if she didn't have the inclination either."

Dig moved over to the desk and sat his ass down on the edge. "Storm?"

"Yeah."

"You really think I could do it? I never aimed for the council because Rex's men are fucking unstoppable up there. I wouldn't have it any other way, you know?"

"I get ya. Enforcer might not be the best job for you, but you can give it a shot, right?"

He nodded.

"Anyway, everyone's in a temporary position for the moment. I want them to learn the ropes, see if they can handle it or, if they can't, see if they can grow into the job. The offer's open to you as well."

"I appreciate that, man. But do you think the others will?"

"Don't give a shit," I admitted dryly. "To be honest, I'd have preferred you as my VP seeing as I trust you, but that position was taken, and Sweet Lips is good at corralling the men. I've seen him in action. I think he'd be good at it. We'll see though. It's all up in the air for the next couple weeks."

He stared at me, his mouth firming as he figured shit out in his head. "I'm down for it, but I just gotta check with MC." He held up a hand. "Don't give me crap for it either."

I shrugged. "Wasn't going to. Sounds like a smart man who'd key his other half in on a decision like this."

His brow furrowed, but he nodded. "Thanks, man."

"No problem. The worst thing that happened to you guys might be the best thing in the end."

Getting to his feet, Digger said, "I'll go and speak with her so I can get you an answer ASAP."

"Appreciate that."

He dipped his chin in farewell and I watched him go, closing the door behind him.

Reaching for my cellphone, I found my message chat with Sin, who was our liaison with the Five Points' Mob and West Orange's Enforcer, as well as a damn good brother.

Me: *What's going on with the Five Points? Are they giving us crap about taking MaryCat in?*

Sin: *Taking her in? She's a Sinners' Old Lady.*

Me: *Preaching to the choir, brother. I just meant what's the status. We both know that was more of a prison break than anything else.*

Sin: *Sorry. Every time I think about what Mom put MC through, I want to tear out her throat.*

I wasn't the only one with mommy issues.

Sin: *Aidan Sr. made a few rumbles, but as far as I can tell, he's backed off.*

Me: *Why?*

Sin: *Fuck if I know. Maybe Lodestar arranged something with her point of contact over there.*

Me: *Who's that?*

Sin: *Tiffany said it was Savannah Daniels.*

Me: *The reporter who broke the exposés on the NWS?*

Sin: *She's Aidan Jr.'s new fiancée.*

Me: *O.o Well, that's fortunate.*

Sin: *Right? Tiffany said that Savannah and Lodestar grew up together.*

Me: *Ever get the feeling the ties that bind the Sinners with the Five Points were destined?*

Sin: *Not sure I believe in fate.*

Me: *Hahaha. Fuck you.*

Sin: *:P*

Me: *Okay, so I don't have to worry about a bunch of Five Pointers tearing down my way?*

Sin: *No, and I'd have warned you first. I'd have been down there so fucking fast your head would have spun.*

Sin: *I'm not about to let my baby sister have her kid snatched away from her.*

Me: *Again, preaching to the converted, bro. FYI, just asked Digger to be my new Enforcer. I think he'll say yes.*

Sin: *He'd be a schmuck if he didn't. Anyway, good for him. Rex'll be pissed. He was great at what he did.*

Me: *Digging. Yeah, fucking waste to have someone that talented at finding shit out not in a council position.*

Sin: *Won't hear me arguing. MC should be with someone high up the ranks.*

Me: *Okay, just keep me in the loop if something changes with the Five Points?*

Sin: *Bet your ass I will.*

Me: *Appreciate it, brother.*

Sin: *Same goes. Thanks for taking her in.*

Me: *You said it yourself—she's a Sinner.*

Sin: *How's shit going down there? You still sober?*

Me: *Yeah. Things with Keira ain't that great, but that's to be expected. Sobriety? Meh. I'm doing okay.*

Sin: *Don't fuck it up again, Storm. Your ass is too far away from the Fridge for Rex to haul it in there.*

I'd wasted too many fucking nights in that goddamn hellhole.

Me: *Got too much to lose if I fuck it up this time, Sin. Don't worry.*

Sin: *I stay up all night worrying about you fuckers. It's my job.*

A knock at the door sounded a couple seconds later, and I rolled my eyes and called out, "Come in."

Me: *GTG. Speak later, bro.*

Sin: *Gotcha.*

Sweet Lips' head bobbed around the door and he said, "Got a minute?"

"I do." I rocked back in my chair. "Got any news for me?"

He waggled some papers in his hand. "Sure do."

"Slayer been over them as well?"

"Yeah. We went through this together. I didn't want to fuck up right from the start."

"I appreciate the care and attention."

I wasn't bullshitting him either. I really fucking did. There was nothing worse than half-baked ideas that hadn't been costed or analyzed.

Poor fucking Rex.

More often than not, my ass had been too strung up to do much more than coast. The only consolation was the fact that I wasn't a dumbfuck so my coasting was someone else's version of a hot shit day.

Sweet Lips made a crinkling noise as he walked toward me, and when he leaned over the desk, something fell out of the pocket in his hoodie.

"Cow Tales? Really?"

His grin was sheepish. "How do you think I earned the name?"

I grinned back, because here I was, thinking his road name was about his skills as a kisser, and it was because the fucker was addicted to candy.

He plunked the files on the table as he snatched up the treat. Hesitating for a second, he asked, "You want one?"

I arched a brow but nodded and accepted it. Shoving open one of the folders, I opened the wrapper and took a bite.

Scanning the details of the first building, I asked, "Why are the owners selling?"

As far as I could see, the diner had a nice little turnover. There appeared to be no reason to sell.

"Because they're retirin'. Fred and Wilma—"

I snorted. "Seriously?"

He smirked. "Seriously. I think they came before the *Flintstones* though. They're fucking dinosaurs, that's for sure."

"I'll bet."

"Like I said, they're real old, and no one's got the money to buy 'em out."

"Why not?"

"Two years ago, there were three factories that served the area. Provided a lot of employment for the county. Then two went broke and dumped a lot of people on their asses. It fucked with things."

"Diner's turnover says otherwise." There hadn't even been a blip two years ago when he said those factories had closed down.

"They're famous."

"What for?"

"That blond guy, the dude with the spikes, from the Food Network, rolled into town five years ago. Put them on the map for their pies." He shrugged. "One of the reasons we get a lot of tourists here."

"You shitting me?"

"Nope. There are folks who go around visitin' all the places he ate at."

"Huh."

Turning another page, I found some numbers that I had to assume *weren't* from Fred and Wilma. Shit like cost breakdowns and estimates of monthly expenditure.

Impressed, I asked, "How'd you work this out?"

"Lot of googling," he said wryly. "Slayer and I might have gone gray trying to do it as well. I tried to get the information from Fred but he can be a close-mouthed fucker when he wants to be. Their pie recipe might as well be a state secret. I mean, don't get me wrong, it's fucking epic so I can't blame them for being cagey."

"But it's why he wouldn't tell you how much sugar, butter, and flour he buys, right?" I laughed a little. "Good old-fashioned industrial espionage. Been classed as many things but not a thief of pie recipes."

"I know, right? I told him, 'Fred, do I look like I wanna undercut you, man? But I got a boss, and he wants to know if this place is profitable.'"

"What did he say?"

"Told me to go and buy a slice of pie and that'd remind me why they're on the map."

"Sounds like a good guy."

"He's a pain in the ass, but he's a town institution. So's *Pies You Like It*."

"I'll bet." I eyed the asking figure, thought about what was in the bank account, and what Rex had said we could use to invest as a means of laundering our dough, and nodded. "You sure they're busy?"

"Always. Always fucking busy. It's why they're retirin'."

"Wait. *Pies You Like It*? That a pun for 'As You Like It?'"

SL blinked. "Huh?"

"Never heard of Shakespeare?"

"That that football player who plays for the Bengals?"

I rolled my eyes. "No. Never mind."

He tipped his chin up as he folded his arms across his chest. "You seen the small print?"

"The part about how they expect five percent of the earnings on all their pies until their demise, and thereafter, five percent goes to the charity of their choice?" I hummed. Definitely an interesting clause in the sales contract.

"Yeah. They're weird as fuck. Never had kids. The diner became their baby."

"They're entitled to ask for whatever they want. Don't mean they're gonna get it. Especially not with that asking price." Though I sounded like a prick, I didn't think it'd be a bad idea. Not considering... "Correct me if I'm wrong, SL, but the Sinners ain't popular around here, are they?"

"No. Not really. Butch had a way of pissing off the locals."

"What did he do?"

He grimaced. "I don't like to speak ill of a brother, man."

"He was a traitor, not a brother," I corrected softly, but with enough bite for SL to get with the program—*don't piss me off.*

SL heaved a sigh. "I know. I just find it hard to get my head around."

"Well, get around it fast. That bastard would have brought the Irish Mob to your door."

"No one wants Aidan O'Donnelly Sr. to come knocking," he admitted gruffly.

"Exactly." Not to mention the fact that the Sinners and Five Points were goddamn allies. If the O'Donnellys had learned one of our chapters was helping the fucking *Famiglia*, it would have destroyed the alliance. Talk about a goddamn disaster waiting to happen. "And that was on the cards. So, tell me, what did Butch do?"

"Nothing major, just a bunch of little things. Would get us all to ride through the town on 4th of July during the mayor's speech. Mostly juvenile shit like that.

"He had a beef with the coach at the high school, so every now and then, we'd ride in the night before a game, wreck the turf." He grunted. "Not our finest hour."

"I can see why that pissed people off." My disapproval must have been clear because his shoulders hunched. "There's a delicate balance in not pissing off your neighbors so they don't come after you with torches and pitchforks.

"They should want you to be here because you'll keep their kids safe from the fuckers who try to come in selling dope and shit. We're their first line of defense. Better than a goddamn sheriff and his deputies." I scrubbed my chin. "This might be a good way of rubbing shoulders with the locals without getting their backs up."

SL's brow had grown progressively more puckered throughout my short speech, and when I was done, he muttered, "Huh."

I shot him a look. "What's that supposed to mean?"

"It means that I get it. I never did approve, but Butch was a fucking head case, so it wasn't like you could say no. The deeper he got into the coke, the more volatile he was."

"Was coke his only vice?"

I couldn't judge the fucker for being hooked on snow, not when I'd been there, but the shit he'd pulled told me he'd been one of those dumbass jocks all his life. Too busy playing pranks to sniff the daisies.

"Yeah. In over his head with it. Spread the infection to a ton of brothers and clubwhores. That's why our numbers are low. We lost a lot to the cull."

"The cull? That's what you guys are calling it?"

"It's why the West Orange chapter ain't all that popular right now."

Then they were going to love my bringing Digger on board…

I grunted. "Well, heads up. I asked Digger if he'd like to take the place as Enforcer on the council. He wants to move down here anyway, and he's a good man. Got a great nose."

"There'll be rumblings," SL warned, but that was as much as he said.

"I'll need you to smooth shit over."

"Call church. Warn them yourself. I can only do so much because they wanna hear from you. You're their Prez. Not me.

"Plus, before, I was nobody, man. They don't trust me, and they don't trust you for picking me as your right-hand man, you know?"

"Then it looks like we gotta prove ourselves." I pursed my lips. "The diner… you know Fred well?"

"Everyone in Coshocton knows Fred, but yeah, more than most. I used to live next door to him when I was a kid."

"Make the call, tell them we'll pay the full asking price."

"What about the stipulation at the end?"

I shrugged. "What's five percent?"

"A lot. You should go to the diner. See what it's like. Try the pies before you buy. They'll make a believer outta you."

His dry retort had me smiling. "I'll take the fam tonight."

SL nodded. "I'll leave you to the others."

"Three businesses? You and Slayer have been busy," I said, opening the other two files up.

"Well, I wanted to impress you, I guess. I'm sick of being Sweet Lips, the guy everyone dumps their shit on. I'd prefer to only have to answer to you, so I'm gonna try not to fuck this up."

"We all fuck up," I told him softly. "It's how we fix our mistakes that defines us."

"Yogi Berra say that or something?"

"Not as far as I know." I tipped my chin at the door. "Thanks for this, SL. You've done a good job."

He grinned at me, his pleasure at the validation clear as he joked, "Don't thank me yet. Thank me after you try the pies. I almost hope we buy it just to get my hands on their peach pie recipe."

"You living up to your name?"

"Hell, yeah."

"Where the fuck do you put it? You're as skinny as a toothpick."

"High metabolism. I'm blessed, what can I say?"

I snickered as he wafted a hand in farewell and left me to it. As I poured over the information Slayer and he had collated, I had to admit to being impressed. I was also curious if Techie had got involved because I was pretty sure some of these figures came from a bank account, and I knew for a fact that the records filed with the IRS definitely weren't something I should be seeing.

Still, it let me know that the diner was the real deal. Let me know we had a decent hacker on board as well.

The second business was a local hair salon. Definitely not MC territory, but I could see why he'd chosen it for me to look at. Low to medium turnover, but he'd included their page on Yelp which had a ton of bad reviews on it. It was on the Main Street, great location, just shitty owners.

As for the last, there was a motel. This one's file was a little thinner, and I understood why—the owners did a lot of their business under the table because if people were riding into town to visit Wilma and Fred's diner, it was unlikely that they weren't spending the night here.

There were six hotels/motels in the area, and this one was near a place called the Historic Roscoe village, and also closest to a park and a couple of lakes. With their Yelp page streaming with reviews—all good—there was definitely something funky going on with the IRS records.

Humming at the thought, I grabbed my cell when it rang. A quick glance revealed it to be Keira.

"Hey," I said huskily, surprised she called. It was the first time in, well, months that she'd reached out to me, not the other way around. "Everything okay?"

"Yeah. I'm just disappointed."

My brow furrowed as my shoulders straightened. "What? Why?"

I knew she was heading to the state college to enroll, but I wasn't sure why she sounded so defeated. Wasn't sure why she was coming to me about it either.

Not that I was about to complain.

Hell, this was exactly the step forward I was hoping for. If not as man and wife, friendship was just as important. I'd missed her so fucking much.

"I was hoping I could just sign up, you know? But not only do I have to apply in March for a fall start, I have a ton of credits to earn." She heaved a sigh. "I guess I didn't think about the fact I'm ancient when I got this crackpot idea of mine."

"It's not a crackpot idea. You want it, you go get it."

Her voice was soft. "What if I'm not good at it?"

"You won't know until you try, will you?" was my calm reply. I rocked back in my seat, trying not to be happy that she'd called me about this.

"It was stupid of me to think I could just dive straight in."

"Why was it stupid? Short-sighted, maybe? But they have courses starting up all the time, right? Is there something you can try out, just to see if it suits you?"

She was quiet a second, and she didn't have to be sitting opposite me for me to realize that she was biting her bottom lip.

"K?"

"I guess."

"You guess?"

"I guess," she repeated, but she didn't sound like she believed it.

"Cyan got into the academy all right. Wish it were closer but it is what it is."

"We can take turns driving her."

"Wonder how she'll settle in?"

Keira cleared her throat. "I'm not jinxing it, but I saw those girls. They reminded me of me when I was their age," she said wryly. "Cyan is nothing like me when I was a kid."

My nose crinkled. "I'm not sure if that's good or not. You were ripe for rebellion."

A soft laugh escaped her. "True. You're living confirmation of that, hmm?"

I pulled a rueful face, but I asked her, "Do you regret it, K? I never asked you that, but... I figure that was because I thought I knew the answer already." I was well aware that if it hadn't been for Cyan, she'd have headed off to college and I'd never have seen her again.

It was one of the reasons I was so fucking grateful to my kid.

"Assuming makes an ass out of you and me," she mocked, but before I could bitch, she muttered, "Of course I don't. You think I wanted what they planned for me?"

"You gave up college—"

"Did I ever tell you about Haiti?"

"In general?" I joked.

She sniffed. "When I was a kid, before we came to West Orange, my dad took us on a mission to Haiti. We were there for two years and had to come back because I caught malaria. It hit me really bad.

"Mom told me once that she thought it was going to kill me, but I made a full recovery, we came back to the States, and he got the position in West Orange where I started attending school.

"I started late but I skipped grades, was on the fast track for an early graduation, then *boom*, it recurred. Suddenly, I was behind in everything. Track and field sports were a thing of the past. There was no way I was getting a scholarship for college anymore—"

"Jesus, you never told me any of this!"

"I didn't really need to. I haven't had a flare up since I was fourteen. Dad said he prayed for me to be healed."

"Apparently it worked," I rumbled.

"Either that or the care was just better here. Anyway, he used to dangle college in front of me like a carrot on a stick. Without the scholarship, he had to pay, but he wanted me to do the courses he chose.

"Nursing was my calling, because I swear, it was the nurses who saved me, not the doctors; they kept me going, you know? However, Dad saw me as a doctor. Said it was pointless being a nurse, and what he wanted he almost always got.

"Only, I wasn't made to be a doctor. I never wanted that," she admitted softly. "I wanted out of there, though. Enough to stick with it? I don't know. I think he thought I'd say no and had a contingency plan."

My brow puckered. "A contingency plan?"

"You remember Ray Leinster?"

"How could I forget?" I drawled, pleased when she laughed.

"Yeah, he had a meeting with your fists if I recall." K snickered. "Dad wanted me to date him because *his* dad was a deacon at his church. Didn't matter he was an asswipe and that he'd slapped Sally Jessop in front of everyone, nope, that was who he wanted me to be with."

"You really think so?"

"I know so. If it wasn't Ray, it would have been someone else. So do I have regrets? About how we ended, sure, but not about how we began." I sucked in a sharp breath as relief whittled away at my bones, but before I could say a word, she continued, "Anyway, we can keep on with this school, but I'm not sure if it'll be a good fit for her. I get why you'd want an all-girls academy, but it's a little obvious, isn't it?"

"I just thought she'd be safe there."

"She'll also grow up uber curious about guys," she mocked. "She's scared now, but she won't be forever. You get someone on the staff to watch over her?"

"Yes."

She sighed. "Who's the poor schmuck that's been following me around the state today? He wasn't the regular one."

"Peanut. He's usually tailing Cyan when she's doing the after-school shit. Your regular guy is Jump. He had to go to the doctor's office."

"I think we should stop wasting gas and get him to ride with me."

"Well, now you know about the guys following you, they don't have to hide. Now people will see you've got an entourage, and they'll be doubly sure to leave you the hell alone."

"You know how crazy that sounds, right?"

"Yeah."

"Not gonna stop you, is it?"

"No."

She sighed again. "Therapy tonight."

"I hadn't forgotten. I'll be there."

"Okay. Just wanted to remind you."

"We'll go out for dinner."

"Yeah? Where?"

"There's a diner in town. Sweet Lips said they serve the best pie in the state."

"Sounds good. Why's he called that? Or do I not want to know?"

I smiled, and even though the truth wasn't sordid, informed her, "Not sure you want to know."

Her snicker shouldn't have lit me up from the inside out, but it did.

It really fucking did, and the bitch of it was, I knew it'd only ever be her who did that to me.

Who made me feel alive.

Who made this goddamn world worth living in.

Righting the wrongs of my past was never going to be an easy task, but for the chance to earn more stolen moments like this? I'd go to hell and back to be the guy who was there for her at the end of a shitty day.

SIXTEEN

KEIRA

PRESENT

I WAS ABOUT ready to tear my hair out by the time we made it to the diner.

The idea of airing our private business in public wasn't ideal, but I didn't want to cook, and I really didn't want to do dishes. Plus, it was a double slice of pie kind of day.

By the time I pulled into the parking lot, Cyan was pouting. She'd been all sass throughout the ride, more attitude than sense, but then Storm's bike rumbled up beside us, and she finished off her diatribe with, "I didn't do anything wrong."

Wishing I had Storm's superpower of getting her to behave, I retorted, "You headbutted someone in your class, Cyan. You have to see that isn't right?"

"Aunt Giulia said the best defense is offense."

Oh.

My.

God.

My kid had taken defense lessons from Giulia Fontaine.

Holy Christ, no wonder she was getting aggressive.

Giulia had more testosterone than any woman on the planet. She was wasted as Nyx's woman because she had the brass balls to be the MC's Enforcer in her own right.

"What did this kid say?"

"I don't know how but they know Daddy is a biker."

I narrowed my eyes at her. "So?"

She sniffed. "They called us names."

"Why didn't you go to the teacher?"

"Because I'm not a snitch." She folded her arms across her chest. "It was my first day, Mom. What was I supposed to do? Look weak?"

Oh, God. Now she was channeling Giulia with me.

Unable to help myself, I plopped my forehead onto the steering wheel. "I need to find you some more classes. Karate or something."

"I wanna do Kraft Magad."

"Kraft Magad? What's that?"

"It's so cool, Mom. I saw it on YouTube."

The parental controls needed checking—stat.

When Storm knocked on the window, I lowered it without raising my head.

"Everything okay?" he questioned warily, sounding just as tired as me but for different reasons.

Family therapy sessions were no fun.

He was better at talking through them than I was, but most of the work fell on Cyan's shoulders which wasn't as bad as all that because she was a Chatty Cathy when the therapist asked the right questions.

We'd learned all kinds of hellish things from her that way.

How London had talked to her, what he'd wanted from her. How he'd sneaked electronics to her so he'd always be there for her when she needed him.

Just the thought made me want to puke.

Constant access to my baby.

Today, she'd even admitted that he'd asked for pictures.

The desire for pie abated, and the need to vomit increased.

A hand moved to the back of my neck, and though I tensed at first, I softened when Storm's thumbs dug into the knot right between my shoulder and throat.

"You know why she headbutted that girl?" I muttered.

"Why?" He didn't sound angry, more amused at her antics.

Was I the only normal person in this car?

Stupid question.

"Because Aunt Giulia," I mocked, "says the best defense is offense."

He didn't have to laugh for me to know he was doing it inwardly. "She has a point."

"No," I hissed, "she doesn't." I rolled my head to the side to glower at him. I'd have shoved his hand off, but it felt too good and it kept the nausea at bay. "Cyan can't keep doing this." After she'd gotten into that fight at the clubhouse, I should have known we'd have problems when she was at school. "She's going to get expelled."

"Mom says I can do Kraft Madag."

"It was Kraft Magad a minute ago," I grumbled.

"You mean Krav Maga?" Storm asked and, this time, he sounded more than tickled, he laughed outright.

God, how long was it since I'd heard that laugh? So carefree and light. Not since before we'd split up that was for sure.

"Yeah!" was Cyan's enthusiastic cry. "Krav Maga. That's it. Dad, can we go? Please?"

"I don't see why not," he said with a shrug. "The next time some old creep comes near you, I think I'd like it if you could break him in two."

A soft silence fell inside the car, and I rocked my head to the other side to see what Cyan's reaction was to that.

She stared at him, all big eyes, and though her bottom lip quivered, she nodded slowly. "I think I want that too."

Trust Storm to see something I hadn't. To understand something I hadn't.

Cyan wasn't being aggressive for the hell of it. *To rebel.* She was defending herself. Protecting herself now where she hadn't before. She was just being a little 'exuberant' with it.

I eyed the bandage on her forehead where there was a nice round goose egg, and murmured, "Only think?"

Her head wobbled from side to side. "No, I know."

"Then we'd better make it happen," was Storm's cheery retort. "What with your gymnastic moves, you'll be able to beat the crap out of me in no time at all."

She giggled. "Daddy, I couldn't do that!"

"Why not? That's how I'll know you're ready for the big bad world, ladybug. The second you knock me on my ass is a day I'll be proud of."

"Really?" was our kid's eager retort.

Before the conversation could get any more disturbing, I muttered, "I seriously need this pie you were talking about before."

Storm laughed. "Me too."

"Me three!" Cyan chirped.

For the past week, she'd been surprisingly cheerful. I assumed that was because her dad was staying with us, and to be honest, I'd appreciated the stay of grace.

I knew I wasn't the only one who enjoyed having a man around the house either.

MaryCat had calmed down a ton since Digger had arrived, and while I didn't doubt he wasn't a cure for postpartum depression, he made her happy. It was clear to see.

When she cried, he didn't chide her, just held her. When she got angry, he talked her down. And when Maddox fussed, he took control, and she watched, a little less despairingly than each previous time I'd seen her staring down at him like she didn't know him, as if he were a stranger to her.

As I watched her, I'd admit to being grateful that I hadn't gone through that. Cyan and I had always been close. Until recently. I just hoped MC and Maddox would get over this hiccup too.

"Mom? You coming?"

I blinked when I realized Cyan had hopped out of the SUV and knew why I'd zoned out—Storm was still rubbing the back of my neck.

Tilting my head to the side, I stared at him, and murmured, "She's definitely your daughter."

His lips curved. "Don't blame me. I remember a certain someone who, instead of giving the mugger their purse like she should have done, hit him over the head with it."

I grimaced. "I forgot about that."

His smile deepened. "I haven't."

"I'm surprised you remembered."

He arched a brow. "Why would you be surprised I remembered

that? Anyway, I had someone take care of that guy shortly afterward…"

Mouth gaping, I whispered, "Taken care of?"

"Yes." Totally unapologetic. Holy crap on a stick.

Seeing as that was more disturbing than my kid mimicking Giulia, I decided that a change of subject was required. "How come, when you were high, you always remembered things like birthday parties and class events?"

"Because I have a phone and a reminder app," he drawled. "And I wasn't high all the time."

"Lots of other men have them too but they forget."

"You two were a priority. Even if it was a skewed priority."

I knew what he meant.

Storm was, in a word, weird.

Why was it that I was only just figuring that out for real?

I mean, I'd always known he was James Dean reborn. Had half suspected and been terrified by the idea of him dying before he reached his fortieth birthday. But I was only just coming to accept how strange he was, how unusual his ideals were.

No wonder we'd struggled as a couple.

He thought I was perfect.

I believed I was to blame for everything he did wrong.

What a pair.

"You know, we'd have had a better chance of making it if you'd been honest with me from the start."

His smile was sad. "You'd never have let me inside if you'd known the truth."

He squeezed the back of my neck in a move that I thought was supposed to soothe but, instead, made me wish he'd haul me into him.

Very inappropriate.

But still. It was Storm.

All of my adult life was entangled with him, and he was showing me a side of his nature that I'd craved for so long.

"Come on, before Cyan bursts."

I shot the front of the diner a look, saw my kid standing there hopping up and down like she needed the bathroom. "You know 'pie' is her magic word."

He smirked. "In this, she definitely takes after me."

I laughed when I thought about the three pumpkin pies I made at Thanksgiving, which I never ate because I hated it, and which always disappeared because these two were pie fiends. Especially for my pastry.

Another gentle squeeze and I sighed, but raised my head, pressed the button to let the window roll up, then carefully pulled the keys out of the ignition as I grabbed my purse and climbed out.

He waited on me.

Like a gentleman.

"Is this your new tactic?" I asked softly. "To charm me?"

He shook his head, but his smile was sad. "Baby, I should always have treated you like this."

I looked away when my throat choked up, because he was right, he should have. That he knew it now triggered a bittersweet kind of agony inside me.

If only we could turn back time. If only we could fix what we'd broken along the way.

Neither of us said anything as we headed into the diner. The shock of heat was like a slap to the face, and I was kind of surprised at how busy it was. Every table except two was full, and the servers were swept off their feet.

One, sweaty and with her hair clinging to her forehead, beamed a smile at me. Her gaze turned a little hotter when she looked at Storm, but he wasn't interested.

I knew this because I looked—he was answering Cyan about Kraft Magad.

I almost snorted at him correcting her again.

"Table for three?"

"Please," I said with a smile.

She guided us to a table, and as we plunked our butts in the booth, I was kind of touched that Storm moved beside Cyan.

He'd been making a real effort to stick close to her, and I knew that was a mixture of this weird contemplative mood he'd been in since Christmas—heck it was a precursor to Bear's passing in all honesty—but also the fact that last year could have ended so differently.

So very, very differently.

Sucking my bottom lip between my teeth, I watched them both, quietly content to listen to them discuss Kraft Madag—I was pretty sure she was doing it to tease him now—not even needing to check out the menu. Just happy to see them together, interacting, and Cyan being her normal self.

Well, a tad bloodthirstier than before, but no longer snappish and bitter and, to be truthful, an asshole.

Bloodthirsty definitely wasn't an adjective I wanted to associate with my eleven-year-old, but it couldn't be helped, I guessed.

I knew what she'd seen even if Storm refused to tell me the details —Amara, the Old Lady of two Sinners up in West Orange, had killed the guy who'd groomed Cyan. In front of my baby and Rachel's baby brother, Rain.

So much violence... it had definitely unveiled a side of the world I'd have spared her from if I could.

"You ready to order?" Storm asked, breaking into my thoughts.

"You want the usual?"

Smiling at him, I nodded. "If they have it."

"Strawberry lattice pie?" he asked the waitress, but his cellphone buzzed and he reached for it. As he did, whatever he read had him growling with annoyance.

Jeeezus.

That growl.

Instantly, I thought of summer nights with me writhing beneath him as he took me from behind.

Of his chest covering my front, his hands tangled with mine over-head, pinning me to the bed.

I thought of slick skin and soft whispers, the memory of a pleasure so exquisite it made strawberry lattice pie seem redundant.

"We have twenty-five different kinds of pie, and that's certainly one of them," the server told me, dragging me from my memories.

When she beamed at me, I almost forgave her for checking out my husband... Damn. *Ex*-husband. That growl had messed with my senses.

Who could blame her, though? He was hot. With that long hair cascading down his shoulders, the shocking gleam of silver contrasting so perfectly against the rich black. He was muscled and thick with it, his plaid shirt sleeves bulging now he'd taken off his leather jacket.

Wearing that alone, he just looked hot. But beneath, once the cut was revealed, it changed him. Morphed him into something else.

Someone dangerous.

Someone delicious.

That growl...

I plucked at my bottom lip, finding it easy to remember why he'd driven me crazy all these years, and why the waitress had looked at him like he was catnip she wanted to rub her face in.

It was a bittersweet kind of truth that had me admitting that my attraction for him had never died.

I wasn't like a lot of women who hit the 'seven-year itch' and wanted to switch up their husbands. If he hadn't cheated, if he hadn't been... well, crap, Storm, then we'd still be together, and I'd still be as into him as I'd been when I was younger.

While I watched him with Cyan, teasing wisps of hope stirred to life, making me wonder if I was just downright dumb or if he was playing me.

How long could he keep up this charade if that was what it was?

We'd been here a little under eight weeks now, and he hadn't let up once. Not a single dinner had he missed, not a single time had he failed to do the dishes. And, even though by his own admission he used to jack off twenty plus times a day, he'd never come onto me.

In fact, it was almost as if he didn't have those feelings at all.

Which, of course, was when I caught his eye, realizing that while I'd been lost to my thoughts, he'd switched from solely entertaining Cyan to looking at me.

The quickest glance at his expression revealed a twisted kind of hunger that seemed to gnaw at him. His cheekbones pulled taut, his nostrils flared, and in his eyes, I saw the feralness within him. A feralness that called to the most visceral part of me. A part that had only stirred to life once before—the day after Rene's death.

The proof of the real Storm, the reminder of him, set me on edge, however. Did this confirm he was playing a role or was it merely evidence that he was castrating himself for my benefit? *Our* benefit. Not just him and me, but Cyan too.

The second he saw I was watching him back, however, his expression changed, turned placid. Calm. He didn't even blink at me, just turned back to Cyan, saying, "There's gotta be a better way of standing up for yourself than headbutting some little bitch, baby."

I winced at the terminology but was grateful he'd broached the subject.

A mini-Giulia wasn't something I needed to be dealing with.

"She deserved it," was the stubborn retort. "Biker princesses don't ever let anyone tear them down."

I grimaced, because I wanted her to have that level of self-worth, but violence wouldn't go down well at a Christian private academy. Something she'd only been able to get into because of my background, her baptism, and my father's position in the church in West Orange.

"You don't let them tear you down—" Storm concurred, until I cleared my throat and shot a glare at him. As he caught my eye, this time, I saw the amusement he was tampering down for my benefit.

I huffed. Of course he wasn't unhappy that she was turning into a termagant.

Was I the only sane person at the table? Lord give me strength.

"—but you can't get into trouble either."

"So, what you're saying is that I need to not get caught?"

I groaned. "Storm!"

Cyan giggled. "Mom, if you could see your face!"

Whatever expression I had, I knew for a fact that it changed at the sound of her giggle.

My baby.

She was coming back to me.

And I knew why.

Storm.

God.

Always Storm.

The server came with our order, and it gave me a second to appreciate the sound of her laughter. To let the joy of it swirl inside me.

Still, I had to temper this before it got out of hand. "You always get caught when you do bad things. No one stays quiet forever."

"Snitches. So messed up."

"Maybe, but it's to protect people too. You can't keep on hurting everyone who gets in your path, Cyan."

It was so difficult, because I wanted her to headbutt the bastards who were intent on hurting her, but hold peace talks with kids in her class.

Whoever said being a mom was easy was a schmuck.

She heaved a sigh as she dug her fork into her pie. "Snitches aren't people."

My brow furrowed. "Ugh, yeah, they are. Amara was a snitch," I told her. "Aren't you glad she saved you?"

Cyan's eyes widened at that as she peered at me, and I knew she'd never thought of it that way.

Slowly, I nodded. "She saved you for us, baby. Without her, you might not be sitting here. So, sometimes, a snitch is needed. Sometimes, they're not all bad."

"They are in the MC," she countered.

Storm cleared his throat, and he nearly broke my face as I smiled with relief when he said, "Baby, my world ain't your world."

"It is! I'm a biker princess!"

"I know, I know," he chided softly, "and you'll always be that, but what I do, baby, ain't what I want you to do. Maybe never, unless, when you're older, that's what you really, really want."

"Why not? You get to rule over all those guys." She peered up at him with so much admiration that I wasn't surprised when Storm squirmed.

Press a gun to his head, I had the feeling Storm would be fine. He'd talk himself out of the situation.

Have his daughter say something admirable about him? He looked like a turkey that was trying to avoid the butcher come Thanksgiving.

That was sad, wasn't it?

How did a man like my husband get to that point? Where he couldn't even accept a compliment from his little girl?

"You have to bear in mind that your school and my MC, they're not... well, they're not on the same level, are they, ladybug?"

"No, the MC is much better," was her stubborn retort, and I almost laughed when Storm grunted in the face of her obstinacy. "I wouldn't have gotten in trouble today if I'd been there. Can't you homeschool me, Mom?"

The irony here being that I'd never even damn well known she liked the MC. There was wanting to wear a cut while she rocked out a tutu—biker ballerina FTW—but I figured she wanted to mimic her father. Wanting to spend time at the clubhouse was another matter entirely.

Praying to God it was like that Pokémon phase back when she was six and that was all I'd heard for months on end before she never mentioned it again, I retorted, "What? So you can headbutt me if I irritate you? Every time I make you do math?"

She grinned at me. "I wouldn't do that."

I clicked my tongue in disbelief. "You forget how well I know you, cheeky monkey."

There was a twinkle in her eye that did my heart good to see. "I don't hate math."

"Since when?" Storm retorted with a laugh.

She blew a raspberry before she shoved a huge bite of pie into her mouth.

"Your mom's going to have classes of her own soon enough anyway," Storm interrupted softly. I cringed at his words. He noticed, of course. His brow furrowed, but he carried on, "So you'll just have to make do. That place will be good for you."

"There are no boys there. It's weird."

"It's not weird. It'll keep you focused."

She blinked. "That makes no sense."

Hiding a smile, I asked, "What do you mean, honey?"

"I mean that boys don't make me lose my focus."

"Who does?"

"Girls." She grunted. "I hate girls. They're mean and nasty and—"

"You liked Katina," I pointed out, referring to the foster daughter of Lodestar, the West Orange chapter's hacker, as well as the younger sister of one of the Old Ladies, Alessa. "She's a girl."

"She wasn't a girly girl though." Her nose crinkled. "I listened to them today. They all want to talk about painting their nails and lacrosse." She scoffed. "What kind of sport is lacrosse?"

Storm's lips twitched. "Canada's national sport?"

Cyan sniffed. "They can keep it. Why would you want to catch a ball with a portable net? What's the point?"

"Wasn't it a traditional indigenous game?" I asked Storm. Track and field sports were more my thing.

"It was," he agreed. "If you get good at it, it can be fun. Be good for your speed, Cyan. Build up some stamina so you can do a thousand backward flips instead of just fifty."

The contemplative look she shot him was deadly serious. "Do you think so?"

He smirked. "Maybe not a thousand."

"How many?"

I laughed. "You'll have to try it to find out."

She hummed, but she was pensive as she turned back to her pie.

Gymnastics was queen in our house. I was pretty sure she'd start at a competitive level soon enough, and before, I wouldn't have really pushed her, but now? I felt certain the challenge would not only be good for her, it was what she needed to keep out of trouble.

With Cyan a little quieter as she was lost to her thoughts, Storm asked, "Why did you look so disappointed when I mentioned classes? After our call, I was hoping you'd be more excited."

"It was just a lot more complicated than I'd have liked," I said on a sigh.

"Whatever you need, Keira, to make it happen, I got your back."

He sounded… earnest.

Was this a part of the charade? Or did he really mean it?

"Thank you," I said stiffly, uncertain of how to take his words.

A part of me felt catty for not taking him at face value, but then, hadn't he proven to me that I couldn't trust him?

I dug into my pie, all of us stuffing our faces with it as if this were appetizer, entrée, and dessert, like my going quiet was a trigger for us to just enjoy the food in front of us. Not that that was hard. It had to be the best pie I'd ever eaten in my goddamn life, that was how good it was.

When the server refilled our coffees and got Cyan another juice, Storm ordered some more, and we all tucked in even though it was the opposite of healthy. But hell, I figured we needed a break after that family therapy session.

"Can we come here next week after visiting Dr. Janowicz?" Cyan asked around a mouthful of s'mores pie, confirming my belief that this was a good way to end a stressful evening.

Storm looked to me, and I shrugged. "I don't see why not."

Hell, it might even make the entire ordeal bearable knowing we were going to eat this afterward.

"Sounds like a yes to me," Storm said with a wink at our kid.

"We should ask MaryCat and Digger to come and eat with us," Cyan chirped. "Maybe she'll let me hold Maddox."

"They'll be leaving or moving into a new house soon, Cy," Storm told her.

"They're leaving?" she whined.

"I don't think so. I think they'll stay, but if that's the case then they'll be settling in at their own place and into a new routine. It's hard with a new baby. We need to give them some time and some space," was his pointed remark.

Though she pouted, mostly I was just glad to hear the news. I really liked MC and hanging out with her was a pleasure. If they stayed, we'd get closer, and there was no denying that Maddox was a cutie-pie.

After we finished up, an old guy came out from behind the counter. He had a dish towel in his hands, and he was drying gnarled fingers on it as he tipped his head to the side while he walked toward us.

Because I was facing away from the door, I took note of his approach first, and shot him a wary smile as he neared the table.

"Spoke with Jaime today. He says you want to buy the place?"

Storm tipped his head back to look up at the owner of the diner— the MC wanted to buy it?

Considering Storm had been integral to Rex's plan over in West Orange to diversify the Sinners' portfolio, which had included the construction of the new mini-mall in the center of town, complete with strip club, diner, garage, and bar—guess which was the odd one out—I wasn't surprised at him looking to mimic the success of that venture here. What surprised me was that he wanted to take over what was, clearly, a mom-and-pop joint.

"I'm guessing you're Fred?" Storm rumbled, getting to his feet, his hand outstretched.

Fred nodded. "That's me." He took his hand, shook it, then asked, "Did you enjoy the pie?"

Storm smiled at the many dishes on the table. "I think you can see we did."

"Jaime said to watch out for you." Fred's gaze dropped to Storm's cut. "No missing a Sinner. All the waitresses get all excited." He shot me an apologetic look, but I just wafted a dismissive hand.

Funny how, when we'd been together, I'd have gotten jealous about that comment. Now I just accepted it as fact.

Storm, however, winced, and his face darkened with annoyance. "I was curious about the pies you want me to pay you royalties on."

Royalties? Huh?

Fred blinked, then he smiled. "That's a good way of phrasing it." He wagged a finger. "I might put that in the real estate ad."

"I don't think you'll need to worry about viewers, Fred. My kid wants to come next week, so I think that's all the approval I need." He dipped his chin. "I'll get in touch with the realtor in the AM."

"As easy as that?"

"As easy as that."

"I always thought the MC was poor."

My eyes widened, especially when Storm didn't rush to defend it. "There's a new boss in charge."

"Heard that Butch did a runner." Fred clucked his tongue. "Bad boy that. Always was, and always will be a bad egg." He squinted at Storm. "You like him?"

"I'm not a good egg, but I won't screw your business up."

Fred shot me a look, as if he were using me as a point of reference who'd back him up. But I wasn't playing.

"If you've got a problem with doing business with the MC, Fred, you'd better tell me now before I waste anymore of both our time," Storm cautioned, a harder edge to his tone as he stared the older man down.

Surprised he hadn't lost his temper at the slights Fred kept making, I had to admit that Storm's volatile nature rarely revealed itself in arguments. Of his many flaws, of the many chinks in his control, his temper wasn't one of them. At least, not with us.

How likely was it that a guy whose road name was Storm, a word that was tempestuous and volatile in nature, didn't have a temper?

And yet, in arguments, I was the one whose voice was raised. Never him. I was the one who got angry, who yelled in his face, who tried to tear at his walls. Me. Not him.

It was a strange time to make that revelation. Stranger still when I watched Fred shake his head and say, "Your money's as good as anyone's."

"My money's the only one buying," Storm retorted coolly. "I've seen that this place has been on the market for a couple years."

"You pay for quality," Fred said with a sniff.

"There's quality and there's pricing yourself out of the market."

I shot Cyan a look, wondering if she understood what was happening here, if she was interested, and I found her spooning up cherry pie as she watched her dad in negotiations.

If this could be considered negotiations, that is.

Storm wasn't arguing about the price, but Fred wasn't exactly being chipper about it.

"We're worth every penny. If you think you can try to get me to lower the price—"

Storm shook his head. "I'm not quibbling."

Fred frowned. "You're not?"

"No."

Fred eyed him suspiciously. "So I can expect a call from Sally Anne tomorrow?"

"You can."

"You think this is a way out of paying for your pie?"

My eyes bugged at that, and finally, I had to speak. "Excuse me, Fred, that's completely out of order. We never suggested that we were trying to get a free meal! We pay our way just fine, thank you very much."

He wriggled his shoulders. "Lots of freeloaders around here," was all he said.

"Well, we're not like that," I said with a huff. *The nerve of him.*

Turning away from the conversation, I eyed Cyan, saw her watching me with surprise, and flickered back to the conversation between Storm and Fred.

"Can we have the bill, please?" I requested.

Fred pursed his lips. "You can. I'll look forward to doing business with you."

With that, he held out his hand to be shaken again, which Storm did, then retreated to the kitchen.

"What a miserable old coot," I grumbled under my breath as he took his seat opposite me.

"I don't think he's ready to let go," Storm mused, tackling Cyan for the last piece of cherry pie which, of course, had her giggling, especially when he let her win.

She surprised me by cutting the piece in half, and saying, "Halfsies, Daddy."

"Thanks, ladybug," he replied, taking it and humming as he chomped away.

"What do you mean?" I asked, trying not to watch him eat the pie. It really shouldn't have been sexy. "Why's he selling if he isn't ready to let go?"

Storm shrugged. "See his hands?"

I blinked. "I guess. I watched him dry them on a towel."

"Did you notice how bad his arthritis is?"

"No."

"The knuckles were fused. No man likes to admit he's incapable of doing what he loves."

"How do you know he loves it?"

He snorted. "He's got two line order cooks and several waitresses, plus it's nearly nine o'clock, honey. No man his age would be here with that many staff on board if he didn't love what he did." His insight had me pausing, but he mistook my curiosity because he said, "I know you worked at the diner in West Orange, so you might not get it. Giulia hates cooking even though she's damn good at it—"

"No, I get it," I denied. "There's something nice about feeding people comfort food. Stuff that puts a smile on their faces. Maybe not when you're slogging for minimum wage and tips, but it's honest work at least."

"Exactly. Imagine if this place was your pride and joy and you'd been working here for forty years?"

"It'd be like getting rid of family."

He nodded. "It would."

As I studied him, surprised by the insight, the waitress came over and said, "Don't know what miracles you worked on Old Fred, but he said you don't have to pay your tab."

Storm just smiled and gave her his thanks, and though we didn't leave immediately, finishing up the rest of the other slices of pie on the table and hanging around until Cyan was yawning and ready for bed, I noticed that when we got up, Storm left a fifty-dollar note under a dish when he thought I wasn't looking.

DEAR KEIRA

I watched you play Helena in that school play today.

I think they miscast you though. At least, I hope they did.

Did you know I never read Shakespeare before you? But when Jimmy told me about the play, told me why you were staying so late after school, I had to know more.

He thinks I'm weird. He doesn't say anything because he's only a Prospect and Rex and I are like brothers, but he probably thinks I'm a creep on top of being weird.

I don't care what he thinks, though. I'm just glad he goes to Jackson High.

You don't know this, but I make him check up on you. I make sure he keeps you safe. One of the clubwhores' girls is in your year. I asked Kendra to watch over you too.

Did you know that Jamie Grier was going to ask you to Prom?

Kendra overheard him talking about you with his friends.

He was going to slip something into your drink, honey. You didn't know that, did you? You'll never know, either. I'll make sure of that. Just like I'll make sure you're always safe.

You should have played Hermia.

She was strong. Helena followed after Lysander like a lost puppy. That ain't you. I know that. I can see the fire in your eyes, but I don't think you know it's there.

I wonder what will make you see yourself how I see you.

I hope I'm around when you realize it. I bet it's a glorious sight.

Just like you on that stage.

Glorious.

Yours,

Storm

DEAR DIARY

SENIOR YEAR

God, I hate being on the stage so much. Now that Midsummer Night's Dream is over, I finally feel like I can breathe again.

I hate that Dad makes me do this stuff. Would Johns Hopkins really not accept me because this wasn't on my application?

Either way, it's done. It was bullshit, and that bitch, Jilly Harlan, was Hermia. I can't believe I had to play Helena. Although… Hermia stands up to her dad, and I can't stand up to him long enough to get out of acting in a shitty play, so maybe Mr. Rogers saw something in me that makes it look like I'm a frickin' pushover.

I hate that Helena got Hermia's leftovers. Demetrius didn't love her. He loved Hermia. But some bullshit love spell gave her her happily-ever-after. What kind of ending is that?

There were two high points to everything, though. Now it's over, I don't have to worry about disappointing Dad, and amid all the anxiety of the performance, I want to say that I saw The Biker there.

At least, I'm pretty sure I saw him in the seats.

Maybe that's just my new obsession talking, though. Maybe I was seeing things. Maybe it was just stupid wishful thinking? Although, why I'd wish for him to be there, watching me in a stupid play, playing a weak ass heroine, I don't know.

There's something about him that calls to me.

You know, I was in the middle of that stupid scene at the beginning where Demetrius is all up in Hermia's business and Helena was just left to watch on like a total moron, and the doors to the theater opened up. The lights are really bright on stage, but I was tilted just so that I saw it open. That's when I'm sure I saw him. It was too hard to catch his features, but that streak of hair—I've never seen anyone but him with that.

Does he have a kid at Jackson High or something? He doesn't look old enough, and I think someone would have admitted to being related to him if he was… It must be my eyes playing tricks on me. Yeah, it must be that.

Although, I'm sure that believing he was there made me put more energy into the character. Mr. Rogers was talking about casting me in the next play, and I backed the hell away from that. Acting is not my calling. No way, no how.

I wonder what The Biker's name is.

If I asked Jimmy, I wonder if he'd tell me. It's not like we're friends, after all. But what's in a name?

SEVENTEEN

STORM

PRESENT

Godspeed - Frank Ocean

"ASHER?"

I jerked my head to the side, relieved when my neck cracked. "Hey."

"Haven't heard from you in a while," Christopher, my new NA sponsor, said calmly.

If he'd been a jackass about it, I'd probably have hung up but the guy had led the Narcotics Anonymous meetings in Manhattan where I attended for a long time, so he knew how junkies worked.

Even if I hadn't had anything more chemical than sugar and aspartame sliding through my veins for two decades, I would always be a junkie.

People who said they were ex-addicts were fucking liars.

We were all in recovery.

All of us just waiting for that one day when shit'd hit the fan and we'd end up drowning in our vices.

I jerked my neck to the side again, needing to feel that crack.

"Storm?"

"I'm here. Thanks for answering. Wasn't sure if you'd be busy."

"I'm glad you called," was Christopher's serene answer. The guy was always like that. It was as if he'd swallowed Gandhi whole or something.

I wanted some of that fucking peace for myself.

"My family moved down to Ohio," I told him abruptly, staring at the plants on the window ledge.

Slowly but surely, they were starting to take over this house as well as my office at the clubhouse. Either Keira hadn't noticed, or she didn't care.

Eyeing the wilting leaf on a geranium plant, I tried to collect my thoughts, tried to figure out why I'd called Christopher in the first place, but my mind was blurry.

Cyan was at gymnastics practice, and because it was a three-hour training session, I'd come home. The house was empty because Keira was on a date.

A fucking date.

My jaw worked again as the desire to crack my neck hit me once more, but I had a feeling the only relief that'd come from that was if I tore my head clean off.

Ever since the MC had bought *Pies You Like It*, Keira had decided that she wanted to work there. I wasn't sure what was going on with that, but I wasn't going to argue because what the fuck did I know about running a diner? It was a relief she wanted to get involved. One more thing off my to-do list.

She liked working there. *Great*. She'd picked up a customer. *Fuck*.

"That's good news, isn't it?" Christopher asked cautiously, breaking into my bad mood with a sledgehammer. "I mean, you were concerned about not seeing your daughter the last time we spoke."

My jaw tensed as I sat up, my elbows hitting my knees as I planted my cell on the coffee table. Head bowing, I stared at the carpet I'd vacuumed earlier, and muttered, "It didn't happen in the best of circumstances, but yeah, I'm glad they're here."

"Want to talk about it?"

"She was..." How did I describe it? I'd spoken about this in therapy but it was harder, somehow, with a man who knew a lot of intimate secrets about me. Plus, I couldn't tell the full truth. That made it more difficult too. "A guy on the internet groomed her and kidnapped her."

"Holy hell!"

I wasn't sure I'd ever heard Christopher swear.

"Yeah," I said gruffly. "Things were... bad."

"Sounds like it. She's okay?"

"We got to her in time."

"I'm glad." His tone was heartfelt, genuine, but that was Christopher, I guessed. I didn't come across altruistic people all that often, but he was like that. Selfless.

It was weird.

Good, nice, kind, but weird.

I thought that was why I struggled talking to him, even as, once I opened up, it was easy to spill my guts.

"Me too," I rumbled before I cleared my throat.

"Is that why you're calling? You want to take a hit?"

"No." I shook my head even though he couldn't see it. "Her mom and I are still broken up, and she went on a date for the first time tonight."

"Okay?"

I knew what he was thinking. My kid had been abducted, but I hadn't wanted to get high, but my ex went on a date, and I did?

It was messed up.

"I had to be strong." It wasn't a justification. It was a reason. "There was no wavering, no indecisiveness. I couldn't be a pussy and think about crack or meth. I just had to be there for them both. I had to get us here, settle us in, then I had to start making amends."

"And why are you triggered now?"

"Because as much as I know that Keira would be better off with someone else, everything inside me rebels at the idea of another bastard touching her."

"Understandable." He paused. "Can I ask you a question, Asher?"

"Sure."

"You were unfaithful, yes?"

"Yes." The admission felt like it was torn from my soul.

"Do you see tonight's date as a form of unfaithfulness?"

"No. We're split up."

"So you're just being possessive?"

"No."

"What is it then?"

"I want what's best for her. I just wish that were me."

"Why did you cheat on her?"

Wasn't that a loaded question? But somehow, it was easier admitting this to him than to Keira. She wouldn't believe me. Christopher had no reason not to.

"First time, it was…" I sucked in a breath. "Pretty messed up."

"Why?"

"She'd left me."

"So, it wasn't cheating?" he asked, confused.

"She was pregnant. It was… Man, I don't even know what it was. But she left me, and like a pussy, I got high.

"I thought she'd come back to me, thought she wanted to make us work so when she came onto me, I didn't think anything of it. I was just happy."

"It wasn't her?"

"No."

"Who was it?"

"The woman who told her I cheated on her repeatedly throughout Keira's pregnancy."

"She lied?" There was no surprise in Christopher's voice. I guessed a guy like him had heard a million sob stories—most of them worse—in his time.

"She did."

"Why?"

"Because she's loved me for a long time."

He sniffed. "That doesn't sound like love."

"No, it doesn't to me either."

"Your love sounds like love. You want what's best for Keira, even though that hurts you to know it isn't you, but it doesn't change anything."

"I guess mine does sound like love." The realization sank into my bones.

"You don't have a very high opinion of yourself, do you, Asher?" He laughed a little. "In fact, don't answer that. I already know you don't, and you'll just give me some BS about it. So, you were raped—"

"That wasn't rape," I scoffed. "My dick was hard."

"It was rape. It was non-consensual," was Christopher's calm retort.

My jaw tensed. "It wasn't rape. I wanted it to be Keira."

"But it wasn't. You were tricked into having sex, and then the woman in question manipulated things further to break you and your wife up."

"She twisted the truth and used it against me."

"Whenever you cheated, was it because you got high?"

"Yes." Jaw clenching, I rubbed at my eyes. I was such a fuck up.

There was silence, for a few beats, then he queried softly, "And each time, did you think it was Keira you were sleeping with?"

Shame hit me. "Yes."

"Interesting."

Shame morphed into bitter anger. "Glad to hear I'm so fucking fascinating."

He clucked his tongue. "I'm just trying to understand, Asher. No harm in that, is there?"

My shoulders hunched as I gruffly admitted, "No. No harm done." Not anymore. The damage had already been done. Years earlier. Wreaking devastation in its wake, unforgivable in its entirety.

The roar of half-pipes put me on red alert so I surged to my feet and headed into the kitchen. Peering out of the window, I got even more pissed when I saw it wasn't Jump—it was Digger arriving home.

From this angle, I could see the front door open, MaryCat standing there with Maddox in her arms. She looked a little wan, pale, but her smile was real and raw as Digger climbed off the back of his bike and headed toward her.

As he wrapped her up in his arms, I wished like fuck I could be back there again. Right to the beginning. To fucking day one.

"Asher? Are you still there?"

Yeah. I'm just busy creeping on my brother as he makes out with his wife who doesn't want to poison him with a tomahawk steak.

"I'm still here."

Christopher sighed. "What are you doing?"

"I thought Keira was on her way home."

"It's barely seven," Christopher drawled. "It wouldn't have been a good date, would it?"

Exactly. "I want her to have a good time."

"Just with you?"

"No. I don't think we can have that anymore." My brow puckered. "Okay, that's bullshit. I think we can, if she can let me in."

"Everyone is worthy of forgiveness, Asher. Don't be too hard on yourself. Everyone has a vice that helps us cope with life—"

"Some just don't destroy their fucking family with it."

"Do you want to be with her?"

"There's nothing more that I want in this world."

"Have you thought about trying to woo her?"

"No. There's no point. I don't want her to end up with me."

"That's taking selflessness too far, isn't it?"

"I'm poison, Christopher. She got out before it was too late to save herself. I'm proud of her because of that."

"That's equally the most depressing, disturbing, and wonderful thing I've ever heard anyone say," Christopher said after a few moments.

I grunted. "Glad I'm entertaining—"

There was a rumble of more half pipes, and as I waited for the sight of the SUV to show up, instead, I saw a new hog.

A bright red one.

My brow puckered and even though Christopher was talking, I muttered, "Great talk, Christopher. Thanks. I gotta go."

Cutting him off halfway through his next words, I studied the bike, wondering who the fuck it was, then headed over to the kitchen cupboard I had locked and loaded with a twelve gauge.

Dragging it out, I walked over to the front door, opened it, and keeping the shotgun hooked over my forearm, I waited for the bastard to turn around and face me.

When he did, my eyes widened. "Rex? Where the fuck have you been, you dipshit?"

If he'd have looked like hell, I could probably have forgiven him. But he was clean-shaven, a little tanned. His eyes were wild with grief, but I understood that. As for the rest of him, he looked like his clothes were clean, his boots were even fucking polished.

I stormed out of the front entrance, and before I knew what the hell I was doing, I punched him in the shoulder. Hard enough to take him back on his ass, even though he'd probably braced for that.

As he went flying, I loomed over him, and aware that he was bracing for a kick now but wasn't willing to fight, I snarled, "Well? Where the fuck have you been?"

When he didn't bother getting up, just lay there looking at me, I heaved a sigh, and though it was insane because the temperature out here made frigid look warm, I twisted around and plunked my ass down beside him.

The snow had pretty much gone but the cold sank into my bones as I laid back on the frozen grass, staring up at the sky.

Screw the cold, screw everything, it was fucking awesome that he was here.

I'd been worrying my ass off, all of us had, so to know he was safe came as a massive relief.

I hadn't even registered how his being missing had been a burden on my back until now, when it went away. That didn't mean I was about to make it easier on him, and silence worked wonders where badgering his ass wouldn't. I knew he'd open up if I was patient.

As we rested there, saying shit, shivering our dicks off, finally, he muttered, "Kendra's my half-sister."

I didn't say anything. Though I was surprised that was where he went first, this wasn't news to me.

"You knew?" Rex rumbled after a few seconds, head rocking to the side.

"Found out a few years back."

"That why you never let me toss her out?"

"Well, it wasn't because I was in fucking love with her."

"I thought that was why."

"I know. It was easier to let you think that."

Rex rolled his head to look at me. "I can't believe it."

"Trust me, Bear didn't believe it either—"

"Why did he confide in you and not me?"

"Because I asked him if he'd ever cheated on your mom, and I wanted to know how he made it right."

"Christ," Rex said with a hiss. "I—I guess I thought he was faithful, which is crazy—"

"Why is it crazy?"

"The point is moot considering he *did* cheat on Mom."

"No. It isn't inevitable that people will cheat. You think Nyx is gonna cheat on Giulia?"

"No, she'd chop his dick off. He ain't as insane as everyone thinks he is."

I snorted. "Link wouldn't cheat on Lily, Sin on Tiff, Mav on Alessa, Steel on Stone… they're in it." I emphasized the word 'it.'

"Never seen a man more all-in than you, Storm. But you fucked it up."

The words hurt worse than how he'd likely felt with the punch I'd landed on his shoulder.

"I did," I agreed.

"Anyway, I thought he'd have wrapped that shit up at least. Christ." He grunted under his breath as he rubbed his eyes with the butts of his hands. "That why you always steered me away from her? Not that I liked her toxic cunt. She was always mooning after you, anyway. Those fucking cow eyes were a turn off.

"Plus I've always been more discerning than most of you bastards."

I grimaced. "You never fucked her? Ever?"

"No. Can't say I picked up on a vibe or anything, just always hated the bitch. Thank God, huh? Man, that'd be fucked up. Even for the Sinners."

"True dat."

"Storm?"

"Yeah?"

"Why did you do that? Why did you fuck it up with Keira?"

My mouth tightened. "Didn't mean to."

"Just fell on Kendra? X marks the fucking spot?"

"No. I didn't fuck around as much as everyone thinks. It happened, often enough that I'm goddamn ashamed, but it was never me just getting off for the sake of getting off. I was always high.

"Don't forget, I wasn't using all the time. Most of my marriage didn't pass by in a fucking blur."

"No. Because I used to throw your ass in the Fridge," he reminded me.

I pulled a face. "Thanks?"

His laugh was short. "Trust me, I hated doing that as much as you hated me for it. Wasn't about to let you ruin your life though."

"I appreciate that, brother," I rasped, meaning it less in the MC way and more fraternally.

He knew that because he rumbled, "I wish you hadn't messed shit up with Keira."

"Me too."

"I don't even know why you fucked them. You had blinders on ever since you met her anyway. Never seen a dipshit so head over heels more than you."

For a second, I lost my voice because it was easier to admit this shit to someone who had no horses in the race, like Christopher, than it was with Rex who'd been there for every up and down.

"I used to think I was fucking Keira," I managed to choke out.

Rex stilled. "You kidding me?"

"No. Wish I were."

"That's messed up."

"I know."

"Jesus."

Silence fell, and I knew he'd just lost a whole hell of a lot of respect for me—I deserved it though.

Jaw working, regret hitting me, I grated out, "You remember when your mom had that miscarriage?"

Rex hissed out a breath. "Yeah. I remember. She froze us all out."

Yeah, that year had been hell.

Rene was the only mother in my life that mattered, but when she'd lost her baby, she'd gone in on herself. So far into that cave of depression that it had felt like we were going to lose her too.

I used to go and sit with her. Not saying shit. Just slipping into her room, lying on top of the covers at her side. I'd been around eight at the time. It was probably messed up that at that age, I understood what she was going through because I felt like that all the time.

Still did.

Just had a better mask now.

"About eleven months into that, your dad got a girlfriend. Got her a place in town—"

"Holy shit," he rasped. "How do you know this?"

"We only ever talked about cheating that once. Second your mom was back to herself, he got rid of her. Paid her to leave. Kendra came back because she said she was the daughter of a clubwhore. She didn't tell him until after Rene died."

"Christ."

"Yeah."

"How old were you when you found out?"

I thought back, and guesstimated, "Twenty-seven? It was a few months after Keira gave birth."

"When Keira left you again?"

I sighed. "Yeah."

"Why *did* she keep leaving you?"

"Because she had sense?"

"Bullshit."

"Because life wasn't as pretty as she thought it would be," I said simply.

"What happened? Why did she come back?"

"I don't know. She just came back like she usually did." 'Did' being the operative word.

"Did he know his girlfriend was pregnant?"

I blinked at the change of topic. "No. He found out when Kendra gave him a birth certificate. I think she knew no good would come of that news being brought into the light while his Old Lady was around. At least, I think so. Never spoken to her about it."

"He believed her?"

"I think Kendra's mom was a good woman."

"Christ, irony."

"Yeah. She bred a viper."

"Probably Dad's intervention. His DNA probably made her a cunt." As I snorted, Rex rolled upward, sitting so that his back was curved, his knees high, his arms resting on them. "Dad's kid or not, she deserved to be kicked out of the club for what she did to Keira."

"I know she did." Getting kicked out of the house, my marriage breaking down, finding out *who'd* whispered in my wife's ear... I'd wanted to kill the bitch.

But, when it boiled down to it, the mistake was on me.

All this shit was on me.

"Then why didn't you let me? Why, when Link raised the subject, did you come to me and tell me not to?"

"I was looking out for future Rex. I knew when you found out, it would mess with your head if you'd kicked her out."

"Maybe," he said slowly. Then, he shook his head. "Being my half-sister don't give her a free pass to be a cruel bitch, Storm."

"You can say that now," I rumbled. "But you might not have done before."

"Why didn't you just fucking tell me?"

"Because Bear asked me not to."

He didn't scoff, but his anger throbbed through his words as he asked, "Do you know what I don't understand about you?"

"What?"

"How someone so fucking honorable can get himself into so much shit with his wife."

"I wish I had an answer to that."

"Me too," he snapped. "Rachel read me Dad's will. It wasn't official because he had a lot of bequests but..." He blew out a breath. "He left you something."

"What?"

"Don't know. Rachel does, but she wouldn't say."

"We've been waiting on the funeral for you."

He rocked his head. "Had to get away." He must have heard my silent criticism.

"Couldn't have left a message?"

"Checked in with Rachel from time to time."

"She never said anything."

He scraped a hand over his jaw. "Talked to her as the club's lawyer."

"Where you been?"

"Does it matter?"

I rolled my eyes because I heard him stonewalling, and I didn't have the patience for that bullshit. "You're lucky I didn't beat your ass."

"Instead, we're gonna freeze it off, huh?"

"Yeah," I retorted as I rolled up and mimicked his position.

The cold was bitter, eating into the plaid shirt I wore under my cut, but it was good to feel something other than goddamn self-loathing and exhaustion.

My phone buzzed, and because it could have been Cyan, I pulled it out of my pocket and checked the notification.

Jump: *Want me to stop this before it starts?*

My throat worked as I looked at Keira kissing the guy she'd gone out with tonight.

His name was Jared Ryker. He worked for a Big Pharma company in R&D. He owed three hundred grand on his house, had the beginnings of a coke habit, and was three months behind on his child support.

However, his divorce had been amicable, and his ex-wife spoke highly of him—aside from the child support issues which, according to her, he was often late paying, but when he was flush with cash, would usually give her extra as an apology.

I'd told Jump to give her what she was owed to keep her quiet, because it wasn't her kids' fault that Jared clearly had financial issues. Jump was looking into him some more, but I suspected a gambling addiction on top of the coke.

He wasn't ideal, but his wife said he'd never cheated, had never hit her, and that he was going places in his job. A good candidate for a first steady boyfriend, especially if he had a woman like Keira at his side who'd encourage him to stay on the straight and narrow.

Rex grunted under his breath as he peered over at my screen. "You still having her followed?"

"What the fuck do you think? 'Course I am."

"Poor goddamn Cyan," Rex muttered. "Let me guess, you got her being tailed as well."

There might have been a brother or two watching over the gym as we spoke, but I wasn't about to tell him that.

"Where the fuck did you go wrong, Storm? Jesus. It's not like you even 'see' other women. Just... Please tell me you weren't like Dad. Please tell me you used a condom."

"Of course. I always use a condom."

His brow puckered as I zoomed in on the picture. "Even with Keira?"

"Especially with Keira."

"Huh." He waited a beat. "Why?"

"Because I don't want to risk her getting pregnant again."

Rex heaved a sigh. "She ain't gonna die in childbirth, Storm."

"How do you know that?" I rumbled. "The U.S. maternal mortality rate is the worst of any developed nation."

"You always wanted a big family," he pointed out.

"Want her alive more."

"What if she'd wanted another kid?"

"She did. We argued about it. A lot."

"You won, obviously."

"She froze me out for six months," I said wryly. "That was painful."

"Did you cheat on her, then?"

"No. Didn't need to get high for that one." *She hadn't walked out.*

"I wish I got what went down in your brain."

"Me too." I hesitated a second, then admitted, "What you feel for Rachel... is it love?"

It took him a good long while to answer. "Yeah," Rex admitted gruffly.

"What I feel for Keira borders on an obsession. I know it's crazy, but that's how it is. I spent half her pregnancy terrified I'd resent the hell out of Cyan. I never wanted to share Keira. Ever. A second kid..." My words waned. "I don't know how I'd cope."

"Your mom did a real number on you, Storm." Rex shook his head. "Not sure why that surprises me, but it's true. Love don't work that way. It's generous, it isn't selfish."

"If you say so," I rasped, but the concern was there.

"I've seen how you are with Cyan, man. Jesus, you're one of the best dads I've ever known."

My shoulders hunched up around my ears. "Thanks."

He heaved a sigh. "Believe me or don't, it's the truth. You should have more kids. You got too much love in you, that's your problem. Anyway, I ain't gonna convince you so what are you going to do about that guy?"

"Nothing." I stared at them kissing. Stared at the kisses that should have been mine. At the mouth that belonged to me...

Me: *Leave it. Just make sure, if things get deeper, and she tries to stop it, that you're there to help out.*

Jump: *Seriously?*

"Seriously?" Rex sputtered at my side at the same time.

I cut him a look. "She deserves to find happiness."

Me: *Seriously. Just make sure she gets out safe. She won't spend the night.*

Jump: *Gotcha. Your funeral.*

My mouth tightened.

"Your honor code is messed up."

"We know that already," I said tightly.

"Did you guys talk about dating?"

"I told her I was proud she dumped my ass, and she told me that we'd never be together." I shot him a look. "Which part of that was supposed to give me hope?"

He pursed his lips. "What if she's supposed to find happiness with you?"

"She'll never find that with me. I'm toxic for her. I'm just lucky she's letting me stay here for the time being."

I saw the exasperation etched into his drawn features. "Martyrs don't get the girl."

"I want what's best for her."

"Dipshit," he grumbled. "Never understood why you treat her the way you do."

I frowned. "What the hell's that supposed to mean?"

"It means you treat her like she's a kid. I told you to keep it traditional, not fucking paternal. Bet you ain't never told her dick about her old man and the games he's pulled over the years, have you?"

"I had it under control."

"I'm sure," was his dry retort. "Just so you know, I'll only let you pull this martyr shit for so long before I snap. Even if you ain't high, I'm not above hurling you in the Fridge to make you drag your head out of your ass." Before I could reply, he demanded, "Anyway, how's Cyan doing?"

"Better now I'm here."

"Maybe Keira will take you back because of her?"

"She shouldn't."

Rex growled and punched me in the shoulder, much as I'd done him. "Maybe she doesn't want you to just passively accept her fucking other guys, Storm. Maybe she wants you to grovel, huh? Maybe she wants you to get in her face and tell her that she's yours and that you're hers?"

I stared at him. "I'm not good for her."

"So? Is Nyx good for Giulia?" was his rejoinder. "The fucker needs to kill people to find inner peace, Storm. Jesus. How he's gone clean for so fucking long I don't know. He's gonna blow at some point. That sound healthy?"

I winced because I knew Nyx needed the kill. It went deeper than addiction. His sanity rested on it.

"Sometimes shit doesn't have to be healthy to be right." He grunted. "I need coffee."

"How long you been riding?"

"Eighteen hours."

"Jesus. What the hell were you doing down on the West Coast?"

"It doesn't matter. How are things going here?"

"Better. We bought a diner, a local motel, and a garage. We're looking into buying a factory as well. They fabricate auto parts."

Rex arched a brow. "You're working fast."

"Most of the plan to legitimize the Sinners in West Orange was my idea," I said dryly. "Just repeating what we did. Why fix what ain't broken?"

"The brothers accepting you?"

"Yeah. Few rumbles from a guy who's pissed I didn't make him VP—"

"He a problem?"

"No. Don't think so."

"What about the Sinners we ran off? Any issues there?"

"No. It's a good chapter. There were just a few bad eggs. It's very family-oriented."

Rex's brows rose. "Really?"

"Yeah. All of my council are family men. I'd say nearly eighty percent of the remaining brothers have kids and Old Ladies."

"Jesus. So, the Ohio Chapter is like the Sinners' version of *The Waltons*?"

I smirked at that. "Yeah, you keep on thinking that, John Boy."

He shoved me in the arm, then fell quiet as the cold sank even further into our bones. Christ, it was better than meth at making me feel awake.

"Storm?" he asked after a few minutes.

"Yeah?"

"Dad... I—"

"I miss him too."

Rex cleared his throat, but he still sounded choked as he grated out, "He woke up before he died."

I straightened up. "Seriously? What did he say?"

He was silent again, and when he spoke, I knew why—he was holding back tears. "He asked me to help him get to Mom."

His words hit me in the gullet.

They hit me in the throat.

They hit me in the gut.

They hit me in the fucking head.

But worst of all, they hit me in the heart.

If he sounded choked, that was nothing to me as I rasped, "Don't tell anyone else."

"I won't."

I reached over, grabbed his shoulder, and whispered, "He was waiting to be with her."

"I know."

And like two pussies, we sat in the dark, on the frozen ground, hunched over, both of us trying not to cry as we mourned the man who'd been our father.

As we mourned the mom we'd lost too young.

And prayed that, if there really was a God, he delivered Bear into Rene's arms.

EIGHTEEN

KEIRA

PRESENT

JARED WAS SURPRISINGLY good in bed.

He knew where the clitoris was, which was definitely a check in the positive column. He wasn't afraid to suck it, and he wasn't afraid to wait for me to get off before he came.

He was clean, had a nice house, a good car and job, and he smelled great.

So why was he so wrong?

I faked my orgasm, because though he'd gotten me off, it had been a tiny peak and that wasn't his fault. He'd really tried, so I'd groaned like I was in the throes, and he believed me because afterward, I sobbed like it was good, spluttering and gasping not with pleasure, but with regret. With loss.

He wasn't Storm.

God, I was so fucking pathetic.

As Jared kissed my tears away, he chuckled softly. "Hey, it's okay," he teased, moving his lips down over the arch of my slick cheekbone.

I felt his pride, though, and was relieved that he didn't think I was defective or something.

I gave him a soggy laugh that I prayed didn't sound fake.

When his lips met mine, it was hard not to back away, not to retreat. He was nice. Kind. A good date. I'd never been in the market for a date before because I'd never had the chance to, but so far, I'd had a good time. What with Dane back in West Orange, and then Jared here, but neither of them did it for me.

I wasn't even sure what it was.

Dane hadn't been good in bed, but Jared was. He was generous with himself, eager to satisfy, and though my body might have peaked a little, my head just hadn't been in the game. He didn't deserve for me to treat him like he was a leper.

"Thank you for dinner," he murmured with a soft laugh, his lips gently pressing against mine before he moved down, onto my throat, down to my breasts.

It felt strange not wearing the leather necklace, not having the solid weight of the key to Storm's padlock tucked into my cleavage, but I'd removed it tonight because I'd intended to have sex. Something I almost regretted now.

My nostrils flared as I worked through my desire to toss him away, and as he sucked on my nipple, I was grateful when my alarm rang. I'd set it, just to be on the safe side. This had happened with Dane, and the last thing I wanted was to be stuck here like I'd been with him.

"Damn," he grumbled, but it wasn't mean, just disappointed. "Guess you need to pick your daughter up, huh?"

I sighed and apologetically murmured, "Sorry, babe."

He grinned at me. "No worries. Hey, I'll be away the rest of the week on a conference, so if you don't see me in the diner, don't worry. I haven't ghosted you."

Well, that made me think he was going to ghost me. Damn, it was definitely a bad sign that I was relieved. A part of me even hoped he wouldn't come into the diner where I was working now… or was that just wishful thinking?

I blinked. "Okay."

He shook his head as he lowered his mouth to mine again. "Seriously, it's a boring team-building exercise. When I get back, we'll go out again, yeah?"

I shot him a smile that I hoped was eager and nodded. "I'll look forward to it."

Quickly rolling out of bed, I grabbed my purse and my phone to turn off the alarm, then shot off a text to Storm.

Me: *I'll be back in time to get Cyan.*

Storm: *You sure?*

Me: *Of course.*

Storm: *I made soup. Or do you want me to order in? Rex came. He's staying the night before leaving tomorrow.*

My eyes rounded with surprise. And relief. I knew how worried Storm had been about Rex. Heck, I'd started to worry too.

Me: *Rex is there?*

Storm: *Yeah.*

Me: *Is he okay?*

Storm: *As well as can be.*

"Everything okay? You look shocked," Jared questioned, his concern clear.

"No, it's all good. Just checking in with the gym where my daughter's got a class."

Storm: *Soup or takeout?*

What was it with him and soup right now?

I was beyond grateful he'd cooked, but I knew he hated it.

Deciding to save him from himself, I typed out:

Me: *Order in. Your choice.*

He sent me a thumbs up, just as MaryCat texted me. We'd grown close over the last couple of weeks, enough that I'd shared the gossip about Jared asking me out.

MC: *How did the date go?*

Me: *I'll tell you later. xx*

MC: *Just tell me if you want to see him again.*

Me: *No…*

MC: *Damn.*

Smiling a little, I shoved my phone back in my purse and started gathering my clothes together. Well aware Jared watched, I tried not to feel uncomfortable with his eyes on me.

Storm… why was it only now that I realized I never actually felt that way with him?

At the beginning, after Cyan, I'd been like this. But over the years, he'd celebrated my body in so many different ways that I couldn't really be self-conscious. He reveled in my tits, loved my ass, and wasn't afraid to tell me so.

No, Keira. NO! He's bad for you. BAD.

I cleared my throat when I was ready, and though it was weird, I rounded the bed and leaned down to give him a quick kiss on the cheek.

He smiled and, afterward, said, "The door locks itself."

If I'd been serious about him, that would have been a red flag, but I was just grateful I wouldn't have to wave bye to him as I drove off.

"Speak later," I told him huskily, hoping I still sounded eager.

Darting out of the bedroom, I managed to find the light switch and headed down the stairs. It was a nice house. Very nice, in fact, for a divorced guy with two kids to pay child support for.

Another red flag if I'd been interested in him.

When I left the house, a light popped on, which was how I saw him.

At first, his presence made me jerk back in surprise, then I recognized Jump.

My throat tightened as our eyes clashed and held.

Storm would know soon.

Or maybe he already did.

Would he have asked me about soup if he'd known I was fucking some guy I'd met at the diner? Who'd bought me a nice meal after work, who'd wooed me?

Jump broke eye contact first, and when I saw a glint of light, I knew he was on his phone, probably informing Storm I was leaving.

My throat was tight as I headed into my SUV and backed onto the road. Jared's home was a few streets away from Main Street, so the rumbles of my engine and Jump's weren't out of place as we rode off.

Mind whirring as I drove to Cyan's gym, I told myself I had no need to feel guilty. Nothing to be ashamed about. I'd done nothing wrong. I was a single woman. I could sleep with whomever I wanted.

Those things were all true, they were all facts, but that didn't stop me from being nervous.

Cyan was bubbling with enthusiasm, talking about the horse and how she'd managed to do a handstand on the barre, and I let her, the white noise comforting me even as I braced myself for what was about to go down.

A weird hum throbbed in my veins. It wasn't excitement, neither was it dread. It was just energy.

I felt alive.

A little nauseated, sure, but alive.

After I pulled into the driveway to my house, Cyan darted ahead, racing to find out who our visitor was seeing as there was a shiny red hog on the road, and I let her.

Behind me, I heard Jump's half pipes as he pulled into his own home, then Cyan's squealing made itself known to me. For a moment, I found her joy discordant with my current mood and carefully climbed out of the driver's seat.

As I moved toward the front door, suddenly hyper aware that I needed to shower off Jared's musky aftershave, I saw why Cyan was squealing as Rex had picked her up and was hugging and twirling her around in a circle all at the same time.

Storm watched on from the kitchen doorway, his amusement clear. His eyes softened when Cyan darted over to him for a hug as well, and I bit my lip, waiting, waiting...

Over her shoulder, he looked at me. He didn't look around, didn't have to find me. He saw me standing on the doorstep, saw me as if he'd known where I was all along, and in his eyes, there was...

Nothing.

No rage. No jealousy. No hate. No bitterness.

I blinked. Taken aback. And then I deflated.

Didn't he care?

Storm murmured, "I got pizza, Cyan."

Whatever I expected his first words to be, they weren't that.

As they whirred away, I was left on the doorstep, and that was when Rex asked, softly, "Hey Keira. How're you doing, honey?"

His kindness was jarring. Not because he'd ever been anything other than that with me, but because I'd expected Storm's reaction to be violent.

Instead, it was passive.

Hell, it wasn't even passive. It was non-existent.

Did he know? Had Jump not told him?

No, that wasn't likely. I'd made no friends at the clubhouse, so why would Jump protect me when I'd made no overtures? Hell, I even made him pay for coffee at the diner.

Had I misunderstood?

Had I...

Guilt hit me.

I'd never thought about it, not actively, but I knew Jump watched over me. It was both irritating and nice to know that I was safe. But I also knew he reported back to Storm. Which meant... God. Had I wanted to hurt Storm? Did I want to make him react?

Make him jealous?

Why would I want that? We were over. Done. Through. Weren't we?

Confused, and suddenly weepy at how cruel I'd been, letting Storm find out about my date through a subordinate, I shot Rex a wobbly smile and murmured, "You're the one who should be answering that, Rex. I'm so sorry about Bear."

He sucked in a breath that he released slowly. "You going to come inside?"

Oddly shaken, I moved into the entranceway, closing the door behind me. That was when Rex was suddenly there, and he surprised me by curving his arms around my waist and holding me in a warm embrace.

I'd just left one man's bed, I didn't need affection from Rex who was as much of a stranger to me as Jared because of how distant I'd always been with the club, but it was easier to hug him back. To have him hold me and to hold him. This was Storm's friend. His brother.

"Don't give up on him, Keira," he whispered in my ear, like he knew my mind and heart and soul were torn in all directions. "You could never hate Storm as much as he hates himself."

I swallowed, because it had taken Bear's death and my learning about his past to recognize the truth in what Rex was saying.

I didn't get it.

How my self-confident, brash ex-husband could have low self-esteem issues, but hell, ya lived and ya learned.

"Some things aren't meant to be," was my raw response, because I didn't know what else to say. I was still getting my head around Storm's issues, and I was feeling like a fool for not having seen them for myself.

I couldn't blame him for that, either. I had personal issues that he'd worked hard to resolve, but apparently, I'd never bothered to reciprocate.

After breastfeeding Cyan, my breasts had changed, and he'd always celebrated them. When a woman at a PTA meeting had called me a whore for being with a Sinner, something he knew was a trigger because of my parents, he'd done *something*, something he'd never shared with me, and she'd apologized to me the next day. Every problem I encountered was never too small or too big for him to handle.

He was always there.

Always.

Yet, somehow, my husband had self-harming tendencies and I didn't know. He had addiction issues, and look at me, being all in the dark.

Christ, maybe I was a worse wife than he was a husband.

The thought had my chewing on the inside of my cheek.

Had he strayed because those women had seen the real him? They'd understood his weaknesses, his flaws? Whereas self-obsessed Keira had just been happy playing stay-at-home Mommy and living in her bubble while he dealt with massive emotional and psychological traumas on his own?

God, had I pushed him away? Why hadn't he considered me a safe haven? A port of calm in the storm that was his life? Why had he fixed all my issues but never let me do the same for him?

Didn't he think I could?

I'd been dumb at the start of our marriage. Always running away, making him chase me. I'd been scared, though, and I could admit now, immature. I hadn't been ready to be a wife or a mother and instead, I'd been both.

Kendra had told me Storm said I was weak. Too weak for another kid. But did he mean that in life too?

"I think we both know that's bullshit," Rex's grumble jerked me from my pity party. He pulled back, but his arms stayed around me. "I saw your expression. You were on tenterhooks."

I shook my head. "No, I—"

"You were waiting on his reaction to him finding out about your hook-up, and you weren't happy about what you got..." He dipped down and pressed a kiss to my temple that was oddly paternal. "My dad cheated on my mom, Keira. Years before she died. They got back together, they came back to one another, and knowing Dad, he wouldn't have lied to her. She'd have known what he did. But they were stronger than before. I know that.

"My dad lived for her and she lived for him, and they were like the dream team. H-He died on Christmas Day, but I know the real day he died was the day the sheriff found her on that road."

Eyes watering in the face of his grief, I choked out, "We're not your parents. We're different."

"Did you know that after a bone breaks, for a short time, it's stronger than it was before? It doesn't last forever, but that's a period of grace worth dissecting, don't you think? Maybe that's something you should think about?

"Instead of hooking up with guys who make you look at Storm with longing and regret, you should focus on what really matters— your feelings for him.

"I get that you want to punish him. Jackass in there deserves it. But I'm telling you now, you will *never* understand the lengths Storm has gone to to protect you, to serve you as a husband." His lips turned white under pressure. "That's on him, because he's a close-mouthed fucker, but just trust me on this, Keira."

I stared up at him. "Like, what? He cheated, Rex—"

"Does that counter every good thing he's ever done for you? For your marriage? Do a handful of acts take away from years of—"

"How do you know it's a handful?" I bit off angrily, jerking away from him. "A handful of times a night, more like. He had a goddamn girlfriend at the clubhouse—"

"No," Rex retorted, shaking his head. "He went crazy after you left him. That I *will* tell you. But you were over. You can't hold him accountable for that, not when you're coming back with a hickey from another guy right this second because you're separated." Flushing, my hand swept up to my throat. I covered it, glowering at him, but he carried on, "Before, no. It happened, but there was no relationship."

Gnawing on my lip, I rasped, "I want to believe you." I wanted so badly to believe him, but that bitch Kendra was still squawking in my head.

We had a baby together, but I had to have an abortion. The baby wasn't... right. Storm was so sad but he was there for all of it. He was so supportive, he held my hand and everything. I know he wants more kids, but he thinks you're too weak to have them. We keep trying but we haven't been blessed yet.

Was it terrible to admit that I could have dealt with the cheating? I'd been raised knowing Dad was unfaithful—his hypocrisy had disturbed me more.

But Kendra getting pregnant?

That was my hard limit.

"Then do," Rex rumbled. "Years' worth of working hard to make sure you can stay at home, of providing for you and Cyan without question—"

"That's what husbands do for their families!"

His laughter scorched me. "Honey, get real. Most men don't even pay their fucking child support. I know for a fact Storm was giving you most of his goddamn take so you didn't have to work after you split up.

"If you didn't accept it, then that's on you, but he gave you most of it because he doesn't need much to live on and he wanted you to have the world." He shrugged. "Maybe in your weird church, men *were* the providers, and I ain't saying that's a bad thing, but either way, you shouldn't take it for granted.

"Then there's the stuff that ain't normal, but that costs. It's fucked up, but he spends a lot of money on guards for you—"

"I don't ask him to do that. It's like being surveilled by the FBI."

"—and how about the fact you always have a new SUV while he rides that old Harley—"

"It's a vintage ride!"

"No, it ain't. It's *old*. The fucker's got a stack of cash but he'll spend it on you and Cyan before ever spending it on himself." He glowered at me. "While we're at it, how about the fact that your dad routinely calls the ATF on us, and we only get out of shit because we have an in with them?

"How about how Storm ain't never said shit to you about that or the fact that your pop manages to get the landlords of every property you've ever tried to live in to throw out the rental agreement before you can sign on the dotted line so he always has to buy a property first… and trust me, honey, he ain't going to Chase Bank for a mortgage to cover it."

"Dad gets us tossed out of our homes?" I gasped.

"No, he makes it so that you won't have a roof over your head in West Orange. Because that's the kind of God-fearin' gentleman he is.

"Why do you think you were on the outskirts, on the border with Verona? Because dear, old Daddy doesn't have reach there. Hell, I don't know what shit he's got over people, but he even had some sellers back out of contracts. That's some power over his flock.

"Never mind the fact that you ain't never come to a family picnic at the MC apart from that first year, or a party or ever tried to be a part of what makes Asher Storm. The Sinners are integral to him, and you never—"

"He discouraged me! He didn't want me there, probably so he could be with his—"

Rex pshawed. "Grow a pair. That man in there would lie down in the middle of a fucking road for you. He'd take a goddamn bullet for you. The shit he's put up with and you're telling me if you'd put your fucking foot down, if you'd given enough of a damn, he wouldn't have given in?

"You trying to tell me that if Nyx told Giulia she couldn't go to a party, she wouldn't roll up there anyway?" Rex shook his head. "You're different, Keira. I get it. You come from a different background, but don't lose sight of reality here. Your background is religious not fucking alien." My mouth worked as I tried to figure out what I was being told, but Rex just smirked at me. "See? You think you know your husband, but you don't. And that's on him, but it's also on you.

"Maybe you should give him a second chance so you can get to know the guy who's put up with eleven years' worth of bullshit just so he can climb into bed with you at night."

He swept away before I could tell him to fuck off, tell him it was none of his business, tell him he was wrong, tell him that he had no right to dissect my character like that, but instead, I plastered myself to the door, knowing he was right.

Knowing it and hating myself for it.

I didn't know Storm. That much was truth. Oh, I knew that he smelled of patchouli because he used a shampoo I liked, and I knew that he loathed soup even though he was making it every day at the moment.

I was aware of his issues with his mom, and how he loved Rene and Bear like they were his real parents.

I knew that he slept on the left-hand side of the bed because, if he was on the right, he always woke up with his back aching.

I knew that he was allergic to cilantro, and that whenever his team lost, he'd pout into a bag of chicharrones that I bought specially and hid in a drawer so that he didn't have to share them with Cyan who gnawed on them like they were cookies…

But that wasn't enough, was it? How could it be when he'd kept so much of himself hidden from me?

A strange pool of grief surged inside me, making me press my fist to my mouth to contain the sob that wanted to escape. I didn't have answers tonight, but instead of heading into the kitchen, I went to my bathroom and cleaned up.

If I cried in the shower, that was my business and no one else's. And if I stared blindly at the shower wall for a good five minutes, trying to wonder if I was as shitty a wife as Rex had made out, that was no one's business either.

But facts were facts, and there was no getting away from one single home truth—it was time for me to grow up. And for a thirty-year-old woman, that was a bitter pill to swallow.

It took two to make a marriage and, there was no hiding from this, two to break it.

DEAR KEIRA

Tomorrow's your birthday.

I'm not sure what I'm supposed to do.

I know you've seen me watching you.

I know that you're not scared.

I know that when you smile at me, it's genuine.

Do you want me to come talk to you? I think I already know the answer.

I wish I were younger. I wish I didn't feel like some creep prowling around a high school Senior. I'm pretty sure every pervert going thinks they're not a pervert. Says they can't help it. But that's bullshit. I can help it. I'm not a pervert. If it means not being able to talk to you for years, I'll wait.

I'll always wait. Because it's not your beauty or your youth that calls to me, it's your smile. It's your soul. It's like a song starts up in my head when I see you and I need to hear that song, because it drowns everything else out.

If I could tell you that, maybe I'd feel better inside.

Tomorrow, it's your birthday. I have no right to wish you a happy one, but I need to. I need you to know I care.

I'll think about it tomorrow.

I'll sit on my bike, and I'll watch you walk into school, then later on, I'll watch you walk back out, knowing that you're safe because my eyes are on you, and I'll come to a decision.

I have your birthday gift.

Maybe you'll never hold it in your hands, but when I saw it, I thought of you.

I always think of you.

Kendra told me that Ray Leinster is going to try something at your birthday party.

Jimmy told me he and the other jocks have a bet going on about who'll get in your panties first.

I'll kill him before I let him steal your virginity from you.

I hope you say no so I don't have to.

I'll be watching.

Always yours,

Storm

DEAR DIARY

It shouldn't feel this good to be nineteen. Eighteen is the age where things change and that was last year, but it was no fun when Josse and Laurie were turning seventeen—I can't wait for their birthdays. We're going to have soooo much fun!

I keep trying to tell myself that age is only a number, but it means I'm one step closer to leaving this house.

It's horrible, really, to think that the second I graduate is the second I'll be out of here.

I don't even want to come back for Thanksgiving. I have no doubt that I'll return because I'll never hear the end of it if I don't, but still... freedom is around the corner.

I've been thinking about that a lot recently.

I don't want to believe that it's because I'm ridiculous and I can't stop watching that biker who waits in the parking lot every day for Jimmy. It's just, when they ride off, he looks that way.

Free.

I don't think I've ever been free.

I know for sure my mom hasn't, and I don't think she ever will be either.

I see him and Jimmy on their bikes, that girl, Kendra, on the back of Jimmy's, and I watch them with envy.

I'd love to feel that way.

That's probably as likely as me suddenly growing wings. Dad definitely wouldn't approve of me bringing home a biker. Just the notion would probably make him have a coronary or something.

I shouldn't find that amusing.

I really shouldn't. Gah, that's evil. I'm just sick of it. Sick of the rules, sick of the strict discipline. I'm nineteen now! I shouldn't have to have a curfew, for God's sake. Mom screams at me when I try to argue. She always screams now.

I can't wait to go to college. Even if it's for pre-med, anything is better than this. Being a good girl is so tiring. Living my life so that Dad's flock can't judge me, doing as I'm told just in case it triggers his disapproval, waiting on Mom to slap me to punish me... I'm so ready for the next step.

Tonight's my birthday party. I'm surprised by how many people are saying that they're coming seeing as I'm the quiet one in our year, but I guess it's any excuse for a good time.

You don't think nobody will show up, do you?

We made arrangements for seventy people, but... it could be a prank, couldn't it?

Ugh.

I hope someone shows up.

Nineteen... freedom is just around the corner.

NINETEEN

KEIRA

PAST

"TRY AGAIN!"

I sobbed at my mother's harsh demand, sobbed even harder when she slapped me after I failed to open the package, snatching it from me to rip out the pregnancy test and to shove it in my hands.

"So help me God, Keira, if you've managed to get yourself pregnant, I won't be able to save you from him this time."

My eyes rounded at her words. "Save me from him?" I swallowed.

It sounded ridiculous, but she was channeling major aggression like I'd never seen before—before or after the moments she slapped me —and when I'd told my parents that I thought I was pregnant, my father had quietly left the room and told Mom to 'deal' with it.

"Do you think he'll kill me?" It sounded so stupid, but...

I knew to tread lightly around him.

He often disappeared, leaving Mom to chastise me whenever I did something he didn't appreciate, but he was the one behind the punishments. He was the driving force behind them.

"Why would he do that when he could just punish you for the rest of your life?" was her bitter retort as she shoved another glass of water at me.

Draining it dry, I stared up at her, the second pregnancy test in one hand, the empty glass in the other, wondering how this had happened. Wondering when this had gone wrong.

He'd used a condom.

I wanted to scream it.

He'd used a condom.

She filled the glass again, twice more, and I drank them. Twice more.

When I finally needed to pee, my mouth trembled as I stuck the kit between my legs, no longer embarrassed about being on the toilet in front of my mom, no longer caring about having to pee in front of her because this was the third time.

The last time.

There was a short row of positive tests on the vanity, but she still kept making me do this. Like one negative was all I needed to finally be allowed out of the bathroom.

My eyes watered when she set the timer on her phone, but I knew.

I was pregnant.

I'd known when my period hadn't come. I'd known when I started bawling at the sight of the photos of the Holocaust we were shown in school. Not just saddened, but moved to actual tears.

How had this happened?

I thought about Storm. About how he'd looked as he kissed me. About how his eyes had softened, that sorrow in his eyes gone as he held me, as he touched me, as he caressed me, reveled in me.

I'd never felt anything like that before.

Ever.

I sometimes knew I'd never feel it again either.

No one would look at me like he did. It was intoxicating, making me giddy with a strange sense of power.

He was a Sinner. He was a brother in an MC that everyone in town said actually killed people and ran drugs and guns and stuff for a living.

But that all faded away, my nerves, too, when he looked at me and that sorrow wasn't in his eyes.

I did that.

Me.

Just by being there.

By kissing him, holding him, needing him, wanting him back.

The memory of the one time we'd had sex made me feel flushed and awkward as I sat on the toilet. It was weird, her looming over me, but I had a feeling she had an arsenal of pregnancy tests just waiting for me to pee on. I didn't know where she thought I got it from, but hell, I was nervous enough that it wasn't a problem.

Storm should be here.

Not her.

I shouldn't be terrified. I wouldn't be if he were here.

I'd be safe.

Safe from everyone. Safe from the world.

"Oh, God," she rasped, breaking into my thoughts a second before the alarm went off.

I knew what that meant.

Another positive.

Shocked silence ratcheted the tension up twofold in the small downstairs bathroom, and I wondered if she was really that naive that she'd put all her prayers on one small test, but... hell if I knew what was happening here.

I'd blurted out the truth over meatloaf. We always had meatloaf on Mondays. As my dad drenched his in gravy, the one vice, of all things, he allowed himself—aside from his parishioner's wives—I'd told them, unable to hold it in, needing their help and not sure what to do.

That was why I was here.

Meatloaf now decorated the peony wallpaper in the dining room, and for the first time in my life, my father had slapped me. I'd been spanked as a child, but slapped? Never by him.

Of course, when Mom did it, she'd hit the same cheek.

Tomorrow, I'd be bruised.

If I lived that long because that was the kind of vibe I was getting here.

That thing kids said, 'My parents are gonna kill me,' felt shockingly real right about now.

"We can fix this," she rambled, her words spitting out like sparks. "We'll tell your father that you were wrong, but we'll go to the clinic tomorrow. The one in Newark so no one will recognize you. He doesn't have to know."

Dumbly, I blinked. "He'll know when my belly shows."

Her mouth tightened. "Don't be ridiculous, Keira. I don't mean the doctor's clinic."

For a second, I could only gape at her. "You want me to have an abortion?"

"Of course." Her nostrils flared. "You're nineteen. You're going to Johns Hopkins. That's what your father wants for you right now."

Why were the last two words the ones that resonated the most?

Right now.

Would I always be living for what he wanted for me *right now?* And if it wasn't him, was it a 'nice' man like him who slapped his wife when she burned dinner that he'd set me up with from his church? Would it be my husband's *right nows* that forged my life? Would I drown my sorrows in drink like Mom because of someone else's *right nows?*

Throat tight, I whispered, "What if I don't want an abortion?"

"It's tough."

"But… the church? They say—"

"If your father finds out," she snapped, reaching down and grabbing my chin, hard enough to hurt, hard enough to leave more marks, "you'll have no choice but to have this baby, and he will make your life hell. Do you want that?"

I gulped. "No." A strange feeling blossomed in my chest. It felt like hatred. It burned like it too. "What about my soul?" I hissed. "You're the ones who tell me how important it is not to sin. But this is the worst—"

"You listen to me, Keira. Your father will…" Her jaw tensed, but I saw terror whisper into being in her eyes. She even shivered before she rasped, "Look, we'll tell him you were wrong—"

A bang sounded at the door and both of us jumped. Heads whipping to the side, I had no idea why we started panting but we did.

"What's going on in there? Why's it taking so long?"

The growl sent shivers down my spine. I'd seen him angry, but never this angry.

My mouth trembled as Mom said, "Nothing's going on in here, Derek. It took a while for her to pee on the stick. Keira's not pregnant. I think it's that PCOS I told you about."

"PCOS?"

"It's a woman's thing, dear, you wouldn't understand."

"She isn't pregnant?" he repeated, his voice more normal now, but my heartbeat continued racing.

I don't want an abortion.

Storm's sad eyes were all I could see, even as I felt sure I was about to hyperventilate. I felt like there was a murderer outside my door, ax in hand, about to break in and do horrendous things to me, but there was Storm.

He'd keep me safe.

He'd keep our baby safe.

I hadn't intended for any of this to happen. I didn't want to go to Johns Hopkins, but that was the only way Dad would pay for college and I—

"Show me the test."

My mother sucked in a sharp breath. "Derek! Why would you ask to see that?"

"Because I don't believe you, Marilyn." He slammed a hand on the door. "Show them to me."

Her nostrils flared, and when our eyes met, I saw something I'd never seen before.

Terror.

I knew she was scared of him, but outright terrified?

My mouth wobbled as I wondered what he'd done to put that look in her eye. I'd never thought they were happy together, had always known she was a Stepford Wife, but I'd never realized that she was petrified of him.

Gulping, she straightened up. "It's covered in urine, Derek."

"Wash it."

"One moment. Keira isn't decent. We'll be out in two minutes."

Silence hummed, and just when I felt sure my heart would explode, he rumbled, "Be quick about it. I'll be waiting in the family room."

We heard his heavy stomping footfall, then she grabbed my arm and hauled me off the toilet. That was when she reached for a kit, peed on the stick, then shoved it on the vanity.

"Come on, come on, come on," she warbled under her breath as she sorted out her skirt, tugged on her cuffs, and made herself look presentable.

It didn't take Einstein to understand what was going on here.

She feared for us both.

Righting my clothes, I watched her woodenly, scared and shocked and lost, and when it finally showed negative, she released a soft breath now the waiting was over.

"Tomorrow," she rasped. "Tomorrow." The words were to herself as she nodded, like if she said them aloud, she'd make them so. "We'll fix it then. He'll never know."

She didn't even look back at me, didn't even ask me if this was what I wanted.

Just acted.

Because she knew the repercussions in a way that I didn't.

Had she protected me from him my whole life and I just hadn't seen it?

The house was big. Big enough that my bedroom was on one side and theirs on the other. I could play my music as loud as I wanted, and they never heard…

Throat tight, thick with emotions, I got to my feet, knowing that I had to get out of here.

I had one chance, but it depended on Storm.

As I sneaked out of the bathroom, the bruises on my arms made themselves known to me.

Dad had shaken me, demanding to know who the father might be, and when I'd told him, he'd called me a whore. He'd slapped me again. Thrown me down to the ground like I was trash.

Mouth wobbling, I carefully slipped down the hall, opened the front door, closed it with my heart in my throat in case it clicked too loudly, and didn't stop treading cautiously until I was on the sidewalk. That was when I took off running.

My flip flop-covered feet slapped against the ground, and it was only when I could duck down an alleyway, that I pulled out my phone.

Dad had said I was a slut. That Sinners used women like their personal whores, and I'd allowed myself to be sullied by one of them.

He said they belonged in jail, that they had no honor, no respect—but Storm didn't look at me like that.

He looked at me like I was precious.

God, had I been stupid?

I found a nook down the alley where I could hide. It stank of trash and urine, but I had the weirdest feeling that Dad would chase after me. That he wouldn't let this go.

This was his reputation on the line.

God, I really *was* in danger.

I connected a call to Storm.

He didn't answer.

I tried again.

This time, he cut the call.

My eyes grew round, tears welling in them as I stared at the screen—*Dad was right.*

Now we'd had sex, he didn't want anything to do with me. He'd said he had to go away on a run. Had that been a lie?

I'd have to do what Mom said. I'd have to—

My cell pinged.

Storm: *Baby girl, I'm in church. What's wrong?*

The relief was so vast that it made me nauseated. I leaned over and puked, but there was nothing in my stomach, hadn't been for three days as I dealt with the fact I had a late period.

Another text came in.

Storm: *Keira? Everything okay?*

With my eyes stinging, I typed back:

Me: *I think I'm in danger.*

His response was immediate.

Storm: *Where are you?*

Storm: *What's going on?*

Storm: *I'm coming—send me your location.*

Me: *I'm pregnant, Storm.*

Silence.

Then my phone rang and I started sobbing the second I picked up. Relief entwining with terror, merging with joy because he cared.

He cared.

My dad was wrong. So wrong.

"Where are you? Are you safe?"

His voice was strong, calm, with no fear—why would he be scared? My dad was a pissant church minister to Storm. A nobody, a nothing. He was a Sinner, and at that moment, he was my dark knight.

"Baby girl?" he prompted.

"Mom wants me to have an abortion tomorrow," were the only words I could get out.

"Do you want an abortion, Keira?" he asked softly, like he was asking if I wanted KFC for dinner. There was no judgment in his tone, not much of anything at all.

My mind whirred as I was faced with a decision I shouldn't have to have. How did women do this? How did they decide? I wanted to be a nurse, I wanted to go to college… I wasn't ready to be a mom, but fate had decided that wasn't my path.

I placed a hand on my belly as I heard the lack of emotion in his voice.

I knew why, too.

Whatever I wanted, he'd go through with for me.

This was my choice because it was my body, my future, and I knew, whichever path I took, my life had changed forever.

I suddenly felt incredibly young, stupid, too immature to raise myself never mind another living person, and then he said, "Baby girl, it's okay. You're breathing like crazy. Inhale with me, and exhale when I do."

Standing in a dirty alley, a grimy brick wall at my back, a chain link fence in front. I smelled crap and my own vomit, and there was a puddle just a few feet away that looked dubious because we hadn't had rain in a few days, but I listened.

I breathed with him.

I exhaled when he did.

And as he calmed me down, I knew that I could do this.

I knew that he'd help me do this.

"I don't want an abortion."

His sharp exhalation, so rushed after the calming breaths we'd been taking, told me everything.

He hadn't wanted me to have one.

"I love you, Keira."

My eyes flared wide at that, at words I really needed to hear right now, and it was so easy to let them fall from my lips as well, "I love you too, Asher."

TWENTY

STORM

PRESENT - MARCH

I SQUINTED AT THE LAUNDRY, blinking a couple times to make sure that my eyes weren't deceiving me.

"Why the fuck is everything pink?"

I wasn't that guy. I knew how to take care of myself, knew how to do the goddamn laundry, and throwing in something red with a white mix was pure idiocy.

Growling under my breath, I dragged out the sheets that were newly fucking neon pink and found the culprit.

"Cyan!" I hollered.

I didn't like to raise my voice at her, but in this damn house, and with the TV on, she'd never hear me otherwise.

A few seconds later, I heard thudding down the hallway, and a quick peek out of the door had me rolling my eyes as she did three cartwheels, two flips and a forward roll to reach me.

This kid.

She'd better be the next Simone Biles was all I was saying.

She beamed at me when she landed perfectly, and I sighed, unable to stay grumpy when she looked up at me as if I were a fucking rockstar. I wasn't sure why she looked at me that way, but she did, and I didn't want to change that.

So, even though I was pissed, I channeled calm and asked, "Cy, what did I tell you about laundry?"

She blinked. "To sort clothes into piles."

"Which piles?"

"Darks and whites."

I pulled out the bright pink leotard, a cotton one that apparently fucking leached color. "You sorted them, so why did you dump that in with the rest of the load?"

Her eyes widened at the pink laundry and she winced. "I needed it to be clean."

"Why?"

She sucked her lips between her teeth. "It was dirty."

"We're doing a dark load tomorrow, Cyan," I grumbled. Would bleach make the pink sheets white again? Christ, okay, maybe I *was* that guy. "Couldn't it have waited?"

"There was—" She ducked her head. "—blood on it."

My brows rose. "Where?" When her cheeks turned pink, *mine* puffed up.

And… I got it.

Of course, she had to get her period the day that her mom was working at the diner. Was fate fucking with me or what? Couldn't have been yesterday or tomorrow that she got her period.

No.

Today.

Fuck.

"Do you need tampons? Or pads?" I asked, trying to sound like I wasn't choking. Like I was cool with this when my little girl shouldn't be dealing with this shit at eleven.

She fidgeted. "No. Mom bought me some stuff and had it ready for me if I needed it."

Crap.

"The blood on the leotard…" I shot her an embarrassed smile. "Everything's okay, right?"

One time, Keira had bled through her pants, and I knew that shit happened more often than a woman would like, but this was my kid's first period and she was going through it without her mom…

It wasn't like I had to call an ambulance or anything.

Right?

Just as I started to sweat, she dipped her chin. "I got it to fit."

Okay, just grab me a fucking shovel so I could dig a hole for myself.

'Got it to fit.'

Jesus.

Boys had it easy with the whole 'voice breaking' and 'wet dreams' shit.

Grimacing on her behalf, I asked, "Do you need some Advil?"

"No."

"What about a hot water bottle?" I'd seen Keira use one of those before. I'd even seen her puke. Cyan didn't look nauseated though.

"No." She shot me a shy smile. "But thank you."

Then I thought about how she'd come rolling down the hallway like she was at the Olympics and called myself a dumbass. Of course, she was okay.

"You could have just told me about you getting your period, honey," I chided softly. "I don't bite. You know that. You can tell me anything."

"Anything at all?"

I nodded.

"Sorry about the sheets."

"Guess we're going pink for a while, huh?"

Her lips twisted. "I like pink."

"Shoulda called you that, not Cyan." Her giggle made me feel better for hauling her in here like she'd committed a crime. "You go finish your homework. I'll figure this out."

She peeped a smile at me before she rushed out of the laundry room, leaving me with a ton of pinks. Because I had zero idea how to fix this, I grabbed my cell from my back pocket and called Keira.

"Hey. You pick Cyan up okay?"

Why did her voice do shit to my insides? Making hunger lash at me, my dick surging into a full, agonizing erection from my self-imposed chastity.

For a second, I couldn't breathe as my cock throbbed with the heavy-gauge piercing's stranglehold on it. I clenched my fists into tight balls, trying to control the ache, but my weakness was just proof yet again that I was a piece of shit, not worthy of her.

So fucking weak.

So goddamn pathetic.

I was a grown ass man. Sex addict or not, my dick shouldn't be twitching just because she greeted me with no loathing in her words.

Talk about being willing to scrape the bottom of the barrel.

Scum. That's what you are, boy. That's all you'll ever be. You're a fucking magnet for it too. No matter what you touch, you'll soil it. You're just like me. Don't look down that pretty nose of yours and think we're any different. We ain't. We're trash.

The memory echoed in my head, making me jerk with surprise. I hadn't thought of Mom in a long time, but it was hard not to at that moment. Hard not to be plagued with memories and regrets and remorse.

The thing about addiction? The thing they never told you? After the suffering and the going cold turkey, and the withdrawals, as well as the rest of the misery that came with it, you never stopped apologizing. You never stopped trying to make shit right. You never stopped trying to earn forgiveness for the things you did when you were under the influence.

It was like being a lost puppy that was asking to be kicked. Sure, you deserved the kick, but it never got easy. The bruises still went deep. The ache didn't lessen. And what hurt worst of all was knowing that what you put your loved ones through was ten times worse than anything you had to deal with.

"Storm? Everything okay?" she questioned, tone changing now, shifting with worry at my extended silence.

"Sorry. Everything's fine." I stared at the clothes again, then grimaced. "She got her period."

"Here's the order for table two," she told someone, but to me, when I heard the background noise dissipate as she walked away, she questioned, "Did I hear you right? Sorry, some guys from a nearby plant came in. Cyan got her period?"

"Yeah."

"She told you?"

"Well, no." The pinks taunted me. "I was doing the laundry—"

"Oh, thank you! God, I needed to do that tonight."

"Don't thank me yet," I muttered, uncomfortable with the gratitude.

"Why?"

"Cyan dumped a pink leotard into the mix of whites."

Keira snorted. "Oops."

"Yeah."

"How bad is it?"

I shot a picture and sent it to her. "See for yourself."

She whistled under her breath. "So she told you about it while faced with the evidence?"

"Yeah. But I asked her if she needed Advil or a hot water bottle, and she has pads and… well, tampons, you know?"

"I do." She laughed a little. "Poor Storm. Wrong day to be the one on pick-up duty, huh?"

"Hey, I handled it okay. She did cartwheels outta here."

"Cartwheels? Then she definitely didn't need painkillers." A sigh escaped her. "Our baby's growing up."

"No, she's not."

"Yes, she is." Keira chuckled. "Get used to it. It's only going to get worse from here."

I groaned. "Don't remind me."

"I won't need to. She'll do that herself." She snickered. "I'll talk to her about periods some more tonight. We already talked about it a year or so ago."

"Why? Don't they teach that shit in schools?"

"You're kidding, right?" She scoffed. "Never enough, and I wasn't going to have her being uncomfortable about asking me that sort of thing."

"I'll have the sex conversation with her."

Silence fell at my declaration, then, "Huh?"

"You heard me. I can tell her all the shit she needs to know about how to avoid boys."

"For a second, I thought my ears deceived me," she said wryly.

"I don't want to talk about it," I clarified, eyeing the pink sheets. "But fuck, she shouldn't be embarrassed with me either."

"She's a girl. You're a guy. She's going to be embarrassed."

"Well, we need to break that stereotype. Plus, I looked this up. Ohio is an abstinence state."

"I know." I didn't have to see her to know she was grimacing. "Not ideal."

"Fucking stupid. Like, what? You tell horny teenagers not to have sex, so they'll listen? Since when do kids fucking listen?"

"You won't hear me arguing."

"I'll teach her all the shit so she'll never want to do it."

Keira laughed. "You want to traumatize her?"

"Well, that's a harsh word. More like keep her on the straight and narrow."

"That bastard probably did that."

My jaw clenched. "Maybe," I conceded. "If he did, then I won't have to scare her, just inform her." As the idea percolated in my head, I asked, aware I was pleading, "I won't need to do this for a while though, right?"

"Maybe in a couple of months?"

"Jesus. So soon? She's only eleven."

"Any later, she could be sexually active. Kids have sex young." At my groan of dismay, a groan that was founded in truth because I'd first had sex at thirteen and hell, Scarlet had a year later, she sighed. "I know, I know. I don't like it any more than you do."

"I'll do it. Maybe in the summer, when we've done a good six months of therapy, yeah?"

"You don't have to," was her dry retort. "I'll talk to her about it."

"No. That's not fair."

"If we'd had a boy, I'd have let you talk to them about sex. And wet dreams. And all the other gross shit that happens to you."

My lips quirked. "You're so kind."

"I know it," was her rejoinder. "Give her a kiss from me, but I need to go."

"Yeah." I heard the bustle in the background. "What should I do with the sheets?"

"There should be a color run remover sachet in the cupboard above the washing machine. Just follow the instructions."

"Sorry, Keira."

"For what?"

"Fucking this up."

Her laugh was soft. "I'm guessing Cyan shoved it in at the last minute?" When I said nothing, her laughter deepened. "Not your fault, Storm. Thank you. Really. It's not the end of the world."

"See you later," I said gruffly. "Drive safe."

"I will."

She disconnected the call, and as she did, her laughter echoed in my head.

I was trying to live like a fucking priest, but I was a sinner. There was no hiding from it. No evading it.

My head bowed as I gripped the sides of the washer.

I felt like I could rip this goddamn thing out of the wall and hurl it across the room, especially when my dick made itself known.

It'd be so easy to grab it.

To hold it.

To jack off.

Just one touch…

Fuck, I swore, that's all it'd take.

I was hurting with need. Aching with arousal. But my fist wouldn't do. Only Keira's pussy would quench this hunger.

For years, I'd fought it. Like a starving man who was fed only scraps, I'd panted after her, never giving her all of me because I knew she couldn't handle it.

What had my consideration gotten me?

Locked out of heaven's gates.

Scum like me was allowed in by invitation only, and I'd flipped that invitation the bird like the moronic motherfucker that I was.

Jaw clenching, dick aching, the tip fucking weeping precum even though the heavy weight of the padlock made me feel like it was cutting off circulation, I growled under my breath.

I could do this.

I'd let her down so many fucking times before.

Even if she didn't know what I was going through, even if she never understood, she was worth the sacrifice.

Worth the pain.

I sucked in a breath, and as reason slowly came back to me, so did something else.

The beast in my head that never let up. The fucking animal that thought of her safety.

What had she said?

A bunch of guys from a local plant had come in?

My mouth tensed.

Sure, I bet they were there for pie, but for a glimpse of my woman too.

All shiny and pink as she bobbed around the diner, all goddamn smiles for those fuckers where she barely shot me a look.

She hadn't been on another date since that Jared guy, but that wasn't to say she wasn't on the lookout for someone else. She and MaryCat had gone out to a local bar to celebrate MC's birthday, but Jump hadn't said that she'd danced with anyone else.

I deserved to beg for scraps, but I resented every bastard she served. I hated them for each smile she bestowed upon them, every fucking glance she graced them with.

Dick under control simply through anger, I reached for my cell after I let go of the washing machine, surprised I hadn't dented it in all honesty. But though the hungers inside me often had me feeling like I was the Hulk, I wasn't that goddamn strong.

Me: *Everything okay?*

Jump: *Diner's busy.*

Me: *Anyone given her any shit?*

Jump: *Nah. It's not like that, Storm. You should chill the fuck out.*

Me: *I'll chill the fuck out when I'm dead.*

Jump: *Prez, it's your dime. If you wanna pay me to sit my ass in the diner, that's what I'll do.*

Me: *Keep me in the loop.*

Jump: *Always.*

Grumbling under my breath, I looked in the cupboard above the washing machine, found the packets she'd been talking about, read the instructions, and put the clothes back onto wash. I had no concerns about my masculinity, but I had a few undershirts in there so I hoped they turned back to being white sooner rather than later.

Heading out of there, I retreated to the kitchen where there was some soup bubbling away that I'd made earlier and pulled out my phone again after I looked at it with distaste.

I fucking hated soup.

Eating that shit reminded me of the times Scarlet and me had been living with Mom. We'd survived on knock off versions of Campbells' soup, so it wasn't exactly a nice memory, but they were easy to make.

Not even I could fuck it up.

Plus, the recipes I followed were Giulia's. She'd sent them to me when I asked for help after school with feeding Cyan, and they were good, just reminded me of worse times.

A couple of pings rang around the kitchen, and I knew why. The motherfucking group chat was driving me batshit. The WO one was active, but this one was crazy. It was good, they were eager, and I needed that, but still, I wasn't used to talking so much. I guessed it meant I could read along without having to interact so that was pretty neat.

Though Bear's death had been officially labeled as natural causes after the autopsy—the news of which had sent shockwaves of relief through me after Rex's confession—the funeral didn't have an official date as of yet.

I wasn't the only one suffering from the lack of closure, and the WO chat was often filled with grief-stricken comments, nostalgic memories, and photos the brothers all discovered after they'd gone through their belongings.

The inability to move on didn't just come from the funeral, but how much I knew we all felt like we'd missed out on.

In the last eight or so years, since Rene's death, Bear had cut himself off from all of us. Scissoring massive chunks into the fabric of our beings as he disappeared for long chunks of time.

I knew Rex had called him and that conversation was the reason he'd come back to West Orange, where, ultimately, he'd died. I wasn't sure if we'd ever know what really happened. Not a hundred percent.

So many people had been killed the night the compound had been bombed, and we still didn't know how explosives had been packed onto Bear's bike. That was definitely a mystery.

What we did know was how the sniper had gotten onto the compound—through a bitter clubwhore who'd been tossed out of the Sinners for causing trouble with Steel's Old Lady.

By trouble, I actually fucking meant she beat the shit out of her while Stone was still recuperating from injuries she'd sustained when she'd been abducted by an Angel of Death at the hospital she used to work at.

As a group, we'd lost so much time with Bear because of Rene's murder. Back then, we'd thought it was a hit and run, which was bad enough. Learning that she'd been targeted by the Sparrows to keep Bear from digging into the crimes his brother-in-law had been sent up for, was another dose of hell entirely.

The knocks kept on coming, and somehow, I was staying strong. The need for relief was a constant but I managed to evade it.

For Keira.

For Cyan.

Still, with grief pounding at me on all quarters, I blew out a breath and decided to check out who'd sent the messages.

Cringing when I saw it was my council and they were talking about the Bengals, I rolled my eyes and retreated to the soup, which, to make matters even worse, was vegetarian for my kid's sake.

As I sniffed it, Cyan stepped into the kitchen, asking, "What type of soup are we having today?"

I pulled a face because I couldn't pronounce this shit. "Giulia called it Whoreso."

Dragging the breakfast bar stool out, Cyan tutted. "Orrrrr-Zoh."

Twisting around, I looked at her. "Huh?"

"Orzo. That's how you pronounce it. She made it for me at home."

I didn't fail to notice that she classed West Orange as 'home.' I couldn't blame her either. I'd been here longer than she had, and Jersey still called to me like a fucking siren song.

Who the hell would have thought that we'd miss the Garden State this goddamn much?

"Did you hang out a lot with Giulia?" I questioned bemusedly, focusing on that rather than the homesickness.

"She cooked, I ate."

"She's really the one who taught you about headbutting?"

"Yeah." She peeped a smile at me, and I saw she'd had a shower because her hair was wet, her face scrubbed.

Was that a little tightness around her eyes? Was she in pain? And was that a bruise on her forehead or just the lighting in here?

"So I can blame her?" I teased, keeping it light even though I was growing more positive she'd been in another fight because she'd been jittery ever since I'd picked her up. The school hadn't said anything... didn't mean it hadn't happened, of course.

She pouted. "No. I liked it."

"The soup or the headbutting?"

"Both."

I snorted. "Well, let's hope your ma likes the soup too. Otherwise I wasted a shit ton of veggies to make it."

I slopped some out into bowls, and she peered into it. "Aunty Giulia's didn't look like this."

"See if it tastes decent."

I grabbed a bag of oyster crackers I'd bought from the store then shoved it at her.

She scooped some up, tasted it, hummed. "Not the same, but very good, Dad. Eight out of ten."

Despite myself, I grinned. "Thanks, Gordon Ramsey."

She giggled. "You're welcome. It really is good. You'll like it."

The only way I could eat it was if I drowned oyster crackers in it, making it more soggy cracker with sauce than a soup.

"If you say so," I grumbled as I hooked a foot around the stool next to hers, dumped my bowl beside hers, then hunched over as I started to scoop it up.

For a second, we were silent as we ate, and then she murmured, "Dad?"

"Hmm?"

"I might be in trouble tomorrow."

I didn't tense up. "That bruise on your head?"

"Uh-huh."

"You headbutted someone again?"

"I did," she said with a whisper. "The teacher didn't know but…"

"Not everyone believes snitches are evil. I get it." Sighing, I told her, "I'll drop you off at school tomorrow."

"You will?"

"I will." I cut her a look. "We really need to get you to those Krav Maga classes." I'd tried to sign her up, but all the classes in Akron were on the same time and days as gymnastics. "We gotta do something, honey. Gotta get that temper under control."

She hunched her shoulders. "I know."

"What happened?"

"She called me trash."

I froze at that, a red wave of fury washing over me.

How many fucking times had I heard that?

How many times had they chanted that at me?

With my own mother being the worst bully of them all?

I ground my teeth together. "They did, huh?"

She nodded.

"This the first time someone's called you that?"

"No. But it's the first time I retaliated. I tried not to get into trouble. I really did!"

"I believe you, baby." I cast her a glance. "You know you're not trash, don't you?"

She was my Keira's mirror image. The only thing I'd tarnished her with was our shared eye color, but hers were so beyond beautiful that whenever I looked into them, I was reminded that I wasn't a total and complete failure.

Cyan hitched a shoulder. "I think so." I didn't rake her over the coals for that, just let her say her piece, as I knew, full well, she'd have something else to divulge. Of course, it shocked me when it went down a path I hadn't anticipated. "Sometimes, I feel…" She swallowed. "Like not enough showers will get me clean, you know?"

"You did nothing wrong," I told her staunchly, looking her square in the eyes. "*He* was to blame."

Her brow puckered. "I don't know why I listened to him."

"Because he was a very clever man, and ladybug, you're young. He knew all the tricks to play that would reel you in." I reached over and pressed my hand to her shoulder. "I'm sorry I let you down, Cyan. I'm sorry I made it so that you went to him instead of me."

She chewed on the inside of her cheek. "I was so mad at Mom for making you go away. Back home, at school, they made fun of me because of the Sinners, but I could, I don't know, deal with that. When you were there. Then you went away, and I felt alone. Mom's not a Sinner. Not like you and me. She doesn't get it."

It hurt to hear her talk like an adult. Hurt even more to hear her isolate her mom that way.

"Your mom's a Sinner, Cyan. You might not think she is, but she gave up so much to be with me.

"That guy who called her a whore, he was your grandfather, honey. When your mom decided to be with me, she lost all her family because they didn't like her for associating with me."

"I just thought they were dead. She never says anything about them." She gnawed on the inside of her cheek. "None of them will talk to her?"

"No." I shook my head to compound the point. "And you know what? She shouldn't want to talk to them, either. People who treat you like that don't deserve to have you in their lives." I winced. "I know what it's like to have a temper, honey. I got one too—"

"You don't get mad at me."

No. I didn't. Rarely, at least.

I barely raised my voice at either of them, and only in an emergency.

The last time I remembered was when Keira had changed the locks on our old place in West Orange. Even then, that was just to make myself heard. I never shouted at them in anger.

"You're both my everything," I said simply. "Can't get mad at my everything, can I?" When she blinked, then smiled, I carried on, "I broke your grandfather's nose."

"When?"

"When he tossed your mom out." My jaw gritted at the memory, but I pressed my finger to my lips and said, "That's a secret between you and me, ladybug. Okay?"

She gaped at me, but nodded.

"She didn't tell me she was pregnant with you until she had to. She told her mom and dad first, like a good girl, but when they found out, they didn't react well.

"When she called me, she was sobbing. I went by to try and make things better, but they'd packed all her stuff and threw it out into their yard. You know what, Cyan? I will never forget that day. Ever. And you know what sucks?"

"What?"

"That I let her down as badly as they did."

She tilted her head to the side. "Why did you? Why did you make her let you leave us?"

"Because I was stupid. Very, very stupid. Selfish too. Some mistakes, honey, you can't make up for. You can't make them right. You need to remember that, so that when it comes time for you to live your life, you don't do what I did.

"You can and should earn forgiveness, but there are some stains that just won't wash out.

"I think, in your own way, you're a little hellion like I was. I didn't have gymnastics though, didn't have anything like that until I was older than you, and Bear—" If my voice choked up, then so be it. "—decided that I needed to burn off some energy. Kinda like you with Krav Maga."

"What did you do?"

"Link, Nyx, Rex, Steel, Mav, and me used to beat the crap out of each other in the basement of the clubhouse."

She gaped at me. "Was that allowed?"

"Oh, yeah. We weren't terrorizing someone. It was just how we used to control our tempers." I shrugged. "It worked for Steel, Rex, Link, and Mav."

"But not Uncle Nyx and you?"

"Nope. Some ya win, some ya lose."

"What happens if I still get really angry after Krav Maga?"

"Then we'll figure it out. You willing to skip a gymnastics class to go?"

Her nod was small, but determined. When I smiled at her, she placed her hand on mine and her small fingers squeezed me tightly. "Dad?"

"Yes, honey?"

"Mom loves you."

I smiled at her, but it was sad. "You know, baby, when you're older and you're her age, I pray that you do what she did. That you have the strength and the confidence and the self-esteem to walk out of that door when a man isn't treating you right."

Her eyes rounded. "B-But—"

"But nothing." I leaned over her and pressed a kiss to her forehead. "Believe in yourself, baby. Your mom and I do, but it doesn't mean anything unless you do too.

"We'll go to school in the AM, and we'll get things sorted. You hate it there, don't you?"

She nodded, and the crown of her head bumped against the underside of my chin.

"We'll see about getting you transferred to one of the schools here." I heaved a sigh, because I really didn't want her in a mixed school, but if she was getting into fights... "It might not be much better here with the kids," I warned, regret lacing my words.

"At least they're normal. They won't be massive snobs who think their poop doesn't stink just because they're rich."

I smiled a little. "I'll talk to your mom tonight. Get her on board then I'll sort it out."

She peeped up at me, darted a kiss to my cheek, then said, "The soup is yummy."

"Thanks, ladybug."

As I dug in, I had to admit, my effort wasn't a total shitshow.

In more ways than one.

DEAR DIARY

The party didn't go very well.

I enjoyed it, until it got weird.

Everywhere I turned, Ray Leinster was there. He never seemed to back off, and if we danced, he kept grinding into me, his hands on my butt and stuff. I didn't like it. It made me really uncomfortable, but I could tell he didn't care.

Ray said something about our dads wanting us to get together before he got in my face and tried to kiss me, but I shoved him away. About a half hour later, he tried to apologize, and stupid me, I listened, before he put his hands on my ass, had the nerve to grope me, before he touched me between my legs.

I didn't have to knee him in the balls because, out of nowhere, the biker was there. The one with the streak of silver in his hair. He was in my house.

MY HOUSE!

He took Ray away.

I don't know where.

I know that no one stopped him, and Ray just squeaked as the biker picked him up off the floor and carried him out by his shirt collar.

I didn't even think that was possible, but, up close, the biker is sooooo much more muscled than I realized. My goodness, I didn't think men like him existed outside of movies.

The party started to fade what with, ya know, people wondering if the school's QB had just been murdered, and after I said bye to everyone, even Josse and Laurie who were going to help me clear up the mess from the party, a knock sounded at the back door.

I was kind of scared it'd be Ray again, but it wasn't.

It was the biker. He told me that his name was Asher.

Anyway, he stood there, looking as clean as before, but his fingers were mussed up. He was wearing those leather gloves without the tips, which made me think he'd used them to cover up the mess he'd made of them as he'd been barehanded before. Whatever had happened, Ray hadn't fought back.

Just thinking about it makes me squirm.

Asher hurt Ray because of me.

Jimmy must have called him. That's the only thing that makes sense. How else would Asher have known to come riding in like the cavalry?

"I just wanted you to know that Ray won't ever hurt you again," he'd said, standing there like a dark knight on my doorstep. So beautiful it hurt to look at him.

Then he turned away. He walked away.

He.

Walked.

Away.

What was I supposed to do?

Let him go?

I don't think so.

I called out, "What's your name? Or do you only answer to Prince Charming?"

Thinking about that now makes me feel stupid because he's a Sinner, not exactly the Disney type, but I didn't want him to go. I really didn't.

He stopped on the path, turned toward me, and his voice was so deep, so rumbly and gravelly as he said, "I'm no one's idea of Prince Charming."

"You saved me tonight," I told him. "And maybe on Monday at school, or another time I go to a party. He was getting hot and heavy no matter how many times I said no." Girls didn't say no to Ray. That was why I'd been scared.

"He won't hurt you again."

"Is he dead?" I'd squeaked.

Just thinking about that smile tears me up inside. It wasn't an answer, it was anything but. "You'll never have to worry about him again." Never? Goodness, had he killed him then?

Before I could ask for clarification, he stepped away and started to leave.

"Please, don't go," I'd called out.

He paused again.

"Please? At least tell me your name?"

Without turning back, he'd said, "Asher."

And that was how I learned his name.

I touched myself last night. Thinking about those hands on me. Hands that would hurt another guy to keep me safe.

He's a biker. He's the exact opposite of the kind of man I should be interested in. Dad wants me to be with a Ray Leinster of this world. On top of his game, heading to MIT to study engineering on a scholarship. Not a criminal.

But when Ray touched me, I wanted to crawl up and hide somewhere.

Just the thought of Asher touching me makes me hot.

I can't wait to see him on Monday. I hope he'll be waiting outside school again.

DEAR KEIRA

Ray won't bother you again. His jaw's wired shut and if his dick isn't broken in two, then my baseball bat deserves to be tossed in the trash.

I'm sorry you had to go through that.

I'm sorry he scared you.

I'll never let anyone scare you again.

I promise you, Keira. I don't have much honor, most would say that scum like me have none at all, and maybe they're right, but what I do have, with it, I vow to you that you'll always be safe.

I had Jimmy and Kendra watching over you, but that's gonna change now that we've met. I'll figure something out, make sure I can be there when you sneak out at parties. I've seen your parents. I know they don't approve. They're not wrong. Angels like you shouldn't be out of the house past ten.

If you were mine…

Who am I kidding?

You'll always be mine; you'll just never know it.

Always yours,

Storm

TWENTY-ONE

KEIRA

PRESENT

WAS I a terrible mom that I loved the shorter commute to school?

Dropping Cyan off at the nearby school was heavenly by comparison to the long drive to the academy, and she seemed happier. She really did.

Less time in the car, more time at home or at the diner with me or at the clubhouse with her dad.

No uniform to have to press every night, fewer fights, no more bruises or calls from the teacher, no more worrying about her being expelled and that being on her permanent record…

I should have put my foot down sooner, but I wanted the best for my kid.

Having St. Angela's Academy for Girls on her resume would have looked damn more impressive than the local public school, but fuck, I'd take it for a happier daughter.

When she twisted around to wave at me, I smiled at her and waved back, only reversing when she'd gone inside. As I waited in line to get out of the parking lot, I checked my cell and grinned at a meme Link had sent me before I shot MC a message, asking her if it was okay to come around for coffee.

As the line gave way and I pulled out onto the road, I let loose a contented sigh. It was her tenth day here, and I was loving the new routine.

In the back of my mind, I knew I had less than two weeks left to make a decision. Enrollment time was approaching at the local satellite college in North Canton, and on top of that, Storm really should be moving back into the clubhouse…

Was I letting down womankind by admitting that I liked having him around the house?

He did the laundry and he cooked. I never had to worry about shit breaking down because he fixed it, and he was always there for Cyan if I had a late night at the diner, and he was doing all that while, in his spare time, redecorating the family room so that it was more to my taste than the older style.

It was like having a live-in handyman without having to put out.

Okay, that sounded bad.

Like I was using him…

I bit my bottom lip at the thought, but appeased my guilty conscience by accepting that Storm wasn't the kind of guy who did stuff unless he wanted to. Which meant everything he was doing was his choice. His decision.

I turned up the radio at the thought, smirking when Nu Breed's "Welcome To My House" blared out loud. This always reminded me of Storm, and maybe a few months back, I'd have switched it over, but now, I sang along with the moody lyrics as I drove away from the town border with West Lafayette, where the school was located, and back into Coshocton's center.

It was really green around here, a lot greener than West Orange. Lots of tilled fields with soggy-looking crops, plenty of trees all interspersed with houses that peered onto the road. It made me appreciate that our place was far out, with a lot more privacy.

As the meager winter sun warmed my face, I accepted the call when it came, tapping a finger on my dash while I drove past a river that lined the road. Its banks were looking a little full, and I wouldn't have been surprised if, with the next rainfall, it flooded.

With Storm's name on the dash, I also turned down the volume and asked, "Everything okay?"

"That *Nu Breed*?"

I laughed. "Yeah. I love this song."

"You know it's my favorite." He chuckled, and that soft, amused, husky sound did things to me that were probably illegal in a state where abstinence was taught to kids... Hell, I knew in some states, anal sex was illegal. Talk about taking the fun out of stuff.

As his chuckle died, his husky voice still made me tingle in all the best places. "It came on and made me smile."

He paused a second. "Really?"

"Really." Before he could read too much into it, I asked, "You need something? Or just checking in on Cyan?"

"Nah, I don't need to ask. She's happier there. Plus, she gets to sleep more. I know that's making me less grouchy," he said wryly.

"Me too," I admitted. "Shit, I feel so bad for admitting it, but I love not having to drive that far."

"You're not alone." He laughed again, this time it wasn't as husky, a lot lighter, and it still hit me in all the wrong places.

I knew arousal wasn't something you could switch off, and Storm had always tripped my buttons. But having him wander around the house, dusty and fusty, a little bit of paint on his cheek, or tools in his hands? Those mental images were like my teenage fantasies come to life.

Because I wanted to hear that laugh again, instead of teasing him some more which would lead to more of that dangerous laughter, I asked, "Everything okay?"

"Can you come to the clubhouse?"

I pulled a face, glad he couldn't see my expression. "Why?"

"I need your help with something."

"With what?"

"Couple things."

"Like what?" I repeated.

He heaved a sigh. "Nothing bad. Just need your advice on some club matters."

I nearly braked at his words, but instead of causing a frickin' accident, sputtered out, "You want *my* advice? What do I know about club matters?"

He grunted. "Yeah. It's not as crazy as it might sound."

"It isn't? You never asked before."

"That was different. I was only VP."

I blinked. "That makes a difference?"

"I was the only guy on the council with a wife and kid, babe. What do you think? That they'd have loved it if you came in and dusted?"

"They accepted Giulia."

"Do you really not see the difference between Giulia and you?"

"What's that supposed to mean?" I demanded, taking affront at his words.

"There's no need to feel like I'm insulting you, honey. I'm not. It's actually a compliment. Giulia wears her street smarts on her sleeve. You… don't."

"I have street smarts," I complained.

"Would you headbutt someone who was bullying you?"

I winced. "No." My eyes narrowed. "I'd hurt London, though. You never did tell me what happened to him."

"Mostly because it'd give you nightmares."

Scoffing, I told him, "I doubt it. I think he could have been boiled in oil, tarred and feathered, and I still don't think it would be enough for what he put our baby through."

"I agree," he said gruffly, but in his voice, there was something deeper. Darker.

It made me lick my lips and, even though it was freezing outside, less than thirty degrees, I seriously needed the bitter chill to shock me out of the churning, tumbling waves of desire that lapped at me as a result of that tone.

I heard the violence within it.

I heard the fury.

I heard the desire to cause pain to the man who'd thought he could hurt our child.

And I loved it.

Hands tightening around the steering wheel, I rasped, "One day, I want you to tell me what happened."

Then he sealed the deal.

He growled under his breath.

Lord.

That noise.

It went straight through my veins like a shot of vodka.

"You should ask Amara. She'll tell you, I'm sure. Word for word."

The thought had me raising my chin even as that growl had every-thing inside me melting. "You wouldn't mind?"

"What you speak about with your girlfriends is your business," was his rumbly retort. "Just try to do it on a secure line only."

I pshawed a little at that because, duh. Even I knew that much.

"I wish you'd served him justice, but I'm glad she did too. It's complicated because she probably deserved to kill him more than we did—"

"Doesn't take away the fact we wish things were different."

I sighed. "Yeah." It was nothing but the truth, and I wasn't even ashamed of it.

"You gonna come to the clubhouse, honey? I wouldn't ask if I didn't need help."

My brow puckered but I murmured, "Sure. It had better be worth my while though. It's my day off."

"I know it is. But, you can always have tomorrow off as well. Perks of knowing the boss?"

"Nepotism makes people hate you."

"There have to be some advantages to being the fucking Prez," he grumbled. "How far away from the clubhouse are you?"

"Fifteen minutes?"

"Okay. I'll be in the garage. Meet me there? I'm avoiding the club-house until you get here."

"What? Why?"

He didn't answer, just cut the call, which pissed me off. Especially when he didn't pick up after I called him back.

Grousing, wondering why the hell I was even going to the club-house when it was the last place I wanted to be, I drove there, well aware that if Cyan found out she'd be jealous.

I wasn't sure why or how, but Cyan loved being at the clubhouse. I'd never noticed before because she was so sulky all the time in Jersey, but here, she was always pestering me to go there. Like it was a day out at the zoo or something.

The next time I messaged the girls back home, I'd definitely have to give Giulia some schtick about her ruining my daughter and making her less biker princess and more biker bitch. Things had been so crazy since the MC had taken over the diner, though, that I hadn't had much time on my hands just to chat. Which, in all honesty, sucked.

MaryCat and I were hanging out when I had some hours to spare, but I missed the self-proclaimed Posse in West Orange. They were good women, loyal and true, and I was lucky that they included me when I wasn't an Old Lady.

Determining that tonight I'd message them, I drove up the narrow, shrub-lined roads that led to the clubhouse. It was a one-way tract, which meant your hands were tied if someone other than a biker was riding down, which was, in my mind, a definite 'fuck you' to anything other than two-wheeled vehicles.

It was a little like the modern version of building a moat around a castle. Bottlenecking traffic in and out of the place would probably allow for guys to escape the law.

If that were required…

Ah, who was I kidding? We were talking about the Sinners. They weren't a riding club. They were one-percenters.

I was relieved when I made it to the driveway, finding the gates open as I pulled straight into the yard. There was barely any room between the gates and the front entrance, so when I parked, I saw the door was open and that the clubwhores—AKA skanks—were all squawking about some shit or other in the hall.

Preferring to ignore them, I moved around the side of the building toward the area where I knew they worked on the bikes.

Not that I'd explored the place that much.

I'd come here a handful of times, stuck around for the bare minimum like I had when I came to help with MaryCat, then retreated home, unable to deal with the clubwhores.

I believed Storm when he said he hadn't fucked them. The damn key to that padlock was around my neck like some kind of locket that housed a promise. It didn't make me like them or what they represented. It didn't make me comfortable around them. It sure as hell didn't make me want to share oxygen with them.

The thought dampened my mood as I parked and caught a glimpse of Storm with a rag in his hands, wiping at his fingers. He twisted around at the sound of the SUV though, and there was no taking away from the fact that he was *fine*.

The plaid shirt was open, revealing his chunky muscles that felt so good against my teeth. I saw Cyan's name on his pec—the letters I'd traced every time we made love—and looked down at his jeans and boots. He was dressed, but there was sweat on him despite the cold, plus a few smudges of grease and engine oil.

He looked, in a word, lush.

Everything about him drew me in, and I felt so much more stupid than a moth when it was close to a flame. This was intense, the need to touch, the desire to hold him—it didn't seem to abate.

Frustrated with myself, I jumped out of the SUV and strode toward him.

His smile was warm, welcoming. It hit his eyes, those sad, sorrowful eyes that had gotten me into trouble in the first place all those damn years ago, and even now, mad at myself, I couldn't hold back.

Happiness pierced that sorrow as he responded to my smile, and it was like a knife to the heart. Seriously. How could he do this to me? How could he look so broken and beautiful all at the same time?

My smile didn't falter because seeing his joy made my heart happy, but I was determined to keep this meeting short.

"Everything okay?"

"Yeah."

He was, annoyingly, a man of few words sometimes.

I peered at his bike, the one Rex said was old because Storm prioritized his family over his ride—which meant some bikers did that, schmucks—and asked, "Is it broken?"

He shook his head. "Just changing the oil."

I took him in, those grease stains and oil marks, and found myself grateful he'd taken over doing the laundry.

Stuff like that was a bitch to get out, and I'd never been all that great with that chore.

My mom could sort through it like she was a pro, but for me, my whites turned yellow fast, stains never came out even if I overdosed a load with product remover, and don't get me started on dryers—they never lasted longer than a year, and they always had to be fixed at least twice in that time.

I tipped my head to the side, wondering why he didn't seem to feel the cold. It was frigid out here, but he was dressed down like it was in the high seventies rather than the low thirties.

"What's going on?" Barely refraining from asking him to put on a sweater before he caught his death, a little because I wanted to carry on appreciating the view, a lot because I didn't want to sound ninety, I peered at the clubhouse behind him and said, "You know I don't like coming here."

He nodded. "I know. I was hoping to change that. Cyan seems to love it here."

"Cyan loves to fight here," I corrected gruffly.

"The kids fight," he admitted with an unashamed shrug. "Maybe they need to get it out of their systems?"

My jaw worked a second, but slowly, I lowered my head. "You're right. She does love it here. She wants to come all the time."

"And you stop her?" He nodded. "I get it, Keira. I really do."

"I doubt that," I told him tightly.

"No, you're wrong, I mean it. I made things very difficult for us by compartmentalizing my life, but I've never wanted you to be involved in this world. I always wanted to keep you separate from it—"

"So you could cheat on me," was my bitter retort, something I couldn't have withheld if I tried.

Only, he shook his head. "No. Not because of that. If you'd ever shown any interest in coming, though, I'd have figured out a way to make it happen."

"Why then?"

"Because somebody once told me that you were out of place there."

My eyes flared wide and the hurt that hammered me was as brutal and as raw as the day that bitch Kendra had confirmed my worst fears.

"What?" I gasped.

Unashamed, he nodded. "They meant it as a negative, but I took it as a positive. And when you never asked, I just didn't bother to encourage you."

I just blinked at him, focusing on the first half of his remark rather than the second. "You took that as a positive?"

His smile made another reappearance, somehow filling up the gaping wound he'd just caused.

I'd always felt out of place.

Be it at home, where my religious family wanted one thing, while I wanted another. In the church, where everyone seemed to get 'it' without question, whereas I was just left wanting more information. At school, where I was different because of who and what my dad did for a living, as well as the malaria that flared up. Then, finally, at the clubhouse.

The only place that had ever felt right to me was standing at his side, but he'd managed to wreck that for me too.

"I did," he confirmed. "Because had I wanted someone in the lifestyle, I'd have married a clubwhore, Keira. I'd have left you alone, but I couldn't do that. You called out to me then, and, to this day, you still do."

Swallowing back some stupid tears, I asked, "Who told you that?"

"It doesn't matter. You don't need another reason to hate the Sinners," he said wryly. "And their opinion meant dick to me anyway.

"My brothers never got a chance to know you, K. I figure, if they had, they'd have realized what a loving person you are." When I just blinked at him, he said, "I asked you here because I was hoping you'd help me fix this place up. Make it more… well, hell, just make it *more*."

The place was rundown, so it wasn't like I couldn't understand what he was asking.

"Me, though? How would I know what you guys need?" I queried uncomfortably, uncertain if I wanted to get that into the club lifestyle.

Maybe a part of it intrigued me. I'd seen a different side of things when I'd moved onto the West Orange compound and had gotten into the Old Ladies' inner circle. Even there, I was an outsider because of having left Storm, but they'd never really made me feel that way.

Mostly, it had been because I worked shifts at the diner unlike the rest of them. They'd included me in most things, though—at least, I thought they did—so starting up a whole new Posse was definitely something I'd have been interested in... if I was still Storm's wife.

Which I wasn't. Right?

"You know better than me," was Storm's dry retort.

But as I looked at him, I slowly shook my head. "I have a lot of work at the diner, Storm," I said uncomfortably. "Plus, there's school. I'll have to come up with a decision soon."

He raised his grease-streaked hands, and though it was ridiculous, I saw them and realized I'd never once seen him come home with dirty fingernails.

Not once.

And I knew his bike was vintage—*old,* according to Rex—so it took a lot of repairs...

"I've never seen you with dirty nails before."

He looked down at his hands. "No, of course not. I wash them. I'm not about to touch you with filthy paws." His lips tightened. "Filthier, anyway."

Annoyed, I asked, "What's that supposed to mean?" Was he talking about the sluts he'd touched over the years? The ones he'd sullied our marriage with?

"It doesn't matter."

"I think you'll find it does," I grated out, slamming my hands onto my hips.

Tilting his head to the side, he frowned, his confusion clear, but slowly, he explained, "I've never been good enough to touch you. Of course, my hands are filthy."

For a second, I could only gape at him.

'I've never been good enough to touch you.'

Each word was like someone hammered a nail into my heart.

He felt that way?

I stared at him in consternation, then rasped, "You felt that way when we first met?"

I could literally feel my walls lowering, my defenses too. Jesus help me.

"Of course." He shrugged that off like it meant nothing, as if his complete lack of self-worth should come as no surprise to me. "Anyway, I get it. It's a big undertaking, but I just thought if you wanted to take over the styling of it, maybe you'd feel more comfortable."

"I think being comfortable here will take more than fancy new drapes and carpets, Storm."

His lips curved. "Not sure how the guys would feel about 'drapes.'"

I smirked. "See? That's why I'm the wrong person for the job."

I took his humor as a chance to escape. Not only from the clubhouse, or from what he'd just said, but from him as well.

I needed to breathe air he wasn't breathing because Storm was one of my worst weaknesses, and I couldn't afford to be weak anymore.

Starting to back up toward the SUV, I said, "I'll see you at dinner."

He nodded. "See you then."

"It's your turn to pick up Cyan," I pointed out.

"I know," was his calm response as he watched me retreat.

And that was how it felt.

Like a retreat. Like I was the one escaping.

In the face of his serenity, I felt chaotic. My nerves and confusion and stupid attraction to him at war.

The bitch of it was, as I looked at him, I knew he saw it and I knew, even though the notion broke something inside me, that he cheered me on as I backed away.

He'd really meant it when he'd said he was proud of me for leaving him.

He'd meant it.

My jaw worked as I raised a hand in farewell once I was behind the wheel, but the second I was out of the gates, I put my foot on the accelerator.

My demons didn't chase me down the dangerous road—Storm's did, and somehow, they were more terrifying than my own.

But, for all that they had wings, as I pulled up at the house, before I headed over to MaryCat's to hang out, I grabbed my phone and fidgeted with it as I thought about the clubhouse, thought about how the bar was right next door to the family room... and then I thought about what I'd overheard Giulia say one time. That as a kid, she'd learned, in her words… "about blowjobs and banging, because I saw brothers boning bitches in the hall and in the bar."

I didn't want that for Cyan. I really didn't. I just wasn't sure if Storm was talking about a little fixin' up or if he meant massive structural changes.

Cyan still needed the sex talk, once she was more settled, so learning *that* way was out of the question.

With that in mind, I knew I had to get involved. Even if it was only peripherally.

Me: *The bar needs to be at the other end of the clubhouse. Away from the family room. We don't really want Cyan learning the birds and the bees from what goes on in there, do we?*

Barely a minute passed before he texted me back.

Storm: *Yeah. I didn't think about that. I'll set SL onto figurin' out how to make that happen.*

Nervous, I gnawed on the inside of my cheek, before I typed out:

Me: *I might not be able to get super involved, but you can always run things by me.*

Storm: *Okay. Whatever makes you comfortable.*

Nothing made me comfortable right now. Rex's words were still floating around my head all these weeks later, what I'd learned was still making me question everything but, when it came down to the wire, like with today, my instinct was still to retreat.

Frustrated, I growled under my breath.

I was dancing around this situation like a fool, and Storm was no help because he'd let me continue in this vein for a century.

The man seriously needed to work on his self-esteem.

Did I want to be the one who helped him with that?

I groaned and butted my head against the steering wheel because the answer, stupid as it made me, pathetic and anti-feminist and weak, so, so, so weak, was yes.

Indefatigably, *yes.*

TWENTY-TWO

STORM

PAST

Girls, Girls, Girls - Motley Crue

THE BONFIRE RAGED at my side, music blared heavy and loud, Whitesnake at war with Motley Crue, while I laid there, staring up at the sky.

The fireworks in the distance weren't exactly real, but that didn't mean I wasn't seeing them anyway. They shot up, every now and then, reminding me of how long ago it'd been since I'd shot up, the firework display getting quieter and quieter with every hour that passed.

"Dad's gonna fucking kill you if he spots you out here like this."

I ignored Rex, humming along to 'Girls, Girls, Girls,' as I zoned the fuck out.

I'd had the day from hell. I deserved to zip in and out of focus.

A steel-capped toe booted me in the side, not hard enough to wind me but to make me peer up at him.

"Wassup?" I grumbled, hitting out at the offending leg. "Why'd you do that?"

"Because you need to get moving before Bear sees you."

My hand flopped onto the ground. "She left me."

"Again?" was Rex's wry retort as he squatted down beside me. "What did you do this time?"

"She wanted a picket fence." I squinted at him. "I can't get her a picket fence because of her fucking father—"

Rex smirked at me. "I don't think that's what she was asking for, Storm."

"She said, 'I want a picket fence.' How am I supposed to misinterpret that?" I slurred.

"Misinterpret, huh? Let me see. I think she was saying she wanted a more traditional place to bring up her kid. Which house did you show her?"

"The condo on Maryland Avenue."

"Well, you couldn't have been much further from a house, could you?" Rex commented with a laugh, rocking back onto his ass so he was sitting beside me before he rolled back as well and laid at my side. "You two are like oil and vinegar. How the fuck did you even get her knocked up?"

"She's perfect."

"No one's perfect."

"She is." I sighed. "She's so fucking clean."

"What skank bitches you been with who don't shower?"

I grouched, "Not clean like that."

"Okay, clean like what?" When I fell silent, he murmured, "From this way of life?"

"I guess."

"Or do you mean your mom or sister?" He elbowed me in the side when I didn't answer. "You visited Scarlet in jail the other day, right? How's she doing?"

"I think she's evil."

Rex snorted. "No 'think' about it. That bitch sucks off Satan for fun."

A cackle escaped me. "Explains why she has bad teeth."

Rex laughed. "I have no idea what one has to do with the other—"

"Satan's cum has to be acidicik."

"Think you mean acidic, bro." He grunted. "Swear that sister of yours could get arrested in a convent. What did she have to say when she found out you were gonna be a dad?"

"Whatcha think?"

"She gave you shit for it?"

"Uh-huh."

"Did you take that out on Keira?"

"Why would I?"

"I dunno. Trying to figure out why your sorry ass is here at tonight's party when you'd much rather be with your woman. Where is she?"

"In a motel."

"What?" Rex spluttered.

"She went to her parents, but her mom wouldn't let her through the door. Doesn't help that her friends don't want anything to do with her now too. Goddamn churchgoers. Never met a bunch of fuckers less Christian than Christians." Disconcerted, I whispered, "I really fucked up her life." The thought was more sobering than I'd have liked.

"Why did you wife her? Why not make her an Old Lady?"

"I want her legally safe."

"Legally safe? That's a weird way of phrasing it."

"Not for someone like her. She lost her family even though I wifed her. What would they have done if I'd just made her an Old Lady?"

"True. Do you think she could handle the club?"

"No. Wish she could, but the other night, I came home with busted knuckles after I beat the shit out of Junker for stealing the petty cash, and she started crying."

"I saw Junker. He was a mess. Think it was more than busted knuckles."

"What was I supposed to do? Drive around looking like death warmed over? My place was two streets away. I had to clean up." I heaved a sigh. "She don't like being alone at night."

"Then why are you here and not with her?"

"Because she left me. Ain't you been listening?"

"I know she's left you six times since you two married," Rex said drolly. "I don't get you guys. You should have left her alone. She's a good girl."

"She is," I agreed, my voice dreamy.

"And I ain't talking about whether she swallows or not."

I scowled. "Don't be talking about my wife like that."

Rex snorted. "Reel it back in, bud. I don't think you could get a hard on right now never mind stand up to beat the shit out of me."

"Damn. I hate it when you're right."

"So you must hate me all the time then," Rex joked, making me cackle.

"Fucking love you, bro."

"Fucking love you too." He groused, "I hate it when you get high. You get all emotional."

"Don't."

"Do too." He huffed. "You got high after you visited Scarlet in jail. What did she tell you?"

"That I was scum. That I was gonna be a shit dad. That I was gonna be a shittier husband. That I should just drive my bike off of Summit Ridge."

"Jesus, she said that?"

"Got high. Slept here. Went home the next morning, Keira started talking about picket fences. So I went to look at condos—"

"What's the logic there? She asked for a fence, so you went high rise?"

"Ain't you listening? Her dad's making it impossible for me to get a house. Plus, she doesn't like being alone at night. Me and Nyx work for Grizzly, Rex. We work at night."

"So?"

"Being in a condo, she wouldn't be alone at night."

"Storm, how are you the smartest man I know and you're the biggest idiot where this bitch of yours is concerned?"

"Hey!" I surged into a sitting position just so I could slam my hand into his shoulder. "Don't fucking call her a bitch."

Rex tackled me, shoving me onto my side and onto my back. "Cool it, Storm," he grumbled. "Why didn't you just go for a house in Verona? Why didn't you get her the picket fence? I mean, it's more metaphorical, but you could have made that happen. So why didn't you?"

"I need eighty grand more before I can put down a deposit on a house."

"Can't you just rent?"

"Nope."

"Why not?"

"Her dad. Got all those fucking do-gooders at his church turning me away. Hypocrites."

"So you gotta buy?"

"Yep."

"And it's cheaper to buy a condo?"

I hummed. "It is. Until I can get the next eighty grand. Saw a nice place in the hills, but I don't think she'd wanna be on her own. It gets dark out there."

"Gets dark out everywhere," he pointed out.

"Nah. I mean real dark. No streetlights or anything. She'd get freaked out."

"Did you tell her about any of this?"

"'Course not. It's my job to protect her."

"You sure she wants protecting?"

"Dead sure."

He grunted. "If you say so. What do you guys talk about?"

"You don't want to know."

"Sure I do," he said wryly. "I'm curious what this angel and this Sinner have in common."

"Politics." I sighed. "Philosophy. Ethics. You name it."

Rex snorted. "That's what you talk about?"

"Yeah. We argue. A lot. It's hot."

"I'll bet," he drawled. "So, what happened this time? Specifically with the picket fence."

"She said we'll never work out when we're too different." I squinted at him. "Which makes no sense."

"What makes no sense is you and her period."

I scoffed. "We make magic together."

"If you're gonna talk with your dick, then I'm outta here."

"Do you wanna know why we started dating?"

"Because your dick did the talking?"

"Nope. Well, a little."

"She's fucking jailbait, bro. It's kinda creepy."

"She's nineteen. Anyway, Keira is an old soul."

"She'd have to be. Shame on her driver's license it says she's under twenty-one."

"You're making it creepy. What's seven years?"

"A lot?" Rex drawled.

"Fuck off. It ain't like that."

"No?" He snorted. "Okay. What's it like?"

"These fuckers at the high school had this bet on her."

"Huh. Christ, I'm so glad I'm out of high school."

"Yeah, me too. Anyway, they were gonna try to bone her. Whoever got there first, whoever took her virginity, was gonna win big."

"You beat the shit out of them?"

I snorted. "Bet your ass I did."

"So you swooped in and took her virginity instead?"

"Fuck off, I didn't do shit. I got the main fucker away from her then beat the hell outta him."

"You being serious right now?"

"Dead serious." I peered at him. "Look at me. Don't I look like I'm being serious?"

"You look stoned. Thought you'd stopped with the drugs for real, man."

"Did."

"Okay, looks like it," he said on a sigh. "What happened then?"

"Nothing. I walked away."

"You're a regular Prince Charming."

"She thanked me for saving her. Told you. She's a fucking angel."

"So you fucked your angel?"

I scowled at him. "You trying to make me look bad?"

"Nah. You're doing that on your own."

"We're soul mates."

"Can you have a nineteen-year-old soul mate though?"

"*I* can. I'm immature for my age."

He barked out a laugh at that. "Storm, if anything, you're ancient for your age, not young."

"Well, maybe she's the same?"

"She's the daughter of a church minister. He's not exactly Rocke-feller, either, so it's not like she can be all that apathetic."

"Apa-what?"

"How much did you snort this time?"

"Too much."

"You're pretty lucid. You know Dad will kick the shit out of you if he finds out."

"He's busy with your mom. They were arguing earlier."

"Mom's pissed about Scarlet getting arrested."

"I'm a shitty brother."

"Why? Because you want her ass locked up for a while?"

"Yeah."

"Me too." He grimaced. "I used to… well, you know I loved her. But since she left, she's turned into such a cunt."

"She's a fucking viper. Just like Mom."

"You said it."

"I did." I rocked my head to the side. "How do I make her love me like I love her?"

"You been drinking as well?" Rex groused. "Since when do you come to me for dating advice?"

"Since I fucked up and since you know what she wants with this whole picket shit fence crap thing."

"Never let it be said you don't have the vocabulary of a poet laureate."

"Just consider me Arthur Miller."

Rex snickered. "You know I hated him."

"Yeah, because he gets in your head. That's why you didn't like Animal Farm."

"That was Orwell."

"Dude, I know. I ain't that high."

"Just give her what she fucking wants. Isn't that what any woman needs in a guy? We both know you listen to her like she's the fallen Madonna. So put that into action." He paused. "Her mom really kicked her out?"

"She did. I wanted to kill her."

"Best not to kill the mother-in-law. Doesn't bode well for a happy future."

I grunted. "I didn't. She's still intact. But how Keira looked? Fuck. I wanted to scoop her up and take her home."

"Things were always going to be hard between you two. You're from different worlds. Romeo and Juliet, except Juliet isn't rich."

"We're not that different. Not where it counts."

"She wants traditional. Nothing about you is traditional."

"She thinks she wants it."

"No, that was how she was raised and she wants to emulate it now that she's pregnant. Give her what she needs. She'll be happier."

I frowned. "You really think so?"

"I know so."

"I didn't want us to be that way. She's my—"

"She's your what?"

"Equal. Not my subordinate. I watched her family interact. Her mom literally stands a couple steps behind her husband at all times. She takes direction from him, she obeys him."

"Didn't you tell me she was gonna lie to him about Keira being pregnant?"

"She wasn't going to, she did. She had it all set up. She pissed on a stick as well, showed him that test."

"Well, you can't count that."

"Why can't I?"

"Her momma bear genes kicked into high gear."

"Why didn't they today?"

"Because baby bear took herself out of the family den."

"If my kid took herself out of the family den, I'd do everything I could to get her back in it. Wouldn't shove her out in the cold."

"You know what these religious whack jobs are like. Once you're out, you're out. It's all a fucking cult to me."

"You think Catholicism is a cult."

"The biggest out there," he confirmed. "All headcases. Why the fuck would anyone support a God who's so goddamn mean?"

"You're an atheist," I discounted. "And I'm too high to argue about existential shit with you."

"This is why I hate it when you take drugs. You're the only fucker who'll debate with me, period. We could be talking about all kinds of shit, instead I'm giving you advice on your love life."

"Is it good advice though?"

"It's logical advice. That's about as much as you need to know. Give her what she's always known, then she'll feel more secure.

"She's pregnant, Storm. She's just graduated high school. She's married. I bet that was never a part of her five-year plan. Her world is in the air, up is down and left is right. Pregnant women need nests."

"But I'm not that kind of guy."

"You love her, don't you?"

"I do. I really fucking do. More than I know how to handle."

"Then you'll do what's best for her. She wants to live in her little Stepford bubble like her mom did, then give that to her. She wants to go to college, give that to her. Just do what your baby momma wants, and sure as shit, you won't need to get high because she won't leave you." He grumbled. "If I have to dump your ass in the Fridge again to stop Dad finding out you're hooked on—"

"It's a one-time deal." I sighed. "Two-time, counting the other day."

"Does this chick know your sobriety hinges on her?"

"She doesn't know I'm an addict."

"Fuck. Why the hell didn't you tell her?"

"When should I have?" I argued. "In between saving her ass from some fuckers who had a bet on who could bone her first and her telling me she's carrying my baby?"

"Jesus, this isn't going to end well, Storm. You need to do something."

"Like what?"

"I don't know. You can't keep getting high. Not when you're going to be a father."

"I know you're right. Just..."

"No, *just*. When you gonna learn, fucker? I'm always right."

As I stared up at the night sky, I whispered, "Not always."

"Always," he retorted. "Do what I say, and trust me, happy wife, happy life..."

TWENTY-THREE

STORM

PRESENT - APRIL

Every You Every Me - Placebo

"WE HAVE A DEAL?"

Tony Myers smirked at me as he reached over my desk and held out his hand. "We have ourselves a deal."

I dipped my chin as I rocked back in my seat, every inch of me pissed off at having to deal with pigs in my office, but this was a lesson I'd learned from Bear.

Always stay friendly with the local Sheriff.

While, of course, figuring out a way to determine if he had something worthy of blackmail in the closet.

It was two days since Bear's funeral, so my mind kept playing tricks on me, prompting me to remember all the random shit he'd taught me over the years. This lesson was high up there because he'd trained both Rex and me to lead. Even if he'd always known Rex would be the general, that didn't mean he'd skimped on life lessons with me.

"I'm going to need you to make it so that the mayor doesn't cause us problems with a liquor license."

Myers nodded. "I can make that happen. It's the most popular bar in the area, so people are already grumbling about it being shut down."

"Good." I rubbed my hands together. "The city council can think what they want about the Sinners, but you need to convince them we're turning legit. Look at what the Hell's Angels did. Use them as an example."

"I know what to do." Myers smirked. "I had an understanding with the Prez before last. Butch was the one who didn't want to play ball, not me."

"Idiot." I shook my head. "As long as we're on the same page, we should have a good relationship."

"I'm looking forward to it," Myers said with a sly smile as he got to his feet. Placing his hat on his head, he stated, "Seems like this is going to be a rewarding friendship, Storm."

"I agree." I got to my feet. "I'll walk you out."

"Thanks."

We didn't discuss anything as we walked down the hall, and when we passed the bar, I heard the throbbing silence that ensued as brothers caught sight of his uniform. Ignoring them, much as Myers did though he glanced inside and peered at the men, we headed toward the door and I guided him over to his vehicle.

Turning toward me after he unlocked the squad car, he murmured, "Rumor has it that most of the bad eggs went running after Butch when he left."

"The brothers who stayed behind have families." I caught Little's eye, his curious gaze drifting over me and the sheriff until he caught me watching him back. "We just want to get rich and make the town richer, Myers. You got a problem with that?"

"No, don't think the city council will either in all honesty. We haven't been doing well since we lost a couple of factories to China."

"Well, let's see what miracles we can reap, huh?"

Myers smirked a little, then he bowed his head. "I'd watch him."

Turning around, I spied Grim who was also staring at us from the doorway. "Oh, I am."

Grim wasn't taking well to not being my VP. Though SL was doing a great job of it, Grim was the biggest dissenter.

"He was Butch's brother-in-law."

"Was?" I queried, well aware that folks around here didn't know the old Prez was deader than the Confederacy.

"Well, whatever it is you call it. Not his last woman, the one before. Don't think they were married but I know when you claim a bitch, it might as well be a marriage in your eyes."

I heard the sneer as well as the slur, but I didn't expect the fucker to understand our way of life—I just needed him to turn a blind eye to any petty crimes that came across his desk where the perp was a Sinner.

"Were they close?" I asked softly. "As far as you know?"

"Not sure Butch was close to anyone. He had a rep for a nasty temper. Very volatile. Spent a lot of nights in the local jail because he was a meaner drunk.

"I had to haul him in so many times I was glad when I heard he fucked off to—" He arched a brow at me, one that said he wasn't buying the gossip train in town. "Where did he fuck off to, again?"

I smiled. "I don't know. He ain't written us a postcard." Because I could feel Little and Grim's attention on me, I wrapped shit up. "Thanks for the history lesson."

"More than welcome." Our eyes met and held. "I can clean up a lot, Storm, but not everything. I ain't a miracle worker."

After he slipped behind the wheel, I placed my hand on the door and loomed over him. "You'll work miracles so long as I pay you enough. Don't fool yourself about that." I clapped a hand to the roof as I backed away.

"As long as we both know miracles come at a premium," he called out as I walked toward the door, raising my hand in a salute without turning.

"We got a problem?" I groused as Grim moved to stand in my path.

"Why you talking to a pig?"

"Since when did you become Prez, and since when did I have to fucking answer to you?" I rumbled, eyeing him up as he made it more than clear that he wasn't about to move out of my goddamn way.

Uncaring that the fucker outweighed me by forty pounds, I took his measure. We were about the same height, with me just eking it out on top, but the bastard lumbered around like a goddamn bear that was drunk on honey.

"Let it go, Grim," someone called out from the bar.

"He's bringing pigs onto our fucking compound—"

"That's exactly what a smart Prez does, you dipshit. You wanna get your ass busted for possession, that's on you, but personally, I prefer to have a deal going with the local sheriff." I tapped my temple. "But then, you've made it quite clear that you ain't got more than two brain cells to rub together." I shoved his chest, surprised when he staggered back—fucker needed to work on his core. "Now back the fuck away."

"You come in here, thinking you can change shit when things ain't broke," Grim growled, shoving his face into my personal space.

"Ain't broke?" I repeated with a laugh. "Look at this shithole. And look at your take now and tell me things aren't changin' for the better."

"He's right," Little called out.

Grim was so wide that he took up most of the doorway, but I saw brothers behind him, nodding as they took in the show. They weren't coming to my aid, which told me they were on the fence where I was concerned.

I got it.

I didn't drink with them, didn't party with them. I just sat in my fucking office, tending to my goddamn houseplants, working the numbers, getting the business on track until I could get home again.

Any drive I had to be Prez seemed to have been left in West Orange.

I was coasting, no doubt in my mind, but there wasn't a snowball in hell's chance that I was about to have this dumbfuck question me, so rather than try to negotiate peace, I decided to do shit my daughter's way.

Ducking low, I surged upward, slamming my head into his face.

It stung like a fucker, but hell, it was worth it. For weeks now, this bastard had been questioning every fucking move I made, eyeing me askance like I was making bad decisions left and right, so the pain was worth it.

Hell, the pain felt good.

Pain was one thing that I could experience without feeling like a goddamn broken bastard.

Blood spurted from Grim's nose, coating my cut and shirt with it. I reached out, slammed my fist into it again, watching with bitter satisfaction as the split in his skin tore even wider apart, cracking like a sun-baked desert floor.

He let out a yelp before he staggered backward, arms raising high, fists furled as he tried to defend himself.

"You don't fucking question me," I snarled at him, stalking nearer to him even as he tried to move away.

I kicked at his shin with the flat of my boot, then curved my foot behind the back of his knee and drew it toward me. As it buckled under the force, I watched with even more satisfaction as he slammed into the ground.

"This ain't a democracy. I'm your goddamn Prez and you do as you're fucking told."

Grim wobbled on his knees for a half-second, then I shook my head as he went down. Face first. Another crack told me that the fucker would need to visit a clinic before the day was over to get that nose of his reset. At least, I hoped he did. Wasn't sure if I could stand the bastard looking even uglier than he already was.

"Lightweight," I muttered under my breath, pissed because I didn't even get a good fight out of that.

Peering around at the brothers who were studying their fallen comrade like the joke he was, I folded my arms across my chest as I demanded, "Anyone else got a fucking problem with me as Prez? Anyone else bitchin' about how I'm doing my job?

"Your asses aren't in jail, you got cash on the hip, and your families are fed and have a roof over their heads. What's your fucking problem?"

When no one said anything, I shook my head and moved past Grim. The sneaky bastard's arm shot out, and he tried to curve it around my leg, jerking me back, but I'd been raised on dirty fights with my real brothers, so I hopped up to escape his bonds, then slammed that same foot into his head.

Steel-toed cap first.

When he was out for the count for real this time, I growled, "Fuckin' pussy." As I headed back to my office, I called out, "SL, follow me."

No one made a goddamn peep, and by the time I reached my door, I saw the small crowd had disappeared, Grim was still on the floor, and SL was doing as I asked.

"You tell me next time if there's enough dissent to cause a fucking fistfight, you hear me?"

SL raised his hands. "Grim's the only one causing problems."

I eyed him, unsure whether I could trust him or not. "Where's Digger?"

"Sorting out security for the titty bar." My latest acquisition.

I grunted. "Okay." Well, I couldn't give him shit when he was doing his job. Studying my VP, I demanded, "You happy with your paycheck?"

"Sure." He shrugged. "Old Lady's even happier. We're moving into a four bedroom house next week."

"Then you'd better watch my ass. I don't expect you to have my back in a one-on-one fight, but a heads up when a dumbfuck like Grim has sneaky moves would be nice in the future."

SL grimaced. "Served you better to stay silent."

"Wouldn't have if I'd ended up on my ass."

"Grim's always pulled shitty moves like that."

"Yeah, well, like I said, a heads up would be nice."

Nodding, he muttered, "Sorry, Prez. You looked good out there. Strong. They won't give you any shit."

"They'd better fucking not. Schedule a church in two hours' time. Wider than the council. We need to see for real if there's a problem with how I'm running shit."

"Thought you said it ain't a democracy."

"And I wasn't lying. But if you fuckers hate that money in your wallet so goddamn much, I'll gladly start cutting back on your wages."

SL grunted. "I'll call the meeting."

"Do it."

Four hours later, as I headed out of the clubhouse and toward my bike, I stretched my back, working out the kinks.

I hadn't threatened to pull any of the fuckers' cuts, but I wanted to get any bullshit out in the open, wanted to see if there were others like Grim amid the ranks.

SL said there wasn't, but he hadn't said shit about Grim either, and I got it. Loyalty went to the men you'd known all your fucking life.

Unless they were morons.

Unless they were upsetting the apple cart.

Unless they were threatening a good thing.

That was when you took the dipshits aside and made them see the error of their ways for their own safety.

Since Christmas, we'd diversified our portfolio to the extent that it was starting to make waves in town. There were rumbles, but we'd been employing outsiders, and next on my list was another of these factories that, upon their closure, had devastated the local economy so much.

With the sheriff on our side, and next the mayor, it wouldn't be long until people were humming about the Sinners, singing their praise, which was exactly how I wanted it. That way, when bikers ran through Coshocton from other chapters, we wouldn't have to worry about getting our asses handed to us. That way, when we started to recruit and get bigger, the notion wouldn't be too jarring for the local churchgoers.

It was hard to get pissy at what looked like a riding club who was intent on making your town better.

I had an end game, and I wasn't afraid to knock every fucking pawn down in my club to make it happen.

Only when Coshocton was fooled would we be able to get the most out of the chapter. Whether that was through laundering like Rex primarily wanted, or through runs that would see brothers riding through this county to get to West Orange.

Riding off the compound, I nodded at Little in farewell. As I rumbled down the road, heading toward home, I was grateful I didn't have to cook tonight.

Keira had softened up some lately. I wasn't sure why, but it meant I was throwing ideas at her for the clubhouse's renos and she wasn't shoving them in my face.

Was it because of that date she'd been on?

It had been back in Feb but...

Had he dicked her so well that it had put a fucking smile on her face that lasted months? I didn't think so because she hadn't seen him again. Jump would have told me.

As of right now, all she was doing was heading to work, the middle school, Cyan's gym, the store, and home—mixing it up by heading over to MaryCat and Digger's place. Rinse, lather, and repeat for the last six weeks, at least.

While I didn't know what was making her soften up, I was grateful for it. It even put a smile on my face as I rode toward the subdivision, where the guard already had the gates open for me, and I saluted him as I drove through, grateful for the lack of delay because I just wanted to get my ass home.

The days were getting a little longer, but the sky was already starting to darken, so I took advantage of the remaining light and headed into the garage and pulled out the lawnmower. Maybe that'd work some of the aggression out of my system that was still there after that non-starter fight with Grim.

When K and Cy rolled up forty or so minutes later, I was well aware that Keira studied me from the driver's seat, well aware that she'd always loved watching me do menial tasks.

Was that why I kept doing shit like this? Trying to get her wet? Trying to remember the good times we'd had together?

Her stare, this time, was prolonged, heavy. I felt it arc between us like a livewire.

I only looked away when Cy waved at me before she let out a whoop, dumped her bag on the ground, then took a running jump on the grass. She leaped into a double salto, the second one morphing into a decent twist, before she landed, then immediately bounced into a sideways salto.

Flecks of mowed grass fluttered around her feet as she pretty much danced from one side of the yard to the other, and I shook my head at her antics, laughing when she let loose a warbling cry worthy of a warrior on a battlefield.

"Thought Coach told you not to pull those moves out of the gym," I pointed out as I shut off the mower. "You could sprain your wrist on uneven ground."

She grinned at me. "Perfect tens don't come easy, Daddy."

I snorted—my kid didn't have self-confidence issues when she was contorting her body into shapes that'd make a fucking acrobat wince.

Maybe all those hours spent in a goddamn armchair with a therapist *were* worth a damn.

Keira scooped down and picked up her purse from the footwell of the passenger seat before she headed for the door with a massive paper bag in the other hand.

Leaving the lawnmower where it was, I moved toward her, scooped it out of her arms, then went ahead.

Neither of us really greeted each other, but sometimes, there wasn't shit to say. Today was one of those days.

I headed into the kitchen, dumped all the stuff on the island, then murmured, "I'll be outside. I just need to finish the sides."

Cyan skipped into the family room, the TV her end destination, and as I made to move out into the hall, Keira's hand snatched my arm. Her fingers looped around my wrist, and she tugged me to a halt. When she did, I peered down at her.

"What is it?"

She drifted onto tiptoe, then reached up and smoothed her fingers along the crown of my head. "You've got a bruise there."

I didn't answer, but my jaw clenched as I tried not to close my eyes so I could savor the feel of the pads of her fingers smoothing over the bruise in a delicate caress.

Christ, she hadn't touched me, not really, since the day I'd learned about Bear's death.

Hands balling into fists, I rumbled, "Sometimes, men only understand shit when they get bruised."

Her brow puckered. "You got into a fight? Dammit, Storm, how are we going to discourage Cyan from getting into fights if you're doing it too?"

"Prefer me to get my ass shot?"

Her eyes flared. "Don't even joke about that."

"I wasn't," I countered, a part of me wondering if she'd even care if

I did die. Not that I said that, just admitted, "My position at the club ain't exactly stable."

"Why? I thought things were going okay. MaryCat says Digger's been accepted by the guys."

"I'm not Digger. Neither am I making much of an effort to get to know the men.

"My ass is staying out of the bar, and I ain't attending parties or shit like that. Plus, my family stays pretty much to themselves." I shrugged. "Ain't complaining, just saying that it's hard for them not to feel like we're outsiders when that's exactly what we are."

She winced. "Do you think we should come up to the clubhouse? Have a party or something for the kids?"

"You'd be willing to do that?" I questioned, tipping my head to the side in surprise.

"Yeah, I would," she said huskily, her gaze on mine.

My brow furrowed as I looked at her. *Really* looked at her.

There were shadows under her eyes as if she hadn't been sleeping, and her cheekbones were a little gaunter than usual.

Keira had been the same weight since she'd had Cyan, always trying to get back to her pre-baby weight and always failing. She bitched about it sometimes, but she never went up or down, just stayed her curvy self and I wasn't about to complain.

I'd fallen for her when she was slender, but I'd never been making love to curves, had never been making love to skinny—I was just losing myself in Keira. She was all that mattered.

"What's going on with you?" I rumbled, surprised when she let her hand move away from the crown of my head which, admittedly, was tender to the touch thanks to my collision with Grim's nose, but instead of pulling away entirely, she dropped it to my shoulder.

"N-Nothing," she said shakily, sounding real convincing. Not.

"Is something going on at the diner? You don't have to work so hard, Keira. Hell, you don't have to work there at all."

For a second, she just stared up at me. I wasn't sure what was going on with her, but her face crumpled as she asked, "Why are you so good to me?"

My mouth tightened. "Baby girl, you'd better tell me right now if someone has hurt you or—"

"No," she mumbled, both her hands slipping onto my chest. "It's nothing like that."

"Then, what is it?" I reached for my phone, about to check if Jump had texted me while I was cleaning up the yard. "What's going on with you?"

Keira wasn't the most emotional of women unless she was under immense strain. I figured that was because of her upbringing so you could bet your ass this had me concerned.

Her forehead came to rest between my pecs, and as she leaned against me, I swore, it felt like the hinges to heaven's gates creaked a little.

My arms wavered as I wondered if she wanted me to put them around her, then I decided to man the fuck up and did as I needed to.

As I embraced her, my concern for why she was doing this was at war with how good she felt.

She fit there, always had. Always goddamn would. No other bitch'd take her place because Keira was my angel. She was my everything.

I leaned my chin on the crown of her head, letting her huddle into me. "Tell me who to kill and I will."

She gulped. "I promise, it's not like that."

I loved that she didn't tense up.

A few years ago, I'd never have been able to say that, but while hanging around Giulia had made our kid really good at head-butting, it had also broadened my wife's horizons.

She knew what the Sinners were firsthand, and I doubted she was afraid of it.

Especially as, the bastard who'd tried to hurt our daughter was dead now, not rotting in a jail cell like the laws of the land would have preferred—just waiting to get back out onto the streets so he could hurt some other little girl in the future.

Amara, Hawk and Quin's Old Lady, might have been behind the kill, but it was the Sinners who'd made sure that fucker's death was covered up. Who'd made sure she was celebrated for what she'd done, not denigrated like the pigs would have.

"Then what's it like, Keira? How can I fix it if you don't tell me what's wrong?"

She gulped, the sound audible. "I-I've let you down, Storm."

Whatever I'd expected her to say, it wasn't that.

My surprise was such that I'd have reared back if that hadn't meant disconnecting from our embrace.

"What?" I barked dumbly.

"I've let you down."

"Why? What have you done?" I asked carefully, reaching up to stroke the back of her head, to hopefully soothe her.

My mind started racing, wondering if she'd done something at the diner—I could fix most problems before they derailed if I was just given enough warning.

"I haven't done anything and that's the problem. I come home today, and you're mowing the lawn. Yesterday, you picked up Cyan from school and took her to gymnastics.

"I haven't cleaned the bathroom in over a month because you've done it. You make soup and you fixed the dryer last week—" She sucked in a breath. "You're so *here* and I'm just... I've just—" Her mouth worked as she pulled back, not out of my arms, just enough for me to see the war in her eyes. "Why do you love me?"

The question had me staring at her in confusion. "Why *wouldn't* I love you? You're—"

"Don't say it! I'm not perfect," she snapped.

I smirked at her anger. "You asked, but if you don't like my answer that's on you."

"I'm not perfect, Asher," she rasped, and I knew she thought she meant business by using my real name. "I'm the opposite."

"Your version of perfect isn't like mine." I pressed a finger to her chin. "You were raised by a Stepford Wife." Her nose crinkled but I knew she agreed. "You were told that you had to do well at school, you had to behave, do as you were told, and the second you didn't, the second you went against the house rules, your dad got your mom to beat you.

"Perfection to you means putting on makeup to hide a bruise so you can attend church.

"Perfect to me is different." I placed my hand on the flat of her chest, only the touch wasn't sexual. "Perfect is someone who fights against the perfection she was raised in to allow our baby to be born." My mouth tightened as I remembered the day I'd found out she was pregnant. Her terror had the power to fuel me with rage all this time later. Her father was lucky she'd pleaded with me to leave him alone because that fucker would be six feet under by now if I'd had my way. "Perfect is someone who sees me and still wants me. Perfect is someone who will clean up my wounds when I come back broken from a fight—"

"Nothing about that speaks of my character," she whispered miserably. "That's probably because all my life I've been spineless."

"Where's this coming from, Keira?"

She swallowed but reached up and tapped her temple.

I had no idea where she was going with this, no idea if I could fix it, no idea if she even wanted to know this, but I murmured, "The first time I saw you, you were smiling, but it didn't die when you caught sight of me. You carried on smiling at me. It changed, turned nervous, sure, but you smiled at me.

"You didn't gape at me, gawk at my bike. You didn't look at me like I was a criminal which, let's face it, I was then and am now, and to your folks and with your upbringing, that's exactly what you should have seen.

"You didn't act coy because you had daddy issues and wanted to walk on the wild side. You just smiled at me. You were so fucking clean, and even though life has sullied you, you're still pure to me."

"I'm not pure," she mumbled.

"You are. But you're judging yourself from a different place than I am." When she peered up at me with watery eyes, I rumbled, "I spent my childhood between Rene and Bear's place and my mom's.

"Whenever she was out of jail, she took us to whatever dive she lived in, and we were surrounded by dirt, eating fucking SpaghettiOs from cans I hacked open so Scarlet and I wouldn't starve.

"She brought guys back so they could shoot up before they fucked and—" I sighed at the look of horror on her face. "I loved you as you became Cyan's mom—a woman who made sure the house was clean, who watched over our daughter, who protected her, cherished her. But I fell for the woman who smiled at a dirty biker like he wasn't scum."

Her breath seemed to freeze, but then, in the tiniest whisper, she asked, "But what about now? Why do you love me now?"

I eyed her warily. "Do you want me to love you?"

"Yes," she breathed.

My jaw worked as I processed that.

Jesus, was she saying what I thought she was saying? Was there hope?

"Is this because some guy you're dating has treated you badly—?"

Her head whipped from side to side. "I haven't dated anyone since the night Rex came."

Mouth tight, I nodded. "You sure?"

I'd shore up her confidence any day of the fucking week, but I wanted to know who'd dented it too. Just so I could dent something of theirs.

"I'm sure." Keira reached up and slid her hand over my cheek. "We've both made mistakes. I've..." She swallowed. "This is hard to admit, but I need to grow up."

Now that had me rearing back. "As far as I'm aware, you're definitely no kid."

"No. I've been acting like a baby. Immature as hell. I'm a mom, but, more importantly, I'm a wife.

"For years, you've been dealing with addiction and I didn't know. You kept that from me, which makes you a jackass, but I should have seen that. I should have known. Why didn't I? Because I didn't look."

"Because you didn't think to look," I rumbled, not happy about her words.

"I should have. You kept me at a distance because you think I'm pure. Well, maybe I don't want to be pure anymore. Maybe I want to be dirty."

My nostrils flared at the same time as my dick twitched, showering my lower half with bittersweet pain.

What I wouldn't give for her hand to cup me, for her to take that key I knew she wore around her neck—the slight bulge of it sometimes visible depending on which shirt she wore—and to release me from my fucking cage...

But I shoved thoughts like that away.

It was shit like that that'd gotten me into this position.

"You don't know what you're saying. I cheated on you, Keira."

"How many times? Can you count? And I don't mean when we were separated. If we count those occasions, then I've cheated on you twice."

Nerve ticking in my jaw, I muttered, "I don't want to talk about this."

"Tough. You talked about jacking off twenty-plus times a day." She gulped. "I need to know. Was it twenty-plus times a day with different clubwhores too?"

Everything in me told me to lie, but I didn't. "Less than five times." I grimaced. "But I didn't exactly count, Keira, and sometimes I wasn't *compos mentis*."

A shaky breath escaped her. "Really? Five times or five women?"

"Different women." My relationship with my fist was another matter entirely. But I had to be honest... "There might have been other times."

Her eyes narrowed in on me. "'Might?' When you were high and you don't remember?"

Shame hit me like a lightning bolt. "Yes."

Her head tilted to the side and something bloomed to life in her eyes. "Kendra told me you were in a years' long relationship."

My jaw tensed as I processed that particular bullshit. "Kendra's been chasing after me ever since she came to fucking West Orange. She'd say my dick was green if it meant you'd believe her bullshit."

Her hand clenched down on my shoulder. "Were you high every time you cheated?"

"That doesn't excuse what I did."

"Not saying it does, but were you?"

I bowed my head. "Yes. Or coming down."

"What triggered you getting high?"

I swallowed, uncertain I wanted to answer that. "Each time?"

"Yeah. Each time."

"I've gotten high throughout our marriage, Keira. It's not like I can give you a reason for every occurrence," I rasped, shame filtering through each word.

"Why?"

"Because sometimes, I need to feel awake. And sometimes, I just need to sleep. They go hand in hand.

"There's always a trigger, but it might not be something you consider as being one."

"Drugs always help you feel awake and always help you sleep?"

"Yes."

"Do you miss it?"

"Yes." My nostrils flared. "I could tell you that I want you and Cyan to be in my world more than I want the drugs, but some days, I don't.

"Some days, I'm just trying not to feel like I'm falling asleep standing up. Some days, I'm just trying to be a little less fucking broken. The only thing that gets me through is you and Cy. That never changes."

"It didn't work before."

"Never lost you before. You never locked me out of my house before. It was a wake-up call." My hands balled into fists. "I hit rock bottom. You destroyed me, sweetheart. It broke me, to the point where I was fucking crying for days on end like…" I released a breath. "Like someone had died. Like *we'd* died."

Her eyes grew round. "You cried?"

"You're kidding me, right? Felt like I was drowning, Keira."

A whispery breath escaped her parted lips and there was something that looked a lot like awe in her eyes—except that didn't make sense. Then, she shook her head. "I don't understand how I never saw you were an addict."

"I worked hard to make sure you didn't."

I'd hit rock bottom so many fucking times in my life, and on those days, I'd just wanted to end it all. Keira and Cy stopped me from taking a little too much marching powder, but shit had changed when she'd thrown me out for good.

I'd seen the writing on the wall.

I'd lost her, and like that, I realized exactly how much of an abyss I was in. Not just standing at the precipice, about to free fall into the blackness. But subsisting inside it.

Every day, I climbed farther out of that abyss, inches at a time. I made slow progress, but at the end of it, they were there—standing in the light. The only thing that stopped me from letting the darkness swallow me whole.

"Is that why you stayed at the clubhouse a lot? You were away too much for it to be runs, but I preferred to think it was that." She swallowed. "Dumb of me."

"Not dumb," I growled. "But yes. We're not supposed to use heavy drugs there, but Rex turned a blind eye when I was—" I exhaled roughly through my nose. "It wasn't so I could fuck anything in a G-string, Keira. I need you to know that. The drugs and the need for sex are two separate problems. I know it sounds crazy, but it's true. I'm not going to lie about this, not now."

Slowly, she nodded. "I wouldn't have understood before, wouldn't have believed you before, but I think I do now."

I reached for her hand, pressed it to my chest. "I don't think *I* understand."

"You don't have to. *I* have to. You're not the one who wanted to break up. I am."

"Are you saying you've changed your mind?"

"I'm saying I'd like to work on getting to know you again." She bit her lip. "I'd like to work on becoming the woman you think I am, instead of some spineless brat who's whining because she tossed her own damn rattle out of the crib."

"Keira, I don't know where this is coming from, but you're not spineless. You had the courage to toss me out, to live your life and make your own path. You reacted. Your mom wouldn't have. She'd have lived with it. That's why I was proud of you. You did the exact opposite of what you'd learned through example."

"I love that you think I'm strong, but I feel like an impostor. I-I wanted to talk to you about this, not because I wanted you to sing my praises, but because I wanted to understand why you feel the way you do about me.

"I don't think I get it, but maybe that's okay. Maybe I'm not supposed to. Maybe love doesn't always make sense." She gulped. "I-I want to be friends, Storm." Disappointment hit me, but before I could take my next breath, she whispered, "If we get back together, I want to know everything. I want to know you. The real you. Your flaws, your strengths.

"I want to know when you're feeling weak, when you think you might relapse. I want your highs and your lows.

"No hiding at the clubhouse on dark days, no hiding when you're craving your next fix—whether it's a chemical one or a..." She licked her lips. "*Physiological* one.

"I come to you with a problem and you try to fix it. I want to be that for you. It's taken me far too long to realize that our marriage has been one-sided in some things, in a lot of things, and, going forward, if we're going to make this work, then that can't be how we proceed.

"I want us to be stronger, I want to fuse what was broken and to make it better."

I slipped my arm around her waist and hugged her to me. "I want that too."

Christ, more than she could know.

Was this a dream? What the fuck had happened that was making her come to this conclusion? I had no idea, but neither was I about to question this.

It might come to nothing, but if baring my wretched, pock-marked, twisted soul to the woman I loved was the price of a future together, then I'd pay it every day for the rest of my life.

TWENTY-FOUR

KEIRA

PRESENT

IT WAS SEEING him mowing the lawn that did it. Dressed like a badass biker, still in his cut, hair flowing and dancing in the bitter, chilly wind. Laughing and clapping even as he was shaking his head at Cyan's antics...

It felt normal.

I wanted it to be normal.

I was tired of it not being our normal.

So I decided to be brave, and I made an overture.

It had stuck, but we were still wary around each other.

Still sliding alongside one another like two ships that passed in the night, except, this time, these ships lingered after dinner. They talked about things other than Cyan.

And one ship bought the other ship some flowers, just because, 'The color reminded me of your eyes.'

Swoon.

He didn't even give me the damn flowers. Just left them on the hallway console beside my bedroom door so I couldn't miss them, much as he placed my clean laundry on there when it was done.

His lack of ass-licking made it seem more sincere, and I guessed I needed that. I needed to believe in him even though I was the one who'd instigated this new normal. But he was showing up. Time and time again. How couldn't I start to have faith in him?

As we rode up to Cyan's middle school for a parent-teacher conference, that faith settled in my bones with a lead weight. Something I'd need tonight because we all knew it wasn't going to be easy.

Cyan's stay of grace had come to an end long ago. New school or not, new people or not, her temper was back in business when she was in class.

Like our minds were in sync, Storm groused, "Cyan, we both know you're going to get called out for aggression."

"I'm not aggressive! They're bullies."

I saw Storm fight to hide a smile so I just heaved a sigh. "There are ways to mediate these situations."

"Like Rachel? Rachel's a mediator."

I arched a brow. "Who told you that?"

"Katina. She said that Rachel was mediating peace between Giulia and Kendra." Both Storm and I tensed up at the same time. "Who's Kendra?"

"You never saw her at the club?" I asked warily, uncertain if that bitch would have tried to seek out my kid to wreak even more havoc on our lives.

"Nope."

Although, why would she? The bitch was always in a brother's bedroom, probably gagging on slut biker cock.

Okay—maybe Cyan wasn't the only one with hair-trigger aggression.

Oops.

"She's just one of the women who help clean the clubhouse."

"Oh. Those women. Why don't they wear a lot of clothes?"

"Because they have low self-esteem and daddy issues," I sniped.

Even if Storm said they hadn't had a relationship, not like the bitch had made out, there was no hiding from that fact. Nor was there any hiding from the fact I loathed her.

"Dr. Janowicz says I have low self-esteem, but I wear a lot of clothes," Cyan pointed out. "Apart from at gymnastics."

Storm cleared his throat. "I don't know how you can have low self-esteem. She must be wrong. You're about as shy as thunder."

Cyan giggled. "That can be my road name! THUNDER!" she boomed.

"Lady Thor," I teased, turning back to smile at her, loving that giggle, and relieved to see her happy considering the situation.

I knew she was nervous about the first parent-teacher conference and, to be frank, I was too. God only knew what the teachers would say about my daughter who headbutted first and asked questions later.

Dr. Janowicz insisted Cyan was improving and the last time she had headbutted someone was over a month ago. That was a good sign, right?

"When's Rachel going to have her baby, Mom?"

Storm and I shared a glance as we pulled into the school parking lot. "She said September."

When we'd returned to West Orange for a two-day weekend celebrating Bear's life with a funeral that could only be described as 'eventful,' we'd come across Rachel with a baby bump, Giulia who looked like she was about ready to pop, and a bunch of the Posse who weren't afraid to make their stamp on the newly constructed clubhouse…

Naturally, that meant the family room was painted pink—I was pretty sure the Posse were being passive aggressive because no woman in their right mind liked that specific shade of baby pink unless it was for a nursery—and there were throw cushions everywhere as well as hot pink candles.

It had been quite amusing actually.

"Can we visit in September?"

"It depends, honey. You'll have school then, remember?"

She huffed. "We have to meet the baby."

"I'm sure we will. We'll figure it out nearer the time," was Storm's gravelly retort, and I was grateful for the finite note to his comment because Cyan tended to wheedle things out of me, but rarely tried that on with her dad.

It was quite nice having him drive as well. Even though the trip was short, I appreciated his driving us through this freak snowstorm in spring—who said global warming didn't exist?—glad he wasn't on the bike so I didn't have to worry about all our asses.

Mostly, it was just nice to sit next to him. To smell his patchouli aftershave. To watch him fiddle with the crucifix around his neck—my gift to him on his first Father's Day. To appreciate that loose hold he had on the steering wheel, the way he was sat back in the bucket seat, driving one-handed, confident and cocksure...

My gaze dipped down to his crotch.

I thought he must have changed the gauge on the padlock because I swore, in certain lights, you could see the damn thing protruding through the denim of his jeans.

Why did that make me squirm?

The visuals had been... interesting. I'd never have imagined that was something I was into, but it was so oddly obscene that everything in me sat up and took notice.

He had a nice dick. Long, thick. He'd always been a tight fit. That he was clinging on to chastity was somehow even hotter, even if I didn't like that he was hurting himself.

I'd seen him when our hands brushed, or felt him if he leaned into the cabinet behind me while I washed something at the sink—he hissed, because the padlock hurt him. That was wrong.

Strangely hot, but wrong.

There was no reason he couldn't get off like that. I guessed he could even jack off, because the padlock wouldn't stop him from getting a boner—it'd just hurt him. As well as keeping other bitches from getting a taste of his dick.

Feeling oddly feral, like I could pull on the nearest clubwhore's hair until it came free from the roots—especially if my target was called Kendra—I tried to switch tracks, tried to back away from the oddly aggressive mood I'd fallen into at the worst possible moment.

Shaking off those thoughts, I left the car once we pulled up, striding into the school with Cyan sandwiched between Storm and me.

All the parents and kids were bundled up against the cold, standing in winter coats everyone had packed away not expecting the bad weather to return.

However, it didn't escape my attention that the kids chatted among each other while Cyan stayed shivering between us in a way that had nothing to do with the recent freak snowstorm and everything to do with anxiety.

I rested my hand on her shoulder as we were directed to her homeroom. As one of the faculty brought us up-to-date on how the evening would work, shortly afterward, we found ourselves facing her teacher.

In the time that took, Cyan's shoulders were so hunched in, she looked like a pretzel. My kid was twisted into knots.

Jarred by the sight, I frowned when I took a seat in front of the teacher, Mr. Caldwell.

"Mr. and Mrs. O'Shea, thanks for joining us."

Storm settled at my side, Cyan between us, and while he nodded, I said, "It's our pleasure."

"Now, as we all know," he murmured, shooting us a displeased glance, "Cyan hasn't adjusted well and hasn't really settled in here."

"Her grades haven't slipped," I pointed out, well aware she was an A- kind of student.

"There's more to school than just grades."

"Wished it had been like that when I was in school," Storm retorted, his hand coming to Cyan's shoulder. When she nuzzled into him, I saw her tension ease some, and found myself angered at how stressed out she was. "As far as I'm aware, the whole point of school is for her to check all those little boxes on your stupid Scantron tests so she can fit herself into a pigeon hole nicely for the rest of her life."

Caldwell narrowed his eyes at Storm, then shot me a tight-lipped smile, apparently sensing that I was the parent to whom he'd be better off directing his commentary. "We're also trying to help Cyan's development. She's incredibly aggressive, prone to snapping at other children, and frankly can make a class incredibly difficult—"

"You mean to tell me you can't handle one child?" I murmured. "One small kid who's quite clearly being bullied? My kid who's happy as a clam the second she's out of school but the moment she's inside these walls is twisted up like a pretzel?"

Caldwell's mouth tightened further. "Her claims about being bullied are unsubstantiated."

"How do you know that?" I prompted, and I'd admit, my mommy radar was on red alert and scenting bullshit.

"Cyan's failed to disclose names or talk about how she's supposedly being bullied."

"I'm not a snitch," Cyan muttered, her shoulders hunched.

Storm frowned. "Isn't the clue that the kid bullying her is the one she headbutts?"

"That isn't a reasonable way to resolve a situation like this," Caldwell said stiffly.

"I don't agree. Not if the end result is that they leave her the hell alone," Storm retorted.

"If you're failing to protect her, then what recourse does she have but to defend herself?" I questioned.

Caldwell shook his head. "I've spoken with the children she fights with. They say that she's the aggressor—"

"Well, they would, wouldn't they?"

"Having seen your daughter's permanent record, Mrs. O'Shea, I'm aware that she had similar issues at St. Angela's." His smile was condescending. "Are we to assume that she was being bullied there as well?"

I blinked at him. "Are you for real?"

Caldwell stiffened up. "I don't believe that's an appropriate question."

"If that isn't, then you saying my daughter wasn't being bullied when she said she was isn't appropriate either." I turned to Cyan who was peering up at me with big eyes, but I saw her appreciation, saw a flicker of the warmth I was used to seeing when we weren't inside these goddamn walls. "Honey, they've left you alone for a month, right? You haven't been getting into fights for a while now."

"They're leaving me alone," she confirmed nervously.

"They weren't attacking her in the first place," Caldwell sniped. "Look, we often have issues with Sinners' children. It's a learning curve for them to realize that fighting isn't—"

"I beg your damn pardon?" I grated out, not letting him finish. "Are you trying to tell me that my little girl is at fault? She's the one to blame for being bullied?" Before he could finish, I turned to her again and asked, "I know you don't want to be a snitch, but your dad's right.

You kind of gave the game away when you fought with them. What did they do?"

She hesitated a second, but I reached out and grabbed her hand. She clung to me. Fuck, she clung to me like she did when she was little, and I was her calm in the eye of a storm.

"Called me names." She licked her lips. "Called you and Daddy names too."

"Cyan, have you never heard of the phrase, 'Sticks and stones may break my bones, but words will never hurt me?'"

Storm grunted. "Are you for real? Words hurt just as much as fists."

Caldwell sniffed. "Not in the school yard. We're having to separate her from a few of the children she's had issues with—"

"I'm sorry if that's inconvenient for you," I retorted. "I'm sorry that you can't protect my child adequately. Have you reprimanded the other kids who are involved?"

"They did nothing wrong. I can't reprimand a child who's been unjustly attacked."

"They called my mom a whore!" Cyan yelled, jumping up, shaking with her outrage. "My mom isn't a whore. *She's married.* You can't be a whore if you're married. Daddy told me that." Her fists furled into tight balls while I dealt with the repercussions of learning that Cyan had gone to Storm about this, and he'd explained that I wasn't a whore. "They said Daddy belonged in jail and that I was a bastard. I'm not a bastard! My mom and dad had a wedding and everything."

"Apparently you need to improve your school system if kids around here think a legally married couple can have an illegitimate child," I said coolly, before I got to my feet. "Come on, Storm, Cyan, we're done here."

Storm cocked a brow at me, but Caldwell sputtered, "We're *not* done here. We've barely even started. In fact, I think we should reschedule another meeting to come up with a plan to stabilize the situation."

"I have a plan to stabilize the situation," I snarled. "I'm taking my kid out of the 'situation'—" I used air quotes and everything, "—and I'm going to homeschool her.

"I'm not bringing her to a place that fills her with dread, where she feels unsafe, where her parents—her safety net—are called names. Where she feels she has to defend herself, and when that happens, she's the only one punished.

"I understand that violence isn't the answer and we have been working on that, however, she was not the instigator." Jaw clenched, I snapped, "If she's going to be treated unjustly for being a Sinner, then—"

"We have other Sinners' kids in class," Caldwell retorted. "They don't get into fights."

"Well, according to you," I mocked with even more air quotes as I loomed over the desk. "'We often have issues with Sinners' children. It's a learning curve for them to stop fighting.'

"Maybe that's because they've been subjected to this kind of trash talk since they were toddlers and now they're too scared to do anything other than be oppressed." I straightened up. "My daughter is a kind, thoughtful little girl. She works hard, is dedicated and determined, and even with her recent troubles, would never strike out at someone unless she felt cornered.

"You've placed my child in an unsafe situation, Mr. Caldwell, one where she feels she has to retaliate.

"I think your repeated inability to protect her makes this a dangerous place for her to be." I glanced at my kid and my husband, feeling empowered when I saw the raging heat in Storm's eyes that told me exactly what he thought of my declaration, and I boomed, "Let's go."

"Mrs. O'Shea! You can't just leave!"

"Watch me," I growled, steering Cyan out by the shoulder, well aware that Storm had my back as we left a still sputtering Mr. Caldwell behind.

"Pencil-pushing prick," Storm grumbled under his breath, loud enough for me to hear, but I didn't say anything. I was too pissed off to speak.

Even now, the second we walked down the halls, Cyan's shoulders practically folded in on themselves.

Storm had been right in the car—it made no sense when Dr.

Janowicz talked about Cyan having low self-esteem when she was a cocky little thing at home. Yet, here, she was fractious and anxious!

I wasn't having it.

Things hadn't been great in West Orange, much for the same reasons. I remembered when I was at school how Sinners' kids were viewed. Outsiders, rebels. Bad eggs. I'd always avoided them, mostly because if my dad had found out I was friends with one, he'd have made me toss them aside.

My shoulders hunched as I realized I was just as bad as these kids here.

I'd locked Sinners' children out, never letting them close, looking down on them when it wasn't their fault that they were their parents' offspring…

Instead, I'd made friends with kids whose folks were in my dad's flock, and look how that had turned out—they'd dumped me the second my relationship with Storm had led to Cyan's existence.

Well, I wasn't about to stand for that kind of BS with Cyan.

My mind raced as we left the school and headed toward the parking lot. Beneath my boots, the snow crunched, and there was the scent of gasoline in the air as some old junker pulled into a space. A woman darted out of the car, then promptly squealed as she fell back on her butt. The thunk of her body colliding with the concrete had me wincing.

"Ms. Shawnee!" Cyan called out, her voice horrified as she stomped through the snow toward the woman who groaned with pain.

Storm and I hobbled after her, but it was Cyan who crouched down and asked, "Ms. Shawnee, do you need me to get the nurse?"

Winded, the woman coughed. "No, it's okay, Cyan. Thank you though." She groaned as Storm held out a hand and helped her sit upright.

"It's slick around here," Storm cautioned us all. "Looks like oil."

She hissed. "Just my luck."

"Let me help you onto your feet."

Ms. Shawnee winced. "I guess I can't sit here all night. I'm late as it is." She grabbed Storm's hand and tried to wriggle into a standing position but each time, she gasped, until she blurted out, "Oh, my back!"

Concerned, I crouched down in front of her. "Do you need an EMT? You fell pretty hard."

Ms. Shawnee shook her head. "No. I'll be fine. I just need a minute." Her smile was tight, creased with pain. "It's okay, you go, I can manage. It's cold."

Storm grunted. "You're right, it is. Cyan, go and sit in the car." He handed her the keys to the SUV. "You too, babe."

"No. I'll stay. But Cyan, you go. Lock the doors after you get in, hmm?"

"But Mom! I want to help too."

"You won't help if you catch a cold. Now, go on. Get."

Cyan huffed but as she scurried away, she muttered, "I hope you feel better in the morning, Ms. Shawnee."

"Thanks, Cyan," the teacher said with another wince.

I knew my little girl had an attitude problem, mostly because I dealt with it, I knew she was headstrong, but I also knew she had a kind heart, and that confirmed it.

"Do you have any water? I have Advil in my purse."

Ms. Shawnee's eyes rounded. "You do? Damn, that would be great. Thank you so much." She reached for her own purse, cringing in pain as she did so, retrieving a bottle of water from its confines. "It's just the bottom of my back, you know?" she mumbled as she accepted the Advil and downed two.

"It hurts like crazy when you land on your tailbone," Storm concurred, finally stopping looming over us both to squat down beside me. "Do you need me to carry you inside, ma'am?"

Even in the spotlit parking lot, I saw the teacher's cheeks flush as she took in Storm. "That's really kind of you, but no. Thank you so much, though."

I knew she'd checked him and his cut out, but I didn't think it was because he was a Sinner she was hesitant to accept help.

"At least let me get you into your car," Storm rumbled, and though she hesitated at first, the teacher nodded.

"That would be so kind of you."

She swallowed as she raised her arms, letting him snag them as he carefully maneuvered so he was lifting her.

Gasps of pain escaped her as I darted forward to snag the keys she'd dropped on the ground then I quickly unlocked the door, so Storm could help her be seated.

Once she was in the driver's seat, she peered up at us both and said, "Thank you so much both of you. You've been so sweet."

"Our pleasure," I said with a shrug, answering for him. "Is there anything else we can do?"

She grimaced as she wriggled in her seat. "No. Thanks."

"Need us to drive you home?"

"I really must head in there. I have conferences scheduled."

"Then the school should have salted the parking lot better." Storm's smile was grim. "I'd sue the jackasses."

Ms. Shawnee snickered out a laugh which morphed into a groan. "I'm sure that would really make them fall for me. They already don't like my brand of teaching." Though curious, I didn't get to ask her what she taught because her phone buzzed. "Damn. That's the administrator. Thanks again, Mr. and Mrs. O'Shea. I really appreciate you helping me out."

"At least let me take you to the front door," Storm argued, and maybe she heard the implacable stance in his words because she seemed to take measure of the distance between her car and the door, then Storm's bulk, before she ultimately nodded.

"Only if it wouldn't be an inconvenience."

Storm snorted. "You arguing with me over it would have been more of an inconvenience."

I smiled as he gathered her into his arms. I locked up the car behind her, then trudged alongside him, being careful to watch out for slick patches, then, as he deposited her at the front door, I handed her her purse and keys.

People gathered around when they saw him carrying her, and I caught sight of a few men in Sinners' cuts who eyed their Prez in surprise. Ms. Shawnee was absorbed into the crowd after Storm let her down.

"Well, that calmed my temper," I muttered dryly as I stared around the front hall.

Storm's arm settled around my shoulders, and I had to admit, I snuggled into him. God, he was warm. Toasty like we weren't standing outside, whereas I was freezing.

Huddling into his side, I didn't flinch when he remarked, "You were fantastic in there."

My nose crinkled. "Not really. I gave him shit when I know Cyan can be difficult."

"You and I both saw the change in her when we walked through those doors," he pointed out. "That's not right."

"No, it wasn't," I agreed.

"You mean what you said about homeschooling?"

I pulled a face. "That was definitely a spur of the moment decision… I'm sorry. I should have consulted you."

"I think it would be a great idea."

"You do?"

"I do. You always were good at teaching her things."

"Back when she was a toddler," I scoffed.

"You happy working at the diner?"

I bit my lip. "I like it. It gets me out of the house and I'm starting to make friends."

"No need for you to stop doing that entirely then. Cyan can always sit in a booth and do some of her classes there if you really want to make it work. Or she could come to the clubhouse. Don't see why she can't sit in my office with me and do some studying there."

I blinked up at him. "People have sex at the clubhouse."

"Not all the time," he said with a short laugh. "Plus, it's not like the West Orange chapter. When there are parties, it's free reign. But not here. There are too many Old Ladies wandering around. Plus, we're changing the layout. On a certain someone's advice…"

My cheeks turned pink, and it had nothing to do with the cold. Then, a thought whispered into my mind. "Why did she talk to you about the whole 'whore' thing? Why didn't she come to me?"

He winced. "Noticed that, did you?"

"I did," I confirmed huskily.

A breath gusted from his lips, leaving a cloud of steam behind as he muttered, "We should get out of here."

I tugged on the sleeve of his jacket. "No. We need to talk about this."

He grimaced. "Someone called you that back in West Orange. I think it's become a trigger word for her. She's defending you—"

"I know that. But who'd—" My mouth worked. "My dad? Mom?"

"I'm sorry, honey."

I swallowed, trying to accept that after all these years of not talking, he could still call me that. After all these years of marriage, that was the one noun he used to describe me.

"Other Sinners' kids have settled in here," Storm pointed out softly, changing the subject, I guessed. "If you've changed your mind now—"

"Cyan's not other kids," was my gruff reply. "I don't think—" I sucked in a breath. "I'm different, Storm. I used to think that I wanted to be a nurse, so I looked into all the courses, but it was just so complicated that it blew my mind. The cut off date to enroll was weeks ago, so I told myself I'd think about it, only I still don't know what I'm doing—"

"You're wondering if this is you procrastinating?"

"Yes? No?" I sighed. "I don't know. Maybe? I've never wanted to be a teacher, and Cyan and I lock horns all the time. She'd probably never learn anything if I was homeschooling her."

He squeezed my arm and pressed a kiss to my crown. "Keira, one thing I've learned about you, once you've got something in your mind, you'll figure out a way to make it happen. Whether that's being a nurse or homeschooling our kid." His nose rubbed against my hairline. "You should probably remember, though, that you wanted to be a nurse when you were a different person.

"You're not the same Keira as the one I met at eighteen, just like I'm not the same Storm, and that's perfectly fine. You're allowed to change. Your goals are allowed to divert course."

"Nursing is a vocation, Storm. It's not something you're supposed to want to give up."

A laugh escaped him. "I'm pretty sure that every single nurse who finishes school doesn't stay a nurse forever."

"She's an A- student. What if I make her worse?"

"Maybe she'll be an A+ student if you teach her. You saw that anxiety that riddled her when we walked through those doors. That has to be affecting her studies. Maybe she's not doing as well as she could be doing because she's so stressed all the time?"

Did he know how he empowered me? I knew he wasn't blowing smoke up my ass—he believed in me. More than I did, that was for sure.

"Do you think I could do it?"

"I don't just think it, I know it, and you wouldn't be doing it alone." When I peered up at him, he smiled, then he lowered his head and pressed his lips to my nose. I gulped, my eyes prickling with tears at the tender gesture. "I used to be boss at geography. Sciences," he said with a grimace, "less so. History, I'm your guy. Math, I was really good at, and I could write the shit out of a story in English."

My smile grew. "Really?"

"Really," he confirmed with a laugh. "Ms. Keira, are you stereo-typing me when you know I appreciate Shakespeare?"

I literally 'felt' the twinkle in my eyes. "Maybe. I mean, I know you're smart as hell, but I never thought English Class would be your thing. Not with all the 'ain't's you drop."

He tapped his nose. "Lots of uncharted waters for us both to uncover still, honey. That's good."

His ease, his acceptance, his support, his belief in me, all of it combined, forcing me into a chokehold that had me reacting with a flightiness that wasn't like me anymore, but which felt right.

I didn't care that we were in the school parking lot. Didn't care that at my back, there were parents in the community. Didn't care that Cyan could maybe see us from the SUV. Didn't care about anything other than feeling his lips on mine.

So I surged onto my tiptoes and kissed him.

And damn, if it didn't feel as right now as it had done when he'd kissed me that first time when I was nineteen.

TWENTY-FIVE

STORM

PRESENT

Welcome To My House - Nu Breed

I KEPT it chaste even though it almost killed me.

Well, it was either behave or have my dick drop off and though that particular organ was out of office until August, that didn't mean I wanted it to fall off in the meantime.

The pain from the padlock as my erection made an appearance had me hissing, pulling back even though the pressure of her lips against mine was like goddamn heaven. Hers were parted as she stayed in place, her head tilted back, her eyes closed so that my breath brushed across her mouth.

"I want you so bad, honey," I rumbled, dropping my forehead against hers. "But I can't. Not yet."

"Not yet?" she asked a little shakily.

"Not until August."

She stared at me dumbly. "August?"

I couldn't blame her for looking confused. It wasn't like I'd ever shared the recovery process with her. She wasn't wrong about how closemouthed I could be. I really needed to start opening up to her more.

As I tugged her into moving across the lot, she let me until we were away from the doors so I knew she'd gathered I wanted some privacy.

Not bothering to prevaricate, I murmured, "I got hooked on sex because I switched addictions. I would jack off instead of getting high. That's because you're not supposed to have sex for the first twelve months of sobriety."

She blinked at me. "Okay."

One word, but she meant it. There wasn't a connotation to the word that made me think she thought I was weird, nor was she adding a tone to it that was like she believed I was dumb.

No, it was an affirmative.

She'd wait.

"Will you—" I pulled back, sighed. "Never mind."

Her hand snagged on mine. "No. What is it? Tell me. Remember, I want to know the highs and lows."

I bowed my head. "I'd like to touch you."

"You think I'm going to argue about that?"

"Only if you don't touch me. I'm on a hair-trigger, honey. It'll be bittersweet fucking agony, but you're my wife, and I want to satisfy you."

A soft sound escaped her and when she paused and burrowed into my arms, hugging me tight, I wasn't sure if I was shocked or just relieved.

"If you think I'm going to turn down Asher orgasms, you're nuts," she mumbled against my plaid shirt, making me snort.

Nice to know I was good at something.

I squeezed her. "Cyan's watching."

"Let her watch."

Some tension escaped me.

She meant it.

She didn't want to sneak around or anything. She was being genuine in her desire to get to know me, although that had apparently just escalated and she was fine with it so there was no way I wouldn't be too.

"She's going to ask about homeschooling."

She squeezed me. "Do you really think I can do it?"

Her voice was different this time. She knew she could, she knew I'd say she could, but she just needed the reassurance, which I was more than willing to give her.

Cy's reaction in there had been horrendous. Moreover, what she'd gone through reminded me of the hell of my own time in school.

I'd had my brothers, but she was alone. That K was willing to homeschool was a weight off my fucking shoulders and no mistake.

"I do. And if it doesn't work out, we'll figure out how to make it happen, okay?" I hesitated. "What about school? Your school, I mean."

She released a breath. "I don't think I want to be a nurse now."

"Maybe that's how you feel right this second, but hell, college isn't going anywhere and hospitals always need nurses. That option will always be open to you, babe."

"You're too good to me," she rasped, squeezing me harder.

"I'll always do what I can to make sure you have everything you need and want," I told her softly, unsure how she'd feel about my telling her that.

I felt like a cat on a hot tin roof, although, I wished it were fucking hot. My balls were about to turn blue for the regular reason of hypothermia out here.

"Thank you, Asher," she told me.

Cyan peppered us with questions when we got back into the car, not about us hugging in the middle of the damn parking lot, but about homeschooling.

That she didn't want to have to return to Sacred Heart Junior High said everything, and the more she talked, the more excited she got, I knew it buoyed Keira.

She'd responded to the teacher's criticisms, had acted on impulse, and was going to go through with it. I could see the resolve on her face increasing as Cyan practically bounced from topic to topic.

I let them talk, content to just listen, feeling like I'd been welcomed back inside the family even if I didn't deserve it.

After driving through the community gates, I pulled up outside our house and slowly turned into the driveway. As I did, my cellphone buzzed at the same time as I heard straight pipes. Not just one set from Jump, but several sets.

Tension whipped up inside me, but I controlled it for my woman and kid's sakes. Both of them seemed to sense it though, because Cy stopped chattering away and Keira watched me with a stillness that was unnatural for her.

"Bikers, incoming," Jump barked as I picked up the phone.

"I hear 'em." To Keira, I commanded, "Get in the house, K. I need you and Cy to go into your bedroom." My jaw clenched as I shoved her car keys at her, having separated out the one she'd need. "I don't have time to show it to you, but if you look, the back wall of the closet is false. There's just a keyhole."

Her brow furrowed. "You built us a safe room and didn't tell me?"

"I didn't want to scare you." My mouth was tight as I dipped down and pressed a kiss to her lips. "Go and get in there. Please."

She studied me for a millisecond, a millisecond I couldn't afford, then she demanded, "Cyan, move it."

Both of them jumped out of the car and dashed over to the house. As I watched them go, I called Digger. "You at home?"

There was a light on at the back of his property, but he could have been out on business.

"Yeah. Why?"

"Don't you hear those straight pipes? We got company."

"I'm listening to music. I don't hear shit. I'll be out in two."

"Bring guns."

"Duh."

After that, I called the security at the gates, and when there was no answer, I had to figure that whoever was on their way had either knocked Paul out or had killed him.

Regret filled me, but I didn't have time for that shit. Instead, I pulled out the handgun I had strapped to my calf and the knife that was tucked in my back pocket.

I felt a little like John Wayne in a western, but I moved to stand in the middle of the road, intent on staring the fuckers down.

Three bikers came to a halt within scant inches from me, and Jump roared around my back, stopping at my side, silently telling me that he was with me, not them.

And when I said them, I meant the fuckers who were definitely no longer Sinners but still wore our motherfucking cuts.

"Trespassing is a criminal offense," I declared, voice bland, my stance relaxed, handgun held loosely in my hand. I wasn't about to start waving it around, but neither was I going to let them think I was an easy target.

In my peripheral vision, I saw Digger make an appearance, a gun in each hand as he walked quietly toward us, each footstep perfectly placed to cause the minimum of noise.

"We ain't the trespassers here. This is our fucking land. You're the bastard who threw us off it—"

"You're the ones who ran away like pussies," I retorted. "I didn't do shit, just came in here to clean up your last Prez's mess." I smirked at them. "If you can't handle the truth, then you'd better just fuck off."

"Can't believe you're siding with this prick, Jump."

"He's good for the club," Jump retorted, but he stepped up to the plate and came to stand at my side. "You fuckers never thought about the MC. Just about stuffing shit up your nose. We got jobs now, there are businesses in town brothers work for. Butch never gave a fuck about our bills—"

"We're goddamn bikers," one of them roared.

"That mean you don't pay utilities?" I mused. "Show your fucking faces anyway. Pussies wear visors."

Growls were my answer, but they did as I asked, removed their helmets, and I quickly scanned their faces, recognizing a couple from photos on the wall in the bar.

"You're Doc, Sticky, and Hook," I said calmly.

"How the fuck do you know that?"

"Got eyes, don't I? And a brain in my head unlike you dipshits." I sneered at them. "What's your problem? Why the fuck are you here?"

"We're about to take back what's ours. We don't recognize you as Prez and—"

"Good thing seeing as you ain't Sinners anymore."

Punctuating my declaration, Digger cocked his guns which had the men jolting, freezing in place.

"Not very smart, are you? What the hell did you think was going to happen? You'd come here, beat the shit out of me and what, leave me to die?" I smirked at them as I took a step forward, inching into their space until, of course, shit hit the fan.

I heard the unmistakable cocking of my twelve-gauge, then a, "Get the hell away from our property."

I'd expected it to be warbled.

I'd expected her to be scared, to find her cowering in the closet safe room.

I didn't anticipate that months with Giulia and her fucking Posse would bring out the beast in my woman.

I didn't turn away, didn't move to look at her, but those fuckers did.

Just as they started to snicker, amused at my woman showing up, not realizing that she was in full-on momma bear mode, she let loose a shell.

I half-expected to feel the tiny pellets digging into my ass if her aim wasn't true, but I realized she fired into the ground because I didn't hear the ball bearings clatter as they sprayed the concrete.

"Think you're outnumbered, boys," Jump rattled off, but I heard his nerves and knew he didn't want to have a face off.

"The next time you bring shit to my home is a day that your momma will see you in the morgue when she's IDing your corpses.

"Now, this is a public place, the cops will be on their way shortly, and that protects us both. It means I can't gut you like fish, and it means you can't do dick to me.

"It's my land, my home. You came here. I think that's a mixture of stand-your-ground and castle doctrine. And seeing as the local law don't particularly like your brand of the Sinners but are in my pocket, I think I know who'd be getting hauled into jail tonight—"

Their engines roared as they took off, but before he slammed on the ignition, Hook ground out, "You ain't heard the last of us."

"Been waiting for you fuckers to darken my door," I retorted. "You're as dumb as I was warned."

Hatred gleamed in the bastard's eyes, even in the darkness there was no mistaking that glitter, as he hacked up some saliva, spat it at my feet, then rode off, straight pipes tearing through the silence of the night.

As I watched them go, I turned to Digger and Jump and said, "Thanks for having my back, brothers."

Jump gulped. "Didn't think they'd show their faces here."

"Them in particular or just the Sinners who ran off?"

"Bit of both?" Edgily, he tugged on his cuffs. "Sticky's on the run from a murder charge in Canada. That's how he got the name—sticky fingers. Someone caught him thieving some necklace or something, and he killed 'em to keep 'em quiet. He ain't the kind of fucker who stays around unless it's worth his while."

I blinked at that news. "Canada? He's not a Sinner?"

"Used to be a…" Jump frowned. "Wolf? Rabid Wolf?"

My mouth tightened. "He did, huh?" In the distance, over the lingering notes of the bikes, I heard sirens. "I won't forget tonight, brothers."

"I'm your Enforcer, ain't I?" Digger retorted, but he was smirking as he put the safety back on his guns.

"You look like you enjoyed that a little too much," I drawled.

"Hey, I've just been dancing around the living room to Barbie Girl. I needed a dose of testosterone."

"There a reason for that?"

"Maddox falls asleep to it."

"You shitting me?" I hooted, though my lips curved as memories assailed me—I'd been there, done that. Motown had been Cyan's preference of choice. "Stop, Look, Listen" had always done the trick.

"I wish. You can blame TikTok for that. I tried to get him hooked on Whitesnake but no dice." His grimace said it all, but he waved a hand. "Here if you need me, Prez." He glanced at Keira. "Although, looks like you've got an Old Lady who'll ride into war with you now." His brow arched. "Color me impressed."

I wasn't.

I just waved a hand at him, telling him to get lost, but to Jump, asked, "Can you check in with Paul on the gates? Make sure he's okay?

If he's—" I grimaced. "Hopefully he ain't dead. Call me if he is. If he's got a head injury, take him to the ER and pay his bill."

"Will do, Prez," Jump agreed before he 'jumpily' walked over to his bike. I guessed I figured out why he got his name—fucker made a newborn puppy look still.

With that in hand, I twisted around and stormed over to my woman's side.

Now that was done, I'd thought she'd be shaky, nervous, but she wasn't.

Our time apart had changed her. I wasn't sure if I liked that or not.

Frowning at her, I grabbed the shotgun, dumped out the used shell and pocketed the full one as I demanded, "What the hell did you think you were doing?"

Her chin tipped up as she got in my face. "You think you're the only one who can protect our family?"

"It's my goddamn job, Keira," I rumbled, even though her heat slammed into me like a wall.

I'd never enjoyed butting up against fire before, but hell, even my dick didn't taste the pain of the padlock, just appreciated her outrage.

"Well, you're not alone anymore, are you?" Her nostrils flared. "You could have gotten yourselves killed. I couldn't call the cops, not without making you look bad at the clubhouse, but I knew a neighbor would call in a shot.

"I saved your ass so I don't have to tell my little girl that her daddy got his butt killed in the middle of the street."

Her words reverberated in my head, making me grab her chin with a gentleness that surprised her, made her jump, but I tipped it high, then slammed my lips against hers.

She groaned, her hands coming up, nails dragging through my hair as she shoved herself into me, tongues tangling as she thrust hers into my mouth, fucking me rather than me fucking her.

She was angry and hot and scared, and I felt each emotion bleed into me with the purity of the finest cocaine.

Having never experienced anything like it, I let the immobilized shotgun stay hooked in the crook of my elbow as, with my other, I hauled her closer, my hand on her ass, kneading the ripe curve as I ground my dick into her.

The pain was fucking delicious as I pulled back, nipping her bottom lip before I moved down, my mouth trailing over the curve of her throat as I sucked and licked and kissed.

"Fuck, I would have given my left ball to watch you fire that shotgun," I growled. My hand tightened on her ass. "My woman. My fucking Old Lady."

She moaned as I sucked down hard, nipping on her throat before making my way to her lips again.

I didn't sup from her, treat her delicately like I usually did.

I didn't make love to her, didn't kiss and cherish, I fucking worshipped her.

I took.

She gave.

I tongue-fucked her.

She fought back.

I tasted her and reveled in her and savored her.

She groaned and tried to claw at my skin, pressing ever nearer to me, like she wanted to get inside me, and I understood. I fucking got it.

As her mouth tore at mine, I heard the sirens getting nearer, and felt the lights flickering behind me.

When the squad car braked to a halt with a squeak that told me the vehicle needed some work, I heard a wary, "Storm?"

Pulling back, I growled, "Mine." Nipping the thick pad of her chin before I tipped it back, I nuzzled my face in the nook between her throat and shoulder, and bit down there too.

A whimper escaped her, but it turned into a groan as I pulled away.

"Sheriff Myers," I rumbled, twisting around before I let myself forget I couldn't fuck my woman until August. Before I forgot there was a Sheriff standing on my property.

One thing I wouldn't forget?

The day my wife graduated as my Old Lady for real.

TWENTY-SIX

STORM

PAST

Bittersweet Sweet Symphony - The Verve

I STARED up at the ceiling, wondering when the light show would stop overhead.

Hundreds of colors merged and flowed together, keeping my attention, holding it like nothing else could.

LSD wasn't my favorite, usually it ended with me puking and suffering night terrors, but it was all I'd been able to score.

Now I was high, the inner peace it brought was like nothing else because my mind was splintered in so many different directions that one thought brought another.

Without Keira, what was the point in trying to stay focused?

Without Keira, I couldn't function.

This way, my mind and body were in accord—chaos. Each thought acting like a game of word association.

My camera lens was having issues—I needed a new one for when the baby was born.

I was going to be a dad.

I needed to be better than my POS sperm donor.

Shit—

Scum.

Scum.

Scum.

That was me.

Mom said so.

Scarlet did too.

Trash.

Worthless.

Keira deserved better—

My kid deserved better.

Should I just end it?

Save them from me?

From my poison?

The colors twisted and morphed, bringing me peace again, bringing me some solace from my drifting thoughts, and that was when the bed jerked as someone climbed onto it.

"Keira?" Hope hit me like it always did when she was there, offering me a chance at a brighter future, at a cleaner world. "Is that you?" I rasped eagerly, blindly seeking her out amid the shadows.

She hummed.

"You came back?" I sighed. "Why you always gotta leave me, baby girl?"

She didn't reply, just pressed her mouth to mine, settled against me and held me like she knew my broken pieces were in danger of shattering even more, before her hold on me changed, morphed...

I fell asleep like that, fell asleep with her close. Somehow right and wrong. Somehow different. My subconscious kept me wary, which turned my trip into a bad one.

The nightmares were extreme.

Memories of Scarlet and me eating ketchup sandwiches with green-spattered bread where the mold talked to us.

The joy of being with Rene and Bear broken when *she* made it out of jail and took us to the next squalid pit where the walls caved in whenever she locked the door behind her, leaving Scarlet and me alone.

Boyfriends I had to call 'uncle' beating me for stealing their chips, their fists ten times the size of regular hands—

My brain wouldn't work.

Couldn't work—

Reel after reel of each year of my life, the misery my mom had brought upon me.

And my father too.

I jerked awake.

Jolted by a soft snore that was definitely not Keira's.

She didn't snore.

Keira talked in her sleep.

The sight of the brassy red hair smoothed over my chest had anger ricocheting inside me, even as the need to puke hit me square in the gut.

"Kendra?" I barked, shoving her away, desperate for her to wake up before Keira came back. "What the fuck are you doing here?"

Her dazed eyes popped open and, sleepily, she smiled at me. "Good morning, baby."

"I'm not your baby," I snapped, shoving her away from me again.

Light splintered in through the shades, making my head ache, but that was nothing to my soul.

"What the hell are you doing in my bedroom?"

Where was Keira?

"You asked me up here."

I'd never liked her.

She wore her hair red right now, and it suited her. Scarlet Lady. Just like my sister.

Her cat eyes gleamed, her mouth curved into a pout, and everything about her should have gotten me hot, but it never had. Never would.

"I didn't," I told her, my tone like concrete. I'd never wanted her. Before Keira, and certainly not after. "Did you sneak into my fucking room?"

"You asked me up here," she repeated with a sly smile. "You wanted me to make you feel better, baby." She started crawling toward me, her tits jiggling with the move, her hair shifting and curling over her shoulders, but she could have been a zombie walking toward me for all that I cared.

"Get the fuck away from me," I hissed, shoving her hard enough for her to tumble off the bed.

I didn't treat women like shit, but fuck if I didn't when they climbed into my bed and made me think—

No, she hadn't said a word.

I remembered that. The fractures of the memory came together, revealing a moving picture I wanted to discard forever.

I'd chosen to believe it was Keira. Keira who I was kissing. Keira who I was loving.

I scrubbed a hand over my face, weariness hitting me. Weariness and sorrow. Then my eyes caught on my cock. A condom covered it.

I'd cheated on Keira.

The only fucking person who mattered to me, and I'd cheated on her.

The guilt, sweet fuck, the guilt. It was like nothing else I'd ever experienced.

Worse than every mistake I'd made when I was high, worse than the disappointment in Bear's eyes whenever he caught me with drugs.

This was like a knife to the belly—

"You wanted me!" Kendra spat. "You can try to convince yourself otherwise, but you did."

I thought you were Keira.

"You wanted me, Storm."

"I thought you were Keira!" I screamed the words at her, wishing each one were a bullet that would kill her stone dead.

"As if she'd grace the clubhouse with her presence," Kendra snarled. "She's too hoity toity for that. God forbid she comes here and actually sullies herself with the peasants.

"When are you going to realize you and her aren't right for each other?"

"Get out of my room."

"She's all wrong for you. She's too good for this way of life, Storm. She was always like that in school." Her top lip curved into a sneer. "She likes to think her shit don't stink."

"Get out."

"You should let her go. You'll only ruin things for her, Storm. She's not made for this life," she pleaded, her hands clutching at the covers. "I am. I'm perfect for you. Why can't you see that?"

Her whispered words ran too close to what I often thought.

I wasn't good enough for her.

Keira *was* too pure for this way of life. Too clean.

I'd only dirty her. Taint her. Sully her.

Scum.

Scum.

Scum.

The word repeated on a litany, just like it had when Mom spat it at me, but I screamed, "Get the fuck out of here before I make you regret so much as looking at me, never mind fucking with me."

Her shoulders straightened, fear entered her eyes, but she shot me a wobbly smile. "You'd never hurt me, Storm," she told me softly. "You just have to see that we're perfect for each other—"

"I wouldn't have fucked you if you were the last pussy on earth and we'd just been hit with an ice age, Kendra.

"In fact, it'd take more than that for me to tap your frigid ass. Now get the fuck away from me before I do more than threaten you, and don't you dare go anywhere near me again or I'll make you regret it."

I watched in bewilderment when, instead of doing as I said, she clambered onto the bed and started crawling toward me once again.

Was she fucking stupid?

I leaped off the mattress, making her jump, and then I grabbed her by the hand and hauled her off it.

When she landed with a thump on the floor, crying out, I didn't listen. I'd warned her, but she'd refused to back off. So I dragged her out of the room and dumped her sorry ass outside the door.

"What the fuck, man?" Link boomed.

I closed my eyes, unable to believe that I'd been caught with literal proof of cheating on my wife, but I snapped at Kendra, "You leave me the hell alone."

She burst into tears then threw herself at Link who, like the sap he was where women were concerned, held her and comforted her.

I didn't stick around to watch the fucking show. I grabbed my cut, hauled it on, pulled off the condom, puked after I did so, at further proof of what I'd done, then dragged on my jeans then my boots.

While people had gathered around a sobbing Kendra, and I knew the news was spreading that I'd been unfaithful to Keira, I didn't wait for her to sell me as the cheating husband.

There were extenuating circumstances, but I saw the gleam of hatred in her eyes.

There was a fine line between love and hate, and I'd just crossed it.

I raced toward my bike, suddenly desperate to find out where the hell Keira was, to reveal the godawful truth, to beg her to forgive me, but just as I started my engine, my phone buzzed.

When I saw her name, I closed my eyes with relief and regret. Remorse too.

But I shoved that aside, instead answered the call with, "Keira, baby, I know Scarlet upset you but I told her she's no longer welcome—"

"Storm," she sobbed out, making my heart jerk in my chest. "I-I think I'm losing the baby!"

And that was when I knew what it was to be punished for my sins.

As I stared up at the sky, bright blue with the sun so piercing it made my drug-addled head pound, tears wet my eyes and I reached up and rubbed at them before I rumbled, "She's going nowhere, baby girl. Where are you? I'm coming right now. We'll get through this."

We had to.

TWENTY-SEVEN

KEIRA

PRESENT - MAY

I See Red - Everybody Loves an Outlaw

"MARYCAT, can you pass me the salt, please?"

Though I'd been keeping a weather eye on Cyan and MC, mostly because MC was still prone to small bouts of tears and moments of spacing out and because Cyan had a tendency to want to play with Maddox rather than learn French, I had to smile at the sight of my eleven-year-old holding the baby while trying to eat a veggie burger and fries.

"She's not giving up, is she?"

I recognized the voice, then jerked in surprise when I saw it was Jared. Uncomfortable, I shot him a tight smile, then said, "Jared! Hi."

His smile was more sheepish. "I know, I didn't call. I'm sorry. Things got crazy."

Oh dear, I hadn't even remembered him to be honest. Rex's little chat with me had kind of erased him from my memory.

"That's fine. I hope everything went well at the conference." *He hadn't lied about ghosting me.* I made sure to keep some distance between me and the counter he was leaning on. "Want a coffee?"

He nodded. "Please. That's your daughter?"

"It is." I smiled.

"She's not at school?"

"I decided to homeschool her."

He arched a brow. "Really? Why would you do that?"

"Because it's my choice?" I retorted wryly. "Because school was causing her anxiety and that's the last thing she needs right now?"

"School shapes minds," he disagreed.

And who the heck had asked for his opinion?

"I don't dispute that it does, but I just wanted a different path for my daughter." If I placed emphasis on the word 'my' well, so be it.

He raised his hands. "Sorry. None of my business."

"No," I told him sweetly. "It isn't."

"Look, I'm really sorry about not calling—"

"Honestly, no hard feelings," I replied earnestly, able to utter the words because there were zero hard feelings.

Hell, I felt nothing whatsoever, just discomfort that he'd come here, period, clearly hoping to get back in with me. Why that was, I didn't know.

"I was wondering if you'd like to go on another date?"

I shook my head. "I can't."

"Come on," he wheedled. "Friday night? I'll drive us to a club in Columbus. You can let your hair down and we can have some serious fun."

"Thanks, Jared, but I'm actually back with my husband."

Husband.

Not ex-husband.

It was the first time I'd said it out loud and it tasted damn fine.

His brows rose. "Seriously? I didn't realize you were even married."

"Seriously." I smiled at him. "We're working on things."

"Oh." His bottom lip popped out in an honest-to-God pout, and he murmured, "Hold the coffee? I just remembered I have to head back to work."

I rolled my eyes at the bullshit segue but found myself relieved he had somewhere else to be as I returned to cleaning the counter down from the lunch rush.

I didn't want to quit working at the diner entirely. Not only because

I found it soothing to be around normal people, doing normal things, but also because it was a chance for Cyan and me to have a break from each other.

The homeschooling was going surprisingly well, especially with Storm doing some of the classes, and now we were paying MC to teach her French, that made things a lot easier because languages had never been my strong suit.

So, while those classes happened, I took some time to just come here and be Keira, really. Not Mom, or Old Lady or wife, not cook or vacuumer, or math teacher or… the list was endless. Just Keira.

It was refreshing.

I worked with the wait staff to manage the place, formulating schedules, helping make stock orders, and did a lot of behind-the-scenes stuff. Today, Franny was out sick, though, so I'd asked MC if we could move tomorrow's class to now, while I worked her shift.

The door opened once more, and I turned to the entrance with a smile that slowly died.

She strode in like she owned the place.

Of course she did.

God, I hated her.

I didn't think I'd ever hated someone so much in my life.

Even though Storm's words were there to comfort me, Rex's too, and knowing full well that she was a liar, that didn't take away from the fact that she'd been the one to break apart my world and had done it with a comforting smile.

Kendra.

"You can walk back out the way you came in," I told her calmly. "You're not welcome here."

Kendra smirked. "I think Storm would disagree with me."

She was everything I wasn't. Always had been.

In high school, she'd been popular, somehow managing to cross the line between the Sinners and the regular kids, somehow being accepted where Jimmy had only been ostracized.

Of course, now I knew why.

She'd probably sucked, fucked, and bent over for any guy who'd get her into a party.

"I think he wouldn't. I think he'd be insane to disagree with me." I shot her a serene smile, even as my temper soared when she further ignored me by taking a seat at the counter.

Dressed to impress—if you were a hooker—she had baby pink platforms on her feet, at least seven inches in height, a tight white skirt, whose only deference to the weather outside was that it was ankle-length. A pink sweater covered her torso, beneath a fluffy pink jacket.

Hooker Barbie.

Especially with her new hair—bright, white blonde that she had in a high ponytail, which swung to and fro, whipping from side to side with each movement of her head.

She couldn't have been more eye-catching if she tried. At least, if she wanted to draw the attention of every guy in every room in every state in the country.

"I'd like a coffee," she murmured, placing her white pocketbook on the table.

"I'd like for you to get VD and die." I smiled. "We don't always get what we ask for, do we?"

"Tsk, tsk. Someone's grown a spine since I last saw you. Probably having to deal with that stupid girl of yours.

"Such a shame. I don't know how Storm managed without me." She shot me a pitying look. "He called me down here, Keira. He pleaded with me because he needs me."

Her audacity had me shaking my head. "Even before, I wouldn't have believed that. You know how?"

"You think I'm lying?" she scoffed.

"I know you are. Because if you ever inferred that Cyan was stupid," I hissed, low enough for my daughter not to hear even if I knew Kendra and I were drawing the post-lunch crowd's attention better than if I'd declared everyone's tabs were on the house, "Storm would decimate you."

Unashamed, unapologetic at being caught in a lie, she hitched a shoulder that somehow tossed the ponytail and set it swaying from side to side.

Like a pendulum, it entranced me, making my hands curl into fists as she declared, "We both agreed your parenting skills are quite weak. I can promise you that if I'd been blessed with Storm's child, I'd take care of her, make sure she didn't prefer to run away with dirty old men. I wish we'd been so lucky, but—"

"You're not wanted here, Kendra. You should leave." I said that with as much calm as I possessed, but I could feel my control starting to break.

Could feel the edges of it starting to turn frayed.

Giulia wouldn't have shown diplomacy in the face of Kendra's outrageous lies. She'd have thrown a plate at her. That would have been for the bitch's audaciousness in coming down to Coshocton.

Indy would have probably stuck a dinner knife in her face and told her to fuck off. Simply because she'd come to the diner.

Stone would have informed her there were a million things she could do with a scalpel and that she wasn't going to let the Hippocratic oath hold her back. That would have been payment for calling Cyan stupid.

And only the Lord knew what Amara would threaten.

Maybe a mixture of the above?

All to avenge the notion that Cyan *preferred* to be molested because I was a shitty mom.

Then there was Lodestar. Christ, I shuddered to think what she was capable of.

Five women. Each of them stronger than me. Every one of them raised not to give a fuck. All of them raised not to be dainty, delicate little girls who'd turn into future Stepford housewives...

"I think you'll find I am wanted here, Keira. What's a woman supposed to do when the love of her life calls her and pleads with her to come help him in his hour of need."

"Hour of need?" I demanded, wondering if she was talking about the padlock. Did she know about that? Did she know what it represented?

"I heard she's not doing well in school."

Wondering what that had to do with Storm's addictions, I asked, "How did you find that out? Listening in on a conversation with Rex while he was on the phone with Storm?" She smirked like she was going to twist my words, but I merely said, "I'm sure Rex would love to know that you're eavesdropping on private conversations."

Her eyes narrowed like I'd finally hit a nerve, and that it was that particular comment told me I'd hit the nail on the head.

Coldly, I informed her, "If you get out of here right now, I won't call Storm and tell him to haul your ass out of—"

"Look at you. You haven't changed a fucking bit," Kendra snarled, leaning into the counter, her tits quivering with her outrage as she planted them on there. I really hoped there was a splat of ketchup I'd missed mopping up. "Still running to Storm to clean up after you.

"Was it any wonder he strayed? Was it any wonder when you were a little fucking girl throughout your marriage? Storm won't haul my ass out of anywhere, bitch.

"He needs a real goddamn woman. A woman who can make him feel, who'll be his equal, not content to stay four paces back, looking at the back of his head because that's what her folks did.

"You disgust me," she said with a sneer. "I'm the whore. At least I own it. At least I know my worth. You? You're just a grown-up kid, unable to do anything herself without his interference. Is it any wonder that Cyan preferred to go and be with some old creep than stay with you—"

That was it—the straw that broke the camel's back.

I could deal with her character assassination.

Over the last few weeks, I'd come to accept that I *had* been like my mom, more than I appreciated, over the course of our marriage.

But I was a better mother than her.

I was and would always be that.

The edges of my control were no longer frayed. They sprang back, busted coil springs that couldn't take the strain anymore.

That swinging ponytail was all I saw, and my hand darted out. I grabbed it, then I hauled her face down into the counter. The heavy thud jolted everyone.

I'd be ashamed later that my daughter saw me do this, that she was a witness to the violence I told her she couldn't keep on perpetrating in school, but I was taken to the edge.

My temper shot after the last couple months of intense emotion.

My control shattered after I'd allowed this vindictive witch's lies to set me on a course of action that led to my daughter being kidnapped.

She screamed as blood spurted, scrabbling for something to hit me with but failing to find anything, so I did it again. And again. Each thud so inherently satisfying that I wondered why I hadn't punched Storm when I'd thrown him out. I'd just sat there, primly, much as my mom would have done, acting like a doll throughout the whole thing.

I got it now.

I finally fucking got why Storm had been proud of me when I'd dumped him.

Because it was me growing up. Me taking my life back into my control.

Me, me, me.

An adult, no longer a child.

Mature, not immature.

Strong, no longer weak.

Independent instead of dependent.

People jumped up unsure of what to do, some called out from the sides, but they didn't get involved. Either because I looked as irate as I felt or because I was the wife of the Prez of the Satan's Sinners' MC.

When I curled that goddamn ponytail around my wrist, her arms flared out, seemingly aware now that I wasn't about to let this lie. She knew I was going to fight her, and she wasn't wrong.

"Keira!" Jump called out.

"Stay out of this, Jump," I snarled as one of her flailing hands finally caught a sugar shaker, and when she hurled it at me, it clipped my shoulder but she was too close to really do much damage.

In retaliation, I dragged her forward, not her face into the counter, but her entire self over it. I hauled her by her hair, hearing that screech of agony, needing to hear that. Letting it feed the rage, letting it feed *me*. Nourish me where her lies had burned into me, decimating me like each one was tipped with acid.

"You think you can talk smack about my kid? You're mistaken," I rasped as I launched a punch at her.

My hold on her hair didn't give me much leverage, but it stopped her from being able to retaliate as well because I just tightened my grip and she screamed.

I kicked at her knees, wanting her to bow down before me, wanting her to look up at me, and as she did, she aimed a punch at my gut.

It figured that she'd be a better fighter than me, but years' worth of pulling my goddamn baby belly in came to my aid. She met with a wall of tensed muscles and though it socked some of the air from my lungs, it didn't incapacitate me.

Dragging her head back, so far back she screamed, I got in her face, and I did the most undaintiest, unladylike thing I could imagine.

I spat on her.

I literally spat.

The globule landed on her face as I hissed, "You're a piece of trash who got between a man and his wife. You're a whore whose only worth is how many cocks she can suck to pay her way.

"You made that decision, Kendra. You made the decision to whore yourself out while waiting on one man who belongs to someone else because, let's face it, you've been sniffing around Storm since we were both in high school.

"You've been the serpent in our Eden once. Well, it worked before, but it won't work this time."

Her arms came around my knees as she tried to push me forward, but it didn't move me. For a second I wasn't sure why, then I felt a hand slide around my stomach, and a wall of heat appeared at my back.

"My Old Lady's spoken, Kendra. I think we both know she's right."

Storm's voice was like a waterfall the size of the Niagara Falls pounding into a small house fire. It drenched everything in sight, my rage, my hurt, my fears, and it strengthened me.

He had my back.

Literally.

Figuratively.

All the ways in between.

And he'd called me his Old Lady.

I felt his protection, I felt his strength, but I didn't need it. Not wholly. I could stand on my own two feet and I could protect myself. Even more, I could defend Cyan and I could defend *us.*

It was wonderful, however, to have him support me. For him not to rage at me for causing a scene in one of the MC's businesses, for him not to weaken my stance in front of Kendra even though our daughter had witnessed something she never should have seen.

Not for the first time in Coshocton, I felt worthy.

I didn't feel like a failure.

"It's okay, baby, you can let go of her hair now."

Booted feet made an appearance in my peripheral vision, but it didn't break the deadlock between Kendra and me as we stared at each other with all the loathing we felt.

If looks could kill, we'd both be on a direct route to the morgue, but I watched as a hand reached out to unfurl Kendra's hair from my wrist.

"Slowly, Digger," Storm soothed, like I was a fractious animal. Like I was a beast in need of taming.

Was this how Giulia felt?

So out of control yet so *in* control too?

It was awe-inspiring, eye-opening, a true revelation.

As the hair disappeared, slipping from my grasp, Storm slowly backed me up by applying pressure through the hand on my stomach.

Kendra, of course, revealed her stupidity. She didn't wait for Digger to help her off her knees—a position she was probably way too comfortable being in—she surged forward like something from that goddamn Naruto show that Cyan loved so much and aimed herself at me.

But I was ready for it.

And not unlike my daughter, I channeled Giulia.

I headbutted her.

Sadly for me, I wasn't as proficient with the move, but as I knocked myself out, I had the delight in seeing that Kendra went down first.

I considered that a win.

TWENTY-EIGHT

STORM

PRESENT

AFTER A CHURCH FROM HELL, where Grim decided to start throwing his pacifier and everything fucking else out of his crib, bitching about how I was turning the Sinners into a riding club instead of a one-percenter MC, about how I was colluding with the sheriff, raking the past five months of my tenure through the coals like he could've done fucking better, it had been a relief to leave the clubhouse and to head for the diner.

Digger had come with, because MaryCat would be there, tutoring my kid in French, and when we walked in, the first thing we were greeted with was the sight of Keira slamming Kendra's face into the counter.

For a second, I wasn't sure where the hell I was. It was like a *déja vu* moment where we were all back in West Orange or something. But nope. This was Coshocton. Ohio. Not Jersey. So what the fuck was Kendra doing here?

Even through my confusion, I was goddamn happy to see my wife defending herself.

Defending us.

Protecting *us* with her fists.

Standing up for herself, and for our marriage and our family, because no way in hell would she have done this if Kendra hadn't said something about Cyan. Knowing how wicked she was, I didn't put anything past her.

Only when she hauled Kendra over the counter did I decide to step in.

Keira had never been in a fight in her fucking life. I made sure of that. She'd been mugged once before a Sinner helped get her out of danger, and a couple of other times it had almost happened, but a brother of mine had taken care of the situation for her before she even knew it. That was as close to danger as she had gotten. Kendra, on the other hand, wasn't of the same ilk, so I knew I needed to do something before my woman got hurt.

Hauling her back, I knew I should have foreseen Kendra's next move, but Keira's words were ringing in my ears, and when the sweetbutt surged forward, I didn't have a chance to twist Keira and me around so that I took the brunt of whatever the clubwhore was going to dole out because my woman acted first.

She headbutted Kendra.

The dull thud, the crack, resounded around the diner like a bullet gone wild, and everyone hissed like it was a boxing match as both women slumped, one in my arms, and one KO'd to the floor.

Cameras were whirring, guys who'd been taking bets groused when their pick lost, and I found myself wondering if the town of Coshocton was more interesting than I'd first thought.

I tipped K back in my arms, careful with her head as I told Digger, "Mop her up."

He nodded, but then approached me to mutter, "What do I do with her?"

"I need to speak with Rex."

Digger frowned. "Why?"

"I just do." I heaved a sigh. "Stash her in one of the rooms at the motel. Put a brother on her." I narrowed my eyes in thought. "Which one is less likely to cheat?"

"Techie."

I lifted my chin. "Put him on the case."

"Will do. You don't want her going anywhere?"

"Not without me telling her *sayonara* first."

"Got it." He didn't. I could tell he was confused, and who could blame him?

I'd have tossed her the fuck out faster than spitting on her like my wife had—dayum, that was a brutal move I didn't know she was capable of and didn't my pride in her just surge a thousandfold—but she was Bear's daughter.

Bear's fucking daughter.

Of all the goddamn bad luck in the world, Kendra was Sinner royalty. How the hell she'd turned into a cum dumpster instead of becoming an Old Lady was beyond my understanding.

Jaw tight, I turned to find MC and Cyan. Both of them were watching with big eyes. MC looked more impressed, whereas Cy just looked spaced. As if she'd turned on the TV expecting SpongeBob and had tuned into a live cage fight instead.

Couldn't blame her, not really.

I walked out from behind the counter, which ran in a circle in the center of the diner, my woman in my arms.

As I passed Jump, I groused, "Well fucking done, Jump."

"She told me to stay out of it! What was I supposed to do? Get in the middle of that catfight? I'd have lost an eye."

"Fucking pussy," Digger grumbled, and I couldn't argue.

Men moved out of my way as I surged through the crowd, some complained as I saw cash being passed over to the guys who'd gambled against Keira, and when I made it to Cyan's table, she jumped up without asking, quickly gathered her things together, then muttered an, "*Au revoir*," at MC.

As we headed out of the diner, Keira still out for the count, I moved over to the SUV before I realized I didn't have Keira's purse.

"Ladybug, can you go and get your mom's things?"

Cy nodded quickly, dumped her book bag on the ground, then ran into the diner, returning with the purse a few moments later. Moments in which I looked at the goose egg on K's forehead, at the delicate silk of her skin, how the lashes brushed against her cheekbones, how her parted lips were a cherry red as she breathed.

Christ, she was beautiful.

I wanted to eat her up like an ice cream sundae.

Making a mental note to teach her how to fight because the next time I saw her pull those moves I wanted to fuck her in the aftermath, I pressed a kiss to her forehead.

Not unlike Sleeping Beauty, she awoke at my kiss, mumbling, "Did I get her?"

I had to grin. "You got her, baby girl."

She harrumphed. "Good. Hurts."

"I know. Cy's getting your purse."

Keira nodded, then hissed. "Ouch."

"Yeah, it's gonna hurt for a while," I soothed.

As I placed her carefully in the passenger seat once Cy opened the car up, she grumbled a little, but as I delved into her purse to find the pills I knew would be in there, I came across a small wallet. It didn't seem to serve any purpose other than that of a photo book, but under the guise of finding the meds, I quickly flicked through it and found baby photos of Cy and me together.

Smiling because I hadn't known she'd taken them on the many circuits I'd danced around the fucking living room to music Cy and I had loved, I decided to stop being a creep and found the meds.

There was a half-empty bottle of water in the cup holder, so I dosed her up, placing the pills between her lips, then pressed the bottle to them as well.

She sighed. "Was worth it."

I snorted and let that be my answer.

"Mom? Are you okay?" Cy whispered, sounding a lot shaken, more than I'd have expected.

I wasn't sure if the nerves were because Keira had KO'd herself, or if it was because she'd seen her mom fight. I hoped it was the latter— mostly because Cy had declared that K wasn't a Sinner, but what she'd just witnessed proved otherwise.

Casting a look at my kid, I murmured, "She's fine, honey. We'll get her home, she'll sleep it off, and tomorrow… Well, in a few days, she'll be as good as new."

With Keira dosed up and squinting which let me know she wasn't drifting in and out of consciousness, I started up the SUV and drove us home. Each bump, she moaned, and if I went past forty miles an hour, she groaned and clutched at her gut like she was going to puke.

It took about twenty minutes longer than usual to get back because of how slow I drove, and we were all relieved when we got there.

As I moved around the fender, she held out her arms for me to carry her as she grumbled, "I can do it myself."

I grinned because her eyes were closed and she couldn't see me. "'Course you can, baby, but why would you when I'm here?"

"Damn straight," she muttered, sighing when I managed not to jostle her into my hold.

"Open the house up, ladybug," I told Cy, pleased when she obeyed, and went a step further—darted inside and opened Keira's bedroom door without my asking her.

I never went in here, not even to drop off Keira's laundry, so it was the first time I'd seen it since before we'd moved in and had the safe room installed. She'd decorated, choosing colors I would never have expected from her.

In the past, our bedroom had always been navy, plaid on the bed, the walls dark, the furnishings darker. Not that I really gave a fuck, of course, but it was clear she'd picked those colors, that style, for me.

That goddamn programming of hers.

I wasn't even sure if I'd known it had been as prevalent as it was until we'd broken up, until here and now where she led her own life and did things her way.

This room couldn't be more different.

The bedspread was a tropical kind of floral with goddamn toucans on it and palm leaves. The walls were a kind of peachy orange, and she had pretty pictures stacked on them. Some were large and central, others were small and she'd grouped them together. Most of them contained photos of our family, but the larger ones were decorative.

The peach rug was patterned with more palm leaves, the nightstands were rattan and there were gold lamps on them as well as some more framed photos, and she had a massive potted plant in one corner which wasn't doing that great, mostly because it needed more sunlight.

"You need to look after that one," Keira said with a sigh as I helped put her to bed.

"Huh?" I asked, unsure what she meant.

"I saw you looking at the palm. You've got a green thumb. How did I never know that about you?"

I twisted around to look at the doorway, found Cyan had disappeared which came as a surprise, but then I heard the door closing and realized she'd gone to lock it.

Because she was absent, I murmured, "I never used to, but it's a recovery thing."

One of K's eyes popped open and she squinted at me. "Like, a responsibility kind of thing?"

I nodded sheepishly.

"That's why you've got so many of them in your office!" she mumbled. "I wondered about that."

"Surprised you even noticed," I said wryly.

She shrugged, then instantly grimaced and reached up to rub her head. "It was a surprise to see so many. What's the next phase?"

"A dog or a cat."

A hum escaped her. "Cy will like that."

"You hate dogs and cats," I pointed out.

"I know I do," was her grumpy retort. "I know my own head, don't I?"

I laughed, enjoying her grouchiness. "That supposed to make sense?"

"I know what I like and don't like, I mean. But she's always wanted a dog."

"And you always said no."

"I did. But if it helps you, then I won't argue."

I licked my lips. "You'd do that for me?"

Both eyes opened, just a smidge, and she murmured, "You know I would."

My nostrils flared, and I told her, "I'm going to teach you how to fight." Her eyes popped open wider, and she winced, which told me her head was hurting bad. "Just so that, next time, you don't knock yourself out and I can fuck you while we're both riding the adrenaline."

A shocked gasp escaped her, and just when I thought I'd stunned her, she rasped, "I'd like that."

"It's a date, then," I told her.

"It is."

"You were hot as fuck today, Keira."

Her lips twitched at the corners. "I don't feel hot now."

"Well, you are to me." I leaned over her and pressed a kiss to the temple that wasn't decorated with a goose egg. "What did she say?"

"Is Cyan anywhere close?"

I peered around and not spying our kid, said, "No."

"That Cyan preferred London to me because I was such a shit mom."

My mouth flat-lined. "I'll deal with her—"

"You don't have to. I did." That she sounded smug had me laughing softly. "It felt good. I should have done that before." She heaved a sigh. "Now we're never going to make Cyan realize fighting isn't the answer."

"One fight doesn't make you Cassius Clay, babe."

She pouted. "I choose to think otherwise."

I leaned over her and pressed another kiss to her temple, murmuring, "You get some rest. I know your head's probably killing—"

"Cy has classes," she argued.

"I can figure it out."

"I want to prove that teacher wrong, Storm," she pointed out, grousing, "Cyan's smart as hell."

"We know she is." I hummed. "Tonight's Krav Maga anyway. You gonna be okay on your own?"

"Yeah." She turned on her side and muttered, "She always wanted you and could never stand that you picked me because I got knocked up."

My brow furrowed at that. "Whether you got pregnant or not, you were always going to be mine, Keira. I was too selfish to ever let you go."

I'd have let her walk away, go off to college, but even then, I'd have followed her. For a girl like her, college towns were dangerous. Who else would have kept her safe?

She sighed. "Kendra never got the memo."

Uncertain if I should continue, I hesitated a second, but then I dared to say, "Would you have let me go? If you hadn't gotten pregnant?"

Her stillness was an answer in and of itself, and as a lifetime of feeling like scum started to hammer at my temples, she rasped, "The first time I saw you, I knew you were trouble. I knew you were different. I knew my parents would never accept you. You scared me because I couldn't stop thinking about you. Never have been able to stop thinking about you since."

Hope started to fill me. "You should probably have walked the other way when you first saw me."

"Now you're just fishing for compliments," she grumbled. "I think the major reason we have such a problem is that women *can't* walk away from you."

"The only one I ever wanted did though," I told her softly.

She peeped up at me. "I did, didn't I?"

My lips curved a little. "You did."

"I'm back, though, aren't I?"

"You are," I confirmed, the words a croak.

"Then you have your answer, don't you?"

And I did.

It was all I deserved right now, but, when the time came, when I earned it, I knew she'd give me the words I needed to hear.

Knowing her head was aching, I slipped out of the room a few minutes later, finding Cyan sitting in the family room. She was on the floor, her knees to her chest, and I moved beside her.

"You okay, ladybug?" I questioned.

"I didn't like seeing Mom fighting."

"Thought you'd get a kick out of it."

"She's always so calm—" She bit her lip. "I guess I like that about her."

Because I understood, I murmured, "I think we both know it's unusual for her control to break. She and Kendra…" I hesitated. "They're not friends."

"I remember that lady. I didn't think I knew who Kendra was, but I do. Why was she here and why did they fight?"

"They went to school together." I stroked the crown of her head, sweeping the messy curls off her sweaty temples. "They never liked each other."

"Were they fighting over you?"

I shook my head. "It's complicated, honey. I think if there was one person in this world who shouldn't have picked a fight with your mom, it was Kendra. Today was her unlucky day."

"Is she okay?"

"Yeah. She just needs to sleep it off. Hurts like hell when you get a headbutt wrong."

Her eyes twinkled. "I wouldn't know that."

I smirked. "You're a born scrapper, ain't ya?"

"Maybe. Are we still going to Krav tonight?"

"If you want to."

"I do."

"Then Krav it is. Want something to eat?"

She pulled a face. "Does it have to be soup?"

I hid a grin. "No."

"I ate at the diner but I'm still hungry."

"Want a PB&J sandwich?"

"Yes, please."

I got to my feet and left her to her cartoons, but before I headed out the door, I said, "Your mom will always be your mom, and you can always go to her for whatever problem you have, but you have to bear in mind, honey, she's a woman too.

"She's not just your mother. She's my wife, she's MC's friend. We all wear a lot of hats, and it's normal that you only see her as 'Mom.' When she falls out of that pigeon hole, though, don't be surprised."

I left it at that, not wanting to make her more confused. Well aware that when therapy rolled around, Dr. Janowicz was going to hear some more crap about our family, crap that I loathed sharing but would so long as Cyan benefited from it.

The moment I'd learned Keira was pregnant, I'd vowed to myself that I'd be better than my mom, would be as good as Bear and Rene at the whole parenting thing. I wasn't sure if I lived up to their standards, but I had to try.

That was all you could do in this life, wasn't it?

Try your fucking best and hope that it was enough.

TWENTY-NINE

KEIRA

PAST

"GOOD LORD, KEIRA!" Mom declared as I burst through the front door, her hand clapping her chest. "You scared the heck out of me."

She'd asked me to go along to the church to take some sandwiches to Dad. He was working late this evening, and those were the best nights because I got to stay up a half hour later and watch TV with Mom.

I'd been pleased before, but now I was just…

I felt sick.

"Repent, Marjorie. You must repent your sins!"

Those words, her moans…

Fornication was bad, according to him.

What was worse?

Adultery.

I didn't like my father, and that had begun a long time ago before tonight. A lot of it was founded in his character, but in other aspects, it was about his hypocrisy.

He preached about turning the other cheek, but he was the first to speak ill of his flock at the dining table.

He talked about being generous, but he never gave the homeless guy who sat outside the coffee shop in town any of his spare change.

I knew his temper was mean, that he drank too much whiskey when the Dolphins played and when that happened, the next day, Mom usually had some bruises to cover up with makeup, I also knew that he didn't practice what he preached.

But this was just too much to process.

I stared at her a second, then, even though it probably wasn't wise, blurted out, "Dad was..." I swallowed, then whispered, "...fornicating with Marjorie Winters."

No surprise appeared in her eyes, but she stormed forward and grabbed me by the arm, hard enough to hurt, hard enough that her fingertips pinched as she held me in her clasp. "Did he catch you spying on him?"

"No!" I dragged my arm out of her hold. "And I wasn't spying. I just overheard them—"

She pressed a finger to her lips. "Don't say those words out loud again, Keira. Not to me, not to anyone, do you understand?"

I stared at her, bewildered and hurt at her tone. "I *don't* understand. How can I? Aren't you going to—" My mouth worked, but I recognized there was little use in finishing the question. Mom wouldn't divorce him. Dad wouldn't allow it. Mom wouldn't leave him. Dad would beat her first. I bit my bottom lip, then said, "It's wrong."

Her hand was softer as she reached up and patted my shoulder. "Men have urges, sweetheart. I'm thankful that he takes them out on someone who isn't me." My eyes flared wide at that, prompting her to tut. "Don't look at me like that, Keira. It's his soul on the line, not mine." She firmed her lips. "You'll understand when you're married. Men have dirty ways about them, ways that make you feel unclean. The day they find someone else to slew them on is a day worthy of celebrating. Now, I made meatloaf for us. Let's go eat."

Blankly, I watched her drift down the hall, as calm as you like, her destination dinner.

Her words disturbed me on a visceral level, but my biggest concern was whether she was right or not.

Was sex disgusting?

It looked… Well, on the videos, it looked messy.

Messy enough that even the memory had my nose crinkling with distaste. And the sounds the women made… were they in pain? Were the men hurting them?

Maybe, like Mom said, it *was* a blessing when a husband stopped wanting 'that' from his wife?

Uneasily, I dragged off my coat when Mom barked, "Keira, hurry! It's getting cold," and I toed out of my UGGs, before retreating to the kitchen.

Dinner awaited me, as did the one show we tended to watch on nights Dad worked late so he couldn't spew his disapproval at us over it—*Private Practice.*

As I zoned out while the episode played, I wondered how Dad could judge a TV show when he acted worse than the characters in the fictional series.

But that was the measure of the man, I supposed.

I was right not to trust him.

THIRTY

STORM

PRESENT

OVER THE FOLLOWING WEEK, Keira didn't pull away from me, which was my biggest fear after having come face to face with Kendra.

We didn't move closer, but that was okay too. She needed time, time to accept some things, time to see herself in a different light.

Life, as always, was busy. What with homeschooling Cy now, then the club and its many businesses, shit never quit, with Kendra remaining as much of a problem as a nagging tooth that needed extracting.

I had a couple of the guys who wouldn't get drunk on her pussy and wouldn't lose their minds watching over her ever since Rex had requested she stay down here for a few weeks until Giulia cooled off.

Apparently, a very pregnant Giulia was more of a hothead than a regular Giulia, which wasn't terrifying in the least.

Kendra had escaped down here, not come for a fucking visit, when Giulia had found her trying to come onto Nyx.

I didn't think Nyx had cheated, didn't think he even had fucking eyes for any other bitch. Hell, he was more whipped than I was for his Old Lady, so I thought Giulia had been jonesing to get rid of Kendra for a while, probably for Keira's sake, and had never anticipated that the snatch would run to Coshocton.

My Old Lady had said it herself—Kendra was the snake in Eden.

Even though Rex had requested I let her stay here for a couple weeks, I thought that was a fucked up thing to ask considering, so I'd had my brothers drive her over to Pittsburgh. With her a state away, I felt better, even if it made us a few brothers short as I had them keep an eye on her.

Still, gimme that over Keira finding out she was in the vicinity. The last thing I wanted was her doubting me. I'd never wanted fucking Kendra anyway, but that didn't mean Keira wasn't sensitive about that shit—rightly so considering our situation.

With all that crap going on, it was a relief to get my hands on something that needed repairing.

What was that saying? Idle hands were the devil's tools? Well, I didn't mind that so long as hard work kept me on the straight and narrow because, fuck, it was impossible to sleep some nights.

A soft wolf whistle stopped me thinking about how goddamn tired I was, and I smiled, peering up at the woman in question as she wandered into the kitchen.

"Well, hello, handsome," she teased, drooling over me like I was a Butterfinger she wanted to devour in two bites.

That soft purr had my cock reacting, but to be honest, I was rocking a semi nearly all the time I was around her. It didn't have the chance to get full blown anymore, because the padlock hurt too fucking much.

I smirked at her, then returned to fixing the garbage disposal unit. Until, of course, I felt her eyes on me. My smirk deepened and I asked, "You watching the show?"

"Never understood how a guy like you could be good at arguing about politics and be able to fix anything you put your mind to." She shook her head. "You never did fit any stereotypes."

"You should probably be glad about that rather than grumbling," I retorted.

"Not grumbling. Not really." She took a seat at the breakfast bar. "Anyway, don't let me disturb you."

I snorted when she settled in, reaching for an apple in the fruit bowl on the counter. The sounds of her teeth biting into the crisp flesh shouldn't have made me ache, but they really did. My body was messed up. My mind even more so.

The bitch of it was, this was like old times.

She'd often done this, watched me fix shit around the house. I knew it got her hot. Knew it and wanted to deal with the aftermath of it, but how could I? Would it be too much temptation? Would I beg her to unlock my cock, to let me slide into the haven between her thighs?

I always managed to sleep after sex, and I needed that something fierce.

But no.

I had to stay strong.

As I fixed the busted unit, I tried to think about what I should do.

This wasn't the first overture she'd made, but it was the first one when we were alone, and in the scheme of things, was pretty innocent.

Okay, her interest didn't feel innocent, but I wasn't about to complain, was I? My mom had raised many things, but a fucking fool wasn't one of them.

"I take it back."

"What do you take back?" I questioned as I finally got the unit parts collated into place.

"That I'm mad about you being the package." She squinted at me. "It's wrong how right you are. You should be in a magazine or something."

I snorted. "What kind of magazine? Addicts Unite?"

She frowned. "Stop it."

"Stop what?" I asked as I started adjusting the unit.

"Being so hard on yourself."

Taking my attention off of the parts, I shot her a look. "Honey, you need to accept that I'm always going to think I'm a piece of crap for letting you down."

"And you have to know that that hurts my heart to believe that you'll do that, Storm."

"Maybe the day I make it up to you is the day my opinion will change about myself."

She huffed out a breath, but simply said, "I don't think there's anything I can do to change that. Aside from loving you, that is."

That boded well, didn't it?

"Where's Cyan?" I asked after she fell quiet.

"At MaryCat's."

I arched a brow at the unit. "Not her day for French."

"Cyan wanted to play with Maddox."

My brows surged as I recognized that Keira clearly didn't think MC needed help with her personal monsters, otherwise she'd have been there to watch over the kids with her.

"It's a good day?"

A smile danced on her lips. "Nah. The PPD is… she's good right now. I knew a girl back in West Orange in the same mother and baby group who just slipped into it and then slipped out. I'm hoping that's how it's going to be for her.

"She's not checking out as much when I'm there, and I know things are easier all round. Digger's been so supportive and I know that's helped a lot."

"I'm glad you didn't have to go through that."

She pulled a face. "Me too."

"I'm surprised Cy likes playing with Maddox so much. I can't imagine her wanting to change diapers."

Keira laughed. "I told MC to give her the full experience."

"Ouch."

"She has to take the rough with the smooth," Keira joked. "Babies are cute, for sure. I just don't want her forgetting that they're not always cute.

"This can be her first sex-ed class. She doesn't have to know about how you get the baby in the first place to know that they're a lot of work."

I growled as a screw dropped loose, but asked her, "You and MC are getting to be good friends, aren't you?"

"She's very sweet." A soft breath escaped her, loud enough for me to hear it and recognize it as my arms strained while I tightened a couple of nuts and bolts.

That breathy gasp told me exactly where her mind was at, and it wasn't MaryCat.

I heard the stool scrape the tiles, felt the soft vibration of her footsteps before I could look away from my work. When I did, I watched her place one foot on either side of me as she swept down into a kneeling position, straddling me like she'd done a thousand times before.

I wanted so fucking badly to watch her lose herself in me. Christ, I wanted to lose myself in her. Nothing, and I meant nothing, felt better than slipping inside her. Than going home. Jesus, I hadn't been back there in a fucking lifetime.

"What you doing, baby girl?" I muttered, even though I knew the answer and kept my gaze focused on the sink and not the temptation she offered.

I knew how Adam fucking felt.

Her hands went to my belly and I realized my shirt had lifted. Her fingers traced the space, filtering through the soft happy trail at the center, before she murmured, "I miss you."

"I miss you too," I rumbled. "More than words can say."

She shivered a little. "Why did you have to go and fix things? Get all sweaty—"

"You'd prefer for the garbage disposal to keep on jamming?" I drawled, tilting my head forward to catch her eye.

"No. But you could have, I don't know…" She sniggered. "…Worn a massive hoodie or something. Covered up to hide all this fineness."

I grinned. "I feel like this is reverse sexism."

"Reverse it however you want, there's some sexing thing going on here for sure."

"Seeing as you're sitting on me, babe, I figured that out fast."

She smirked. "Quick thinker, that's you."

"The quickest."

"Just not with everything."

I arched a brow at that. "Is that a complaint?"

"Nope." She popped the P. "I never realized—"

Her words waned, and her cheeks turned pink. "Never realized what?"

"Nothing."

"Keira," I grouched. "Just tell me."

She shrugged, but her cheeks stopped being pink and flared into bright red.

"Keira?" I repeated. "You can tell me anything." Even something I didn't want to hear. "New phase in our relationship, right? We're working on something better, something different?" Something less like the marriage model her parents had lived.

Huskily, she mumbled, "Well, you always get me off twice. You know? Minimum?"

My dick went from a semi to rock hard, agony be damned.

God, I loved making her come. The lady turned into a vamp when she was choking on my dick.

"And you're hard a while…" She choked that out. "…so, I get to come that way as well."

"You're spoiled for my dick, huh?"

"Storm!" she declared melodramatically, making me laugh as her hand flared up to her chest.

"I swear, you were born to be a Southern belle, baby girl."

Her nose crinkled, but she muttered, "I think I'm just spoiled for you. I-I shouldn't talk about these things, but you always made me feel like your equal. I realize that now. It was on me for deferring to you when you lifted me up."

"When did I do that?"

"You do it with Cyan a lot. I'm not so noble."

I put down the wrench, resting it on my belly, well aware that put our fingers within inches of each other. "I just want to make sure she appreciates you, baby. She's so lucky to have you as her mom. I'm not about to let her treat you badly on my watch."

She shot me a shy smile. "Thank you."

"No need to thank me. It's the truth. I'll always be in your corner, even if you won't fight for yourself."

Her lip was sucked in between her teeth, and she gnawed on it before she rasped, "I really want to bone you right now."

"I'd kill for that to happen, honey. But Christ, August. I have to wait until August."

She pouted as her hand went to my dick. "This says otherwise."

"Bet your ass it does." I gritted my teeth. "You didn't know I made you that goddamn promise, but I did. I won't let you down again."

Her brow furrowed and I sensed her awkwardness, her hesitancy. It made me want to make things better. To take away all her worries. But that was the old Storm talking. Not the new one.

She didn't need me to come along and make everything better. She needed me to let her take her own stand. To have her own voice. To do her own shit.

More than that, she had to learn that my promises meant something. She had to come to accept that I wasn't the same man she'd married—I was stronger. I fought my demons rather than caving into them.

So, I sucked in a breath and waited. And waited. I stared at her with heated eyes, giving her the safe space she needed for her to ask me to get her off, but she just got pinker and pinker and more embarrassed.

When she scuttled to her feet, I slipped out of the cupboard, jumped up, and stalked toward her.

With big eyes, she looked up at me, her back to the breakfast counter, and I rumbled, "What's our rule?"

She swallowed. "Whatever I want, I can have."

"That hasn't changed, Keira."

When she licked her lips, my dick started weeping precum. I literally goddamn felt it. Fuck, the pain was so pure, it made me feel high. Which was a massive fucking problem.

I shuddered, holding back barely as I placed my hands either side of her on the counter, pinning her in place. "I will always give you what you need."

Her mouth quivered. "What if that's you?"

"Then you can have me." I tipped my head. "That why you've gone all shy on me, sweetheart? Thought you stopped turning pink on me back when you were twenty."

Her nose crinkled at the bridge once more. "When I got pinkeye because cum got in it? Yes. That solved me of all embarrassment. Standing there stark naked, Cyan latched onto my breast because we woke her up, you pouring saline into my eye—"

My lips curved. "If memory serves, didn't you get your period?"

"Yes, because God was kind to me that evening."

I snickered. "We survived that, though, didn't we? Although I'll admit I was sure you wouldn't look at me in the face ever again."

She snorted. "I was mortified."

"You never have to feel that way with me."

A sigh escaped her, and she stepped closer to me, pushing her forehead against my chest. "I've spent so many months hating you, Asher. It's… I feel like I'm letting myself down, but then I look at you and I'm like, 'Girl, why the fuck haven't you hopped on that dick of his?'" She rocked back to scowl at me. "You ruined me for orgasms."

My lips twitched. "I didn't mean to."

"Well, it's not something one aims for in a marriage, is it?" She huffed. "Ruination of a wife by sex?"

"Every man should aim for that," I said dryly, but I leaned down and pressed a kiss to the top of her head. "We take this at your pace, K."

"I know that," she grumbled. "I'm the one who started this, and now I'm backing off like I'm nineteen again." She rolled her eyes. "I'm supposed to be growing up—"

"Yeah, you've got that in your head. I never asked you to do that. I love you as you are."

Her brow furrowed. "What if I don't love me as I am? And that sounds whiny. Jesus. I'm not whiny. I refuse to be whiny—"

"You need an orgasm. It's been a tough couple of weeks. You're stressed about classes with Cy and everything that's going on with Dr. Janowicz." 'Everything' being yesterday's recommendation that we start couple's therapy. "Then there's the diner and the club—"

She nodded. "Maybe I wasn't born to be First Lady."

I grinned. "You were born to be mine. That means you were born to be First Lady."

"I love it when you say things like that." She shivered. "But that was never the problem between us, was it? I was always yours, you were never mine."

The words stung because they weren't true. I licked my lips, needing to share something with her. "This isn't going to make it any better, Keira. But every time I cheated, I thought they were you. I thought I was reaching for you, I thought we were together..." My mouth twisted. "I've only ever seen you. That's what makes it so fucking laughable.

"I should never, ever have cheated, but I did because I'm a fucking idiot. Because you're perfection, and I've knocked your self-confidence and your self-esteem, and all because I got high, some clubwhores took their chances and—"

"Their chances?"

I arched a brow at her, surprised that was the one thing she picked up on. "You know what they're like. They were hoping I'd brand 'em."

Her mouth tightened. "And you wonder why I hate the club lifestyle."

"It's better here," I appeased. "I think you'd like it. There are more Old Ladies than clubwhores, and I think Cyan needs to have more of a social life outside of gymnastics and Krav. Maybe she could make more friends there.

"We can't cut her away from kids entirely, and it's not like they're gonna bully her for being a Sinners' kid when they're Sinners themselves."

"True. We can try." Her lips parted. "I think we need to promise not to keep secrets from each other anymore.

"The reason you were at the clubhouse was to get high. If I'd known you needed to get high, I could have—" She swallowed thickly. "I'd have been there. I'd have been what you needed, Storm."

"I didn't want to taint you with that."

"You tainted me anyway." Her eyes were big in her suddenly pale face. "You've always wanted me to stay pure, but I think we both know I don't want that anymore.

"You said something back at Rachel's house. It made me think you held back on me—"

"I did," I admitted. "I never wanted to scare you."

"Then I don't want you to do that. I want the real Storm."

My jaw tensed. "I can't give you that. Not until August. But I can give you as much of me as I'm able.

"My promise to you supersedes my pleasure, but it doesn't supersede *yours*. Whatever you need from me, you can have—"

"Just not penetration."

"Yes. No penetration."

"Funny how this promise is for my sake, and I'm the one suffering."

"Trust me, babe, you're not the one suffering."

Her nostrils flared at that. "Show me your dick," she demanded.

I narrowed my eyes at that bossy tone, surprised and kinda turned on. Enough that I backed off and said, "Let me wash my hands."

She nodded. "Be quick about it."

Chuckling at her sass, I retreated, soaping them up before I twisted around, returned to her side, and unfastened my pants, freeing my cock.

I'd never worn boxer briefs until recently, so I saw her surprise when I reached into my Calvins, pulling out my shaft, revealing a cock that looked fucking outraged at being caged.

Bright red, silky white precum slathered around the tip, making the padlock gleam in the light. It was a fucker to keep clean, but I considered that another punishment.

Handling the bastard was hell on earth.

"Oh, God, Storm," she said thickly, wobbling back against the counter as she stared at it. "August?" she rasped.

"August." I allowed myself the only touch I permitted—I reached down, grabbed my balls, and yanked on them hard. Hard enough to clench my ass, hard enough to hiss and rock onto my toes with the pain.

"Why do you have to hurt yourself?" she moaned. "I hate that you're doing this to yourself."

"Because I need to break the habit. I need to be grounded, and this works." I swallowed. "I will probably always wear this, K—"

Her eyes rounded. "You can't be serious. Forever?"

"I'll chop the fucker off before I cheat on you, and this way, you'll always know I stay true to you because you'll have the key."

Something flickered in her gaze, something hot and needy, something that looked very much like *want*. She liked the idea of that, so I ramped it up.

"This dick is yours, K. Every fucking inch of it. Your goddamn toy, no one else's—"

She released the softest of moans, and precum dripped from the tip onto the kitchen floor. When she licked her lips, I yanked on my balls again, before I manned up and stepped toward her.

Gravity made my cock bob with the weight, which was an extra kind of pain, and each time it did, she tracked it with her eyes.

I felt her gaze like a lick to the tip so knowing that I needed to change the narrative before I fucked up my promise to her, I rumbled, "Is that pussy wet, baby girl?"

"It's always goddamn wet around you."

Music to my fucking ears. "You gonna let me christen this kitchen by eating you out on the counter?"

Her mouth pursed, but she surprised me by hauling her ass onto it, plunking herself down and narrowing her eyes at me. "Well?"

I grinned at her, then reached for the waistband of her yoga pants. "Want me to cut these off you?"

Her eyes flared wide in surprise. "No! I like these pants."

"I do too. Your ass looks fine in them. Would still cut them off just so—"

"No. No cutting," she hissed, her hand splatting against my chest. "I'll get some shorts you can wreck next time."

Next time.

Confident I could give her what she needed, I let the elastic pop against her stomach, then rolled it down. She put one foot on a stool, then the right one on the other, and made a bridge so that I could drag them over her ass.

When her pussy was bare to me, my nostrils flared at the juicy cunt that should never have known another's touch but, thanks to my own idiocy, had.

Well, I'd fucked up. I begged for second chances. But Storm 2.0 would never make the same mistake twice.

As I dragged them clean off, I demanded, "How many do you want?"

A whimper escaped her. "Do we have to do this?"

I caught her eye. "How. Many?"

She gulped. "Three."

I nodded. "Three orgasms it is."

A shaky moan escaped her as I loomed over her, and when my finger traced over her folds, she released a high-pitched sob that had her planting back onto the counter, her fist to her mouth.

I reached up, grabbed that fist and said, "Cyan ain't here, baby girl. You can scream as loud as you want."

"Fuck," she said thickly.

God, I wished.

Her hips started rocking with just the barest touch, and I knew why she'd asked for three.

One to take the edge off.

One to feel good.

One to savor.

Mouth watering as much as her pussy, relieved that I could still inspire this kind of need in her, that I hadn't broken us that fucking much, I let my finger rub over her slick clit.

"I fucking love this pussy, K," I rumbled, "so wet and hot and always so fucking juicy for me. My dick misses its home so goddamn much.

"I wanna fuck you so bad, baby girl. I want in you more than I want my next breath." She gave off a soft mewl as I pressed harder on her clit. "You thinking about that?

"About me sliding into you? Filling you full? Or are you thinking about how my dick will only ever belong to you? About how you own it, about how you have the key and only *you* can unlock it—"

She groaned as her hips bucked upward.

My supposition confirmed, I knew that most dirty talk in the future would revolve around her owning my dick.

Duly noted.

As her pelvis rocked back and forth, I slipped those fingers down to slide into her. Her muscles clung on as I ground the base of my hand against her clit, knowing she'd feel empty and would need some pressure there now.

She heaved a sigh, her ass still high as she ground against me, rocking harder and harder, getting herself off as much as I was.

"I want to own your dick," she whispered, voice fierce, surprising me because she'd never been a very verbal kind of lover. She squeaked and moaned, but I knew that having Cyan around had made her naturally quiet in the sack.

God, I wanted to make her scream so fucking bad.

It was time to rip her inhibitions away, time to worship this woman how she'd always deserved.

"You do own it."

"I hate that you— I hate that it's there, but I want this key—" She groaned, long and low, hips bucking faster and faster as I fucked her with my fingers, giving her what she needed as best as I could.

Hell, I'd grab a dildo next time.

Making sure that my woman was satisfied was my number one priority.

"I need your mouth on me, Storm. Please, love. Please. I need your—"

Love.

How the fuck I didn't detonate then and there was a miracle in itself.

I grabbed her ass with my free hand, gripping the firm curves and letting my fingers bite into her ripeness. I urged her back down against the counter, and she groaned as I hovered over her cunt, letting my breath wash over it.

"You smell divine, Keira. You smell like mine."

She squealed when my lips dropped onto her clit, and as I sucked on it, hard and heavy, the squeal morphed, turning high-pitched and hungry. She didn't beg, but she rode my face, not passively taking my kiss, but actively demanding more.

This was new.

I fucking loved it.

She wriggled against me, taking everything she needed, and I wasn't surprised when the power trip had pleasure bombing her inside out.

Her cunt squeezed my fingers hard and I moved faster, scissoring them wide, fighting that tight clench to make her feel fuller, wanting to give her as much as I could to satisfy the need I knew had been growing.

Twisting.

Writhing inside her.

Unfulfilled for over two years because I'd fucked up.

I snacked on her cunt, slurping up her juices, savoring them, the taste of them, the taste of her because I'd been so fucking sure I'd never get a taste of this again.

I fucking drowned in her, wished I could drown like this for real because this would be the way to fucking go.

She came again, but I ignored her request for three total and took her up to the fourth one. That she got there told me how fucking horny she'd been and as she peaked that fifth time, I vowed I'd never make her wait that long again.

As she screamed herself hoarse, her hands came to my hair and she tore at it, one hand dragging me against her cunt, the other pulling me away.

Realizing she was greedy for more but was still sensitive, I started to pull back. Dropping kisses to her clit, nibbling on her labia, letting my tongue circle her slit as I retracted my fingers, pressing a biting kiss to her inner thigh before I slowly moved into a standing position.

That had been hell.

Purely, blissful hell.

I wasn't sure how I hadn't come other than the fact that my willpower was getting stronger, but as I stared at my Old Lady, saw that spaced out look on her face, I knew I'd endure this torture every day until August, because sometimes, being the best man you could be involved taking one for the team, and making sure the woman you adored didn't suffer for your mistakes.

STORM

PAST

"WHAT THE FUCK did you do this time?"

Scarlet scowled at me before she flipped me the bird. "I didn't ask you to come down to the jail."

"Unlucky for you, the club lawyer knows my fucking number." Even unluckier, Scarlet seemed to have a season pass for this place. "Anyway, I'm not here about that. I'm here about Keira."

"What's your bitch wife got to do with anything?"

I growled under my breath. "How many goddamn times do I have to tell you not to call her that?"

"What are you going to do, Storm?" she taunted. "How are you going to make me stop calling her exactly what she is? That head of hers is so goddamn big it's a wonder she can suck your dick without—"

"Shut the fuck up, Scarlet. If you want me to bail you out of here, shut the fuck up," I snarled.

Her smirk didn't die, and that was what drove me crazy about her. She never gave up. She was relentless. Like a demented Energizer bunny who spat nails and harsh words.

"Maybe I got other people who'll get me out of jail, hmm? Maybe I don't need my pussy big brother to bail me out. Remember, I wasn't the one who called you."

I ignored her taunts, and demanded instead, "What are you even doing in here?"

"None of your business."

"Where are these other fuckers who are supposed to be bailing you out, huh?"

"They'll be along soon enough."

"Who are they?"

"My employers."

"Your bosses?" My eyes bugged. "You expect your bosses to bail you out of jail?" Jesus H. Christ, and I thought she was insane before.

"It's none of your business," she repeated. "Now fuck off. I don't want to deal with your shit today."

"What did you say to Keira, Scarlet?" I demanded, ignoring her. "She fucking left me again."

Scarlet snorted. "How many times is she going to leave you before you get a goddamn clue, Storm? You're not good enough for her.

"I don't know what the hell it is about your dick that gets all the chicks panting, but fuck, quit it with her, let her go back to that ivory tower she lives in, and bang someone who's as much of a no hope as you."

"Keira and I will work out fine if you'd keep your nose out. Hell, you only ever come around to make trouble. Trust me, if I'd been there, I wouldn't have let you through the front door."

"That's brotherly love for you," Scarlet mocked with a false yawn. "You should be grateful I got rid of her for you."

"Grateful?" My heart started pounding and, I swore to fuck, that if she wasn't six feet away and behind bars, I'd have throttled her.

Scarlet was the only woman who made me forget she possessed a vagina.

If I could have beaten the shit out of her, I would've. But I'd never beat a woman.

Never.

Only around her did I have to repeat that mantra.

"Why the fuck do you hate me so much, Scarlet? Why the fuck do you think you can just wander into my life to stir shit? I never see you unless you're hanging around to cause trouble."

She smirked at me. "What did Prince used to say?"

"That if you were a guy, your road name would be Troublemaker." I grunted. "Not hard to understand why. The hell are you bringing that fucker up for anyway?"

Her smirk deepened. "Mom never told you?"

"Told me what?"

"Ha! She didn't. Christ, she hated you more than she hated me, which is really saying something."

Her words didn't rake at me like they once might have done. It was only when I'd cut the old bitch from my life for good that I'd come to realize I'd have taken my mother's hatred over her love any day of the fucking week.

Against the cinder blocks, Scarlet's hair was currently her natural color—a rich, glossy black. She didn't have the streak like me, but the rich obsidian looked like silk against the coarse concrete.

Dressed in an orange D.O.C jumpsuit, she wore it with a panache that spoke of someone who'd worn it many times before. Her feet were crossed at the ankle, her hands tucked into the pockets as she leaned against the wall.

Her expression was that of tedium, like I was boring her. Like my presence didn't matter worth a damn to her.

It didn't hurt, not when I knew it to be true. Knew it, in fact, and was glad about that.

We'd always fought like cats and dogs. For all that she tried to tear me down, there was a reason I had a family back at the clubhouse and she was barely tolerated.

"What did you say to Keira?" I repeated, trying to keep shit on track. Mostly, that was why I was here.

Keira wouldn't answer her phone, and I was getting sick of trying to figure out where she was at. I'd hit up her friends, but they weren't saying shit—it was desperation that had me calling, because I knew they'd dumped her when news of her pregnancy had spread around school before graduation. I knew her parents wouldn't let her in. She wasn't even at the motel where she'd taken to hiding out the last few times she'd run off.

Now she was out of school, and stayed mostly at home, I'd stopped using Jimmy to trace her, but I knew I had to keep an eye on her again. She'd proven herself to be a runner, and while that was her prerogative —you couldn't stop an angel from flying—I had to know where she was.

I needed to know she was safe.

That meant, on top of the prospecting, Jimmy was going to have to start following her around when I was too busy with club business to trail her.

Shit with Grizzly was getting intense right now. We were having problems with the *Famiglia* buying up parcels of land in Jersey and thinking that they owned the keys to the kingdom as a result.

That wasn't how territory worked.

"I said what had to be said," she retorted, wafting her hand and disrupting my thoughts. "That she'd be better off without you in her life, of course. Apparently she agreed if she left you. Again." She snickered. "What is that now? Four times?"

"She's adjusting."

"That's what happens when you aim for someone who's too good for you. You have to stay among your own pond slime. You won't be disappointed that way."

"Spare me your opinions. If you've got something to say, say it."

"What do you see in her?" Scarlet queried, her confusion clear. "I don't get it. She's not your type at all, and she's that kind of boring bitch who'd stay a virgin until she found Mr. Right so she can't have been good in the sack and couldn't have twisted you around her finger with her cunt. What is it about her that makes you forgive her for making you look like a joke?"

"You wouldn't understand."

She hopped to her feet, loping over to me with all the grace of a predator on the hunt. I recognized that expression, recognized it and gripped my hands to the bars so that I didn't try to strangle her.

"Wouldn't I?" she intoned softly, staring up at me, eyes gleaming with curiosity.

"Have you ever loved anyone or anything other than your-fucking-self, Scarlet?" I retorted.

"Only person in this world who'll look after me is me, Ash."

"You're so wrong. If you'd been anything other than a bitch, I'd have loved you instead of being glad your ass is in jail." I scoffed. "Remember how fucking happy I was when Mom landed up in here? Yeah, that's how I feel about you now. It's not like you can mess with my goddamn life if you're behind bars."

"Oh, don't try to challenge me. You know how much I love a dare," she mocked. "Come on, Asher. Tell me what it is about Ms. Goody-Two-Shoes that gets your dick in a knot. I wanna know."

"Why? So you can use it against me?"

"I wanna know," she barked. "What is it? You're ashamed of your feelings for her, is that it? You think that—"

My mouth twisted into a snarl. "She's the exact fucking opposite of you," I spat. "She's the exact opposite of Mom. She's no bitch in the clubhouse. No whore or Old Lady. She's good, Scarlet. *Good.* You should understand that seeing as you're the complete goddamn opposite.

"You know when she sees some homeless guy in the street? She gives him money, doesn't pour her coffee into his cup of quarters. She holds her friend's hair back when they're puking up their guts, doesn't dunk their face into the toilet. She doesn't do drugs, doesn't smoke, doesn't whore herself out.

"She's normal, Scarlet. She's normal. And she's good. And she's kind and sweet and doesn't have a goddamn criminal record." I leaned into her, aware her eyes were surprisingly big and that, for once, her trap was shut. "So yeah, I love her. I ain't afraid to admit that. I ain't afraid to chase after her when she spooks because anyone in her right mind would tear off at the shit I have to offer her.

"A bitch who wants me, who wants a Sinner, who wants to be tied to me, is the exact opposite of what *I* want in a wife, so if that makes me goddamn whipped, I'll take it.

"But whatever you did, whatever you said, whatever you're thinking of doing to destroy my marriage in the future, keep it locked in your head, because if you ever come between Keira and me again, I *will* kill you.

"See, all this time, I've been acting like you're my sister. Like I should care about you. Like I should watch out for you. But you said it yourself—you don't look at me like that. You think everyone's out to get you, but guess what, Scarlet? They only fucking hate you because you're the biggest cunt in the Tri-State area.

"You're meaner than a rabid fucking raccoon, and everyone hates you. They always have, and that's on you. It's always been on you. So, come between Keira and me again, I'll end you and no one will give a fuck. They'd probably be happy that you're dead.

"I'm telling you here and now, I see you again? I'll make sure you regret it. You ain't my sister anymore, Scarlet. You just cut the ties that bind, because bitch, I'm sick of your sorry ass. You're as much of a liability as Mom, and I got rid of her years ago, I don't need a miniature version fucking up my life. Not when I've got a kid on the way. So, nice knowing you, Scarlet, but the next time I see you, I hope it's in hell."

She waited until I was standing in the door to rumble, "If it is, then I guess we'll be able to play happy families with Mom and Dad when we're all down there."

Like a dumbfuck, I frowned and twisted around to look at her. "You say that like she even knew who donated sperm to the sorry cause of making us."

A fly in her web, I saw it too late. "Oh, I know. He told me."

I narrowed my eyes at her as I returned to the bars. "Who?" Then, I scoffed. "As if you fucking know. You and your goddamn games, Scarlet—"

"Let me guess, you're hoping it's Bear, ain't you? Hoping that's why he took us in." She grinned, smug and precocious because she knew something I didn't.

I refused to admit that I had always hoped Bear was my biological father, even if it was the truth.

"As if she'd know who knocked her up."

"Oh, apparently they were quite tight for a while. Exclusive. Never his Old Lady, but definitely his bitch."

"Who the fuck are you talking about?"

She smiled at me. "Prince."

"Prince is our father?" I pshawed.

"Yep."

She believed it. That much was clear. The malice in her eyes was eager, hungry. The predator in her scented prey, but I was done with being her whipping boy.

"What's the end game here, Scarlet? Why are you telling me this?"

"Wasn't he the one who got you hooked on meth?" She tapped her chin. "I'm pretty sure that's the same guy."

My jaw worked. "Why are you telling me this? You think I give a shit about who our father is?"

She shrugged. "Nah. Just wanted to rip away any hopes and dreams you had of dear old dad being Bear... instead he's the junkie VP who got you hooked on the same stuff as him." A laugh escaped her. "Your poor kid. She's got a real prize for a dad, hasn't she?"

My fingers slipped through the bars faster than she expected, but years of working for Grizzly, of fighting with my brothers, hadn't exactly made me slow. I grabbed her wrist, jerked it out from between the bars, then pushed it backward, using a bar as a fulcrum to bend it further.

As she let out a yelp, her eyes wide as, with the other hand, she tried to claw at me, I rasped, "When you die, Scarlet, I hope you remember me. I hope I'm the last person you think of. The one man who'd have loved you unconditionally. Who wouldn't have wanted you in his life for your snatch. Who'd just have loved you and would have been there for you regardless of the crap you pulled—" I put more pressure on her wrist so that the bone was close to snapping. "—instead, you treated me like shit so I should treat you like shit too..." She moaned with pain as I took it deeper, to the brink, before I leaned in and whispered, "Leave my family alone, Scarlet. If you don't, I'll end you."

THIRTY-TWO

KEIRA

PRESENT - EARLY JUNE

I Promise - Radiohead

WITH AN EVENING of watching Storm's favorite movie—*Die Hard*—for the tenth time behind me, I was deeply asleep and resting like a champ after Storm had gotten me off before bed. As a result, the shrill cry didn't penetrate my dreams, but the scream did.

I jerked awake, sitting upright, eyes flaring wide as my feet hit the floor and I pretty much flew out of the bedroom. Storm was already there, his back to me as he tunneled through the door to Cyan's room, and that was when I saw her thrashing around like she was in the middle of a fight.

A howl escaped her.

A howl that would haunt me until my dying day.

Unlike me, who froze in the damn doorway, Storm was there. He didn't touch her, didn't try to calm her, just barked, "Cyan. He's dead! He's dead and gone and he can't hurt you."

Whatever I expected him to say, it wasn't that. I surged forward, wanting to help, but he grabbed me and held me back.

She started sobbing and the sounds of her terror had me cursing Dr. Janowicz.

This week had been hell.

Literal hell.

And it was that bitch therapist's fault.

They'd been revisiting the day that London had taken her, and the hardest thing of all? Telling Cy that the thing she needed to discuss with a therapist to get over it, she couldn't. If she did, she'd implicate Amara in a murder charge.

I'd never felt so guilty, but Amara had saved Cyan, she'd goddamn saved her, and my kid was too smart not to understand but that didn't mean it wasn't messing with her.

Patient privilege would protect her, but... I understood why Storm wasn't about to let things rest on that. He'd been raised not to trust anyone in authority, and that he was going to see a shrink at all was a testament to the love he had for his daughter.

Huh.

How did I just realize that?

A little mad at myself for failing to spot the massive sacrifice Storm was making by talking about things brothers in an MC didn't share with anyone in a position of power, I studied Cyan once more. This was the fourth nightmare, and each was getting progressively worse, like her subconscious wasn't happy about being denied.

"Cyan!" Storm barked, jolting me from my thoughts. "Cyan, it's Dad! It's time for school."

Surprised by the tactic, I found myself awestruck as it calmed her down.

"School's starting in twenty minutes, ladybug. You need to wake up or we're going to be late." As he spoke, he took a seat at her side. "You don't want to be late for school. We'll get in trouble."

After a couple minutes, time spent with my heart in my throat, a groggy sound escaped her. "Daddy?"

He hummed. "Yes, honey."

She blinked sleepily. "What time is it? Are we late for school?"

"No, Cy. You were having another nightmare."

Silence, then... a sharp sob escaped her. "I remember."

I bit my lip as I stepped forward. "It's over now, sweetheart. It's all done."

When she started crying, hurling herself against her dad's chest as he absorbed her into his embrace, I wanted to sob with her, but that wouldn't do her any good.

I needed to make this better, but how could I do that when the one thing she really needed to get off her chest was the one thing she couldn't talk about?

Agitated, lost, and heartbroken, I rasped, "Baby, would you talk about that day with your dad and me?"

It took her a few minutes to reply, and when she did, her voice was soggy and pain-filled. "W-Will you hate me if I tell you?"

Storm's voice was fierce, ferocious as he snarled, "We will never hate you. Never. Do you hear me, Cyan? You could kill a man and I wouldn't hate you. I'd help you dig the bastard's grave.

"You will never earn my hatred. I will love you no matter what you do or say and, until the day I die, I will always make sure you have a safe place with your mom and me. Do you understand?"

Her cheeks were raw from tears, her eyes still wild from her dream. "I understand. I love you, Daddy."

"I love you too, baby."

"Mommy—" I loved it when she called me that because she used it so rarely, but it was bittersweet because it came when she was at her most vulnerable. "—I love you too."

"Sweetheart, I love you," I told her, just as fiercely as her father.

Storm hefted her into his arms, and I knew what he was doing so I backed away, watching as he headed down to my bedroom, the only room with the bed big enough for all three of us.

I darted around him to quickly sort out the duvet, and then as he walked in, I turned back to switch off the light in her room and in the hall.

When I made it back, he was on his side of the bed, the left, Cy in the middle, and I closed the door behind me as I headed to my side. Switching off the light as I sank between the sheets, Storm drew them over us.

It had been a long time since we'd had to do this, but it was totally the right call.

Cyan turned to face me. "I don't want Amara to go to jail, Mommy."

I hated that she had to be silenced to protect Amara, but I—

God.

I was so fucking lost with this.

"You're protecting her, like she protected you," Storm told her gruffly, somehow knowing exactly what to say. He turned on his side, too, curving his body around our little girl, murmuring, "I wish you could tell the truth, Cy, but this is a safe space. We won't judge you, and you can tell us anything and everything you want."

It took her a while, so long I would have assumed she'd fallen asleep if she hadn't been as tense as a board at my side. Just as I started to fear that she wasn't going to say anything, she released a shaky breath.

"He started touching me on the ride to the motel. He'd done it before but not like this, and he started talking about things I didn't want to talk about.

"When we got there, he took all his clothes off and told me that I needed to nap, but I didn't want to—" She gulped. "He started touching me, and I screamed, I screamed so loud." A sob escaped her. "He shoved a hand over my mouth and he punched me."

"God, he must have hurt you, darling," I whispered, moving nearer to her, wanting to hug her but knowing, as much as Storm did, that she didn't want to be touched. We were within touching distance, but not that close where skin met skin.

"He did," she whimpered. "He punched me between my legs."

A snarl escaped Storm but he softened it toward the end when she tensed. "You did good for screaming, baby."

Only, she shook her head, whispering, "It hurt so bad that I couldn't scream, and I started sobbing on the bed, but he left me alone.

"When I was better, I started screaming for real, and that was when someone knocked at the door." Cyan sucked in a shuddery breath. "Amara came in like, like, like Wonder Woman. She just took over, and he didn't know what to do.

"She hit him and hit him and hit him, then Rain was there, and he held me as she carried on hitting him. He held me so tight and I didn't feel so afraid anymore.

"My mind was all over the place, but when he held me, it was like he squished all my thoughts together again. Amara was… I don't want her to get into trouble because of me."

"She won't," Storm promised.

My eyes were wet as I leaned in and pressed a kiss to her forehead. "You can talk about this any time you need to with us." I might need a quart of vodka afterward, but that wasn't her problem, just my liver's.

"I don't want to talk about it."

"You say that but your mind says otherwise. Why would you be having bad dreams if you weren't thinking about it?"

She wriggled on the bed, moving higher and closer toward me. Her mouth went to my ear, and she covered it with a clammy hand as she whispered, "I-I touched myself there. Where he did."

"With a tampon? Or because it feels good?" I whispered back once Storm rolled off the bed, leaving the door open as he headed toward the bathroom, giving us the privacy Cyan clearly wanted, but didn't know how to ask for.

Cy nodded. "I didn't mean to, but it did feel good."

I released a shaky sigh. "You need to tell Dr. Janowicz that, baby. The bit about touching yourself."

"Why?" she whined. "I don't want to."

"Because when you touched yourself there, something in your head created a connection between what happened with… that day. You need to break that connection because in the future, there'll come a time where you want to do that freely.

"You don't want to associate the bad things with that, because it's a wonderful feeling and I'd hate for him to spoil it for you." When she stayed silent, I prompted, "Will you promise to talk about it with Dr. Janowicz? It's something about that day you can discuss."

"I never talk about how I got away."

"Does she ask?"

"Yes. But I say I can't remember."

I nodded. "I wish you could tell the truth, baby."

"I don't want Amara to have to leave. I want her to be happy."

"She is. She's with Quin and Hawk now," I told her easily.

"Why does she have two boyfriends?"

My lips curved. "Because she wants to?"

A 'huh' escaped her, then the door to the bathroom opened and we both heard Storm's padding footsteps. I was certain he'd return to his bedroom, but he didn't.

"Please, don't tell Daddy about me touching myself."

"I won't. Not if you don't want me to, but he knows all about that kind of thing. You can talk to him about anything and everything. He'll never be embarrassed. Did he act funny when you got your period that first time?"

"No," she conceded.

"Well, then."

Storm shut off the hall light, closed the door again, then climbed in beside her, all in silence.

"Can I stay in here tonight?"

"Of course you can."

"With both of you?"

"Of course," I repeated.

For a moment, none of us said anything, we just wriggled around and settled down for the night.

I was pretty certain that I'd never fall asleep, not with my mind whirring. Then, she whispered, "Mom?"

"Yes, baby?"

"Will you tell me about how you and Daddy got married again?"

Storm snorted and before I could do more than chuckle softly, he murmured, "Again, ladybug? How many times you wanna hear that one, huh?"

His voice was soft, teasing, and it eased the ache in my soul from her revelations.

That bastard had punched her between the legs. I wanted to kill him myself and was beyond grateful that Amara had slaughtered him like the pig he was on my behalf.

I still wanted to know the details, and not just because I wanted to understand what my daughter had witnessed that day. I wanted to relive his suffering, wanted to know that he'd endured agony for what he'd put her through…

"It's one of my favorite stories!" Cyan declared with a huff, before she wriggled around to face her dad. "Plleeeasssee," she wheedled.

I didn't say a word because I knew he'd cave in—he always did.

"The first time I asked your mom to marry me, it wasn't really romantic, so the second time, I did it with my arms wrapped around her belly, so that you got some love too—"

"I don't think I felt it," Cyan said with a pout.

"Well, I tried," was his retort. "And she said yes, but she was crying."

"Happy tears?"

"Nervous tears," I inserted because that was my prompt. "Your dad always made me feel jumpy inside." Cyan's presence in my belly hadn't helped matters either.

"Like when I need to do three forward saltos in one go?"

Storm laughed. "Something like that."

My lips curved. "You'll understand when you're older, sweetheart."

"If you say so."

I didn't tell her I'd been nervous about being a single, unwed Mom… she didn't need to know that.

"On the day itself, I made her wear white—"

Harlots didn't wear white.

That had been our first argument.

"—and we went to this hill where we always used to meet."

"I picked wildflowers for my bouquet," I whispered softly, remembering how the sun beat down on my hair as I gathered them, and I smiled. Much as I'd done back then. Even nervous, even *terrified*, I'd still had to smile.

"Wild roses and daisies, right?"

I hummed. "Right."

"I want to see them tomorrow."

"I'll find the Bible. It's probably in the basement right now with the rest of the unpacked boxes." I'd pressed two of the flowers between its sheets.

"Uncle Digger really married you?"

"He did, and he wasn't happy about it."

"What's Digger's real name?"

"You know that already," I chided.

"Mom! Don't spoil it."

"He was Jimmy back then," Storm answered her. "Just Jimmy."

"He was a Prospect, wasn't he?"

"Yep, and that's why you have to think long and hard about being a Prospect for the Sinners, ladybug, because you get asked to do all kinds of weird jobs."

"I'd do that job. I'll marry all the Sinners," she chimed in.

He cleared his throat. "Sinners don't need to get married, baby. Remember?"

She hesitated at that. "Does that mean the Old Ladies are whores?"

I tensed, but I knew where that came from—fucking school. God, I hated kids.

"No, it doesn't," Storm rumbled. "And if an Old Man ever heard you call their Old Lady that, you know there'd be hell to pay, right?"

"Because Sinners protect their own," she declared, sounding proud as all get out.

My lips curved, my tension abating as she sighed. "I wanna get married like you two."

Christ, I really hoped the circumstances of her marriage were better than ours.

From being tossed out of my parent's home for good to the day when I'd been stuck in a bed because the pregnancy became high risk, those months had been fraught with tension.

Most of it of my own making.

The memory had me wincing.

I'd given Storm a hard time from the start, and he'd only ever tried to do his best by me.

By us.

As Storm described the weather, what he wore, and how my dress had ruffled in the wind—he was quite good at telling stories that had her transfixed—she heaved a sigh and gradually, I felt her tension lessen until she drifted off to sleep.

"Night, baby girl," Storm rasped as she quieted down, the endearment was mine. One he only used for me.

"Night, Storm," I whispered back, thinking of that day, of how warm it had been, and how I'd puked four times that morning, terrified that he wouldn't go through with it.

For all that, he'd made it special.

Our place on the hill... Warm and sunny, loaded with memories, with good times before things had soured. Peaceful and tranquil—Cyan wasn't wrong. It had been an idyllic setting. The perfect place.

Not once, after we were married, had we visited it. A thought that saddened me and made me want to go back the next time we were in West Orange.

Eventually, mind racing, I fell asleep, finding that I rested better than I had in months with both of them at my side. Sure, they took up a ton of room, but it felt good. Like we were united again, bound with secrets that we wouldn't share outside of this room.

When I woke up, I was well aware that Cyan wasn't between us, but the faintly tinny sound of the TV at the other end of the house, even with the door closed, told me she was awake and in the family room.

Yawning and stretching, I rolled onto my side and came across the glorious sight of Storm sleeping in a pool of sunlight. It picked out the silver in his hair, making the glossy locks look like a crown around his head, but I could see the fatigue on his face, saw the strain that shouldn't be there when he was resting, and I felt it in my marrow.

Cyan's pain was our pain.

God, being a parent never let up. Not when what she endured would probably haunt us more than it did her. There'd come a day when her mind would gloss over things to protect itself, whereas for us, we'd never forget. *Ever.*

A shaky breath escaped me as the urge to find comfort in his arms hit me.

We hadn't shared a bed in so long.

Even before I'd tossed him out, we hadn't. He'd spent more and more time at the clubhouse, and if his word was to be trusted, it hadn't been him getting laid, he'd been getting high.

In the grand scheme of things, neither was all that great, was it? Still, he was here now. He stacked the dishwasher, did laundry, fixed things, and took care of the yard. He even cooked!

He was trying.

But was it still trying when he'd been here for months?

When he'd done this repeatedly? Over and over so that it became less about impressing me, trying to get into my good graces, and was more of a sign of him as a husband?

For the first time, I was grateful we were away from West Orange.

Our friends and family were there, but I wasn't sure if the place was good for Storm. I could imagine us rolling back into bad habits swiftly, whereas here, we had to depend on each other for everything. We were alone among strangers, with no port of safety outside of within these walls. That had to make a difference.

Nibbling on my lip, I rolled over to him, and when he stretched, his arms coming around me, I sighed, snuggling into him, loving how right it felt, how good he felt. "Morning."

"Morning," he rumbled.

"Storm?"

He hummed sleepily, and the sound filled me with warmth.

Maybe it was talking about our wedding day, or maybe it was just waking up with him like this, but I couldn't withhold the words. They burst free from me, and I had no desire to keep them in.

"I love you."

He tensed, then a long exhalation escaped him. "I love you too."

"I miss you."

"I miss you too."

The immediacy of his responses soothed something inside me.

"I choose you, Keira," he whispered, surprising me. "I will always choose you from now on. I won't pick the drugs over you; I won't let myself fail you.

"You have all of me. Just like you should have from the start. I let you down, but I won't do it again, and I sure as hell won't let Cyan down."

I closed my eyes, the power of his words enhanced all the more by the sleep-ridden huskiness to his voice. "I wanted to—"

"I know." He pressed a kiss to the top of my head. "I know. I'm jealous of Amara. I'd serve time to have the honor of butchering that bastard."

Squeezing him, I said, "I'd prefer to have you here." Before he could say another word, I told him, "I think we should spend the day at the clubhouse."

"It'll be busy," he warned me. "There's going to be a BBQ for the families."

"I know. MaryCat told me. I think… you were right. Cy needs to make friends. She needs to get out of her head, and if she gets into fights, at least we don't have to worry about her being expelled."

"The school of Mom and Dad," he teased softly, making me grin.

There was nothing I wanted more than to let him kiss me, to take my mind off the night before, to sink into his arms and escape the world for a half hour, but that was what he meant when he said he chose me, and I had to honor that.

Especially when, every night, he'd been eating me out like I was a pint of Ben & Jerry's on a post-breakup binge with the girls.

So we laid there, and we talked, and it felt good.

We discussed the fact that Cyan's skills with math were something he'd have to tackle because she was advancing in leaps and bounds, and we talked about the diner and how it was doing better than ever since I'd introduced savory pies that the diners seemed to be adoring. We discussed the clubhouse renovations, and he told me that he hadn't heard from those bastards that had shown up on our street, and we talked about life.

Just life.

No regrets, not the past, just the present.

And it was beautiful.

Later on, with a buzzing Cyan in the SUV beside me, I drove to the clubhouse with Storm at my back.

It was almost as if last night were a distant memory, but it *had* happened and there was no escaping it. I knew what had happened to her, and so did Storm, but Cyan was bright and breezy, like the weight off her chest had transferred successfully onto us. I'd take that burden any day of the damn week that was for sure, especially if it helped her in the long run.

When we made it to the clubhouse, I felt awkward. I wouldn't deny it. But I was so glad MC was there, Maddox in her arms, and both of us sat in the sun under a parasol that someone had stuck in the ground, watching the chaos of the new club.

"It's different here," MC said after a few minutes.

She'd spent even less time at the clubhouse than I had—which was really saying something.

"Family oriented," I agreed as I took a sip of Bud Light which Storm had given me twenty minutes ago. He'd disappeared, returned with the beer, given me a kiss that made my toes curl, before disappearing again.

"Yeah. You can still spot the clubwhores though."

"They're dressed better than in Jersey."

"Trashy instead of like hookers."

I snickered and tapped my beer bottle with her glass of juice.

"God, I'd kill for a non-alcoholic beer but they don't have any," MC admitted. Then, a little defensively, explained, "Beer stimulates milk production. Just FYI."

"Don't worry, honey. I'm not a Karen. Anyway, I thought with your past you'd be all about the white wine," I teased.

"I am, but Digger's corrupted me."

"That must be nice. To be corrupted." My nose crinkled. "Storm wouldn't let me drink alcohol until I turned twenty-one. That tells you how corruptive an influence he's been on me, doesn't it?"

She blinked at me. "You're kidding me, right?"

"No," I said on a soft laugh.

"You mean to tell me that he breaks all the laws under the sun, but with you, he makes you abide by them?"

"Yep."

"I don't know why I'm shocked," she muttered to herself, laughing the next second. "That man is nuts for you."

Yeah. He was.

I grinned, not unhappy about that fact, and on the brink of telling her so, when someone plunked herself down beside us before I could defend my husband's twisted morals. Well, they were twisted where he was concerned, strict for me.

I guessed I should have seen before how he kept me on a pedestal. Talk about myopic.

"Okay, ladies, I know you don't know me, but I gotta ask… what the hell is it with your Old Man and all the houseplants?"

I blinked at the woman, who had rainbow hair teased up into some kind of bouffant, mixing a modern and a vintage look together, had cat eyes to die for, and the shiniest red mouth I'd ever seen. "Excuse me?"

"Sorry," the woman said sheepishly. "The name's Darla. Pleasure to meet you both."

I shot her a smile. "I'm Keira. This is MaryCat."

MC murmured, "Pleasure to meet you."

"Likewise." Darla beamed at me, then leaned over the table. "Seriously, Keira, his office is like a jungle."

Arching a brow, I merely asked, "How do you know?"

"My Old Man, he's Jump… He's the guy who…?" She pulled a face. "We're neighbors. I just ain't had the courage to come and say hey. But Jump was telling me how every time he goes in there, there's another plant."

"Storm's a recovering addict," I told her calmly.

It wasn't my secret to share, but I knew my husband had been getting shit for not attending parties, for not hanging out at the bar. Maybe if she told her Old Man, Jump would spread the word around.

"The houseplants are his way of taking responsibility of something else's care."

"That's a thing?"

"Sure is."

I'd made sure to research it the last time we'd discussed it. I'd learned a whole host of things about NA. Sex addiction was trickier, though.

After hours of investigation, I wasn't surprised he'd come up with something so drastic as the padlock.

It was distinctly medieval in nature, but desperation often led to dramatic overtures.

"Why?"

I told her about what I read online. "They look after the plant for, like, a year, then they graduate to a pet. I guess it's about looking after someone other than themselves and being selfless."

"You sure he's not addicted to buying plants?" Darla asked, but before I could reply, she hollered, "Kelly O'Bryan! What in the hell do you think you're doing? You leave that girl alone."

I twisted around at her holler, trying to see what was going on, but all I saw was Cyan facing off with a boy about her age.

Darla muttered, "Sorry about this, he has issues." She stalked off, her direction Cyan, which keyed me into the fact that Kelly was a boy, not a girl.

Before she reached them, however, Cyan punched Kelly.

Groaning, I hid behind my beer for a second, then hid some more when I saw Storm appear out of nowhere and make a beeline toward the fight.

"You gonna let him deal with that?" MC joked, snickering as Kelly and Cyan started rolling around on the ground like it was a bar room brawl.

Apparently, last night's conversation hadn't eased her anger issues.

"You bet your ass I am," I said with a huff, then I sank back the Bud Light, got my butt up off the chair, and found myself a second bottle.

The family party had started off with such promise, as well...

THIRTY-THREE

BEAR

PAST

"WHAT'S GOING on with you, boy?"

Storm had made it to the grand old age of twenty-seven because of Rene and me. There wasn't a doubt in my mind that was true. Only, there was surviving, there was subsisting, and there was living.

He'd met that Keira girl, and suddenly, it was like he was living.

But something had changed recently, and I didn't like it.

Not one bit.

Storm tilted his head to the side, and in his eyes, deep within them, I saw that same old sorrow that had haunted him since birth.

"You ever fuck up so badly that nothing you do can make it right again?"

"We all fuck up," I told him quietly. "It's how we fix our mistakes that defines us."

His lips rolled inward as he stared at the bonfire. I knew he'd taken a couple of hits this past week, hits that had made him score some pot. That usually led to goddamn crack or meth. I was watching him because he couldn't pull the same shit he used to.

He was a daddy now.

"Some mistakes are too big to fix."

"Nah," I disagreed. "Just takes a big enough man to shoulder the burden." I took a deep draw of beer and asked, "What did you do?"

"Pretty fucking sure you know already."

I grunted. "That snafu with Kendra?"

I didn't like that girl, but I wasn't about to toss her out. She was popular with the men, and though no clubwhore was important enough to cause a mutiny, I didn't need dissent in the ranks right now.

Not with the goddamn *Famiglia* buying up parcels of land that were starting to encroach on our territory.

A war was brewing.

Goddamn, I was too old for that shit.

Some days, I just thought about getting on my hog, Rene at my back, and riding down to Florida, but Rex wasn't ready to lead yet.

We had time.

"Wasn't a snafu," Storm muttered. "Was a fucking disaster."

"Ain't gonna disagree with you."

"Didn't even know she was the one I was fucking," he whispered brokenly, his hand tightening around the can he was holding, crushing it in his fist.

"You were high," I said flatly. "Them fucking drugs, Asher. When you gonna quit that shit?"

"I-I try—"

"Tryin' ain't fucking good enough. You talk about fixing shit, but you gotta fix that first." I grabbed his shoulder. "The sickness has been in you since birth. It's why I cut you slack, but Jesus, you gotta grow up. You got a kiddy now. You're a father."

He sucked in a breath. "I know I do." He twisted to look at me. "I know I am."

Christ, I wished he were my boy. If he were, then he wouldn't be so goddamn broken.

I should have killed Ellen. Should have had someone finish her off when she was inside, then she'd never have been able to taint him worse than she already had.

How couldn't I cut him some slack when she'd brought him into this world craving a high?

"You told her what you did?"

"No." His jaw tightened. "Was going to, but then she nearly miscarried."

I winced. "Shit."

"Yeah." He hurled the can across the way. "Now, Cy's not gaining enough weight and her dad managed to pull some strings so that the owner of the fucking house I was gonna buy her in the hills has backed out."

"You got money for someplace else?"

"I do, but I showed her that one. She loves it. First thing I've done as her husband that made her happy, and I can't goddamn give it to her.

"I can't break another fucking promise to her, Bear. Fuck, I just can't."

"How much was the house in the hills?" When he told me the amount, I said, "Call him up and offer him fifty grand over the asking price."

He frowned. "Huh? I can barely afford the asking price, Bear, never mind—"

"Consider it a gift from Rene and me."

"What?" He gulped. "No—"

"Yes." I squeezed his shoulder, then hit it home, with, "Yes."

"I can't thank you enough, Bear."

"The pleasure's mine, son."

"I wish you were my real dad. Maybe I wouldn't be so fucked up if you were. Instead, I got that bastard Prince's DNA jacking up my system—"

"Prince is your dad?" I sputtered.

"You didn't know?"

"Bet your ass I didn't fucking know." I scrubbed a hand over my face. "He got you hooked on meth."

"I know," was his flat retort.

"Fucker."

I slammed to my feet, hurling the lawn chair my ass had been sitting on across the yard, watching as it collided with the fire, burning up the second it made contact.

Some squeals came from the sweetbutts, brothers peered at me, but no one approached.

"Thank you, Bear," Storm whispered, and I saw he was looking up at me. "Thank you for being pissed."

I was more than pissed. I was fucking outraged.

I'd never liked Prince, but the council had voted on him as VP, and Grizzly was friends with the fucker so I'd pushed him through when I should have been exiling him.

"It's a good thing he's dead," I snapped, "or he'd be about to meet his maker tonight."

Storm's laugh was cold. "He'd have died a lot earlier than this if I'd had my way."

Jaw clenched, I crouched down at his side, ignoring the roaring of the flames, the whispers from the sweetbutts and the men, and rasped, "Storm, you're a better man than him. Don't let that shit about his DNA jacking up your system mess with your head. You're your own man. You make your own destiny, son."

"My destiny don't mean jack when I keep on messing up. I fucked another woman, Bear. How am I supposed to make up for that?"

"By never doing it again." I cleared my throat. "I messed up too, Storm. Remember when Rene lost our second kid?"

"Yeah, I remember."

"She was…" Shame hit me. "She pushed me out, and I gave up. I-I got a girlfriend, got her a place in town. I thought my marriage was over, but that was no excuse. I regret it. Every fucking time, I regret it."

"Does she know?" I saw anger on Rene's behalf in his eyes, but I also saw relief.

I wasn't perfect.

I'd just given him proof.

And my Old Lady was still at my side.

I'd given him hope.

"She does, and she forgives me. In time, when you tell Keira, she'll forgive you too. But you can't do it again, Storm."

"I got so much shit to fix, Bear, some days, it feels like it's gonna drown me. The drugs, the sleeping, this shit with Keira's dad, but she's the only thing that makes me happy—"

I knew he was obsessed with her, but I didn't like to tell him that she was as much of an addiction as the crack and the pot.

Fuck, this marriage was a disaster waiting to happen.

I knew it'd never work. The drugs were too potent a siren's call, and Storm, well, he needed a partner. Not an innocent.

He needed someone who'd call him on his BS, who'd have his back, who'd wade into Hades itself for him, not one who'd been spoon-fed hellfire and damnation since birth.

So I chose my words carefully, because he had to change that. Just because she'd been raised naive, didn't mean she had to remain that way.

I liked the girl, but she wasn't right for him.

Not as she was.

"Storm, there'll come another day when you need a hit, you and I both know that. Every time you let it conquer you, you're taking a step away from a future with Keira.

"Now, life happens. Shit goes down, and you're not always gonna be strong. That's okay, boy. I'm not always strong. But you gotta lower those walls—"

"I can't do that, Bear. She's not like us. She isn't one of us."

"You need to bring her into the fold."

"I can't," he repeated. "Rex was right. She needs picket fences. She needs what her mom and dad have."

"Yeah, she might do, but what about you, son?"

His mouth tightened. "I-I'll be what she needs."

I shook my head. "That ain't the way forward."

"It has to be," he rasped.

"If you say so, Asher," I said softly, hoping that, when the day came and his marriage fell around his feet, Rene and I were around to pick up the pieces.

THIRTY-FOUR

KEIRA

PRESENT

Blurry - Puddle of Mudd

"DAMMIT TO HELL," I snapped under my breath as I jumped behind the wheel and quickly darted out of the diner's parking lot.

I was due at the therapist's ten minutes ago, and while MC was looking after Cyan, I was late because Franny had cut out on us today. This was getting to be a bad habit of hers.

Sweating, still wearing my uniform, I drove to the edge of town where Dr. Janowicz's office was located.

When I hit a red light, I ducked into my purse for a make-up wipe to clean up some of the grease on my skin, and as I twisted, I happened to catch a glimpse of a face in the window of a coffee shop.

For a second, I was pretty sure my eyes weren't working. I even blinked a few times, thinking the sweat that had been dripping into them on a freakishly and unseasonably hot day was making me see things, but nope.

That was Kendra.

Sitting in a coffee shop.

In Coshocton.

In my goddamn town.

What the hell was she still doing here?

I swear to God, I'd have climbed out of the SUV and headed in there just to see what the hell was going on, but someone honked their horn behind me and I lit it out of there before she, or the guy she was with, could spot me.

That guy was a biker—I recognized the cut. I hadn't caught much else about him…

Was it stupid that I was just glad he didn't have long hair? Not that Storm could be in two places at once seeing as I knew he was at the couples' session at the therapist's on his own right now.

I rubbed my forehead, wondering what the hell she was still doing in town. Had she been here all along? Surely Storm had made her go back to West Orange? The Posse hadn't mentioned her return, but after what had gone down, why would they mention her, period?

I hadn't seen the bitch at the BBQ, so I knew she wasn't staying at the clubhouse, and trust me, Kendra was self-destructive enough to have shown her face at the party. She was the kind of brazen cow who didn't give a shit about authority, just did what she wanted to serve her own purpose.

As I raced toward the therapist's office, I found a space fast, then darted inside, making it to the appointment twenty minutes late. The receptionist tutted her disapproval but let me dart in past the doctor's next patient.

Sinking into the chair, flustered and overheated, annoyed and not in the mood to be dissected when I had questions for my husband, I apologized, "I'm so sorry I'm late, Doctor. It's been a busy morning."

Dr. Janowicz arched a brow at me, which, of course, made me feel more flustered. She was in her early forties, fit in with her magnolia decor like a champion, and I was pretty damn sure she had a crush on Storm.

All in all, she irritated the hell out of me, however, she was good with Cyan.

There were no kiddy shrinks in Coshocton, but she'd been helping Cyan so far so I didn't see a need to travel further to Cleveland or

Columbus just yet. Maybe if Cy outgrew Dr. Janowicz, we'd have to revisit the subject, but my suspecting she had a crush on Storm wasn't enough of a reason to change psychiatrists.

And yes, I was well aware that I sounded crazy.

Maybe I was.

Maybe I always would be.

Hell, if Storm could have me followed for almost twelve years and get his dick padlocked to prove himself to me, I was allowed to think anything with a vagina would crush on my husband because he was that hot.

"You're still liking the position at the diner, Keira?" she asked me quietly, not referencing how late I was.

I shot Storm a look. His gaze was on his boots, which was unusual. He'd glanced at me when I walked in, and while I didn't think he was angry at me for being late, he was definitely pouting about something.

"I am. It's harder now that I've got Cyan's schooling to worry about, but it stops me from going stir crazy."

She nodded. "Storm and I were just discussing the recent developments in your relationship."

"What developments?"

My mind scuttled along to Kendra.

God, I hated her.

Even slamming her face into the counter at the diner wasn't enough to make me feel better about her.

Had I broken her nose? Had it seemed a little crooked in the coffee shop?

I really hoped it was.

"The fact that you're identifying as a couple now?" Dr. Janowicz explained, breaking into my bloodthirsty thoughts. "With his predilection for addiction, and considering this is still a recovery in the early days, I was explaining how it isn't wise for him to be getting entangled once more."

I frowned at her. "Entangled? We're married."

"You separated for a long time, Keira," she told me calmly. "This could constitute a new relationship. Storm's recovery has to be his priority right now. Have you researched the twelve steps?"

"I have." *You sanctimonious bitch,* I tagged on.

"Then you'll know I'm right."

"We've been attending couple's therapy for over a month, and you've just decided that we can't be a couple now?" I sniped.

"You were attending as Cyan's parents. There's a difference."

"I don't think there is," I argued, turning to stare at Storm, waiting for him to leap into the argument.

Were we really being rebuked by our daughter's shrink? Seriously?

I didn't do well with therapy. In my family, we kept things tightly held up in a ball, repressing the hell out of them until they gave us an ulcer when we were fifty. I was more than okay with that. I thought Storm was too. The only reason we were so proactive now was because of Cyan.

I'd deal with a lot to make things better for my kid, but it pissed me off to be reprimanded by this bland bitch with her holier-than-thou attitude, who thought she had the right to split us up.

But my temper merely surged when he stayed quiet.

When he didn't say a goddamn thing as she rebuked us for making the massive step of coming back together again.

And because he didn't defend us, and because, apparently, Kendra was back in fucking town and he didn't think I should be told, I stayed quiet as well.

But I got madder, and madder, and madder.

My temper boiling and bubbling away until I thought I was going to burst all while, over the remaining twenty minutes, both of us gave her one-word answers, barely elucidating on any of our responses as we sat there like naughty children.

I was well aware that romantic partnerships weren't a part of the twelve steps. The whole section about the houseplants was tied up in that. You had the plants for a year, then you got a dog once those were flourishing, and then after a year with the dog, that was when you were ready for a relationship.

But Storm and I were different.

Most guys didn't tie up their dicks for their wife, did they? I had a feeling he hadn't shared that salient part with her during the time they'd spent alone while I was running late.

Nor did most men have a biker tailing their woman and child at all times.

Storm had massive trust issues, but we never talked about any of that during our sessions. We didn't talk about a lot of things.

Conclusion: therapy was bullshit when you didn't tell your therapist the full truth.

As we rounded off the hour, her chiding us once more for diving into the deep end when we had many issues up in the air, my temper blossomed as I stared more and more out of the window where nasty storm clouds were brewing. It was too perfect. Like watching my own anger take shape.

The clouds were big and dark and loomed over the town, casting visible shadows everywhere. The power was intense, and I felt it simmering away inside me, just waiting to break open.

After the intense heat, I guessed I shouldn't have been surprised there was a rainstorm heading toward us—it even explained my tension headache—and once the session was over and Storm settled up, I headed over to the door, watching big, fat raindrops land on the fender of my SUV.

Storm moved over to me; I knew it without having to turn my head. His scent hit me square in the chest. Normally, I'd have sucked it and him in, absorbing him as much as I could in a public place. But after we'd just been reprimanded like we were horny teens who'd been caught making out behind the bleachers, and after he'd *allowed* that, I was in no mood to suck anything in.

"Keira, I—"

I didn't wait for him to finish, just shoved the door open and darted toward the SUV. Not bothering to wait for him, I leaped behind the wheel then took off, too fast for him to join me, too quickly for Jump to follow.

The journey back to the subdivision wasn't overly long but the rain begun teeming down in a way that broke my mad with him. The downpour was so strong it made me cringe because Storm would be soaked through by the time he made it home. He wasn't following me, because there was no single ray of light beaming through the shadows from the overcast sky in my rearview mirror, which added to the concern hitting me in the gut.

Goddammit, I'd acted like a child again.

Instead of speaking out in the session, I'd bottled it up. Instead of telling him how I felt, I'd run off.

Seriously, about now, Cyan was showing more maturity than I was.

Though visibility was low, I found a place on the road where I could do a U-turn and decided that I'd find him in the rain. Praying to God that he hadn't crashed because I was a bitch and hadn't let him ride with me, I was about to turn around when the tire popped.

I rarely swore, not this bad, but I growled, "Motherfucker!"

Of all the times to get a flat tire, it had to be now?

"Really, universe?" I snarled to myself, unsure of what to do.

I didn't want to get wet and, I was ashamed to admit, I didn't know how to change a tire anyway.

Wanting to ram my forehead into the steering wheel for my stupidity, I determined that Cyan and I would be taking a class on how to do basic shit for ourselves. Storm would have to teach us, of course, and he might bitch about it because the man liked it far too much when I depended on him, but in a crisis, I really needed not to be this goddamn useless.

Growling again, I grabbed my phone and looked through the glove compartment for the papers Storm had put in there. I knew there'd be the number for a mechanic he'd want me to use, so I started hunting one down.

That was when I heard it.

The rumble of a bike.

I peered up, saw that single beam of light I'd come to rely on when we were riding together, and saw him dash over to the SUV's passenger side. He slammed on the door for me to unlock it, which I did the second I saw his face, then he hopped in.

Thanking God that he was okay, I took him in, accepting that I'd seen dryer people come out of the shower.

Rather than fuss over him when it was my fault, I slammed on the heat as he slicked his hair back. A part of me expected his anger, but of course, he wasn't angry.

This man.

"You okay?" he demanded, making me aware that his primary concern was me.

Always me.

I was so selfish sometimes.

Guilt hit me like a two by four to the temple as I turned to him, reaching over to cup his cheek. "I'm sorry I let you get wet."

He tilted his head to the side. "Is that why you stopped?"

"No. One of the tires blew." I huffed. "I was turning around to come and find you."

He swiped water off his face. "Why?"

"Because I wanted to give you a ride. Like I should have done at the doctor's office." I cringed, prepared for his annoyance, but I didn't get it.

"I didn't need a ride." He sniffed. "This ain't the first time I rode in the rain. I'm just pissed I couldn't catch up to you, not when Jump wasn't tailing you."

I bit my lip. "I'm so sorry, Storm. I need to stop being a baby."

"You're not a baby," he scoffed. "I wasn't gonna leave my bike at the edge of town. I wouldn't have taken a ride anyway. I'm not a pussy like Jump." He grumbled, "Fucker texted me to let me know he was on his way home when the storm came in."

Though his admission that he'd have ridden his bike home anyway appeased my guilt some, the malice behind my move made me realize I had to step up my game. I also had to be honest with him about why that malice was there in the first place.

"Am I damaging your recovery?"

He snorted. "Is that what has your panties in a bunch? That bullshit Janowicz was spouting? Baby girl, I wouldn't have a recovery if it weren't for you. I'd have OD'd years ago—"

Terror filled me. "Don't even joke about that!" I slapped my hand over his mouth to shut him up.

His fingers curled about my wrist as he tugged it away. "I'm not joking. I tried to overdose a lot when I was younger. The guys never let me."

"Well, I owe them a debt of gratitude." Not the shit I usually wished on them. "You were really suicidal?"

"A part of me still is." He shrugged like it was nothing when it was everything. Before I could protest, he told me, "You're my reason for waking up in the morning, baby girl. Janowicz can go suck rotten eggs. I just let her spout that BS because it's easier than arguing." He rolled his eyes. "Bitches like that, they think they're preaching God's word. They ain't never been addicted to anything other than shopping channels and coffee. I got a sponsor of my own. We talk about this shit on a daily basis now. I'm gonna listen to him more than I would her."

"You have a sponsor?"

He hummed. "Yep."

"Why didn't you tell me?"

"Because you—" He blinked. "To be honest, I just thought you'd know. Sponsors are things people have on TV, you know? I just thought you'd put one and one together."

"You know you can talk to me, right?"

"Of course, but a sponsor's different. I've fucked up our lives by being an addict. It's on me to fix things how the program says."

"Storm," I rasped, "I haven't helped the situation. I know things… I know I must have made things difficult along the way."

He frowned. "No."

"Yes." I blew out a breath. "I need to get better at seeing to your needs as well as my own. We need to work on this together. We talked about this—I can't do that if you cut me out." I straightened my shoulders. "I need to step up to the plate."

He started to argue, "You've stepped up plenty—"

"No, I haven't. It's still too one-sided." I tipped up my chin. "I need to become more at ease with the Sinners. I need to get to know what it takes to get you clean." Then I cringed. "I need to know how to change a damn tire too."

His lips curved. "You'll never change a tire in your life while I'm around."

His words had fear hitting me. "You can't change 'em if you take yourself out of this world."

"I'll stick around so long as you and Cyan are here with me. You don't need to worry about that." He angled his head to the side. "Don't be worrying about that. I ain't been that bad since I met you. The last year was pretty dicey..." He pulled a face. "I did shit I wasn't proud of—"

"You did stuff you should be proud of too. Lily and Tiffany told me about how you saved them, Storm. You put yourself out there. You..." I gulped. "You could have been hurt."

"Wasn't about to let them get snatched," was all he said. Then, he reached over and cupped my chin, his thumb sliding along my bottom lip. "I won't do anything to myself."

He said it so matter-of-factly.

"You know I'll be pissed?"

He grinned a little. "I know you'll be pissed. It's hot when you curse."

I sniffed. "Well, get used to it. I had to grow up sometime."

"Big words for big girls," he joked, making me grin back at him.

"Something like that." I peered out of the window and said, "I don't want you changing the tire when it's raining so hard. We could be here for a while."

"I'm okay with that. Cyan's safe, and you're my favorite person in the world. Where else do I wanna be?"

His words, the meaning behind them, the depth of feeling, all of it made me hot and fidgety.

How had I not seen his devotion before?

How had I just taken it as my right?

I'd let him down as much as he'd let me down.

Just in different ways.

I turned to him and murmured, "You're my favorite person too."

His grin was beatific, like a kid being handed a three-pound bag of Sweet Tarts. "Really?"

He sounded so surprised, and so happy, all at the same time. Damn. That hurt my heart as much as it healed it.

"Really," I confirmed.

"You wanna tell me what had you spittin' feathers when you walked into that old bitch's office?"

A smile curved my lips. "You know she's like a couple of years older than you, right?"

He just sniffed.

"I saw something on the way to the appointment."

"What?"

"Kendra. In that coffee shop over on Kennedy Street."

His eyes flared wide, and he stunned me when he boomed, "What?"

Okaaaay.

He was as surprised as me.

He snatched his phone out of his pocket, grimaced when it was wet and didn't turn on, then snatched mine from the hands' free unit on the dash and dialed in a number.

"SL? You wanna tell me why that cunt was in Coshocton?"

I studied him as he snarled at his VP, curious about the curl to his lips, the sneer of hatred.

He hated Kendra.

He really did.

How had she managed to pull the wool over my eyes? Was it because I'd been willfully blind? Or was it because she'd tapped into my own insecurities where Storm was concerned?

For so long, he'd led two lives, and that was on me. Part of his life had been the Sinners and the other part had been Cyan and me. Instead of letting those merge, I'd allowed them to remain separate, and that was a weakness that was easily exploited by any bitch who wanted to cause mischief and mayhem in our marriage.

"She's supposed to be in Pittsburgh. Fuck, even a state away ain't enough—"

Why Pittsburgh?

"You'd better find out how she slipped her fucking tail, SL, or there'll be shit to pay. We've got a viper in the nest and she's currently waltzing around our town like she has every goddamn right to be here." SL replied, then Storm muttered, "You do that."

When he put down the phone, I murmured, "You were mean to him."

"He's my VP, he can take it." His top lip curled up some more as he slammed his hand against the dash. "Goddammit, that bitch just doesn't know when to quit."

"Why was she in Pittsburgh?"

"Because I didn't want to share a state with her?" He grumbled 'cunt' under his breath. "And Rex didn't want her ass in West Orange."

"Why didn't he want her there anymore? Thought she was part of the stable?"

He snorted. "You make 'em sound like cows."

"Aren't they though?" I mocked. "You have clubwhores here too—"

"I ain't even looked at their tits, never mind thought about fucking them," he defended. "I don't just stick my dick in anything, Keira. I told you, it happens under very specific circumstances."

"When you think they're me," I said wryly, surprising myself with the lack of bitterness to the words.

He cringed. "Fuck, that sounds so bad."

"Well, it doesn't sound good," I confirmed with a laugh.

It was his turn to be shocked. He arched a brow at me. "You just waiting to slap me or something?"

"No. But I'm not going to keep flogging a dead horse, either. You know you're lucky I'm letting you back in my life. You know you're lucky that I forgive you. You know that if I even catch a sniff of your dick going anywhere near another woman, I won't ever let you back into our home."

"Our home?" he repeated softly, like that was the only thing I'd said that mattered.

"You know it is."

"I felt that way, but I didn't... I just didn't want to presume," he rumbled, his voice deep and dark and, Jesus, tantalizing.

I had to watch out for his sobriety too now, and August had never seemed so goddamn far away.

August—I needed to make a countdown on a calendar so I could count off the days.

Was it the first of the month?

Or a day in particular?

"I have no desire to fuck any woman but you."

"I know."

"You do?"

"What did Kendra do to piss Rex off? I know she was listening in on his conversations—"

"How do you know that?"

"She knew about Cyan having trouble at school. Said you told her that, but I know you wouldn't."

"Ain't spoken to the bitch since the last time I was in West Orange, and even then it was to tell her to get the hell away from me."

"I know."

"Good." He grunted. "Giulia's more moody than usual. Apparently just looking at Kendra makes her projectile vomit."

A laugh escaped me. "I have good friends."

His nose crinkled at the bridge. "Projectile vomiting on demand? I don't think so—" My arched brow said otherwise. He rolled his eyes. "That goddamn Posse."

"My friends," I corrected.

"Your friends," he grouched. "SL will deal with Kendra."

"I'm sure he will."

"She won't be darkening our doors again."

"Good." I studied his wet clothes. "We need to get you into something drier."

"I'll be fine."

Of course, he wasn't.

Over the next few days, he caught a cold, which turned feverish. It was when he wouldn't accept pain or cough meds that I really recognized his dedication to his sobriety, when I accepted that I had to watch out for him as much as he did for me, and it was also then when I realized that Dr. Janowicz was wrong.

Storm was working to his own schedule, his own timetable, and I knew why as well.

Cutting me out of his life would only cause harm, because more than the drugs, more than sex, more than anything else in this world, *I* was Storm's addiction. The one thing he couldn't live without. And when it boiled down to it, going cold turkey from me would hurt him worse than anything else could. Do more damage than anything else ever would.

I saw that when I moved his feverish butt back into my bedroom, and he curled around me like I was a living teddy bear.

I saw that when, even though he was back in my good books and he got back to normal, he didn't stop doing laundry or mowing the lawn and taking out the trash.

He showed up.

Every day.

And I knew, now we'd gotten over this blip, he always would.

THIRTY-FIVE

STORM

PAST - TWO YEARS AGO

Comin' Home - City and Colour

"I TOLD you never to contact me again."

I stared at my mother, hatred in my eyes because it burned through my soul.

She was acid. She tore through everything, wrecking whatever she touched, destroying what she neared.

"Your sister's stopped answering her cellphone."

I stared at her, trying to resonate that this was the beautiful woman who'd given birth to me.

It had always seemed so crazy that such an evil bitch could be so beautiful. Now, however, she looked like the hag she was. Only fitting. Maybe there was some justice in the universe, after all.

"She's got sense, then." I snorted out a laugh as I leaned into my handlebar. "I don't know why she didn't cut you off years ago."

"You hate her as much as you hate me, but the difference is, you came when you thought she called."

"I told her to fuck off, but when have you ever known Scarlet to obey?" My mouth tightened.

I didn't like that Scarlet was one of my weaknesses, but as much as I loathed her, I couldn't see her out on the street. So when I'd received a text telling me that she was homeless and had no money, I'd had to act.

As for this bitch, I didn't share the same loyalty.

"Should have realized something was fucked up about this meeting when you wanted me to come here." I stared down the narrow alley that, even though it was midday, was dark enough to make me squint at her. "What's the plan? Hit me on the head and take off with my bike then sell it?"

"That sounds like a good idea, son."

"Thought it might. Was hoping you were dead."

"Only the good die young, Asher," she taunted, stepping closer to me, close enough that I could see the way her skin hung on her face, how the bones were prominent, her eyes sunken.

She looked like a corpse in the middle of decomposing.

Not a pretty sight.

"That's true. Did you hear Rene died? Not sure why she was taken and you fucking weren't, but hey, you'll die soon by the looks of you."

"Rene's dead?" She cackled. "Never did like that sanctimonious bitch. Always sticking her fucking nose in. Never could keep it out of things that weren't her business."

My hands tightened on the bars. "She kept your kids alive when you were rotting in jail." Although this new look gave rotting a whole different definition. "For nothing else, you should be grateful. Of course, that's if you were a regular mother who gave a damn about her kids in the first place." I scoffed just as she scrunched up her face.

"Just like her. You always were a sanctimonious fucker too, Asher. Always thinking you were something better because you were book smart—"

"That's a fucking lie," I drawled. "I never thought I was something better. Thanks to you and dear ol' Dad screwing shit up for me."

She stilled at that. "Scarlet told you?"

"She did. Prince." I shook my head. "Fucking bastard. He's the one who got me hooked on this shit." I laughed a little. "I guess he wanted to see me suffer as well. Every addict loves a fellow sufferer."

Mom ground her teeth together. "I didn't want her to tell you that."

"Why not? Doesn't make a lick of difference to me."

She sniffed. "Because it's my business. If I'd wanted you to know who your father was, I'd have told you myself."

"Not sure why it was a big secret, but you do you, Mom. Like you don't always do that anyway." I grunted. "I ain't got all day. Got shit to be doing that don't involve you. So, get moving with the conversation. Tell me what you want so I can tell you to go fuck yourself."

She cackled. "Now who's acting like they're something better." Her eyes dropped to the VP patch on my cut. "Thought you didn't do that?"

"I'm a grown ass man. Just like you're a grown ass woman. We went our separate ways a long time ago—"

"I got cancer, Asher. I ain't got long left to live."

I studied her, really studied her. She made a pile of shit look good, but, in all honesty, I didn't see anything other than damage from substance abuse. That wasn't to say she didn't have both, of course.

"What do you want from me?"

"I know you got a daughter. Scarlet told me."

I tensed up. "You'll never meet her if that's what you want."

"You'd deny your mom the chance to see her only grandchild?"

"To hell and back. Don't you dare go anywhere near my family, Ellen. Or I'll make you fucking regret the day you were born," I snapped. "Now, if we're done, I got things to be doing."

"Heard you were the VP now. Seems as if the rumors were true." She hummed under her breath. "Like father, like son, in more ways than one. Trash always reveals itself. You'll never run past that. Though, I'll admit, I didn't expect you to make it to the council."

"That's because of Bear and Rene. It has jack shit to do with you." I scrubbed a hand over my chin. "You know where Scarlet is?"

"No." She tipped her head to the side. "Heard she was doing something in Manhattan."

"You hear a lot, huh?"

"Always got my ear to the ground, boy."

"Looks like it," I said with disgust, even as I wondered why Scarlet was in Manhattan.

I couldn't see her serving turkey subs in a diner, nor could I see her sitting behind a desk in an office, typing boring emails for a boss or working construction. She wasn't the kind of woman who did menial very well, but thanks to bombing high school, it wasn't like she had many options open to her.

"You can't let go, can you?" Mom murmured snidely.

"She's my sister." That was all the explanation she deserved.

I cut her out a long time ago, but I kept an ear to the ground, just wanted to hear that she was alive and keeping her ass out of jail. As of right now, I hadn't heard a whisper of her in years. Neither had I known about her being in Manhattan.

"I'm your mother," she hissed. "Don't I deserve some loyalty too?"

"You deserve to burn on a fucking bonfire. Hell, if you were on fire, I wouldn't piss on you to put out the flames—"

She grunted, then she did the damnedest thing.

I thought she'd back off. I thought my words would have her shuffling backward, retreating to whatever shithole she'd been living in.

But she didn't.

She struck me.

It didn't hurt.

Not really. Pain tolerance shifted the more you had the shit kicked out of you and under Grizzly, I'd had that happen plenty of times.

It was a needle.

It quivered in my forearm.

I stared at it, unable to believe what I was seeing, unable to believe what she'd done.

"If I'm gonna die, then I don't see why I shouldn't bring my hellspawn with me."

I didn't hear her. Not at first. I just stared at the needle. The dirty fucking stick that was in my arm. That could be carrying only the fuck knew what. Which was when it registered that this was why she'd brought me here.

This.

She cackled at me, baring yellowed teeth that were tinged black, most of them missing. Her stringy hair fluttered a little with her laughter, and she crowed, "You should see your face, boy—"

My hand snapped out, faster than she anticipated. As it closed around her throat, I grabbed the needle, tossed it aside, then climbed off my hog. I didn't give a shit that it clattered to the ground, didn't even fucking notice when it sank onto a pile of trash.

She had my full focus.

She had every bit of it.

As I squeezed her throat, choking her, she didn't fight me. Her nails didn't drag or claw at my forearm, no, in the meager light, I saw her smile.

The bag of bones that was Ellen O'Shea rattled as I pushed her against the wall, and her smile seemed to beam at me. So bright that it seemed to cut through the shadows, illuminating the murky alleyway, taunting me with her glee.

I felt the grim rictus of my jaw, frozen as I accepted what she'd just done to me.

Infected me with something.

Killing me with something.

I wanted to ask her why she had to do that, why she'd fucking destroy me, but that was my mother.

Poison.

From beginning to the end.

She'd poisoned me.

First with crack, and then this.

"It's almost poetic," I whispered, staring into her eyes, eyes that were mirror images of my own, squeezing hard, not enough to kill her, just enough to hold her in place.

"Knew you wouldn't let me see my granddaughter," she choked out.

"So you could infect her too?" A laugh escaped me, one as bitter and twisted as she was. That was when I raised my second hand and brought it to her throat. This time, I squeezed with the intent to kill.

But as I did, a shimmer of light pierced the gloom, just as Keira's ringtone buzzed through the alley.

It jolted me. Not just because it made me think she was there, but that light, made me see the desperation in my mother's eyes.

She wanted me to kill her.

That was when I accepted she had cancer.

That was when I truly accepted she was dying, not lying.

She wanted to die, just not by her own hand. Not by the cancer eating away at her flesh.

She wanted me to do it.

Which was when I let go of her. When I watched her crumple to the ground.

"No!" she barked, but her voice was a croak. "No! You want me to die, I know you do."

"Oh, I do," I agreed, my heart pounding in my ears, my lungs burning as if I'd been running ten miles. "But I think I'll let whatever shit you've got eating into you do the job.

"Always knew you were a coward. The amount of times you OD'd accidentally and didn't do us the fucking honor of dying, but this time, you can't do it, can you?" I scoffed. "I hope you die in pain. I hope you die in agony and alone—"

I stopped speaking, stopped listening, stopped seeing and feeling as I backed off.

Maybe she wouldn't be the only one to die in agony?

Terror slalomed through my veins.

What had she infected me with?

I backed off, hauled my bike into an upright position, and as I kicked it into gear, I saw her clamber to her feet. When she threw herself in front of me, I swerved out of the way.

"I won't be the only one dying in agony!" she screamed, mirroring my thoughts but vocalizing them, wishing that on me.

As I gunned the engine, I knew I had to find a clinic, had to uncover whatever the hell it was she'd poisoned me with. As if being born addicted to crack because of her wasn't bad enough, she wanted to taint my death too.

Like a taunt, a siren song, Keira called me several times.

Ed Sheeran's "Thinking Out Loud" raced along with me until she gave up trying to get through to me.

Which was when I accepted that I wouldn't be around to see her grow old. I wouldn't be around to taste her lips at seventy…

I was a dead man walking.

And as the thought filtered through my mind, I whispered under my breath, "Happy birthday to me."

THIRTY-SIX

KEIRA

PAST - SEVEN WEEKS LATER

AS I PULLED up outside the compound, the gates opened when the Prospect, Jaxson, caught sight of the SUV and registered who it was behind the wheel. I waved at him in thanks then carefully headed up the driveway.

When I heard music pounding from the clubhouse, even from this distance, I grimaced. I hated parties, and there always seemed to be one happening here—day or night. Didn't matter that it was eleven AM right now, that most people were at work and kids were at school, the party never stopped.

Though I'd intended on going inside, finding Storm, and asking him what the hell was going on with him recently, the noise made me shrivel up and shrink away from going in there.

I'd never felt comfortable here and had never understood how Rene had fit in so seamlessly. She was like me. Quiet, shy. Retiring. She loved needlepoint and had done the most beautiful beadwork that took hours upon hours…

Thinking of her made me miss her.

Thinking of her made me realize how little I missed my own mom.

The urge to visit Rene's grave compelled me to park the SUV and to head over to the compound's private cemetery.

I never came here without Storm, and without there being a hundred other men and women in the vicinity, so the dead silence filled me with raw relief in comparison to the noise from the clubhouse.

Wading through the many gravestones of brothers and Old Ladies who'd passed over the years since the club's inception, I found Rene's.

The entire place was neat, the grass trimmed, no trash anywhere. But Rene's sparkled somehow. From that alone, I knew Rex came here, I knew he tended to it personally.

The thought had me biting my lip, guilt whispering through me as I thought about how infrequently I visited her. Sinking down to my knees, I sat there, just staring at the words on the tombstone.

Loving Mother, Old Lady, and the original First Lady.

I reached forward and traced the engraved words with my fingertips even as I whispered, "Rene, I think I'm losing Storm."

Something had happened a month ago. Around his birthday. I didn't know what, but he'd changed.

He slept away from home for runs. That was it. All of a sudden, he was barely at the house.

Cyan missed him, I missed him. Our home felt empty without him. It was hell waking up in bed to an empty space after years of him always being there. Of having him curled around me.

"I just..." I gulped. "I don't know what I did wrong."

She gave me no answer, of course. But verbalizing it helped.

Yesterday, after he missed a parent-teacher conference, I knew that was it, I had to take a stand. I had to come here, I had to confront him, but I was scared.

Just like my mom.

My head buried firmly in the sand.

It was safer that way, after all.

What you didn't know, didn't hurt you, but I was hurting regardless so that wasn't true.

A soft sprinkle of rain sputtered overhead, drenching me through, but I needed it. It made the scent of the grass stronger, more pungent, and the flowers laid here sprinkled their perfume throughout the area.

When it stopped, I didn't move, but a sudden blaring of sound had me jerking in surprise.

A few minutes later, I heard footsteps crunching through the grass, and just as my heart leaped with hope that it was Storm, and that he'd noticed the SUV, I turned around and saw Kendra walking toward me.

I frowned when I saw her wearing a cut, because Storm hadn't told me she'd become an Old Lady. Brothers never took off their cuts, and if anyone dared wear it, they'd only survive if the person was their Old Lady.

Christ, I never even touched his. I always left it where he laid it, like it was Babe Ruth's jersey at Cooperstown.

Kendra and I had never been particularly friendly. I got the feeling she'd tried to become an Old Lady over the years, but when that hadn't worked out, she had, instead, become a clubwhore. The years of that lifestyle hung heavily on her face, but who was I to judge? Maybe she enjoyed it. Maybe she had fun?

"Hi Kendra."

She didn't greet me back. "I saw your SUV, then saw you sitting out here… What's going on?"

"Just visiting Rene." I bit my lip, figuring I had a chance of finding out if Storm was acting as weird at the clubhouse as he was at home without having to confront him.

Everyone had a little breakdown from time to time, right?

"Why?"

"I felt like it. I miss her."

Kendra sniffed. "Don't know what there was to miss. The old bitch wasn't exactly a pleasure to be around."

Shocked, I gasped. "She was! She was such a sweet person."

"Maybe to you," she sneered. "She treated clubwhores like we're second-class citizens."

I found that hard to believe but, at the same time, knew it wasn't outside the realms of possibility. Rene had told me once that Bear had cheated with a clubwhore, so it wasn't as if she'd like the women who routinely targeted men who had partners and tried to be with them just so they'd get branded.

It was very much a dog-eat-dog kind of environment; one of the many reasons I hated it.

"Nothing to say to that, Keira?" Kendra snarled.

"No. I don't know how she treated you," I admitted, her aggression surprising me. "I never really got the chance to see her interacting with any of you."

She sniffed. "Well, trust me, she wasn't sweet and lovin'."

I frowned at her, but then I looked at her cut, really looked at it, and my mouth tensed when she started stroking one of the patches on the front.

Heart in my throat, I took in the VP's patch, and registered she was wearing Storm's cut.

A smile curved about her lips, so cat-like in its form that, for a second, I found it hard to believe that she took such pleasure in hurting me.

"Why are you wearing Storm's cut, Kendra?" I asked softly.

"I picked up the first thing I could find on the bedroom floor," she told me, trying and failing to be coy.

I jerked up my chin. "You're sleeping with Storm?"

"Oh, we're doing the exact opposite of sleeping, honey." She leaned back against the fence that circled the perimeter of the cemetery. "He's been acting strangely since his birthday. Have you noticed that?"

I gulped. "Yes."

"Do you know what happened? He's been..." She smiled again. "... rampant."

The adjective would have made me snicker at any other time. Instead, it was like a hammer to my heart.

"I don't know," I muttered blankly, reaching up and pressing my knuckles to my temple where an ache was starting to bloom.

She started rubbing her fingertip over the patch again. "I think your days as his wife are over, Keira. I'm sorry to have to tell you that, but I'd prepare myself if I were you for that 'goodbye, it's been fun' talk."

Woodenly, I stared at her. "How long's it been going on?" I rasped, suddenly feeling the cold sink into my bones, suddenly feeling the dampness from the rain filter through to my skin, making me feel as if I were freezing from the inside out.

"Oh, years," Kendra said airily, wafting her free hand.

My eyes flared wide. "Years?" My temper stirred, the embers starting to flicker into flames at her gumption, but then she nodded, and her tone was a bewildering combination of sorrowful and catty as she told me:

"Yes. While you were busy resting your fat ass in bed, I was keeping *my* man satisfied. Least you could have done was sucked him off, but nope, you couldn't even do that. Don't worry, I did that for him when you were too lazy to."

My fat ass in bed?

Was she talking about when I'd been put on bedrest? When my pregnancy had turned high risk?

"He should have left you years ago. We had a baby together, you know? No, I don't suppose you would know, would you?" Her smile was sympathetic, but in her eyes, I saw her scorn. "I had to have an abortion. The baby wasn't…right. Storm was so sad, but he was there for all of it. He was so supportive; he held my hand and everything.

"I know he wants more kids, but he thinks you're too weak to have them. We keep trying, but we haven't been blessed yet." Then, she patted her stomach, and murmured, "Maybe after trying for the past month, we'll be lucky."

My hands curled into fists as I surged into a standing position. She stopped leaning against the fence, a sudden awareness adding a tension to her form as if she were preparing herself for an attack, but I twisted away from her, and I ran.

Like a child, like that goddamn ostrich with its head in the sand, I ran away, but as I did, she laughed. It echoed in my head, ricocheting around and around, deafening me with her gleeful amusement at my horror.

When my foot got snagged with something on the ground, I wrenched it, growling as I twisted it. The pain was nothing in comparison to the agony inside me.

The cheating… that was one thing.

But he'd gotten her pregnant?

Was trying to get her pregnant again?

My brain wasn't computing the blows to my system, but that one fact remained—he didn't want us to have another kid. Hell, we'd argued a few weeks before his birthday about it!

He didn't want me to have another of his children, but he was okay with Kendra getting pregnant because I was too weak?

Too weak?

I'd been bedridden toward the end of carrying Cyan, but...

I wasn't weak.

I'd brought my baby girl into this world. I'd stagnated on a mattress for months to save her.

Was that a sign of weakness?

No.

That was a sign of strength. Of love. Of hope. Of *faith.*

As I hobbled back to my car, the journey seeming to take twice as long as it had been to get to the graveyard, something that had nothing to do with my ankle, my brain whirred.

Storm thought I was weak.

He thought Kendra was the right person to carry his child.

Because I was too fragile. Too delicate.

I thought about when we made love, how he cherished me and was careful with me. Even when I dug my heels into his ass and growled against him, when I tugged on his hair and bit his lip, trying to trigger what he'd shown me that one time after Rene's passing... But he always calmed things down.

Always.

Because I was weak.

Because he didn't think I could take him.

All of him.

And maybe he wasn't wrong—I'd never told him about what happened here at the clubhouse between us. Had never shared that I'd seen a different side of him.

My hands curled into fists as righteous anger washed through me. An anger that was aimed at both of us. An anger that made me feel small and pathetic—exactly like my mom.

I'd turned into her.

Knowing Storm was one thing, completely avoiding the truth because it didn't suit my narrative was another.

I was her.

Storm was Dad. Cheating. *Lying.*

Things had turned full circle. Somehow, we'd morphed into them as spouses.

Mind racing as I asked myself if we were like them as parents, I wondered if the toxic stain had already made its way into Cyan's DNA.

I wanted to be a better mom than mine, but… it had taken Kendra to make me see the woods for the trees. Maybe I was a *worse* mother. What else was I burying my head in the sand over?

That Cyan could repeat my mistakes had terror whipping at my insides.

That she could be okay with cheating, okay with a man treating her like a second-class citizen—

"No. *No,*" I whispered to myself as I jumped into the SUV, speeding off down the driveway, uncaring if Storm saw me now. "I won't let that happen, Cyan, I won't let that happen."

THIRTY-SEVEN

STORM

PRESENT - JULY

TWO WEEKS after Kendra made an appearance in Coshocton, before disappearing like a fucking ghost, North, Giulia and Hawk's brother, showed up.

At first, I thought it actually was Hawk standing in my doorway, Little behind him, shadowing the fucker like he was haunting him. But then I took in the fact Hawk wasn't wearing a cut, which would never happen. Hell, I'd worn mine to the school parent-teacher conference.

"What are you doing here?" I demanded, not exactly pleased to see him.

Fucker had run off with his dad's Old Lady. If that wasn't the shadiest fucking thing, then I didn't know what was.

"You know him, Prez?" Little boomed.

"I know him." *Unfortunately.* Scowling, I waved a hand. "Come in."

Little grunted as North slipped into one of the seats in front of the desk. When the palm frond beside the door got caught as Little closed it, he heaved a sigh, shoved it away, then closed it again. I almost smiled, but the guys already thought it was fucking weird that I had a green thumb—unlike my Old Lady—so I didn't need to add to the rep.

"Didn't say you could sit down, but I guess that's okay," I grumbled. "I repeat, what the fuck are you doing here, North?"

"I wanna be a Sinner again."

"You mean you want to Prospect for the Sinners," I sniped, rocking back into my seat as I watched him.

He nodded. "I do."

"You're the one who left West Orange, fuckface. You'd be a brother like Hawk now."

His eyes flared with interest, and he leaned forward. "How is he?"

"You coulda called him yourself."

North shook his head. "He'd never understand. Seriously, how is he?"

"Got an Old Lady now."

North's mouth dropped open. "What? What the fuck? He's got a woman?"

"And a dog," I mocked. "Probably a couple fucking dozen pets as well."

"I don't get it." His head swayed slowly from side to side as if he were in a daze. "He wasn't ready to settle down."

"Takes the right woman. As you well know," I said pointedly. "What happened with Dog's Old Lady?"

He just shrugged. "Didn't work out."

"You left your family behind for her," I remarked, then I pursed my lips and said, "You're an uncle now. Did you know that?"

"Jesus. Giulia had a kid?"

"She did."

"Fuck."

That pretty much summed it up. "Why the hell should I let a dumbass like you into my club, North? Someone who don't give a shit about family?"

"I do give a shit about family. I just..." He sighed. "I'm a Sinner through and through, Storm, but I know what the MC life is like. Dad was beating the shit outta her." He wriggled his shoulders. "I fucked up, but I did it for good reasons. I just wanted to keep her safe and didn't think anyone in the MC would help her."

"You do remember Nyx, don't you? If she'd gone to him, he'd have put a stop to Dog's bullshit."

"She was scared."

I hummed, a little disbelievingly. It wasn't on me to judge a victim of domestic abuse, but something about this had rung false with me from the start.

"You know most of the club think you killed Dog—" North's eyes flared even wider at that, which was when I realized he hadn't known his dad was dead.

"Dad… he was murdered?"

I didn't tell him Lodestar was behind that particular job, one undertaken because she knew about Dog beating his woman up as well. Unfortunately for North, he'd been cast as scapegoat when he'd done a fucking runner.

This was going to shit up Rex's plan majorly. Last thing we needed was North or Hawk getting all up in Lodestar's face about putting that piece of shit father of theirs six feet under.

Ah, fuck.

I scratched my chin, well aware that Coshocton was gonna become the dumping ground of all the Sinners who pissed off Rex or were defective brothers in that they couldn't do shit right.

Great.

"You can stay and Prospect, but you ain't getting any special treatment from me," I told him gruffly.

His brow puckered. "Really?"

"Yeah. Really."

"No questions asked?"

"I already asked questions. You gave me mediocre answers. That's why I'm gonna let you slide right back to the beginning. You have to work up to my good graces," I said wryly, slotting my fingers together so I could crack my knuckles. "You got someplace to live?"

"No."

"We have a bunkhouse out back. It ain't pretty. You might wanna live in the MC's motel. There's a cheaper rate for brothers." Mostly because I wanted to knock down the bunkhouse seeing as it was an environmental fucking health hazard.

Not just because of the asbestos in the walls either—that was where the brothers took the clubwhores to fuck, and I sure as hell didn't want Cyan playing out back and hearing them screwing.

He nodded. "Okay, sounds great. Can you give me directions?"

I grabbed my phone, demanded, "Your number?" I inputted it, then sent him a link. "There."

North chewed on his lip a second as he stared down at the text, before he rasped, "You know someone called Sticky?"

Curious, I tipped my head to the side. "Yeah. I know someone called Sticky. Why?"

"I heard these guys talking about you in a bar while I was riding through Pittsburgh. They were talking about the new Prez in Coshocton. It's why I slid over this way."

"Just to meet little ol' me?" was my dry rejoinder.

"Maybe. I knew you'd cut me more slack than Rex would."

"What'd make you think that?"

"You're a man who appreciates second, third, fourth chances. Rex's so fucking perfect, it's like he never makes a mistake. As a Prez, I respect him, but I know better than to ask for any leniency from him. You?" He shrugged. "You're human. Probably will make you a better Prez than him—"

"You don't need to butter me up," I rumbled. "I already said I'd take you in."

"Yeah, but I'm worth it," he muttered. "I just… Without Hawk, I had to grow up. It sucked. But I did it. I got a job and I kept it and put a roof over my woman's head, and it still wasn't enough, you know?"

"What went wrong?" I questioned.

"I don't think anything did. I just think she wanted to get away from Dad, and I was her way out. I can't even be mad. He treated her like shit, exactly how he used to treat Mom… that was who he was. A jackass." His mouth tightened. "Sticky has a grudge against you."

"I know. It's a dumb grudge. I didn't do shit to him."

"Doesn't matter. You pissed him off and he wasn't afraid to run his mouth about it."

"When did you hear him bitching off?"

"Yesterday."

"Whereabouts?"

"Jimmy's Bar & Grill on the I-70." He stared me down. "He's staying at a motel nearby."

"How d'you know that?"

"I followed 'em. They were as pissed as skunks. Watched 'em go inside. They each had a room, and they were dumps—I checked. They'd been living there a while."

The intel was surprisingly helpful.

"Thanks for the info, North." I pursed my lips as I thought about what those fuckers were planning, well aware that it wouldn't be anything good.

"Storm, I know I fucked up in West Orange so, I mean, I know I have to prove myself. I'm willing to do that though. Any shit jobs, I'm your man, okay?"

I laughed a little. "Trying to buy your way into a cut, huh?"

He pulled a face. "Maybe."

Rubbing my bottom lip, I told him, "Pick your poison."

"Huh?"

"Pick your poison. Before, you used to let Hawk do every-fucking-thing for you. That ain't gonna slide here, North. So, where do you want to work?"

"You're giving me a choice?"

"Let's just say I'm fond of your sister."

"Giulia?" His eyes bugged.

"You got more than one sister?"

"No, but dude, no one's fond of her."

"Think Nyx would disagree. Think he'd also punch you in the *cojones* for talking smack about his Old Lady."

"True." He whistled. "Okay, so, if I have a choice… under the Road Captain."

"Doesn't always mean you get to go on runs and pick up a bonus," I pointed out wryly. "One last offer, North, pick something you want or I'll just give you the shittiest jobs in the place like you asked, and they'll make your idea of crappy tasks look fun."

His eyes bugged again, but then he smirked. "Okay. Under the Enforcer."

"Digger's the Enforcer here. I'll tell him I got him extra help." I sat up. "Go and move into the motel, then check back in with Dig. He'll tell you what he needs from you."

North nodded, then got to his feet. "Thanks, Storm. I appreciate it."

"Make sure that any other pieces of information that come your way slide over to me too, huh?"

"For sure."

He saluted me, which made me roll my eyes, and as I watched him go, my cell buzzed but I called out, "There's a party tonight, North. You're welcome to join us."

He grinned. "I'll be there."

Nodding at him, I glanced at the Caller ID and smiled. "Hey, babe. Everything okay?"

"Your dog just pissed on the rug. Again."

I grimaced. "Fuck." I didn't fail to notice the 'your' there, either. When he was cute, Fraction was *our* dog. Whenever he disobeyed, he was mine.

"Yeah. Fuck. You're gonna have to fix this, Storm. He won't stop doing it! This reminds me of why little things are so annoying."

Despite myself, I had to laugh. "Little things?"

"Yeah. Humans, animals. Why didn't we just adopt an older dog? One who knew not to piss on rugs?"

"I don't think they come preprogrammed."

"Ya think?" She huffed. "Couldn't you and Cyan have picked a small one? One that didn't pee a fountain every time he goes to the bathroom?"

"She picked Fraction, not me." I paused. "You ready for tonight?"

"As ready as I'll ever be," was her retort. She didn't sound all that excited, and before disappointment could hit me, she growled, "Fraction! Don't you dare—"

She was distracted.

Good.

I'd prefer that to her being nervous.

It was the first party she'd be attending at the clubhouse in years. Hell, it was my first party as Prez seeing as I'd avoided all the others, but August was approaching, and I had to start integrating better. I'd accepted that before North had informed me that the old guard Sinners were hovering in the background.

Scratching my jaw, I listened to her bark at the dog, before I said, "Just shove him in the yard."

"I can't. Cyan lets him back in."

"She loves him."

Keira groaned.

I grinned, but conceded, "I'll work on training him some more over the weekend. It's been crazy this week what with signing on the dotted line and getting started on construction with the diner expansion."

"I can't believe you bought the lot next door because I suggested it," she said, but it wasn't the words, it was her tone that had me arching my brow at my potted asplenium.

"Are you running?"

"No, I'm scrubbing the rug," she grumbled.

"Ah. Why wouldn't I have listened to you? You showed me the accounts, showed me statistics… you're right. The diner does need expanding. Fred and Wilma were Flintstones. They didn't move with the times."

"How long have you been waiting to use that pun?"

"Since I learned their names."

A soft laugh escaped her, but she confirmed, "MC says Cyan can sleep over so I'm yours all night long."

"That sounds good to me. I knew I got Digger to be my Enforcer for a reason."

"What? Because I'd trust MC to be our babysitter?"

"Well, yeah, and you're friends now."

"True. We are." I heard the smile in her voice.

"Shame she isn't coming to the party."

"She's coming to the BBQ tomorrow."

"Are things okay between her and Digger?"

"Oh, yeah. He's very supportive. He reminds me of you, actually. You never used to get mad at me for not wanting to go to those parties."

"You meet the right woman the parties are only fun if you go together."

"I'm sure you didn't used to be this romantic."

"Well, I never said I wasn't a dumbass before."

It took losing her to recognize that I had to get my head out of my ass. But of all the shit my mom had accused me of, being a fucking idiot wasn't on my list of shortcomings. Now I had my second chance, I wasn't going to mess things up.

North was right—I was a man who could appreciate that people weren't perfect, they made mistakes, but how they went about fixing them defined them more than the mistake ever could.

She tutted. "I don't like it when you call yourself names."

"It's all good, baby girl."

"No, it isn't. We need to work on your self-esteem."

I grinned a little. "Same as Cyan? You gonna tell me I don't need to wear makeup to look pretty? And that short skirts won't make me feel better about myself?"

A laugh escaped her. "Shut up, you. Anyway, I can't make your self-esteem better until August."

That robbed the breath from me. "Does that mean what I think it does?"

Her laughter turned sultry. "It does."

A growl rumbled from my parted lips. "I'm gonna make you come so hard, baby girl."

"You'll probably last two seconds," she teased, but I heard her shaky breath. "I want to see that too though. Want to see you shatter into a million pieces just so I can put you back together again."

My dick started throbbing. "Fuck," I rasped, leaning over, then rocking back. Neither position helped. "I wanna bend you over this desk so bad—"

She sighed. "August."

"The eighth," I told her quietly.

"The eighth. It's gonna be a good day."

"Yeah." I cleared my throat. "Do you think MC would look after Cyan again? For two nights, maybe? Saw this place called Corkscrew Falls—"

"Just happened to see, huh?"

Sheepishly, I smiled. "Well, you know. I might have googled it."

She snickered. "I can ask."

"It's beautiful. I think you'd love it. We can spend the night there. It's less than two hours away so we're close by in case of an emergency, but… what do you think?"

"I think I'd love that," she confirmed, her contentedness whispering down the line.

A knock sounded at the door, and for a second, I thought it was someone outside my office, but it wasn't.

"Coming!" Keira called out. "Two seconds, honey," she told me, which made me smile. I heard the click of the lock, took in the sound of the door opening as she called out, "MaryCat, I told you to come around the back—"

The undeniable sound of someone pumping a shotgun came down the line.

There was a thudding noise, and the sounds of footsteps boomed in my ears. One pair, three. *Five*. Shit.

Jerking to my feet, I snarled, "Who the fuck is that? What's going on?"

I didn't expect an answer because I thought Keira had dropped her phone, but someone must have snagged it, because a purr whispered in my ear. "Guess who?"

Kendra.

"What do you want?" I spat.

"I think you know the answer to that."

Then, she disconnected the call.

THIRTY-EIGHT

STORM

PAST

"LET GO OF ME," I snarled as my brothers pinned me in place.

Even Maverick was in on it—they'd hauled in his help while he was on leave.

Nyx grabbed one arm, Steel the other. Link and Rex dealt with my feet, and Maverick was the one who slipped his hands around my waist as, on the count of three, they all hauled me into the air.

A yelp escaped me as I wriggled out of their hold, but it was no good. They weren't letting go. They were holding on tight.

A couple Sinners saw our antics, laughed and jeered as if it were a joke, not realizing that this was serious.

That my brothers were intending to dump me in the Fridge again.

That they were going to force me into withdrawals.

Panting and gasping for breath, they hauled me over to a waiting cage. I buckled one knee in an effort to kick my boot in Rex's face—this was all his fucking idea, and seeing as it worked, they kept on goddamn doing it—but as I did, a soft gasp caught my attention.

A woman stood there. Young. Her eyes on us. Taking in the situation.

My mouth tightened as I ignored her, not giving much of a shit that she was hot, just needing to get free.

"Who are you, honey?"

Link.

Always the fucking flirt.

"I'm Kendra," the woman replied softly. "I-I just—"

"The party's in the bar," Rex said, his tone flat, dismissing her without words while also containing Link from heading after her.

I took advantage of the distraction to pull my arm back, and when I managed to clock Nyx in the side of the head, he went down with a grunt, straight onto his knees which knocked out the stability of their hold on me.

With a yelp, I felt myself falling, but then Maverick was there, under my gut, holding me up while the others managed to swing me toward the cage.

As I was tossed in the back, my head collided with the metal framework, and groaning, I didn't even notice when they clambered into the cage, some leaping into the trunk with me. The engine just rattled, and I felt the aches pounding through my system as we roared off the driveway, past the cemetery, and onto the land that separated the clubhouse from the Fridge.

The guys were talking, laughing, bitching.

This was a regular occurrence now. It wasn't as traumatic. At least, not for them. For me?

It was hell.

I tried to get up, tried to roll onto my knees so I could clamber off the side of the truck, but my body wouldn't let me.

Lying there, curled up in a ball, I groaned as we went over a nasty ridge that jerked the vehicle, and I puked, almost choking on it until Maverick hissed and grabbed me by the hair, then tugged me away from it and over onto my back.

The journey could have taken a decade and it wouldn't have been long enough.

When we pulled up, I started crying, not giving a shit about looking like a pussy. I just sobbed as they dragged me out of the cage, then hauled me into the place where we tortured enemies, killed 'em, and cut up their bodies to hide the evidence.

They threw me in there like I was trash, locking the door before I could scamper forward and escape.

The pitch black of the walls had me closing my eyes, and finally, I got enough strength to crawl over to the door, to lean against it, to bring my knees to my chest as I huddled in on myself. Then, I pressed my head to the door, *listening*. Always listening.

I heard them set up a fire, heard them laughing and joking, Link talking about Kendra and how hot she was and how, later, he was gonna tap that. I heard them opening cans of food and popping bottles of beer, sitting around like they were Boy Scouts at summer camp.

And even as the fear hit me for what was about to come; even though the pain was a specter just waiting to consume me whole; even though the withdrawals would tear my sanity to shreds, I was grateful for them.

Closing my eyes, aware that I'd never be left alone for one minute, that I'd be here for weeks, that they'd be the only people I spoke to for days, who'd give me food and drink, I accepted what I couldn't change.

Cold turkey was about to make me its bitch.

THIRTY-NINE

STORM

PRESENT

THE SOUNDS OF THAT SHOTGUN, of Kendra's voice, of the implications of what was happening at my house, didn't send me into a tailspin.

In fact, the rationale that settled over my brain was similar to when I took a hit of coke. The alertness, the hyper focus, it was beautiful. So fucking crystal clear that I recognized how hard life was without the ability to concentrate intensely.

But it made sense.

My woman was in danger.

My kid was in danger.

My fucking *everything* was in danger.

My hands curved about the edge of the desk as my brain clicked into gear.

Men—I needed men.

Guns—I needed guns.

Blood—I needed to shed it.

I slammed my fist into the table, not even feeling the pain as it soared through my knuckles. I needed *my* brothers. My fucking people. Rex, Nyx, Sin, Steel, Maverick, Link, Cruz.

As tunnel vision took over everything else, I ignored the flurry of notifications I'd received during my conversation with North, and sent out a chapter-wide text with two words in it:

Code Red

Following it up with my address, I shoved my phone into the back pocket of my jeans, then pivoted on my heel toward the cabinet where I housed our weapons.

Arming myself with as many guns as I could fucking carry, I headed to the door and out into the hallway, ready to direct the troops to the armory so they could arm themselves.

As I moved down the hallway, though, the silence within the clubhouse resonated hard.

It wasn't possible that they'd reacted so swiftly to the Code Red, but when I reached the bar and found it empty, my jaw clenched, my eyes widened, and I took the hit as much as I would a bullet to the gut.

The fuckers had defected.

Jesus, you could have heard a pin drop in the silence of the room, a silence that seemed to buzz over the music that was playing on the speakers, music that—even at top volume—usually could barely be heard over dozens of brothers shooting the shit.

Hell, even the clubwhores had absconded.

I ran outside, found the gates wide open and North standing there, perplexed as he hovered by the gatehouse. He kept twitching, jerking from side to side like he wanted to do something but didn't know what.

"Where is everyone?" I snapped, mind racing back to our meeting. Had I heard them ride off?

Bikes drifted in and out at all hours of the fucking day and night. Hearing the rumble of a dozen bikes wouldn't have caught my attention because it was white noise by this point.

Christ, I was used to dozens of bikes coming and going at West Orange. They barely caught my attention now.

North sputtered, "I-I was gonna leave but with the gates wide open, I didn't think I should—"

"You did good," I told him stonily. Because he had. The fucker hadn't left, even though he knew something funky was going on.

Bastard had just proven himself to be more loyal than the entire fucking chapter. "I need you with me."

"What's going on?" he shouted as I ran over to my bike.

"Keira's been…" I couldn't get the words out, so instead I hollered, "My house has been hijacked."

His eyes flared wide in astonishment, but he earned himself another brownie point by running over to his hog and kicking it into gear without another word.

Was it fucked up that I'd prefer this dipshit at my back than my council anyway?

Fucking Coshocton assholes. West Orange brothers were the only ones who goddamn mattered, anyway.

Although, where the hell was Digger? Where the fuck was my Enforcer?

Racing down the single track that led to the main road, I gunned it once we were off the uneven ground then headed toward my subdivision.

Traffic swerved, horns blaring as I rode through them like the hounds of hell were biting at my ankles, but I ignored the fuckers, not even giving them enough attention to flip them the bird.

The wind whistled in my ears, but the white noise was cleansing. It let me think about my next steps. About how I was going to resolve this fuck up when it was likely that, by the end of the day, my family and I, North as well, would be goddamn dead.

If the entire chapter was against us, if they were just waiting to reclaim their club, then we were screwed. In more ways than one. Cyan hadn't fucking survived that bastard just to die today, and there was no way in hell any of those fuckers were going to touch my Old Lady.

Rage filled me, cleansing me, strengthening me. Awakening me even more. This was like a dose of meth and coke at the same time, only without the fatal consequences.

I clenched my fingers around the handlebar, riding toward my death, prepared for it so long as they goddamn lived. Those fuckers wanted me. Not my woman and kid. I was the end goal. I could handle that, would easily trade myself for their safety.

That, I realized, was how I'd get them out alive.

An exchange.

Simple.

My heart settled. A trade. That was all we needed here.

As I raced toward the gates, out of nowhere, the whistle of the wind changed, shifted, turning into a roar that sent my heart pumping again. It shivered over my skin, bringing every single nerve ending in my body to life.

Praying that I wasn't wrong, I twisted my head around, careful not to whirl into traffic and felt a relief more fucking pure than newly processed heroin shift through me.

The chapter was there.

In the distance.

Dozens of bikes, of men… *my* brothers.

Riding to me, not already at my house.

Not waiting to kill my family and me.

The rumble on the ground was sweeter than any high I'd experienced in my fucking life. It shot through my limbs, sank into my bones as they rode into war *with* me, not against me.

I released a full breath, the first since I'd heard Kendra's voice, and more confident now, if still confused as to where they'd all goddamn been, I made it to the subdivision.

The sight of blood in the gatehouse had my nostrils flaring with anger. I'd suspected this was likely, but that didn't mean I was happy to be right.

It dripped down the back wall of the booth, blood and brain matter splattered there like some kind of modern work of art.

Jaw clenched, I rode through the open gates, spotting a crumpled Paul on the ground as I passed.

The idiocy of the fuckers behind this told me they had no business being anything other than grunt workers, never mind the leaders of an MC.

Who the fuck took out an unarmed security guard?

Then, if that wasn't bad enough, left the body and the evidence behind and didn't expect the cops to be called?

"What a fucking waste," I rasped under my breath, feeling bad for

Paul because if I hadn't picked this subdivision, he'd still be goddamn alive.

Someone else I feared for?

Jump.

As I raced through the streets, well aware that how fast I was riding and the number of brothers roaring up behind me were drawing attention from the neighbors, I hoped to fuck the sheriff would be heading toward us sooner rather than goddamn later. I'd never call 'em, but I didn't have to when old bats had one finger on the '9' and the '1' whenever I rode by alone, never mind when I brought my whole chapter with me.

When I pulled up to my street, I absorbed all the information my eyes shot my way. Digger's house looked shut up, no sign of life there, but Jump's? He was flat out on the front yard, face down. I ground my teeth, accepting another soul's loss on my conscience, before I saw someone in the doorway.

His woman.

Darla, I thought her name was.

She was dead too.

The fucking bastards had killed his Old Lady.

Was it too early for school to be out? I genuinely didn't know what time it was, but I just hoped to Christ it wasn't, otherwise his kid could be dead as well.

Aside from the bikes parked on the lawn I fucking mowed week in and week out, all looked quiet at my house. There was no one in the windows, no one by the door. As I pulled up on the road, I climbed off and stared at what had been, until this afternoon, my home.

Hands clenched at my side, I started on the walkway as North pulled up behind me.

"Storm? Where the fuck are you going?" he called out.

"They want me," was my calm reply, but my voice was quiet enough for the roar of my brothers' hogs to drown it.

I scanned the building's façade, coming up with nothing apart from a shadow in the kitchen window that made me think someone had their eyes on me.

When they didn't shoot, I figured this was what they wanted, although what their plan was, I didn't have a fucking clue.

Thudding footsteps pounded behind me, and someone dragged my arm, twisting me around and bringing me to a halt. As they did, the scent of smoke hit my nostrils and I frowned, peering up at a soot-covered Digger.

"There was a fire at the warehouse over in Lafayette. Called in as many brothers as I could. We'd have been here sooner—"

"You got here plenty fast."

Digger let out a gruff exhalation. "What the fuck's going on, man? What's the Code Red?"

"Kendra and those ex-Sinners are in there. They're holding my family hostage."

He sucked in a breath. "You can't go in there. Not if they're leveraging them for you. The second they get you, is the second they'll blow you all apart. You saw what they did to Paul."

"Jump and his Old Lady too."

Digger's mouth tensed but he nodded. "Fucking bastards."

"Where's MC?" I rasped.

"She's at the diner."

"You sure?"

"Positive. She checks in."

"Whatever happens today, Digger, I need you to promise me something."

"Anything, man. Any-fucking-thing."

Just thinking of Kendra had my heart pounding. "You kill that bitch. You make sure Kendra dies—"

He grabbed my arm. "I'll leave that job to you."

"I'll do whatever they fucking want to make sure K and Cy are safe, Digger. I don't expect to make it—"

"Shut the fuck up." He grunted, smashed a fist into my shoulder, then growled, "What's their end game here?"

"I don't know. North gave me intel on that Sticky fucker. They were talking about overturning me as Prez. They want the clubhouse back. No idea why they brought the war to my home, unless it's because of Kendra."

"Would she have that much power over them?"

"Maybe, maybe not."

I twisted around and caught a sight of a dirty SL who hovered a few feet away. It seemed too much of a coincidence for the fire not to have been set by these bastards as a diversion and I just hadn't gotten the memo.

"SL, what happened with Kendra?" I demanded as I checked my phone, finding a couple of messages in the council's group chat that, fuck me, I'd muted because they drove me nuts with their talk about the Bengals.

If I survived this, I'd never mute a goddamn chat again.

SL wrung his hands together at my question which didn't put my nerves on edge at all... Not. "I sent her back to Pittsburgh and set three different brothers on to guard her."

"She was meeting with Grim, wasn't she? That day when I called?"

SL nodded. "Yeah."

"You find out what they were talking about?"

"Grim just said he bought her a coffee."

"I really believe that," Digger mocked.

"Kendra took a risk coming into Coshocton. It had to be for a reason."

"To give Grim something?" SL asked.

"Maybe." I scowled. "Please tell me he wasn't one of the fucking brothers you used as a guard—"

He scowled at me. "Do I look like that big of a dipshit?"

"I dunno, man. I really don't fucking know right now." I scraped a hand over my face. "I didn't get more involved because I didn't think she was a threat. Should have known that, even in Pittsburgh, she'd find a way to fuck with me."

All I'd done was check in with SL to make sure she was still in the motel room we'd shoved her in after Keira had beaten the crap out of her that day at the diner.

"Grim's been acting weird all week," Digger said gruffly. "And I was in on the scheduling of her guards, man. Grim couldn't get to her, but we didn't keep her fucking prisoner. She had a phone. No reason why one of her guards wouldn't give that number to Grim if he asked."

Anger lashed at me, but I thought about what North had said. "You heard of Jimmy's Bar & Grill, SL?"

He scrubbed a hand over his dirty face. "Yeah, it's near the motel where she was staying. It's the only place for a couple of miles where you can grab decent food."

I wanted to scream, but instead, I just cursed fate and coincidences. "North said he heard those fuckers talking in that same bar. That's probably how they met.

"If he overheard 'em talking, no reason why Kendra wouldn't too." I narrowed my eyes on my VP. "SL, you find out if that's what happened."

His shoulders hunched up around his ears. "Will do, Prez."

Wondering why the ex-Sinners weren't throwing demands at us, I turned back to look at the house, which was when I saw Kendra in the bedroom window, a goddamn gun to Keira's head. She had duct tape covering her mouth and wrapped around her wrists too.

The rage that filled me made me think of the time I OD'ed on meth. I knew what it was like to embrace death, understood the feeling of letting the life in my body be drained away, but this was different.

I'd die a thousand times if it meant keeping her safe.

K's eyes clashed with mine, and the lack of fear in hers had my heart leveling out.

She was angry.

I could deal with that. Anger was something I was accustomed to stirring in her. Her fear would break me.

"SL, pick ten men and get them going around the back of my neighbor's house," I rumbled, a plan kicking into gear. "Keira keeps the French doors open now because of the dog." Christ, if Fraction had even survived—

"Okay, Storm, I'll do that."

"Make sure they go in stealthily."

"Will do."

"What's the game plan?" Digger demanded.

"Shift the focus of the fuckers in there so we can get to Keira—"

The window tilted open and Kendra's grating voice shimmered out, "Storm, whatever you're planning, stop it. You know what I want."

I cast the bitch a look. "I know what you fucking need—to be shoved in a mental asylum, you crazy cunt." My gaze shifted over the room at her back. "Where are the brothers?"

She smirked. "Trying to find your kid."

"Takes five men to find one kid?" Digger taunted.

"There are only four—"

Digger laughed when she bit back her words, cursing at having given us concrete numbers, confirming what I'd heard on the phone.

Though she was as big a moron as I already knew, rage still flushed through me. "Kendra, what the fuck is your game?"

"They want to be Sinners again, Storm."

"It's not the fucking Boy Scouts. You can't just come and go within the MC as you goddamn please." Gritting my teeth, I demanded, "Why did you jump in with them?"

"Overheard them talking in a bar—" Well, there I had my confirmation I was right. "—heard your name, thought I'd play along." A smile tipped up the corners of her mouth. "Don't worry, Asher, I'll never let them hurt you."

"You mean to tell me you got four bikers wrapped around your fucking finger? What did you put in that snatch of yours, Kendra? Fucking molly?"

Her mouth twisted. "Ain't never met a man I can't twist around my finger—apart from you, Storm."

Scoffing, I said, "You rewriting the last twelve years, Kendra? Where every day you whored that skank pussy out to any willing brother in the West Orange chapter?"

"I only did that for you!" she screamed, her face turning hot pink as she jutted her chin out with rage.

"Did that for me?" I retorted. "Since when did I ask you to do dick for me? Jesus fucking Christ, Kendra, I ain't given a shit about whether you lived or died even knowing who your pa is. You're the one who stuck around when I made it fucking clear that I didn't want you—"

"You did want me," she snarled, shoving the gun harder into Keira's temple, with enough force to make her stagger, knees buckling in response. "You just let her pussywhip you, trap you with that kid. I freed you, baby. You should be grateful to me." The last came out as a scream.

"Keep her calm, Storm, Jesus. She's gonna pistol-whip her soon."

I didn't ignore Digger's advice, because sweet fuck, I wanted Keira harmed less than he goddamn did, but something weird as shit was going on here and I needed to figure out what the fuck it was.

Brothers, ex-MC or not, didn't get snagged up by clubwhore cunt. That wasn't how shit worked.

Bitches turned into clubwhores hoping that they'd snag a brother who'd brand 'em, but that rarely happened.

"What did you do, Kendra? What did you offer them?" I rumbled, not focusing on the personal. There was nothing personal between us whatsoever.

She wanted me alive, I knew that. But the brothers would want me dead. Her goals and the brothers' were divided.

"Nothing," she retorted, her arm tightening around Keira's throat until my woman's face turned a mottled red.

My hands clawed into fists at my sides. "Let her go. She ain't done dick to you."

"She stole you from me," Kendra raged. "You're mine. You were always fucking mine."

"I ain't never been yours." I narrowed my eyes at her. "You creatin' some kind of delusion about us being together don't make it so. I ain't never been yours and I never fucking will be either."

"Easy, Storm," Digger muttered.

"Ten brothers have reached your back yard," SL whispered softly behind me.

"You will be mine. Once this bitch is dead!" Kendra snarled, pushing the gun harder into Keira's temple. "I should have killed you years ago, you sanctimonious bitch," she spat at her. "You should have left him alone. He's mine. *Mine*, do you fucking hear me?"

I caught Keira's eyes, urging her to… Jesus. I didn't know what. I'd never taught her fucking self-defense, had always relied on brothers to protect her for me.

Sweet fuck.

She needed to do Krav as well.

If we made it out of this hell, she'd be joining Cyan and me at those classes too.

I clung to that hope with every fiber of my being. Praying that'd happen, pleading with whoever the hell would listen to make it so.

When Keira's knees buckled, Kendra's attention split a bare second and I took the opportunity to rush closer to the window while her focus was shot, but I didn't get there fast enough.

Kendra shoved Keira against the window, using the glass to prop her up. With her face shoved into it, I knew it had to be hard to breathe, but this close, I could smell Kendra's godawful perfume and knew that if I was fast enough, I could shoot her, but that was only one-fifth of the problem resolved.

"What's the end game here, Kendra?" I rumbled, close enough now that I saw the beads of sweat on her temple, little droplets that rolled down into her eyes, making her blink double time. Those godawful beetle eyelashes fluttered as fast as the pulse in her throat and prompted me to continue, "You're just pussy, Kendra. Just pussy. You don't have a clue what you got yourself wrapped up in."

Her knuckles blanched under the pressure of her grip on the gun. "I know they wanted you to hand yourself over. I knew that the only way you'd do that was if this fucking cunt was in danger. Why the hell did you have to be so predictable, Storm?"

"If love's made me predictable, then so be it."

"You don't love her. You're obsessed with her—"

"Like you're obsessed with me?" I scanned a look behind her, trying to see if there was any movement.

This was Keira's bedroom, *our* room more recently, so I had to pray that Cyan was tucked up in the safe room.

"I love you, Storm. I've always goddamn loved you and you never saw me once you clapped eyes on this bitch."

"Want to know a secret, Kendra?" I rasped, taking a step closer to the window, so close that we were almost within touching distance.

Our room wasn't on ground level, it was like a half floor up, so I stared up at her with about four feet of height difference. It meant I couldn't launch myself into the room without Keira getting hurt, but that didn't mean I couldn't mess with Kendra's head.

"I want to know anything you've got to tell me," she whispered, the puppy voice making me want to hurl.

"You stuck to me like superglue because you thought I was the weakest of my brothers—"

"No," she whined.

"Yes," I drawled. "Do you remember that day you rolled into town?"

"No. 'Course I don't. That was years ago. And baby, that's a lie, I never thought you were weak—"

My skin crawled at her term of endearment. "I know you saw them dragging my ass off to the Fridge. I know because I saw you watching me." I tapped my nose. "Not gonna lie, I checked you out. But you saw an easy ride, and when I never rolled over, you got more and more hooked on the idea of an easy score. But there's nothing easy about me, Kendra, and the biggest secret of all?

"I hate you," I told her softly, letting my hatred for her filter into the words like venom, wanting it to kill her, hoping it choked her. "I've always fucking hated you. Every last goddamn thing about you.

"It's why the only way I tapped your ass is when I was so fucking high I'd mistake you for the only goddamn woman I've ever truly wanted."

"No, no, no," she warbled, punctuating every word I uttered with one of her own. "You love me, you just don't understand what we mean to each other."

"I understand that you're fucking insane," I retorted, which was when I heard a crash and the shattering of glass at the other end of the house which told me my brothers were storming in through the family room.

Kendra twisted around at the noise, I grabbed one of my guns, but before I could do anything, Keira swept her arms to the side, using her bundled fists to slam them into Kendra's temple.

The move jolted Kendra, pushing her over just as Doc rolled in. Without even a second's thought, I pulled back so I could get a better aim, then depressed the trigger, watching with satisfaction as blood spurted from his forehead and he froze in space and time, hovering endlessly before he dropped to his knees.

When another brother rolled in, Sticky, spying Doc's fallen body, yelled, "You motherfucker!" That was when I took aim again, getting the fucker in the throat. As he choked on blood, his body flopping around like a dying fish, I heard Keira's war cry when she started hammering into Kendra who was fighting back with tooth and claw.

Needing to get in there, I hurled myself at the window, grabbing the sill and throwing my body through the space. It was a tight fit, and I almost bit a bullet for it when Keira knocked the gun out of Kendra's hands and it went off.

The blast was excruciatingly loud because the shot went wide, hitting the brickwork beneath the window while the weapon landed near the closet. Dust plumed and exploded, and I swallowed a fuck ton of it, hacking it off my chest.

Before I could stop the ringing in my ears and get the dust out of my eyes, out of nowhere, Cyan appeared.

Coughing, I stared at her in shock, not having seen her leave the safe room, but the doors to it and the closet were wide open.

"We got two down here," a brother hollered from the other end of the house.

"Grim and Hook," another shouted, confirming that everyone was accounted for.

That was when Cyan clicked the safety on the gun she was holding, and that was when Keira and Kendra froze in place.

"Ladybug, what are you doing?" I rasped, determined that I'd kill Giulia the next time I was back home. She'd taught my kid how to hold a fucking gun? Who the fuck did that? "Put the gun down, baby."

Her eyes were surprisingly calm, and what was worse, her hands weren't shaking.

It looked obscene.

My fairy-like daughter holding a weapon that butchered men.

That slayed them.

I gritted my teeth, managing to grate out, "Put it down, Cyan."

I heard a soft curse as Keira reached up and tugged at the duct tape on her mouth. "Baby, do as your daddy says," she slurred, half of the tape still stuck to her lips.

Cyan shook her head. "She killed Fraction, Mommy."

My jaw tensed just as Keira's brow puckered.

"She didn't have to do that. She didn't have to." Her head swayed from side to side, then her bottom lip trembled. "Why would you do that?" she screamed at Kendra, bouncing on the balls of her feet like she had too much energy to contain.

But still, her goddamn arms didn't waver.

Her hands didn't tremble.

And that scream after her calm? She was fading fast.

"Who taught you how to hold a gun, honey?" I rasped, trying to distract her.

She blinked, but didn't take her eyes off Kendra who, ironically enough, looked scared.

Fucking typical.

Maybe she saw what I saw—that my baby was a lot more damaged than we'd realized. Maybe she saw that Cyan, for all she looked like a skinny kid, was holding that weapon with more confidence than Kendra herself had.

"Lodestar," Cyan said, her voice sweet and so incongruous by comparison to her stance. "Every woman should know how to defend herself," she murmured. "That's what Star says."

I was gonna kill that motherfucking psycho.

Who taught an eleven-year-old how to hold a gun?

And that was pure Lodestar. I could almost hear her voice as she taught my kid how to 'defend' herself.

I gritted my teeth and rumbled, "Kendra will die, baby. But I don't want her blood on your hands."

"She killed Fraction," Cyan said, an odd hollowness to the words this time. "She didn't have to do that. He wasn't going to hurt her. He was a puppy. He was little. He peed himself when they came in. He was so scared." Out of nowhere, she screamed, "SHE DIDN'T HAVE TO DO THAT!"

"He was a pitbull," Kendra whimpered.

"He was a puppy," she growled. "A baby. Why do people think they can hurt babies? Why?"

"Ladybug, maybe Fraction's still alive," I attempted to soothe. "If you put the gun down, we can check on him. Get him to the vet."

She finally looked away from Kendra. "I called the vet. He's on his way."

Her rationale had me tensing up. It was so discordant with the sheer madness of her holding a weapon.

"Put the gun down, baby," I repeated, unsure of how to appeal to her.

"You don't need to do this," Keira whispered softly. "You don't need to—"

Cyan's arms wobbled, but not because she was putting them down. No, she moved them to the side, pointing at Sticky. "He used words that Martin used. I heard him. He was going to hurt Mommy, and Kendra laughed." Her eyes turned rounder, so wide that she looked like they were going to pop out. "She laughed," Cy repeated, then I saw her hands tighten around the gun, just as I heard the sound of sirens in the background.

Kendra sobbed, "Please, don't—"

And that was when Cyan pulled the trigger.

FORTY

KEIRA

PRESENT

IT SEEMED incredible to me that the entire episode took less than ninety minutes from beginning to end.

It felt like a lifetime as I endured it.

As I was pistol-whipped, tied up, felt up. As I was hauled into my room, all the while praying that Cyan had hidden in the safe room like she'd done the night these bastards had barged their way into our lives the first time.

As Storm negotiated with Kendra, revealing his hatred of her. As men were shot in front of me, killed by my husband. As my kid held a gun on us all…

With the silver foil blanket wrapped around my body and Cyan's, I held her close.

Cyan's fragility was… as expected as it was unexpected.

I pressed a kiss to her temple, and murmured, "He's still alive, baby."

Fraction had bled out a lot. Whether he survived the night was another matter entirely.

Storm dropped down to a crouch in front of her. "The vet says we should go home, ladybug." He reached for her hands which stopped her from rocking herself back and forth.

"I can't leave him," she denied. "You wouldn't leave me."

I winced because she had a point.

"We need to get you to bed, honey," I said instead. "You've had a… difficult day." I almost choked on the words.

She turned her face into my throat. "Am I going to get in trouble?"

"No, ladybug. It's all been sorted with the sheriff."

I pressed a kiss to her hair, reveling in that sweet, sweaty smell. The fear was… well, it was strong in me.

Strong because I'd thought Cyan was doing okay, had thought she was dealing well with all the changes, and then I'd seen my little girl holding a gun with the confidence of someone who knew what they were doing.

When she was running around the clubhouse in West Orange, I'd just been grateful that she was keeping herself out of trouble and not giving me sass. Never thinking she'd been hovering around Giulia and Lodestar, two of the most volatile women I'd ever met.

Cyan whispered, "She deserved it."

"She did," Storm agreed, his hand tangling with hers, before he reached for mine, forging a small triangle between us. "But I'm still glad you missed anyway."

Not that it had done Kendra any good.

They said that when you took a life, it changed you.

I agreed.

I felt different. Just not in a bad way, like they made out on TV.

I knew cops who'd only had to fire their weapons needed counseling, but me? Taking out the trash was cathartic.

Better than eight months of therapy with Dr. Janowicz that was for damn sure.

Things had blurred after Cyan's bullet went wide, grazing that whore's arm, and my side, but I'd taken advantage of the chaos to snatch Sticky's gun, to shove it under Kendra's chin, and to let that bitch's brain blow.

Her lies, her malice had devastated our family, had led to the worst things imaginable happening to us.

She deserved my wrath.

She deserved for it to end like that.

Just as another person has received injury from him, so it will be given unto him.

Dad would be proud that I hadn't forgotten my scripture.

"I'm sorry I hurt you, Mommy."

Her words took a while to penetrate, and I knew I'd spaced out a little. "I'm sorry you had to see what happened," I told her softly, regret filtering through me.

My baby had seen too many people die in front of her.

God, she was going to be in therapy until she was a hundred.

Guilt and shame at what she'd witnessed tangled with the pride I felt in ending that bitch, in finally releasing us from her toxicity, and I pressed another kiss to her forehead, aware I had to cauterize the situation and fast.

"I need you to promise me something, Cyan." At her fervent nod, I murmured, "I need you to promise that—" I heaved a sigh. Needed her to promise what? That she wouldn't defend herself? When twice in the last twelve months that had been imperative?

Storm cleared his throat. "What your mom wants you to promise, Cy, is that you won't use a gun unless it's in a situation like today, where you had to defend yourself. But, and this is a big but, when you've got two people there who are in control of things, you don't arm yourself with a gun you don't know how to use."

"But I do know how to use it!"

"If you knew how to use it, ladybug, you wouldn't have missed."

Her shoulders hunched. "She moved."

"She didn't," he said dryly, and I shot him a glare. Nothing about this was funny.

He heaved a sigh. "You pick up a gun when you know you can use it. When you know that you can hit a target. You didn't hurt Mom today, but you could have, couldn't you?"

She bit her lip and tears bubbled in her eyes. "I could have."

"So, when you're ready, we're going to go through with gun handling classes." He grunted when I glowered at him. "You can't do that until you're eighteen years old, baby. Lodestar had no right to teach you that—"

"Katina knows how to shoot," Cyan muttered.

Jesus Christ.

I rubbed my forehead. "How did the state let her foster anyone? She couldn't look after a cat!"

Storm winced, but I knew he was in agreement. "The guns in the house are all under lock and key anyway, ladybug, but I don't want you thinking you can play with them—"

"They're not toys, Dad," she grumbled. "I know that. But I wasn't… I mean, when I… I only came out of the safe room when I heard him."

I thought back to the chaos that had gone down in my bedroom and asked Storm, "The second man?"

"Must be. Doc didn't speak."

"He was the one who said he was going to hurt Mommy."

Storm's mouth tightened, and I knew he was thinking that he was glad he'd shot the fucker in the throat. The second guy had still been sputtering as he bled out on my nice pale peach carpet.

The thought of sleeping in that house tonight made me want to puke, but the only alternative was the clubhouse.

Could I do it?

Could I stay there?

The MC owned a motel, that would be a better option.

So many deaths today.

So many people lost.

The thought of Jump, of his wife, of the security guard on the gates —they all died because of us.

I knew the threat was gone because brothers had swept the guys who'd broken into the house away, taking them to only God knew where, but could I deal with anyone else being hurt because of us? There'd be a lot more innocents at the motel…

Nervously, I asked, "Storm, is there somewhere for us to sleep at the clubhouse?"

His eyes settled on mine, and I didn't know why, but he imbued a level of calm in me that made me blink.

He was alive.

I'd thought for sure…

I clenched my jaw at the thought. Of the things I'd heard them say, similar things to what Cyan had, but worse. About her daddy.

About how they were going to hurt him. About what they wanted from him.

Even when Kendra had taken such pleasure in slapping me as the guys held me down and taped my hands and feet together, I'd mostly feared for Storm. They wanted back into the Sinners, and they weren't afraid to kill him to achieve that goal.

By the end of the day, I'd felt certain he'd be the one dying, not me. At least, not until they were done with me.

It hit me hard then. Hit me hard enough to make the breath sough from my lungs, for the panic to overwhelm me. Not even the calm in Storm's eyes took it away but what worked?

When his hands reached up and he cupped my face.

When he pressed a kiss to my forehead.

And when he said, "You're safe now."

Would we always be though?

We didn't live a regular life. Today had proven that. We'd brought chaos to the suburbs.

I wasn't made for this, but... I blew out a breath. I was made for Storm so that meant we had to wend this path together.

"Your father tells me you don't want to leave?"

The vet's words had me jerking in surprise because I hadn't realized he'd stepped out of the OR.

Cyan nodded. "I want to be here when he wakes up."

"We don't normally do this, but you've had a difficult day, honey. So, would you like to see him?"

"Yes, please!" The eagerness in her voice hurt my soul. The desperate need for her dog to be alive had me praying that he didn't die.

God, I'd spent half the time bitching about the damn thing that peed everywhere like we were living in a litter box, but that didn't mean I wanted him to die.

"You need to promise that once you've seen him, you'll go home, though. Fraction doesn't need you to be sick because you're so tired. When he's able to go home, he'll need a lot of TLC."

Cyan's head bobbed so fast it was a wonder she didn't give herself whiplash. "I promise!"

As she darted to her feet, trailing after the veterinarian as he took her to see Fraction, I closed my eyes and shuddered, able to let go now that she wasn't in the vicinity.

"I'm sorry, baby girl." Storm dropped onto his knees before he slid his arms around me and held me tight.

I swore he was the only thing that kept me together as he allowed me to break down in his embrace.

"You're safe, you're both safe," he rumbled, the words triggering a soft vibration in my ear that made me shiver a little. "I'm so sorry you had to do that—"

Swallowing, I whispered, "I'm not pure anymore, Storm."

Was it messed up that that concerned me? He'd always made such a big deal out of it—

His eyes tangled with mine and for the longest time, I felt certain he was going to get up, walk into that room with Cyan and…

Jesus, what?

Take her away from me because I wasn't a suitable mom anymore?

Storm would never, ever do that.

"You'll always be my angel," he remarked gently, that penetrative stare making me feel like he was looking into my damn soul.

I'd never felt anything like it. Nothing more invasive but loving all at the same time.

"I've never been an angel," I countered, surprised to see a smile dance around his lips.

"Some angels are demons too," he rasped, and those words had a shaky breath escaping me, as if, at long last, I could inhale and exhale to the full extent. I almost sagged on the seat, annoyed at myself by how much those words resonated.

I'd killed a woman who'd made it her life's mission to destroy me, to steal my husband, to devastate my family, and to decimate my world.

She'd brought enemies into my home, had allowed men who wished to do my family harm to breach our safe place, and had done it all with a smile.

She needed to die.

And I needed to be the one who sent her back to her maker.

That was nothing to be ashamed of, but Storm…

He was so hooked up on my purity.

His hands cupped my face again, and slowly, gently, he pressed his lips to mine. "I want to brand you, Keira."

My eyes flared wide at that. "Huh?"

"You heard me." His chin tipped up. "Do you want that?"

Bemusement, bewilderment, astonishment, each of them encompassed what I felt about his declaration. None of them explained why I felt the most beautiful sense of joy. Of wonder. Of relief.

"Please."

One word.

He dipped his chin.

One reaction.

I was going to be his Old Lady in truth, which was when I accepted how jealous I'd been of my Posse sisters.

They were branded, but I wasn't.

That was going to change.

I heard a soft sob coming from the room where the vet had taken our daughter, and it brought me back down to earth with a bang. The realization of what had happened, what she'd seen and what she'd done… God, she was a baby who'd experienced a war zone.

"S-She was so okay with shooting her, Storm," I said around a gulp. "What the hell are we going to do to—" Fix her? To make her better? Was she already too broken?

His jaw tensed, I felt it turn to obsidian against my cheek, as he stated, "I'll talk to Stone. See if there isn't something we can do in-house."

I swallowed. "Does she need to see more shrinks?"

"I don't know, baby, I don't know." He moved slightly, shifting so that he could rest his chin on the crown of my head. "We'll work it out. She's been fine so far. Maybe under pressure, that's when things change."

"If she'd been a boy, you'd have been proud of her, wouldn't you?"

He cringed. "Maybe."

"Then maybe, we shouldn't worry?" I asked hopefully.

"I think we need to talk with Stone. See what she has to say, okay?"

I nodded. "You said something today..." I paused. "You said that you didn't give a damn about whether Kendra lived or died even knowing who her dad is... Who was he?"

"Bear."

Both Rene and Rex had told me that Bear had cheated. He'd said that his parents' relationship had come back stronger than before, and I'd seen for myself how tight they were, but I'd never learned that Bear had another kid.

Christ.

Kendra was Bear's daughter?

"Are you okay?" Storm asked. "I know it must come as a shock."

I shook my head, but not wanting to dwell on this, even though I'd admit the idea of Kendra being Bear's made my head spin, I muttered, "What next?"

"I'm going to take you both to the clubhouse, then I have business to attend to."

"With the sheriff?"

"No. There'll be questions and interviews, but you don't have to be scared. Two armed men with a grudge—that a dozen or more brothers are willing to swear on oath for—against me acting as their Prez, forced their way into our house. They shot our dog, who nearly died, and they were killed by me defending my family on my property." He squeezed me. "You've nothing to worry about where the law is concerned."

I released a shaky breath. "That should make me feel worse, not better."

His chuckle was soft, sad. "I'm sorry, sweetheart. This is why I always wanted you to stay separate from the MC, but... in this instance, there wasn't much I could do..."

"Poor Jump and Darla," I whispered. "They died because of me."

"Because of me," he corrected gruffly. "Don't you dare blame yourself. You've done nothing wrong."

I bit my lip. "Maybe we should live nearer to the clubhouse so other people won't get hurt?"

"There are no houses near the clubhouse," he replied softly. "Unless we build them."

"I don't want to live in that property again."

"Who could blame you?"

"I don't want people to get hurt because of us. Paul... he should never have been a casualty of this. Never mind Darla." I swallowed. "Is their son okay?"

"Yeah, he's staying with MC tonight."

Shakily, I nodded. "I don't want to live in the clubhouse."

"I wouldn't make you," he soothed. "I'll figure something out, baby girl. I know you have no reason to trust me, but I promise you, I won't let you down."

My brow puckered as I pulled back, his words hitting me hard. "Storm, do you know what resonated the most today?"

"What?" he asked cautiously, like he was waiting for me to kick him in the gut.

"How scared I was that you'd show up at the house, even as I knew you would."

"*What?*"

"I heard them talking about you. If you didn't do what they wanted, they were going to kill you. Storm, in all the time I've known you, I've not seen you do anything the 'normal' way. You never do what anyone demands of you. But I knew, point blank, that you'd come.

"I trusted in you, and I prayed that you'd let me down because I knew that if you came to the house, you'd die. You'd die and I'd never —" I gritted my teeth and this time, it was me who raised my hands and cupped his jaw. "I love you. I love you and I need you and I want you to stay by my side.

"I need you not to die, Asher. I need you to stay with me for a very long time—"

His lips crashed against mine and I bit back, fighting him for control as I thrust my tongue into his mouth, needing him to know that I was as deep in this as he was.

Needing him to realize that he wasn't alone anymore.

There was no more testing the waters, no more dipping my toes in to see if I could make this work.

He could have died today.

He could have died and I could have lost him, and what kind of a fucking world would that be without him in it?

While we kissed, he straightened up on his knees as his hand came back to cup my nape. Supporting me even as my hands moved around his chest, hugging him and holding him and feeling him and registering just how alive he was. How safe.

I thought about those bastards' intentions, and I let out a sob.

"They were going to drug you," I rasped, pulling back and dropping my forehead against his. "They were gonna get you high and hooked and they were gonna make you do what they wanted and then they were gonna kill you."

He pressed a softer kiss to my lips, letting his mouth trail along my cheek, up to my eyebrow. He didn't stop until he pressed another kiss to the center of my forehead.

"Sounds like they wanted more than to take back the club. Do you know what they wanted from me?"

"I heard them talking about Butch. He was the Old Prez, right?"

Storm hummed. "He was."

I gulped. "They mentioned something about the Rabid Wolves. About Butch having a deal with them."

"You know what deal? I'm sorry to ask, baby girl, but—"

I shook my head, silencing him. "I didn't hear anything else, just them griping about Butch and the Rabid Wolves."

His eyes were narrowed, but before he could say another word, Cyan was there, running forward to slam into his back. "Dr. Ricardo says that he thinks Fraction will be fine. He lost a lot of blood but that he's young and they managed to fix him."

The vet tutted. "I said that it was likely he'd make a full recovery, Cyan."

"That means he'll be fine!" she argued.

"*Likely* is doctor speak for we don't want to make you a promise that could be broken," I told her softly. "We'll see how things are in the morning, honey." I got to my feet and said, "Thank you so much for all you've done."

He smiled at me, and because it seemed genuine, I believed that Fraction *would* live to pee on one of my rugs another day.

Relieved, even if I remained silent on the subject, I left Storm to deal with the bill as I grabbed a firm hold of Cyan's hand and tugged her outside. Leaving the foil blanket behind because Storm had warmed me up from the inside out with that tender, possessive kiss.

As we made it outside, I blinked in surprise at how dark it was then turned to Cyan and said, "We're going to stay at the clubhouse."

Her eyes widened. "We are?"

I didn't need to ask if she was okay with that. She looked more excited than when I'd told her we were going back to West Orange for her birthday.

"We are," I confirmed, sucking in a breath as I opened the back door to the SUV to shepherd her in before I climbed into the passenger seat.

As she talked about what the vet had told her, I reached for my phone which I'd left in the glove compartment, then winced when I saw a couple hundred messages from the Posse.

Giulia: *What the hell is going on down there, Keira? I heard Nyx telling Rex about something Storm had said.*

Indy: *Sounds like a game of telephone to me.*

Lily: *You're not supposed to listen in to their conversations.*

Giulia: *Stop being such a goody two shoes.*

Lily: *I'm not! The last time I did it, I got the completely wrong story.*

Giulia: *I know when Nyx is concerned or not.*

Indy: *Yeah, seeing as you concern him the most.*

I rolled my eyes at that, then scrolled down, seeing the women's worry with my own two eyes and feeling it, really feeling it. It was good to be included. Five hundred miles away, and they still considered me a part of it.

Me: *Posse, I'm fine. I'll talk to you in the morning though. Things were crazy today, but Storm, Cyan, and I, we're all safe and well. Thank you for caring.* <3

I saw the little dots as they started to reply, but I needed to message Lodestar first.

Me: *Lodestar? You and I need to have a conversation about what you've taught my daughter.*

It took barely five seconds for her to reply.

Lodestar: *I apparently taught her just enough to keep herself safe.*

Me: *She almost shot me.*

Lodestar: *ALMOST is the key word there.*

Fuming, I growled under my breath.

Me: *You had no right to teach her that!*

Lodestar: *I didn't teach her. I taught Katina. Cyan watched. I would never impose lessons upon another person's daughter, but upon my own, that's different. I want Katina to know how to handle a weapon.*

Me: *She's a baby!*

Lodestar: *Babies don't stay babies for long in this world. And I'm not just talking about the MC world either. In general.*

Lodestar: *I was raised in an unorthodox way, but I had security all around me. Someone still got to my mom, and to this day, I regret not knowing how to fire a gun. Not knowing how to protect myself and her, because if I'd known, I'd have been able to save her.*

I felt the truth in her words, felt them resonating inside me like the ringing noise of a tuning fork as it whistled in my ears.

She meant it.

Her mom had been murdered.

If she'd been able to fire a gun, she could have saved her.

I accepted that kids saw things differently than adults, but Lodestar truly believed what she was saying.

Me: *I'm sorry.*

Lodestar: *Don't be. Happened a long time ago.*

Me: *I'm still sorry that you lost your mom.*

Lodestar: *I'm glad you're alive.*

A soft laugh escaped me.

Me: *Me too.*

Me: *Don't expect Storm to be as easily persuaded as me about this.*

Lodestar: *I'm prepared to butt heads with him. Don't worry.*

Grimacing as I expected him to come away with more bruises than her, I just typed out:

Me: *Don't be too hard on him. She nearly took ten years off both our lives.*

When she didn't reply, I turned to my other chats.

As much as the others had drawn me into their gang, I was a part of my own growing Posse down here. Maybe it was just a two-woman thing right now, but after today, after Darla had paid the ultimate price, I felt obligated to her, obligated to do something. To be more at ease with the Old Ladies, to seek their acceptance.

She'd died for me.

Sure, she hadn't meant to, but that didn't take away from her sacrifice.

Her kid was going to grow up without a mom and a dad now.

Because of us.

The thought had tears pricking my eyes as I read MC's chat:

MC: *You need anything, K, I'm there. Okay?*

MC: *I can't believe that Kendra bitch.*

MC: *Digger says she's dead. I'm really glad.*

MC: *I'm here if you need me.*

MC: *If Fraction dies, I'm going to ask Digger where he's keeping those SOBs so I can stab them myself.*

I replied:

Me: *I'm fine, MC. Please, don't worry. Good news re. Fraction. The vet seemed hopeful about him making it through the night.*

MC: *Phew! I'm so glad, K. Cyan didn't need that on top of everything else.*

Thanking God that only Storm and I knew about what had gone down in my bedroom, I just replied:

Me: *We're going to stay at the clubhouse for a few days. Tell me if you have a problem with Kelly. He might be better off at the clubhouse, too, with friends and family around.*

MC: *He cried himself to sleep. I tried to help but he wouldn't let me.*

Me: *Understandable.*

MC: *I know, but I just wish there were something I could do.*

Me: *I'm so relieved you weren't there, MaryCat. I don't know what I'd do if you'd gotten hurt as well.*

MC: *<3 I hope you know I feel the same way. These past months have been bearable because of you and Cyan. You've both helped me so much. You didn't have to take me in as much as you did.*

Me: *Hush. We moms have to stick together.*

MC: *I guess we do. <3*

MC: *What a crazy day.*

Me: *That about sums it up. I gtg but talk later.*

MC: *Night, K xox*

The second I finished that convo, another text chat popped up. Link.

A smile danced around my lips.

Link: *Heard someone took out the trash tonight.*

Me: *Well, you guys didn't leave me much choice.*

Me: *Typical men… always forgetting the basic chores.*

Link: *Lol. I'll accept that. Proud of you, sweetheart. So fucking proud of you.*

Me: *Link, Storm offered to brand me.*

Link: *Wow, that's awesome, honey!! I'm so glad.*

Link: *Maybe now he'll figure shit out in his head. Not saying you don't have a beautiful soul, Keira, but babe, the dude thought you walked on fucking water. Shit got creepy years ago.*

Me: *It feels good not to be on a pedestal anymore.*

Link: *I'll bet.*

Me: *GTG, Link. Thank you for always being there.*

Link: *Honor's all mine. I always will be, Keira. Now Storm's there, and Lily's here, that don't change our friendship.*

Oddly relieved, a sigh whispered from my lips.

Me: *I'm glad.*

I thought back to that day after Rene's death. When the brother who hung around the house sometimes, who never left dirty dishes on the coffee table and brought them into the kitchen to help me out, had turned into a friend.

Me: *Never want to lose you as a friend, Link.*

Link: *And you never will. Give Cyan a kiss from me, yeah?*

Me: *Will do. xo*

"Mom?"

Realizing she'd stopped talking about Fraction, I cast Cyan a look in the backseat. "Yes, baby?"

"You and Dad… you're not going to send me away, are you?"

My brow furrowed. "Why on Earth would you think that, sweetheart?"

"I don't know. I just… I don't want to go anywhere. I-I, please, don't send me away. I know I'm trouble. I know I'm bad, but please, I don't want to—please, I can't—"

When she scrabbled forward, wriggling through the space between the front seats so she could clamber onto my lap, surprise had me jumping when she nearly elbowed me in the head, but I let her crumple up and release her fears and her tension in my arms.

Accepting that this was simply the release of the day's many stresses, I cried with her, not loud enough to disturb her but just letting it out because her fear was tangible.

When I saw Storm coming out of the vet's office, I whispered, "You're not bad; you're not trouble. You're perfect. You're mine, and you're going nowhere that I'm not, baby. You're staying right here with us and we're going to…" My words waned. Because what were we going to do? Make her better? Was there anything wrong with her? Or were her reactions not the most normal thing for a child who'd been traumatized as badly as she had? "We're going to make sure things are better from now on," was what I eventually settled on as Storm opened the door.

Cyan tensed in my arms, but I hugged her tighter as he settled behind the wheel.

I wondered if he heard me, because he rumbled, "I'm going to make sure you're not in danger like this ever again, do you hear me?"

She sniffled against me, then turned her face to the side. "I knew you'd come for us, Daddy. I just… I was scared they'd hurt you."

Was I surprised when she flung herself at him and sobbed in his arms too?

But that was when I broke down, because this world was fucked up. Lodestar was right. It had everything to do with the MC today, but how London had groomed her was the real world. The reality that sucked.

There was danger everywhere.

There was peril in all corners.

And for the first time, I recognized that Storm was right to have someone watching us.

Today, however, that hadn't worked. Today, we'd lost our guard. Which meant, tomorrow, we'd have to figure out a new plan of action. But we'd do it together because I was no longer on the outside looking in.

FORTY-ONE

STORM

PRESENT

IT WAS hard leaving Cyan and Keira behind at the clubhouse. Even though I knew they were safe there, even though there were over a dozen bikers at the compound who'd protect them, dragging myself away had never felt more impossible than it did at that moment.

I knew the Coshocton compound had its own version of the Fridge. I didn't have a clue why it was called the Lockbox, and wasn't sure if I wanted to know either, but I walked over to it, Digger and SL at my side with spotlights guiding our path as we crossed to the other end of our territory.

Having been here when I first arrived and scoping out the lay of the land then, I asked SL, "You know what's on the other side of the border?"

"Nothing. Just fields."

"Owned by a farmer?"

"Nope," SL replied, scratching his stubble. "We own it."

"Why?"

"I dunno. Maybe to make sure no one could overhear what went on in the Lockbox?"

Pulling out my cellphone, I googled our address and scanned the area around us. Seeing the tract of land, I grunted. "Could be. I'm gonna need you to get an environmental impact survey done on it."

"Huh?"

"Environmental impact. It needs to be surveyed to see if we can construct on there or not."

"You wanna build shit on there?" Digger asked.

"Keira won't want to stay in the clubhouse for long," I murmured. "And she talked about something today that resonated. When we rode past Paul, I had to accept the only reason he was dead was because I lived there. Otherwise, he'd never have been dragged into this mess."

"You want to build houses there?"

"Is that ideal when the Lockbox is close by?"

They both spoke at once, but I just said, "The Lockbox can be moved, and yeah, I'm thinking about it."

"How big's the land, SL?"

"Plenty big. Couple developers came calling a few years ago, trying to buy it."

I arched a brow. "Really?"

"Yeah."

"Never thought this would be what we were talking about, Storm," Digger said wryly. "Thought you'd want to know what we found out."

"Keira overheard some of it. They were gonna shoot me up, get me high, then use that to get information outta me. Of course, Keira just thought they wanted me to die by day's end, but you can't get answers out of a man that way in twenty-four hours." My jaw clenched. "Spent plenty of time in withdrawals to know how that shit works."

"I'd judge 'em for using that as their method of torture, but who the fuck am I kidding? We ain't going in there to tickle their feet," Digger drawled.

"No, we goddamn ain't," I agreed with a laugh. "She mentioned the Rabid Wolves. This ain't the first time I've heard talk of them. Sticky was a Rabid Wolf, SL, right? On the run?"

"Yeah, Butch took him in because of Cassandra."

"Cassandra?" That was the first time I'd heard that name mentioned.

"Cassandra Shawnee? She works over at the junior high. She's a guidance counselor. Sticky is, well, *was* her brother."

My brow furrowed as I wondered if the woman who'd fallen on her back in the parking lot of the junior high while we'd been there for the parent-teacher conference was one and the same.

I pursed my lips. "Why was she down here and why was he a Rabid Wolf? What the hell did Butch have to do with this?"

SL pulled a face. "You really want me to gossip?"

"Ain't gossip if it's pertinent to the facts," Digger retorted, his curiosity piqued as much as mine.

I knew he'd been up in Canada, hunting something down about the Rabid Wolves. I'd never asked why because he'd been serving another Prez at the time, and Rex would've shared the information with me if he'd wanted me to know.

I had plenty enough of my own problems without adding to them.

SL groused, "It's pretty fucked up. Butch was boning this bitch over in Columbus. This is pre-Peggy. He brought her over to Coshocton, got her settled in as his girlfriend."

"Not his Old Lady?"

"Naw. Not then. She had two kids, one was a teenager. He didn't get along with Butch so she sent him to live with his father."

"A brother in the Rabid Wolves?"

SL nodded. "Sticky joined the ranks, then he got involved in an armed robbery. Killed a couple guards in a bank. His girlfriend ratted him out, so he took her down too." He grimaced. "Butch brought him in when Cassandra pleaded with him to watch out for her bro after he made it back across the border."

"And he listened?"

"Their mom died of an overdose. Butch took it hard because he gave her the drugs."

"What happened to Cassandra?" I asked softly.

"She was sixteen when this happened—they were together a long time. She went back to Columbus, and I think Butch helped her get an apartment so she wasn't taken in by the state.

"Anyway, fast forward to two years ago, she moves back here and starts working at the junior high. Not much later, Sticky comes down, and Butch brings him in.

"Never liked the fucker. Had a hair-trigger temper the likes of which you wouldn't believe. Butch used to find him funny, but no one else did. He was nuts."

Even more curious now, I queried, "Did Grim and Hook talk yet?"

Digger shook his head. "Nah. I left them to you."

With a hum, I murmured, "What kind of gear we got down here?"

"All kinds of shit. I laid it out," Digger told me.

Nodding my thanks, I took the last few steps toward the Lockbox which was a lot larger than the Fridge, and cast a glance at the two men guarding the door.

Surprised to see North was standing there, I arched a brow at Digger who shrugged, "Fucker waded into war with you without a second's thought. Figured he deserved to be in on this."

Smirking a little, I didn't argue, just nodded at North. "Thanks for having my back, brother."

I'd seen pictures of the destruction of the warehouse over on the edge of the county and was wicked pissed at what we'd lost in the fire and how the fuckers in the Lockbox had used that as a diversion. Still, I decided that'd be my inspiration.

They'd regret it for as long as they lived.

Which wouldn't be for long.

I turned the door handle and found both men duct-taped to a chair, their heads bowed, their clothes soaked through with sweat because it was fucking hot in here.

There was a naked lightbulb overhead, revealing the grimness of this place in its entirety as well as a table full of gear that was laid out —it made a Lowe's look understocked.

Still, I didn't need much for my plan.

I peered around on the hunt for a faucet, finding a fucking fire extinguisher of all things attached to the wall.

"Didn't know we had to pass the fire safety code in here." I drawled as I walked over to it, unclipping it from its holster on the wall as I hefted it in my hand.

The door opening hadn't made them lift their heads but my voice did. I caught a glimpse of Hook, saw that his scruff of before had turned into a full-fledged beard of ZZ Top proportions since spring, and I smiled.

His nostrils flared as his head reared back at the sight of my smile, and right he fucking was to be scared.

I held out my hand and asked, "Either of you got a lighter?"

SL cleared his throat but slipped a Zippo lighter onto my palm. I twisted it in my fingers then stepped over to Hook.

"Heard from my kid's lips that your brothers were going to rape my Old Lady."

His eyes flared wide as his head shook from side to side. "Naw, that wasn't in the plan."

"No?" I questioned. "You calling my kid a liar? You think she talks about men rapin' her ma every day of the fucking week?"

His Adam's apple bobbed. "Sticky, he… Kendra, she wanted that. It was all her idea."

"You're in the habit of listening to club snatch?" I mused, flicking the roll top on the lighter and watching the flickering flame.

"Sticky, he really liked her."

I shot Grim a look. "Think you must have liked her too, considerin' Keira saw you cozying up to her in town."

"Knew you were a dumbfuck, Grim, but never realized how big of a fool you were," SL groused.

"Shut the fuck up, Sweet Lips. You're the one who's a goddamn turncoat. This bastard comes swaggering in like he's king shit and you all just drop to your fucking knees and start sucking his dick—"

"Never asked you to suck my cock. Just my balls," I mocked, then I made a prong with two fingers, stuck them up his nose then yanked back. "You're a fucking dipshit. Only dipshits stick with the losing side when their ass is safe with the victors."

He screamed as I dragged his head all the way back, until the chair was tipping over and I let it fall, let his head clatter against the concrete floor, his scream cut off short as the move knocked him out before I turned my attention to Hook.

"Now, what's going on with the Rabid Wolves?"

"Nothing." He blinked. Then blinked twice more, really fast.

"You got some kind of Morse Code going down with your lashes?" I retorted, flicking the lighter again. "And if you're just gonna keep on saying fucking nothing, I'm going to get bored, and I'm going to have to entertain myself."

Digger cackled. "When Storm's bored, you're not gonna like it. There are legends about the guy back in West Orange."

Hook gulped, and I twisted back to look at Digger. "Legends?"

"Hell, yeah. Among the Prospects, for sure."

"That true, North?" I called out.

"Sure is, Storm. They say you're worse than Mother Nature at causing havoc."

I smirked. "Bet your ass I am. Had to tone it down when I got married though. Got a kid. Can't be raising her that way." Not that it had worked. I had a mini fucking terrorist on my hands. That was all Keira goddamn needed—two of us under the same roof. I flicked the lighter again. "Now, you got one chance to tell me something interesting—"

"I don't know anything," Hook rambled, the words tumbling out of his mouth like he had the verbal shits. "I really don't! Sticky was the leader! He just told me about some safes, nothing else."

Safes? Curious for real now, I ignored his remark about not knowing anything else and said, "Grab some water, SL."

He nodded, then headed deeper into the Lockbox. There was a door there, which told me a faucet existed somewhere in this place. He returned with a mop bucket that sloshed as he wheeled it over to my side.

I moved closer to Hook, the light from the flame flickering under his breath. His feet scuttled against the concrete floor, and he started to tilt the seat back, but Digger was there, stopping him and I grabbed some of his beard, held it tight, then wafted the flame beneath it.

He started screaming before the fire even raged into being, and Digger took a step back at the same time as I did after I set his face alight.

FORTY-TWO

CYAN

PRESENT - THREE DAYS LATER

"WHAT'RE YOU DOING?"

Twisting away from the window, where I was watching a bunch of kids playing with water guns, I turned and found Kelly looking at me. He was wringing his hands together, pleating his fingers into knots.

Guilt hit me hard.

The last time I'd seen him had been when we'd played in the street four days ago. I'd called him a wuss, and then I'd pinned him in a headlock. He'd cried afterward.

Now, his eyes were bright pink, but for a different reason.

My mouth wobbled when I thought about how easy it'd have been for me to have lost my mom and dad. In the blink of an eye, everything could've changed.

Everything.

Again.

Most of the time, when Kelly made his way over to me, we ended up fighting. But today, I didn't have it in me to pin him in another headlock. He didn't know that though, did he?

He tensed up when I patted the window seat beside me. "No, Kelly. I don't want to fight."

His mouth quivered. "You always want to fight."

He wasn't wrong. But neither were his words an accusation. More of a sniffled statement.

"Usually, yeah, but I don't feel like fighting right now."

"How's your dog?"

"He's still sick."

"Did your folks tell you when they'd be bringing him home?"

I shook my head. "He got better, but then something went wrong and he got sick again. Mom said it was an infection."

"Infections are easy. I had a chest infection last year and I got better."

"I had one of those a few years ago." Relief filtered through me. "You're right. Infections, they have meds for that."

"They do. Good ones." Kelly reached up and rubbed his nose on the back of his hand. "I hope he gets better."

"I do too." I turned back to look at the kids playing in the water as if nothing had happened. "I'm sorry, Kelly," I continued, my voice quiet. "Everything changed for us, but they're all acting like nothing did."

Kelly sniffled some more. "Did they hurt you?"

"They were going to."

"I'm glad they didn't."

"Me too. I wish your mom and dad weren't hurt. MC's real nice though. It's not the same, but…"

"I'm not staying with her."

"You're not?" I turned to look away from the playing. I could have taken part, but it didn't seem right.

Everything was wrong at the moment. I didn't know why, and even worse, I didn't know how to fix it.

"No. I'm going to stay here for a while."

He rubbed his nose again, and it was gross enough that I pulled out a paper napkin from my pocket. It had ketchup stains on it, but it was better than him using his hand as a handkerchief.

"Here. Use this."

He wiped it. "Your dad fixed it so I wouldn't go away."

Tugging on my bottom lip, I whispered, "I'm glad. I don't want to go away, either."

"Why would you? Your mom and dad are alive."

I swallowed. "I-I did something bad."

"What kind of bad? Did you beat someone up again?"

Grimacing, I muttered, "I don't always beat people up, Kelly." We'd started hanging out in my yard and his since the day we fought at the BBQ here. Playing usually involved games of tag and hide and seek, as well, I'd admit, more fighting.

"You do most of the time. Sarah Jessica's scared to play with you in case you give her another black eye."

"That was her fault. She called my mom a whore. And anyway, that was in December. That was ages ago."

Kelly grumbled, "People don't forget. Especially girls."

"True. We have long memories." I squinted out the window and found my target. I didn't like Sarah Jessica. She hadn't called Mom a whore again, but that didn't mean she didn't look down on me. "I'm glad you're staying."

"You are?"

Surprised at his shock, I cast him a glance. "You're the only person I like playing with, Kelly. Duh."

His smile was shaky, but it was real for all that. "I like playing with you too, Cy."

I dipped my chin. "That's settled then. If you're here and I'm here all the time, then we can play more. It won't make up for what happened, but at least we can take your mind off things." I reached over and grabbed his shoulder. "And Kelly, whenever you want, you can cry with me. I won't make fun and I won't tell anyone."

The phone in my pocket started ringing before he could reply. I pulled it out as he asked, "Whose phone is that?"

"My mom's."

"Why do you have it?"

"She's taking a bath."

"It's hot out. Why's she taking a bath?"

"I don't know. She takes baths when she's all over the place."

"How is she all over the place? She's here. At the clubhouse."

I squinted at him. "Don't be dumb."

"I'm not dumb. What you said makes no sense."

I huffed. "Boys." Then, I eyed the cell and whispered, "I wanted to read her texts but I can't get into it." The call died, as did the screen that flashed with Rex's name.

"You don't know her passcode?"

"Nope."

"Then why did you think you could get into it?"

"She didn't have one before."

I didn't want to think about why she'd added a lock to her cell. A part of me was sure they really were going to send me somewhere, but at the same time, we were staying at the clubhouse. She wouldn't want just anyone being able to open her phone, would she?

When a message popped up on the screen, I caught sight of the first couple lines.

Rex: *When you have a second, Keira, I'd like to speak with Cyan.*

My brow furrowed. Why would the Prez of West Orange's chapter want to speak with me?

It rang again and this time, I connected it.

"Rex?" I asked softly.

"Cyan?" His confusion was clear. "Is that you?"

I hummed. "Mom's in the bathroom. I saw your text."

"Should you be reading her phone?"

"No. I shouldn't."

"Then why did you?"

"Because I wanted to read her texts."

Rex was silent a second. "I thought you were going to lie."

"Daddy says a brother never lies to his Prez."

A soft laugh sounded down the line. "He's right. Sisters don't either."

Pleased, I straightened up. "Nope. And they don't snitch."

"They surely don't. Why do you want to read her texts, Cyan? And remember, don't lie to your Prez."

"You're not my Prez," I said immediately, even though I knew I was contradicting myself. "Daddy's my Prez."

"I'm the head of all the chapters. That means you can't lie to me or your father."

I grunted. "Do you think, sometimes, if you say something out loud that it will come true?"

Kelly's head nodded swiftly, bobbing up and down like he was high on Kool-Aid.

"No. That's not how life works."

"I've already said it once. If I say it again, maybe it'll come true for real."

"Tell me what it is. I might be able to ease your fear."

"I wanted to read what Mom was saying to the Posse."

"Why?"

"Because I-I don't want her to send me away and I think she'd tell them if she was planning on it."

Rex was quiet a second. "Why do you think they'd send you away?"

"Because I did a bad thing."

"I don't think you did. Not really. I don't think you did something ideal either. I know your dad's not alone in thinking that you should have stayed in the safe room, but you didn't do anything that would make them send you away. And the question is, where do you think they'd send you to?"

I bit my lip. "Azkaban."

Kelly hiccuped. "Azkaban doesn't exist."

"Maybe somewhere like it for kids does."

He scowled at me. "Harry Potter isn't real. Azkaban was for bad people too. You're not bad."

"I have no idea who's talking to you," Rex said, "but he isn't wrong. I read Harry Potter to Rain when he was younger. I know all about Azkaban. It doesn't really exist, honey."

"I know it doesn't. But I just… places like that do exist. I know they do. I know Quin was in prison—"

"There were no Dementors there," Rex teased softly. "Assholes, for sure, but no Dementors."

"I know he got hurt bad."

Rex heaved a sigh. "Didn't think I'd be talking about allegories today. Look, Cy, you don't have to worry about your mom and dad sending you away. If anything, that's why I want to talk to you."

"You do?"

I didn't think Rex would lie to me. Rex was straightforward. Everyone knew that, and that was why they looked up to him.

Mom said they weren't going to send me away, but parents did that. Didn't they? Told you one thing and then did another. Mom and Dad weren't terrible for doing that. They were usually honest with me, but that was before I'd grabbed a gun and fired it.

"Yes. I wanted to see how you were doing?"

I swallowed. "That's all?"

"That's all. It was pretty intense what you went through."

"It was horrible," I whispered, turning to look at the kids in the yard again while Kelly wandered over to the other side of the family room and started filtering through the board games stored in one of the toy chests.

I was glad he gave me some privacy. Gladder still that he stuck by me.

"Do you know what Rain's doing?" I asked, out of the blue.

"Rain? He's getting ready to enlist."

Brow puckered, I asked, "What does that mean?"

"It means he wants to be in the Army."

I'd seen Captain America. "Are we at war with someone?"

He cleared his throat. "No. I mean, not on American soil. But technically we've been at war for the past sixty—" He sighed. "Never mind."

"Then why does he want to join the Army?" He'd be putting himself in danger. I didn't like that.

I thought about his arms, the protective shelter of them the last time I'd seen him...

The idea of him getting hurt had my eyes watering with dumb tears.

"It's what people do." I heard the shrug in Rex's voice. "He was going to college, but then he changed his mind."

"Why?" I asked, my voice raw with pain, like I knew—

No.

I didn't know that.

I didn't know that he'd get hurt.

He wouldn't. Sinners didn't get hurt. They got knocked down, but they always got back up again. Rain might not be a full-blown Sinner, but that didn't take away from his heritage.

If I was a biker princess, well, he was a biker prince, wasn't he?

"I don't know. Things have been different for everyone since you were taken that day, Cyan."

"You mean, since I got into that car with Martin."

Shame whispered through me. Shame and self-loathing. I raised my legs and pinned my knees to my chest. Hauling one arm around them, I huddled in on myself.

Rex grunted. "I knew a man like Martin before."

"You did? One who wanted to hurt little girls?"

"Yes. Unfortunately. I wish I didn't know him. I wish that I'd never known him. He was Nyx's uncle."

"He's dead?"

"Yes."

"Like Martin."

He hesitated. Seeming to sense what I meant. "Yes, he's like Martin."

A small puddle of relief filled me. "So he can't hurt anyone anymore?"

"No." Rex sighed. "Would you say I'm smart, Cyan?"

"I would. I think you, Daddy, Maverick, and Mommy, oh, and Star, and Stone, too, are all super smart. I think Alessa and Amara are as well. They talk two languages! How cool is that?"

"Very cool. But… You mentioned me, and your dad, Maverick, too, Stone as well… we knew Nyx's uncle. We knew him, and he hung around the club a lot, and my dad, he was so smart. *He* was smarter than me, but he didn't know that Nyx's uncle was like Martin. That he was hurting Nyx's sister, Carly. You know how much cunning that takes?"

"A lot."

"Exactly. A lot. But he did it. He pulled the wool over my dad's eyes. Now, honey, I have a feeling that when you're older, and when you've finished school and you're ready to take on the world with whatever you want to do, you'll be as smart as my dad.

"But, and it's a big but, you're only eleven, Cyan. You're not supposed to think that a man would want to hurt you like that. You wanted to see your dad. Martin was going to take you there. That was what you believed."

"I'll never believe it again," I mumbled.

"Good! I should hope you wouldn't."

It shamed me to admit it, but I whispered, "I thought he loved me. I thought he wanted to be my uncle."

Rex blew out a breath. "You don't need uncles outside of the club, Cyan. Whenever you need to talk, I'm here."

"Really?" I frowned. "No, you're too important—"

"Never too important for you. You're like my niece anyway. Did you know your dad and I grew up together?"

"Of course, I did, silly. You all did."

"Well, we did, but your dad lived in my house with my mom and dad and me."

"Why?"

"Because his mom, your grandmother, used to get into a lot of trouble and he needed somewhere to stay."

I stared at Kelly who was fiddling with a jigsaw puzzle, and murmured, "Do people do that? Take in kids that don't belong to them?"

"They do. Storm and I grew up fighting and having fun. We're brothers in more ways than one. Sometimes, you can feel more attached to a person you choose to love than one who's tied to you by blood."

His words had me blinking. "I think I know what you mean."

"Cyan?"

"Yes, Rex."

"Your dad told me that yesterday, you didn't want to speak to your psychologist. So, I want you to know that whenever you need to talk, I'm here. You can tell me anything. Anything at all. Good, bad, ugly."

"Really?"

"Yes. Really."

I didn't know why, but my eyes prickled with tears. "You won't think bad of me?"

"No. I won't. I promise."

I wasn't sure why, but I knew we were talking about the other day. Not Martin, anymore.

"She shot my dog."

"I know she did, sweetheart," Rex said softly.

"I-I wanted to shoot her. Make her hurt like he hurt." I licked my lips. "He got better and now he's sick. Kelly says that infections are normal. Do you think Fraction will make it?"

"I don't know, Cyan. I don't know, but we can hope so, can't we? And if not, well, my dad and mom probably need a pet in heaven. So they'd look after him for you."

My throat was thick. "You think they would?"

"I know they would."

"I'd still prefer him to live."

Rex snorted. "Well, sure, of course you would. I do too. But if not, if things turn bad, then you know they're there for him."

That made me feel better. I didn't want Fraction to be alone.

"I only had him two weeks. But he used to sleep with me, and I know for sure that he made me have fewer nightmares. He kept me safe at night."

"I wish I could promise that he'd make it, Cyan, but I can't."

I was both sad and happy that he wasn't willing to lie to me. "Will Rain be okay?" I whispered, needing Rex's assurance. He knew every-thing. He was the Prez.

His voice was gruff, not reassuring, just honest. "He's going to be a soldier, Cyan. A lean, mean fighting machine."

"I thought he wanted to do what Rachel does."

"That day changed him."

I knew the day he was talking about.

The day my life had changed too.

I bit my lip. "Rex?"

"Yeah, honey."

"You really mean I can call you whenever I want to talk to you?"

"I do. I'm going to speak with your mom and dad, make sure they're okay with it, because I know you don't have a phone.

"But whether it's me you want to talk to or Stone or Lodestar or whoever, you can talk to us. We might be in West Orange, but we're still family. You got me?"

Warmth filled me. "I got you, Uncle Rex."

FORTY-THREE

KEIRA

PRESENT

I HATED FUNERALS.

I mean, nobody liked them, but this year, there'd been too many. Way too many.

Fraction lumbered out of his bed, clearly thinking I was playing fetch when I tossed my purse onto the dresser, but then he squatted on the rug in the universal signal for 'I'm gonna pee.'

I peered at him.

He peered at me.

"Don't do it," I warned. "Fraction, don't you dare—"

He dared.

He goddamn dared.

"Storm!" I screamed, which I swore made him piss even more. "Come and take care of your dog!" When he ambled into the room, pulling a face at what Fraction was frickin' doing, I grumbled, "I was not put on this Earth to wipe up your dog's mess, Storm. You fix it."

He headed over to the bedroom door and hollered, "North!"

I had to smile. "You're supposed to do it."

"What's the point in having Prospects if they don't get to handle the nastier aspects of club life?"

"How will they learn?" I agreed drolly, rolling my eyes, but to be honest, I didn't give a damn so long as I didn't have to clean up more piss. "I think they were signing up for grittier jobs."

"Ain't nothing grittier than cleaning up dog shit." Storm kicked the rug with his toe, rolling it up into a sausage. When North appeared at the door, frowning, he clicked his fingers and said, "Rug needs hosing."

North groaned. "Again? What the hell is it with this dog?"

"Fraction can't help it," Cyan said primly, clearly having overheard the conversation and come to weigh in on matters. Where Fraction was concerned, she was beyond defensive. "He has to stay inside until his stitches are all cleared up."

"I don't see why he can't pee in the yard," North muttered. "Hell, I'd pick him up just so I didn't have to clean this damn rug again."

Content now I didn't have to deal with this, I turned away from them all and headed into the bathroom, tugging at the pins in my hair and letting it flow.

Today had been hellish.

Watching Kelly throw himself on his mom's casket, before sobbing at the side of it broke my heart. He was currently sleeping it off in the bedroom beside ours, but I felt each tear he shed as if it were my own.

He didn't know this, but no one in his extended family wanted to take him in, so I'd told Storm that we had to keep him here with us. When we eventually moved out, he'd be coming too. There was no way I could have that boy on my conscience when he was left languishing in foster care after he had a perfectly good, if odd, family here.

I placed my hands on the edges of the sink as I stared into the vanity mirror, wondering why I didn't look as exhausted as I felt. The day had been long, the week had been longer, and the month was shaping out to look just as tedious as the rest.

Eight days.

That was the one thing that was keeping me going through all these transitions.

August Eighth.

I blew out a breath just as a tap sounded at the door. "Come in," I said softly, watching as Storm's face peered through the crack.

"Oh, you're decent," he rumbled, sounding disappointed.

I snorted. "I mean, if you want, I can take a seat on the toilet."

His eyes twinkled. "That's not my kink."

"Thank God for that," I grumbled, even as I turned around, butt on the sink, and folded my arms across my chest.

He eyed me, my stance, tilted his head to the side. "You okay?"

"What do you need?" I asked, not wanting to get into it.

I wasn't okay, but I would be.

That was as much as I could hope for after burying two innocent people who'd died because some psychos didn't understand that murder was a worst-case scenario.

Storm didn't tell me much about club business, but he'd told me that Kendra had latched onto the ex-Sinners when she'd overheard them talking in the bar & grill where they were eating.

A plan had been concocted to reel him in. Kendra—knowing Storm's biggest weaknesses, i.e. Cyan, drugs, and me—had been of great use to the small band of exiles.

Their end game? Safes. Apparently, there were hidden safes in the clubhouse that they wanted to access. Safes they felt sure Storm knew about.

He didn't. But now that he was in the loop, he'd started tearing the clubhouse apart for them.

What Storm wasn't saying was that their plan hadn't been to twist his arm into letting them back on board.

I had a feeling that Kendra, though she loved Storm and wanted him for her own, would have found herself dispensable if she tried to fight for the man who was her living, breathing obsession. I figured if that had happened, she'd have saved her own skin first. Damning Storm into the hell in which she'd invited him.

They'd have tortured him, gotten him hooked on the drugs again, and then killed him. God only knew what they'd have done to Cyan and me…

Of course, none of that took into account the fact that this chapter believed Storm was their Prez now, believed *in* him as a leader.

The exiles' plan was one thing, but I had to wonder how far they'd have gotten before the club came tumbling down on them like a ton of bricks.

Regardless, innocents had died, I'd killed someone, Storm had murdered and tortured the exiles, my daughter had fired a weapon, our dog was a walking miracle, Kelly was without his parents, and all because a bunch of headcases had sought weaknesses in our family, our chapter, where there were none to be found.

We were solid.

More than we'd ever been before.

"Wanted to check if you were coming down to the wake."

His words had me frowning at him. "Of course," I muttered. "I just wanted to get changed."

He brightened up a little, which told me he'd thought I was going to hole up in our room. "You look hot as is."

I rolled my eyes. "Yes, because that was the look I strove to achieve this morning when I knew I had to attend a funeral."

It would take time for him to accept that I was going to involve myself with club life more. So there was no need to get snippy with him. Just yet.

His lips twisted as he stepped into the bathroom, shutting the door behind him. As he pressed his back to it, he held open his arms and without a second's thought, I flew into them.

He held me tight, so tight that I felt like all the loose threads in my being were suddenly bonded together, and I nuzzled my face into the pocket of space between his throat and chin, glad he'd done this because I hadn't thought to ask.

That would be another habit we needed to break. That I could call on him for what I needed, be it a hug, a lesson on how to break a man's nose, or that I was worthy of taking his time.

For too long, I hadn't made waves because I was scared of what the repercussions would be. That needed to change, but we had time. Time to grow, to evolve, to become even more solid than we were now with all the writing on the wall, all our secrets laid bare for each other.

I'd never let Asher drown in his sins, and he'd never let the tsunami of self-doubt pull me under.

In the storm that was life, we'd be each other's life rafts.

If nothing else, the 'episode' had taught me that.

"It's going to be okay, Keira."

Nervously, I rasped, "How can it be? We have another kid now."

His mouth pressed to my temple. "Never thought I could be prouder of you, baby girl, then you go and claim one of my brother's children."

I swallowed. "We've made a mess with Cyan. What if we fuck him up too?"

He growled under his breath then pulled back to grab my chin. "We haven't fucked Cyan up. She's perfect as she is. Sure, she might be a little rusty around the edges, but with a bit of polishing, she'll be as good as new."

"You didn't just say our daughter was rusty, did you?"

Storm grinned—I felt it when his beard scraped me. "It felt fitting."

I pushed my forehead against his chest. "Kelly's traumatized. What if we don't do right by him?"

"Then we don't. What we can do, baby girl, is our best."

"And if that's not good enough?"

"Nothing is."

The simplicity of his words as well as the staunch truth in them had me peering up at him once more.

I was this man's everything. He'd proven that to me time and time again, and now it was my turn. I was going to become a worthy First Lady, one who'd make Rene proud. Not just for Asher, but for our family, for Kelly, for the chapter who'd ridden into war to defend us.

He deserved a strong First Lady, but so did they.

"Eight days." It was all I could think to say.

His lips curved. "Eight days."

When he pressed his forehead against mine, I murmured, "I miss you."

"I miss you too. Eight days."

That was our mantra.

In the following hours, as we celebrated Darla and Jump's lives, as the brothers partied and drank too much before sobbing into their JDs as they reminisced, and as the women sat there soberly, guzzling tequilas through tight lips, I watched him.

He didn't attend many parties, a choice I knew stemmed from his predilections, but I watched him and enjoyed it because with every hour that passed, he confirmed that I was right to trust him.

He didn't drink, didn't so much as sniff the air when joints were handed around. There were clubwhores in here, too, not acting like hussies but just sticking to themselves as they grieved a brother as well, and he didn't look their way once.

I wasn't monitoring him because I didn't trust him, but because I found the greatest joy in watching him. In seeing him move around, in seeing him be accepted, in seeing the ranks close around him, in seeing the man he should always have been as he led the chapter into glory.

The days slithered past as time had a habit of doing—slipping out from under our fingertips.

Fraction peed everywhere. North grumbled.

Cyan and Kelly argued about *Operation,* while Cyan aced her math test to the point where I knew, in the next couple of months, we'd need a tutor for that as well as French, while Kelly struggled at school, and got into a fight that had me adding him to the roster at the Krav Maga classes in Akron.

With the funerals over, Storm set about tearing the clubhouse apart on the hunt for the safes the exiles had wanted, and as he did, I worked a couple shifts over at the diner, finding comfort in the humdrum routine, especially during the lulls where Cyan and me talked about lessons.

Storm came to me with an idea to build a property on the land behind the clubhouse, and because I loved the idea of being on the compound, safe from harm and keeping others safe from the harm we perpetrated, he got to work on making that happen.

Eight became seven, six became four, and three became one.

I'd never been so nervous in all my life.

As much as I wanted August Eighth to happen, it was like the countdown to the vacation of a lifetime… you both longed for the day to come and feared when it was over.

I went to bed, wondering if he'd be there at 12:01, hoping he would but… he didn't show up. I knew why—he was in his office, the architect was here, and they'd been fine-tuning the plans for the development.

Was I disappointed?

Yes.

Did I get my ass out of bed and head down the stairs to grab him?

No.

I stayed there.

Staring up at the ceiling, my heart racing, my body throbbing with a need only he could assuage.

Over the last couple months, he'd gone down on me enough that I pitied the man's jaw, but that wasn't enough.

I needed him.

I wanted our union.

But still, I stared up at the ceiling.

I watched the lights flicker over it, heard the noises in the clubhouse start to wind down as it became one AM then two. My presence, as well as Cyan and Kelly's, was a definite hindrance to the guys who lived here.

All-night parties were no more, and that'd continue to be the way of it until my new house was built and my family was living elsewhere.

"That's probably why he has the architect staying so late," I muttered to myself. "He wants to get the development done."

But when it rolled around to three AM, that was when I realized I was acting like the old Keira.

The Keira who waited. But didn't act.

That wasn't me anymore. I wasn't that person.

More proof that I still had habits in need of destroying.

Now, I went after what I wanted.

I slammed Kendra's face into counters and I homeschooled my kid because that was what she needed. I did Krav now so that, in a pinch, I could defend myself if anything happened to my guards, and where my husband was concerned—I didn't let him get away with handing out bullshit.

He owed me his time, and I wasn't afraid to take it.

Just like I'd expect him to do the same if the tables were turned.

That was why I climbed out of bed. That's why I ripped off the Band-Aid instead of wasting more hours lying in the dark.

The clubhouse was quiet aside from a couple of moans that were coming from the bar, and I shoved them aside because they were pretty standard at this hour.

Yet another reason to get the housing development underway because, dear God, if my kid happened to learn about BJs how Giulia had, then I'd scream.

When I made it to Storm's office, I saw the light was on underneath the doorway.

I didn't knock, I just opened the door, coming across a room that had changed since I'd started staying here.

What with him tearing his office apart to find the hidden safes, I'd taken the opportunity to paint the walls again, get a new carpet, and a new sofa that didn't look like it had chlamydia.

For whatever reason, Storm had decided to keep the painting of the dogs playing poker—I never said he was an art connoisseur—and his menagerie of plants was taking over a good three-quarters of the room, mostly because he'd brought in the ones from the old house too.

I was seriously waiting on the day for him to decide to grow weed. Merging a hobby with business seemed to be pretty standard for the MC way of life.

At first glance, he wasn't in here, then I found him, standing in the chaos of leaves from a thriving fishtail palm, a false aralia plant, a rubber plant, and a lacy leaf rhododendron—yes, I knew the names now. He had his phone out and was taking a picture of something.

"Cyan will like this."

Jolting in surprise because I hadn't realized he knew I was there, I queried, "What will she like?"

"Come see," he directed, shooting me a look from eyes that were... well, they weren't as sad as the first time I'd ever seen him, but they were definitely tired.

I trod over to his side, then peered at where he was looking before I let out a snort. "A ladybug for a ladybug." Well, in this case, a little huddle of them on a leaf.

"Exactly." He smiled at me. "I took a picture for prosperity."

"Surprised you even saw them."

"Was just making sure they were okay for the night."

I cast him a look. "You putting them to bed?" I teased.

He grinned at me, looking surprisingly boyish. "Maybe."

His eyes darkened when he took me in. I guessed it was dumb not to have dressed up for the 'occasion,' but I didn't wear lingerie or anything lacy, just sleep shorts and a loose camisole. Didn't stop him from drooling over me like I was wearing Victoria's Secret, though.

The sudden hunger in his eyes, one that overtook his fatigue, more than made up for the hours of waiting in our bed, but still, it prompted me to ask, "Were you nervous too?"

He let out a short laugh. "Crazy, right?"

I shrugged. "Nothing's crazy if that's how you feel."

"You know I'm gonna come the second you put your hand on me."

"I don't know. If that was true, you'd have broken your promise months ago."

He blinked. "True."

Was this really about performance anxiety?

Call me stupid, but I found that endearing. So I backed off, begun to retreat, that was when he grabbed my hand and hauled me against his side. I yelped in surprise, but then tumbled into his arms. Amid the leaves, he held me close as he walked backward so that he could lean his butt on the windowsill.

"Where do you think you're going?" he rumbled.

I smiled. "Nowhere?"

"Exactly." He arranged me so that I could sit on his thigh while still leaning into his chest. I placed a hand over his heart, and he tipped his chin over my head. "I'm sorry we couldn't go to Corkscrew Falls."

"Things are too crazy here. I get it," I disregarded, sighing as I twisted a little more so I could better hug him. "I just need to be with you," I admitted softly.

"Truer words, baby girl, truer words." He pressed a kiss to the crown of my head. "I guess I'm scared."

Eyes flaring wide at the admission, I asked, "Scared? Of what?"

"That once I let go, I'll fuck up."

"You won't fuck up."

"I might. I don't want to let you and Cyan down but I've been doing that since the beginning."

I frowned and pulled back to stare at him, just so he could see me scowl. "You didn't fuck up everything."

"No? Well, that's something then." He rolled his eyes.

Squinting at him, I demanded, "We had plenty of good times and we'll have plenty more. You're not going to be bearing the burden of our marriage on your shoulders alone anymore. We'll be stronger going forward, and I'll be better prepared to deal with whatever comes our way."

He swallowed. "Everyone's dead now who could cause a problem."

"God, you're right. Your mom too?" He'd never mentioned her dying, but neither had he said she was still living.

"I need you to know something, Keira. Before we do this."

"Okay?" I asked warily.

"I would never touch you if I was unclean."

"I quite like it when you're sweaty," I teased.

His nose crinkled. "I didn't mean that kind of unclean."

"You mean STDs?"

"I do."

"I never thought you would. Me or another woman." I shrugged. "Was I wrong to think that?"

"No! You weren't wrong to trust me. I just—" He reached up and scrubbed a hand over his face. "Two years ago, couple months before we broke up—"

"When you started acting weird on me?"

He nodded. "Mom called me to meet up with her. I didn't realize it was her. She pretended to be Scarlet. I went and saw her, talked to her, found out she was sick. Dying, by the looks of her. She gave me a birthday gift."

Why didn't I think it was a nice gold watch?

"What was it?"

"She stuck me with a dirty needle."

I jerked to my feet. "Jesus Christ! What the fuck?"

He tilted his head back to look at me. "You don't say 'fuck' a lot."

"I think this merited it." I slammed my ass back down on his thigh. "What happened?"

"She implied that, well, I was going to die too."

My throat felt thick. "She's dead, right? So I can't go kill her?"

"She's dead," he murmured, no small amount of satisfaction lacing his words. "I went and had every kind of blood test under the sun, but HIV tests take time. It's detectable between one and three months after potential exposure so—"

"You were in limbo."

"I was." He dipped his chin. "I was clean though. It was too late by that point. I'd already wrecked things with you."

"Wait. This went down around your birthday, didn't it?"

He blinked, nodded. "Yeah. On my birthday."

It hit me then, why he'd been so weird. Why he'd been so distant. Not because he was cheating and pulling away, but because he thought *he was dying*.

He'd thought his mother had killed him.

"Why didn't you tell me? If you were dying, didn't you want to be with us?"

"I didn't want to let my poison touch you. I-I spent weeks high, Keira. Those days passed in a blur. It was the only way I could cope." When tears pricked my eyes, he reached up, rasping, "Hey, what is it?"

"I-I went to the clubhouse," I told him softly, "the day after you missed a parent-teacher conference at the school. Kendra came and talked to me. Fed me a lot of bullshit. Said…" I gritted my teeth, but I was determined to get this out. Determined to lay this all on the line so there was nothing, no lies, between us. "She said that you'd had a kid together, that you'd been trying for years, that you didn't trust me to have another baby because I was too weak. Said that you'd had sex while I was bedridden—"

Rage had him turning to stone beneath me. "I wish I could kill her again."

Me too.

"She seemed to slip into every single crack in my confidence, making me think I was like my mom. I-I had no choice but to react, Storm. I needed to make sure I did right by Cyan when she never did that for me."

"And to my dying day, I will never stop being proud of you for doing that," he rumbled, his assurance filling me with relief. *He didn't hate me for believing her lies.* "Baby girl, this is the last time we're going to talk about this because it's in the past, and we have a beautiful future ahead of us.

"Do you remember the day you almost miscarried?"

"I do. I'd left you," I told him in a small voice.

"Yeah, and I couldn't fucking find you. Where did you hide?"

"I went to Verona, stayed in the motel there."

He closed his eyes. "'Course you did. Dumbass—why didn't I look there?"

"It was twelve years ago, Storm, I think you can cut yourself some slack."

"No. I can't." He shook his head. "I couldn't find you, so I fell back on old habits."

"You got high," I said softly, reaching up to pet the cross he always wore.

"I did. I could only get LSD and it always fucks me up, and when you came into my room, I never questioned it. I was just too happy. Just too fucking relieved." I tensed. "Then I woke up, and it wasn't you."

"She pretended to be me?"

"I believed it was you. She just never said anything to break the belief." Guilt had him gulping. "I threw her out, told her if she came near me again I'd kill her, then I stormed off, determined to find you and to confess, but... you called and you were on bedrest from that moment on."

"You never slept with her again?"

"Never."

"When I was bedridden?"

"No. I swear." He hunched his shoulders. "You left me, I got high. That was when it usually happened."

The truth settled into my bones, filling up all the places Kendra had corroded with her lies.

"If you go on Ross's logic in *Friends*, you didn't cheat."

"I did," he said firmly, taking full accountability. "You deserved better from me, and I let you down; well, I won't do it again."

"What about after what happened with your mom? Did you cheat then?"

"No! Hell, no. I thought I had HIV! Christ, I never touched any of the clubwhores while I waited on the results, and only touched any of them after you threw me out and I started hardcore with the drugs again. I need you to know that. I also need you to know that I'm clean now."

"You really didn't have to tell me that, Storm. You wouldn't have gone down on me if you had an STD. I know that you think you're the villain, but have you ever thought that, to me, you might be the hero?"

"Don't think I'll ever believe that, baby girl."

"Then, it's on me to spend the rest of our lives proving that you are."

Storm slid his hand around my cheek, tilting my chin down. "That sounds really fucking good. 'The rest of our lives.'" His smile was shaky. "I remember thinking that I wouldn't get to see you when you're old and gray, and that I'd never walk Cyan down the aisle, and just… for a long time, my head was whirring with what I was going to lose and getting high seemed to be the solution to that. It was my only escape.

"I never imagined that Mom would have just been messing with me. I truly believed I'd be sick. And by the time I got the results, I'd already lost everything that mattered to me anyway."

"I love you, Asher. I've always loved you, and I know that I always will. We'll work our way back to each other, no matter what's thrown in our path because now that we've survived this, we'll survive anything."

The most joyful of smiles creased his jaw, making those eyes of his gleam with it and prompting me to realize I'd been waiting to see this ever since the first day I'd met him.

He went to push his forehead against mine, but I slipped out of his hold before he could. Kneeling between his thighs, I reached for his fly and carefully unzipped it.

As I did, his cock surged out, like he'd just been waiting for me to do this.

The gauge was thicker than before, and I glowered at the sight. "No more making this bigger. Jesus, Storm. In fact, you don't have to wear it—"

"I'll always have to wear it. I just won't up the gauge anymore."

Was that supposed to be a concession?

"I want you to always know that I'll be true to you. I *need* you to know that."

"What about when you go for health checks?" I joked. "Will you wear it then?"

He snickered. "Look at you, deciding to forget that I'm a lion not a pussy cat."

Wow.

My pussy clenched at that, which completely changed how I thought this would go.

But, by God, I needed it.

Just us. Always us. Perfectly imperfect.

I stroked the leather necklace I wore, watching as his nostrils flared as I rolled the key between my fingers, then I drew it over my head and moved over to the padlock to release him.

"How do you change the padlocks?" I questioned as I slipped the key into the lock. "And why do they always use the same key?"

"They're custom built by this guy online and my piercer down here changes it. He has a master key." He gave me a severe look. "Not once did I own that key. You're the only one who possesses it."

I tried not to feel a flare of delight at that, instead, grumbled, "Why did you have to make it bigger?"

"Because I started to like the pain. That was when I had to increase it."

"You know how messed up that sounds, don't you?"

"More messed up than jacking off twenty-five times a day just to forget about needing to get high?"

His arched brow called me on my bullshit. "True," I said on a huff as I unclicked the lock and freed him.

Carefully, I slipped the shank out of his glans, and when the heavy weight was gone, we both released a relieved breath. The tip was distorted now with a hole that I could peep through if I tried— which I so wasn't going to—but I guessed if this was a scar he wore that was proof of his sobriety, in the grand scheme of things, it wasn't too bad.

Now the pain, the deterrent, was gone, his dick bloomed to full mast.

I eyed it, then looked up at him and said, "You don't wear this to bed anymore. Just through the day."

He bowed his head in agreement, then his nostrils flared as I reached down and dragged off my camisole.

"Fuck," he ground out as I grabbed a hold of my breasts and played with my nipples. "I love your tits, K."

I smiled at him. "I know."

Pinching the nipples, I leaned down and pressed a kiss to the tip of his shaft. As I did, he groaned, and the sound was so animalistic, so pained and tormented that I swore it made my pussy clutch at the emptiness inside me again.

Taking note of his hands which were clenched down around the windowsill, I carefully tongued the slit, tasting the precum that was already slipping free from it, then I sucked the tip in between my lips.

"Holy fuck," he ground out, his hips bucking.

I sank my mouth further down his length, palpating it with my tongue, stroking the underside of the vein with it, then when he released a pained grunt, I let go of my breasts and sank one hand between my legs.

Through the gusset, I could already feel how wet I was just from the noises he was making, and I squirmed, rocking my ass against my heels as I began to bob my head up and down his cock.

Sucking hard whenever I made it to the tip, each tortured sound that escaped him made me work harder because I wanted to break him. Not make him come. Just to break him.

I wanted those hands of his in my hair.

I wanted him to do what he'd only ever done once before—*let go*.

With each suck, I felt him shake because he wanted to come, but I figured he was testing himself here, not my skills. Maybe he didn't want to be a two-pump chump, though he'd already proven that ten sucks ago.

A groan escaped me as the need to touch my clit hit me hard, but rather than focus on me, I grabbed my tits again as I pressed his dick back against his belly with my tongue.

Letting it flop there, I reached around and let him slide between my breasts, and slowly jacked him off that way, kissing the tip, flicking it with my tongue with every pass.

"Holy fuck," he rasped again.

"Christ, shit—"

"Keira, baby—"

"Please, fuck, don't stop."

His words were a litany, and that he swore at all was a huge breakthrough.

When that didn't get him to grab a hold of my hair, I let my tongue rim the holes from his piercing, which made him jerk. Then I reached down and grabbed a hold of his balls, and instead of twisting them like I'd seen him do so often, I sank my mouth around his shaft as far as I could before pulling back and sucking one in too.

As I palpated my tongue against the much-abused organ, I cosseted it with affection before I pressed one hand to his knee, urging him to spread them wider, as I let my tongue roll down his perineum.

Ass clenching before I could get further, that was what had his hands grabbing my hair, and the bite of pain was so sweet that I almost burst into tears.

"Where do you think you're going, baby girl?"

The threat, the delicious hint of a growl, the taunt and the demand had me shuddering as he guided me back to where he wanted me, and that right there changed everything.

He no longer just took, he directed.

If this was a symphony, he was the conductor, and I was more than happy about that.

"Suck me hard, K," he grated out, hissing when I obeyed.

"Lick the tip, let me see my cock in your mouth."

"Look at me as you take my dick, baby girl."

"That's right, deeper. Deeper. You can do it, Keira, you can—"

His hands tightened, pulling on my hair, forcing a squeal out of me which made him grunt, "Fuck," before he came.

He came and he came and he came.

Jesus, he'd never come so much in his life.

I gagged on it a little as his cum filled my mouth, running out of the sides, spilling down over my cheeks as I tried to swallow but holy hell, for as long as he climaxed, he groaned like he was suffering, like he was in pain and that was the sweetest sound of all.

He didn't let go of my head, his hold in my hair, for one second, not even when he was done, so his softening shaft stayed in my mouth, cum dripping everywhere, and I let it. Because this was, in nearly twelve years of marriage, the first time he'd ever let me swallow.

When he finally let go, urging my head off, he stared at the cum around my lips, on my chin, the mess he'd made, and his dick stunned me by getting hard again. Was that because of his addiction? Or just because he was turned on by looking at me?

His fingers slipped through his cum, spreading it over my mouth then thrusting the tip of one between my lips.

As I sucked on it, he rumbled, "Did I scare you?"

"You only scare me when you pull away."

He blinked, clearly surprised by my admission, but he merely said, "No more holding back?"

I shook my head. "No more holding back."

"Are you wet?"

Blinking, I nodded.

"Take off your shorts." He held out his hand for me to take as he helped me onto my feet. I shimmied out of them, then did as he asked, "Give them to me." My cheeks flushed when he pressed the crotch to his nose, and he smirked. "Soaked through."

"I-I'm turned on," I said hesitantly.

He threw them aside, then asked, "How many, baby girl?"

His question had me rocking my hips, relieved that this little ritual wasn't being swept out with the old.

"Two."

His lips quirked up in a cocky smile. "Only two? I think we can do better than that, don't you?"

A breathy moan escaped me as he surged to his feet, and in one smooth move that somehow managed to avoid our skulls from colliding, he ducked down slightly, grabbed my ass then hauled me against him. As he did, my pussy lips spread, and a small gust of air drifted along my slit which had me laughing as I buried my face in his throat.

"What's got you giggling?" he teased.

"Nothing," I replied, still snickering, then, I stopped when his fingers gripped my ass harder, pulling the cheeks wider apart.

He uh-huhed me like he didn't believe me, which told me he knew exactly what had made me laugh, then he moved us to his desk.

"Know how many times I've wanted to lay you out on this and feast on you?" he growled as he tipped me back against it.

"Prepared for this, did you?" I whispered shakily when my back collided with bare space, not the usual papers and other crap he kept on here.

"Bet your ass I did. Need to knock this off my list."

I leaned back on my elbows. "How long's this list?"

He grinned at me, looking so beautifully boyish that it made my heart sing. "Long. There's at least one or two things I have to knock off it every day for the rest of my life."

Snickering, I reached for the edge of his cut and murmured, "You gonna talk or give me what I need?"

"Never let it be said I kept my Old Lady waiting," he rumbled, his voice dark and deep and, best of all, dirty.

Loaded with a promise that I didn't think he'd break.

One that I'd make sure he didn't—that he'd stop holding back. That he'd stop treating me like I was porcelain.

Maybe, when I was younger, I'd wanted that. Now, I didn't. Now, I wanted more. I wanted everything he had to give, and I knew what that looked like.

The one time he'd fucked me.

When he'd claimed me like he was an animal claiming his mate.

I wanted that again.

God, I wanted it so badly.

When he loomed over me, keeping space between us, I arched my back, making sure we connected. When my breasts rubbed against his cut, I bit my lip but couldn't stop myself from moaning because it felt so decadent to be naked when he was, all told, fully dressed.

"Do you know," I whispered, "since that first time, you've only ever —" I swallowed back the word. "—fucked me in a bedroom?"

"No, no way."

Shakily, hopefully, I nodded.

His head wobbled from side to side. "No."

"Yes." I smiled at him, wondering if it looked as broken as I felt. "It's okay," I tried to appease.

His hands reached for mine, and when he bridged them then raised them over my head, he stated, "That was on me. Not you. I-I genuinely didn't realize—"

As his words waned, I found myself believing him. He hadn't realized.

Licking my lips, I asked, "You lost control with me once."

"I lose control every time with you, baby girl," he rumbled, but again, I shook my head at him.

"No. You don't. I don't want you to think I'm complaining, because I'm not, but if you'd like to lose control around me more often, I wouldn't be upset about that."

His lashes drifted closed. "I let you down—"

"No," I snarled, not willing to let him take the blame. "I could've brought the subject up, Storm. I didn't. In fact, I sneaked away from it.

"I was a coward, but that was in the past. The old me was like that. I'm not that Keira anymore. This is me, asking for what I need, willing to take it if you won't give it to me."

His smile broke my heart then put it back together again. "I really believe that."

"You should. You should believe it. It's true. I want you, Storm. All of you. Good and bad. I want you to want me too—not just the parts that you think are pure, but the parts that have really, really, really impure thoughts about you too."

"About me, huh?" His grin was dopey. "I think I like that."

I knew my eyes twinkled as I looked up at him. "So you should. I have really great, dirty thoughts."

"Like what? Care to share?"

Grinning at him, I repeated his words back to him, "There's at least one or two things I have to knock off my list every day for the rest of my life."

He laughed, then he stopped looming over me and pressed his weight into me. When his mouth hovered over mine, I knew why.

He was waiting.

Waiting for me.

So I raised my head, let our lips collide and I sank into him as much as he sank into me.

With a groan, I let him take the lead because I had no desire to rule over him, I just wanted him to shatter over me as much as I shattered beneath him.

My nails dug into the spaces between his knuckles as he supped from my lips with the tenderness I was used to, but it lasted for a split second before he was biting into me, grabbing my bottom lip and tugging it back and down, thrusting his tongue against mine, devouring me like I'd always craved. Like I'd always needed.

With a high-pitched mewl, I felt the bonds of his control begin to snap, and it felt so good that I arched my hips, then spread my legs, letting them come to his ass, digging my heels into his butt as I rocked against him from underneath.

Every time I did so, my pussy dragged against his dick, and the throbbing silk felt so good against me that I pulled back and moaned, "I missed you so fucking much, Storm."

He snarled against my mouth, "Every second without you felt like a fucking lifetime, baby girl."

I let out a sob as I felt his words resonate with me, and while tears pricked my eyes, I was so glad when he pulled back, then started kissing down the length of me.

As he did, his mouth curved over my nipples, tasting first one, then the other, biting the flesh with his lips, then raking his teeth over them. As he nibbled, I groaned, thrusting them further into him, then wriggled against him some more, digging my heels harder into him, getting myself off more than him.

When I came, it happened so fast that I didn't expect it. It was a small burst, but it felt so good that I cried out, my body tensing with delight as my nerve endings shimmered with the release.

Moaning through it, it took me a while to realize he'd come. I felt the slickness of it, the heat, and I blinked dazed eyes open and whispered, "You just came on me."

I wasn't disgusted, just shocked.

He laughed. "You looked so beautiful, baby girl. How couldn't I?"

Still dazed, I groaned, "You've never done that before either."

"A day for firsts?"

"Many firsts," I rasped, loving how slick I was now, how wet and messy—damn, it felt so good. So delicious. So wonderful.

When he untangled our fingers, I was almost disappointed, but then he moved down my body again, going further, until he was between my legs, his knees on the ground and he was staring up at me, over the curves and divots of my body, his face so close to my cum-slicked pussy.

A shocked breath escaped me when he shot me a smirk, then his mouth moved to my clit. I screamed when he sucked down hard on it, sliding his tongue around it, circling before suckling and tormenting it. He hummed as he did, moaning like he was getting off on it, and as shock and surprise made love to each other, my body was busy being ridden hard to the stars.

When he fluttered his tongue along the edge, then moved down, sucking on my pussy lips, then flickering around my slit, I rumbled, "No more condoms."

He paused. "What?"

"No more condoms. I'm on the pill. We don't need them."

The pause turned into a hesitation. "Are you sure?"

"I'm sure."

"But after what we just talked about—"

"Gives me even more reason to trust that I'm safe with you." I rocked my hips. "Don't stop. That felt good."

He didn't answer, but after a few seconds, his mouth returned to my pussy, and when he got me off, a hard and fast one, he jumped to his feet, then slapped his cock against my slickness.

"Fuck, do you know how much I've wanted this?" he whispered, looking down at us, bare, as if we were a magic box he was only now just allowed to open.

As he ground his dick into me, his cock rubbing over my clit, I muttered, "I want everything, Asher. I want everything you have to give. The gross stuff and the beautiful stuff and the raw stuff and the needy stuff.

"If you need to jack off, I want to see it, and if you want me so badly that you think you're going to burst, I want to be there when that happens—no more denying me what's my right. Do you understand me?"

He nodded, but his fascinated gaze was where we were both on the brink of coming together.

I surged upward, surprising him when I grabbed his cheeks, forced him to look at me, and demanded, "Asher, do you hear me? No more denying me what's my right."

"I hear you, baby girl." Then he pressed his dick to my slit and slowly pushed in.

I stopped caring about rights and started caring about how thick he was. How long.

My spine arched as I slumped against the desk, and I tipped my pelvis up and back so that it was easier for him to fit.

Jesus, I'd missed him.

I'd missed him so much.

When he filled me, all the way, when his thickness pushed the folds of my sex apart and it exposed my clit, when he started to thrust into me, slow at first, I watched him watch us.

And I knew, crazy though it was, he'd never forget this moment.

The first time he was allowed back home—for real.

And I melted.

I just melted.

I let him enjoy himself, let him savor, and then, I started to tease.

Clutching at him, I squeezed my pussy around him, urging him into moving, into remembering, into reacting. Slowly, it worked. He came back to me, and when he looked at me, the joy in his eyes morphed into the feral hunger I recalled from before.

I saw it eat into every other emotion, saw it tear at the bounds of his control, and I reveled in it.

I savored it.

He fucked me, then. He fucked me hard and raw and brutal, and it was like everything I needed, and everything I'd forgotten.

He pounded me so hard that, tomorrow, I knew I'd be sore, and I gloried in it, because this was my man. My personal Storm.

When he came, he filled me with his cum, but carried on thrusting into me, wild and hungry, until I was bucking back. Until he reached for my sensitive clit and dragged me up to the top just to shove me, face first, into an orgasm.

And when I fell, it consumed me.

The flames ripped into me and ravaged me.

Until I knew I had only one choice—to burn in those flames and to be reborn as the woman he craved.

The wife he wanted.

And the Old Lady he needed.

FORTY-FOUR

STORM

FOUR WEEKS AFTER AUGUST 8TH

"CHRIST, KEIRA," I muttered thickly, trying not to shoot my wad because I didn't want this to fucking end.

When my eyes were ready to roll back into my head and with my hands tangled in her hair, I didn't have enough sense to grab my phone when it started pinging, message after message after fucking message.

I was semi-concerned, but a lot more interested in my dick, and then, I recalled how I'd received the same Code Red text from Digger alerting me that one of our warehouses was on fire but the chat was muted… Shit.

Shit.

Double, triple, quadruple fucking shit.

"Baby girl, I gotta get that."

She pulled back, her lips making a popping sound as she released me, but she surprised me by murmuring, "So get it?" Then she dove back in, and I growled even as I untangled one hand just so I could reach over and grab it.

With her tucked between my knees under my desk in my office, the one place that was soundproofed, I blindly sought my phone then groaned when I saw all the fucking messages.

"Think Rachel gave birth," I rasped. Then, I squinted at the screen. "Or is going into labor. Or her water broke."

She snickered around my dick which definitely had my eyes rolling back into my head. "Is it just one or all of the above?" she asked when she pulled back.

"They all happen on the same day. So…"

"True. The first one is pretty important though," she said mildly, but she sucked on the tip, hard enough to have me growling. "Best get you off fast, huh?" were her next breathy words as she licked her way around my shaft like it was a sucker.

When she started jacking me off, too, I was a fucking goner, and as she swallowed every drop of cum, my head rocked back as I processed how goddamn awesome that felt.

I'd never let her do it before, mostly because that seemed dirty to me, but I liked her dirty. I liked her dirty *a lot*.

When she wiped the corner of her mouth with a fingertip, I hummed as she reached for the padlock and carefully inserted the shank into the pierced hole before she locked it up nice and tight.

"I'd have preferred you to hop on it rather than lock it," I grumbled.

"Me too," she replied dryly, "but I have a Posse to call."

My nose crinkled, but as she got to her feet once she fastened up my zipper, too, I hauled her onto my lap, hugging her close to me.

I reached for her chin, pressed my lips to hers, then kissed her until she was breathing hard and she was limp and docile against me.

I loved the taste of me on her and couldn't get enough of it. We were working things out, slowly. The urge to fuck was hard. As hard as fighting the drugs. Now I'd been let loose, and now she was a goddamn wild cat who'd let me bend her over any and everything, I wanted it all.

Now.

But that way led me back down the path I'd already left behind.

I didn't want to trigger old habits.

Our new rule was that every time I needed her, she was there.

If it was twice or three times, she was there.

And when the urge to jack off hit me, she was there.

It was hot, but oddly enough, it was the accountability I needed.

It'd be easy just to whack one out, but when she was there, when I dragged her into whatever private space I could get, it reminded me that I couldn't do that twenty plus times a day. She had shit to do, our kid to teach, a life to live. She couldn't spend her fucking life bent over a desk, on her knees, or with her legs spread.

I loved her too much to put her through that, and as such, though I wanted to bang her from one minute to the next, I controlled it. It helped that, with her, I could lose control now. It helped that she took me as is, no holding back, accepting every part of me—good and bad.

A knock sounded at the door, and I grumbled under my breath. "No fucking privacy."

"They're breaking ground soon, aren't they?"

I hummed. "Next week."

"Good."

The plans were all in, the construction firm was one I'd had the Sinners buy into, and five houses were being built simultaneously.

It was a massive project, one that I had a couple of councilors as well as brothers managing. If it all went well, we'd be building more houses once this set was complete, and slowly but surely, every brother with an Old Lady could have a property on there. Some smaller than others, with the club footing the deposit to give them a starting chance, while they saved up the rest.

"Come in," I called out, tugging her back into me when the door opened.

Her cheeks were flushed as Little peered over us both, a wide grin on his face, as he declared, "Mailman was just here."

I arched a brow as he lumbered over, dropping a pile of letters onto the desk before ambling out.

"Did you know he has a twelve-egg white omelet for breakfast?" Keira whispered as he closed the door behind him.

"Not surprised. You should see what he bench presses," I joked as I reached for the pile and started sorting through the letters.

"Your phone's going crazy," Keira said softly as she watched me.

"I know, I know," I muttered, finally reaching one that had me frowning because it was from the woman of the hour—Rachel.

Curious, I tore the letter open, and found there was a sheet of paper and an envelope inside it.

Bear wanted you to have this.

At the right moment.

Rachel

"Wonder what it is."

"I don't know. Guess we're about to find out," I replied, staring at the envelope. It didn't look new, in fact, it looked battered around the edges, as if it had been handled many times. Nervous, I passed it to her. "Read it to me?"

"You sure?"

"Yeah."

Oddly choked up, I turned my face into her hair, unashamed to admit that I was hiding as she tore open the envelope. As she did, she pulled out another envelope. A smaller one this time.

"Dearest Asher,

You'll always be Asher to me. I know you earned the name Storm—remember when you were called Lightning? Because of that streak of hair? Storm suits you much better even if it saddens me how you got it.

Still, I'll always see you as the baby we brought back from the correctional facility. You were so fucking small, Ash. We tried you on the bottle at first, but nothing soothed you.

Probably too much information, but Rene ended up nursing you because that was the only thing that brought you any peace. Right then, I knew you'd mean more to us than just a kid we had to look after until that bitch mother of yours got her ass out of jail.

I always wanted to adopt you, but Ellen wouldn't stand for it. I hope you know that, in my heart, you were my son too. Not just Rex.

I had a lot of hopes for you, but your past stuck its claws in tight and it didn't seem like it was going to let you go. Then Keira came along. She sideswiped us all. I never imagined that you'd fall for a girl like her, and when Rex told me you guys split up, I was probably more devastated than you. Which is saying a lot because I know you worship the ground she walks on.

I left Rachel with two letters, and it was at her disposal to choose which one to send to you.

This one, I asked her to send if you guys ever looked like you were getting back together.

I don't think I'm long for this earth, Asher. I'm ready to be back with Rene. I miss her. She's my soul mate and she was torn from me. I know you met your soul mate too—" Keira released a sharp sob at that, before she sucked it in while I hugged her harder, and continued, "I just hope she isn't torn from you by your own stupidity.

We talked once about how dumb I'd been when I cheated on Rene. After looking around my brothers, I realized how what I did, what you did, wasn't just dumb—it was masochistic. A trait we both share.

The love we feel for our Old Ladies is rare, Storm. We both know that. But we betrayed them, we let them down, and they might think that they know how badly we regret it, however *we* know they couldn't possibly understand what it is to hurt the one person who makes up your entire universe.

So, yes, I'm praying this is the letter you're reading. I'm praying that Keira let you back in, that she doesn't punish you forever because, let's face it, you'll punish yourself far worse than she ever could. That's how it should be though.

There has to be balance.

Such a massive gift of a soul mate has to be tempered in other ways. It's in man's nature to start to take something for granted, but having made that mistake once, I know, like me, it's not something you'll be repeating. So, I wish you a happy life together, with many wonderful years, and that big family I know you always wanted. You'll make a great father, son. Just trust in yourself like I do.

There's one thing in particular I'd like to impart to you.

You set your own worth in this world.

I've watched you struggle for years with your value. The only place you've ever looked right was as VP, but even that wasn't enough. How could it be? I raised both you and Rex to be leaders. No wonder you faded under his leadership, you were supposed to strike out on your own, but that's not exactly possible in our world, is it?

I hope that you find your way, I hope that you set out and take a path and make it your own—rule over your own kingdom on your own throne. You deserve that, son. And by that right, so does Keira. She'll make a fine First Lady. If you'll stop pulling the wool over her eyes and let her see the real you.

Not sure why she likes that pansy version you sell her, but I'm hoping that over time, she'll learn the mettle of the man.

Know that I think you're worthy.

Know that I love you.

Know that Rene loved you.

And know that, when shit comes to shit, and you ride into any battle, you do so as my son. As my heir as much as Rex.

One regret I'll always have is that I never got your mom to sign over those adoption papers, but that's on me, not you.

Now, to business.

Kevin Sisson.

When Nyx was done with him, I took his body and dumped him in the Hudson. Call me paranoid, but with global warming, and bad luck —let's face it, it follows me like a specter—if his corpse ever comes to light, there's a letter here. It's my confession. When I got rid of him, I put my dad's old WW2 revolver in there. They're pigs—they're dumb and like cold cases wrapped up nice and fast. They shouldn't look past the signed confession and the discovery of the murder weapon. Fuck, I couldn't have tied this up nicer for them.

Rex's brothers… you were all my kids. I'd kill for each of you, would have gone to the electric chair to save Nyx. I watched over you, let you down, built you up, and saw you all grow, but it's only you and Rex that I call 'son.'

So, son, I'm sorry this is goodbye. Even as I'm glad to be going into the goop of the universe where, hopefully, Rene will be waiting on me, I wish we had more time, but that's another life lesson.

There's never enough time.

I love you, son. Tell that grandkid of mine I love her too.

While I can still boss you around, make sure you take care of that wife of yours—she's going to make a fantastic Old Lady if you'll just give her a shot.

Bear

Ps. Rex inherited most of my assets, but you're my boy too. Speak with Rachel. She'll tell you where to find your inheritance.

Pps. Don't be like me. Don't waste your life wishing you were with Keira if fate shines its shit upon you and takes her first. When the time comes, join her. Don't suffer like I did."

And when Keira broke down in tears, she wasn't alone.

I held her tight, tight enough that it had to hurt but it was the only way I wouldn't cave in.

For all that I'd thought of Bear as my dad, he'd thought of me as his son, and though I hid my tears in my Old Lady's hair, though they were loaded with sorrow and grief, peace filled me too.

Peace.

Because he was back with his First and only Lady now, and my parents were together again.

FORTY-FIVE

KEIRA

FOUR MONTHS AFTER AUGUST 8TH

Finale B - Cast of the Motion Picture: Rent

"CYAN!" I hollered her name because she was busy fighting with Kelly. "Leave him alone!"

When she scrubbed her knuckles in his hair, I shook my head as Storm replied, "Let them be. They're only playing."

"She's going to give him a complex."

"He's learning an important life lesson," Storm drawled.

"What's that?"

"It's okay to be beaten by a girl." His lips quirked up at the corners. "Anyway, look at him, he's having a ball."

I winced when Cyan threw him over her shoulders and he landed with an audible 'Ooooofgh.'

"Don't discourage her," Giulia agreed.

I scowled at her. "Don't even get me started on you, missy."

"What the hell did I do?" she retorted, wincing when baby Bear tugged on her nipple. "Dude, there's no more milk there," she told him grumpily. "You drained me dry. Let me recharge my batteries and give the tits a break."

Storm snorted. "Not sure he speaks 'Posse.'"

"He will by the time he's older." She jerked her chin up and pinned me with another glare. "Come on, you. What have I done now?"

"You gave her pepper spray."

Giulia shrugged. "She should be protected."

"It's illegal."

I received another shrug for my pains. "All the good stuff is. But, duh, bitch, I checked. You think I'm gonna hook mini-Giulia up with the bad shit? Ohio is lax as fuck where that stuff is concerned. Check your laws."

"She's not wrong," he told me when I glowered at his snicker of amusement.

"You're lucky she's homeschooled, because if she wasn't, then we'd be screwed when she tried to take that into class with her."

Giulia grinned. "Yeah, okay. I'll give you that. I forgot about that stuff not being allowed in schools."

"No, 'course you didn't," I mocked, rolling my eyes.

"Come on, babe, chill."

I grumbled, "I am chilled."

"You don't look chilled."

I peered up at him. "*I'm chilled,*" I growled.

Lily laughed as she wandered over to this end of the porch. "You really sound like it, Keira."

"Back off, Lily," Giulia rumbled, but her tone was teasing. "We got ourselves a lean, mean, shootin' machine on our hands."

My nose crinkled at the reference to what I'd done that day.

Giulia whacked herself on the chest. "Proudest day of my life. Learning our little pigeon turned into a blood-covered dove."

"Well, that imagery isn't disturbing," Lily drawled with a snort, but it died off as she turned to grant Link a smile as he tucked her under his arm. Damn, they looked right together.

Link, my oldest Sinner friend, finally seemed at peace. We all had our demons, but Lily and his seemed to be in perfect accord.

It kind of hurt to admit how jealous I'd been of all these women at one time or another.

For as long as I'd known them, I'd been fighting the pull Storm had on me, but seeing them all cozied up, settled in their Old Men's lives, at ease with club life... I could have let that impact my interactions with them.

I wasn't sure why I hadn't, but I was grateful for them.

Friends like these were for life. They were sisters. As linked and bonded as Storm was with his brothers.

Once you went Posse, I realized, you never came back.

Had knowing I had my family's love, and that the Posse had my back, given me the courage to do what I'd done that day?

To take that gun, to shove it under Kendra's chin, and to rasp, "This is the last time you'll hurt my family, bitch."

Rather than dwell on what was, essentially, a stain on my mortal soul, I grumbled, "Shuddup," at Giulia, hiding my face in my hot drink, grateful for the warmth it imparted to my fingers.

It was freezing out here, but the girls had put up those heaters so we could all sit outside and watch the kids horse around. Of course, the few West Orange kids there had snowmen on their mind. Cyan and Kelly were fighting.

I'd worry for them both if, outside of play-fighting, they weren't friends.

I'd decided that Kelly, after his grades plummeted, could be easily homeschooled, too, so the pair of them were classroom buddies. Kelly's grades weren't as high as Cyan's, but his English papers had the ability to move me to tears. He had a poet's soul. I just couldn't compute that he'd love brawling as much as Cyan when he could write what he did.

Because neither of them attended school, we'd stayed an extra week after Christmas to be with our family up here, leaving Sweet Lips to rule the roost in our absence.

MaryCat and Digger were here somewhere as well, and I had to admit, it felt good to be back. Good to be with our people. The folks in Coshocton were becoming that, too, but it was impossible to forget your roots.

When a bike pulled up, I didn't think much of it until Rachel sat up hard enough to make Lisandra squawk as Rachel jerked the bottle out of her mouth.

"What is it?" Tiffany asked, concern lacing her words.

"Rain? Is that you?" Rachel called out.

When the biker hauled off his helmet, revealing a close-shaved buzz cut and a wide grin, Rachel laughed. "My God! You'd be late to your own wedding, wouldn't you? I asked you down for Christmas, not New Year's."

Rain chuckled as he climbed off his hog, but before he could even think about moving toward the porch, someone ran at him, nearly barreling him over.

Cyan.

That was her signature move.

"Rain! OMG! Your hair! What did they do to it? Daddy says you're a soldier but you're not wearing a uniform! Have you shot anyone yet? I shot someone last year, well, *almost*—"

At the blur of questions and statements, the only one that had Rain rearing back was the last one.

Understandably.

He shook his head down at my daughter, revealing two cute dimples in his cheeks that, I knew, were going to be a big problem, in a big way, especially with how Cyan was looking up at him as if she had stars in her eyes.

I was pretty sure she hadn't looked so excited when Miley Cyrus had come to Columbus.

"Oh, dear," Lily murmured softly, catching my eye.

I grimaced. She smiled.

Cyan tugged Rain along to the porch where we were all gathered, leaving him alone long enough for Rachel to hug him, for him to meet his niece, and to greet everyone on the deck. Then, she demanded again, "Why did they cut your hair?"

Brothers waded out, each of them greeting Rain, some hauling him in for a hug, others just slapping him on the back. All the while, Cyan sat there, looking up at him with puppy dog eyes as Kelly hovered around them, as curious as she was, asking him questions when Rain turned his attention toward them.

It was sweet.

Dangerous, but sweet.

Especially when Kelly stared up at Rain with the same look as Cyan, except with hero worship rather than blind adoration.

I had to admit, though, the evening passed by in a blur. We ate too much, drank too much, laughed and talked, and it was good. So good. As I sat in the clubhouse I'd hated for so long, with brothers I'd been scared of throughout my marriage, it was like a graduation, of sorts. I returned here an Old Lady, not a wife, and this was confirmation of that.

Definitely tipsy on happiness if not alcohol when I made it to the stairs with Storm propping me up, we headed to the bedroom that we were borrowing for the next couple nights. Rex said it was Storm's bedroom, though, so I didn't know if that meant no one else was allowed to use it or not, but it left me feeling like we still had roots here in West Orange, and that warmed my heart.

As I dropped my sweater on the floor and shrugged out of my jeans, I called out, "Guess who I saw at the drugstore today."

Storm, in the middle of checking his messages from the Coshocton chapter, asked, "Who?"

"My mom."

His head whipped around so he could look at me. "Your mom?"

I nodded.

"Did she acknowledge you?"

I smiled. Shook my head.

His brow puckered as he clambered to his feet, and within seconds, he was hugging me, and I was right where I needed to be. "It's her loss, baby girl."

"I know."

"Did she see Cyan?"

"No, I went alone."

He hummed. "I'm not sure if I'm glad about that or not. I'd hate to think that she'd have blanked Cyan as well." He gave me another squeeze. "I mean it, Keira. It's her loss."

"Truly, I know. Before Coshocton..." I shrugged. "I'd probably have been upset but not now."

He grunted. "The old bitch is too stupid to realize what she's missing out on." He pressed a kiss to my lips and when I let my tongue dart out to ensnare his, he shifted a little, grinding his dick into my belly, letting me feel both his hardness as well as the padlock.

For Christmas, he'd bought a gold chain and had had a jeweler weld the key to his padlock onto it alongside the first birthday gift he'd ever given me—the pendant with the Midsummer Night's Dream quote on it. Touched as I was, it still amused me to think that his dick-lock was studded with diamonds.

I reached up and rubbed it between my fingers, murmuring, "Wish it wasn't too cold for us to visit our spot on the hill."

He grinned. "There's plenty of time for that. I'll have to make sure we visit in the summer."

I grinned back, then let go of the lock and let my hands come up to cup his cheeks, holding him in place as I surged onto tiptoe so I could nip his bottom lip.

"Them's fighting words," he mumbled against my mouth.

"I didn't say a thing," I taunted with a soft laugh, releasing a shriek as he hauled me into his arms then tossed me onto the bed.

As he crawled between my legs, I smiled at him as I slipped my hand underneath my panties. When I played with my clit, he growled and grabbed the crotch then dragged it away so he had the perfect view of my pussy.

My hips rocked as I touched myself, enjoying it even more when he dragged his cock out and started jacking off. The visual obscenity of the padlock was something I was used to now, but seeing the tip, leaking precum, and an angry red, had me moaning at the sight.

Jerking upright, I snagged the key around my neck, then slotted it into the lock as he held his cock firm. He tossed it to the side as I bucked upright, tumbling us around so that I was on top. Grabbing his dick, I held it fast in my hand as I slipped it through my juices, before I notched it into my slit.

As I sank onto his thick, fat shaft, my head tipped back.

As I rode him, I let loose a garbled laugh that was a mixture of joy and love and need.

As I sped up, I let the freedom of being with Storm like this overtake me.

As I clutched at him with my pussy, I felt the bindings that tangled us together tighten even more.

And as I came, and his cock spurted inside me a bare half-second later, as I cried out my orgasm and he roared with his own, I felt a secret smile drift about my lips.

Tomorrow, I'd tell him we were going to have a baby. A baby that, before, he wouldn't have wanted but I felt sure he would now.

Tonight was for us. Tomorrow was for our family.

FORTY-SIX

KEIRA

FOUR YEARS AFTER AUGUST 8TH

Wake Me Up When September Ends - Green Day

A HISS ESCAPED me when he spread my pussy lips apart, and I groaned when his damn phone was suddenly between us, and he started clicking.

"If you ever get hacked one day," I whispered, "I'll kill you."

He snickered, but nipped my inner thigh before he moved my legs further apart. As he did, I felt his cum slipping out of me and, of course, he took another shot.

When he encouraged me to roll onto my belly, to go on all fours, I did, arching my back and peering at him over my shoulder as he took shot after shot once he'd pressed a kiss to his brand on my ribcage. It read, 'Some angels are demons too.' And I thought it fit us to a tee.

After Phoenix's birth, I'd been, well, self-conscious. Of course, Storm had let me get away with that for about five minutes. Like always, he worshipped every inch of me, filling up the spaces in my self-esteem with the truth—at least, in his eyes.

Eventually, I'd started believing him, and, a little while later, I'd agreed to let him take pictures of us.

Ever since, his phone was usually close to hand whenever we had sex.

I'd admit that knowing he got such a visceral pleasure out of my body was a massive turn on. Two kids hadn't been kind to it, but he still looked at me like I was a porn star.

Of course, to him, I was.

With a baby and two teens, it wasn't always possible to be as accessible as he needed, and I'd agreed that if he needed to jack off, he could, so long as he sent me a photo in return. As a result, he used the pictures he took of me and then, later, for extra accountability, told me what in particular had made him come.

It worked. The lock and that seemed to keep him under control, and with the expansion of the chapter, how the businesses he'd invested in at the start of his presidency had exploded under his watch, with two teenagers and a toddler, life couldn't really have been more stressful and yet, he was doing okay. Better than okay, I thought. We were strong. Stronger than ever.

"Put your fingers in your cunt," he rumbled, and I groaned but did as he asked.

My clit was still sparking with the pleasure he'd gifted me a few minutes ago, but I was used to this. Waking up to an orgasm and a photo shoot in the morning was pretty much how I started every day.

As I toyed with my pussy, I replied, "You know I hate that word."

"I love it. I love your cunt."

I grumbled but didn't complain. Not when he leaned down and tongued my slit, not when he sucked my clit into his mouth again and got me off hard and fast. By the time I was humping his face, he was sliding back inside me and I groaned, pushed to the limit as he stuffed me full of his shaft.

The phone was flung aside, forgotten, as his hands clawed at my hips when he dragged me back onto his dick. I reached between us, fingering my tender clit again, knowing he wouldn't get off until I did, and I worked myself harder, higher, faster, trying not to let the endless to-do list filter through my concentration.

Storm needed me, all in. If I wasn't focused, he'd know, and he'd feel like a piece of shit. I was done with him feeling that way. It had taken three years and the birth of our son to get him to admit that Bear was right—that he was worthy. And in that time, I'd worked hard to show him how I loved him, how I didn't want to live without him. How we were it for each other.

Soul mates, just as Bear had called it.

So I shoved aside the desperate state of our fridge, which was severely lacking groceries, and the schedules that were needed by the diner staff. I focused on us. Just us. Forever us.

Like always, it worked.

Pleasure cascaded through me, enough to make me hold my hand over my mouth, to restrain myself from screaming with the explosion that was an orgasm with my Old Man.

His fingers dug into me, biting hard into my flesh and I groaned, overwhelmed and joyous all at the same time. As he dragged me into him for one final thrust, as he came in me, marking me, branding me, I sank into the sheets, a limp and soggy noodle that was done for the day before it even started.

As I splatted into the sheets, he nestled close to me, flat on his back, both of our chests heaving as we just laid there, trying to come down from the cataclysm that never ceased to amaze me.

After a good ten minutes of silence, where we both knew the other was awake but we were just glad to be in each other's company, I murmured, "What do you want for your birthday?" He snickered, and I whacked him on the stomach. "What?" I complained. "You have to tell me unless you want me to get you something you don't need? It's not like you're a necktie man, is it?"

That had him snickering harder.

"I don't need anything," he said after he managed to stop laughing. "Just you."

I grumbled, "Don't say that. It makes me feel bad when I have a list of things I want for my birthday."

"Ah, so it's guilt that has you asking," he teased, turning his head to the side so we could look at each other.

And as simply as that, he stole my breath.

I reached over, tracing that smile with my thumb—even though it was kind of awkward in my current pancake position—all while his sparkling eyes held mine.

"You know, when I was eighteen, and I saw you outside of school, I was pretty sure that I hadn't seen eyes sadder than yours. I never realized how right I was." I smiled. "They're not sad now, though."

He shook his head. "Nothing to be sad about." His gaze drifted to another point of the bedroom, a point I couldn't see, but I knew he was taking it in.

We'd lived in smaller houses for most of our married life—I knew why now. *Thanks, Dad*—but this place was large. Five bedrooms, a massive family room, an office for him, a schoolroom for the kids, a room for me. Five baths, three half-baths, a kitchen, a separate dining room, and all of it beautifully decorated. Like it belonged in a magazine. Well, that was after the housekeeper had finished tidying it up. Mostly, it looked like a bomb had dropped what with so many people roaming around the place.

Beside us, Digger and MaryCat had a property for them and their three kids, Sweet Lips was on the other side, as were Picasso and Slayer with their Old Ladies. There were eighteen properties in total, with North and his Old Lady building one right now.

The Coshocton chapter was less illegal and more legal than its other Satan's Sinners' counterparts. They were still one-percenters because of the runs that traveled through our compound, but Storm's speciality, so it had turned out, was laundering money and creating thriving businesses that worked.

He'd recruited a further thirty brothers over the years, each with families and lives of their own, and while he sat at the throne, I stood by his side. Club life wasn't alien to me anymore. I wasn't frightened of clubwhores or of the parties in the bars. In fact, the sweetbutts were frightened of me, and the brothers respected me. I had friends here, of which MaryCat was my BFF, and more importantly, we'd put down roots, made our own family among the Coshoctonites.

As he looked around the room, I knew that was what he saw, what he was thinking.

In four years, we'd achieved more than we had in the previous twelve.

A solitary warble sounded down the hall, jerking us both out of our contemplative thoughts, and recognizing it as the godawful ringtone of Cyan's that she'd put on to piss Kelly off, I frowned in surprise because it was a little too early even for Cyan and her Krav buddies.

Yeah, Cyan was still practicing Krav, as well as a whole host of other activities I'd never have imagined her taking part in. Gymnastics had gone the way of the dodo. Martial arts were her thing, with two black belts in Judo and Taekwondo making every brother in the club-house respect her because she could, and would, put them on their asses.

When a sharp, short scream sounded down the hall, I immediately clambered to my feet. It had been years since she'd had a night terror, but we both reacted as if it were yesterday.

Unlike me, Storm didn't wait to grab a sheet. Nope, that would be too easy. He just took off at a fast clip, dragging his shorts off the floor and hauling them on, as he lived up to his name as he stormed down the hall to reach our kid.

I raced after him, nearly tripping over the sheet in my haste. When I caught up, Cyan was sobbing in his arms.

"What is it?" I demanded, wondering what the hell was going on.

Cyan's sobs tore at my heart, ripping it to shreds. Kelly came tumbling out of his room, some paper stuck to his head which told me he'd been cramming for the test we were going to have today and had fallen asleep at his desk, and in the next room over, I heard Phoenix start to wail as he heard his sister and responded to her pain.

"Jesus, what's going on?" Kelly rattled out, huddling close to us all, creating a triangle in which Cyan stood at the center.

"I don't know," I rasped, looking to Storm for answers.

His mouth was tight as he held our devastated daughter against his chest. "That was Rachel."

"Rachel?" Kelly mumbled sleepily. "Why's she calling?"

"Rain's MIA."

DEAR DIARY
KELLY'S SENIOR YEAR

Today was perfect. So, so, so perfect. All Kelly's hard work has finally come to fruition. Watching him get up on that stage, dressed in his graduation gear and accepting his degree was one thing—summa cum laude, dontcha know— but watching him give the valedictorian speech is something I'll never forget.

We were all there for him, the whole chapter rode down, the Posse and their Old Men came with, and we took over this motel on the I-80. Literally **everyone** *is here. We took up nearly the entire auditorium, and that was before they asked some of us to leave to make room for other families.*

It was hilarious, though.

Storm or some other brother must have texted them to let them know when he made it on stage because a fucking riot of horns blared outside when he accepted his diploma.

I swear everyone jumped in their seats.

Not the chapter, of course, and not me.

I think today was the first day I've actually realized how integrated I am with the club. It hasn't exactly snuck up on me, but I'm just... well, I guess when you do something every day, you don't know it's happened until something reminds you.

Giulia would slap me upside the head, call me a dumbass for taking this long to figure it out, but I'm glad she didn't. I'm glad I worked it out for myself.

Hey, never let it be said I'm not slow to process things. Took me twelve goddamn years to stop being flighty, but once the lesson is learned, that's it for me.

Sitting by Storm's side today, his arm around my waist, his fingers tracing my brand on my side—I remembered what it was like when I was younger and we first met, I remembered when we married, and I remembered when Cyan was born. I'd imagined myself at a place like this, grabbing a diploma, getting cheers from friends and family, but that hadn't happened. Not yet. There was time still. And life hands you different kinds of achievements, doesn't it?

Raising a foster kid so well that he becomes as essential to your family as your own flesh and blood—I'm so proud of that. So proud of Kelly. I guess... when I see him, I see parallels with Storm. When he was young. When Rene and Bear took him in. I wished they'd been able to get full custody, and I wished, even more, that Jump and Darla hadn't had to die, but life is what life is and now, I just know I did them proud.

Seeing him here, seeing what he's achieved and knowing he's going onto great things doesn't take away my regret, but it makes me happy to know that his folks are looking down on him, as proud as we are, and undoubtedly relieved knowing that he's loved.

It was a brilliant day, and I'll write some more, but Storm's just wandered out of the bathroom, and if he shakes that padlock in my face one more time... well, let's just say I'm about to celebrate the only way him and I know how.

FORTY-SEVEN

STORM

FOURTEEN YEARS AFTER AUGUST 8TH

Say You Won't Let Go - James Arthur

"LOVE ISN'T the only thing I can give to you," I told Keira, grabbing her ass and hauling her into me.

She laughed, chuckling as I groped her on the dance floor, in full sight. But I didn't see the harm in it. Most of the people here were doing the same, hell, even Cyan was with her groom.

I smiled at the sight of them both, the glee on her face, the outright love on it, and I shot her husband a grim stare, one that was a promise. A promise he already knew and understood because I'd threatened him last night in the Lockbox.

He nodded at me, and I nodded back, just as Keira grumbled, "Stop scaring our son-in-law."

Snickering, I peered down at her. "A man's got to have his fun. It's a rite of passage."

She rolled her eyes. "I'll give you a rite of passage—" She leaned up on tiptoes and gave me a kiss that still had the power to knock me off my feet.

Twenty-five years.

Fuck.

Twenty-five.

It still seemed crazy how quickly the time had passed, and yet, I'd lived it to the fullest, Keira had too. We had four kids now. Cyan, Kelly, Phoenix, and Brook, and each of them were content to drive me crazy on the regular, but I wouldn't have it any other way. Brook had been a surprise baby, popping up after a birthday gift had gone awry.

I'd never thought I'd be having another kid at forty-two but hell, who was I to complain?

Shit wouldn't have felt right without the little monster.

Speaking of, I recognized Brook's particular wail from the other side of the fucking dance floor.

"Your spawn is causing hell," Keira muttered as she broke our kiss.

"My spawn?"

"It's that damn dog. I swear, the next one I'm choosing. He gets all the kids riled up."

"If you choose it'll be a chihuahua."

"What's wrong with that? They're not hell on four paws."

I grinned. "You know you love it."

"Do I?" she grumbled, but her eyes were twinkling with joy as well as the thousands of fairy lights that had been strung up all over the place.

She'd done Cyan proud with this reception, a feat that had taken all the Old Ladies, from Coshocton and West Orange, to pull off.

It was a kind of street party on our subdivision, except, in the road, there were dozens of tables and chairs, a dance floor, a bandstand, the gazebo where my eldest had said her vows with Digger as her officiant, much as he'd been ours, as well as play areas for the younger kids, and all other kinds of shit that told me my woman would have made a great wedding planner in another life.

When she'd told me her plan, I'd just rolled my eyes, handed her the checkbook, then let her get on with it. I was a smart man, and a smart man knew when to back the hell away and let his Old Lady have free reign.

Wasn't like we couldn't afford it.

I'd made a small fortune over the years, more than enough for us to retire to Florida or California when Brook hit eighteen, and I was looking forward to that as much as I loved my life as is. And if I didn't have enough, Bear's inheritance would have paid for this party ten times over.

God love a man who invested in gold.

I'd sold it and had made a steal five years ago when prices rocketed.

I twisted around when I heard a holler, seeing Nyx's hellions mixing with mine, then Link's and Sin's joined the fray. I wasn't sure what they were doing, didn't really want to know. There were plenty of adults, I figured someone else could parent for once—wasn't every day that I was father of the bride, was it? I deserved a night off.

Spying Rex dancing with his daughter, Cruz and Indy twisting around the dance floor, him with one kid on his hip, then Stone and her son shuffling around as well, I had to shake my head.

Somehow, we'd made it past our forties.

Somehow, we were in our fucking fifties.

When did that happen?

"You look maudlin."

"Not maudlin. Just..." I smiled. "Thinking. It's been grand, hasn't it?"

"What? The day? Yeah." She blew out a breath. "I'm so glad it's over, babe. Fuck, if I had to worry about corsages and vegetarian entrées and making sure that Giulia didn't have to sit next to whoever she'd offended last for one more day, I'm pretty sure I'd have gone crazy."

I smiled at her, though that hadn't been what I meant, and instead, I murmured, "I got a present for you."

She froze. "You did?" Her eyes narrowed. "Does this end with me on my back?"

I snickered. "I'm more than willing if you are."

Her lips formed a pout. "You owe me one."

"And one you'll get." I raised a hand. "Scout's honor." I dipped my head and pressed a kiss to her lips. "Never left you hungry for long, have I?"

"Nope. You'd better not start, either."

"Greedy," I chided, even though it thrilled me to know she was still as hungry for me all these years later as I was for her.

The hunger never abated.

If anything, it increased.

My need and love for her expanded with it, growing and growing, filling me full. I'd never be satiated, not really, and I knew she felt the same way.

We couldn't get enough of each other.

"It isn't an orgasm, though."

"What is it?"

I wriggled my shoulders at her surprise, smiling at Little when he collided into us. Dude had only just gotten Cinnamon to agree to being branded. Because he was on cloud nine, he'd forgotten that he was a tank in a body and kept trampling on us all. His happiness was infectious, though, so who was I to bitch at him for standing on everyone's fucking toes?

"Nothing special," I told my woman with a grin as her fingers traced the brand on my throat, one that matched hers, "but I wanted you to have them. Rex found them in that old warehouse they were selling. Bear had dumped a lot of boxes there after he sold the house."

"Ooh, I didn't realize! He brought them down with him?"

"Yep. Didn't know what they were, thank God, but the box had my name on it, so bring it to me he did."

She tugged on my hand. "I'm curious now."

"Good." Leaving Nat King Cole to sing about L-O-V-E, I tucked her into my side and started the retreat to our house.

It still boggled my mind that the kid who'd been raised on moldy ketchup sandwiches and who'd lived in dives, had a house like this. I'd earned it, sure, but still, there'd never be a day where I wasn't grateful. Grateful for every fucking thing I'd gotten.

Some people might have hoped that I'd never have this. They might think I wasn't worthy of a future because of the mistakes I'd made in the past, but my woman wasn't those people.

My woman had seen something in me, something she saw to this day, and I was so fucking thankful for her. For every day she'd blessed me with. For every kiss and for every caress. Of a future she'd gifted me when she'd owed me bupkis. Instead of sending me to hell, she'd brought me to heaven.

We'd survived a breast cancer scare last year, and I was on meds for my cholesterol and severe high blood pressure, and I knew, along the way, there'd be more challenges, but we'd survive those too.

That was what we did.

We strived.

I waved at people as they greeted me, some walking over, chatting with us about the event, congratulating us both, so much so that it took over an hour to get to my fucking front door.

By the time we were there, Keira was giggling over something MaryCat had told her, and I twirled her into the doorway, letting her in first before I guided her to my office.

There, she splatted herself on the sofa in front of the desk, wafted her hand at a frond from one of my ferns that danced over her from the pot I was gonna have to transfer soon because it was getting unruly, then huffed when Two-Fourths, AKA Twofer, made an appearance. Bounding over to her, he landed on her lap as if he were a Shih Tzu when, instead, he was a Mastiff.

She grunted, but let him settle there, and I smiled, even as I picked up the notepad.

"I completely forgot about these," I admitted.

"What is it?" she asked, clearly curious.

"Letters I wrote to you."

"Letters?" Her eyes widened.

"Yeah, when I first saw you at Jackson High." I smiled at her. "They're probably depressing as fuck, but I dunno, thought you might get a kick out of seeing them." When I passed her the notepad, I saw that her eyes welled with tears. "Hey!" I chided, "less of that."

"Sorry, I'm being silly."

I grinned at her. "Sure are. Trust me, I wasn't a wordsmith with these."

She hugged them to her. "I'll love them all the same. Thank you for letting me have them."

Leaning over, I chucked her over the chin. "Read them another night? Tonight's for smiling, for thinking about the now, not the then."

Her eyes were soft as they danced over my features. At first, I thought she was going to argue, but she patted the seat at her side and murmured, "Sure."

I made a space for myself on the sofa, Twofer huffed and growled but he let me weasel in beside her, and I raised an arm that she immediately settled under.

She heaved a sigh as we sat together, among my plants, photos on the wall of me and her, of our kids, music from the street party serenading us as we took a moment to just be.

To process.

Our little girl wasn't so little anymore.

She'd overcome so much, become so fucking strong that, some days, I didn't recognize her as the frightened, scrawny fairy who'd come down to Coshocton in desperate circumstances.

She was an Olympian.

My kid, a fucking Olympian.

Screw you, Mom.

"Think she'll be happy?" Keira asked, breaking into my thoughts.

"He'd better make her happy," I grumbled. "I have a twelve-gauge, and I ain't afraid to use it."

DEAR KEIRA

This is going to be the last letter I ever write to you because, baby girl, I don't have to write shit down anymore. You're at my side, so that means I can just tell you.

You probably don't know how freeing that is for a man like me. I don't have to be ashamed, I don't have to hide, I can just speak with you because you're there. You're not on a pedestal—even though you're still my fucking angel—you're my Old Lady.

My woman.

My fucking life.

These letters aren't to upset you, just to make you realize the dipshit I was back then, and hopefully for you to see how much I've changed. For you. Always for you, baby girl.

You took a piece of shit, some scum, and transformed him into a man you believe is worthy to stand by your side because I know that if I wasn't good enough, you'd have tossed me out years ago.

I'm proud of myself. At long fucking last. I'm honored that you're my Old Lady. I'm honored that you're my wife. But more than that, I'm so thankful that you're mine. That you forgave me enough to give me another chance. That you loved me enough to see us through.

I will cherish you until the day I die; know this, know that I adore you, know that I will kill and walk through hell's fire itself for you, and know that there is no Storm without his Keira.

I love you, baby girl.

Asher

** TRIGGER WARNING **

If you want to find out how Storm and Keira's story ends, you can keep reading.
If you'd rather imagine it for yourself, you can stop right here.

If you don't wish to carry on…

REX IS NOW AVAILABLE ON PREORDER!
Grab it here: www.books2read.com/RexSerenaAkeroyd
You've met him, you think you know him, but does anyone *really* know the aloof Prez of the West Orange chapter?

Need to know how MaryCat and Digger got together?
Learn how the Five Points and the Satan's Sinners got their wires tangled in this exclusive prequel!!
A Very Naughty MC Christmas!
PREORDER NOW LIVE!

EPILOGUE

FORTY YEARS AFTER AUGUST 8TH

Sarah Cothran - As The World Caves In
Never Let Me Go - Florence & The Machine

I WATCHED her take her brush and slowly drag it over her hair. It was thinning out, and I knew she was losing it in clumps. She hated that, and I hated it for her. I didn't care if she was bald, but she did. She'd lost it all back when she got breast cancer at fifty, but my Keira was a fighter. She'd come back stronger than ever. There was no fighting it this time though.

We both knew it.

Pancreatic cancer. Stage four.

She was dying.

And though I had my illnesses, for which I took a pharmacy worth of meds, I wasn't there yet. Which was cruel considering the way I'd treated my body over the years. That she should be taken first told me that there was no justice in this world.

That didn't mean that today wasn't my day to die though.

She had it all set in her head, enough so that I'd found her with a bottle of pills, which was when I'd told her my plan. I'd never have verbalized it, not if I hadn't seen her with the Valium, but I'd already mapped out how I was ending it. Though she'd begged me to reconsider, that wasn't going to happen. I wasn't about to live in a world without her. I wasn't about to suffer like Bear had without his Rene.

No one knew.

Not my brothers, not her sisters. Our kids were in the dark. Our family wouldn't know until they found the letters we'd left them.

I wasn't sad about it. What saddened me was watching her fade away.

A few more weeks, the doctors told me. A few more weeks of watching her get frailer and sicker, of watching her leave me.

I'd told her the second she died, I was gonna end it.

She didn't like that. And my Keira, after all these years, was a bossy miss. She'd gotten used to calling me on my shit and wasn't afraid to talk back.

Fifty-three years together.

Christ, we'd had some good times.

All our kids were married and had little monsters of their own. Hell, some of those even had their own kids.

We'd retired young, had come to California because my Keira had her heart set on living on the West Coast when Cyan had moved out here with her family to be nearer to Kelly. The two of them had always been inseparable, so close it was almost like they were born to be siblings.

With his thriving practice in Cali, she'd made the move, then we had. Shortly after, Phoenix had joined us, but Brook hadn't and now ruled over Coshocton. I'd never imagined my youngest would take over as Prez, but the chapter was in safe hands.

They were all as settled as they could be, and with their inheritances, they'd be set for life. So would our grandkids. And maybe even *their* grandkids.

My mom might have thought I was trash, but she'd never realized how much money trash could make.

One man's trash was another man's treasure, after all...

"You having second thoughts?" she asked me.

I shook my head as I got to my feet with a grumble. Moving around was harder now, and to be honest, getting old sucked. I was ready for the next phase. I wasn't scared because I knew we'd be together. I could handle anything so long as we had that.

"Of course not. I'm not the flighty one."

She narrowed her eyes at me then prodded the air with her hairbrush. "I'm not flighty."

I scoffed. "You keep telling yourself that, baby girl."

A soft laugh escaped her. "All these years, and I'm still that?"

"Don't ask dumb questions."

"There are no dumb questions, just dumb people."

She'd gone to school to be a teacher when we'd moved out here and had spent a couple of years teaching kids with special needs.

That was my Keira. Always helping others.

"Don't turn into a teacher with me. I'm a little old for your lessons."

Her beautiful smile still lit up the room. "You're never too old. Didn't I prove that?"

"Oldest undergrad at Berkeley." I pumped the air. "Still proud as shit."

She beamed at me as I settled my hand on her shoulder, then placed her fingers over mine.

"We packed each year with memories, didn't we?"

"We sure did."

Our eyes clashed and held in the mirror, and I grinned at her, trying to show her that I wasn't afraid. Trying to show her that the only thing that mattered in this world was her, and our love, and I wasn't about to live without either—not for a week, never mind an hour. A minute without her was too damn long.

"You don't have to do this, Asher."

"Baby girl, if you think, for one minute, I want to be on this shithole planet without you, you're mistaken."

A shaky breath escaped her. "The kids… they'll never forgive us for it. And you... They could still have you for a while longer."

"We both know you're kidding yourself thinking that." I shrugged, unafraid to admit that the second she passed over was the second I'd end shit too. There was no Storm without his Keira. "That's on them if they don't forgive us. They can argue with us when we meet up again. If they'd have preferred to see you fade—" I broke off. "No. I don't care what they think. We left them notes. They know we love them. They'll never stop knowing that."

I'd placed the cross Keira had bought me on my first Father's Day, one I'd worn throughout my life, so much that the engraving had faded long ago, into the envelope for Cyan. I hoped she wore it.

Much as I hoped my other kids would wear the pieces that mattered most to us. My wedding band, her first birthday gift. All the myriad things we'd collected over the years.

"Won't make it easier on them."

"No, but they had to lose us at some point."

"True." She sighed like she was concerned, but I felt her relief as if it were a visceral entity between us. She was tired. So tired. "Help me up?"

I leaned over and settled her on her feet. She needed a walker now, but the doctor had told me that in the next few days, she'd have to stay in bed permanently. That was why we were doing this today. While she could still walk by herself, albeit slowly and painfully.

It took us a while to make it to the front door, but I savored every moment. Outside, my three-wheeler trike—easier on the bones and the old ass—sat waiting. It wasn't as sleek as my Harley, but it was either that or give up riding bikes and neither me nor Keira had wanted that.

I was supposed to settle her on the backseat, but I wanted to be near her. So, instead, I indicated that she should lean against the trike as I took my place on the front seat, and said, "Your carriage awaits."

A laugh escaped her, one that took me through the years of our marriage. The good times, the best times, the highs and the surprises. It settled in my chest like a solid weight, and it powered me. Spurred me on.

I wanted to remember that.

I wanted that to be ringing in my ears as I died. Not her desperate gasps for breath. Not the beeps of the monitors as she left me.

Her laughter. Her joy. Markers that defined my life, that had made me the man standing here today instead of the desperate nobody I'd have been without her.

She was so tiny now that she settled between my thighs with ease, and that was when it occurred to me.

"Do you think you could sit on my Roadster?"

"How far is it to Gray Whale Cove?"

"Twenty minutes."

She thought about it, then nodded decisively which told me it'd be hard on her but she'd do it.

I sorted it so she was waiting for me on the trike as I dragged out the bike I hadn't ridden in years. Cyan's youngest, Louis, came out here and rode on it—a secret between me and him because his mom didn't think he was old enough to ride yet. I could have told her he wouldn't be old enough at thirty, but she wouldn't listen. Cy was as stubborn as her mom and grandmother—and though it took a feat of strength to get my old leg over it, I managed.

Rolling out of the garage, I drove up to her, and the rumble between my thighs felt right. This all felt right. Now, I just had to get her on it.

It took us a long time, a lot of strength, patience and a few tears from her, but we got there. She settled in front of me, leaning most of her weight on mine. I knew her strength was fading already, so I made short work out of heading off.

The journey to the beach was beautiful. A part of me expected to be hauled off the road by a busybody pig, but we made it without interruption. Passing miles of coastline, the ocean glittered in the warm summer evening, and it was a joyous sight to behold. With each minute, weakness had her settling more into me and though the judders of the engine rocked through my system, exhausting me with each moment, I absorbed it.

This would be our last ride.

It was worth it.

Then we made it to the cliffs.

"I told you I meant it when I said 'til death do us part.'" I buried my face in her throat as I tucked myself low, one arm tight around her as she clung to me as much as I did to her, and whispered, "I love you, baby girl."

A soft sigh escaped her, one that I shouldn't have heard but that the wind gifted me. "I love you too, Asher."

Always Asher at moments like these.

That was when I revved the engine, that was when I slipped off the asphalt and onto the rocky terrain at the side of the road, and that was when both of us flew free into the unknown.

But we did it together.

This wasn't our last goodbye, but the start of something else.

Something just as beautiful as the last fifty-three years.

Eternity wasn't frightening when you had your soul mate at your side.

** BONUS SCENE **

WHEN HOOK'S screams were loud enough to pierce my eardrums as I watched the flames consume his beard, I grabbed the extinguisher, took off the cap, then sprayed it all over his head.

Digger snorted out a laugh, SL coughed with surprise, and North muttered, "Jesus."

"Don't breathe in, Hook," I taunted. "This shit can be deadly when you inhale it." I motioned at SL who stood there, hovering, and I sniped, "Pour it on his head, SL. Fuck's sake."

SL grimaced. "Ain't never done this stuff before, Prez," he grumbled, but he did as I asked, revealing a pretty scorched-looking Hook.

"Now, I can keep on doing this, Hook. You got plenty of other shit I can burn off ya, and you can die in a beautiful bonfire worthy of a funeral pyre, or I can slit your throat. Nice and fast. Your choice."

His breathing was labored, pained but he managed to get out, "Slit my throat."

"Thought as much. Now, talk to me about the Rabid Wolves."

He sucked in air, the rasping sounds reminding me of someone with emphysema, but he spluttered, "Sticky stole something from them when he came down here. It's one of the reasons why Butch let him stay."

"Wasn't out of the kindness of his heart, then," I drawled.

Hook frowned. "No. Worth a lot of money."

"What was it?"

"A necklace."

Whatever I'd expected him to say, it wasn't that.

"You shitting me? A fucking necklace?"

Hook nodded, then repeated, "It's worth a lot of money."

"Would have to be, Christ."

"Pearls or something. Butch took it, but we know he never sold it."

"Fucking pearls?" I scowled. "How?"

"Butch would have told his council."

"Would he? Wouldn't he have had to share in the spoils?"

"Butch wasn't like that," Hook gasped.

"From the state of your accounts when I got here, I can tell you that's BS," I drawled.

"And you fuckers were loyal to him?" Digger muttered. "Bigger idiots than I thought."

"Hey!" SL groused.

"It's true. Jesus. That kind of shit would get split with the chapter back in West Orange, wouldn't it, Storm?"

"Bet your ass it would," I replied, folding my arms across my chest. "What was so special about this necklace?"

"It belonged to a crime family in New York," Hook rasped, before he started coughing. Before our eyes, pink welts started to appear on his skin, and I knew that was from the irritants in the retardant spray. "The Wolves stole it about a decade ago from this rich tycoon."

"What's this necklace gotta do with today?"

"Sticky wanted you to let us back into the Sinners so he could get access to the safes. Everyone's been loyal though. We couldn't get in otherwise."

"You genuinely thought that taking the Prez's family hostage would get you reinstated into the Sinners?" Digger demanded. "Are you fucking shitting me? Or have you just been taking stupid pills?"

Hook shook his head, wiping his cheek against his shoulder to ease the irritation on his skin. "It'd have worked with Butch. And with the Prez of the Rabid Wolves. Might is right."

My brow puckered. "If you seriously believe that, then I'm glad the world won't have to deal with your shits for brains for much longer."

"You wanted the necklace to sell it? Or to take it back to the Rabid Wolves?"

Hook shrugged. "Sticky said we'd be made welcome back at the Rabid Wolves."

"I think you'd have ended up dead the second Sticky got his fucking mitts on that necklace," Digger retorted with a cackle. "He wasn't about to split the money with you fuckheads."

My Enforcer wasn't fucking wrong.

Something about what he'd said resonated with me though. "You said safes. Plural." I had two in my office. One for guns, the shit that was legal and that the sheriff could call on to see, and then one for money.

Hook blinked, then what appeared to be some sense slivered into his eyes. "Yeah. There are some hidden in the clubhouse. I'll show them to you if you let me go."

Because I knew he was bluffing, I smirked. "I'd prefer for those safes to burn the fuck down than to let your moronic ass live to see another goddamn day. Now, you can carry on talking or I can slice your throat and let you bleed out slowly. Your choice."

Never let it be said that I wasn't diplomatic.

REX IS NOW AVAILABLE ON PREORDER!
Grab it here: www.books2read.com/RexSerenaAkeroyd
You've met him, you think you know him, but does anyone *really* know the aloof Prez of the West Orange chapter?

Need to know how MaryCat and Digger got together?
Learn how the Five Points and the Satan's Sinners got their wires tangled in this exclusive prequel!!
A Very Naughty MC Christmas!
PREORDER NOW LIVE!

EXCLUSIVE TEXT CHATS

PLEASE FIND some exclusive text chats between the Sinners and their Old Ladies here…

https://dl.bookfunnel.com/nxoiaquus5

AFTERWORD

REX IS NOW AVAILABLE ON PREORDER!
Grab it here: www.books2read.com/RexSerenaAkeroyd
You've met him, you think you know him, but does anyone *really*
know the aloof Prez of the West Orange chapter?

Need to know how MaryCat and Digger got together?
Learn how the Five Points and the Satan's Sinners got their wires
tangled in this exclusive prequel!!
www.books2read.com/FilthySinnerSerenaAkeroyd
PREORDER NOW LIVE!

How are you feeling, darlings?

Broken? Raw? Angry?

I'm sure you are all of these things and more.

But I like to think of it this way—there is no Storm without his
Keira.

And in this, his final act, Storm proved to you, *yet again*, that he will
always show up. That Keira will always be his priority.

I needed you all to read that. I needed you to see it.

This man, broken no longer, because his Old Lady has his back.

I hope, by the end, you feel he redeemed himself.

<3

While you're here…

No lies—non-alcoholic beer really does help stimulate milk production. Source

And if you're struggling, if your book hangover is beyond real, then be sure to join my Tea & Spoilers' room on Facebook. Come and cry in the community. I know I will. <3

Join here: www.facebook.com/groups/SerenaAkeroydsTeaAndSpoilersRoom

For a comprehensive reading order of the crossover universe, start here:

FILTHY

NYX

LINK

FILTHY RICH

SIN

STEEL

FILTHY DARK

CRUZ

MAVERICK

FILTHY SEX

HAWK

FILTHY HOT

STORM

THE DON

THE LADY

FILTHY SECRET (COMING NOVEMBER 2021)

Thank you, so much and as always, for your support.

Remember if you'd like to join my Diva reader group on FB for all the latest news on my releases, especially if it's still release week, there'll be some goodies to grab in there. Join here: www.facebook.com/groups/SerenaAkeroydsDivas

Love you, guys, and thanks for reading!

Serena

xoxo

START THE FIVE POINTS' UNIVERSE FROM THE BEGINNING...

FILTHY

FINN

Obsessive habits weren't alien to me.

They were as much a part of me as my coal-dark hair and my diamond-blue eyes. Ingrained as they were, it didn't mean they weren't irritating as fuck.

As I rifled through the folder on the table in front of me, staring down at the life of one pesky tenant, I wanted to toss it in the trash. I truly did.

I wanted not to be interested in her.

Wanted my focus to return to the matter at hand—business.

But there was something about her.

Something. . .

Irish.

I was a sucker for my own people. When I was a kid, I'd only dated other Irish girls in my class, and though I'd become less discerning about nationality and had grown more interested in tits and ass, I'd thought that desire had died down.

But Aoife Keegan was undeniably, indefatigably Irish.

From her fucking name—I didn't know people still named their kids in Gaelic over here—to her red goddamn hair and milky-white skin.

To many, she wouldn't be sexy. Too pale, too curvy, too rounded and wholesome. But to me? It was like God had formed a creature that was born to be my downfall.

I could feel the beast inside me roaring to life as I stared at the photos of her. It wanted out. It wanted her.

Fuck.

"I told you not to get those briefs."

My eyes flared wide in surprise at my brother, Aidan O'Donnelly's remark. "What?" I snapped.

"I told you not to get those briefs," he repeated, unoffended. Which was a miracle. Had I been speaking to Aidan Sr., I'd probably have lost a finger, but Aidan Jr. was one of my best friends, as well as a confidant and fellow businessman.

When I said business, it wasn't the kind Valley girls dreamed their future husbands would be involved in. No Manhattan socialite, though we were wealthy as fuck, would want us on their arm if they truly knew what games we were involved in.

My business was forged, unashamedly, in blood, sweat, and tears.

Preferably not my own, although I had taken a few hits for the Family over the years.

"My briefs aren't irritating me," I carried on, blowing out a breath.

"No? You look like you've got something up your ass crack." Aidan cocked a brow at me, but his smirk told me he knew exactly what the fuck was wrong.

I flipped him the bird—the finger that I'd have lost by showing cheek to his father—and he just grinned at me as he leaned over my glass desk and scooped up one of the pictures.

That beast I mentioned earlier?

It roared to life again when his eyes drifted over Aoife's curvy form.

"She's like your kryptonite," he breathed, tilting his head to the side. "Fuck me, Finn."

"I'd rather not," I told him dryly. "Now her? Yeah. I'd fuck her anytime."

He wafted a dismissive hand at my teasing. "I knew from that look in your eye, there was a woman involved. I just didn't know it would be a looker like this."

I snatched the photo from him. "Mine."

My growl had him snickering. "The Old Country ain't where I get my women from, Finn. Simmer down."

Throat tightening, I grated out, "What the fuck am I going to do?"

"Screw her?" he suggested.

"I can't."

He snorted. "You can."

"How the fuck am I supposed to get her in my bed when I'm about to bribe her into selling off her commercial lot?"

Aidan shrugged. "Do the bribing after."

That had me blowing out a breath. "You're a bastard, you know that, right?"

Piously, he murmured, "My parents were well and truly married before I came along. I have the wedding and birth certificates to prove it." He grinned. "Anyway, you're only just figuring that out?"

I shot him a scowl. "You're remarkably cheerful today."

"Is that a question or a statement?"

"Both?" The word sounded far too Irish for my own taste. My mother had come from Ireland, Tipperary to be precise—yeah, like the song. I was American born and bred, my accent that of someone who'd been raised in Hell's Kitchen but, and I hated it, my mother's accent would make an appearance every now and then.

'Both' came out sounding almost like 'boat.'

Aidan, knowing me as well as he did, smirked again—the fucker. "I got laid."

Grunting, I told him, "That doesn't usually make you cheerful."

"It does. I just never see you first thing after I wake up. Da hasn't managed to piss me off today."

Aidan was the heir to the Five Points—an Irish gang who operated out of Hell's Kitchen. It wasn't like being the heir to a candy company or a title. It came with responsibilities that no one really appreciated.

We were tied into the life, though. Had been since the day we were born.

There was no use in whining over it, and Aidan wasn't. But if I had to deal with his father on a daily basis? I'd have been whining to the morgue and back.

Aidan Sr. was the shrewdest man I knew. What the man could do with our clout defied belief. Even if I thought he was a sociopath, he had my respect, and in truth, my love and loyalty.

Bastard or no, he'd taken me in when I was fourteen and had made me one of his family. I'd gone from being his kids' friend, the son of one of his runners, to suddenly being welcome in the main house.

All because Aidan Sr.—though I was sure he was certifiable—believed in family.

I shot Aidan Jr. a look. "Was it that blonde over on Canal Street?"

He rubbed his chin. "Yeah."

Snorting, I told him, "Hope you wore a rubber. I swear that woman has so many men going in and out of her door, it should be on double-action hinges."

He scowled at me. "Are you trying to piss me off?"

"Why? Didn't wear a jimmy?" I grinned at him, my mood soaring in the face of his irritation. "Better get to the clinic before it drops off."

Though he flipped me the bird as easily as I'd done to him—I was his brother, after all—he grumbled, "What are you going to do about little Aoife?"

I squinted at him. "She's not little."

That seemed to restore his humor. "I know. Just how you like them." He shook his head. "You and Conor, I swear. What do you do with them? Drown yourself in their tits?"

Heaving a sigh, I informed him, "My predilection for large tits is none of your business."

"And whether or not I wore a jimmy last night is none of yours."

"If it turns green and looks like a moldy corn on the cob, who you gonna call?"

"Ghostbusters?" he tried.

I shook my head, then pointed a finger at him and back at myself. "No. Me."

Grunting, he got to his feet and pressed his fists to the desk. "We need that building, Finn."

"The business development plan was mine, Aid. I know we need it. Don't worry, I won't do anything stupid."

He snorted. "Your kind of stupid could go one of two ways."

That had me narrowing my eyes at him, but he held up his hands in surrender.

"Fuck her out of your system quickly, and then get started on the deal," he advised. "Best way."

It probably was the best way, but—

He sighed. "That fucking honor of yours."

I had to laugh. Only in the O'Donnelly family would my thoughts be considered honorable.

"If I'm fucking someone over, I want them to know it," was all I said.

"That makes no sense."

"Makes for epic sex, though," I jibed, and he shot me a grin.

"Angry sex is always good." He rubbed his chin, then he reached over again and flipped through the photos. "Who's the old guy to her?"

"To her? Not sure. Sugar daddy?" The thought alone made the beast inside rage. I cleared my throat to get rid of the rasp there. "To us? He's our meal ticket."

Aidan's eyes widened. "He is?"

I nodded. "Just leave it to me."

"I was always going to, *dearthái*." He tilted his chin at me, honoring me with the Gaelic word for brother. "Be careful out there."

"You, too, brother."

Aidan winked at me and, with a far too cheerful whistle for someone whose dick might soon be 'ribbed for her pleasure' without the need for a condom, walked out of my office leaving me to brood.

The instant his back was to me, I stared at the photos again. Flipping through them, I glowered at the innocent face staring back at me through the photo paper—if only she knew.

Hers was a building in Hell's Kitchen. Five Points Territory. One of many on my hit list.

Back in the 70s, Aidan Sr., following in his father's footsteps, had bought up a shit-ton of property, pre-gentrification, and it was my job to either sell off the portfolio, reconstruct, or 'improve' the current aesthetics of the buildings the Points owned.

This particular one was something I'd taken a personal interest in.

See, I was technically a legitimate businessman.

This office?

I had views of the Hudson. I could see the Empire State Building, and in the evening, I had an epic view of the sunset setting over Manhattan. This office building, also Points' property, was worth a cool hundred million, and I was, again technically, the CEO of it.

On paper?

I looked seamless.

The businessman who sported hundred thousand dollar watches and had a house in the Hamptons. No one save the Points and my CPA knew where the money came from. I liked that because, fuck, I had no intention of switching this pad for a lock-up in Riker's Island.

Still, this project cut close to home, and the reasoning was fucking pathetic.

I'd never admit it to any of the O'Donnellys. The bastards were like family to me, and if I admitted to this, they'd never let me hear the end of it.

Extortion?

I usually doled that out to someone else's to do list. Someone with a far lower paygrade than me, someone expendable. But the minute I'd heard of the troublesome tenant who was refusing to sell her lot to us? After not one, not two, not even three attempts with higher prices?

Five outright refusals?

The challenge to convince her otherwise had overtaken me.

See, I liked stubborn in women.

I liked fucking it out of them.

Throw in the fact the woman's name was Aoife? It had been enough to get me sending someone out to follow her.

If she'd been fifty with as many chins as she had grandchildren, she'd have been safe from me.

But she wasn't.

She was, as Aidan had correctly stated, my kryptonite. All milky flesh with gleaming auburn hair that I wanted to tie around my clenched fist. Her soft features with those delicate green eyes that sparkled when she smiled and were like wet grass when she was mad, acted like a punch to my gut.

Now?

My interest hadn't just been piqued.

It had fucking imploded.

Yeah, I was thinking with my cock, but what man, at the end of the day, didn't?

I'd just have to be careful. Just have to make sure I put pressure on the right places, make sure she'd bend and not break, and the old bastard in the pictures was my key to just that.

See, every third Tuesday of the month, Aoife Keegan had a habit of traipsing across Manhattan to the Upper East Side. There, at three PM on the dot, she'd enter a discreet little boutique hotel and wouldn't leave until nine PM that night.

Five minutes after she arrived and left, the same man would leave, too.

At first, when Jimmy O'Leary had told me that Senator Alan Davidson was at the hotel, I hadn't thought anything of it.

Why would I?

Senators trawled for donations in fancy hotels every fucking day of the week. It was the true luxury of politics. Sure, they made it look real good for the press. Posing in derelict neighborhoods and shaking hands with people who did the fucking work . . . all while they lived it up large with women half their age in two thousand dollar a night suites.

My mouth firmed at that.

Was Aoife selling herself to the Senator?

The thought pissed me off.

I couldn't see why she'd do such a thing. Not when I'd looked into her finances, had seen just how secure she was. But maybe that was why. Maybe the Senator was funneling money to her.

The only problem was that the lot Aoife owned—did I mention it was owned outright? Yeah, that was enough to chafe my suspicions, too, considering she was only twenty-fucking-five years old—was a teashop in a small building in a questionable area of HK.

I mean, come on. I loved Hell's Kitchen. It was home. But fuck. Where she was? What kind of Senator would put his fancy piece in *that*?

My jaw clenched as I studied the Senator's and Aoife's smiling faces as they left the hotel. Separately, of course. But whatever they'd been doing together, it sure put a Cheshire Cat grin on their chops–that was for fucking sure. Jimmy being a dumbass, hadn't put the two together, had just remarked on the 'coincidence,' but I was no fool.

How did I know they were together in the hotel?

Jimmy had been trailing Aoife for four months—told you I was obsessive—and every third Tuesday, come rain or shine, this little routine had jumped out, and when Jimmy had picked up on the fact Davidson had been there each and every time, I'd gotten my hands dirty, bribed one of the hotel maids myself—and fuck, that had been hard. Turned out that place made even the maids sign NDA agreements, but everyone had a price—and I'd found out that my little obsession shared a suite with the old prick.

My fingers curled into fists as I stared at her. Butter wouldn't fucking melt. She was the epitome of innocence. Like a redheaded angel. Could she really be lifting her skirts for that old fucker? Just so she could own a teashop?

Something didn't make sense, and fuck, if that didn't intrigue me all the more.

Aoife Keegan had snared one of the biggest, nastiest sharks in Manhattan.

She just didn't know it yet.

***

Aoife

"We need more scones for tomorrow. I keep telling you four dozen isn't enough."

Lifting a hand at my waitress and friend, Jenny, I mumbled, "I know, I know."

"If you know, then why the hell don't you listen?" Jenny complained, making me grin.

"Because I'm the one who has to make them? Making half that again is just . . ." I sighed.

I loved my job.

I did.

I adored baking—my butt and hips attested to that fact—and making a career out of my passion was something every twenty-something hoped for. Especially in one of the most expensive cities in the world. But sheesh. There was only so much one person could do, and this was still, essentially, a one-woman-band.

With the threat of Acuig Corp looming over me, I didn't feel safe hiring extra staff. I'd held them off for close to six months now. Six months of them trying to tempt me to leave, to sell up. They'd raised their prices to ten percent above market value, whereas with everyone else in the building, they'd just offered what the apartments were truly worth. Considering this place wasn't the nicest in the block, that wasn't much.

Most people hadn't held out because, hell, why wouldn't they want to live elsewhere?

Those who were landlords hadn't felt any issue in tossing their tenants out on the street. The tenants grumbled, but when did they ever have any rights, anyway?

For myself, this was where my mom and I had worked to—

I brought that thought to a shuddering halt.

Mom was dead now.

I had to remember that. This was on me, not her.

My throat thickened with tears as I turned to Jenny and murmured, "I'll try better tomorrow."

The words had her frowning at me. "Babe, you know I'm not the boss here, right?"

Lips curving, I whispered, "I know. But you're so scary."

She snickered then peered down at herself. "Yeah, I bet I'd make grown men cry."

Maybe for a taste of her. . . .

Jenny was everything I wasn't.

She was slender, didn't dip her hand into the cookie jar at will—the woman had more willpower than I did hips, and my hips seemed to go on forever—and her face looked like it belonged on the cover of a fashion magazine. Even her hair was enough to inspire envy. It was black and straight as a ruler.

Mine?

Bright red and curly like a bitch. I had to straighten it out every morning if I didn't want to look like little orphan Annie.

I'd once read that curly-haired women straightened their hair for special events, and that straight-haired women curled theirs in turn, but I called bullshit.

Curly-haired women lived with their straightening irons surgically attached to their hands.

At least, I did.

My rat's nest was like a ginger afro. Maybe Beyoncé could make that work, but I sure as hell didn't have the bone structure.

"I think grown men would cry," I told her dryly, "if you asked them to."

She pshawed, but there was a twinkle in her eye that I understood. . . . She agreed with me, knew it was true, but wasn't going to admit it. With anyone else, she might have. She had an ego–that was for damn sure. But with me? I think she figured I was zero competition, so she felt no need to rub salt in the wound, too.

I plunked my elbows on the counter and stared around my domain as she bustled off and started clearing the tables. It was her last duty of the day, and my feet were aching so damn bad that I didn't even have it in me to care.

This owning your own business shit?

It wasn't easy.

Not saying I didn't love it, but it was hard.

I slept like four hours a night, and when I wasn't in bed, I was here. All the time.

Baking, cooking, serving, and smiling. Always smiling. Even if I was so sleep-deprived I could sob.

Jenny's actually a life saver.

My mom used to be front of house before. . . .

I sucked down a breath.

I had to get used to thinking about it.

She wasn't here anymore, but just avoiding all thoughts of her period wasn't working for me. It was like I was purposely forgetting her, and, well, fuck that.

She'd always wanted to have a teashop. It had been her one true dream. Back in Ireland, when she was a little girl, her grandmother had owned one in Limerick. Mom had caught the bug and had wanted to have one here in the States. But not only was it too fucking expensive for a woman on her own, it was also impossible with my feckless father at her side.

I didn't want to think about him either, though.

Why?

Because the feckless father who'd pretty much ruined my mother's life, wasn't the only father in my life. My biological dad hadn't exactly cared about her happiness, but once he'd come to know about me, he'd tried. That was more than could be said for the man who'd lived with me throughout my early childhood.

"You look gloomy."

Jenny's statement had me blinking in surprise. She had a ton of dishes piled in her arms, and I'd have worried for the expensive china if I hadn't known she was an old pro at this shit. Just as I was.

We could probably earn a Guinness World Record on how many dishes we could take back and forth to the kitchen of *Ellie's Tea Rooms*. I swear, I had guns because of all that hefting. My biceps were probably the firmest part of my body.

More's the pity.

I'd have preferred an ass you could bounce dimes off of, but, when it boiled down to it, there was no way in this universe I could live without cake.

Just wasn't going to happen.

My big butt wasn't going *anywhere* until scientists could make zero calorie eclairs and pies.

"I'm not glum."

"No? Then why are your eyes sad?"

Were they? I pursed my lips as I let the 'sad eyes' drift around the tea room. I wish I could say it was all forged on my own hard work, but it wasn't. Not really.

"I was just thinking about Mom."

"Oh, honey," Jenny said sadly, and she carefully placed all the dishes on the counter, so she could round it and curve her arm around my waist. "It was only seven months ago. Of course, you were thinking of her."

"I just—" I blew out a breath. "I don't know if I'm doing what she'd want."

"You can't live for her choices, sweetness. You have to do what you think is right for you."

I gnawed at my bottom lip again. "I-I know, but she was always there for me. A guiding light. With Fiona gone and her, too? I don't really know what I'm doing with myself."

This business wasn't something that made me want to get up on a morning. It was my mom's dream, her goal. Every decision I made, I tried to remember how she'd longed for a place like this, but it wasn't my passion. It was hers, and I was trying to keep that dream alive while fretting over the fact my heart wasn't in it.

"I think you're doing a damn fine job. You have a very successful teashop. Your cakes are raved about. Have you visited our TripAdvisor page recently? Or our Yelp?" She squeaked. "I swear, you're making this place a tourist hotspot. I don't think Fiona or Michelle could be more proud of you if they tried."

The baking shit, yeah, that was all on me, but the other stuff? The finances?

I'd caved in.

I'd caved where my mom had always refused in the past.

With the accident had come a lot of medical bills that I just hadn't been able to afford. Without her help, I'd had to take on extra staff, and out of nowhere, my expenses had added up.

Mom had been so proud of this place, so ferociously gleeful that we'd done it by ourselves, and yet, here I was, financially free for the first time in my life, and I still felt like I was drowning because my freedom went entirely against her wishes.

"Is this to do with Acuig? I know they're still pestering you."

Jenny's statement had me wincing. Acuig were the bottom feeders who wanted to snap up this building, demolish it, and then replace it with a skyscraper. Don't get me wrong, the building was foul, but a lot of people lived here, and the minute it morphed into some exclusive condo, no one from around here would be able to afford to live in it.

It would become yuppy central.

I'd rejected all their offers to buy my tea room even though I didn't want the damn thing, not really. Mostly I wanted to keep mom's goals alive and kicking, but also, it pissed me off the way Acuig were changing Hell's Kitchen. Ratcheting up prices, making it unaffordable for the everyday man and woman—the people I'd grown up with—and bringing a shit-ton of banker-wankers and 1%ers to the area.

So, maybe I'd watched Erin Brockovich a time or two as a kid and had a social conscience . . . Wasn't the worst thing to possess, right?

"Aoife?" Jenny stated, making me look over at her. "Is Acuig pressuring you?"

I winced, realizing I hadn't answered—Jenny was my friend, but she also worked here and relied on the paycheck. It wasn't fair of me to keep her hanging like that. "They upped the sales price. I guess that isn't helping," I admitted, frowning down at my hands.

Unlike Jenny who had her nails manicured, mine were cut neatly and plain. I had no rings on my fingers, and wore no watch or bracelets because my wrists were usually deep in flour or sugar bags.

I spent most of my life right where I wanted it—behind the shopfront. That had slowly morphed where I was doing double the work to compensate for Mom's loss.

Was it any wonder I was feeling a little out of my league?

I was coping without Fiona, grieving Mom, working without her, too, and then practically living in the kitchens here. I didn't exactly have that much of a life. I had nothing cheerful on the horizon, either.

Well, nothing except for next Tuesday, and that wasn't enough to turn my frown upside down.

The money was a temptation. I didn't need to sell up and start working on my own goals, but that just loaded me down with more guilt and made me feel like a really shitty daughter.

Jenny squeezed me in a gentle hug. But as I turned to speak to her, the bell above the door rang as it opened. We both jerked in surprise— each of us apparently thinking the other had locked up when neither of us had—and turned to face the entrance.

On the brink of telling the client we were closed for the day, my mouth opened then shut.

Standing there, amid the frilly, lacy curtains, was the most masculine man I'd ever seen in my life.

And I meant that.

It was like a thousand aftershave models had morphed into one handsome creature that had just walked through my door.

At my side, I could feel Jenny's 'hot guy radar' flare to life, and for once, I couldn't damn well blame her.

This guy was . . . well, he was enough to make me choke on my words and splutter to a halt.

The tea room was all girly femininity. It was sophisticated enough to appeal to businesswomen with its mauve, taupe, and cream-toned hues, and the ethereal watercolors that decorated the walls. But the tablecloths were lacy, and the china dishes and cake stands we used were the height of Edwardian elegance.

Moms brought their little girls here for their birthday, and high-powered executives spilled dirt on their lovers with their girlfriends over scones and clotted cream—breaking their diets as they discussed the boyfriends who had broken their hearts.

The man, whoever the hell he was, was dressed to impress in a navy suit with the finest pinstripe. It was close to a silver fleck, and I could see, even from this distance, that it was hand tailored. I'd seen custom tailoring before, and only a trained eye could get a suit cut so perfectly to this man's form.

With wide shoulders that looked like they could take the weight of the world, a long, lean frame that was enhanced by strong muscles evident through the close fit of his pants and jacket, then the silkiness of his shirt which revealed delineated abs when his bright gold and scarlet tie flapped as he moved, the guy was hot.

With a capital H.

"How can we help, sir?" Jenny purred, and despite my own awe, I had to dip my chin to hide my smile.

Even if I wanted to throw my hat into this particular man's game, there was no way he'd choose me over Jenny. Fuck, I'd screw her, and I wasn't even a lesbian. Not even a teensy bit bi. I'd gone shopping with her enough to have seen her ass, and I promise you, it's biteable.

So, nope. I didn't have a snowball's chance in hell of this Adonis seeing *me* when Jenny was in the room.

Yet. . . .

When I'd controlled my smile, I looked over at the man, and his focus was on me.

My breath stuttered to a halt.

Why wasn't his gaze glued to Jenny?

Why weren't those ice-white blue eyes fixated on my best friend's tits, which Jenny helpfully plumped up as she preened at my side?

For a second, I was so close to breaking out into a coughing fit, it was humiliating. Then, more humiliation struck in a quieter manner, but it was nevertheless rotten—I turned pink.

Now, you might think you know what a blush is. You might think you've even experienced it yourself a time or two. But I was a redhead. My skin made fresh milk look yellow, and even my fucking freckles were pale. Everything about me was like I'd been dunked into white wax.

But as the heat crawled over me, taking over my skin as the man looked at me without pause, I knew things had rarely been this dire.

See, with Jenny as a best friend, I was used to the attention going her way. I could hide in the background, hide in her shadow. I liked it there. I was comfortable there. Sometimes, on double dates, she'd drag me along, and even the guy supposed to be dating me would be gaping at Jenny. As pathetic as it was, I was so used to it, it didn't bother me.

But now?

I just wasn't used to being in the spotlight.

Especially not a man like this one's spotlight.

When you're a teenager, practicing with your mom's blush for the first time, you always look like a tomato that's been left out in the sun, right?

I was redder than that.

I could feel it. I could fucking feel the heat turning me tomato red.

When Jenny cleared her throat, I thanked God when it broke the man's attention. He shot her a look, but it wasn't admiring. It wasn't even impressed.

If anything, it was irritated.

Okay, so now both Jenny and I were stunned.

Fuck that, we were floored.

Literally.

Our mouths were doing a pretty good fish impression as the man turned back to look at me.

Shit, was this some kind of joke?

Was it April 1st and I'd just gotten the dates mixed up again?

"Ms. Keegan?"

Oh fuck. His voice.

Oh. My. God.

That voice.

It was. . . .

I had to swallow.

Did men even talk like that?

It was low and husky and raspy and made me think of sex, not just mediocre sex, but the best sex. Toe-curling, nails-breaking-in-the-sheets sex. Sex so fucking good you couldn't walk the next day. Sex so hot that it made my current core temperature look polar in comparison. Sex that I'd never been lucky to have before, so I pined for it in the worst way.

Jenny nudged me in the side when I just carried on gaping at the man. "Y-Yes. That's me." I cleared my throat, feeling nervous and stupid and flustered as I wiped my hands on my apron.

Sweet Jesus.

Was this man really looking for me while I was wearing a goddamn pinafore?

Even as practical as they were, I wanted to beg the patron saint of pinnies to remove it from me. To do something, anything, to make sure that this man didn't see me in the red gingham check that I always wore to cover up stains.

And then I felt it.

Jenny's hand.

Tugging at the knot.

I wanted to kiss her. Seriously. I wanted to give her a fucking raise! As I moved away from the counter and her side, the apron dropped to the floor as I headed for the man whose hand was now held out, ready for me to shake in greeting.

There are those moments in your life when you know you'll never forget them. They can be happy or sad, annoying or exhilarating. This was one of them.

As I slipped my hand into his, I felt the electric shocks down to my core. Meeting his gaze wasn't hard because I was stunned, and I needed to know if he'd felt that, too.

From the way those eyelids were shielding his icy-blue eyes, I figured he was just as surprised.

It was like a satisfied puma was watching me. One that was happy there was plump prey prancing around in front of him.

Shit.

Did I just describe myself as 'plump prey?'

And like that, my house of cards came tumbling down because what the hell would this man want with me?

I was seeing things.

God, I was so stupid sometimes.

I cleared my throat for, like, the fourth damn time, and asked, "I'm Ms. Keegan. You are?"

His smile, when it appeared, was as charming as the rest of him. His teeth were white, but not creepy, reality-TV-star white. They were straight except for one of his canines, which tilted in slightly. In his perfect face, it was one flaw that I almost clung to. Because with that wide brow, the hair so dark it looked like black silk that was cut closely to his head with a faint peak at his forehead, the strong nose, and even stronger jaw, I needed something imperfect to focus on.

Then, I sucked down a breath and remembered what Fiona had told me once upon a time. When I'd been nervous about asking Jamie

Winters to homecoming, she'd advised me in her soft Irish lilt, "Lass, that boy takes a dump just like you do. He uses the bathroom twice a day and undoubtedly leaves a puddle on the floor for his ma to clean up. I bet he's puked a time or two as well. Had diarrhea and the good Lord only knows what else. Just you think that the next time you see that boy and want to ask him out."

Yeah. It was gross, but fuck, it had worked. Her advice had worked so well I hadn't asked anyone out because I could only think of them using the damn toilet!

Still, looking at this Adonis, there was no imagining *that*.

Surely, gods didn't use the bathroom.

Did they?

"The name's Finn. Finn O'Grady."

My eyes flared at the name.

No.

It couldn't be.

Finn O'Grady?

No. It wasn't a rare name, but it was a strong one. One that suited him, one that had always suited him.

I frowned up at him wondering, yet again, if this was a joke of some sort, but as he looked at me, *really* looked at me, I saw no recognition. Saw nothing on his features that revealed any ounce of awareness that I'd known him for years.

Well, okay, not *known*. But I'd known his mother. Our mothers had been best friends. And as I looked, I saw the same almond-shaped eyes Fiona had, the stubborn jaw, and that unmistakable butt-indent on his chin.

At the reminder of just how forgettable I was, my heart sank, and hurt whistled through me.

Then, I realized I was *still* holding his hand, and as he squeezed, the flush returned and I almost died of mortification.

CHAPTER 2

FINN

GOD, she was perfect.

And when I said perfect, I meant it.

I'd fucked a lot of women. Redheads, blondes, brunettes, even the rare thing that is a natural head of black hair. None of them, not a single one, lit up like Aoife Keegan.

Her cheeks were cherry red and in the light camisole she wore, a cheerful yellow, I could see how the blush went all the way down to the upper curve of her breasts.

She'd go that color, I knew, when she came.

And fuck, I wanted to see that.

I wanted to see that perfectly pale flesh turn bright pink under my ministrations.

Even as I looked at her, all shy and flustered, I wondered if she was a screamer in bed.

Some of the shyest often were.

Maybe not at first, but after a handful of orgasms, it was a wonder what that could do to a woman's self-confidence, and Jesus, I wanted to *see* that, too. I wanted a seat at center stage.

My suit jacket was open, and I regretted it. Immensely. My cock was hard, had been since we'd shaken hands, and her fingers had clung to mine like a daughter would to her daddy's at her first visit to the county fair.

Fuck.

Squeezing her fingers wasn't intentional. If anything, I'd just liked the feel of her palm against mine, but when I put faint pressure on her, she jerked back like she'd been scalded.

Her cheeks bloomed with heat again, and she whispered, "Mr. O'Grady, what can I do for you?"

You can get on your fucking knees and sort out the hard-on you just caused.

That's what she could fucking do.

I almost growled at the thought because the image of her on her knees, my cock in her small fist, her dainty mouth opening to take the tip. . . .

Shit.

That had to happen.

Here, too.

In this fancy, frilly, feminine place, I wanted to defile her.

Fuck, I wanted that so goddamn much, it was enough to make me reconsider my demolition plans.

I wanted to screw her against all this goddamn lace, which suited her perfectly. She was made for lace. And silk. Hell, silk would look like heaven against her skin. I wouldn't know where she ended and it began.

When her brow puckered, she dipped her chin, and that gorgeous wave of auburn hair slipped over her shoulder.

If we'd been alone, if that brassy bitch—who was staring at me like I could fuck her over the counter with her friend watching if I was game—wasn't here, I'd have grabbed that rope of hair, twisted it around my fingers, and forced her gaze up.

Some guys liked their women demure. And I was one of them. I wasn't about to lie. I liked that in her, but I wanted her eyes on me. Always.

It was enough to prompt me to bite out, "Can we speak privately?"

She jerked at my words, then as she licked her bottom lip, turned to look at the waitress. "Jenny, it's okay. I can handle the rest by myself. You get home."

Jenny, her gaze drifting between me and her boss, nodded. She retreated to a door that swung as she moved through the opening, and within seconds, she had her coat and purse over her arm.

As she sashayed past—for my benefit, I was sure—she murmured, "See you tomorrow, Aoife."

Aoife nodded and shot her friend a smile, but I wasn't smiling. There were dishes on every table. Plates and saucers and tea pots. Those fancy stands that made any man wonder if he could touch it without snapping it.

Aoife was going to clear all that herself? Not on my fucking watch.

When the bell rang as the waitress opened the door, I didn't take my eyes off her until it rang once more upon closing.

Aoife swallowed, and I watched her throat work, watched it with a hunger that felt alien to me, because, God, I wanted to see my bites on her. Wanted to see my marks on that pale column of skin and her tits.

Barely withholding a groan, I asked, "Do you often let your staff go when you still have a lot of work to do, so you can speak to a stranger?"

Her cheeks flushed again, and she took a step back. "I-I, you're not —" Flustered once more, she fell silent.

"I'm not what?" Curiosity had me asking the question. Whatever I'd expected her to say, it hadn't been that.

She cleared her throat. "N-Nothing. You wished to speak with me, Mr. O'Grady?"

My other hand tightened around my briefcase, and though seeing her had made my reason for being here all that more necessary, I was almost disappointed. There was a gentle warmth to those bright-green eyes that would die out when I told her my purpose for being here. And her innocent attraction to me would change, morph into something else.

But I could only handle *something else*.

Some men were made for forever.

But those men weren't in my line of business.

I moved away from her, pressing my briefcase to one of the few empty tables. I wasn't happy about her having to do all the clearing up later on, and wondered if Paul, my PA, would know who to call to get her some help.

There was no way I was spending the rest of the night alone in my bed, my only companion my fist wrapped around my cock.

No way, no fucking how.

I paid Paul enough for him to come and clear the fucking place on his own if he couldn't find someone else.

I wanted Aoife on her knees, bent over my goddamn bed, and I was a man who always got what he wanted.

In this jungle, I was the lion, and Aoife? She was my prey.

I keyed in the code and opened my briefcase. The manila envelope was large and thick, well-padded with my documentation of Aoife's every move for the past few months.

It had started off as a legitimate move.

I'd wanted to know her weaknesses, so I could put pressure on her and make her cave to my demands.

Now, my demands had changed. I didn't just want her to sell the tea room we were standing in, I wanted her in my bed.

Fuck, I wanted that more than I wanted to make Aidan Sr. a fucking profit, and Aidan's profit and my balls still being attached to my body ran hand in hand.

Aidan was an evil cunt.

If I failed to deliver, he'd take it out on me. Whether I was his idea of an adopted son or not, he'd have done the same to his blood sons.

Well, he wouldn't have taken their balls. The man, for all his psychotic flaws, was obsessed with the idea of grandchildren, of passing it all on to the next generation. He'd cut his boys though. Without a doubt.

I knew Conor had marks on his back from a beating he refused to speak about. Then there was Brennan. He had a weak wrist because his father had a habit of breaking *that* wrist.

Without speaking, I grabbed the envelope and passed it to her.

She frowned down at it and asked, "For me?"

I smiled at her. "Open it."

"What is it?"

"Leverage."

That had her eyes flaring wide as she pulled out some of the photos. A gasp fell from her lips as she grabbed the photos when she spotted herself in them, jerking so hard the envelope tore. Some of the pictures spilled to the ground, but I didn't care about that.

Leaning back against one of the dainty tables once I was satisfied it would take my weight, I watched her cheeks blanch, all that delicious color dissipating as she took in everything the photos revealed.

"Y-You've been stalking me. Why?"

The question was high-pitched, loaded down with panic. I'd heard it often enough to recognize it easily.

I didn't get involved in wet work anymore. That wasn't my style, but along the way, to reach this point, I'd had no choice but to get my hands dirty. Panic was part of the job when you were collecting debts for the Irish Mob. And the Five Points were notorious for Aidan Sr.'s temper.

He wasn't the first patriarch. If anything, his grandfather was the founder. But Aidan Sr. was the type of guy that if you didn't pay him back, he didn't give a fuck about the money, he cared about the lack of respect.

See, you owed the mob and didn't pay? They'd send heavies around, beat the shit out of you, and threaten to do the same to your family, and usually, that did the trick. You didn't kill the cash cow.

Aidan Sr.?

He didn't give a fuck about the cash cow.

Only the truly desperate thought about borrowing money from Aidan, because if you didn't pay it back, he'd take your teeth, and your fingers and toes as a first warning. Then, if you still didn't pay—and most did—it was death.

Respect meant a lot to Aidan.

And fuck, if it wasn't starting to mean a lot to me. The panic in her voice made my cock throb.

I wanted this woman weak and willing.

I wanted it more than I wanted my next breath.

Ignoring her, I reached for my phone and tapped out a message to Paul.

Need housekeeping crew to clean this place.

I attached my live location, saw the blue ticks as Paul read the message—he knew better than to ignore my texts, whatever time of day they came—and he replied: *Sure thing.*

That was the kind of reply I was used to getting. Not just from Paul, but from everyone.

There were very few people who weren't below me in the strata of Five Points, and I'd worked my ass off to make that so.

The only people who ranked above me included Aidan Jr. and his brothers, Aidan Sr. of course, and then maybe a handful of his advisors that he respected for what they'd done for him and the Points over the years.

But the money I made Aidan Sr.?

That blew most of their 'advice' out of the window.

The reason Aidan had a Dassault Falcon executive private plane?

Because I was, as the City itself called me, a whiz kid.

I'd made my first million—backed by the Points, of course—at twenty-two.

Fifteen years later?

I'd made him hundreds of millions.

My own personal fortune was nothing to sniff at, either.

"W-Why have you done this?" Aoife asked, her voice breathy enough to make me wonder if she sounded like that in the sack.

"Because you've been a very stubborn little girl."

Her eyes flared wide. "Excuse me?"

I reached into the inside pocket of my suit coat and pulled out a business card. "For you," I prompted, offering it to her.

When she turned it over, saw the logo of five points shaped into a star, then read Acuig—in the Gaelic way, ah-coo-ig, not a butchered American way, ah-coo-ch—aloud, I watched her throat work as she swallowed.

"I-I should have realized with the Irish name," she whispered, the muscles in her brow twitching as she took in the chaos of the scattered photos on the floor.

Watching her as she dropped the contents on the ground, so she was surrounded by them, I tilted my head to the side, taking her in as her panic started to crest.

"I-I won't sell." Her first words surprised me.

I should have figured, though. Everything about this woman was surprisingly delicious.

"You have no choice," I purred. "As far as I'm aware, the Senator has a wife. He also has a reputation to protect. I'm not sure he'd be happy if any of those made it onto the *National Enquirer's* front page. Not when he's just trying to shore up his image to take a run for the White House next election."

She reached up and clutched her throat. The self-protective gesture was enough to make me smile at her—I knew what the absence of hope looked like.

There'd been a time when that had been my life, too.

"But, on the bright side," I carried on, "this can all be wiped away if you sell." As her gaze flicked to mine, I added, "As well as if you do something for me."

For a second, she was speechless. I could see she knew what that *something* was. Had my body language given it away? Had there been a certain raspiness to my tone?

I wasn't sure, and frankly, didn't give a fuck.

There was a little hiccoughing sound that escaped her lips, and she frowned at me, then down at herself.

"Is this a joke?"

"Do I look like I'm the kind of guy who jokes, Aoife?" Fuck, I loved saying her name.

The Gaelic notes just drove me insane.

Ee-Fah.

Nothing like the spelling, and all the more complicated and delicious for it.

"N-No," she confirmed, "but . . ."

"But what?" I prompted.

"I mean . . . you just can't be serious."

"Oh, but I am." I grinned. "Deadly. You've wasted a lot of my time,

Aoife Keegan. A lot. Do you think I'm normally involved in negotiations of this level?"

Her eyes whispered over me, and I felt the loving caress of her gaze as she took in each and every inch of me. When she licked her lips, I knew she liked what she saw. I didn't really care, but it was helpful for her to be eager in some small way—especially when coercion was involved.

Aidan had called it bribery. I preferred 'coercion'. It sounded far kinder.

"No. That suit alone probably cost the mortgage payment on this place."

I nodded—she wasn't wrong. I knew what she'd been paying as rent, then as a mortgage, before some kind *benefactor* had paid it all off. Free and clear.

"I had to get my hands dirty, and while I might like some things dirty . . .," I trailed off, smirking when she flushed. "So, as I see it, we have a problem. I want this building. You don't want anyone to know you're having an affair with a Senator. Or, should I say, the Senator doesn't want anyone to know he's having an affair with someone young enough to be his daughter . . ."

If my voice turned into a growl at that point, then it was because the notion of her spreading her legs for that old bastard just turned my stomach.

Fuck, this woman, the thoughts she made me think.

Because I was startled at the possessive note to my growl, I ran a hand over my head. I kept my hair short for a reason—ease. I wasn't the kind of man who wasted time primping. It was an expensive cut, so I didn't have to do anything to it. Even mussing it up had it falling back into the same sleek lines as before—a man in my position had to look pristine under pressure. And very few people could even begin to understand the kind of strain I was under.

The formation of igneous rock had less volcanic pressure than Aidan Sr.

She licked her lips as she stared down at the photos, then back up at me. "And you want me to sell the place to you, even though this is my livelihood and the livelihood of all my staff, and then sleep with you?"

Her squeaky voice, putting suspicion into words, had me crossing my legs at the ankle. "We wouldn't be doing much sleeping."

Another shaky breath soughed from her lips, then, those beautiful pillowy morsels that would look good around my cock, quivered.

"This is crazy," she whispered shakily.

"As far as I'm concerned, all of this could be avoided if you'd just sold to me a few months back. Now you have to pay for my time wasted on this project."

"By spreading my legs?"

Another squeak. I tsked at her question, but in truth, I was annoyed at her using those same words I had to describe her with that old hypocrite of a Senator.

I didn't move, though. Didn't even flex my arms in irritation, just murmured, "Small price to pay. And, even though it's ten percent above market price, I'll stick to the last offer Acuig gave you. Can't say anything's fairer than that."

She shook her head, and there was a desperation to the gesture as she cried, "I need this business. You don't understand—"

"I understand that some very powerful and very dangerous businessmen want this building demolished. I understand that those same powerful and dangerous men want a skyscraper taking up this plot of land. I understand that a four hundred million dollar project isn't going to be put on hiatus because one small Irish woman doesn't want to go out of business . . ." I cocked a brow at her. "You think I'm coming in hot and heavy? These kinds of men, Aoife, they're not the sort you fuck around with.

"Take my check, and my other offer, before you or the people you care about are threatened." I got to my feet and straightened my jacket out. "This suit? These shoes? That briefcase and this watch? I own them because I'm damn good at what I do. I'm a financial advisor, Aoife. Take my word for it. You're getting the best deal out of this."

She staggered back, the counter stopping her from crumpling to the floor. "You'd hurt me?"

"Not me," I repudiated. Not in the way she thought, anyway. "But the men I work for?"

Her gaze dropped to the one thing she'd retained in her hand—my card. "Acuig," she whispered. "Five in Gaelic."

My brows twitched in surprise. She knew Gaelic?

"The Five Points." Her eyes flared wide with terror. "They're behind this deal."

I hadn't expected her to put one and one together, but now that she had? It worked to my advantage.

Nodding, I told her, "Any minute now, there'll be a team of house-keepers coming in here to clear up for the night." When she gaped at me, I retrieved the contract from my briefcase, slapped it on the table, and handed her a pen as I carried on, "I suggest you let tonight be your last night of business."

What I didn't tell her, was that my suggestions weren't wasted words. They were like the law.

You didn't break them, and, like any lawmaker, I expected imme-diate obeisance.

***

Aoife

SO, the beautiful man just happened to be an absolute cocksucker of a bastard.

Still, this couldn't be real, could it?

The dick could have anyone he wanted. Jesus, Jenny was panting after him like a dog in heat. She would have gone out with him if he'd so much as clicked his fingers at her.

But he'd had eyes for me.

Like he wanted me.

He thought he'd bought me. Or, at least, bought my silence, and yeah, to some extent he had. But . . . why buy me, why not just drop the price on the building if he wanted me to pay for the time he'd wasted on me?

The arrogance imbued in those words was enough to make me pull my hair out, but that was inwardly. I was a redhead. I had a temper. But that temper was mostly overshadowed by fear.

Senator Alan Davidson wasn't my boyfriend, my lover, as this dick seemed to believe. He was my father, and as Finn O'Grady had correctly surmised, he was aiming for the White House.

How could I put that in jeopardy?

My dad was a good man. He'd made a mistake one summer when he'd come home from college, one that only some careful digging by his campaign manager had uncovered. Dad himself hadn't known of my existence, not until his CM had gone hunting for any nasty secrets that could come out and bite him in the ass.

This had been five years ago when he'd run for Senator. Now, Dad's goal was the presidential seat, and I wasn't going to be the one who put a wrench in the works.

When Garry Smythe had approached me back then, I'd thought he was joking. I was out on the street, heading home from work. At the side of me, a black car had driven in from the lane of traffic, just to park, or so I'd thought. As he'd held out his hand with a card, one of the car doors had opened up, and I'd been 'invited' inside.

Had I been scared?

At first.

But when Garry had told me my country needed me, I hadn't been sure whether to laugh or tell him to fuck off. He hadn't shuffled me into the car, though, hadn't tried to coerce me. He'd just asked if I'd voted for Senator Alan Davidson in the elections, and because he was one of the only politicians out there who wasn't a complete douche, and that was the name printed on the card in my hand, I'd shuffled into the back of the car.

Where the Senator himself had been sitting.

Now, when I thought about that day, I realized how fucking naive I'd been to get into the back of a limo for such a vague reason. But I'd been fortunate. Alan *had* been waiting for me. Waiting to tell me a story that still shook me to my core.

I'd made a promise to my dad that I wouldn't tell anyone. He'd offered me money, and I hadn't accepted it. I guess I should have, but back then, I'd been haughty and proud, and because the good guy I'd thought him to be hadn't been so good when he tried to buy my silence, I'd told him to fuck off. I'd been disappointed in him, frightened by the lifelong lie I'd been living, and equally hurt that the man who'd sired me was just concerned that I was a threat to his campaign.

I'd walked out of that car never expecting to see my dear old Dad ever again.

Then, the day after he'd been elected, he'd been sitting in the booth of the cafe where I worked part-time to get me through culinary school.

Seeing him, I'd almost handed that table off to one of the other waitresses, but I hadn't. Not when every time I'd passed the table, he'd caught my eye, a patient smile on his lips, one that said he'd wait for me all day if he had to.

Ever since that second meeting, I'd been catching up with him every three weeks.

And this bastard thought he could use our limited time together against my father? The one politician who could make a difference in the White House? One who didn't have Big Oil up his ass, a pharmaceutical company sucking his dick, or any other kind of corporation so far up his rectum that he was a walking, talking lie?

No.

That wasn't going to happen.

Which meant I was going to have to sleep with this stranger.

Before this conversation, hell, that hadn't been too disturbing a prospect. Because, dayum, what woman wouldn't want to sleep with this guy?

Even with an ego as big as his, he was delicious. Better than any cake I could bake, that was for fucking sure.

More than that, I knew him.

And I now knew that the life Fiona would never have wanted for her son was one he'd been drawn into.

The Mob.

The Five Points were notorious in these parts. Everyone was scared of them. I paid protection money to them, for God's sake. I knew to be scared of them, and having been raised in their territory, it was the height of stupidity to think paying them wasn't just a part of business.

Still, Fiona had never wanted that for Finn, and her Finn was the same as the one standing before me here today. In my tea room, which looked far too small to contain the might of this man.

She'd be so disappointed. So heart-sore to know that he was up to his neck in dirty dealings with the Five Points, and as he'd pointed out, the cost of his shoes, his clothes, and his jewelry, was enough to speak for itself.

If he wasn't high up the ladder in the gang, then I wasn't one of the best bakers of scones in the district.

Like Jenny had said, I had five star ratings across most social media platforms for a reason. I was good. But apparently, this man wasn't.

Before I could utter a word, before I could even cringe at how utterly sorrowful Fiona would be about this turn of events—not just about the Five Points but what her son was making me do—the door clattered open.

Like he'd predicted, a team of people swarmed in.

Finn motioned to the floor. "Want anyone to see those?"

With a gasp, I dropped to my knees and collected the shots, stuffing them back into the envelope with a haste that wasn't exactly practical.

Two shiny shoes appeared before me, followed by two expensively clad legs, and I peered up at him, wondering what he was about. He held out his hand, but I clasped the photos to my chest.

"You're making more of a mess than anything else, Aoife." His voice was raspy, his eyes weighted down by heavy lids.

For a second, I wondered why, then I saw *why*.

He had an erection.

An erection?

I peered around at the staff, but they were all men. Not a single woman in sight, well, save for the seventy-year-old with a clipboard who was barking out orders to the guys in what sounded like Russian.

So that meant, what?

The erection was for me?

The blush, the dreaded, hated blush, made another goddamn

appearance, and to cover it, I ducked my head, then pushed the photos and the envelope at him.

For whatever reason, I stayed where I was, staring up at him as he calmly, coolly, and so fucking collectedly pushed the photos back into the torn envelope—it was some coverage. Better than none at all, I figured.

Being down here was. . . .

Hell, I don't know what it was.

To be looked at like that?

For his body to respond to me like that?

It was unprecedented.

I'd had one sexual experience with a boy back in college, and that had not gone according to plan. So much so I was still technically a fucking virgin because, and this was no lie, the guy had *zero* understanding of a woman's body.

Craig had spent more time fingering my perineum than my clit, and every time he'd tried to shove his dick into me, he'd somehow managed to drag it down toward my ass.

I'd gotten so sick of him frigging the wrong bits of me, that I'd pushed him off and given him a blowjob. It had been the quickest way to get out of that annoying situation.

Yeah, annoying.

Jenny, when I'd told her, had pissed herself laughing, and ever since, had tried to get me to hook up with randoms, so I could slough off my virginity like it was dead skin and I was a snake. But life had just always gotten in the way, and I'd had no time for men.

Shortly after *that* had happened, we'd lost Fiona. Then, I'd graduated, and after, Mom and I had set up this place thanks to some insurance money she'd come into after her husband had died. It had been crazy building the tea room into an established cafe, and then mom had passed on, too.

So, here I was. Still a virgin. On my knees in front of the sexiest man on Earth, a man I knew, a man whose mother had half raised me, one who wanted me in his bed as some kind of blackmail payment.

Was this a dream?

Seriously?

I mean, I'd been depressed before Finn O'Grady had walked through my doors. Now I wasn't sure whether to be apoplectic or worried as fuck because he wasn't wrong: you didn't mess with the Five Points.

God, if I'd known they'd been behind the development on this building, I'd have probably signed over months ago.

The Points were. . . .

I shuddered.

Vindictive.

Aidan O'Donnelly was half-evil genius and half-twisted sociopath. St. Patrick's Church, two streets away, had the best roof in the neighborhood and the strongest attendance because Aidan, for all he'd cut you into more pieces than a butcher, was a devout Catholic. His men knew better than to avoid Sunday service, and I reckoned that Father Doyle was the busiest priest in the city because of Five Points' attendance.

"I like you down there," he murmured absentmindedly.

The words weren't exactly dirty, but the meaning? They had my temperature soaring.

Shit.

What the hell was I doing?

Enjoying the way this man was victimizing me?

It was so wrong, and yet, what was standing right in front of me? I knew he'd know what to do with that thing tucked behind his pants.

He wouldn't try to penetrate my urethra—yes, you read that right. Craig had tried to fuck my pee-hole! Like, *why*?

Finn?

He oozed sex appeal.

It seemed to seep from every pore, perfuming the air around me with his pheromones.

I hadn't even believed in pheromones until I scented Finn O'Grady's delicious essence.

It reminded me of the one out of town vacation we'd ever had. We'd gone to Cooperstown, and I'd scented a body of water that didn't have corpses floating in it—Otsego Lake. He reminded me of that. So green and earthy. It was an attack on my overwhelmed senses, an attack I didn't need.

With the envelope in his hand, he held out his other for me. When I placed my fingers in his, the size difference between us was noticeable once more.

I was just over five feet, and he was over six. I was round and curvy, and he was hard and lean.

It reminded me of the nursery tale Mom had sung to me as a child —Jack Sprat could eat no fat, and his wife could eat no lean.

Did it say a lot for my confidence that I couldn't seem to take it in that he wanted *me*? Or was it simply that I wasn't understanding how anyone could prefer me over Jenny?

Even my mom had called Jenny beautiful, whereas she'd kissed me on the nose and called me her 'bonny lass.'

Biting my lip, I accepted his help off the floor. My black jeans weren't the smartest thing for the tea room, but I didn't actually serve that many dishes, just bustled around behind the counter, working up the courage to do what Mom had done every day—greet people.

I wasn't a sociable person. I preferred my kitchen to the front of house, hence the jeans, but I regretted not wearing something else today. Something that covered just how big my ass was, how slender my waist *wasn't*.

Ugh.

This man is blackmailing you into his bed, Aoife. For Christ's sake, you're not supposed to be worrying if he likes the goods, too!

Still, no matter how much I tried, years of inadequacy weighed me down as I wiped off my knees.

"Do you have a coat?" he asked, and his voice was raspy again. "A jacket? Or a purse?"

I nodded at him but kept my gaze trained on the floor. "Yes."

"Go get them."

His order had me shuffling my feet toward the kitchen, but as I approached the door, I heard his strong voice speaking with the old woman with the clipboard: "I want this all cleaned up and boxed. Take it to my storage lot in Queens."

With my back to him, I stiffened at his brisk orders. *Was I just going to let him do this? Get away with it?*

My shoulders immediately sagged.

Did I have a choice?

If it was just him, just Acuig, then I'd fight this, as I'd been fighting it since the building had come to the attention of the developer. But this wasn't a regular business deal.

This was mob business, and it seemed like somehow, I'd become a part of that.

FML.

Seriously, FML.

CHAPTER 3

FINN

SHE WASN'T AS fiery as I imagined.

Did that disappoint me?

Maybe.

Then I had to chide myself because, Jesus, the woman had just been *coerced* out of her business. What did I expect? For her to be popping open a champagne bottle after I'd forced her to sign over her building to me?

Sure, she'd made a nice and tidy profit on her investment—I hadn't screwed her that way. But this morning, she'd gone into work with a game plan in mind, and tonight? Well, tonight she was out of a job and knee deep in a deal with the devil.

Of course, she hadn't actually agreed to my other terms, but when I guided her out of the tea room and toward my waiting car, she didn't falter.

Didn't utter a peep.

Just climbed into the vehicle, neatly tucked her knees together, and waited for me to get in beside her.

Like the well-oiled team my chauffeur and car were, they set off the minute I'd clicked my seatbelt.

The privacy screen was up, and I knew how soundproofed it was—

not because of technology, but because Samuel knew not to listen to any of the murmurs he might hear back here.

And if he was ever to share the most innocent of those whispers he might have discerned? We both knew I'd slice off his fucking ear.

This was a hard world. One we'd both grown up in, so we knew how things rolled. Samuel had it pretty easy with me, and he wasn't about to fuck up this job when he was so close to retirement. If he kept his mouth shut, did as I asked, ignored what he may or may not have heard, and drove me wherever the fuck I wanted to go, Sam knew I'd set him and his missus up somewhere nice in Florida. Near the beach, so the moaning old bastard's knees didn't give him too much trouble in his dotage.

See?

I wasn't all bad.

Rapping my fingers against my knee, I studied her, and I made no bones about it.

Her face was tilted down, and it let me see the longest lashes I'd ever come across on a woman. Well, natural ones. Those fucking false ones that fell off on my sheets were just irritating. But as with everything, Aoife was all natural.

So pure.

So fucking perfect.

Jesus, Mary, and Joseph.

She was a benediction come to life.

I wasn't as devout as Aidan Sr. would like me to be, but even I felt uncomfortable thinking such thoughts while sporting a hard-on that made me ache. That made my mental blasphemy even worse.

"Why did you let him touch you? Was it for money?"

I hadn't meant to ask that question.

Really, I hadn't.

It was the last thing I wanted to know, but like poison, it had spewed from my lips.

Who she'd fucked and who she hadn't, was none of my goddamn affair.

This was a business deal. Nothing more, nothing less. She'd fuck me to make sure I kept quiet, and I fucked her so I could revel in the copious curves this woman had to offer.

Simple, no?

She stiffened at the question, and I couldn't blame her. "Do I really have to answer that?"

I could have made her. It was on the tip of my tongue to force her to, but I didn't really want to know even if, somewhere deep down, I did.

"You know why you're here, don't you?" I asked instead of replying.

Her nostrils flared. "To keep silent."

I nodded and almost smiled at her because, internally she was furious, but equally, she was lost. I could sense that like a shark could scent blood in the water. This had thrown her for a loop, and she was in shock, but she was, underneath it all, angry.

Good.

I wanted to fuck her tonight when she was angry.

Spitting flames at me, taking her outrage out on me as she scratched lines of fire down my spine as she screamed her climax. . . .

I almost shuddered at how well I'd painted that mental picture.

"When you're ready, you have my card."

"Ready for what?" she asked, perplexed. Her brow furrowed as she, for the first time since she'd climbed into the car, looked over at me.

"To make another tea room. I've had them move all the stuff into storage."

She licked her lips. "I want to say that's kind of you, but I'm in this predicament because of you."

A corner of my mouth hitched at that. "Honestly, be grateful I was the one who came knocking today. You wouldn't want any of the Five Points' men around that place. Half that china would be on the floor now."

Her shoulders drooped. "I know."

"You do?"

"I pay them protection money," she snapped. "Plus, I grew up around enough Five Pointers to know the score."

That statement targeted my curiosity, hard. "You did, huh? Whereabouts?"

Her mouth pursed. "Nowhere you'd know," she muttered under her breath.

"I doubt it. This is my area, too."

She turned to me, and the tautness around her eyes reminded me of something, but even as it flashed into being, the memory disappeared as I drowned in her emerald green eyes. "Why are you doing this?"

"Why do you think?" I retorted. "You're a beautiful woman—"

"Don't pretend like you couldn't have any woman under you if you asked them."

I wanted to smile, but I didn't because I knew, just as Aidan had pointed out to me earlier that day, that Aoife wasn't exactly what society considered on trend.

She'd have suited the glorious Titian era. She was a Raphaelite, a gorgeous and vivacious Aphrodite.

She wasn't slender. Her butt bounced, and when I fucked her, I'd have some meat to slam into, and her hips would be delicious handholds to grab.

If I smiled, I'd confirm that I was mocking her, and though I was a bastard, and though I was enough of a cunt to blackmail her into this when it hadn't been necessary—after all, before I'd told her who I was, I could have asked her out and done this normally—there was no way I was going to knock this glorious creature's confidence.

"Some men like slim and trim gym bunnies, some men like curves." I shrugged. "That's how it works, isn't it?"

Her eyes flared at that. "But Jenny—"

"Would you prefer she be here with me?" I asked dryly, amused when she flushed.

"Of course not. I wouldn't want her to be in this position."

I laughed. "Nicely phrased."

"What's that supposed to mean?"

Leaning forward, I grabbed her chin and forced her to look at me. "It's supposed to mean that you can fight this all you fucking want, but deep down, you're glad you're here. Your little cunt is probably sopping wet, and it's dying for a taste of my dick. So, simmer down. We're almost at my apartment."

And with that, I dipped my chin, and opening my mouth, raked my teeth down her bottom lip before I bit her. Hard enough to make her moan.

***

Aoife

THE STING of pain should have had me rearing back.

It didn't.

It felt. . . .

I almost shuddered.

Good.

It had felt good.

The way he'd done it. So fucking cocky, so fucking sure of himself, and who could blame him? He'd taken what he wanted, and I hadn't pulled away because he was right. My pussy *was* wet, and even though this was all kinds of wrong, I did want to feel him there. To have his cock push inside me.

Jesus, this was way too early for Stockholm syndrome, right?

I mean, this was . . . what was it?

It couldn't be that I was so horny and desperate for male attention that I was willingly allowing this to happen, was it?

Fuck. How pathetic was I if that was true? And yet, I didn't feel desperate for anything other than more of that small taste Finn had given me.

As a little girl, I'd watched Finn. It had been back in the day when his old man had been around and Fiona had lived with her husband and son. He'd beaten her up something rotten. Barely a week went by when Fiona, my mom's friend, didn't appear with some badly made-up bruise on her face.

I was young, only two, but old enough to know something wasn't right. I'd even asked my mom about it, wanting to understand why someone would do that to another person.

I couldn't remember what my mother had said, but I could remember how sad she'd been.

For all his faults, my dipshit stepfather had never beaten her, he'd just taken all her tips for himself and spent every night getting drunk.

Well, Finn's dad had been the same, except where mine passed out on the decrepit La-Z-Boy in front of the TV, Gerry had taken out his drunk out on Fiona.

And eventually, Finn.

Even as a boy, in the photos Fiona kept of him, Finn had been beautiful.

I could see him now, deep in my mind's eye. His hair had been as coal dark then as it was now, and not even a hint of silver or gray marred the noir perfection. His jaw and nose had grown, obviously, but they were just as obstinate as I remembered. Fiona had always said Finn was hardheaded.

When I was little, I hadn't had a crush on him—I'd been a toddler, for God's sake—but I'd been in awe of him. In awe of the big boy who'd been all arms and legs, just waiting for his growth spurt. Sadly, when that had happened, he'd disappeared.

As had his father.

Overnight, Fiona had gone from having a full house to an empty nest, and my mom had comforted her over the loss of her boy.

To my young self, I'd thought he'd died.

Genuinely. The way Fiona had mourned him? It had been as though both men had passed on, except we'd never had to go to church for a service, and there'd been no wake.

As kids do, I'd forgotten him. I'd been two when he'd disappeared, so I only really remembered that Fiona was a mom and that she was grieving.

We'd barely spoken his name because it could set her off into bouts of tears that would have my mom pouring tea down her gullet as they talked through her feelings.

As time passed, those little scenes in our crappy kitchen stopped, yet Fiona hung around our place so much it was like her second home.

One day, my stepfather died in an accident at work. The insurance paid out, Fiona moved in with us, and Mom had started scheming as to how to make her dream of owning a tea room come true. With Fiona living in, I'd heard Finn's name more often, but the notion he was dead still rang true.

Yet, here he was.

Finn wasn't dead.

He was very much alive.

Had Fiona known that?

Had she?

I wasn't sure what I hoped for her.

Was it better to believe your son was dead, or that your son didn't give enough of a fuck about you to contact you for years?

I gnawed on my bottom lip at the thought and accidentally raked over the tissue where Finn had bitten earlier.

"We're almost there," the man himself grated out, and I could sense he was pissed because the phone had buzzed, and whatever he'd been reading had a storm cloud passing behind his eyes.

"O-Okay," I replied, hating the quiver in my voice, but also just hating my situation.

This was. . . .

It was too much.

How was it that I was sitting here?

This morning, I'd owned a tea room. Now, I didn't.

This morning, I'd been exhausted, depressed about my mom, and *feeling* lost.

Now?

I was the *epitome* of lost.

A man was going to use me for sex, for Christ's sake.

But all I could think was: *did I still have my hymen?*

God, would he be angry if he had to push through it?

Should I tell him?

If I did, it would be for my benefit, not his, and why the hell was I thinking like this? I should be trying to convince him that normal people did not work business deals out by bribing someone into bed.

But, deep down, I knew all my scattered thinking was futile.

I wasn't dealing with normal people here.

I was dealing with a Five Pointer.

A high ranking one at that.

It was like dealing with a Martian. To average, everyday folk, a Five Pointer was just outside of their knowledge banks.

Sure, they thought they knew what they were like because they watched *The Wire* or some other procedural show, but they didn't.

Real-life gangsters?

They were larger than life.

They throbbed with violence, and hell, a part of me knew that Finn was cutting me some slack by asking to sleep with me.

Yeah, as fucked up as that was, it was the truth.

He could have asked for so much more.

He'd have a Senator in his pocket, and to the mob, what else would they ask for if not that?

Yet Finn?

He just wanted to fuck me.

My throat felt tight and itchy from dryness. I wanted some water so badly, but equally, I wasn't sure if it would make me puke.

Not at the thought of sex with this man—a part of me knew I'd enjoy it too much to even be nervous.

No, at what else he could ask of me, that had me fretting.

Was this a one-time deal?

How could I protect my dad from the Five Points when . . .?

I shuddered because there was nothing I could do. There was no way I could even broach any of those questions since I wasn't in charge here.

Finn was.

Finn always would be until he deemed I'd paid my dues. Whether that was tomorrow or two years down the line.

Shit, it might even be forever. If my dad hit the White House, only God knew what kind of leverage Finn could pull if my father tried to carry on covering up my existence. . . .

"We're here."

Something had *definitely* pissed him off.

He'd gone from the cat who'd drank a carton full of cream, to a pissed off tabby scrounging for supper in the trash.

"We're going to go through to the private elevator, and I'm going to head straight down the hall to my living room. You're going to slip into the first door on the right—that's my bedroom."

"O-Okay," I told him, wondering what the hell was going on.

"You're going to stay quiet, and you're going to try to not hear any fucking thing I say, do you hear me?"

"I hear you."

"You'd better," he ground out, his hand tightening around his cellphone. "Coming to Aidan O'Donnelly's attention is the last thing a little mouse like you wants."

A shiver ran through me.

Aidan O'Donnelly was in his apartment?

Fuck, just how high up the ranks was he?

CONTINUE
THE FIVE POINTS' MOB COLLECTION
HERE:
www.books2read.com/FilthySerenaAkeroyd

CONTINUE
A DARK & DIRTY SINNERS' MC SERIES
HERE:
www.books2read.com/StormSerenaAkeroyd

FREE BOOK!

Don't forget to grab your free e-Book!
Secrets & Lies is now free!

Meg's love life was missing a spark until she discovered her need to be dominated. When her fiancé shared the same kink, she thought all her birthdays had come at once, and then she came to learn their relationship was one big fat lie.

Gabe has loved Meg for years, watching her from afar, and always wishing he'd been the one to date her first and not his brother. When he has the chance to have Meg in his bed—even better, tied to it—it's an opportunity he can't refuse.

With disastrous consequences.

Can Gabe make Meg realize she's the one woman he's always wanted? But once secrets and lies have wormed their way into a relationship, is it impossible to establish the firm base of trust needed between lovers, and more importantly, between sub and Sir…?

This story features orgasm control in a BDSM setting.
Secrets & Lies is now free!

CONNECT WITH SERENA

For the latest updates, be sure to check out my website!
But if you'd like to hang out with me and get to know me better, then
I'd love to see you in my Diva reader's group where you can find out
all the gossip on new releases as and when they happen. You can join
here: www.facebook.com/groups/SerenaAkeroydsDivas. Or you can
always PM or email me. I love to hear from you guys: serenaakeroyd@
gmail.com.

ABOUT THE AUTHOR

I'm a romance novelaholic and I won't touch a book unless I know there's a happy ending. This addiction is what made me craft stories that suit my voracious need for raunchy romance. I love twists and unexpected turns, and my novels all contain sexy guys, dark humor, and hot AF love scenes.

I write MF, menage, and reverse harem (also known as why choose romance,) in both contemporary and paranormal. Some of my stories are darker than others, but I can promise you one thing, you will always get the happy ending your heart needs!

www.ingramcontent.com/pod-product-compliance
Lightning Source LLC
Chambersburg PA
CBHW050944210726
48287CB00004B/1124